I, WHO 3

The Unauthorized Guide to Doctor Who Novels & Audios

Lars Pearson

mad norwegian press | new orleans
www.madnorwegian.com

INTRODUCTION

There always comes a point when the sheer magnitude of a researcher's work makes them sit down, pause for breath, shakily gulp down a scotch and consider their actions from outside the fishbowl.

In the course of *I, Who 3*, that happened just once—when I was compiling the Uber-Timeline, and realized that canonized "Doctor Who" [i.e. what's commonly accepted as "real," which is a bizarre concept] now incorporates more than 450 stories—TV stories, novels and audios included.

Naysayers will often blather about the impending demise of "Who"—and certainly, the halving of the novel line was a blow to morale—but really, we've all got *nothing* to complain about.

As I write this, the BBC, audio maker Big Finish and book publisher Telos alone are expected, within the next year, to release at least 37 original novels/audios with the official "Who" logo on them. And that's before you even start counting all the wealth of spin-off lines, such as Bernice Summerfield, the Daleks, "Doctor Who" Unbound, BBV's audio output and—dare I shamelessly whore myself?—Mad Norwegian's *Faction Paradox* novels and comics.

We're spoiled, and we often don't realize it. By nature, books and audios dealing with established sci-fi properties are typically lazy, abhorrent pieces of pulp—a festering boil on the face of literature [look no further than the *Farscape* books—or vast chunks of the *Star Trek* range, even though it occasionally produces nice stuff—for examples of *that*]. Yet the ghetto-ized "Doctor Who" industry continues to pump out a wealth of stories—and often quite *good* ones—like there's no tomorrow.

Indeed, keeping up with everything's such a gargantuan task, it's easy to fall behind. Life interferes, and suddenly you've got eight novels, two novellas and five audios on the shelf, all untouched.

So, as we always say: "Since you've been busy, we've read—and listened to—this stuff for you."

WHAT I, WHO 3 DOES FOR YOU

In a dazzling display of Pulitzer-worthy material, *I, Who 3* continues the task of cataloguing the "Doctor Who" novel and audio lines.

Although I've made the *I, Who* series as friendly and accommodating to newcomers as humanly possible, I'm forced to freely admit this isn't the place to learn about the "Doctor Who" TV series. I can only direct you to the re-released *Television Companion* from Telos, and—once you're slightly more proficient with the ins and outs of "Who"—*The Discontinuity Guide* by Paul Cornell, Martin Day and Keith Topping.

Failing all that, you can always resort to a *hell* of

a lot of video parties. If you watch one "Who" TV story a week, you should get through the series in 2 1/2 years. Feel free to check back with us then.

SPOILER WARNING

Spoilers, it must be said, often do to certain fans what the smallpox-riddled blankets did to the American Indians. But as always, let's be honest: Guidebooks that keep certain details secret aren't worth the paper they're printed on.

THE "WE" of I, WHO 3

Mad Norwegian's staff is a team of "Doctor Who" fanatics who've spent dozens of hours debating the finer points of "Who" mythology (such as "If Gallifrey is a utopian society... do they sell Twinkies?").

Whenever you see the word "we" in a review, it indeed denotes a group opinion—usually hashed out over conference calls after we're through talking about women, booze and sex. However, there's the rarest of rare instances where—as this book's author and publisher—I've channeled the wisdom of Rassilon and trumped the group opinion with my own. I mention this not out of arrogance, but because it's desperately important for any publisher to take responsibility for his actions [even if this leaves him/her open to assassination at times].

THE CATEGORIES

Most categories are self-explanatory, but a few probably warrant further description:

MEMORABLE MOMENTS: The utterly glowing moments that make a novel/audio worth the price of admission. If you're like us, the *X-Men* motion picture was worth it just to hear Wolverine deliver his infamous "You're a dick" line to Cyclops. Similarly, *Memorable Moments* chronicles the choice bits of these works—the breathtaking bits you remember long after you've forgotten the relevant novel/audio's name. Or your own.

SEX AND SPIRITS: *Doctor Who Magazine* reviewer Vanessa Bishop once cited this as "a checklist of zipper action," and that's fairly accurate. In short, this catalogs any time the TARDIS crew [and other relevant characters] indulge in carousing, cavorting and other bits of naughtiness.

ASS-WHUPPINGS: Less pleasurably, this serves as a rundown of the series' shootings, stabbings, maimings, throat-slittings, horsewhippings, keel-haulings and more (i.e. the stuff you really care about), typically centered around the TARDIS crew and other weighty characters.

TV/NOVEL/AUDIO TIE-INS: We need to keep stressing: These sections do not chronicle every time a character opens their mouth about a previous adventure. If Jamie mentions, "That escapade with the Quarks," we don't bother citing it as "The Dominators" [which we know you've seen five or six times, dreadful as it is]. But if Jamie references, "That escapade with the Quarks... where I lost my kilt when your back was turned," we cite it. In other words, we try to restrict this section to new information.

TIE-INS: After a certain point, "Doctor Who" references get so cross-pollinated, everything winds up in a delicious Gordian Knot of continuity. In instances where references got much too convoluted to cleanly fall under the TV/Audio/Novel categories, we lumped 'em under a general *Tie-Ins* header.

We hope this causes more enlightenment than confusion—although frankly, it seems like the "Who" readership these days is so hardboiled, they'd probably understand perfectly if, say, Roz Forrester and Iris Wildthyme had a lesbian love affair during a Bandril raid on the Nosferatu II.

CHARACTER DEVELOPMENT: Again, a list of new information about prominent "Who" characters. We omit previously established stuff—such as the fact that Daleks now have rocket pads for maneuvering up stairs—or we'd be here all day.

TOP 10 AND 5 LISTS: It's worth noting that for the purposes of our Top 10/5 lists [or shall we say, our rundown of "The Best of..."], we lumped Big Finish's Benny and Dalek material in with the main "Who" stuff, as Benny and the Daleks [which oddly enough, makes us think of Elton John's "Benny and the Jets"] simply didn't publish frequently enough to warrant their own lists.

Also, we should state early on that the novel range frequently gets Top 10 lists, but the Big Finish audio line usually gets Top 5s. That is not a slight against Big Finish, however—it's simply indicative of the fact that, until Sept. 2002, the novel range was publishing twice as frequently, thereby giving us more material to play with.

AT THE END OF THE DAY: Ah, the review section, meting out pleasure and pain with regards to the novels/audios indexed therein. We'd hardly claim that our opinions rule supreme—and there's certainly no penalty if anyone wants to disagree—but if we somehow manage to point readers who cherry-pick their books and audios in the direction

MISCELLANEOUS STUFF!

HOW WE GOT HERE

I, Who 3 continues the colossal—nay, almost Herculean—task of being a concordance to the "Doctor Who" original novel and audio ranges. To this end, *I, Who 3* concerns itself with the following arenas of off-screen "Doctor Who":

• **The BBC "Doctor Who" novels**—Chiefly composed of the Eighth Doctor Adventures (the EDAs, centered around the Paul McGann Doctor) and the Past Doctor Adventures (the PDAs, focused on Doctors #1-#7). [Note: *I, Who 3* indexes the EDAs *EarthWorld* to *Time Zero*, and the PDAs *Rags* to *Ten Little Aliens*.]

• **The Big Finish "Doctor Who" Audios**—Original audio stories featuring the fifth through eighth Doctors. [Note: This book chronicles "Loups-Garoux" to "Neverland."]

As stated in *I, Who 2*, we defy the notion that the "Who" novels and audios exist in different universes. Ultimately, they're chiefly produced and written by the same people, and the few contradictions between them (notably "Dust Breeding" and *First Frontier*) can be solved without too much hassle. So they're equal.

• **Related Universes**—... chiefly Big Finish's Bernice Summerfield audios/novels, which feature Benny—a former TARDIS companion from the novels. Also included; Big Finish's "Dalek Empire" audios [and we trust the *Daleks* need no introduction].

• **Apocrypha**—Stuff that doesn't count as canon, although this time out, we only need index the webcast [later released on CD] seventh Doctor story "Death Comes to Time."

There's been craploads of debate about this, but ultimately, we couldn't find any sensible way of viewing DCTT as canon. Because really, there's no way to incorporate its details—such as the deaths of the seventh Doctor and the Time Lords, plus the revelation that pretty much every Time Lord has godlike powers—without splitting "Who" continuity open like an overripe cantaloupe.

As "Who" researchers, our job is to chronicle and index the novel and audio stories—*not* completely invent crackpot explanations why *everything* should count as canon. If your personal continuity is better off claiming that DCTT actually happened, more power to you. But since DCTT doesn't make the slightest effort to mesh with the rest of "Who" continuity, we're ruling it apocrypha until proved otherwise.

of the really good stuff, so much the better. Because ultimately, that's what we're here for.

—Lars Pearson, New Orleans.

TABLE OF CONTENTS

The Doctors Who

TIME AND RELATIVE

By Kim Newman

Release Date: November 2001
Order: Telos "Doctor Who" Novella #1

TARDIS CREW The first Doctor and Susan.

TRAVEL LOG Coal Hill School and 76 Totter's Lane, London, March 27 to April 4, 1963.

CHRONOLOGY Some months before "An Unearthly Child."

STORY SUMMARY Trying to acclimate to London, 1963, the Doctor's granddaughter Susan enrolls at Coal Hill School. Susan makes a number of friends including Gillian Roberts, John Brent and a youngster named Malcolm, even as England experiences a mysterious cold snap. An intangible intelligence animates a number of killer snowmen, whom Susan dubs "the Cold Knights," to murder any human they happen across. The Cold Knights skewer a number of Coal Hill students with their ice lances, but Susan rounds up her friends and races to find her grandfather for help.

At Totter's Lane, Susan's group becomes dismayed to learn that the Doctor has already spoken with the Cold, the central intelligence animating the Cold Knights, and decided to leave it alone. The Doctor explains the Cold evolved during Earth's last ice age, but became inactive as the climate warmed. Now, having awakened eons later, the Cold plans to kill off humanity and reclaim Earth for itself.

However, the TARDIS inadvertently started bleeding off some of the Cold's energy, prompting the intelligence to commune with the Doctor, asking him to end his unintentional interference. Holding little regard for humanity, the Doctor agreed and cobbled together a device to halt the energy loss. Susan's friends implore the Doctor to intervene and save humankind from extinction, but he stubbornly refuses, insisting he cannot break his people's cardinal rule of non-interference in history.

Impressed by little Malcolm's youthful imagination, the Doctor decides that humanity possesses a uniqueness worth saving whatever the risk. Relenting, the Doctor adjusts his device to siphon the Cold's intelligence into a single lump of ice.

Pleased, the Doctor pilots the TARDIS to Pluto, the distant future, and deposits the Cold there. The TARDIS returns to Totter's Lane after many false starts, but the Doctor notes that a key TARDIS filament burnt out from restricting the Cold. The Doctor makes reassurances, but Susan nonetheless fears the Ship won't function properly in future. Meanwhile, life at Coal Hill School returns to normal.

MEMORABLE MOMENTS Susan ponders that for all she knows, the TARDIS might still be on Gallifrey, and that she and the Doctor only stole the door.

During a debate about the merits of the Cold vs. humanity, the Doctor claims: "The Cold built living ice cathedrals, and could sculpt on the level of an individual snowflake. Have you ever seen anything as perfect as a snowflake?" In response, Susan replies "Yes"… and points to little Malcolm.

When the Doctor stubbornly refuses to defeat the Cold, Gillian threatens to twist Susan's head off. The Doctor initially seems unconcerned, unwilling to yield to violence, but starts to acknowledge the force of her passion for mankind.

John asks if the Doctor's an alien, and the Doctor responds: "No… there's no such thing. There's only life." Susan indirectly agrees with the Doctor by claiming: "We aren't human, but we are people."

SEX AND SPIRITS Gillian pads her bra with handkerchiefs, then takes Susan with her for a Saturday night on the town. A young stud named Flash offers drinks, but Susan lets slip their age, causing Flash to take off. Gillian meets gang member Zack and, after this story, takes up with him.

Susan's diary decries thoughts of sex, but she's notably quiet regarding John. Sadly, Susan's extra-terrestrial nature creates a gulf between them, and the fact that John's father dies fighting the Cold pretty much sours their relationship.

John's visited The Pump bar, which has entrances on the High Street and Totter's Lane.

ASS-WHUPPINGS The Cold Knights spear ice lances through Coal Hill teacher Mr. Okehurst and several schoolboys. But in the tradition of *Buffy the Vampire Slayer*, the public somehow doesn't question this *too* hard.

Francis Minto, a bully, also gets stabbed, but recovers. John's dad Captain Brent dies saving Gillian, as the Cold Knights snap his spine. The Knights also crush a waitress named Dolly, who tries to help Susan's party.

THE CRUCIAL BITS...

- **TIME AND RELATIVE**—First recorded instance of the Doctor interfering with history. The TARDIS gets damaged, leading to the Ship's unreliability in "An Unearthly Child."

TV TIE-INS *Time and Relative* explains the TARDIS' unreliability in "An Unearthly Child," claiming the Ship burnt out a rare filament while restraining the Cold. Also, Susan implies the Time Lords will know about the Doctor's time meddling and pursue them all the more vigorously (leading to the Doctor's trial in "The War Games").

In something of a jumble, "An Unearthly Child" claims the Doctor and Susan have resided in London for five months. Yet, *Time and Relative* implies they arrived a year previous to the TV story.

Susan notes she has a Vidal Sassoon hairstyle— a jape on Newman's part, since Sassoon genuinely tailored actress Carole Ann Ford's unearthly hairstyle in the debut "Who" story. Student Wendy Coburn's name obviously evokes "An Unearthly Child" author Anthony Coburn.

Susan currently calls the TARDIS "the Box." [Either a term of affection, or Newman's way of suggesting that she hasn't coined the word TARDIS yet—when the term clearly pre-dates the Doctor leaving Gallifrey.]

NOVEL TIE-INS *Lungbarrow* details the Doctor and Susan's flight from Gallifrey and the exact nature of their relationship. The Cold in *Time and Relative* is unrelated to the ice creature in *Drift* and the similarly named Cold in *Interference*.

TIE-INS John and Gillian's names hail from the first Doctor's companions in the *TV Action!* comic strips.

This story claims Susan has two hearts. *City at World's End* concurs with this, although *Managra*, *The Man in the Velvet Mask*, "The Edge of Destruction" and "The Sensorites" all suggest the pre-regenerative Doctor only had one heart. A possible explanation lies in *Lungbarrow*, which cites Susan as the last natural-born Gallifreyan. It's possible that only Loom-spun Time Lords such as the Doctor have one heart in their first incarnation, whereas natural-born Gallifreyans innately had two. [Or this could all be a tremendous clusterfish.]

CHARACTER DEVELOPMENT

- *The Doctor:* The Doctor's not yet fond of humanity, but gradually warms to it. He's not actively aiding the Cold, but doesn't want to get in its way. He ignores Susan's friends unless they speak to him. He's never broken the Time Lords' non-interference rule before now.

- *The Doctor and Susan:* Susan opens this story unable to recall her homeworld's name, how the TARDIS' physics work, or how Time Lords reproduce. She can't recall her parents. She claims she *should* know the Doctor's name, suspecting it got taken away from him. The Doctor's actions undo a number of these blocks (*see Alien Races*).

The Doctor faked school enrollment forms for Susan, randomly adding the surname "Foreman" [from Foreman's junkyard, "An Unearthly Child"] because the documents required two names.

He tested Susan with an Eleven Plus exam but she failed, so he placed her in Secondary Modern School. He keeps forgetting to attend parents' night. The Doctor lets Susan do what she pleases on Saturday night. She worries that if she stays out too long, he might forget about her. It's implied she can empathically scan the Doctor's moods. She gets frightened when he's consumed by work, when he's least himself.

The two of them know of a more rational place than Earth, but don't want to live there. Susan's the only person in the Universe to whom the Doctor's got any attachment. She suspects he let her attend school to test humanity's mettle. She's pleased he didn't outright kill the Cold, afraid of saddling him with guilt for killing a lifeform.

Susan says they are "political exiles" from Time Lord society. She sometimes lies to the Doctor about how she's getting on in school. Susan considers herself and the Doctor honorary Brits, because they like tea and grumble about officials.

- *Susan:* Susan hates a number of things including herself, her whiny voice, her awkward face, school rules, school games, cooked liver, bully Francis Minto and the cold (generally speaking).

She particularly despises her form master and Geography teacher, Mr. Grange, and once got lines for calling him, "Ghastly." She's in 4G—4 for the Year Four, G for Grange.

She doesn't hate the Doctor. She likes celebrities Peter O'Toole, John Lennon and Patrick McGoohan. She's probably got a crush on Albert Finney, but doesn't like Cliff Richard.

Susan's tops in math and science, but bottoms out in everything else. She's woeful at geography, because she keeps forgetting the names of countries and capitals in this time zone. She got top score on a history test about Renaissance Italy. Mademoiselle "Madame Weasel" Quelou teaches Susan French, but Susan keeps mixing it with Latin [a symptom of her time in the Middle Ages].

Susan looks upon meddling as an obligation, a case of those with power acting benevolently to make things better. She's in her first incarnation.

She keeps a diary. Her weekend job babysitting Malcolm (for five shillings a time) dries up after this story. She's never had detention time.

Susan's afraid of the Time Lords. She has a half-memory of a highly regarded truant officer [presumably the Master], who attended class with the Doctor. In Susan's dream, the truant officer got assigned to track down the Doctor down.

The strenuous events in this book alienate Susan from John and Gillian.

• *Susan and Gillian Roberts:* Gillian befriended Susan their first day at school. She calls Susan "Forehead." [Susan examined her face for hours as a result.]

• *Gillian Roberts:* Gillian's mother took off when she was young. Her dad obviously abuses her, but her boyfriend Zack makes him think twice about it. Gillian misbehaves a lot, the only Coal Hill schoolgirl to get caned.

She's currently 15, and hopes to leave home [and school] next year after getting engaged to Zack. She's lousy at math.

• *John Brent:* He's nicknamed "John the Martian," considered the class oddity. John's Army captain father enlisted him in after-school ROTC training, but he dropped it after his dad's death. John's knowledgeable about the solar system. The Doctor says John's a name to be reckoned with, in some futures.

• *The Cold:* The Cold isn't malicious, but regards humans as the worldwide equivalent of algae. The Cold can turn snowflakes into tiny, meticulous razors. It can trigger avalanches, and create giant rolling snowballs.

The Cold declines to harm Susan out of respect for the Doctor. In time, the Cold could have dropped Earth's temperature, covering the world in ice and snow.

• *The TARDIS:* The Ship requires five attempts to reach Pluto in the future, and more than a dozen shots to return to Foreman's Yard. The Cold can drop the temperature inside the Ship.

The TARDIS contains an elephant's foot umbrella stand full of *assegais* and a chrono-synclastic infundibulator. Ironically, Susan's never found a telephone inside the Ship.

ALIEN RACES *Time Lords:* The Time Lords seem to mentally condition their own people against meddling with history. Time Lords who successfully break one of their mental blocks usually shatter the remainder. [The Doctor's first act of interference, removing the Cold from Earth,

removes a number of mental blocks in both himself and Susan.]

Susan worries that if the Time Lords catch her and the Doctor, they might erase their memories ("The War Games"), or worse, retro-engineer it so they were never related.

ALIEN PLANETS *Gallifrey:* Susan implies that it's not part of the Universe's standard timestream.

STUFF YOU NEED *The Cold Knights:* The Cold can either animate human-made snowmen, or generate its own to create the Cold Knights. They require freezing temperatures to function. By day, they function like an army. At night, when the temperature further drops, they become even more forceful, like a hostile, malign glacier.

PLACES TO GO *Coal Hill School:* A youth club's located at the foot of the school, attached to a church. High Street's located five short bus stops from the school. The school's staff common room stinks of tobacco.

Susan's assorted Coal Hill classmates include Sadie Lederer, Gibson [who's Year Five], Ape Okehurst and the nice Wendy Coburn. Her teachers include Mr. Carker, who banned snowballs and turned down dozens of petitions for girls to wear trousers to school.

ORGANIZATIONS *The Novosibirsk Project:* A Russian undertaking, the purpose of which remains unknown. The Novosibirsk Project's possible agendas entail cryogenic experiments for cosmonauts, storing populations underground to survive a nuclear war, or deploying a freezing ray against America and Britain.

HISTORY Millennia ago, during the first great ice age, the Cold was Earth's dominant lifeform — an evolutionary experiment with intelligence. It went dormant as the climate warmed, but recently awakened for an unspecified reason. It's speculated the Cold revives due to the Russians' Novosibirsk Project (*see Organizations*), drilling in Alaska or simply another climate shift.

• In future, pens will become obsolete, with everyone mind-dictating into machines.

AT THE END OF THE DAY The crowning achievement of the Telos line, breathing life into an old formula and setting a standard that puts most other 2001 PDAs to shame. Set before the TV series, *Time and Relative* plays the show's core concept of an old man, a junkyard and a police box

that's a portal to other worlds to the max, dramatically hinging itself on the Doctor and Susan's *alien* nature. As such, it sparkles with great moments, triumphantly celebrates the immense innovation that got "Doctor Who" underway 40 years ago, and reminds us why we love this series so much.

DID YOU KNOW?

- Author Kim Newman likes tying his stories and novels together, to the extent that *Time and Relative* bleeds over into his other works. Mlle Quelou, the French teacher who gets a mention, appears equally briefly in his novel *Life's Lottery*. Also, a character in Newman's novella *Swellhead* was a Coal Hill School pupil in the 1950s.
- *Time and Relative* actually marks Newman's second bash at writing a William Hartnell part. *Teddy Bears' Picnic*, a novella that Newman co-wrote with Eugene Byrne (in the book *Back in the USSA*), features Sergeant Grimshaw—whom Hartnell played in *Carry On Sergeant*.

BYZANTIUM!

By Keith Topping

Release Date: July 2001
Order: BBC Past Doctor Adventure #44

TARDIS CREW   The first Doctor, Ian, Barbara and Vicki.

TRAVEL LOG   Byzantium, March 14, 64 AD. *Byzantium!* covers the TARDIS crew's early adventure in this time zone, eventually leading them to Nero's burning of Rome, July, 64 AD ("The Romans"). Also, the British Museum, London, November 1973.

CHRONOLOGY   Between the TARDIS plunging off a cliff ("The Rescue" Part 2, repeated in "The Romans" Part 1) and the main events in "The Romans."

STORY SUMMARY   Emerging from the toppled TARDIS ("The Rescue"), the first Doctor and his companions find themselves near the city of Byzantium, 64 AD. The travelers spend a week exploring the city, finding it torn by political and religious strife between the occupying Romans, the Pharisee Jews, the extremist Zealot Jews and the early Christians. The Doctor's crew stops at a market for supplies, and inadvertently gets caught

in the crossfire between a pack of Zealots and some Roman soldiers.

The Doctor's quartet survives the melee, but gets separated in the process. Vicki lodges with the benevolent Greek shopkeeper Georgidias for a time, but flees after repeated abuse from his wife Evangeline. Barbara shelters with Pharisee Jew leader Hieronymous, then departs upon realizing he intends to marry her.

The Doctor fares much better, finding refuge with Christians in some caves outside Byzantium. The Doctor meets scribes Rueben, Rayhab and Amos, who're busy translating early Christian writings into Greek. In due course, the Doctor lends assistance, helping to translate an early version of the Gospel Mark.

The Romans mistake Ian for a contemporary Briton and accord him some respect as a citizen of the Empire. Ian eventually befriends Roman General Gaius Calaphilus, and his political opponent, city praefectus Thalius Maximus. With help from Maximus' advisor Gamellus, Ian encourages the rival Calaphilus and Maximus to settle their differences for the good of Byzantium.

Hatred between the various factions in Byzantium finally bubbles over, leading to a massive amount of bloodshed between the Romans and the Zealots. In turn, Calaphilus and Maximus unite against corrupt elements in Byzantium, instigating a purge. Amid the chaos, the Doctor's quartet miraculously reunites and heads back to the TARDIS, knowing from history that Byzantium faces a turbulent period of reform.

Unfortunately, the TARDIS has gone missing from its landing site. Upon hearing rumors that Roman Senator Germanicus Vinicius found the Ship two weeks ago and lugged it back to his villa as a curiosity, the Doctor's group begins the arduous trek to Rome to retrieve their property (leading to "The Romans").

MEMORABLE MOMENTS   The Doctor agrees to visit Byzantium, but cautions: "No doubt, some terrible fate will befall us. It usually does."

Vicki finds herself orphaned, starved, an object of curiosity and the victim of brutality. In short, she labels herself a Dickens character.

The TARDIS' loss makes the Doctor feel very old, tired and alone. He claims they have a long journey to Rome, but that, "at the end of it, a carriage to the stars awaits us."

SEX AND SPIRITS   Ian spends a great deal of time trying to *avoid* getting laid. That's not a misprint. Lady Jocelyn and Felicia, respectively City Praefectus Thalius Maximus' wife and maid, both

try to seduce Ian. He resists because: A) he's naturally reserved, B) he hopes to avoid a political scandal, C) it would put his life at risk, and D) it's fairly well established, especially in *More Short Trips:* "Roman Cutaway," that he's in love with Barbara by this point.

Nonetheless, Jocelyn naughtily spies Ian sleeping naked, and he stumbles out of the bed, warding off her advances while wrapped in a sheet. Felicia also tugs at the hem of her skirt provocatively, making Ian recall schoolgirls who've performed the same stunt.

Ian also turns down a third proposition from Maximus' ex-wife Antonia, asking her to spread the word that he's not interested in wild nookie. By showing such restraint, Ian gains General Gaius Calaphilus' respect.

Barbara rejects a marriage proposal from Hieronymous, the Pharisee Jew leader. Hieronymous somewhat graciously gives Barbara safe passage out of Byzantium, but vents his frustrations by more ruthlessly prosecuting Christians.

Vicki prevents a legionnaire from raping her friend Iola by threatening to scream. The Georgidias family trains Vicki as a good housewife, probably intending to marry her off.

From here, we present oodles of side notes, related to Ian and Barbara's pre-TARDIS days: Ian distinctly recalls hitting puberty, waking up to suddenly prioritize girls over rugby. He went drinking on Friday nights in the West End with friends from teaching college. He recalls Saturday night fist fights down the Old Kent Road. He formerly drank pints of Theakston's and a whisky chaser in Pages Bar.

Ian previously spent a wretched weekend in Colchester with a girl from Guildford. It rained the whole time, so he now hates the town. Barbara notices that quiet [or rather, subtle] women attract Ian's attention better than brazen hussies.

Barbara still curses fellow student Herbert Effemy, who introduced her to gin and tonic 15 years ago. She got drunk for her first (and only) time, perilously negotiating a 1.5-mile trek through Cricklewood at night. She once spent New Year's Eve alone with a small box of Quality Street and a bottle of Babycham, plus endless turkey sandwiches.

ASS-WHUPPINGS Vicki cuts her arm on the TARDIS console as the Ship crashes. Ian gets large bruises on his face.

The Doctor and Ian witness a Zealot slitting a Roman soldier's throat. During the marketplace scuffle that separates the TARDIS crew, a Roman soldier mistakes Ian for a Zealot and attacks him.

Ian wrests a sword from the soldier's hand and, in accordance with his bayonet training (during his National Service days), expertly thrusts forward and kills the man. The melee overall kills more than 160.

Political intrigue boils over at book's end, with Ian's friend, an old librarian named Fabulous, taking an assassin's sword meant for Ian. A united Maximus and Calaphilus purge Byzantium of corruption. Ambitious tribune Marcus Lanilla and his friend Fabius kill Hieronymous for political advantage, but Calaphilus in turn offs them.

A crazed Zealot named Yewhe tries to kill Barbara and Vicki, but Ian stabs him in the back with a Roman gladius sword. Ian's evidently more comfortable with the idea of self-defense, because he readily shrugs off the killing.

TV TIE-INS The TARDIS food dispensor's currently on the fritz ("The Daleks"), prone to giving out boiled eggs and toast if you ask for porridge. The Doctor claims Vicki's destiny was mapped thousands of years before her birth, suggesting he knows her fate in ancient Greece ("The Myth Makers").

The TARDIS' exterior is specifically dated as a 1952 London telephone box ("An Unearthly Child"). Ian and Barbara don't understand the TARDIS' translation ability ("The Masque of Mandragora").

The Doctor spent time in a tavern on Rigel, during the early years of the Draconian Purges ("Frontier in Space"). He's recovering from bruised ribs inflicted by the Mountain Mauler of Montana ("The Romans"). He's already collaborated with Shakespeare about *Hamlet* ("City of Death").

Byzantium! dates "An Unearthly Child" as November, 1963 (rather than the TV show's more vague "winter" dating).

Post-TARDIS Ian is associates with Greg Sutton ("Inferno").

NOVEL TIE-INS The Doctor left Gallifrey nearly 60 years ago (*Lungbarrow*).

In a post-TARDIS scene, Barbara in 1973 befriends Dr. Julia Franklin at the British Museum's Roman Archaeology exhibition. Per tradition, Julia and her husband Robert have encountered various Doctors and their companions in every Keith Topping novel, never realizing their common connection. Julia and Robert previously appeared in Topping's *The Devil Goblins From Neptune*, *The Hollow Men* and *The King of Terror*.

TIE-INS *Byzantium!* and the short story *More Short Trips:* "Roman Cutaway" compete with one

BYZANTIUM! SONGS

As anyone who's read a Keith Topping book knows, he always names his chapter headings after song titles and lyrics. Accordingly, we got Topping—good sport that he is—suitably liquored up at Gallifrey convention and drug out of him, kicking and screaming, his source material for the chapter titles that appear in *Byzantium!*

Prologue: Once in a Lifetime (Talking Heads, from *Remain in Light*, 1980)

Episode 1: LXIV, And All That... (an allusion to *1966, And All That* by Half Man Half Biscuit)

Chapter 1: Direction, Reaction, Creation (The Jam 5 CD box-set, 1996)

Chapter 2: There Are 7 Levels (strangely enough, not a song title)

Chapter 3: Through the Past, Darkly (Rolling Stones compilation LP, 1969)

Chapter 4: Naming All The Stars (lyrics from "Met Your Sister" by Jeff Hart and the Ruins, from *Glancing from a Nervous Groom*, 1996)

Chapter 5: Babylon's Burning (The Ruts, from *The Crack*, 1979)

Chapter 6: The People Who Grinned Themselves to Death (LP and song title by The Housemartins, 1987)

Chapter 7: Cephalic Symbol (yet again, not a song title)

Chapter 8: Right Here, Right Now (Fatboy Slim from *You've Come a Long Way, Baby*, 1999)

Episode 2: Four Sides to the Circle (not a song title)

Chapter 9: The Culture Bunker (The Teardrop Explodes from *Wilder*, 1981) and Heliocentric (Paul Weller LP, 2001)

Chapter 10: Spies Like Us (Paul McCartney, single 1985)

Chapter 11: Going Underground (The Jam, single, 1980)

Chapter 12: Everybody's Been Burned Before (misquote of lyrics from "Everybody's Been Burned," The Byrds, from *Young Than Yesterday*, 1967)

Chapter 13: The Enemy of My Enemy is My Friend (not a song title)

Chapter 14: He Not Busy being Born is Busy Dying (lyrics from Bob Dylan's "It's Alright Ma (I'm Only Bleeding)" from *Bringing it All Back Home*, 1965)

Episode 3: Window Shopping for a New Crown of Thorns (*The Teardrop Explodes*, B-side, 1981)

Chapter 15: Pale Shelter (Tears for Fears, from *The Hurting*, 1982)

Chapter 16: True Faith and Brotherhood (respectively a 1987 single and a 1986 LP by New Order)

Chapter 17: How Soon is Now? (The Smiths, single, 1985)

Chapter 18: Searching for the Young Soul Rebels (Dexy's Midnight Runners, LP, 1980)

Chapter 19: Some Call It God-Core (Half Man Half Biscuit, LP, 1997)

Chapter 20: What Did Your Last Slave Die of? (not a song title)

Episode 4: Infamy, Infamy They're ll Got it in for me (not a song title)

Chapter 21: Perfume (All On You) (Paris Angels, single, 1991)

Chapter 22: Jehovahkill (Julian Cope, LP, 1992)

Chapter 23: You're History (Shakespeare's Sister, single, 1988)

Chapter 24: Rust Never Sleeps (Neil Young, LP, 1979)

Chapter 25: Give 'em Enough Rope (The Clash, LP, 1978)

Chapter 26: Jigsaw Feeling (Siouxsie and the Banshees from *The Scream*, 1978) and A Poem for Byzantium (Delerium, from *Poem*, 2001)

Episode 5: Four Lane Ends (not a song title)

Chapter 27: Losing My Religion (R.E.M, from *Out of Time*, 1990)

Chapter 28: The Passage of Time Leaving Empty Lives Waiting to be Filled (a misquote of lyrics from The Smiths' Rubber Ring, from *The World Won't Listen*, 1986)

Chapter 29: One Man Clapping (James, LP, 1989)

Chapter 30: Coping (Blur, from *Modern Life is Rubbish*, 1992)

Chapter 31: Just Another Greek Tragedy (not a song title)

Chapter 32: A New Dawn Fades (from "New Dawn Fades" by Joy Division, from *Unknown Pleasures*, 1979)

Chapter 33: Here's Where The Story Ends (The Sundays, from *Reading, Writing and Arithmetic*, 1992)

Chapter 34: ... And Miles to Go Before we Sleep (not a song title)

Epilogue: Two Thousand Light Years From Home (The Rolling Stones, from *Their Satanic Majesties Request*, 1967)

another to fill in the gap of the TARDIS plunging off a cliff ("The Rescue" Pt. 2) and when we next see Barbara and Vicki wandering through a Roman marketplace ("The Romans" Part 1). If push comes to shove, *Byzantium!* wins out over "Roman Cutaway" as canon, simply because a novel's, harder to ignore than a short story.

Even so, much of "Roman Cutaway" can be preserved if one simply dices the arrival scene and a few other details. [Of course, *Byzantium!* fails to explain how the TARDIS ends up back in a ditch in "The Romans" Pt. 4, but one thing at a time.]

Goth Opera first mentioned that a post-TARDIS Ian and Barbara got married. They birthed a son, John Alydon Ganatus Chesterton (named after two of their Thal friends, "The Daleks") in 1967 (mentioned in both *The Face of the Enemy* and Topping's *The Hollow Men*). Here shown in 1973, young John longs to become a pop star like Julian Blake or Mr. Big Hat of Slade. *Timewyrm: Revelation* revealed Johnny's future career as rocker "Johnny Chess." Topping previously showed Johnny as having married (and divorced) Tegan after her TARDIS days in *The King of Terror*.

The Doctor's already visited the alien planets Mondas (explaining his foreknowledge in "The Tenth Planet") and Cassuragi (elaborated on in Topping's *Ghost Ship*).

CHARACTER DEVELOPMENT

• *The Doctor:* The Doctor finds religion worthy of considerable study. He can read Biblical writings in the original Aramaic/Greek. He's previously done translation work.

The Doctor witnessed the third battle for Ypres (a.k.a. The Battle of Passchendaele) in World War I. He was also present at Dunkirk in World War II, sailed around the Caribbean in a pirate galleon and saw the assassination of President McKinley. He witnessed *King Lear*'s debut performance. He deems Richard Burbage a good actor, but thinks he's horrible at portraying old men crushed by life's uncertainties.

He's seen the first movement of French composer Erik Satie's *Trois Gymnopedies* as played by a green-skinned, three-armed creature (probably a Venusian) using a unique keyboard instrument.

He thinks goodbyes get in the way of departing. He can diagnose a cancer growth in the throat. He rarely gets upset at people dying, because he witnesses it so often.

The Doctor recalls growing up.

• *The Doctor and Susan:* They previously visited Rome, Antioch and Jerusalem during brutal periods in history.

• *Ian Chesterton:* Ian was born in Reading. During Ian's childhood, his brother and sister fished and played cricket. At night, they studied the stars with their father's telescope, learning about constellations. Mr. Dumbie taught Ian some Latin, but the topic baffled him (although he recalls useful phrases such as "You stink like the worst toilet," "nymphomaniac whore" and "ugly old bag who can't keep her trap shut").

Mr. Quibbs was Ian's form tutor. Ian attended school with a Jewish lad named Goldfinkle and a pipsqueak named Perryman, who's now a journalist. He liked a Greek schoolteacher who also sold second-hand jewelry on Portobello Road.

Ian served two years national service in the RAF, receiving an honorable discharge. He spent six months whitewashing doorsteps at RAF Lynham.

He vacationed at a remote cottage in North Wales. He was formerly a wing-three quarter for Harlequins Third XV.

Ian taught science, English and occasionally PE. He's far less knowledgeable about history. He's studied oriental disciplines, including karate, ju jitsu and unagi.

Ian's more of a rationalist and humanist than a Christian. He's skeptical about religion, but thinks Christianity's as good as any other dogma.

He once owned a Ford, but hated it. He's never been to Cirencester. He's seen magician Tommy Cooper perform at the London Palladium.

Ian gets his shirts from John Collier, a tailor's shop on Bond Street in the 1950s and 60s.

• *Ian and Barbara:* They first met in a quaint little tea shop on Tottenham Court Road. They've now traveled with the Doctor for a year, but feel as if they don't know him. At Coal Hill School, Ian and Barbara worked with a Scottish form mistress who terrified her students and most of the staff.

• *Barbara Wright Chesterton:* Barbara's nearly 32. At age 10, she read a Ladybird book on Captain Cook while stuck in bed with whooping cough. It inspired her to bring history to life in class.

She was Form 2A at Cricklewood Grammar School. Her teacher, Mr. Dolphin, wasn't impressed by Barbara's "simplistic and banal" work, but was otherwise likeable. Barbara's father took her, age 13, to visit the Tower of London.

After her TARDIS days, Barbara gave up history teaching no later than 1973 [possibly in 1967, when she had Johnny]. She specialized, among other things, in Roman and early Christian archaeology.

Barbara doesn't speak Latin, and only knows a smattering of Greek. She doesn't like football matches, Odeon cinemas and fashionable Knightsbridge dinner parties in 1960s London.

• *Vicki:* Vicki previously lived in Liddell Towers of the South Circular Road, New London, Earth. Her mother wanted to call her "Tanni," but her dad preferred "Vicki." She considers it a stupid name.

Vicki's currently 14 years old. She was 11 when her mother died. On Earth, Vicki was born into an era of space travel, interactive learning, virtual reality, chemical stimulation and instant maturity. She was 14, "going on 108."

She studied the Romans in Britain a little bit, but Barbara helps out with verbal essays on the topic.

THE CRUCIAL BITS...

• **BYZANTIUM!**—Details of the TARDIS crew's landing in Roman times (during "The Romans").

In Byzantium, Vicki traffics by the name Vickius Pallister. She likes Byzantium, save for being entirely clueless about what to say.

She can't identify singer Alma Cogan ("I Can't Tell a Waltz from a Tango").

• *John Alydon Ganatus Chesterton:* At age 6 1/2 (in 1973), he's pretending to be footballer Tony Green of Newcastle United and Scotland. Last week, he wanted to be an astronaut.

• *Julia and Robert Franklin:* They live in Reborough. Their youngest just turned three.

• *Thalius Maximus:* Byzantium city praefectus, executive to Emperor Nero. His father knew Pontius Pilate.

• *General Gaius Augustus Calaphilus:* Commander of Nero's forces in Byzantium, previously served with Claudius and Aulus Plautius when they took England in 54 AD.

• *The TARDIS:* The TARDIS' telepathic matrix means that when the Doctor's party speaks Latin, it sounds like Latin. But whenever someone speaks Latin *to* them, it sounds like English. The Ship translates anachronisms for clarity's sake.

HISTORY Byzantium's more than 250 years from getting re-named Constantinople [circa 330 AD].

• The Doctor helps with translating rough notes of the Gospel Mark—primarily written in Aramaic and Hebrew, with parts in Greek—into just Greek. Along with scribes Reuben, Rayhab and Amos, he works with an unedited version of Mark [the first-written of the Gospels, possibly as early as 60 AD], producing a version to complement the writings of Matthew the tax-gatherer. Mark either resides in Miletus or was executed by Nero.

• The Doctor meets James, a second-generation Greek Christian whose uncle witnessed the Sermon on the Mount. James located Mark's writings, found as completed scrolls in Babylon some months ago. James' family friends include Mary of Jerusalem and Mark's mother, at whose house Jesus and his disciples gathered. The Doctor also meets Hebron, a former companion of Paul.

• In Roman times, Maximus gives Ian a short sword with the initials "IC." The weapon goes missing, but eventually winds up in the British National Museum. Historians erroneously date the sword to the end of the first century, and it amuses Ian to know it's actually 35 years older.

AT THE END OF THE DAY A book that laudably wants to come off as TV's "The Romans" done seriously, but suffers for its lack of plot. Understand: One cannot call the plot "bad," because it's missing entirely. Basically, the TARDIS crew gets separated, experience adventures of little import (barring the Doctor helping to bring the Gospel Mark to fruition), then meet up again. That leaves *Byzantium!*, as a fellow reviewer put it, as "a good book struggling to get out," in dire need of two or three revisions to become the striking piece it deserves.

DID YOU KNOW?

• The *Byzantium!* cover was originally conceived to look like a poster from a Cecil B DeMille-style Biblical epic, such as *The Ten Commandments* or *Ben Hur*—only this time featuring a rippling-chested Ian Chesterton instead of Charlton Heston. Topping claims that for some reason, he got it into his head that such the posters showed the movie's title with an exclamation mark—so he titled the book *Byzantium!* rather than the more sedate *Byzantium*. When the cover concept got changed, Topping left the exclamation point simply because it looked different. (And he later learned, to his dismay, that the Hollywood posters in question actually didn't have exclamation points.)

• Topping loosely ties *Byzantium!* and *More Short Trips:* "Roman Cutaway" together by making Ian mention a dream in which he owns a Ford Anglia. The same car gets mentioned in "Roman Cutaway"—which is Topping's way of suggesting readers can view the short story as a dream on Ian's part.

TEN LITTLE ALIENS

By Stephen Cole

Release Date: June 2002
Order: BBC Past Doctor Adventure #54

TARDIS CREW The first Doctor, Ben and Polly.

TRAVEL LOG Unnamed planetoid in orbit around Vertigan Majoris, bordering the Earth Empire and the Morphiean Quadrant, circa May 23, 2890.

CHRONOLOGY Between "The Smugglers" and "The Tenth Planet." Actually, *Ten Little Aliens* exists in something of a continuity void, since

This book is not endorsed by the BBC. Doctor Who and TARDIS are trademarks of the BBC.

13

there's no gap between Ben and Polly's entering the TARDIS (at the end of "The War Machines") and the first Doctor's regeneration ("The Tenth Planet"). A *possible* explanation entails hypnotizing yourself that the frigid area the TARDIS arrives at in "The Smugglers" Part 4 *isn't* the South Pole ("The Tenth Planet"), allowing for a break between stories. Whatever the case, *Ten Little Aliens* says a "few adventures" have occurred since the crew left London.

STORY SUMMARY In the distant future, Marshal Nadina Haunt takes nine trainees, members of Earth's Anti-Terror Elite, into a mock battle against robotic Kill-Droids. Haunt's crew sets down on a supposedly barren planetoid, only to find a complex with architecture from the Earth-conquered Schirr homeworld.

Meanwhile, the Doctor, Ben and Polly arrive in the TARDIS, and begin examining a central chamber within the Schirr complex. Haunt's troopers blink at finding the Doctor's trio present, and nearly lose it upon discovering the corpses of the Ten-Strong, a magic-wielding Schirr terrorist cell, sealed behind a force field. Haunt's group explains the Ten-Strong previously learned black magics from the discorporeal Morphieans, then assaulted Earth forces with various spells. The assembled humans ponder how the Ten-Strong came to be lying dead on a planetoid, but their brainstorming session gets unceremonially interrupted when the complex breaks away from the planetoid and rockets toward the Morphiean Quadrant.

Eventually, the Ten-Strong revive, having faked their demise behind a time-stasis field. The Doctor realizes that Haunt, a Schirr sympathizer, deliberately led her troopers to the asteroid as fodder for the Ten-Strong. Weakened from their recent escapades, the Ten-Strong plan to magically convert Haunt's soldiers into Schirr flesh, then absorb them to regain their health.

If successful, the Ten-Strong intend to cast their greatest spell to date—a ritual that will let their allies, a group of Morphiean extremists, seize control of the Morphiean host mind. United, the Ten-Strong and renegade Morphieans will crush the Earth Empire, gaining the Schirr revenge and the Morphieans a plethora of physical hosts. But because a specific number of beings must be present for the final spell, the villains kill a few of Haunt's troopers, including a cyborg named Shel. The Ten-Strong then usurp the troopers' neural net, a means of looking through each others' perspective, to forcibly link the minds of everyone present. Finally, Ten-Strong leader DeCaster consumes Haunt and readies for the final incantation.

The Doctor discovers that when the cyborg Shel previously interfaced with the network, a trace element of his personality remained behind. As the Ten-Strong make their final casting, the Doctor begs the Shel's digitized persona to mentally resist the incantation. Shel's disruptive presence ruins the chant, causing an energy backlash that obliterates the Ten-Strong. Additionally, the energy surge ruins the Morphiean extremists' protection spells, allowing the proper Morphiean authorities to detect the renegades and eliminate them. With the threat to Earth ended, Haunt's remaining troopers steer the wayward complex for home.

MEMORABLE MOMENTS With Earthmen held in ill repute during this era, Ben ponders claiming he's a Martian and hoping for the best.

There's a jaw-dropping moment (literally) when DeCaster uses his magical powers to eat Haunt whole and absorb her into his being. Finally, the Doctor exerts his own willpower to its limit, imploring Shel to help him during the action-packed finale.

SEX AND SPIRITS Trooper Matthew Shade seems more than a little friendly to Polly in confiding he gained some facial scars while shielding children from grenade shrapnel. However, Polly later learns Shade actually gained his scars after cowardly deserting soldiers under his command. Naturally, this douses any possibility of romance between them. Also, Polly gets the dawning awareness that Shade looked upon her merely as a source of comfort, and that Ben's one of the few men to treat her like an individual.

Ben gets jealous about Polly's attention to Shade, a bit hypocritical since he's busy getting cozy with female trooper Mel "Frog" Narda. Little comes of it, however, and Frog ignores Ben to have—unsuccessfully, given the rampaging Schirr and Morphieans—sex against a wall with fellow trooper Joiks.

Trooper Joseph Creben also seems taken with Polly, but it fails to gel.

When the Doctor's party searches each other for signs of Schirr flesh, everyone gets felt up. [The Doctor notes: "This is most demeaning."]

ASS-WHUPPINGS The Ten-Strong fake their deaths, although DeCaster's second, Pallemar, tries to betray his overly ambitious leader to Earth Central. DeCaster accordingly bludgeons him to death, then feeds him—along with a few humans—into the complex's propulsion drives.

The Ten-Strong magically remove various impurities from the humans present, a pre-cursor to

their becoming Schirr flesh. Accordingly, trooper Matthew Shade feels shrapnel emerge from his facial scars, soldier Frog's traumatized when damaged vocal chords regrow and Haunt loses a cyst.

The Morphiean renegades manifest themselves by congealing billions of fleas into stone-like giant figures, tearing the cyborg Shel apart. Ben gets a wounded knee while scuffling with the giants. Conversely, he takes a rifle and blows apart a Kill-Droid at point-blank range.

DeCaster eats the very yummy Marshall Haunt. Ben and Polly start turning into Schirr flesh, but the Ten-Strong's demise reverts them to normal. Already dying, DeCaster gets hurled into the complex's engines.

Appalled by his transformation into Schirr flesh, trooper Dax Roba kills himself by swallowing an expandable force-mattress [initially about the size of a boiled sweet]. This marks, so far as we know, the first instance of "death by expandable couch" in "Doctor Who." [And the plastic chair smothering in "Terror of the Autons" doesn't count.]

TV TIE-INS As "Doctor Who" outright rejects the existence of magic ("The Daemons"), the Morphieans/Schirr's magical arts are perhaps best couched under Clarke's Law, that any advanced form of technology is indistinguishable from magic and vice versa ("Battlefield"). Alternatively, the discorporate Morphieans and their Schirr counterparts might use an advanced form of psionics.

CHARACTER DEVELOPMENT
• *The Doctor:* With effort, the Doctor can mentally block the Ten-Strong's paralyzing pulse, enabling his allies freedom of movement. He can wall off his mind from the troopers' webset (*see Stuff You Need*).

He has good hearing, but not so good eyesight. He can decipher Schirr navigational equipment.

The magic-using DeCaster smells youth in the aged Doctor.

• *The Doctor and Polly:* Polly briefly contacts the Doctor's mind via the troopers' webset, and feels like she's touching a raw flame. She senses the Doctor's young and vital, but trapped inside an "awful, ancient corpse" of a body. Finally, the Doctor blocks Polly's telepathic contact with a bicycle image ("The Space Museum").

• *The Doctor and Ben Jackson:* The Doctor reminds Ben of his father, who fixed the family vehicle by haphazardly flinging parts around.

• *Ben Jackson:* Ben's self-conscious about his height, especially since Polly's an inch taller than him. His formal rank is "Able Seaman." He joked

with colleagues aboard his sailing ship, the *Teazer*, that he'd go AWOL when the perfect island came along.

• *Polly Wright:* On New Year's Eve, 1963, Polly made a resolution to work in a Notting Hill charity shop for the benefit of cancer research. However, she ended up hating the store's squalor and walked out after a week, making her mum ecstatic. Polly donated a pricey pile of clothes to assuage her guilt.

• *Ben and Polly:* Polly automatically categorizes people as cat or dog people. She thinks Ben's definitely a dog person, but her independent streak makes her a cat person.

Polly acknowledges that Ben, thanks to his Navy service, knows how to handle himself. By comparison, Polly's only known Beaujolais Nouveau parties, poncy nightclubs and finishing school in South Ken.

• *Marshal Nadina Haunt:* Earth Central, questioning her loyalty to some degree, sent the cyborg Shel to spy on her.

ALIEN RACES *The Schirr:* Schirr have broad, round, mottled pink heads. They also have thick, rubbery lips and milky white, bulging eyes. Their ears are virtually melted onto the sides of their head.

Earth Central brands Schirr dissidents with a long, thin rectangle crossed with a diagonal line—a symbol in their language meaning "dissident." They wear the mark with pride.

Schirr navigational technology uses cartographic crystals. They have dark blood. They smell like sweat, perfumed soap and soiled diapers all rolled into one.

• *The Morphieans:* Certain factions on Morphiea are pressing to expand their race's territory on a corporeal level. All things being equal, the Morphiean central command favors leaving the Earth Empire alone, operating on intangible planes.

Morphieans can take corporeal form by amalgamating billions of fleas [or any miniscule form of life such as bacteria, etc.].

ALIEN PLANETS *Earth:* Supposedly ships its poor out to half the galaxy. Being born on Earth now carries special privileges, even with the empire's military.

• *Vertigan Majoris:* Located barely a thousand miles within Earth space.

STUFF YOU NEED *Neural Net Websets:* A means of sharing and recording perceptions. The device relies on the optic nerve, and thus doesn't

This book is not endorsed by the BBC. Doctor Who and TARDIS are trademarks of the BBC.

15

function well in total darkness. It doesn't accord its users outright telepathy, although memory sharing is possible.

- *Schirr Time-Stasis Field:* The stasis field device has components similar to ones in the TARDIS. Schirr inside the field scan as dead, because they're outside the flow of time.

ORGANIZATIONS *The Earth Empire:* Renames subjugated planets after Earth cities and states, such as Beijing, Idaho and New Jersey.

- *Earth Military:* Directed by Pentagon Central. Its forces include the Pauper Fleet [a disparaging name based on their lack of equipment], the Royal Escort, Peacekeeper Volunteers and the Anti-Terror Elite. Androids sometimes perform military intelligence work.
- *Earth's Anti-Terror Elite:* Train their troopers in a no-hope scenario involving the starships *Ardent* and *Harbinger*.

The Elite wear intelligent armor, sculpted from carbon nanotubing, designed to dampen vital signs and mask its wearer from enemy sensors. The armor also automatically constricts around wounds to staunch blood flow.

PHENOMENA *Morphiean/Schirr Rituals:* Probably an advanced form of psionics, but requiring certain amounts of flesh as fuel [presumably following standard conservation of energy laws].

Schirr flesh works best for such rituals. Schirr spell-casters can transform other species into Schirr meat, but must first heal their victims' injuries and impurities (tumors, etc.) to achieve the purest possible conversion.

The most powerful Morphiean/Schirr rituals require at least 10 members. Humans transform to Schirr flesh faster as they approach Morphiean space.

HISTORY Centuries ago, the Morphieans and the Schirr enjoyed diplomatic relations, but fell into disfavor with one another.

- Fifteen years ago, Earth repatriated the Schirr homeworld, renaming it Idaho.
- The Earth Empire is currently crumbling, taxing the crap out of its subjugated populations.
- At some point, the Ten-Strong stole the Morphieans' knowledge of the black arts, intending to vengefully use them against the Earth Empire. The outraged Morphieans—identifying the Schirr as part of the empire—retaliated against various Earth worlds, including Beijing Minor, threatening further destruction to retrieve their secrets. Earth settled into a Cold War phase, unable to retaliate against the rebellious Morphieans with

conventional weapons.

- Using the stolen rituals, the Ten-Strong spent a decade committing terrorist acts against Earth interests. They committed atrocities on worlds including the Argentines. Two years ago, the Ten-Strong tried to destroy a Pentagon sub-router on New Jersey, leading to heavy casualties.
- Nadina Haunt joined the service when Schirr dissidents eradicated the Earth embassy on Idaho. At age 29 or 30, she witnessed a Schirr assault on Toronto, a fertile seafood exporter to a dozen colony worlds. Earth forces razed the planet—since the Schirr had located the secret Pentagon Central Headquarters—inadvertently wounding Haunt in the process. They subsequently saved Haunt's life, secretly implanting her with a tumor to guarantee her loyalty in future.

Haunt went on a rampage across 20 worlds, trying to exact vengeance on the Schirr, but only wound up killing many innocents. A cataclysm on New Jersey resulted in a nuclear detonation that claimed a million lives. Haunt was retired to training duties afterward. Once informed of the tumor's existence, she consented to betray her trainees to the Ten-Strong, both to get her tumor removed and hopefully to give the Morphieans, whom Haunt tagged as the real enemy, the means to become corporeal—and therefore vulnerable to assault.

- The Japanese Belt is currently working to develop teleport technology.
- A Codes and Ethics of War is in place.

AT THE END OF THE DAY Very nicely polished, taking an [ironically] almost *Aliens* approach and grafting it onto a Hartnell period that technically doesn't exist (*see Chronology*). *Ten Little Aliens* unfolds as well-steeled sci-fi novel—adeptly introducing a lot of questions, staying focused, and driving the pigskin into the end zone. As such, it's a surprise win for the PDAs of 2002, packed with a good amount of drama and unashamedly putting magic, normally dismissed in the "Who" universe, to stellar use.

DID YOU KNOW?

- Cole started percolating the core concept for this book while editing an Agatha Christie partwork—which entailed his reading Christie's *And Then There Were None* for the first time. During discussions with editor Justin Richards, Cole's book got named *Ten Little Aliens*. Cole later turned in the storyline with the title *A Coherent Hell*, but BBC range editor Ben Dunn bemoaned the title change, feeling *Ten Little Aliens* was too good to not run with.

DYING IN THE SUN

By Jon de Burgh Miller

Release Date: October 2001
Order: BBC Past Doctor Adventure #47

TARDIS CREW The second Doctor, Ben Jackson and Polly.

TRAVEL LOG Los Angeles, October 12, 1947.

STORY SUMMARY In Los Angeles, 1947, the Doctor attempts to see an old friend, movie producer Harold Reitman, only to find Reitman was recently murdered at his home. Sorrowful, the Doctor looks into his friend's death, learning details about the case from police Captain Charles Wallis.

Meanwhile, a budding, independent studio named Star Light Pictures makes ready to debut its intended masterpiece, *Dying in the Sun*. As part of his investigation, the Doctor meets Star Light movie producer Leonard De Sande, who casually invites him to a private *Dying in the Sun* screening. The Doctor labels the film mediocre, then grows disturbed by the abnormally high, almost mesmeric praise it wins from the audience.

Curious, the Doctor snatches a *Dying in the Sun* film reel, finding it tainted with alien creatures that affect human perception, leaving the viewer open to telepathic suggestion. In time, the Doctor identifies the creatures as "Selyoids," a race of creatures who long ago fled their homeworld's destruction, only to get frozen into dormancy on Earth. While shooting footage in Alaska, De Sande revived some Selyoids—who can inhabit liquids such as blood or movie film chemicals. The Selyoids merged with De Sande, and "convinced" him to help them acquire other hosts.

The Doctor deems the Selyoids reasonably benevolent, but realizes De Sande hopes to use their emotion-swaying power to create a peaceful world order. In short, De Sande plans to mentally enthrall the *Dying in the Sun* viewers, then make them ingest Selyoids in liquid form. If successful, millions of people will become Selyoid hosts under De Sande's sway, spreading the Selyoid infection. On a more personal level, the Doctor deduces Reitman was murdered so the Los Angeles charity FOCAL, a front for De Sande's operations, would inherit his estate.

De Sande marches ahead full steam, debuting *Dying in the Sun* to the public. Enthralled Los Angeles moviegoers drink Selyoid-laden liquid as planned, but the de facto Selyoid leader learns to better appreciate humanity, its emotions and independence. The Selyoid ranks fall into disarray, compelling De Sande to regain control by absorbing even more Selyoids into his own body.

Forced to start anew, the Selyoid-loaded De Sande flees aboard a distribution plane loaded with *Dying in the Sun* reels. The Doctor cobbles together a movie projector and focusing crystal, casting horrific images onto the departing plane. De Sande's pilot loses control and crashes, causing an explosion that kills De Sande and disperses the Selyoids in his body over Los Angeles. The other Selyoids die off without De Sande's influence, but the Doctor realizes the dissipated Selyoids will keep emotions in Los Angeles running high for decades to come.

SEX AND SPIRITS Polly dines with MGA Studios producer Leon Zane, but discovers he wants a casting couch session and storms out. She's smitten with Selyoid-induced celebrity Caleb Rochefort, who's happily attached [and winds up dead].

Later, Polly downs three drinks—including a Flaming Hero—in a half-hour at a Regent Hotel bar. She later switches to rum and Coke.

De Sande absorbs massive amounts of Selyoids by kissing everyone present. Even the men.

ASS-WHUPPINGS Years ago, Robert Chate's father blackmailed Wallis, who in turn killed Robert's parents in a gas explosion. Police Captain Charles Wallis guiltily adopted young Chate, then married a woman with no interest in baggage and ejected Chate from the house.

Chate later becomes a drug dealer, and Wallis frames him for Reitman's murder, leading to a confused shoot-out at LA's Silent Gold restaurant [the *LA Times* dubs it one of the biggest police blunders of 1947]. Several customers get shot, including Selyoid-tainted celebrity Caleb Rochefort. Eventually, Wallis falls to his death after a rooftop struggle with Chate.

Polly herself gets infected with a Selyoid, leading to Rochefort handing her a gun to shoot the nosy Doctor. Mentally resisting the Selyoids' influence, Polly shoots Rochefort instead—marking the first time that she's killed someone, albeit under unusual circumstances.

Some Selyoids solidify themselves as movie-protected Roman legionnaires and horse-mounted Klansmen, leading to a brawl with the LAPD.

The Doctor's final gambit kills De Sande, his

This book is not endorsed by the BBC. Doctor Who and TARDIS are trademarks of the BBC.

17

pilot and assorted Selyoids. A wealth of Selyoids, including the one in Polly, die from shock.

CHARACTER DEVELOPMENT

• *The Doctor:* The Doctor first met Harold Reitman during a visit to England in the 1920s, but they weren't very close.

The Doctor prefers reading books to watching movies. He likes Danish pastry and roses. The Selyoid empathic influence doesn't affect him. He hasn't been to America in some time.

• *Ben Jackson:* Ben's in his mid-20s. He's seen *Jason and the Argonauts*.

• *Polly Wright:* Polly loves movies. Her mother especially enjoyed *The Sword of Damocles*, directed by De Sande.

ALIEN RACES *The Selyoids:* Selyoids are vastly intelligent, but get bored easily, wishing to experience life through someone else's eyes. They can live in humans by blending personalities with their hosts. Selyoids can enhance their hosts' personality traits, empathically making them act and look like celebrities. Selyoid-infected people gain a good deal of empathy, and can sense emotional shifts in others. They also gain an enhanced healing factor, though it can't save them from major gunshot wounds or severe falls.

The Selyoids prefer to animate corpses, through which they retain their true personalities. Liquid Selyoids can duplicate themselves a million times over while retaining a single consciousness.

Using a special projector crystal, Selyoids merged with film emulsion can mentally enhance a tepid motion picture to blockbuster proportions. The audience gets caught in a psionic feedback loop, convinced the motion picture's got a lavish amount of special effects, when it's actually quite ordinary. Their belief only strengthens the Selyoids' telepathic hold.

Given enough of a psionic charge, film-projected Selyoids can manifest themselves as solidified movie characters such as Roman soldiers. The transition to solid matter essentially wipes the Selyoid intelligence, leaving them as drones. Too much light or darkness ruins this effect, because the audience can't see the projections and stops believing in them.

Liquid Selyoids can also coat billboards, mentally nudging people to see whatever they're advertising.

STUFF YOU NEED *Dying in the Sun:* Directed by De Sande, *Dying in the Sun* concerns a man who keeps glimpsing terrifying monsters. The man singularly witnesses the monsters killing people, but nobody believes his wild claims. After ending his romantic relationship, the man confronts one of the monsters. The monster chases the man down a city street, with the entire scene melting away into a fire-riddled vision of hell. The man discovers he committed the murders himself, concluding that true monsters come from within. He returns from hell to begin life anew in Los Angeles.

ORGANIZATIONS *Star Light Pictures:* Budding studio that uses the Selyoids' character-enhancing traits to resurrect the careers of washed-up celebrities. Much of Star Light functions as a legitimate company, with little clue they owe their success to the Selyoids. James Hensleigh serves as Star Light head of distribution.

• *FOCAL (a.k.a. Friends of the Community of Los Angeles):* Supposedly a charity to help actors going through hard times, De Sande usurped it to further his agenda with the Selyoids. Using FOCAL, De Sande promoted a philosophical practice called "Way of Light," a quiet means of indoctrinating people to the Selyoids' influence. "Way of Light" conducts itself like a quasi-religious order, although most of the members simply view it as a chance to network.

With De Sande and Wallis' deaths, control of FOCAL's assets passed to Chate. He pledged to make it a truly charitable organization, sans secret agenda.

HISTORY Some time ago, the Selyoid homeworld plunged into darkness. Many Selyoids, existing as magnificent beings of light, died out. Others, calling themselves "the Children," transferred themselves to a rock on course for Earth. They eventually reached our world and condensed into rain, but got frozen in Alaska.

• FOCAL was founded in the 1890s.

• De Sande unearthed the Selyoids three years ago in Alaska, while filming *The Cold Blooded*. He coined the term "Selyoids" as a joke.

• Thanks to the Selyoids' influence, Star Light Pictures became one of the fastest-growing studios in Hollywood. They contracted top celebrities such as *A Piece of Sunset* star Maria Coleman, whose career later flopped with *Cowgirls Abroad*, and the late Caleb Rochefort. After De Sande's death, the studio presumably collapsed.

• Nearly all Selyoids on Earth died with De Sande, but at least one lived on benevolently inside police detective William Fletcher.

• The dispersed Selyoids ramped up emotions in Los Angeles such as ambition, hysteria, selfishness and compassion for decades to come, perhaps permanently.

AT THE END OF THE DAY Full of good intentions, attempting to present a Troughton tale that would've never been done on TV. But really, *Dying in the Sun* just doesn't take well to its setting, with not enough intrigue for a crime novel, and insufficient high-concept ideas for a science-fiction book. Landing somewhere between those two extremes, the book's slow to action and realization—much like a tour guide abruptly halting his group to go, "Look at this…"—and finally just leaves you cold.

DID YOU KNOW?

• De Miller originally pitched *Dying in the Sun* as part of the eighth Doctor "Earth Arc" saga, but editor Justin Richards instead favored *Endgame*, which occurs in roughly the same time period. However, Richards liked some ideas from the story, causing de Miller to re-draft it as a seventh Doctor/Ace story. Finally, Richards suggested that Miller's themes favored the second Doctor, Ben and Polly, so the outline again underwent substantial revision.

• After a Jade Pagoda discussion board member suggested it was impossible to write a Past Doctor Adventure without continuity references, Miller vowed to write a PDA where the TARDIS isn't even mentioned. Indeed, this book never states that the Doctor, Ben and Polly are time travelers.

• Miller nicked the title from a lyric in *Cannon Fodder*, the title song to the 1993 Amiga computer game.

• Thanks to the miracle of www.imdb.com, Miller named every character in *Dying in the Sun* after an actual actor, director and crewmember in 1947 Hollywood.

RAGS

By Mick Lewis

Release Date: March 2001
Order: BBC Past Doctor Adventure #40

TARDIS CREW The third Doctor, Jo Grant and UNIT.

TRAVEL LOG Chiefly Dartmoor, Cirbury, Bristol, Princetown and Stonehenge, England, May 8, circa mid-1970s. [Dating the UNIT years has never been precise, although *Rags* takes place with an election "drawing near." As *Rags* notably falls on May 8, that makes 1974 the immediate suspect, as elections were held on October 10 of that year. The only other 1970s British elections occurred on June 18, 1970 (less likely, given *Rags* clearly falls in Season 8 or 9) and May 3, 1979 (impossible, given *Rags*' dating as May 8).]

CHRONOLOGY Roughly between "Colony in Space" and "The Three Doctors." [The Doctor's stuck on Earth, but the Brigadier mentions his playing truant, probably alluding to "Colony in Space."]

STORY SUMMARY In Dartmoor, England, a B-level punk band pulls over to answer the call of nature, stopping directly next to some ancient standing stones. A group of drunken, upper class Exeter students crash into the band's vehicle, leading to a lethal brawl. Amid the chaos, a psionic force trapped within the standing stones stirs to life, telepathically feeding on the class violence. Before long, the combatants kill each other off, providing enough bloodshed to free the psionic force entirely.

Soon after, the psionic force re-animates the band members' bodies as zombie mummers, compelling them to travel throughout the country on the seedy "Unwashed and Unforgiving" tour. At each stop, the undead mummers telepathically incites bloody class warfare, yet psionically keeps the slaughter from attracting too much notice.

Meanwhile, at UNIT Headquarters, the TARDIS detects an anomalous energy reading from Dartmoor, prompting the Doctor and Jo Grant to investigate. The Doctor fails to witness the mummer band in action but gets an uneasy feeling about them, cautiously summoning reinforcements from UNIT. The Doctor leaves Jo to monitor the band's activities, then continues tracking the anomalous energy signature.

Locating a secondary energy trace in Cirbury, the Doctor hears local legends regarding a malevolent entity named "the Ragman." The Doctor learns that the Ragman briefly flared to life and wreaked havoc in the 17th century Cirbury, until the townsfolk re-imprisoned it in some standing stones, later relocating the rocks to Dartmoor. With regret, the Doctor acknowledges the Ragman's return to life, finding the creature nestled in a cattle truck.

The Doctor enters the cattle truck to confront the Ragman, but the fiend batters him with a telepathic assault. In resisting, the Doctor experiences visions depicting the Ragman as an alien psionic force, born in the depths of space. The Ragman long ago traveled to the Sol System in a meteoroid, attracted to Earth's ley lines of power. In 17th century Cirbury, it briefly awakened and acclimated to feed on violence created by class warfare (*see*

History). Now, if left unchecked, the Ragman's mummer band will telepathically stimulate class warfare, murder and eventually total anarchy throughout England, then the world.

On Gallifrey, the Time Lords grow worried that the nihilistic Ragman could eventually threaten their ordered society. Acting swiftly, the Time Lords telepathically help the Doctor snap the Ragman's psionic hold. The Doctor staggers out of the cattle truck, even as the Ragman's mummers perform at Stonehenge, inciting all-out warfare between UNIT forces and the local townsfolk.

As events reach a fevered pitch, the Ragman summons journalist Charmagne Peters and deadbeat Kane Sawyer—two of its direct descendants, sired from its brief freedom in 17th century Cirbury. The Doctor convinces Charmagne to acknowledge the Ragman's true aspect, fracturing the Ragman's mesmeric hold over the crowd.

The mob turns against the mummers, even as Kane—blaming the Ragman for a lifetime of lost opportunities—body-tackles the fiend against the standing stones that formerly imprisoned it. The standing stones absorb both the Ragman and Kane, trapping them within for all eternity. The mummers die off without the Ragman's power, allowing the assembled combatants to finally end the violence.

SEX AND SPIRITS   A mummer-entranced Jo Grant smokes a joint, then wonders what she'd look like with short spiky hair and fishnets. She also downs some booze. She recalls flirting with Mike Yates, but here thinks he's a bit wet [possibly the mummers' influence talking]. A Chinese girl named Sin, impulsively caught in the moment, kisses Jo. Afterward, an enthralled Jo wants to smooch her again.

UNIT Corporal Hannah Robinson, under the mummers' sway, gets horny for Sergeant Benton.

Far more innocently, the Doctor drinks Newcastle Brown Ale. He knows a pub in Princetown, the Devil's Elbow, which serves good breakfast.

ASS-WHUPPINGS   Setting aside the fairly mundane killings [save for a band member wiping a bloody sword on his tuxedo] that spark the Ragman's return, the undead mummers motivate the crowd to kill authority figures. To wit, civilians murder policemen with shovels, stab them with garden shears, or simply smash their heads in.

Additionally, the mummers compel a landlord to snap an animal leg trap around his tenant's neck. A resident bludgeons his wife to death with a golf club, then dismembers his teenage daughter. There are instances of suicide, beheadings, a

throat getting slashed with a rusty machete, ribs getting kicked in and eyes gouged out. There's also a dismemberment and two instances of people getting impaled on a pitchfork.

During the final UNIT brawl, a private gets skewered with a spiked codpiece. Gunshots take out privates Hooper, Whitcombe and an unnamed colleague. Private Councell gets strangled. Corporal Hannah Robinson snaps a hippie's neck, but dies, stabbed while choking the mummers' chief roadie.

The Doctor suffers horribly under the Ragman's telepathic assault, made to witness a dais of rotting human bodies, surrounded by a moat of blood. He also envisions Jo's decapitated head, and worst of all, an image of his granddaughter Susan, which makes him feel shamed for abandoning her ("The Dalek Invasion of Earth"). She's also seen carrying her old, diseased husband David (a conceit, since he actually dies young in *Legacy of the Daleks*).

The Ragman makes the Doctor see images of his former companions as tattered, bloodthirsty fiends. Zoe in particular dances wild and naked.

Mike Yates cracks a hostile punk's head against an obelisk. Another attacker smashes a bottle of Newcastle Brown across his head. Yates also endures a car wreck, getting criss-crossed with glass, then bowled over while fleeing from the exploding vehicle. Later, he takes out a zombie by unloading a gun into its mouth. He also takes a gunshot wound in the shoulder. For a finale, he grenades the mummers, but only singes the singer and bass player.

The Ragman threshes some mob members like wheat. Kane finally puts paid to the whole adventure, trapping himself and the Ragman inside the standing stones for eternity.

If you haven't guessed, *Rags* perhaps wins for the most methods of death in a "Who" novel. We didn't count, but it's surely high on the list.

TV TIE-INS   The Doctor's still fiddling with the TARDIS dematerialization circuit, examining it with twin alloy cones cannibalized from the guts of the TARDIS console (a good chunk of Seasons 8 and 9).

NOVEL TIE-INS   Mike Yates has read the works of *The Jungle Book* author Rudyard Kipling (*Evolution*).

CHARACTER DEVELOPMENT
• *The Doctor:* He's dined at some of the Universe's most exotic restaurants. He finds being in the middle of nowhere a rewarding experience.
• *Jo Grant:* She's excited by, but nervous about,

the seedy feelings the mummers awaken in her. Jo never really adjusted to punk, deeming it too violent and nihilistic.

• *Brigadier Lethbridge-Stewart:* The violence in *Rags* makes him consider, for the first time in his life, his motives for becoming a soldier.

• *The Brigadier and Sgt. Benton:* The Brigadier wonders if Benton's getting too soft with his troopers—and Benton knows it.

• *Mike Yates:* He's pretty conspicuous as an undercover agent on the concert tour, badly pretending to smoke.

• *The Ragman (a.k.a. The Great Leveller, The Great Pretender):* The Ragman's core essence manifests itself as a dead-looking gaunt figure, dressed in tatters, with blank eyes, a crooked nose and a protruding chin. He smells like blood, hay and garbage. Worms compose his hair. He's a bizarre mismatch of British accents and period talk, having witnessed various eras of history from his rocky prison.

The Ragman's immeasurably psionic, able to read the Doctor's memories. He's also telekinetic, but chiefly exerts this power by re-animating the mummers.

The Ragman's humanoid form affords him some protection, but also limits his psionic influence. He could, given sufficient death trauma, psionically blanket the entire globe with his influence, but not without reverting to his true, amorphic state.

It's suggested the Ragman's slightly afraid of Kane and Charmagne, probably because, as his descendants, they have some natural resistance to his influence.

Conspicuously, *Rags* makes no mention of how the Doctor disposes of the Ragman's standing stones after this story.

• *Kane Sawyer:* He's about 31, and a lout.

• *Charmagne Peters:* Journalist for the *Plymouth Chronicle*. Five years ago, she visited Romania as a student and witnessed its sewer children. Charmagne's father died while she was young.

ALIEN RACES *The Time Lords:* They project an image of the TARDIS' exterior to snap the Doctor back to sanity, speaking with him through its outside telephone.

STUFF YOU NEED *The Ragman's Cattle Truck:* The interior's actually an internal vortex shaped by the Ragman's essence. There are no walls or floor inside the truck, merely an endless dreary tract of black weeds. There's a slight breeze with a sick flavor, described as a decomposing lover's kiss.

• *The Ragged Fellow / The Ragged Staff:* An assortment of unrelated pubs, located in Bristol, Bath and other cities. The name perhaps hails from some subliminal influence on the Ragman's part, or [more likely] it's just coincidental.

ORGANIZATIONS *The Mummers:* The bodies of a modern-day punk band, telekinetically molded to resemble some 17th century mummers who were executed after the Ragman's original rampage (*see History*). They're a hodgepodge of flesh and bone, immune to gunshot wounds.

The mummers' actual performance is secondary to their psionic influence, so their lyrics mostly entail, "Scum, scum, scum…", and other nonsensical stuff.

PHENOMENA *Earth's Ley Lines:* Run under Cirbury and Stonehenge, among other places

HISTORY Long ago, the Ragman was born at the other end of the Universe, in a region littered with dead stars and the dust of forgotten worlds. It was conceived within a rock womb, spinning through the radiation horizon of a black hole without rhyme or reason. Eventually, it psionically detected energy pulsing through Earth's ley lines, and began a long, arduous journey through space.

• Primitive man witnessed the Ragman's rocky fall to Earth, subconsciously compelled to erect a field of stones and worship it. The primitives erroneously believed the meteor was born of Earth, got lost and had somehow returned.

• The ley lines under the Ragman's rocky prison nurtured the creature, but it remained dormant. The English town of Cirbury was founded near the standing stones, although a class conflict in the 17th century facilitated its awakening. In short, the local magistrate's son and the mayor's daughter, Emily Sawyer, had sex by the standing stones. Afterward, a destitute mummer asked the magistrate's son for coins, annoying him to the point that he cracked the mummer's skull open against the stones.

The class-based violence molded the Ragman's ego and appetites, making it flare to life. It possessed the dead mummer's body, then ripped the magistrate's son apart and violated Emily. The Ragman wreaked havoc, but the Cirbury townsfolk eventually drove it back into the stones. The magistrate wrongly blamed the dead mummer's four colleagues for the chaos, authorizing the townsfolk to execute them against the standing stones [which only amplified the Ragman's lust for class warfare and bloodshed]. Afterward, the townsfolk disposed of the stones at Dartmoor.

• Emily Sawyer's assault left her pregnant. Her father abandoned her, but the church raised her child. Emily herself died in poverty, but her child later sired the bloodline that produced Kane Sawyer and Charmagne Peters.

• The British government shushed up the UNIT/civilian slaughter at Stonehenge, but Heaven only knows how.

AT THE END OF THE DAY   While we normally applaud books that push the envelope, *Rags* unwisely crosses a certain line of grossness that voids the experiment. Basically, it sullies the wholesome Pertwee era of "Doctor Who" for no good reason, then acts perplexed as to why readers would fail to appreciate a book where the characters—albeit often against their will—eat slugs, vomit maggots, behead one another, kill their fellows with any handy sharp instrument, sing "scum, scum, scum" and sleep in their own offal. [You think we jest—verily, we do not.] For all that, we cannot fault the richness of Lewis' prose—but for actual content, *Rags* has nothing to say other than "Everything is shit," existing only to wallow in its own gore. And that's simply unacceptable.

NIGHTDREAMERS

By Tom Arden

> **Release Date:** *May 2002*
> **Order:** *Telos "Doctor Who" Novella #3*

TARDIS CREW   The third Doctor and Jo Grant.

TRAVEL LOG   Forest moon of Verd, orbiting planet Galaxis Bright, time unknown but during "Perihelion Night."

CHRONOLOGY   Shortly after "Planet of the Daleks." [Jo says she could "use a good holiday" after her adventure on Spiridon.] *Nightdreamers* might well take place immediately after "Planet of the Daleks," but *Catastrophea* already claimed that slot.

STORY SUMMARY   On the planet Galaxis Bright, Emperor Exis Umane quarrels with his brother-in-law, Duke Altero, regarding a proposal to resume trade with the neighboring, sinister Galaxis Dark. Altero decries the trade agreement, unwilling to trust the Darklings, but the Emperor in response exiles Altero and his servants to the forest moon of Verd. Altero's followers settle down

there in a castle-shaped spaceship, but in time, a mesmeric force called "the Nightdreamer King" turns several of them into entranced thralls named "Nightdreamers."

Meanwhile, the Doctor and Jo attempt to return to Earth, only to find Verd's abnormally high gravity field pulling the TARDIS off course. On Verd, the Doctor resists the Nightdreamer King's mental sway, studying the moon's deviant gravitational effect. Eventually, the Doctor deduces that Verd's ultra-powerful gravity stems from a Norebo Worm, a legendary psychevore that has taken root within the moon. Intensely psionic, the Norebo Worm—the true identity of the "Nightdreamer King"—has been subsisting on the dreams of Altero and his supporters.

Suddenly, a warship from Galaxis Dark arrives on Verd, coveting the moon's "gravity rocks"—actually flecks of the Norebo Worm's skin—as a cheap source of artificial gravity. The Emperor's son Tonio uses a powerful Vorgon ray, fitted to his spaceship, to eradicate the Darklings. The Norebo Worm feasts on the resultant explosion, absorbing a massive amount of energy. The Nightdreamers return to normal, even as the Doctor—sensing the Worm about to undergo metamorphosis—launches the Duke's spaceship/castle away from Verd.

Moments later, the Norebo Worm matures into a trans-dimensional winged creature and leaves for parts unknown. The Emperor allows the exiled Duke to return home, conceding the Darklings cannot be trusted. After turning down the Emperor's offer of becoming court adviser, the Doctor sets out for Earth with Jo.

SEX AND SPIRITS   Much of *Nightdreamers* concerns itself with the romance between Duke Altero's daughter Ria and the Emperor's son Tonio. The two become lovers, but Altero insists that Ria marry Esnic, the captain of the guard.

In what's emulative of Shakespeare's "A Midsummer Night's Dream," Ria, Tonio and Jo encounter some Nightdreamers and get mentally lulled to sleep. Soon after, Nightdreamer puck Sly squeezes juice from an Atinati flower on Ria and Tonio's eyelids, making them fall in love with the first person they see. Tonio starts lusting for Jo while Ria becomes enamored with Peterkin, a performer wearing an orange, bulbous, "monstrous" costume head. Jo seems a bit taken with Tonio of her own volition, but restrains herself.

The spell eventually wears off, with Ria marrying Tonio after the revelation that Esnic's a Darkling agent. Jo gives Tonio a lingering glance as she enters the TARDIS to leave.

ASS-WHUPPINGS The Doctor endures two psionic attacks from the Norebo Worm. Peterkin, the play actor in a monstrous costume, gets a lucky shot and stuns the Doctor with a phaser.

Initial mental contact with the Norebo Worm knocks Jo cold. The Nightdreamers make Jo swoon, *swoon* unconscious. The Norebo Worm channels energy through Esnic's eyes and nails the Doctor. The worm also "hatches" out of Verd, destroying it, then goes off into parts unknown.

TV TIE-INS Jo was indeed tempted to leave the Doctor for a new life with Latep ("Planet of the Daleks"). The Doctor strangely doesn't recognize a recorder left lying about the TARDIS, even though his second incarnation recently used it in "The Three Doctors" [and much before, for that matter].

CHARACTER DEVELOPMENT

• *The Doctor:* He hasn't swum in a low-gravity zone for years. He considered Norebo Worms the stuff of myth.

• *Lady Ria:* She grew up on Verd, suggesting her father's been exiled there for some time.

• *Emperor Exis Umane (a.k.a. Munex Axis):* He masqueraded on Verd as one of Altero's butlers, watching for any potential to reconcile with him. Endowed with scientific know-how, the Emperor developed the powerful Vorgon ray for use against Galaxis Dark and fitted it to his son's Lightship.

• *The Nightdreamer King (a.k.a. the Norebo Worm):* Supposedly a granter of wishes, but actually a fanciful identity for the Norebo Worm. It acknowledges the Doctor as a Time Lord.

• *Sly (a.k.a. Green Sly):* Special minion of "the Nightdreamer King," a little man in green who channels the Worm's power to entrance others and cause mischief. Sly can become invisible.

ALIEN RACES *Norebo Worms:* Look serpentine and monstrous in their larvae form. The worms develop enormous gravity fields to better snare their prey [and presumably to propel them through space]. Norebo Worms are intensely psionic, and can communicate through the more entranced of their victims.

The Norebo Worm matures into a winged, multi-colored creature seemingly clad in flashing jewels. Innumerable, translucent tentacles—*tentacles*, people—hang beneath it. Parts of the creature vanish as if slipping into another dimension.

• *The Darklings:* They have an empire in all but name, with a fair amount of economic power. They possess ways of exploiting gravity rocks.

• *Nightdreamers:* Persons under the Norebo Worm's sway, able to mentally lull others to sleep.

ALIEN PLANETS *Galaxis Bright:* Not exactly the haven it sounds, economically inferior to its sister planet, Galaxis Dark. There's talk of insurrection against the Emperor.

• *Verd:* Smaller than Earth's moon, and largely covered by dense vegetation. Thanks to the Norebo Worm, parts of Verd have Earth-like gravity.

STUFF YOU NEED *The Tragical and Comical History of Boreas and Thamia or The Complications of Love:* A Galaxis Bright play, concerning a beautiful young princess named Mazy Grace, imprisoned by her father behind a high wall. She eventually winds up with a prince, who spends a time magically transformed into a mouse. [Author's Note: Obviously, this reflects the Pyramus/Thisbe play from *A Midsummer Night's Dream.*]

SHIPS *Altero's Castle:* Actually a "sanctum ship," used by colonists in this quadrant of the galaxy.

PHENOMENA *Cosmic Rays:* 8,005,366 different types of cosmic rays exist.

HISTORY The Norebo Worm infested Verd centuries ago.

• Duke Altero and Emperor Exis Umane were childhood friends. Altero married the Emperor's sister, but the two friends quarreled over Galaxis Bright, leading to Altero's exile.

AT THE END OF THE DAY Little more than a travesty, *Nightdreamers* sounds like it's written by someone who remembers watching "Doctor Who" decades ago, but couldn't explain for spit what made the series *work.* The *Midsummer Night's Dream* element adds nothing—repeat, nothing—to the proceedings, devolving parts of the book into a Harlequin romance novel (a fawning Ria: "But that was before Tonio—Tonio, Tonio!"). Overall, a book that made our collective stomachs churn, dripping with dialogue that sounds like an eight year old wrote it. [If you think we jest, try reading it aloud.]

DID YOU KNOW?

• *Nightdreamers* was originally called *The Gravity Moon.*

• Arden's five-book fantasy epic *The Orokon* is about a quest for some crystals of power, doubly inspired by "The Key to Time" storyarc (Season 16) and "The Seven Keys to Doomsday" stageplay.

• The Norebo Worm and a magical flower—the Atinati weed—take their names from anagrams of

"Oberon" and "Titania," the quarreling faerie king and queen in the Shakespeare's *A Midsummer Night's Dream*.

• Arden's favorite in-joke in *Nightdreamers*: A scene where the Doctor hides behind a sofa.

AMORALITY TALE

By David Bishop

Release Date: April 2002
Order: BBC Past Doctor Adventure #52

TARDIS CREW The third Doctor and Sarah Jane Smith.

TRAVEL LOG London, December 3 to 8, 1952.

CHRONOLOGY Between "The Monster of Peladon" and "Planet of the Spiders."

STORY SUMMARY While researching an article, Sarah Jane investigates the mysterious smog that killed thousands of Londoners in December, 1952. Sarah's eyes bulge out when, during the course of her research, she discovers an unpublished 1952 photograph of the Doctor shaking hands with gangster Tommy Ramsey. The Doctor examines the photo, taken outside the ruins of St. Luke's Church in London's East End, but fails to recognize it. He does, however, note a "warpshadow"—a residual temporal effect—rippling in the picture of the church's remains.

The Doctor stresses to Sarah that the London die-off is historically unavoidable. Regardless, he advises they investigate the event, hoping to potentially avert a greater tragedy. Accordingly, the Doctor and Sarah TARDIS-travel to 1952, arriving two weeks before the smog appears so they can better melt into the community. The Doctor sets up shop as a watchmaker, while Sarah starts waitressing at the Red Room restaurant—a illegal gaming facility owned by Ramsey.

Sarah worms her way into Ramsey's confidence, monitoring a growing conflict between his mobsters and the rival Callum gang. Hostilities between the two groups quickly increase, leading to a street brawl in which Ramsey severs Callum's left arm with a sword. Callum shrugs off the injury, revealing himself as an alien Xhinn. Bristling with life energy, Callum projects energy bolts that atomize several gangsters.

The surviving mobsters flee, and the Doctor later identifies the Xhinn as a race of alien conquerors. Meanwhile, in their hidden scoutship, a

Xhinn triumvirate punishes Callum for prematurely revealing their presence on Earth. The Xhinn re-absorb Callum's life energy, killing him, then push forward their time table. In short order, the Xhinn activate a device that starts creating a lethal fog in London, hoping to quell Earth resistance to a full-blown Xhinn invasion.

Running out of options, the Doctor decides that eliminating the scouting party might convince the Xhinn warfleet to avoid Earth. He constructs a forbidden time bomb, engineered to accelerate time thousands of years per second. The Doctor finds the Xhinn scoutship hidden under St. Luke's Church and, after a tremendous struggle, detonates the temporal warhead. Just in time, the Doctor flees St. Luke's, even as the device eradicates the church and the Xhinn.

Afterward, the Doctor and Ramsey shake hands in front of the gutted church, allowing a passing *Bethnal Green News* reporter to photograph the moment and fulfill history. Mourning the thousands of Londoners who died from the Xhinn fog, the Doctor and Sarah depart for home.

MEMORABLE MOMENTS Gangsters torch the Doctor's watchmaker shop, *Fixing Time*, then paint over its sign until only "Fixed" is visible. Callum's severed arm screams as Tommy's allies toss it into a fire—a rare instance, even for a science-fiction book, of an arm screaming.

Violence-prone Tommy draws back a fist to bash Sarah at one point, but her refusal to flinch makes him back down. Later, Sarah Jane hugs gangster Arthur Brick when the Xhinn smoke kills his pet pigeons.

SEX AND SPIRITS Sarah finds Tommy an infectious personality, and tries to ignore his occupation as a gangster. Tommy's associates mistake them for lovers, but nothing happens beyond Tommy spying a nightgown-clad Sarah and offhandedly commenting, "Nice nightie." Sarah's potential attraction for Tommy further dissipates with each display of violence.

Tommy's lieutenant, Jack Cooper, killed Tommy's last girlfriend on his behalf. Cooper claims dibs on Sarah if anything happens to Tommy, but she knees him in the groin. Tommy defends Sarah against abuse from his lackeys.

In 1952, Sarah stays at a boarding house where the landlord's husband keeps catching her bathing "by accident." [A fed-up Sarah starts bathing in the TARDIS].

ASS-WHUPPINGS When the Doctor refuses to pay protection money for his watchmaker shop,

Fixing Time, Tommy's lackeys torch the joint.

Tommy slices off Callum's arm with a sword, but an unaffected Callum in turn slaughters lots of mobsters. The Xhinn later kill Callum for revealing their presence.

The Xhinn cloud has less effect on Gallifreyans than humans, but still makes the Doctor ill. A Xhinn teleportation system also gives the Doctor the dry heaves.

The Doctor disarms rival gangster Bob Valentine to save Tommy's life, but Tommy—capitalizing on the moment—upsets the Doctor by plugging Valentine in the head.

As part of the Xhinn's offensive against Earth, Father Xavier Simmons—unknowingly a Xhinn himself (*see Alien Races*)—founds a bread-making business named *Bread of Life*. Against his will, Simmons laces his bread products with a psychotropic drug, leaving his customers susceptible to the Xhinn's telepathic prompting. After a certain point, the drug kills the brain of anyone who eats it, but animates their bodies as a zombies.

Many East End policemen fall prey to this, creating a zombie workforce which engineers a conveyor belt and death chamber for the Xhinn. Amid the smog, the zombies round up East End residents and process them, via the conveyor belt, into a pre-packaged food supply for the Xhinn. Something like the last third of *Amorality Tale* features battles between Tommy's mobsters and the undead policemen. Tommy's second Jack Cooper deems everything lost, sets himself afire, and jumps a zombie policeman.

Arthur Brick, one of Tommy's more compassionate operatives, dies taking a Xhinn energy bolt meant for Sarah Jane. Rather simplistically, the Doctor eradicates the Xhinn with a time bomb.

TV TIE-INS Sarah's Aunt Lavinia ("The Time Warrior") wore pink flannelettes when Sarah stayed with her on summer holidays. The Doctor needs little sleep, but dozes off as if to suggest his body's getting old (foreshadowing his regeneration in "Planet of the Spiders").

CHARACTER DEVELOPMENT
• *The Doctor:* The Doctor claims he's a doctor "of science, mostly." He's heard of the Xhinn, but hoped to avoid encountering them. He can skip eating for days.

Talking out loud helps shield the Doctor's thoughts from telepathic intrusion. The Doctor once met military strategist Pyrrho. If caught in the time bomb's blast radius, the Doctor would burn through his remaining regenerations in a second.

• *Sarah Jane Smith:* Sarah's been a city dweller all her life. 1952 London seems shockingly quiet compared to her day. She doesn't take to the era's sexist and racist views. Sarah hates stiletto shoes. She gets slightly disoriented every time she enters the TARDIS, since her senses rebel upon experiencing its internal dimension. She once tried exploring the TARDIS' interior in detail, but got confused.

She likes her vegetables a bit undercooked. She reveals her existence as a time traveler to Tommy.

• *Tommy Ramsey:* Tommy was stationed in Egypt during World War II, and spent a stretch in military prison for violent behavior. Tommy's recently released after a six-month stay in Wandsworth Prison. He should have gotten the chair for murder, but his boys systematically eliminated witnesses and paid off the jury.

Tommy's gang chiefly controls illegal activities in Old Street, Shoreditch, Spitalfields Market, and even as far as Finsbury and Bethnal Green.

He lives at 15 Tabernacle Street in London with his mother Vera. His father Herbert died while fighting in World War I, never knowing his wife was pregnant.

Tommy has receding brown hair. He smokes to calm his nerves. He acknowledges his fear, but refuses to let it rule him.

• *The TARDIS:* The Doctor's installed a new directional finder, increasing [for now] the Ship's accuracy.

ALIEN RACES *Xhinn:* The Xhinn have dominated thousands of worlds. Like most alien conquerors, the Xhinn subjugate or exterminate a planet's natives, then plunder its natural resources to fuel further colonization and even more plundering. They're very methodical, sending scout missions to a potential target years before bringing an invasion fleet to bear. Primarily designed for pre-emptive strikes, the scouts are ill-prepared to hold an entire city, let alone a planet.

Xhinn are humanoid, but have glowing tendrils instead of hair, and a hundred small eyes on their heads. They have no mouths, speaking telepathically. They cannot telepathically invade waking minds, but can scan sleeping ones, even those of Time Lords.

They never travel alone. They think they're acting as missionaries, bringing "salvation" to the lesser species, when they're really just cutthroats and murderers. Xhinn can live for a thousand years, cannibalizing energy from other Xhinn as they die.

Xhinn possess teleportation technology. They deem the Time Lords as impotent.

The Xhinn can infuse humans with their life energy, killing them and transplanting their memories into human-looking Xhinn. Such sleeper agents have no knowledge of their service to the Xhinn. They have an immense healing factor. They can regrow severed limbs, which remain animated even when cut off.

The agents can let their Xhinn aspect become dominant, then use their Xhinn energy for attack and defense. In such states, they look Xhinn rather than human. They can also project enough heat to melt incoming bullets. The sleeper agents are particularly vulnerable to fire.

STUFF YOU NEED *The Doctor's Time Bomb:* It contravenes all known weapons treaties.

PLACES TO GO *"Fixing Time":* The Doctor's watchkeeper shop in the East End, featuring a front parlor with dozens of timepieces. The TARDIS is parked on Whitecross Lane, just around the corner.

POSSIBLE HISTORY According to legend, the Xhinn appeared five million years before mankind and rebelled against their maker. For their pride, they were banished into our Universe.

HISTORY In 1946, US army officer Xavier Simmons started illegally selling army surplus to London's gangsters. Simmons killed one of his customers on the steps of St. Luke's, but immediately afterward encountered the Xhinn scouts, who murdered him and grafted his memories into a Xhinn sleeper agent. Unaware of his Xhinn aspect, the new Simmons repented his original self's crimes and became pastor of St. Luke's. He also founded *Bread of Life*, inadvertently furthering the Xhinn cause (*see Ass-Whuppings*). Simmons eventually escaped the Xhinn's influence and survived at least until August, 2000, nervously watching for signs of a follow-up Xhinn invasion fleet.

• Historically, a killer smog in London killed between 4,000 and 12,000 people in December, 1952, with a disproportionate number of deaths occurring in the East End. Later, the Clean Air Acts of 1956 and 1958 curtailed coal burning which, along with industry relocation out of London, helped alleviate the problem.

• *Bethnal Green News* reporter Terry Sharp and his photographer, Bob Cohen, took the picture of the Doctor and Tommy shaking hands. It was purchased for inventory and never saw print.

• *The Metropolitan*, Sarah's chief employer, started publication in 1967.

• St. Luke's Church [an actual building, closed

in the late 1950s due to subsidence] was still a wreck in August 2000, but operations were underway to renovate it.

• A main Xhinn fleet was to follow the scouting party in 50 years time [circa 2002], but to date, there's no record of it approaching Earth.

AT THE END OF THE DAY Entertaining, if woefully slight in parts. *Amorality Tale* sets up a nice cast, neatly placing the Doctor and Sarah alongside the promising gangster Tommy Ramsey. However, it slits its own gullet for its generic science-fiction elements, notably the run-of-the-mill Xhinn and their simplistic desire to overrun Earth. Also, it's not as if the London smog die-off of 1952 was a mystery that particularly needed solving. We'll grant that *Amorality Tale* has foundation, but it needs a house atop it—and isn't it a shame that David Bishop, author of the investigative *Who Killed Kennedy?*, didn't put Sarah Jane's journalist skills to greater use?

DID YOU KNOW?

• Author David Bishop worked in London's Old Street area when he first immigrated to Britain in 1990. He walked past St. Luke's church, promising to use it in a future story.

• That's an actual image of the St. Luke's church steeple on the *Amorality Tale* cover. The original cover featured an image (from "Planet of the Spiders") of Sarah Jane looking over her shoulder while wearing a horizontal-striped top. However, this was swapped with a more generic Season 11 photo.

• Teenage versions of real life East End gangsters, the Kray twins, show up in this book.

GHOST SHIP

By Keith Topping

> *Release Date: August 2002*
> *Order: Telos "Doctor Who" Novella #4*

TARDIS CREW The fourth Doctor.

TRAVEL LOG The *Queen Mary*, sailing toward New York, October 21, 1963.

CHRONOLOGY Immediately after "The Deadly Assassin."

STORY SUMMARY Pondering the mixed results of his battle against the Master ("The

Deadly Assassin"), the Doctor grows increasingly introspective aboard the TARDIS. Refusing to let the Doctor keep moping, the TARDIS materializes aboard the *Queen Mary* ocean liner, bound for New York City, in October, 1963.

The Doctor mingles among the passengers, but finds a disturbing number of ghostly and demonic images dogging him. Sufficiently spooked, the Doctor races back to the TARDIS, only to find an unidentified force locking the Ship in place. As a result, the Doctor heads for Cabin 672, long-rumored to be the *Queen Mary*'s most haunted part.

The scarf-wearing Time Lord finds Cabin 672 occupied by a mad quantum physicist named Peter Osbourne, who took advantage of the cabin's ill reputation to conduct fiendish experiments in private. Osbourne quickly recognizes the Doctor as his intellectual equal, and explains that he has crafted a time-space visualizer to let him witness events throughout history. But as a side effect, the visualizer's main component—a bell jar—has captured psionic residue from the ship's passengers. In effect, the bell jar has bottled "ghosts," i.e. psionic carbon copies, of the ship's passengers from past, present and future.

The Doctor decries Osbourne's unethical work, but Osbourne slips into outright madness, determined to further science even if the ghosts suffer as a result. The Doctor abandons diplomacy and hefts up the bell jar, smashing it to pieces. The ghosts burst free in a gush of psionic energy, knocking the Doctor unconscious for hours.

Awakening later, the Doctor fails to find any trace of Osbourne and heads for the TARDIS, finding the liberated, grateful ghosts in front of the Ship. The Doctor recognizes that the ghosts, with Osbourne among their number, will remain bound to the *Queen Mary* forever, then departs in the TARDIS.

MEMORABLE MOMENTS In the middle of the book, the Doctor makes sure to don his floppy hat because the worsening situation "somehow requires it."

The Doctor strikes up a friendship with the fearful passenger Irene Lamb, but she later drowns while taking a bath. With the Doctor already reeling, Lamb's dead eyes stare at him through the water as if to ask: "Why didn't you come sooner? You said it would be all right."

Mad genius Peter Osbourne laments his inability to acquire UK funding: "I could have ruled the world. If only I'd been eligible for the government grant."

When the Doctor smashes Osbourne's bell jar, he gets knocked unconscious by the energy back-

MISCELLANEOUS STUFF!

GHOST SHIP SONGS

As with most of his previous books, Keith Topping intended to make the chapter titles in *Ghost Ship* all song titles. However, he soon ran dry of suitable cinematic songs (having used too many in *Byzantium!*, he claims), and eventually just resorted to a bundle of ghost references and puns such as "Dispossessed" and "A Warning to the Curious." Below is a full list of the songs' source material.

Prologue: The Void (the, alleged original title of The Beatles' "Tomorrow Never Knows," from *Revolver*, 1966)

Chapter 1: Once Upon a Midnight Dreary (not a song title)

Chapter 2: I'll Sail This Ship Alone (The Beautiful South, single, 1994)

Chapter 3: Dead Souls (Joy Division, from *Still*, 1981)

Chapters 4-6: Cabin 672, Atlantic Ocean Drift and A Warning to the Curious (not song titles)

Chapter 7: Behind That Locked Door (George Harrison, from *All Things Must Pass*, 1970)

Chapter 8: Dispossessed (not a song title)

Epilogue: Oh, How The Ghost of You Clings (lyrics from "These Foolish Things" by Cole Porter).

lash and experiences a bizarre lucid dream. To wit, he's sitting on the lawn of Christ's College, Oxford, enjoying ham and cheese, cakes and lemon tea with French King Louis XIV, Nazi propaganda master Joseph Goebbels, philosopher Bertrand Russell and art historian Sir Kenneth Clark. The Marquise de Pompadour, an 18th century mistress to the French king, turns up after getting stuck in traffic on the M3.

SEX AND SPIRITS The depressed fourth Doctor tells himself, in a double entendre: "I need company. Badly. I needed to meet people who were young and lively."

ASS-WHUPPINGS The ghosts grant the Doctor two images of impending fatalities. First off, Irene Lamb drowns in her bath. Later, ship steward Simpkins, unbearably haunted aboard the *Queen Mary*, snaps and commits suicide by bringing down a bulkhead to slice him in half.

The specters' psionic force inflicts great pain on the Doctor. He's blasted unconscious twice while

simply approaching Cabin 672. He's also staggered by supernatural images, thinking he's drowning in a corridor of blood.

Back in 14th century France, the Knights Templar once dosed a drapery dye with a powerful narcotic, catching the rival Doctor by surprise. As a result, he experienced frighteningly strong visions of devils and demons.

TV TIE-INS The Doctor broods in the TARDIS cloisters, finding a bare brick wall that hasn't seen any light in decades ("Logopolis").

NOVEL TIE-INS The Doctor seems acquainted with Lord Byron (either the genuine article, or the "Reprise" version that appeared in *Managra*).

He's previously experienced manifestations at Auderley House, pulse spirits in the Cave of Horrors on Cassuragi III (*Byzantium!*) and haunted castles on the planet Kambalana.

TIE-INS With the TARDIS immobilized aboard the *Queen Mary*, the Doctor tries escaping by using the Fast Return Switch ("The Edge of Destruction," *The Witch Hunters*)—its first use in "a lifetime or three."

CHARACTER DEVELOPMENT

• *The Doctor:* The Doctor flat-out doesn't believe in ghosts, deeming them the result of scientific stuff such as temporal anomalies, etc. Still, this adventure makes him reconsider that view.

He spent many pleasant evenings with composer Henry Purcell (1659-1695), in which they downed wine and cheese while Purcell fiddled with his violin and wrote, "Arise ye Subterranean Winds."

The Doctor once had a lengthy bedside conversation with French novelist and critic Emile Zola concerning remorse, redemption and regret. He once stood on a rocky shore with *Lord of the Flies* author William Golding. He spent a day in Calcutta with *Vanity Fair* author William Thackeray, observing the decadence of the English abroad. He gazed at rainbows in Malmesbury with English philosopher Thomas Hobbes.

He spent much time down by the Siene River in Paris with Charles Baudelaire (one of his favorite poets) and French painters Edouard Manet and Eugene Delacroix.

He's scrambled up a blasted planetscape, pursued by menacing fox-like creatures. He enjoyed a Hong Kong sunset, with semi-drunken sailors giddy for surviving a cannonball hit to their ship.

The Doctor believes some wars, especially World War II, are justified. At a settlement near Conder-

cum, in Northern England, he once failed to sway a Roman centurion's opinion about the ethnic genocide of the barbarian Caledonians.

He considers the Time Vortex his home, in the philosophical and literal sense. He experiences rare moments when he questions his individualism, wondering if he should do something mundane like fish in a Cornish village.

The TARDIS seems empty without his companions. A pessimistic voice in his head constantly warns of danger, but he keeps ignoring it. The Doctor likes people who call a spade a spade.

He gives obscure answers when asked if he believes in God.

• *Dr. Peter Osbourne:* A maverick quantum physicist, looking for American backing after the English government cut his grant. Osbourne's an unimposing man in his mid-30s. He drinks tea with white-gloved hands. He wears polyester and tweed clothes, along with thick, black, horn-rimmed spectacles.

He's completely insane, believing his science makes him akin to God. He by-and-large doesn't give a damn about the consequences of his work.

• *The TARDIS:* The TARDIS sits immobile during much of *Ghost Ship*, refusing to leave until the Doctor frees the trapped, victimized specters.

ALIEN RACES *The Time Lords:* A Gallifreyan bedtime story claims that excessive time travel causes dementia or hallucinatory schizophrenia.

STUFF YOU NEED *Jelly Babies:* The red dye in jelly babies comes from the crushed bodies of tiny Mexican beetles. [Author's Note: The dye's called cochineal, and is used in lots of UK sweets.]

PLACES TO GO *First Class Cabin 672:* Located on Deck Four, near the grand ballroom.

Cabin 672 likely earned a reputation for being haunted because Osbourne's visualizer, located there, sucked in negative emotions from all over the ship. The Doctor speculates the effects will ripple through time, lasting from the *Queen Mary*'s construction until many generations later, when the hull finally rots into oblivion.

SHIPS *The Queen Mary:* The ship's innately cold, due to the ghosts' presence. Deck Four has a First Class swimming pool.

PHENOMENA *The Ghosts:* Osbourne's visualizer (*see Stuff You Need*) works by scanning space-time and trapping what one might call "fragments of reality." In short, it bottles up psionic residence left by the *Queen Mary* passengers of past, present

and future. The ghosts have a measure of consciousness, but exist in a state of suffering, since adrenaline-charged negative emotions leave a much deeper residue than positive ones. The visualizer trapped thousands such ghosts. Because they were pooled from the whole of the *Queen Mary*'s existence, they can predict future events onboard the ship.

The ghosts to some degree are co-dependent, not a group mind as such, but sometimes speaking with one voice. They can write on the walls in blood [a mental projection, or possibly the real thing]. Once freed, they remain with the *Queen Mary* mostly because they've nowhere else to go.

They have a pungent, sickly sweet aroma that simultaneously smells like burning rope, rotting skin, rosemary, oranges and wet autumn leaves all rolled into one. It's more unsettling than unpleasant or disgusting.

There's no explanation for what happens to Osbourne's body, but his mind certainly joins the ghosts in the "afterlife."

• *The Universe:* The Doctor cites the Universe as containing an incalculable number of inhabited worlds [a fact which, if properly pondered, makes one feel small and vulnerable].

HISTORY Suicides and mysterious deaths have plagued the *Queen Mary* over the years. [It's possible that Osbourne's visualizer concentrated the ship's negative emotions in Cabin 672, making the passengers/crew more prone to acts of violence.] In 1938, The *Queen Mary* crewmembers suspected a bursar of trying to scare the passengers. They locked him in Cabin 672 for safekeeping, but later found him dead, literally frightened to death.

During World War II, the *Queen Mary* served as a troop transport. An explosion ripped through lower decks, killing some soldiers.

AT THE END OF THE DAY We must ask ourselves: What's the point in having a novella narrated by the fourth Doctor, if the text ends up sounding almost—but not quite—entirely unlike the fourth Doctor? And so *Ghost Ship* fails to pass muster, bizarrely lacking a drop of the Tom Baker Doctor's lunacy, yet supposedly showing us the world through his eyes. Against that, it's decently spooky, and sure to please those who innately love ghost stories. But ultimately, even its ghostly element never much comes to fruition, making this book climax in a terribly obvious fashion.

DID YOU KNOW?

• Topping was moved to title Chapter 7 after a

George Harrison song (specifically, "Behind That Locked Door") as Harrison died on November 29, 2001, while Topping was writing *Ghost Ship*.

ASYLUM

By Peter Darvill-Evans

Release Date: May 2001
Order: BBC Past Doctor Adventure #42

TARDIS CREW The fourth Doctor, with Nyssa.

TRAVEL LOG Oxford, 1278; Nyssa's abode, unspecified planet, autumn, 3488. [Lance Parkin's *A History of the Universe* dates "Terminus" as circa 3483. Darvill-Evans more-or-less retains this date, as *Asylum* opens, for Nyssa, "about six years" after she left the TARDIS.]

CHRONOLOGY For the fourth Doctor, between "The Deadly Assassin" and "The Face of Evil." For Nyssa, "about six years" after "Terminus."

STORY SUMMARY Banished from their wartorn homeworld, a group of non-corporeal beings—snug in their "Ikshar" alien host bodies—set out in a dimension-hopping spaceship. The beings land in England, 1346, but unfortunately, their Ikshar bodies perish enroute. After mentally subduing a few humans as hosts, the beings use their vessel's time scanners to search for danger. But with mounting dread, the entities realize that, in the all-too-near future, the Black Death will annihilate most of Europe.

With their spaceship low on power, the entities find they lack the means to leave 14th century Earth—or shift hosts fast enough to outrun the oncoming plague. In desperation, the entities scan history for signs of a cure to the Black Death, learning that in the recent past, a philosopher named Roger Bacon researched an "Elixir of Life." Using their dwindling resources, the entities shunt one of their number into a 13th century host, hoping the agent can further Bacon's research and retroactively create a plague defense.

Meanwhile, in the 35th century, the Doctor's ex-travelling companion Nyssa becomes a university teacher specializing in technography, the study of writings about science. Nyssa works on a thesis about Bacon as an "early scientist," but the alien presence in Bacon's era puts history—and the contents of Nyssa's thesis—into flux. Simultaneously, the TARDIS detects the Bacon anomaly, materializing in Nyssa's home so the fourth Doctor can

This book is not endorsed by the BBC. Doctor Who and TARDIS are trademarks of the BBC.

29

learn more. Nyssa turns, shocked to meet an earlier incarnation of the Doctor, then provides some details about Bacon's seeming "double" life as a scientist/philosopher. The Doctor consequently sets off for 13th century England to investigate, but Nyssa, bored stiff with academia, stows herself aboard the TARDIS.

In Oxford, 1278, the Doctor and Nyssa track down an aged Bacon, currently a member of the Franciscan order. After the duo stumbles across the murder of a Franciscan named Brother Godwin, the Doctor leaves Nyssa with a town enforcer, knight Richard of Hockley, for safekeeping. The Doctor then learns that Brother Thomas, Bacon's assistant and a host for the alien intelligence, murdered Godwin when he learned of Bacon's blasphemous, "scientific" research.

A string of events lands the Elixir Manuscript in Richard's possession, bringing the knight to the attention of Thomas, who summarily murders him. Thomas tries to conceal his crime by permanently silencing Nyssa, but she bravely grabs Richard's knife and deals Thomas a minor head injury. The metal blade dissipates the non-corporeal alien within Thomas, freeing his mind from possession.

Afterward, Bacon confesses that "the Elixir of Life" doesn't exist, and that he only worked on the project to humor Thomas. Bacon burns his "Elixir Manuscript," fully aware that the Franciscans will arrest him for heretical studies. The Doctor quietly informs Nyssa that Bacon will only be renowned as a great philosopher, not a scientist, as history intended. As the Doctor returns Nyssa to her home the 35th century, the Black Death (presumably) wipes out the aliens.

MEMORABLE MOMENTS Brother Hubert inquires after the Doctor's identity, to which the Time Lord replies, "I'm just me. I don't fit into any of the categories you have available."

SEX AND SPIRITS Knight Richard of Hockley spends most of *Asylum* smitten with Nyssa. He deems her a work of perfection because she's fair, noble, elegant and not afraid of the dark. Even better, she's a good horsewoman.

Richard makes extremely chivalrous advances toward Nyssa, hoping to "guard the temple of her soft, warm body." But Nyssa, uninterested in a 13th century romance, tells him to shut up and leave her alone. She comes to *like* Richard, but mostly just wants peace and quiet.

At one point, Richard accidentally enters Nyssa's chamber and catches her undressed, but nothing happens. He finally sits down to compose a love letter to Nyssa, but Brother Thomas interrupts and murders him. Nyssa feels grief, if not *romantic* love, for Richard's passing, appreciating him as someone who sought to protect her.

Nyssa has taken some unspecified lovers since leaving the TARDIS. In *Asylum*, she merely takes a steam bath naked. She's dodging advances from Professor Nydan, her head of faculty. Brother Alfric somewhat looks at Nyssa with desire, then remembers he's a friar.

ASS-WHUPPINGS Brother Thomas surprises Richard, who hardly expected an attack from a Franciscan monk, then stabs Richard in the chest and throat. In turn, Nyssa strikes Thomas on the forehead with Richard's knife.

Thomas kills five people to protect Bacon's illicit research, including Brother Godwin, who happened to spy Bacon, clearly up to no good leaving his observatory. Brother Thomas also kills Hubert, the minister of the Franciscan house, as part of his efforts to reclaim Bacon's lost "Elixir Manuscript."

TV TIE-INS The fourth Doctor here meets Nyssa for the "first" time and—if we're to take *Asylum* at face value—he apparently remembers this adventure while traveling with her younger self from "The Keeper of Traken" through "Terminus." For better or worse, the entire problem of the fourth Doctor meeting the older Nyssa gets glossed over with him commenting, "When I meet your younger self, I'll remember not to recognize you."

From Nyssa's perspective, she left the TARDIS six years ago. She departed Terminus in quiet euphoria, after developing a vaccine against Lazar's Disease ("Terminus," *see Character Development*).

Nyssa never figured out how the TARDIS translation net ("The Masque of Mandragora") worked. The TARDIS lets Nyssa and the Doctor both speak French, although the Doctor occasionally lapses into Latin. The Ship automatically switches Nyssa's language to aid with her cover identity, sometimes making her talk in elegant English.

Nyssa's family kept a crypt on Traken ("The Keeper of Traken"). Her father, Tremas, owned extensive gardens while Nyssa's mother was alive. Nyssa remembers avenues of trees with golden leaves on Traken, plus islands of flowers and fountains. To large degree, she's always felt empty since the loss of her parents, childhood and homeworld ("The Keeper of Traken" again, and moreso "Logopolis").

Nyssa claims she spent "about two years" travelling in the TARDIS, somewhat curtailing speculation (*The Discontinuity Guide*) that she and the fifth Doctor spent a much longer period together

THE CRUCIAL BITS...

> • **ASYLUM**—Nyssa, now older and working as a university teacher in the 39th century, shares an adventure with the fourth Doctor.

(between "Time Flight" and "Arc of Infinity").

The Doctor furrows his brow as if foreseeing one of his companions (obviously Adric, "Earthshock") will die, making Nyssa wonder if he possesses some sort of Time Lord foresight—the result of living several lifetimes throughout history.

The Doctor initially suggested the line of, "To exist or not to exist, that is the question," for *Hamlet*, but Shakespeare later changed it ("City of Death").

CHARACTER DEVELOPMENT

• *The Doctor:* He's met engineer Isambard Kingdom Brunel, circa 1770s, noting that he smokes "the vilest cigars." The fourth Doctor has blue eyes.

• *Nyssa:* After Terminus, Nyssa wandered the Universe, performing a wide variety of philanthropic missions. She undertook microbiology research to kill a deadly fungus, initiated 11th-hour diplomacy to avert a war and raised funds for medical supplies after a flood.

Conversely, she witnessed some catastrophes. She was the last nurse to leave a field hospital on Brallis, cutting open patients' pustules while feeling leech grubs growing under her leg skin.

On Exanos, Nyssa joined a group of volunteers who airlifted food to Parety, a town surrounded by warlords during a vicious civil war. Nyssa later caught a teenager trading some of the airlifted food for a homemade pulse weapon. She thwarted the deal, but the boy run away and later got shot. Worse, a particularly insane warlord detonated a rival's nuclear power plant. Nyssa witnessed the resultant mushroom cloud from a departing cargo shuttle.

After Exanos, Nyssa arrived in a planetary system with no war, oppression or hunger. She took a university post there, turning her back on hardcore scientific disciplines to teach technography. She's barely older than her students, who sometimes change their skin pigmentation.

Nyssa is currently trying to find her place in life, and her academic work is suffering as a result. Professor Nydan, her head of faculty, judges her current performance as "lukewarm." Nyssa doesn't like to alter her metabolism much, preferring to naturally experience what she's feeling.

Nyssa's despondency reaches the point that she wonders if she wants to live or not. She's not suicidal, but when Brother Thomas attacks Nyssa, she's not convinced she wants to fight back. She eventually rises to the occasion, becoming more self-actualized by story's end.

She lives alone, burying herself in work. She sometimes walks in the mountains, wanting to feel at peace. She remains acquainted with Earth history. She doesn't know Latin. She considers the fourth Doctor less sensitive and understanding than the fifth.

• *Richard of Hockley:* He serves Guy de Marenne, kin to Philip of Seaby, the Oxford university chancellor. De Marenne owns lands in England, Normandy and Gascony, and serves as counselor to the king.

• *Home:* Voice-interactive computer that regulates Nyssa's domicile. Home contains multibillion-synapse organic circuitry, blessed with an almost infinite capacity for research. Home can reconfigure rooms and doors in Nyssa's house according to her taste.

ALIEN RACES *The aliens:* Their ability to transfer from host to host seems artificial, not inherent to their being.

PLACES TO GO *Bacon's Private Observatory:* Contains an immense volume of knowledge. Regrettably, when Bacon joins the Franciscan Order, he lets his private library go to rot. Eventually, a fire destroys it.

ORGANIZATIONS *Technographers:* They study the writings of science, but usually after the scattering of humankind throughout the galaxy. Nyssa is perhaps the only technographer of note who remembers Earth's pivotal contributions to science.

SHIPS *The aliens' spaceship:* It's capable of scanning the timeline, although looking into the future requires more power than viewing the past. The spaceship is solar powered, but would require centuries of recharging to travel again.

PHENOMENA *History Revision:* The uncertainty of the timeline makes the topic of Nyssa's thesis waiver between Bacon and Isambard Kingdom Brunel, an engineer from Earth's early industrialization period. The timeline fluctuation also affects Nyssa's memories, although her computer, Home, better remembers previous drafts.

HISTORY Roger Bacon was born in 1220. He taught at Oxford, starting in 1247, and became one of the foremost philosophers of his era.

• Bacon joined the Franciscan Order in 1257, possibly because he blew his family wealth on unproductive scientific experiments. The brotherhood initially celebrated Bacon's addition to their ranks, but increasingly found themselves at philosophical odds with him. In 1266, the Pope asked Bacon to formulate methods to thwart the Antichrist.

• From 1278 to 1290, the Franciscans imprisoned Bacon, bringing his work to a standstill. The exact charges remain unknown, although it's possible that Bacon's writings—scientific or otherwise—were somehow deemed an embarrassment to the Order. He died in 1292, age 72.

• In *Asylum*, the Doctor discovers that Bacon had theories about aircraft, submarines, telescopes, metallurgy, gravity theory and more, putting him 200 years ahead of his time. However, a fire ravaged Bacon's private observatory, destroying most of his theories. As with real-life, Bacon goes down as a gifted scholar who briefly dabbled in astrology, alchemy and other arcana. But he left little to science, barring some theories regarding optics.

• The unnamed aliens evidently hail from thousands of years in the future. A militaristic race called the Narbrab overran the aliens' homeworld, then banished the group that shows up in *Asylum* in a solar powered ship. In Earth, 1346, the aliens tried to blend in among the human population. They shunted their intelligences into human hosts, then melded with their personas. The hosts to large degree seemed unaware of their possession, but were compelled to gather near the aliens' module at regular intervals.

• Brother Thomas lived to at least age 90. After Nyssa drove the alien intelligence from his head in 1278, Thomas felt drawn to the alien spaceship in 1346. Thomas warned the aliens about the futility of their efforts, but they deemed him a lunatic priest and proceeded with their plans.

• The 35th century remembers Aristotle, Hobbes, Shakespeare [in translation only] and Sophocles. The era knows little about the Industrial Revolution.

• Circa 3488, an outbreak of war loomed in the Staktys System. Talks between the Tet-Gen Confederacy and the rival Jamlinray System sporadically occurred, but conditions in Staktys deteriorated, leading to widespread famine. Jamlinray refused to accept the Staktys refugees. The outcome of the conflict remains unknown.

AT THE END OF THE DAY A seemingly fruitless endeavor, given that *Asylum* squanders Nyssa's return by making her lounge about and wallow in self-pity for most of the book [so what's the point of bringing her back?]. Just as odd, the boggle-eyed fourth Doctor comes off completely flat, without a drop of Tom Baker's wit, and Richard, whatever his touching love for Nyssa, essentially seems like a wet loaf of bread. At the end of the day, a book that's *too* divorced from the "Doctor Who" mythos, and poorly lays its cards on the table.

PSI-ENCE FICTION

By Chris Boucher

Release Date: September 2001
Order: BBC Past Doctor Adventure #46

TARDIS CREW The fourth Doctor and Leela.

TRAVEL LOG University of East Wessex, Norswood, England, modern day.

CHRONOLOGY Likely between Boucher's *Corpse Marker* and "The Talons of Weng-Chiang." *Psi-ence Fiction* sets itself up as Leela's first journey to Earth, placing it before "Talons" and *Drift*.

STORY SUMMARY As normal, the TARDIS completes its journey through the Time Vortex by scanning all possible realities, then collapsing the potential timelines into a single inevitability—i.e. "our" reality—and materializing within. But upon detecting an external time/space anomaly, the TARDIS deliberately changes course and arrives at the University of East Wessex in England. There, the Doctor and Leela find university researcher Barry Hitchins testing students for psionic powers. Hitchins makes little progress, unaware that one of his subjects—engineering student Josh Randall—has already become telepathic and is merely playing possum. Regrettably, Randall's talents also make him deeply psychotic, motivating him to mentally torment his classmates with horrific visions.

Eventually, the Doctor discovers that wealthy physicist John Finer secretly funded Hitchins' experiments as part of a mad bid to travel back in time. Finer has already created a haphazard time machine, but requires a powerful psionic to mentally monitor and anchor any such traveler on their journey. If successful, Finer hopes to travel back in time six years and prevent his daughter's accidental death (*see Ass-Whuppings*).

The Doctor examines Finer's machine, realizing that—like the TARDIS—it can collapse an infinite

amount of timelines. Unfortunately, the apparatus lacks the TARDIS' ability to reintegrate our reality, meaning that if left unchecked, the device will simply compress the whole of existence into nothingness. The Doctor implores Finer to reconsider, but the physicist—having obtained Randall's help—sets the machine into full motion.

To Finer's terror, the machine runs amok. Simultaneously, Randall turns completely insane, wanting to let the machine annihilate the Universe, then psionically set himself up as god. Finer repents and tries to self-destruct his temporal engine, but Randall telepathically kills him.

Thankfully, the TARDIS senses the Doctor's plight and materializes within Finer's machine, using its own control systems to stabilize the reaction. The Doctor hustles Leela into the TARDIS and dematerializes, leaving Randall behind. Leela grows confused, but the Doctor explains that although the TARDIS saved the Universe, some damage occurred to the localized timeline. A new history has developed in which Finer never started his time experiments, Hitchins became a successful media pundit and Randall is a normal engineering student. Indeed, the Doctor and Leela won't even remember the adventure upon leaving the isolated TARDIS, bringing all memory of the university's psionic experiments to an end.

MEMORABLE MOMENTS A student innocently comments that "nobody uses a public phone box these days—except to pee in."

The psychotic Randall tries to terrify his classmates by making a Ouiji board spell out, "U D-E-D. U D-E-D. U D-E-D...", but it merely makes student Meg speculate: "My guess is we're in contact with a defunct budgerigar. Or possibly a dead tape recorder."

The Doctor realizes officials wouldn't question him so much if he'd stop giving his name and address as "the Doctor, no fixed abode," which inevitably causes a lot of futile background checks.

The Doctor to a Clearspring Water Company worker: "I'm from Gallifrey." The worker: "What line are they in? Don't tell me it's bottled water." The Doctor: "No, no. Nothing like that. Travel."

SEX AND SPIRITS A student bar worker offers to buy Leela a drink, but nothing comes of it.

ASS-WHUPPINGS Six years ago, physicist John Finer lost his temper with his daughter Amelia, then accidentally killed her. He dumped her body in the nearby Norswood, causing a low-profile police investigation that went unsolved. The telepathic Randall kills Finer simply by plant-

ing the illusion of death in his brain. In the new timeline, a guilt-stricken Finer turned himself in for slaying Amelia.

A confused Leela thumps a student, trashes the student cafeteria, kicks a campus security guard seven ways to Sunday and pulls a runner.

Randall psionically makes his classmates and Hitchins experience soul-freezing images of blood, *lots* of blood, during a deprivation tank experiment. He telepathically torments student Joan Cox, making her commit suicide by slitting her wrists, then her throat for good measure. [She's resurrected in the new timeline.]

TV TIE-INS The Doctor here introduces Leela to cows ("Image of the Fendahl"). He also cites Earth as the most probable home of her forefathers ("The Face of Evil").

The Doctor again refutes the concept of magic, believing that ignorant people apply the term to stuff they don't understand ("The Daemons").

NOVEL TIE-INS The Doctor claims he used to experience "temporal shift lag," the equivalent of jet-lag for time travelers, but eventually developed the mental discipline needed to counter it. Leela doesn't feel temporal shift lag, possibly owing to her primitive nature. All of this somewhat clashes with some New Adventures books, which suggest the TARDIS automatically counter-acts such temporal jet lag.

CHARACTER DEVELOPMENT

• *The Doctor:* The Doctor thinks he's in his fourth "reincarnation," but claims it's difficult to remember at times. He hasn't been on a university tour since a pre-knighted Issac Newton showed him around Cambridge.

The Doctor hopelessly jumbles references to physicist Issac Newton, fisher Issac Walton (author of *The Compleat Angler*), composer William Walton and Walton Hummer, a popular, three-feet-tall kazoo and wiffle-synthesizer player in the 21st century.

He claims that South American guerrilla fighter Che Guevara once advised him: "If in doubt, don't stir up [the authorities]."

The Doctor doesn't take drugs, instead getting his "recreation" simply from trying to understand things. Calling the Doctor a shaman insults his integrity and honesty.

The Doctor finds jelly babies—particularly green ones—of great comfort in times of stress, because they boost his blood sugar. He deems blackberries almost as good as jelly babies. He can't recall what a "stitch in time" saves. He likes cows,

This book is not endorsed by the BBC. Doctor Who and TARDIS are trademarks of the BBC.

33

thinking them good-natured.

He knows about sensory deprivation tanks. The Doctor sometimes pines for the past, including his previous incarnation. He's not claustrophobic. Unlike Leela, he can't sleep anywhere he likes.

The Doctor deems paranormal research an embarrassment for a serious academic institution.

In all of the Doctor's travels, he's only encountered one entity who came close to answering the philosophical question, "Who are you, exactly?" — a planet-sized fungus whose name was a small electric shock and a rather unpleasant smell.

• *Leela:* In times of crisis, Leela grabs her knife hilt as a security reflex. She's attuned to the TARDIS' functions, sensing when the Ship's about to land. Leela's belt pouch contains a sharpening stone, a high-energy food bar and a comb.

She doesn't like the Doctor's jelly babies. She finds the Doctor's choice of food non-poisonous, but un-tasty. She finds a typical English "fried breakfast" greasy, but not unpleasant.

Her mentors in the Sevateem taught her to avoid fear, because it distorts the senses. She's never heard of the Welsh. She insists on using a person's full fighting name (such as "Doctor Ghostbuster Bazzer Hitchins" for Barry Hitchins) as a mark of respect.

Leela knows the phrases "Time Lord" and "Time and Relative Dimensions in Space" respectively refer to the Doctor and the TARDIS, but don't understand their meaning.

• *The Doctor and Leela:* The Doctor tries to explain the concept of Earth fashion to Leela, but she decides he doesn't know what he's talking about.

The Doctor considers Leela one of the bravest people he's ever met. Unlike the Doctor, Leela doesn't like Earth at all.

• *John Finer and Josh Randall:* Finer, a wealthy physicist, owns the Yorkshire-based Clearspring Water Company. He laced Clearspring water bottles on sale at the East Wessex university with cognition enhancers from his biochemical business, hoping to boost the students' higher brain functions. The drug stimulated formidable psionic powers in Josh Randall, but it also made him dangerously psychotic.

• *Josh Randall:* Randall can telepathically read the Doctor's mind. He can also amplify people's thoughts, driving them mad. He continues using ordinary speech, a means of curtailing unwanted telepathic contact.

In the new timeline, Randall is a normal engineering student with a passing interest in the paranormal.

• *The Doctor and the TARDIS:* The Doctor often doesn't know how to fix the TARDIS, unable to simply take her to Gallifrey for a tune-up. He tries to avoid mucking around with the TARDIS' parts, because it makes the Ship resentful. In turn, this makes him feel her resentment, causing a feedback loop. If that happens, it takes time for the Doctor and the TARDIS to get comfortable with one another again, leaving the TARDIS more unpredictable than normal in the interim.

The more the TARDIS steers, the less the Doctor knows where they're going. Leela hears the Doctor variously talking to the Ship like it's a friend, then hurling insults.

• *The TARDIS:* The Ship's time-line flux adjusters help detect temporal anomalies (*see Phenomena*). The probability compensators sometimes correct such space/time weaknesses.

Finer's machine doesn't work because it lacks the TARDIS' trans-dimensional containment and semi-sentient control systems.

ALIEN PLANETS *Earth:* Blackberries, hose hips, finches and squirrels are only found on Earth.

STUFF YOU NEED *Basic field-effect detector:* A hand-held device that scans for temporal breaches. The Doctor can build a basic model by cannibalizing parts from the TARDIS' viewing screen, central console and electric sandwich toaster.

• *Finer's Time Machine:* A chamber, about 10 times the size of the TARDIS' console room, powered by positive and negative pulses in collision. The TARDIS interrupted the machine by simply imposing itself in the pulse stream, then letting its control circuits kick in.

PHENOMENA *Imagination:* A theory holds that anything imaginable must exist — else, you wouldn't be able to imagine it.

• *Temporal Breach:* In layman's terms, a temporal breach often occurs due to an overlap of multiverses, space-time loop anomalies, temporal inversion, etc. Leela observes a temporal breach that looks like a sliver of blackness. It's a bit like a black hole, but proves infinitely more destructive if it expands.

Persons near a space-time breach often experience personality shifts — even violent behavior — accompanied by pervading feelings of paranoia, fear or obsession. Even the Doctor isn't immune. It's possible that temporal breaches cause this effect by partially suppressing the higher brain functions, directly inhibiting logic and rationality.

Failure to seal a temporal breach would essentially collapse history, bringing about chaos and

infinite darkness. It wouldn't be the end of every-thing, in the sense that time would no longer have a beginning.

AT THE END OF THE DAY One of those nov-els that's hard to review, given that it's entertain-ing enough in the moment, yet fails to leave much lasting impact. The fourth Doctor and Leela cer-tainly fit Boucher like a glove, but by contrast, *Psi-ence Fiction* also concerns itself with some university co-eds who—barring the insane Randall—eventually blend together. Yes, *Psi-ence Fiction* carries some understandable gripes, but it's notable as Boucher's best book (especially when stacked against the woeful *Last Man Running* and decent *Corpse Marker*), and, at the end of the day, is best viewed as a glass half full.

DRIFT

By Simon A Forward

Release Date: February 2002
Order: BBC Past Doctor Adventure #50

TARDIS CREW The fourth Doctor and Leela.

TRAVEL LOG Melvin Village, New Hampshire, America, modern day.

CHRONOLOGY Likely between "The Robots of Death" and "The Talons of Weng-Chiang."

STORY SUMMARY Purely for fun, the Doctor decides to let Leela run free with some native tribes in North America—except that the TARDIS arrives in snowy New Hampshire, several cen-turies too late. Shortly afterward, the travelers find White Shadow, an elite military division, engaged in operations to retrieve a missing alien gadget. As the Doctor discovers, the military was field-testing the Stormcore, supposedly a weather control device retrieved from a downed spaceship 30 years ago. The test somehow went awry, and caused a modified Raven jet carrying the Stormcore to crash near the pedestrian Melvin Village, New Hampshire.

Flashing his UNIT credentials, the Doctor offers to help the military locate the alien gizmo. How-ever, a malevolent ice creature, akin to a small storm, attacks Melvin Village and destroys the nervous system of anyone it touches. The White Shadow troopers do their best, popping white phosphorous charges into any house where the ice creature appears, but the monster racks up a num-ber of casualties.

In time, the Doctor concludes that the Storm-core—actually a spaceship navigational device, not a weather control instrument—inadvertently allowed the ice creature access to our dimension from another reality. The Time Lord determines that the instinctive, emotive ice creature isn't out-wardly hostile, but merely seeks to make contact with others, unable to comprehend that its touch proves fatal to humans.

As the ice creature's low-level intelligence rules out meaningful communication, the Doctor cob-bles together a means of isolating it. With the crea-ture's nucleus located in the Stormcore—and with the Stormcore hovering above the TARDIS, res-onating with its psionic forces—the Doctor primes a string of C4 explosives beneath the Ship. As the Doctor expected, the TARDIS' force field deflects the force of the explosion upward, flinging the Stormcore into a nearby frozen lake.

Simultaneously, the Doctor's allies trigger a sec-ond string of charges, cracking the lake and plung-ing a two vehicles into it. For a grand finale, the electrified vehicles—hooked up to some nearby power cables—serve as a giant anode and diode, causing the ice creature's nucleus to crystallize around it via electrolysis. The Doctor turns the im-prisoned ice creature over to the military for safe-keeping, and slips away with Leela in the TARDIS.

MEMORABLE MOMENTS The Doctor offers a bag of jelly babies to Lieutenant Hmieleski, who looks inside despite her years of adulthood and military training.

When two CIA operatives show up, the Doctor greets them as "more people to argue with." He later inquires after Leela: "Have you seen a young lady with limited social graces go by?"

The Doctor tosses his coat over an armchair, for-getting that it's already occupied. He says in all se-riousness that after drinking so much Scotch (*see Sex and Spirits*), he'd better not operate the TARDIS for awhile—because he'd have no idea where he's going.

SEX AND SPIRITS Realizing that alcohol slows the ice creature's effect on the nervous sys-tem, the Doctor downs 12 Scotches, single malt, nothing under 12 years old, to prepare for his final gambit. He declines to take the drinks on the rocks, but allows a splash of water to take the edge off. Lieutenant Joanna Hmieleski looks at the Doctor's row of Scotches and wonders if he's brac-ing himself for a suicide mission. He lets White Shadow prime his explosives, unwilling to trust

This book is not endorsed by the BBC. Doctor Who and TARDIS are trademarks of the BBC.

35

his demolition skills under the influence. Macho CIA agent Parker Theroux deems the Doctor a wuss, arming himself with a bottle of Jack Daniels.

ASS-WHUPPINGS The ice creature rips several troopers and townsfolk apart, appearing as a swarm of ice shards that consumes its victims like electric maggots.

A tremendous explosion pounds Leela. CIA agent Theroux thinks about hitting Leela to halt her interference, but finds himself unable to slug a woman. Having no such compunction, Leela knees Parker in the nuts.

Leela's friend, the psionic Kristal Wildcat, burns out her mind trying to establish contact with the incompatible ice creature.

The ice creature mildly infects Leela and Lieutenant Hmieleskiseki at one point, but the Doctor's blood (*see Character Development*) counteracts their infection.

TV TIE-INS When the Doctor gives Lieutenant Hmieleski a blood transfusion, she feels like she's infused with energy rather than blood (probably the Doctor's innate artron energy, "The Deadly Assassin.")

NOVEL TIE-INS The brain-blitzed seventh Doctor remembered a scene from *Drift* in the preceding PDA *Relative Dementias*. The ice creature bears no relation to similarly frosty entities (i.e. the Colds) in *Time and Relative* or *Interference*.

CHARACTER DEVELOPMENT

• *The Doctor:* The Doctor's blood, containing regenerative properties, can cure individuals who're minorly tainted by the ice creature. [Which proves his blood's compatible with Leela.]

He doesn't like the dark. He eats jelly babies by biting their heads off first. The ice creature negates his empathic link with the TARDIS. In a previous incarnation, he drove a snowmobile. He can identify alien blood—even red-colored alien blood—on sight.

We'd be remiss without mentioning: The Doctor leaves an awful lot to chance, assuming the military will nobly and without ill intent put the ice creature "somewhere safe." [Although to be fair, he comes to trust White Shadow leader Morgan Shaw.]

• *Leela:* A Sevateem legend claims that a hero of the tribe journeyed with some companions to confront the Tesh. The excursion led into a frozen land, forcing the group to retreat. The hero gave out his rations, asked his friends' forgiveness and

remained behind to die. Leela fails to see the point of the story because she's more fascinated by the white landscape imagery.

She likes the name "White Shadow." She's an excellent scout, even in snow. She doesn't recognize the terms "tail-pipe" or "metabolize."

• *Lieutenant Kristal Owl Eye Wildcat of the Pasamaquoddy:* A Native American who doesn't like what the American settlers did to her people, but works for the military to change the system from the inside. Kristal was psionic enough to pilot the Stormcore-modified Raven jet by remote, only losing control when the ice creature manifested in our reality.

• *Melody Quartararo and Parker Theroux:* Stranded extra-terrestrials working for the CIA, who hope to one day find a means of escaping from Earth. They're just about the most human-acting aliens you'll ever meet, having about a decade of practice by this point. They set aside their own concerns about leaving Earth and aided the Doctor against the ice creature, ending this story by realizing that back home, they were ordinary—but as CIA agents, they're something special.

They possibly have a sexual relationship. They possess a graviton distortion sensor that's helpful for locating the TARDIS. They uncovered files on UNIT and the Doctor and determined his race of origin.

Their red blood looks human norm. They can wear sunglasses without bumping into things. Parker carries a .357 Desert Eagle.

• *The Ice Creature:* The creature's not sentient enough to allow meaningful communication, but certainly possesses enough emotion to spare a little girl's life, sensing a kindred loneliness in her.

It tries to make contact via the nervous system, corrupting the cerebral cortex and spinal system of anyone it touches. Some factors which slow the creature's infection: A) alcohol, which hampers the creature's ability to crystallize in the human body, and B) pretty much anything that reduces neural activity, such as mild concussion or the Doctor's hypnosis. Conversely, a psychic barrier might speed neural traffic and quicken the creature's progress.

The creature exhibits a crystalline structure, but shares only some characteristics with ice. It manifests as short spurts of ice storms, eventually burning out and needing to consume biomass to reintegrate itself. Liquids, especially water, render the creature unable to crystallize at will.

The ice creature can cause drifts the size of Moby Dick. It doesn't care much for inanimate materials, but can eat through them.

STUFF YOU NEED *The Stormcore (a.k.a. Prism):* More formerly called a Dimension Phase Multiplexer. It's designed to multiplex energy streams and draw them into a central nexus—whatever that means.

PLACES TO GO *Melvin Village:* Located near Route 109.

ORGANIZATIONS *White Shadow:* American military division, formed to recover and research alien artifacts. The White Shadow platoon seen in *Drift* features leader Captain Morgan Shaw, second-in-command Lieutenant Beard, the late psionic Lieutenant Wildcat, the similarly dead demolitions expert Ben McKin, medical expert Lieutenant Joanna Hmieleski [who considers resigning after this story, having endured one too many close shaves] and engineer Corporal Pydych.

The group's name conveys stealth and nobility. It operates in the field with three squads and a command crew of specialist personnel. White Shadow troopers sometimes use M203 grenade launchers.

HISTORY In the early 1960s, the American military shot down an alien vessel carrying the Stormcore. Afterward, the government initiated Operation Afterburn to adapt the Stormcore, originally code-named Prism, to human technology. Researchers determined that a psionic operator was needed, forcing the government to wait until after the Cold War to find such an individual. With time, Grill Flame—the government's ESP/Remote Viewing program—located Lieutenant Kristal Wildcat and other suitable persons.

• At some point, a clairvoyant reconnaissance of a National Security Agency facility forced relocation of Operation Afterburn to Fort Meade. Finally, Operation Afterburn reached fruition, re-designating the Prism as "the Stormcore" and mounting it onto a Raven Electronic Warfare aircraft. The White Shadow team monitored flights out of Pease Air Force Base, New Hampshire, before this incident.

• The government possibly covered up the Melvin Village incident by claiming that coyotes—which the ice creature freely consumed—brought an infection to town.

AT THE END OF THE DAY Imagine you're playing dodgeball and get presented with two targets. You fail to properly focus and impotently sail the ball straight between them. That's essentially the problem with *Drift*. On the one hand, it's a militaristic thriller involving the White Shadow group; on the other, it's styled after Stephen King's quiet, moody pedestrian New England stories. As both of these threads get equal emphasis, the muddled result spares little time on the Doctor, and makes Leela become almost non-existent for long stretches. Best described as, "some people wander in the snow and occasionally get frightened," *Drift* ends in a white haze much like its name implies.

DID YOU KNOW?

• *Drift* started out as a third Doctor/Liz Shaw book but got remolded into a fourth Doctor/Leela novel. Ghosts of the first version would seem to remain, as the fourth Doctor relies heavily on his UNIT credentials and goes snowmobiling.

• Author Simon Forward lives near a village and reservoir named Drift, but assures that had nothing to do with the book's title.

• Forward's fiancée hails from Northfield, Massachusetts, but he's yet to visit the United States.

• Many character surnames in *Drift* were taken from a local New Hampshire newspaper.

• Forward based "Operation: Afterburn" on several recorded UFO sightings across New Hampshire, along with genuine articles about Grill Flame and military research into psi-spies, etc.

• Shaw is the maiden name of Forward's mother, and he adds that when he found a Mount Shaw on the map, right next to Lake Winnepesaukee, he immediately knew where to set *Drift*.

• Forward had several ideas about Melody and Parker's origins at time of writing, and might explore them in another book.

PRIMEVAL

By Lance Parkin

Release Date: November 2001
Order: Big Finish "Doctor Who" CD #26

TARDIS CREW The fifth Doctor and Nyssa.

TRAVEL LOG Traken and Kwundaar's warfleet (at the edge of the Traken Union), some 3,000 years before Traken's destruction.

CHRONOLOGY Several weeks after "Kinda," between "Time-Flight" and "Arc of Infinity."

STORY SUMMARY In the TARDIS, Nyssa's psychic defenses unexpectedly collapse, threatening her physical health. Desperate to find medical

This book is not endorsed by the BBC. Doctor Who and TARDIS are trademarks of the BBC.

37

help, the Doctor materializes on Traken—Nyssa's homeworld—some 3,000 years before its annihilation. There, a biologist named Shayla tries, and fails, to stabilize Nyssa's condition. Out of options, Shayla reluctantly advises the Doctor to seek help from Kwundaar, a self-proclaimed god.

Shayla explains that Kwundaar has positioned his warfleet just outside the Union for millennia, afraid to come closer lest the Source—the supercomputer that regulates all life on Traken, powered by a "sentient" sun—incinerate him instantly. The Doctor travels to Kwundaar's flagship and begs the godling to save Nyssa's life.

Immeasurably telepathic, Kwundaar offers to aid Nyssa temporarily, promising a complete recovery if the Doctor brings him an unspecified item from the Source vault. The Doctor pressures Kwundaar for specifics, but the godling merely insists the Time Lord will "know the item when he sees it." The Doctor returns to Traken, even as Kwundaar boosts Nyssa's psychic defenses.

Nyssa recovers, but the ruling Consuls, afraid her illness might contaminate the whole of Traken with "evil," order her and the Doctor to leave. The duo takes off in the TARDIS, but the Doctor, suspicious of Kwundaar, rematerializes near the Source vault to check its defenses. Purely as a precaution, the Doctor boosts power to the Source's main electromagnetic shield. The Doctor and Nyssa return to the TARDIS, failing to realize that the reinforced shield—in addition to further protecting the Source—has also bottled up the supercomputer's energy.

Unopposed, Kwundaar's invasion fleet rolls forward and captures Traken. Horrified, the Doctor realizes that Kwundaar gave Nyssa her sickness in the first place (*see Tie-Ins*), thus manipulating the Time Lord into sealing off the Source. Desperately improvising, the Doctor tells Nyssa a Source override code. Eventually, the two of them confront Kwundaar, who—as the Doctor expected—telepathically rips the override code from Nyssa's mind. Kwundaar inputs the code into the main Source console—only to find the Doctor deliberately lied to his companion. Rather than putting the Source at Kwundaar's command, the code reroutes control to a central command chair.

Already sitting in the chair, the Doctor masters the Source, becoming the first Keeper of Traken. Unfettered, the Source's energy rips outward—incinerating Kwundaar and much of his army. Soon after, the Doctor surrenders his post to Shayla, founding the line of Keepers on Traken. The more benevolent of Kwundaar's troops remain on Traken, even as Nyssa—viewing her homeworld as a thing of the past—departs with the Doctor.

MEMORABLE MOMENTS The Doctor introduces himself to Shayla and Sabian—two medics—then realizes the irony of the situation. He also whimsically suggests that if the slow-witted Tegan can handle seeing her planet's past and future, then surely Nyssa, with her scientific training, can cope.

A lively debate between the Doctor and the ruling Consuls spotlights the Trakenites' arrogance, illustrating—as the Doctor contends—one can strive for perfection but never attain it.

Finally, Part 1 offers one of Big Finish's best cliffhangers, with Kwundaar warning the Doctor, "Don't turn around," lest the Time Lord experience the full force of Kwundaar's telepathy and go mad. The Doctor bravely declares, "I'm not frightened of you," leading Kwundaar to impishly reply, "No. But then, you haven't turned around, have you?"

SEX AND SPIRITS Nyssa carries on a brief flirtation with Shayla's assistant Sabian. It's mostly innocent, although there's a steamy spa scene where a recovering Nyssa encourages Sabian to join her in the water, coyly claiming that, "I might faint and drown." Sabian wishes he could see the ailing Nyssa "at her best," then mopes when she departs.

The Doctor and Nyssa don bathing suits in Part 3, although the Doctor quickly re-dons his normal clothes afterward. Nyssa isn't so lucky, forced to spend most of the audio's second half in her swimsuit, although the Doctor lends her his coat for modesty's sake.

In Part 4, an annoyed Nyssa tells one of Kwundaar's troopers: "It's not as if I can conceal a weapon in this [swimsuit]... I'm barely concealing myself."

ASS-WHUPPINGS Psionic vulnerability makes Nyssa's temperature fall dramatically, frequently putting her into shock. This mostly results from Nyssa's brain fighting Kwundaar's influence (*see Tie-Ins*), as it'd rather die than yield. Mostly, Nyssa simply experiences weakness, although she recovers—thanks to Kwundaar's boosting her mental shields—in Part 3.

As part of their negotiation in Part 1, Kwundaar tries to forge a telepathic dialogue between himself and the Doctor. Unfortunately, the Doctor's mental defenses do him a disservice, forcing Kwundaar to *hammer* them down to effect simple communication. The Doctor finishes Part 1 screaming as a result, but eventually recovers.

Kwundaar's troops ransack Traken, rout its fosters ("The Keeper of Traken") and annihilate the Traken spaceport.

THE CRUCIAL BITS...

• **PRIMEVAL**— Early history of Traken explored. Nyssa un-becomes telepathic. The Doctor briefly becomes the first Keeper of Traken. The villainous Kwundaar sends out a summons to various cosmic beings to our Universe, facilitating the Doctor's adventures in Season 20.

Nyssa tricks Kwundaar follower Anona into jumping into water energized by the Source, thereby scalding her [clearly, even minute amounts of Source energy incinerate some aspect of Kwundaar's power]. At story's end, the Source obliterates Kwundaar and presumably hundreds, if not thousands, of his soldiers.

TV TIE-INS The fourth Doctor previously visited Traken (and met Nyssa) in "The Keeper of Traken." The story also debuted the Source, the Consuls of Traken and the Source Manipulator— a device here constructed by Kwundaar as a means of regulating the Source's functions. Traken was destroyed in "Logopolis." Nyssa comments that the Source was far more active in her era ("Keeper of Traken" again).

Shayla here becomes Keeper of the Source, although "Keeper of Traken" claims that Keepers enjoy extended lifespans of up to a thousand years. Ergo, it seems likely that only three or four Keepers existed before Traken's obliteration.

Nyssa tries to teach medical assistant Sabian the Charleston ("Black Orchid"). The Doctor also knows the dance, but insists a true gentleman "knows how to Charleston, but doesn't."

As if things weren't bad enough, Kwundaar very briefly uses the Source to summon a variety of higher powers—many of them banished from our Universe by the Doctor—intending to enslave them to his will. At story's end, Kwundaar somehow marks the Doctor, allowing said higher powers to pick up the TARDIS' scent in future. Parkin uses this twist to explain the return, in Season 20, of the Doctor's old foes ("Arc of Infinity" through "Enlightenment"), although he's posted that it's fine if a future writer comes up with an alternate explanation.

TIE-INS Seeking a means of subtly bringing Traken to ruin, Kwundaar swept his mind through time and space for any Trakenites outside the Union—hoping to make them his agents. He tagged Nyssa shortly after she started travelling with the Doctor ("Logopolis"), then diminished her psychic defenses, hoping to manipulate events and make the Doctor his pawn.

For this reason, Nyssa collapsed at the end of "Four to Doomsday," although the Doctor seemingly fixed the problem by giving her 48 hours of D-sleep ("Kinda"). Even so, Nyssa remained receptive to psionics, demonstrating limited telepathic ability in the TV's "Time-Flight" and the Big Finish audios "The Land of the Dead" and "Winter for the Adept." Kwundaar here restores Nyssa's psychic defenses to normal, explaining why she never shows telepathy from "Arc of Infinity" onward.

CHARACTER DEVELOPMENT

• *The Doctor:* The Doctor doesn't recall earning a doctorate in theology, but possibly earned an honorary one. He wouldn't let Traken get destroyed, even to save Nyssa's life. [Indeed, given the resulting time paradox, he really *couldn't* let Traken get obliterated in this time zone.]

He has difficulty relaxing in tranquil locations, because evildoers almost inevitably show up to wreak havoc. He could build a Source supercomputer of his own—given a century to work. The Doctor left Gallifrey to escape "a certain conformity." He can pilot a merchant shuttle, and thinks he should write a paper on getting knocked unconscious.

The Doctor coins the term "Keeper" to better denote an advisor and confidante—not a controller— to the Source. [Parkin doesn't specify, but it's possible the Doctor bases the term on "Keeper of the Matrix" ("The Ultimate Foe").]

The Doctor sometimes uses artificial gills (a diving aid) and laser cutter. He associates the sun with rising in the "East," even on alien planets.

• *The Doctor and the Consuls of Traken:* The Doctor decries the Consuls' sweeping definition of virtually everything non-Trakenite as evil, stressing that evil often depends on one's perspective.

• *Nyssa:* Nyssa wasn't raised with religion. She can swim.

• *The Doctor and Nyssa:* The Doctor believes he could teach Nyssa Gallifreyan mental techniques, given time.

• *Kwundaar:* Kwundaar's able to read minds throughout time and space. However, he's *not* omnipotent. He's particularly sensitive to Trakenite minds, enough to dominate their individual wills [but not *en masse*]. Kwundaar can directly speak through others, but the effort drains him. To some degree, he's too telepathic, laboring to screen out unwanted thoughts.

Kwundaar's followers regard him as a "living god," although he moreso runs operations like a pirate, sharing the spoils of war. He teaches his soldiers that it's evil to repress their feelings and

desires—rather ironic, given his iron-fisted rule. He forbids most of his soldiers from remembering their past lives, save for a few trusted officials such as his chief of staff, Captain Narthex.

Kwundaar's second commandment to his troops: Serve Kwundaar, then serve yourself. His fourth commandment: Kwundaar helps those who help themselves.

His warships possess transmat capabilities. His soldiers use armored vehicles [fairly useless among Traken's gardens]. He sells conquered races to a slaver's guild.

Looking upon Kwundaar's face triggers insanity [although it's never specified why]. On Traken, Kwundaar's psionic abilities increase, granting him telekinesis.

• *Shayla:* Nyssa has never heard of Shayla. The Doctor only knows Shayla through the TARDIS databanks, which cite her as the greatest authority on Trakenite medicine (although that's not saying much, *see Stuff You Need*). As a senior physician, Shayla can revoke trading permits for medical reasons. She carries a small medical computer.

• *The TARDIS:* The TARDIS can scan nearby architecture. However, it cannot lock onto the Source interface chamber and materialize there directly. Shayla suggests that Consuls could destroy the in-flight TARDIS using the Source, but she probably doesn't appreciate the trans-dimensional physics involved.

ALIEN RACES *Time Lords:* Can innately sense an object's relative age.

• *Trakenites:* Trakenites are extremely insular, convinced that the rest of the Universe envies their science and harmony. They view evil as a radiation or cancer of sorts, worrying that outsiders carry it into the Union. Few races meet Traken standards enough for trade purposes.

Trakenites have only one heart. Nyssa equates the 2,532 years since the Union's formation as "100 generations," suggesting the longevity of a Trakenite is roughly human norm. [But then, the length of a Trakenite year isn't specified.]

ALIEN PLANETS *Traken:* Traken possesses the death penalty. D-sleep ("Kinda") is beyond its current medical level. A small spaceport [here destroyed] lets Traken conduct limited trade.

"Crested avar" birds are native to Traken. The planet possesses a communications center and an undefined area designated the Northern Shores, presumably located close to the Source interface chamber. Traken possesses a courts system with some authority over the Consuls.

PLACES TO GO *The Traken Union:* Kwundaar's ships hold position just beyond "the All Cloud," a barrier of sorts. Virtually nobody leaves the Union. Instead, a few beings smuggle themselves into it.

STUFF YOU NEED *Hyperdrive Engines:* Engaging any type of hyperdrive in a confined space (say, a hanger bay) makes the local atmosphere temporarily toxic.

• *The Source:* Actually an enormous computer matrix fashioned with light instead of silicon chips, then grafted onto Traken's sun.

As such, the Source channels almost unlimited energy and information resources. It regulates Traken's climate. It can direct its energies to incinerate invaders or turn them to stone.

The Source boosts the Trakenites' psychic defenses, meaning any natural resistance they possessed has long since withered. [Nyssa would likely have fallen ill upon leaving Traken with or without Kwundaar's help.] Conversely, the Source heals virtually all physical illness on Traken [although Trakenites are *not* immortal, suggesting they still die from old age]. Medics such as Shayla mostly just pass out fever drugs and let the Source do its work.

The main Source interface chamber holds an inner sanctum containing an avatar—a representation—of the true Source (i.e. the Traken sun). The interface generates heat that warms an underground stream, endowing a nearby spa with healing properties.

The Source isn't *alive* as such, but its sophisticated databanks function with some degree of sentience and at times seem to withhold information from the Consuls.

The Trakenites don't actively worship the Source, but come precariously close [Nyssa's claim, "The Source is just a machine!" draws gasps]. Technically, they respect it as a piece of "perfect" engineering.

Before the Keepers, the Source regulated and repaired itself. Sabotaging the Source would largely prove fruitless.

Input code 245680 lowers the Source's defensive shields. Code 257890 maximizes the shields, bottling the Source's energy. Code 17539 re-routes the Source's command functions to the Keeper's control chair.

• *Falconian Plague:* A lethal disease, although curable with Trakenite science. A dose of Atolix inoculates against it, whereas a tincture of "liquid gallas" treats existing cases.

ORGANIZATIONS *The Consuls of Traken:*

Trakenites Janneus and Hyrca currently serve as Consuls. Membership is restricted to Traken's elite. The Consuls possess secret knowledge about Kwundaar's past (*see History*).

HISTORY Kwundaar existed on Traken early in the planet's history. The first Trakenites revered him as a god. He helped the Trakenites develop science and architecture; in turn, they built temples in his honor.

• Circa 2,532 years before "Primeval," Kwundaar "inspired" the Trakenites to create the Source as the ultimate expression of science. The Source came online, formally marking the beginning of the Traken Union—and Kwundaar's fall from grace. The Trakenites used the Source's energy to banish Kwundaar. [Kwundaar claims he ruled the Trakenites benevolently, which seems somewhat implausible.] He retreated to the edge of the Traken Union's edge with his warfleet.

• In Kwundaar's absence, the Trakenites ditched religion in favor of science. They converted Kwundaar's inner sanctum into the main Source interface vault, making the surrounding temple into a healing spa. Kwundaar's priests became the governing Consuls of Traken.

• By Nyssa's era, the idyllic Trakenites stopped studying their past, figuring history couldn't teach them anything.

AT THE END OF THE DAY A nostalgic, colorful work that's criminally misunderstood at times. "Primeval" makes tremendous use of the fifth Doctor and Nyssa, holding every bit of potency you'd expect from a Lance Parkin script. But because no "Keeper of Traken" sequel can occur in a vacuum, this audio disappointed fans who unreasonably whipped themselves into a frenzy, expecting cosmic-level bells and whistles that it can't possibly deliver. That's a damn shame too, because once you ask, "Yes, but is it interesting?", "Primeval" more than passes the test—finishing as an audio that's worth revisiting.

EXCELIS DAWNS

By Paul Magrs

Release Date: February 2002
Order: Big Finish "Excelis Series" CD Part 1

TARDIS CREW The fifth Doctor, with Iris Wildthyme.

TRAVEL LOG Mountain Excelis and surrounding wilderness, planet Artaris, the end of winter (year unspecified).

CHRONOLOGY Concurrent with "Frontios" Part 4. More specifically, "Excelis Dawns" occurs during the fifth Doctor and Tegan's TARDIS-trip to drop off the sleeping Gravis on the planet Kolkokron.

STORY SUMMARY Enroute to Frontios, the TARDIS stops for a rest on the planet Artaris. There, the Doctor leaves Tegan in the Ship and goes exploring, randomly encountering a local warlord named Greyvorn. The Doctor learns that Greyvorn seeks to locate "the Relic"—a sacred object of unspecified power—and claim total rule over Artaris. Intrigued, the Doctor accompanies Greyvorn on his quest.

The Doctor and Greyvorn travel up the lofty peak of Excelis, the highest mountain on Artaris, to consult texts at a local nunnery. Once there, the Doctor cringes to unexpectedly re-meet Iris Wildthyme, a whimsical Gallifreyan who's smitten with him. Unable to remember how she arrived on Excelis, Iris agrees to help the duo find the Relic.

The convent's Mother Superior provides Greyvorn with a map of the Relic's location, allowing the Doctor, Iris and Greyvorn to drive off in Iris' TARDIS [disguised as a double-decker bus]. Along the way, the Doctor studies local myths that claim the Relic contains a portal to the afterlife. Disturbingly, the Doctor concludes that the Relic might genuinely hold powers over the hereafter.

The fellowship finds the Relic in a zombie village, hurriedly nabs the artifact—which bizarrely looks like Iris' handbag (*see "Unearthing the Relic" Sidebar, "The Plague Herds of Excelis"*)—and beats a hasty retreat back to the convent. Unfortunately, the greedy Mother Superior tries to take the Relic for herself, grappling with Greyvorn. The Doctor tries to intercede, but the two combatants—along with the Relic—fall off the nunnery's bell tower into the swamps below Excelis.

Believing Greyvorn, the Mother Superior and the Relic lost, the Doctor and Iris go their separate ways. Unbeknownst to the Gallifreyans, the Relic's energy saturates Greyvorn, making him immortal, but also grafts the Mother Superior's mind into Greyvorn's consciousness. Greyvorn awakens soon after, unable to find the Relic and hearing the Mother Superior's voice in his head. The warlord turns anguished for having to share his mind, even as the ambitious Mother Superior encourages Greyvorn to rise up and shape Artaris' future.

MEMORABLE MOMENTS Warlord Greyvorn hysterically shares a shopping trip to Excelis market with the older Iris. [He refers to himself as, "Lord Greyvorn, reduced to carrying the hag's shopping basket."]

When a combative Greyvorn tries (and fails) to kill Iris aboard her bus, she gets upset because: "Oh, there could have been blood anywhere, and it's so tough to get out of them seats."

Best of all, an incredulous Doctor asks Iris, "You had no idea your handbag contained all of Heaven and Hell?"; to which a clueless Iris replies, "I only wore it for show…"

SEX AND SPIRITS Iris causes all manner of commotion at the Excelis convent, mostly by cackling, smoking, playing music, prattling about men, promising to take the nuns on exciting excursions in her bus, general carousing and heavy boozing.

Iris' TARDIS contains a well-supplied drinks cabinet. The Doctor never drinks and drives, but serves Iris a vodka and tonic while she's behind the wheel. Also, Iris marks down "Bombay Saffire Gin" on her shopping list during a trip to Excelis market. [The befuddled Doctor asks: "How are we going to get that *here*?"]

Iris insists that the Doctor's proposed on three occasions, but that's probably nonsense. It's *highly* unlikely the Doctor harbors romantic thoughts for Iris, although he does dodge a question about whether he loves her at one point.

ASS-WHUPPINGS Surprisingly few. Greyvorn previously murdered his previous master (*see Character Development*) and slew some local rabble for sport. The insidious Sister Jolene eradicates the Zombie King, presumably with a futuristic weapon.

TV TIE-INS The Doctor's become more circumspect and cautious since Adric's demise ("Earthshock"). Iris here learns about Adric's death and sympathizes with the Doctor's pain, but encourages him to live for the moment.

Iris infuriates the Doctor by writing herself into his adventures, insanely claiming she helped defeat the Sontarans ("The Invasion of Time") and the renegade Omega ("The Three Doctors"), who by her account was "exiled" to a bed and breakfast in Bournemouth. She also insists that Morbius ("The Brain of Morbius") time scooped seven of her incarnations into the Death Zone, instigating a "Five Doctors"-style adventure where her selves fought the Voord ("The Keys of Marinus"), the Zarbi ("The Web Planet") and the Mechanoids ("The Chase"). She's supposedly visited "Frontios."

THE CRUCIAL BITS…

- **EXCELIS DAWNS**—First audio appearance of boisterous Gallifreyan Iris Wildthyme. First appearance of the warlord Greyvorn, who unexpectedly becomes immortal. The Doctor's first visit to Excelis. First appearance of the Relic, a pan-dimensional artifact shaped like Iris' gold lamé handbag.

Naturally, the Doctor decries Iris' claims as complete and total bunk.

NOVEL TIE-INS Iris Wildthyme, described by the Doctor as a "trans-temporal adventuress and cabaret star," first appeared in Paul Magrs' short story, *Short Trips*: "Old Flames." She also turned up in *The Scarlet Empress*, *Verdigris* and *The Blue Angel*, although "Excelis Dawns" marks her audio debut.

The Relic bears no resemblance to the notorious object in *Alien Bodies* (the Doctor's corpse, actually) bearing the same name.

AUDIO TIE-INS Greyvorn here turns immortal, encountering the sixth Doctor 1,000 years in Artaris' future in "Excelis Rising." Iris here leaves the Doctor's company, but turns up in "The Plague Herds of Excelis."

In a bit of foreshadowing, Iris' TARDIS runs wild at one point, catapulting itself more than 1,000 years into the future. The Doctor, Iris and Greyvorn witness a barren, blasted desert where Mount Excelis once stood, although Iris tries to pass off the vision as "a possible future" (*a la* the post-apocalyptic Earth in "Pyramids of Mars," no doubt). Even so, Excelis' destruction comes to pass in "Excelis Decays."

Prior to this story, Greyvorn experiences visions that suggest he'll live to see the far-distant future—which proves true in "Excelis Rising" and "Excelis Decays."

TIE-INS The Doctor elaborates on his regeneration in "Logopolis," acknowledging that he spoke with his wraith-like future self (i.e. "his watcher"). At the time, the dying fourth Doctor experienced a vision of talking with his past and future selves in Gallifrey's Death Zone ("The Five Doctors"). The current Doctor feels haunted because his previous incarnations looked *older* than when they regenerated, suggesting there's more to the afterlife than he thought. [It's unstated, but this largely pares with the New Adventures' assertion, starting in *Timewyrm: Revelation*, that the Doctor's previous selves exist in his mind as avatars.]

Iris thinks she acquired the handbag-shaped Relic at a bazaar on Hyspero (*The Scarlett Empress*), although "The Plague Herds of Excelis" clarifies her involvement with it.

CHARACTER DEVELOPMENT

• *The Doctor and Iris:* Iris can't recall [probably due to booze or her general flakiness] how she and the Doctor met. The Doctor simply "prefers not to remember."

The Doctor regards Iris as a "deeply deluded and dangerous woman" with a talent for "annoying virtually everyone." Even so, he begrudgingly marks her as a friend, protecting her when necessary.

Iris enjoyed sharing Christmas dinner at her bus one year with the Doctor, Nyssa and Adric, but spectacularly failed to get along with Tegan [whom she deems, "that swill Australian woman"].

Iris refers to the Doctor's people as "a snobby, over-privileged bunch," suggesting that she's a Gallifreyan, whereas the Doctor's a full-fledged Time Lord.

She last saw the Doctor [and the Daleks] in the diamond mines of "Marlion." At the time, she traveled with Jenny, a traffic warden who got the runs every time they went through the Time Vortex.

• *Iris Wildthyme:* Iris arrived on Artaris a month ago, drawn to the Relic for reasons she doesn't understand (*see "Unearthing the Relic" Sidebar, "The Plague Herds of Excelis"*).

Gardening bores Iris to tears. She's not much of an engineer, and can't fix the multiple things wrong with her TARDIS. She keeps a bazooka on her bus' luggage rack.

• *Greyvorn:* Greyvorn hails from one of Artaris' swamplands, born to a pragmatic, primitive people who were "terrified of lizards." Eventually, a "charismatic stranger" coaxed a youthful Greyvorn away from his people and enslaved him. Greyvorn later murdered his master, becoming a self-made warlord.

Greyvorn's prone to violence but carries an air of intelligence about him. He claims to command several "filthy cohorts," although it's questionable exactly how much territory/people Greyvorn actually rules. Still, Greyvorn supplies the Excelis convent with elementary construction, plumbing, plus contraband meat. The nuns view him as a protector, granting Greyvorn access to their private library.

• *The Doctor, Greyvorn and Iris:* Greyvorn has little use for the Doctor [calling him a "sandy-haired devil in striped trousers with some kind of vegetable pinned to his lapel"] beyond getting beyond his help in obtaining the Relic. In turn, the Doctor views Greyvorn as a roughneck and a thug.

Iris largely agrees, calling Greyvorn a "savage, bloodthirsty and rapacious warlord."

• *Iris' Bus:* Actually a TARDIS, disguised as a No. 22 double-decker bus bound for Putney Common. The defense systems don't work properly, and the bus isn't dimensionally transcendental. The Ship doesn't handle brief jaunts very well. It contains a kitchen and drinks cabinet, and dematerializes with the older, 1960s TV TARDIS sound.

ALIEN PLANETS *Artaris:* Most of the population lives on perilous mountainsides for defensive purposes, thereby breathing thin, poisonous air and going—as Greyvorn puts it— "gently mad."

Artaris' superstitious communities celebrate the "Festivals of Appeasement" in the Spring, making sacrifices to "the goddess" for the lost Relic's return. Outsiders are frequently sacrificed during this period. Dangerous wildlife, including sabre-tooths, inhabits the Artaran woods.

PLACES TO GO *Excelis:* Name for both Artaris' largest mountain and a settlement located there. The Excelis convent lies among the mountain's highest recesses.

• *The Time Vortex:* Iris whimsically describes it as the "natural environment" for the Time Lords, although she's likely speaking figuratively.

STUFF YOU NEED *The Relic:* Superstition-prone Artaris regards the lost Relic as the stuff of legend. Some people wanted it to commune with their dead loved ones, while others—notably Greyvorn—sought it for power's sake.

HISTORY Numerous civilizations have risen and fallen on Artaris, leaving little sign of their existence. The nuns inhabit a time-lost fortress, suggesting a previous society.

AT THE END OF THE DAY A hell of a lot of fun, taking its time and crafting a frolicking "On the Road…" tale. Magrs' script blends together a truly audacious mix of personalities and performances—Davison as the repressed fifth Doctor, Anthony Stewart Head (Giles from TV's *Buffy*) as the stiff Greyvorn and especially the adrenaline-tanked Katy Manning, sweetly upstaging everyone as Iris. All in all, a lively little story that kicks off the "Excelis" trilogy with hysterical results, unabashedly marching to its own drummer.

> ### DID YOU KNOW?

• The Iris Wildthyme that appears in the Excelis trilogy isn't the older incarnation of Iris, who

regenerated in *The Scarlet Empress*, even though it's easy to imagine her as such. Asked which incarnation of Iris pops up in the Big Finish audios, producer Gary Russell merely replied in a discussion board posting: "A new one."

LOUPS-GAROUX

By Marc Platt

Release Date: *May 2001*
Order: *Big Finish "Doctor Who" CD #20*

TARDIS CREW The fifth Doctor and Turlough.

TRAVEL LOG City carnival, Ileana's ranch and outlying areas, Rio de Janeiro, 2020.

STORY SUMMARY In Rio de Janeiro, 2020, a striking middle-age woman named Ileana de Santos, the de facto head of all werewolves, tries to enjoy a local carnival. However, Ileana finds herself stalked by her ex-lover, the ancient werewolf progenitor named Pieter Stubbe, who seeks to re-claim Ileana as his mate. Swiftly, Ileana gathers her associates and boards a chartered train for her ranch, intending to call a werewolf council to deal with Stubbe.

Simultaneously, the Doctor and Turlough try to holiday in Rio, frightened by the sight of the gray-furred, wolfen Stubbe amid the crowd. The duo spy Stubbe chasing after Ileana's train and materialize the TARDIS onboard, intending to warn the passengers. Ileana gradually learns to trust the Doctor, revealing she mainly hopes to protect her son Victor, who's overcome by his werewolf aspect, from Stubbe's influence.

Herr Lichtfuss, one of Ileana's suitors, jealously views the Doctor as a rival for her affections. Unable to directly confront the Doctor, Lichtfuss uses a hypnotic trick to make Turlough confront his inner darkness. Turlough panics and throws himself off the train, but luckily survives. Soon afterward, Turlough happens across the young Rosa Caiman, a young Amazon Indian on an initiation ritual.

Turlough and Rosa share an assignation, even as Stubbe exerts dominance over Ileana's werewolf council. The Doctor challenges Stubbe's authority, inadvertently offering himself up as a potential mate for Ileana. As a mystical creature bound to the Earth, Stubbe finds himself unable to swallow the extra-terrestrial Doctor. Nonetheless, Stubbe flexes his might by encouraging the werewolf pack to besiege Rio, ordering them to

bloodily tear the city apart.

With Stubbe overlooking the city, the Doctor heads for the lower regions and summons the werewolf pack with K9's ultra-sonic whistle. The Doctor berates the werewolves for readily following Stubbe like timid mongrels, convincing them to roam free. The werewolves agree, abandoning Stubbe and departing before human soldiers arrive in force.

The Doctor rejoins Turlough and Rosa, but Stubbe pursues them all inside the TARDIS. Hurriedly, the Doctor slams the doors shut, dematerializes the Ship and reappears in Earth orbit. Cut off from the Earth, the elemental source of the werewolves' power, Stubbe weakens and dies. As a final gesture to a fallen enemy, Rosa calls upon her tribe's guardian spirits to guide Stubbe to a forest-covered afterlife.

The TARDIS returns to Earth, allowing Rosa to depart and continue her initiation. The Doctor shares final words with Ileana, admitting that as a Time Lord, he can't properly love her. Saddened, Ileana bids the Doctor farewell, allowing him and Turlough to head for parts unknown.

MEMORABLE MOMENTS A defiant Stubbe in Germany, 1589, sentenced to death: "Will you dance for me, magistrate? Shall I set the whole of Cologne dancing to my tune?" In 2020, he menacingly tells Ileana: "My strength of will remains implacable. Age and enforced absence only make it stronger, my long lost love. I'll cut out every rival."

Turlough asks the Doctor what he wants from life, and the Doctor can only reply that he'll know when he finds it. More tellingly, the Doctor tells Stubbe: "I explore possibilities. I look for things I could never imagine."

Platt provides some lovely imagery involving the TARDIS, with Turlough commenting, "While the outside's always changing, some of us are lucky enough to be allowed in here, looking out through a door that's never in the same place twice." He also asks the Doctor if the Ship runs on imagination.

The Doctor haltingly asks Turlough for advice on his lovelife, catching the listener off-guard with the realization that romance constitutes a real blind spot for the Time Lord. Finally, Stubbe meets a memorable end, with his consciousness entering some kind of forest [either death or another realm, but certainly not our reality].

SEX AND SPIRITS Rosa Cayman notably invites Turlough under her blankets at night, under the excuse of keeping warm. [Right.] It's lit-

tle more than a one-night stand, and afterward, Turlough warns Rosa he's not very trustworthy.

Simultaneously, Ileana takes a liking to the Doctor, pleased when he challenges Stubbe and (unknowingly) offers himself up as her mate. The Doctor subtly asks Turlough for romantic advice, erroneously assuming he and Rosa are together. The Time Lord claims to have little experience with women [although this contradicts novels such as *The Infinity Doctors*, *The Dying Days* and certainly *Cold Fusion*], other than being simple friends with his female companions. He finally concludes that, although he would enjoy Ileana's company, he isn't capable of loving her. In the final scene, she acknowledges this and bids him well.

In Rio, a random prostitute offers herself to the Doctor, but he declines, despite Turlough egging him on.

Stubbe and Ileana are clearly ex-lovers, having run together through Russia and Italy. Ileana claims she left Stubbe years ago. And on that note...

ASS-WHUPPINGS Stubbe sets about killing Ileana's werewolf suitors, beheading one Mr. Chaudhry and easily slaying Herr Lichtfuss in open combat.

Lichtfuss and another werewolf get Turlough drunk, then use a mental "mirror trick" and hypnotically make him view his inner darkness. Turlough consequently throws himself off a train, but [implausibly] survives.

Rosa slays three werewolves, including one Mr. Torbut, with her silver blade. Her grandfather died, of natural causes it seems, previous to this story, and she buried him in a creekbed.

Stubbe swallowed a tax gatherer once, Joshua of Dullstad, and was spitting out coins for days. He also gulps down Turlough at one point, but a silver blade that Turlough carries makes Stubbe barf him back up. Years ago, Stubbe and Santos ate the Grand Duchess and Lord Lucan of Anastasia.

The werewolves wreak unspecified havoc in Rio. The Doctor discovers that Dr. Hayashi, hired by Ileana to tend to her son Victor, secretly intends to cure lycanthropy. For better or worse, the Doctor exposes Hayashi's scheme (*see Sidebar*), then protests futilely as the werewolves hunt Hayashi down and eat 'em.

At story's end, the Doctor materializes the TARDIS 500 miles above Earth, blatantly killing Stubbe. His body vanishes, and his psyche either crosses over into death or becomes trapped in a forest within Rosa's mental landscape.

CHARACTER DEVELOPMENT

MISCELLANEOUS STUFF!

THE DOCTOR'S WEREWOLF MORALITY

"Loups-Garoux" somewhat questionably makes the Doctor defend the werewolves' right to exist, as if mirroring his regard for the reptilian Silurians in "Warriors of the Deep." In this, audio writer Marc Platt concurs with TV scribe Johnny Byrne's view of the Doctor as a well-seasoned traveler who acknowledges that all races, not just humanity, are worthy of respect.

That's all well and good, but whereas the Doctor in "Warriors of the Deep" ultimately views the Silurians as honorable but kills them off anyway, preventing them from destroying Earth, he almost willfully ignores the werewolves' innate bloodlust in "Loups-Garoux."

Essentially, when the Doctor discovers that geneticist Matzo Hayashi, Victor's caretaker, is working on a cure for lycanthropy, he vows to stop Hayashi whatever the cost—claiming werewolves have an ancient culture worth preserving. But that seems incredibly naïve, considering the werewolves' "culture" consists of little more than eating humans. Following that logic, the Doctor might as well claim that serial killers have every right to practice their culture, no matter how many innocents die in the process.

In part, the Doctor almost becomes like Barbara in "The Aztecs." He's convinced that Stubbe is the serpent in the garden, and that surely the werewolves would be pacifistic creatures without his influence. Yet, the Doctor fails to recognize that werewolves are geared by nature for slaughter. For every werewolf (i.e. Ileana) who hates their animal aspect, several more surely enjoy the life, and what precisely does he imagine they're going to do, if left to their own devices? Take up needlepoint?

More strangely, Hayashi isn't trying to *kill* the werewolves. He simply wants to make them human again, thus stopping them from harming anyone. Our response: That's a damn good idea, and the Doctor himself usually concurs with this view (such as his goal to cure vampirism in "Project: Twilight," etc.). But as things stand, the Doctor botches Hayashi's undertaking and atypically rallies to the werewolves' cause, making him partly responsible not only for Hayashi's eventual death, but to some degree the death of every human the werewolves slaughter in future.

• *The Doctor:* The Doctor last visited Rio in 1700, before the enormous Christ statue on Corcavado Mountain was built.

Werewolves claim the Doctor smells like several types [presumably non-terrestrial] of unusual musk—and death. The Doctor's familiar with werewolves. He can shield his mind from werewolves, and notably resists Stubbe's hypnosis by reciting *The Rhyme of the Ancient Mariner*.

He's got exceptional eyesight. He thinks discussing money is vulgar. Despite his youthful incarnation, he sometimes feels very old. He can fly a Spitfire. He once met Cleopatra, judging she didn't have much wit.

The Doctor holds some questionable morality concerning werewolves (*see Sidebar*).

• *The Doctor and Turlough:* Turlough thinks the Doctor means well, but that he's too cautious.

• *Turlough:* Turlough's internal greed and darkness makes him especially vulnerable to the werewolves' hypnotic influence. He's distrustful, stealing Rosa's silver knife and later claiming she gave it to him. The grandeur and costuming of Rio parades fascinates him. Turlough hates Earth, believing himself superior to humans. He never watches television.

• *Ileana de Santos:* Her late, human husband Frederico owned the Santos Cattle Empire. They were married for 42 years. Ileana outlived him, unable to age, and inherited his wealth. Atypically for a werewolf, she despises her inner darkness and feral aspect. She hasn't seen Stubbe in years.

• *Pieter Stubbe (a.k.a. "the gray one"):* He predates humanity and therefore doesn't have a human aspect. All werewolves are his progeny. He's consumed by appetite, and legendary among his people. He's strong enough to bite the head off another werewolf. He's touted as a master of different shapes and illusions.

Stubbe can keep pace with a 200-mph train. He hates to talking to someone via phone, because he can't smell them. He got his fill of grandmothers years ago.

Other werewolves experience heightened emotions—as if smelling the scent of lightning before thunder—when Stubbe comes into town.

• *The Doctor and Stubbe:* Stubbe thinks the Doctor stinks of sanctimony, and sees nothing in him.

• *Victor:* Ileana's son. After Victor's human father died, he lost touch with humanity and surrendered to his werewolf side. He slightly regains his humanity by story's end.

• *Dr. Hayashi:* Geneticist at the Institute of Genomic Surgery, Kamikura University. Ileana hired Hayashi to help treat her son Victor, but he sold her out to Stubbe.

• *Rosa Cayman:* Member of the Morano tribe, which largely died off when the Amazon forest perished (*see History*). Rosa's late grandfather served as the tribe's last wise man. He carved Rosa's silver blade and gave her a jaguar pelt, denoting her as the tribe's headman.

Rosa's adept at hunting werewolves and trapping other animals such as armadillos. Rosa calls herself "the Jaguar Maiden," and seems to channel the spirits of her tribe. They supposedly inhabit a virtual forest within her mind. She records a great deal of her thoughts on a computerized wristwatch, but leaves it behind to continue her initiation.

• *The TARDIS:* The TARDIS can materialize in front of a fast-moving train, then time-shift just enough as the train passes by to arrive onboard. The Ship can also hover three inches above the ground. It can park itself in the Time Vortex, according the Doctor extra time to think.

ALIEN RACES *Werewolves:* Werewolves refer to humans as *cutclaws*. They're virtually immortal, but can be killed.

Werewolves hypnotically deceive the senses, appearing invisible to humans and Trions [but not Time Lords]. The brain knows they're present, but the eyes don't. They can mentally spur their victims to run, igniting a hunt.

Becoming a werewolf seems to entail a mental awakening as much as a physical transformation. The "mirror trick" makes a budding werewolf acknowledge their feral side, considered a precious and sacred event. However, it's sometimes used to torment people into seeing their inner darkness.

Werewolves are inherently bound to the Earth, meaning they could never fly in an airplane. Even being in a first floor apartment makes them queasy. Silver's the best defense against werewolves, but they're also vulnerable to fire. They're lightning fast, and super-strong.

Most werewolves can assume human form at will. They become human when they die. They prefer hunting at night, but aren't hampered traveling by day.

A werewolf hierarchy technically exists, with Ileana ruling over a council, but it's almost never exercised. Given their mesmeric ability, werewolves in sufficient quantity could topple a society.

ALIEN PLANETS *Trion:* Has forests, three times as tall as Earth trees. The trees have blood-red trunks. They also have thick, plate-sized mauve and purple leaves, big enough for people to walk on. Large sapphire-colored moths appear in droves during the spring. Trion has more than one sun.

PLACES TO GO *Rio de Janeiro:* Under Amazonian state law, it's an offense to not display genome-ID implants when asked. Robot inspecting officers check such chips. The fine's no less than 5000 credits [the current currency in Brazil, it seems] or a prison term of less than six months. Ident implants also work for financial transactions, like credit cards. It's also an offense to have a nil credit rating within city boundaries.

Rio now features hovercar traffic, whisking along at 30 feet overhead. The city also boasts a monorail system. Parades there use holograms.

ORGANIZATIONS *Santos' Werewolf Council:* Numbering about 20, includes such legendary figures as Mr. Ianst Boxhill of Morebarch, Selena of Glyphstaff, Mr. Moregrim, Mr. Torbut and Billy Redtooth of the Cherokee. [Author's Note: That's all phonetic, and probably misspelled.]

PHENOMENA *Lycanthropy:* Takes many forms, including weresharks.

PROBABLE HISTORY In summer, 1812, Ileana fled with her father, a wealthy merchant from Smolensk, as Napoleon invaded Russia. [The Doctor recalls the event as having stormy weather.] Along the way, Ileana's party ran into bandits, who stole their belongings and shot her father. A handsome partisan, actually Stubbe, found her huddled over a frozen corpse and turned her into a werewolf. She was bound to him for somewhere between 100 to 200 years.

HISTORY Stubbe supposedly pre-dates humanity, evidently born as an avatar of the Earth's power.
- In Cologne, Germany, October 28, 1589, the people condemned Pieter Stubbe to public execution for sorcery, lewd villainies and murders. He somehow escaped.
- About 20 years ago, the Amazon's eco-system collapsed, displacing a number of werewolves and Amazon Indian tribes. The so-called "Lung of the World" became a dust bowl stretching from Rio to the Andes. Thousands of unique species, birds, animals and plants died off. A war nearly erupted because of this, but Earth's governments focused on exploiting the moon and the asteroid belt, and therefore stopped caring. Shantytowns, inhabited by displaced Amazonian Indians, have overrun Rio beaches.
- A spaceport now exists in the former rain forest. British Rail is no longer in service. Hologram amusement parks are in operation.

AT THE END OF THE DAY Passionate, daring, and a brilliant effort from writer Marc Platt ("Ghost Light," *Lungbarrow*). The highly adept "Loups-Garoux" goes about its business with blood dripping from its fangs, painting a werewolf-filled landscape so rich, it makes you forget the story's flaws (notably the Doctor's questionable morality, *see Sidebar*). Overall, "Loups-Garoux" works because it's just so damn *interesting*, not to mention uses both the Doctor and Turlough to full effect, and displays the sort of innovation one hopes from "Who" these days.

SUPERIOR BEINGS

By Nick Walters

> *Release Date: June 2001*
> *Order: BBC Past Doctor Adventure #43*

TARDIS CREW The fifth Doctor and Peri.

TRAVEL LOG An Eknuri-owned planetoid, circa 2994; a remote, unnamed garden planet, circa 3100.

STORY SUMMARY Weary from their travels, the Doctor and Peri try to vacation on a private planetoid with some Eknuri: a race of benevolent, genetically augmented humans. The Doctor also passes the time with visiting xenobiologist Aline Vehlmann, who manifested psionic abilities on a previous expedition (*see Character Development*).

A pack of fox-like Valethske—raiders combing the galaxy as part of a "Great Mission"—appear to capture the partygoers as a ready-made food supply. The Doctor and Aline escape, but the Valethske raiders cryo-freeze some Eknuri—and Peri—in their ship's larder. Mission complete, the Valethske depart into space, also putting themselves into cryo-sleep for their journey.

The Doctor scans the Valethske ship and finds it uses a primitive faster-than-light drive, preventing the TARDIS from materializing onboard. As an alternative, the Doctor triangulates that the Valethske ship will arrive at its next target—a remote, unnamed planet—in roughly 100 years time. The TARDIS accordingly time-skips ahead, arriving simultaneous to the Valethske vessel.

Aline and the Doctor free the Valethske's hostages, then find the planet inhabited by "Gardeners"—enormous, mobile plant creatures protecting sedate herds of giant beetles. Additionally, the Doctor learns the Valethske's "Great Mission" entails tracking down the Khorlthochloi, their for-

This book is not endorsed by the BBC. Doctor Who and TARDIS are trademarks of the BBC.

47

mer gods, to punish them for limiting the Valethske's development.

Eventually, Aline hears a psionic siren call from an engineered plasma stream—a final message from the long-lost Khorlthochloi. Aline irresistibly merges with the plasma stream, geared for use by higher evolutionaries, and suffers terminal cell damage as a result. Aline survives long enough, however, to mentally scan the plasma stream and learn the Khorlthochloi's fate.

As Aline details, the Khorlthochloi long ago abandoned their physical forms, mentally evolving onto a new plane of existence. As a precaution, the Khorlthochloi left behind their insectoid bodies in case they needed to return. Soon after, an unspecified threat forced the Khorlthochloi to reunite with their physical forms. But as the Khorlthochloi's bodies had devolved during the interim, they were no longer compatible with their former minds. The unnamed threat consumed the Khorlthochloi minds, but not before they constructed the plasma stream as a warning to out-of-body travelers.

Aline succumbs to her injuries, even as the Valethske hunt down and kill the escapees. The Doctor and Peri survive, but the Valethske pound the planet from orbit, leveling the giant beetles' feeding grounds. Afterward, Hunt Marshal Veek becomes convinced of the futility of "the Great Mission," realizing the Khorlthochloi, in truth, have already died out. Veek loads up the surviving Valethske and heads for home, allowing the Doctor and Peri to bury Aline, then depart.

MEMORABLE MOMENTS Aline ponders if the Doctor's celery is a symbiote, as it isn't so much pinned on his lapel as it's just *there*.

SEX AND SPIRITS A hunky Eknuri named Athon begs Peri for cheap sex, but she repeatedly declines. She accidentally brushes his butt at one point, and they hug for comfort while in captivity, but that's all.

The Valethske strip their captives—including Peri—and dump 'em into a pit. They briefly ponder getting their captives to breed and produce more meat, deeming Peri's pelvis as especially ripe for child bearing.

Peri fought off a lot of dumb jocks in college. When the Doctor puts a protective arm around Peri, the rest of his body instinctively leans away. Furthermore, the Doctor suspects that Peri might leave him someday because he can't accommodate her youthful [i.e. sexual] needs.

The Eknuri view sex a communal event, almost a sport. They don't bond for life, but get jealous.

ASS-WHUPPINGS Peri endures a jarring skimmer impact. She actually gets off easy, since the Valethske cook some of the vacationing Eknuri. She takes a Valethske bullet at one point and pukes after her draining, cryo-frozen journey to the garden planet.

Hunt Marshall Veek quells [i.e. slits from stem to stern] some rebellious crewmembers. She catches the randy Eknuri Athon in the act of boning female captive Lornay, killing her for sport. Athon commits suicide—with a grenade, of all things—to avoid the Valethske eating his toned body.

Valethske Scourblaze missiles strike home on the garden planet, guaranteeing the Khorlthochloi's eventual starvation. Xenobiologist Aline dies, her body dry up like a raisin from plasma stream exposure.

TV TIE-INS The TARDIS' temporal grace (chiefly "Earthshock") still isn't working, which surprises the Doctor.

In the summer before Peri went to Lanzarote ("Planet of Fire"), she witnessed religious zealots prophesizing on TV and at summer festivals.

The TARDIS wardrobe ("The Twin Dilemma," etc.) is a wall-less area filled with racks of clothes, hats, shoes, tailor's dummies, a half-dozen wedding dresses and more.

Eknur 4's cited as a Wonder of the Universe ("Death to the Daleks").

A Valethske named Ruvis once survived a disastrous skirmish with the Sontarans ("The Time Warrior," etc.), only to get stranded for three years with nothing to eat but Sontaran flesh—a notoriously tough, tasteless and carcinogenic meat. Ruvis lived, but his left leg and lower jaw later needed prosthetic replacement.

NOVEL TIE-INS An unspecified threat kills off the Khorlthochloi, possibly the same malevolence that hounds the Vortex Wraiths (*The Slow Empire*) and the clock people (*Anachrophobia*).

CHARACTER DEVELOPMENT

• *The Doctor:* The Doctor's impressed with the Eknuri's accomplishments, and often visits them to let off steam. He's invited to Eknur 4 to give a series of lectures on temporal physics.

He knows Aline by reputation. He's heard the Khorlthochloi mentioned in myths and legends. He's currently carrying a golden TARDIS key rather than a silver one. Peri marks the Doctor's age as about 800.

• *Perpugilliam Brown:* She's 19, green-eyed, and views the TARDIS as home.

THE CRUCIAL BITS...

- **SUPERIOR BEINGS**—Peri spends more than a century in cryo-stasis.

As a child, Peri endured terrifying hurricanes on her uncle's farm. She likes coffee and doughnuts.

- *The Doctor and Peri:* The Doctor fails to understand why his companions don't remain with him longer. Conversely, Peri wonders how many companions have left the Doctor, scarred by their adventures.

- *The Doctor, Peri and the TARDIS:* From time to time, the TARDIS mysteriously leaves Peri welcome-aboard gifts, including bits of clothing, a first edition of *The Catcher in the Rye*, etc. The Ship doesn't leave the Doctor such gifts anymore. Peri wishes the TARDIS would produce a pair of sunglasses, because she left her only set behind on Lanzarote ("Planet of Fire"), but none appear.

- *Aline Vehlmann:* Renowned xenologist and bio-astronomer, currently writing a paper on the Eknuri for the Hamilton Smith Institute. She's read about the Valethske in Institute's brief *Xenolog* entry.

Previous to this story, Aline encountered an unspecified alien presence that awakened her latent psionic abilities. She's still a bit jittery in the presence of alien beings. She's visited Eknur 4. Her civilization knows about the Time Lords, but has nothing published on them. She holds a doctorate. Aline visits the TARDIS wardrobe and dons a jacket that belonged to Amelia Earhart.

- *The TARDIS:* The Ship keeps moving its rooms around. The wardrobe's currently second door on the right from the console room, with a bathroom opposite, but that could easily change. The Ship also houses a potting shed and a room full of bicycles. The room next to Peri's quarters contained a coffin, which the Doctor uses to bury Aline.

ALIEN RACES *Time Lords:* Their advanced palates detect even minute amounts of toxins. The Doctor claims the Khorlthochloi's achievements even outweigh the Time Lords' [although that seems unlikely].

- *Khorlthochloi (a.k.a. Korlevalulaw, the ebon ones):* An extremely long-lived species, cited before their mental upgrade as "ebony giants with eyes of fire, the size of mountains."

The Khorlthochloi's degenerated bodies look like many-legged, bulbous bugs about the size of cows. Their heads are almost afterthoughts, protruding from a thick, ridged thorax. Deformed-looking antennae sit above plate-sized compound eyes.

- *Valethske:* Fox-like humanoids with tall, long muscular legs, elongated bodies and golden-yellow, slanted eyes. They evolved to hunt herd animals on their homeworld, the forested Valeth Skettra.

The Valethske hold little regard for other species, viewing them as food. They have notions of honor regarding their own kind, with edifices such as the Hall of Glory and the Hall of the Dead.

Deadly rights of combat determine the Valethske command structure. The Ten Trials of Azreske, named after a Valethske progenitor, serve to cull the unworthy. Eating a fallen Valethske's organs is the worst possible insult, since it symbolically reduces the hunter to prey.

The Valethske sent about 30 ships, crewed by a few hundred, on the "Great Mission." Most of them work without question [Hunt Marshall Veek is a rare dissenter]. They've always coveted time travel, but never achieved it.

They have excellent night vision. They usually awake from cryo-stasis hungry, eating synthetic meat if needed.

- *Eknuri:* Genetically altered humanoids who hail from Eknur 4, and theoretically have no enemies. They've never endured a war, and exist within a technocracy. They've combined their knowledge of genetics, physics, philosophy, literature and sport to enhance the human condition.

The Eknuri enjoy a life of unfettered hedonism. They're highly athletic, well above human norm, and have pacifist tendencies. They can live for up to 200 years. Servitors diagnose and heal rare instances of illness. They can self-regulate their gastric juices. There's little exterior difference between Eknuri males and females.

ALIEN PLANETS *Eknur 4:* Contains effective but unspecified defenses.

STUFF YOU NEED *The Khorlthochloi Plasma Strand:* It's pre-programmed to regulate the Khorlthochloi homeworld's climate, tend to its gardens and feed the Gardeners. The Khorlthochloi probably used the plasma stream as a navigational aid to return from their higher dimension.

- *Valethske Stasis Pod:* Able to cryo-freeze humans for at least 500 years with no ill effects. The pod revives its subjects via use of nanites pumped into the bloodstream.

SHIPS *Valethske Ship:* Composed of three bulbous tubular engines, like blackened cigars. The main body sweeps upward into a blunt nosecone, which looks strikingly like the upside-down Valethske head. The ship comes equipped with

151 Scourblaze missiles, typically used to purge planets of disease, or as a last resort when attacked.

HISTORY According to Valethske myth, the Khorlthochloi—allegedly the oldest race in the galaxy [but actually not, as that honor goes to the Time Lords]—acted as shepherds to developing species. Many thousands of years ago, the Khorlthochloi decided the Valethske were getting too dominant. The Khorlthochloi smashed Valethske warfleets out of space and further devastated their civilization with a plague. The Khorlthochloi mentally departed for a higher plane of existence soon after, leaving the Valethske survivors to rebuild their society.

• Some centuries ago, the Valethske initiated the "Great Mission." Since then, they've been a nuisance, raiding alien settlements to capture food supplies.

• Circa 2495, territorial disputes plagued the Thynemnus System. Additionally, boar-like aliens attacked the human colonists there. The Korsair finally established a military outpost in Thynemnus to police the system, driving away the boar-like aliens. However, the Valethske showed up soon after, capturing soldiers and colonists alike for use as food stocks.

AT THE END OF THE DAY A book that's just... bland, really. Whatever its boastful title, *Superior Beings* fronts an incredibly loose structure, with *lots* of characters simply dashing about and getting offed in a fairly boring fashion. Also, the fox-like Valethske aren't much more than the "monster of the month," and it's hard to say that the Doctor actually wins or loses this one, so much as the aliens simply go home.

WARMONGER

By Terrance Dicks

Release Date: May 2002
Order: BBC Past Doctor Adventure #53

TARDIS CREW The fifth Doctor and Peri.

TRAVEL LOG Chiefly planets Karn, Aridius and Sylvana, some years before "The Brain of Morbius" (circa 2375); Gallifrey, some time before "The Deadly Assassin"; unnamed planet with dangerous wildlife, time unknown.

CHRONOLOGY Between "Planet of Fire" and

"The Caves of Androzani." The fifth Doctor and Peri here recover from their "latest" adventure, suggesting *Warmonger* takes place immediately after *Superior Beings*.

Continuity warning: If you're not up to speed on the fourth Doctor's encounter with the mad surgeon Solon, the Sisterhood of Karn and the disembodied Morbius in "The Brain of Morbius," trust us—there's no time to explain it here.

STORY SUMMARY In the past on Gallifrey, the warmongering President Morbius seeks to lead the Time Lords to conquer the Universe, prompting the more conservative High Council to depose him. The High Council resists executing Morbius, likening exile to a fate worse than death. But once away from Gallifrey, Morbius pools mercenaries and space pirates from various planets into a formidable army.

Meanwhile, the fifth Doctor and Peri land on a temperate planet, hoping for a peaceful vacation. Unfortunately, a flying pterodon attacks Peri, nearly biting off her arm. Desperate to help, the Doctor places Peri in stasis and deliberately pilots the TARDIS to the past on Karn. Once there, the Doctor implores a younger Mehendri Solon, a genius surgeon, to save Peri's life.

Currently the Surgeon-General of the Hospice, a neutral healing center, Solon fails to recognize the regenerated Doctor and easily restores Peri to health. The Doctor breathes easy, but soon afterward, Morbius sends a platoon to overrun the Sisterhood on Karn, hoping to secure their immortality-granting Elixir of Life. The psionic Sisterhood repels the attack, but Morbius simply takes his main army elsewhere and conquers a frightening amount of worlds.

Soon after, the Doctor travels to "modern-day" Gallifrey (i.e. before "The Deadly Assassin"), warning the High Council of Morbius' growing threat. The Time Lords favor military action against Morbius, fearing that assassination would martyr him. But as Gallifrey lacks an army, the Time Lords quickly propose uniting the major races of the Universe into a fighting force.

The Time Lords choose the Doctor, as one of the most imaginative and daring Gallifreyans, to lead the new army. The Doctor reluctantly accepts the post, swiftly convincing the Draconians and the Sontarans that Morbius poses a mutual threat to their empires. The various races form a military "Alliance," with the Doctor acting as the group's supreme authority (a.k.a. "Supremo").

The Alliance forces take the battle to Morbius, liberating a number of conquered worlds. Eventually, Morbius abandons his territory, bringing his

remaining forces to bear against Alliance forces near Karn. The Doctor despairs as all seems lost, but reinforcements from the liberated planet of Fangoria arrive and win the day, crushing Morbius' army.

The Time Lords capture Morbius, authorizing his execution. To fulfill history, the Doctor secretly enables Solon—one of Morbius' followers—to remove Morbius' brain before his atomization. With Morbius believed dead—and his brain privately in Solon's keeping—the Alliance disbands while the Doctor travels onward with Peri.

SEX AND SPIRITS As some critics correctly point out, *Warmonger* seems chock-full of rape [and even gang rape] threats.

Morbius, cited as a "fast worker," reported violates some of his female prisoners, then passes the leftovers around to his crew. He also turns smitten with Peri and kidnaps her, but she eludes his advances by scraping her skin and faking that she's got some type of contagious jungle rash. [Morbius falls for the ruse, ranking him among the stupidest Time Lords in history.] One of Morbius' troopers considers raping the younger Sisterhood members before killing them. A toothless soldier named Sammie threatens to have a quickie with the captive Peri.

Solon supposedly fools around with his female patients, and takes a passing fancy to Peri. His assistant Drago moreso gets obsessed her, and mandates a lot of frivolous "check-ups." Solon operates on a drugged, naked Peri, but doesn't take any liberties.

On the planet Sylvana, Peri declines several offers to marry farmers. She variously downs *akkeen*, a potent Sylvanan brandy and a cool, white lemony wine and a green Arcturan wine. She gets tipsy during the Alliance campaign. Peri uses flirting to her advantage, telling a security guard she needs access to the TARDIS because, "I've got nothing to wear…" She dons a low-cut red gown at a Hospice reception.

The Doctor drinks vintage champagne from Copernicus Two with Hawken, the head of Hospice security. He knows Sontaran toasts and has steaming *vrag* with Battle-Marshall Skrug.

In celebration of their final victory, the Sontarans get completely schnookered. The Draconians customarily sip tiny glasses of exquisite liqueurs, and exchange witty and poetic epigrams.

ASS-WHUPPINGS A pterodon nearly bites off Peri's upper arm. In turn, the Doctor clamps his own teeth into creature's neck and finally snaps it. Solon heals Peri's wound with bio-flesh. As lever-

age against the Doctor, Solon briefly gives Peri an injection that reactivates her infection.

Peri briefly succeeds as a freedom fighter on the planet Sylvana (*see Character Development*), but her dozen-strong guerrillas—including Marko (killed), Brand (killed), Lon (killed), Gina (raped and killed) and Kyrin (killed) meet a less-than-benevolent end. In escaping from detention, Peri wounds Lieutenant Hakon with a bullet.

Time Lord Ratisbon commits small acts of sabotage/murder and pins the crime on Morbius, swaying various races to the Alliance's cause. Ratisbon snuffs out some of his own agents to cover his tracks.

The Sisters of Karn drop rubble on some advancing Gaztak mercenaries. Sisterhood leader Maren blinds Morbius' pilots with her ring, making them crash. The Sisterhood also deploys psychic attacks.

Whirlwind battles between Alliance forces and Morbius' troops consume the book's final third. Notably, Sontaran battle-commander Streg dies eliminating a cannon aimed at the Doctor and Peri.

TV TIE-INS *Warmonger* serves as a prequel to "The Brain of Morbius." As mentioned in "Brain," Sisterhood leader Maren here witnesses Morbius' "atomization." The fifth Doctor goes by "Smith" so the younger Solon won't recognize his name "in future." After the fall of Hospice, Solon takes up residence in the ruins of Castle Karn's hydrogen planet ("The Brain of Morbius").

The fifth Doctor readily ventures into Gallifrey's past—something previously forbidden except under the gravest of circumstances (such as Gallifrey losing the War, *Alien Bodies*).

The fifth Doctor here encounters President Saran, killed in "The Deadly Assassin" and remembered as a minor figure, and Borusa ("The Deadly Assassin") as a Junior Cardinal.

It's erroneously stated that Borusa here meets the Doctor for the "first" time, although this refers to his not recognizing the disguised, regenerated Doctor. By this point, Borusa has already served as the Doctor's tutor ("The Deadly Assassin").

Members of the Alliance include: Sontarans ("The Time Warrior," etc.), Draconians ("Frontier in Space"), Cybermen ("The Tenth Planet," etc.), Ice Warriors ("The Ice Warriors," etc.), Ogrons ("Day of the Daleks" and "Frontier in Space") and Gaztaks ("Meglos"). The Alliance races go their separate ways, but their cooperation perhaps furthers the founding of the Federation ("The Curse of Peladon").

The Doctor knows the codes to Gallifrey's transduction barriers ("The Invasion of Time"). He

This book is not endorsed by the BBC. Doctor Who and TARDIS are trademarks of the BBC.

51

keeps an oak-paneled, book-lined study in the TARDIS (which presumably becomes the new console room, "Doctor Who: Enemy Within"), and already possesses an autographed copy of H. G. Wells' *The Time Machine* ("Doctor Who: Enemy Within").

Tracking a ship once it's gone into hyperspace ("The Stones of Blood") is virtually impossible. The Doctor places a wounded Peri into stasis with a flat metal disc ("Planet of the Daleks") during the journey to Karn. The Blinovitch Limitation Effect ("Day of the Daleks") makes short temporal hops tricky—meaning the Doctor can't just scoot ahead a couple of weeks in the TARDIS and pick her up, fully healed.

The Alliance bases itself on Aridius ("The Chase"). The Doctor claims that Time Lord trials don't include juries ("The War Games," although that changes somewhat by "Trial of a Time Lord"), since verdicts are invariably rigged.

Sergeant Benton watched hospital soap operas during his UNIT days (the third Doctor era).

CIA member Ratisbon offers to drop standing charges against the Doctor in exchange for his leading the alien armies—rather generous, since the Time Lords already pardoned the Doctor in "The Three Doctors." The Doctor currently views the Time Lords as ethical, which doesn't exactly match their history (although admittedly, this story occurs before "Trial of a Time Lord"). The Capitol Guard ("The Deadly Assassin") hasn't done any fighting in generations.

If the Doctor hadn't stolen the TARDIS (pre-"An Unearthly Child"), it would likely have been scrapped.

NOVEL TIE-INS The fifth Doctor confusingly claims that Adolf Hitler is an old friend of his, mucking up continuity, as he doesn't meet Hitler until his sixth (*The Shadow in the Glass*) and seventh (*Timewyrm: Exodus*) incarnations.

Peri whines that she hasn't been shopping in "awhile" (*The Ultimate Treasure*).

CHARACTER DEVELOPMENT

• *The Doctor: Warmonger* paints a picture of the fifth Doctor that's hard to credit. He atypically burns with hatred, *three times* threatening to kill Solon and Drago if Peri dies. He's callous about the deaths of Morbius' troopers, deeming prisoners a liability. He outright despises Solon. He recognizes that there's no such thing as a "good war," but in many ways likes being the Alliance leader. He considers knifing himself (and Peri) to death when Morbius' troops near total victory.

The Doctor's formal title is Alliance "Supreme

Coordinator," but the slow-witted Ogrons corrupted the term to "Supremo." In such a post, he wears black uniform with gold epaulettes and an embroidered gold "S." As "Supremo," he's guarded by a group of benevolent Ogrons, headed by Vogar.

He carries an Intergalactic Platinum card, and has access to gold, jewels and virtually any form of galactic currency. He can either shield his mind from the Sisterhood or, alternatively, telepathically communicate with Maren.

The Doctor considers publishing a guide called *Cells and Dungeons I Have Known.*

He can build an anti-jamming device with a triple-band frequency feedback oscillator. A certain drug darkens his skin for disguise purposes.

• *Perpugilliam Brown:* Briefly kidnapped by Morbius, Peri escapes to the planet Sylvana. She initially works as a waitress, becoming a rebel leader when Morbius' forces occupy the planet.

Over the course of a year, "Commander Peri" earns a number of victories, becoming known as "the Scourge of Sylvana." [Author's note: Before you can mention it, the thought of Peri as a resistance leader is completely without merit.]

Stereotypically, Peri needs more than three hours to prepare for a party/reception. She can quote from Douglas Adams.

• *Morbius (a.k.a. The General, Rombusi):* Morbius' supporters in the Gallifrey CIA embezzled funds to help him during exile. He primarily pooled his armies from mercenaries on Fangoria, Romark, Darkeen and Martak.

Morbius is slightly under medium height but intensely handsome and vain. Mirrors line Morbius' war room because he likes to look at himself. He wears a scarlet and gold uniform. He knows something of the Time Lords' quarrel with the Doctor.

• *Reverend Mother Maren:* She acknowledges the Pact of Rassilon and the Vision of the Eye, words of authority spoken by Time Lords. She acts as adviser to Hospice.

• *Mehendri Solon:* Relatively young at present, but consumed with ego. Solon holds little regard for patients, merely wanting them to survive to prove his success.

Solon met Morbius at an intergalactic medical conference in which the renegade Time Lord—in another identity—was a patron. On Karn, Solon instigated "Project Z," an undertaking to create an army of re-animated corpses for Morbius, but little came of it.

• *Ratisbon:* Gallifreyan High Council member and high-ranking CIA operative. Ratisbon's older, with gray hair, gray robes and bright green eyes.

• *Borusa:* He claims to dislike unscrupulous methods, [but readily agrees with a lot of them].

THE CRUCIAL BITS...

- **WARMONGER**—Details revealed about Morbius' exile from Gallifrey and subsequent military campaign against the universe. Solon pockets Morbius' brain, leading to events in "The Brain of Morbius."

ALIEN RACES *Time Lords:* The Time Lords ironically deem execution as more merciful than exile from their homeworld.

Time Lords usually exchange a brief mind-touch [the equivalent of a mental handshake] upon meeting, perhaps explaining how they sometimes recognize one another in different incarnations. They can also shield their minds from such casual contact, hiding their Gallifreyan origins.

Time Lords deem prison cells crude, instead preferring to toss their captives in a well-stocked oubliette suite to go mad, kill themselves or simply die. They authorized Morbius' execution on Karn, fearing that his supporters might pull off a *coup d'etat* on Gallifrey.

- *Draconians:* Draconians consider Earth language crude. They play instruments that look like bagpipes. A Draconian delicacy looks like crystallized grasshoppers.
- *Sontarans:* As Sontarans age, their skin becomes increasingly corrugated. Their vestigial bristles turn white. Sontarans care little for décor and seldom smile, except with regards to an enemy's death-throes. They never bury their dead individually [although the Doctor insists on it for the late, heroic Streg].

Skrug currently holds the highest Sontaran military rank, analogous to a president or prime minister.

- *Draconians and Sontarans:* Their empires typically leave each other alone.

ALIEN PLANETS *Gallifrey:* Keeps a small conventional spaceport outside the Panopticon ("The Deadly Assassin").

- *The Ogron Homeworld:* Largely barren, barely capable of supporting its population. Young male Ogrons go off world as soon as possible, earning a living as mercenaries.
- *Sylvana:* An incredibly fertile planet, serving as a breadbasket in its quadrant. The capital city's imaginatively called "Sylvana."

STUFF YOU NEED *The Elixir of Life:* Has a pungent smell, not unlike stewed apricots.

- *Zargil:* Swamp fish, a rare delicacy if smoked, but which tend to eat fishermen.

PLACES TO GO *Hospice:* Financed by private patients, but moreso funded by planetary governments who employ their medical services.

Hospice largely relies on its neutrality for protection. None of the major powers would allow their rivals to encroach on the medical facility, for fear they might lose access to its services.

Commander Aylmer Hawken serves Hospice as Head of Security, with Lord Delmar acting as the Governor.

ORGANIZATIONS *The Celestial Intervention Agency ("The Deadly Assassin"):* Has enormous financial resources.

- *The Alliance:* High-ranking officers include High Commander Aril (for the Draconians), Battle-Major Streg (Sontarans), Ice Lord Azanyr (the Ice Warriors), a Cyberleader and Vorgar (the Ogron chief).
- *The Sisterhood of Karn:* Possesses sizeable mental power, but often needs time to recharge.

SHIPS *The Alliance:* The Doctor's flagship, fresh from the shipyards on Copernicus Three. The Time Lords arranged for its construction retroactively.

HISTORY At some point, Gallifrey signed the Treaty of Rassilon with the Sisterhood, offering protection in exchange for the Elixir of Life. [Which seems odd, since when Morbius' forces attack the Sisterhood, the Time Lords don't lift a finger to help.]

- On Karn, a band of aristocratic warlords waged a series of internal and interplanetary wars. The warlords' bloodline eventually thinned, with their descendent, the harmless Lord Delmar, retiring [after these events] to a tropical planet to write his memoirs.
- Over the years, Karn gained a reputation as a place of healing, undoubtedly due to the Sisterhood's presence. An Intergalactic medical association set up Hospice, only to discover that the guarded Elixir of Life, not the climate, promoted healing.
- On Gallifrey, the High Council deposed Morbius with a unanimous vote. Vice-President Saran became Acting President.
- Morbius' forces captured Fangoria, Romark, Darkeen [a planet prone to trade wars], the wooded Martak [inhabited by hunters], Tanith [famous for its canals and exotic gardens] and the Ogron homeworld, but the Alliance liberated them. Freedonia allied with Morbius and overran the neighboring Sylvana, but later broke from Morbius' control. President Makir took charge of Fangoria.

This book is not endorsed by the BBC. Doctor Who and TARDIS are trademarks of the BBC.

53

• *Warmonger* entirely fails to explain how the Doctor, after commanding the Alliance, cannot help but become one of the most infamous figures in history.

AT THE END OF THE DAY Absolutely one of the greatest travesties ever perpetuated on the "Who" book line, pretty much violating the whole of the fifth Doctor mythos with the stupid, stupidest of justifications. Among its many sins, *Warmonger* entails the fifth Doctor embracing violence (he threatens to kill Solon more than once), Peri leading a successful career as a guerrilla fighter, alien races who couldn't possibly get along getting along and the "genius" Morbius falling for Peri's "I will scrape my skin and pretend I'm diseased" ploy. As an "Elseworlds"/"Unbound"-type story, this just *might* work, but as canon, it almost redefines "bad."

DID YOU KNOW?

• *Warmonger* originally began life as a sixth Doctor/Peri story called *Prelude* [which might, to some degree, explain the fifth Doctor's abnormally violent tendencies].

THE EYE OF THE SCORPION

By Iain McLaughlin

Release Date: September 2001
Order: Big Finish "Doctor Who" CD #24

TARDIS CREW The fifth Doctor, Peri and Erimem.

TRAVEL LOG Thebes, Egypt, circa 1400 BC.

CHRONOLOGY Between "Planet of Fire" and "The Caves of Androzani."

STORY SUMMARY Travelling harmlessly through the Time Vortex, the TARDIS suddenly changes course, materializing in Earth's solar system. The Doctor double-checks the controls, raising his eyebrows to discover that the Ship allegedly changed direction on his instructions. Hoping to find an explanation, the Doctor slips the TARDIS back in time a few days and arrives in Egypt, circa 1400 BC.

Once there, the Doctor and Peri happen upon a band of mercenaries attacking an Egyptian chari-

ot detail, trying to capture a young woman named Erimem. The time travelers help Erimem elude her attackers, shocked to learn she's slated to become the next pharaoh of Egypt. Unfortunately, the Doctor fails to recall any mention in history of Erimem's rule—suggesting something will prevent her from ascending to the throne.

Shortly afterward, the Doctor learns that a man named Yanis, commanding a mercenary army, intends to conquer Egypt. The Doctor infiltrates Yanis' camp to learn more, discovering that some years previous, an alien prison ship crashed in Egypt. The crash opened a stasis box containing a mental parasite, capable of infecting multiple hosts through mere touch. Having possessed Yanis' mercenaries, the creature intends to dethrone Erimem and dominate Egypt, thereby gaining access to thousands of host bodies.

The Doctor pockets a telepathic inhibitor from the abandoned stasis box. Simultaneously, the parasite mentally compels a priest named Horemshep to politically oppose Erimem's ascension. Horemshep brings forward allegations that Erimem's father secretly sired Fayum, a young priest and one of the parasite's thralls, putting the male Fayum in line to become pharaoh ahead of his "sister."

Improvising, the Doctor encourages Erimem to ask the sun god Ra for favor, then contacts the TARDIS—via the inhibitor—to retroactively arrange the unexplained course correction. The TARDIS materializes between the sun and Earth, momentarily causing an eclipse (*see Character Development*) that "proves" Erimem's authority.

Abandoning subtlety, the parasite brings Yanis' mercenaries to war against Erimem's Egyptian warriors, infecting Peri. Realizing this, the Doctor deliberately lets slip about an "ancient weapon," supposedly hidden by the people of Atlantis, under the Sphinx. The Doctor and the tainted Peri examine a hidden chamber under the Sphinx, but the creature telepathically assaults the Time Lord, lusting after his knowledge of the Atlantean weapon and the TARDIS.

The Doctor resists the creature's attack with his telepathic inhibitor, forcing the parasite—as expected—to abandon its hosts and concentrate itself in Peri. As the Doctor guessed, Peri's single mind proves unable to hold the hundreds of memory sets gleaned from the parasite's hosts. The parasite endlessly fractures, lodging itself in a cat.

Mentally freed, Yanis' mercenaries retreat. Yanis assaults the Doctor for besting his army, but Fayum rushes to the defense. During the struggle, Yanis stumbles against a pillar and brings the entire chamber down, killing him while the heroes

retreat. Afterward, Erimem accepts the Doctor's word that—even in victory—she isn't fated to become pharaoh. With Erimem too well known throughout the civilized world, the Doctor invites her aboard the TARDIS. Accepting that she can never return home, Erimem abdicates the throne to Fayum and joins the Doctor and Peri on their travels. As a final precaution, the Doctor uses the TARDIS' telepathic circuits to wipe the mental parasite from the cat's brain.

MEMORABLE MOMENTS When the Doctor mentions that historically speaking, there's no chance of Erimem standing as pharaoh, Peri retorts that the Doctor "really knows how to kill an evening."

During the finale, the Doctor and Erimem stir up a maelstrom of memories from the parasite's former hosts, encouraging them to remember their past lives and resist the creature.

SEX AND SPIRITS One of Erimem's banquets includes topless dancers and a "black-toothed" priest leering at Peri. The Doctor mentions that some of the palace servants are employed in the oldest profession, making Peri whisper in response: "You don't mean… hookers?"

Erimem would probably have wed her older brother, if he'd lived. Her father had more than 60 wives when he died. Yanis threatens to bed "that brat pharaoh" before he disembowels her.

Erimem oddly vows that she should have castrated her would-be assassin "if he had lived"— while he's still alive. She struggles to understand that Peri isn't the Doctor's wife or concubine.

Peri's attended at least one toga party.

ASS-WHUPPINGS Erimem became heir to the throne because her three older half-brothers died in a series of mishaps. Her eldest brother kicked it when his chariot axle snapped and the conveyance rolled over him. A fever took her youngest brother. An asp bit her last-surviving brother inside the palace [he took five days to die]. Finally, Erimem's father croaked a mere five months after his kids started pushing up daisies, slain by mercenaries while out riding in his chariot.

The Doctor takes a poisoned knife cut at the end of Part 1, spending the whole of Part 2 in a healing coma. The assassin who stabbed the Doctor poisons himself, but oddly survives to endure interrogation. Conspirators finally murder the "poisoned" assassin (a bit redundant, really) to silence his tongue.

Yanis' mercenaries open this story by killing, off-screen, six or 10 chariots of men escorting Er-

imem. The Doctor and Peri upend a chariot pursuing Erimem with a tripwire.

Conspirators poison Varella, Erimem's former nursemaid and one of her father's wives, to further the intrigue of Fayum against Erimem.

Yanis' rebels sack Thebes, leading to a bloody battle with Erimem's archers. Erimem dons armor and participates in battle herself.

At story's end, Peri's mind briefly shuts down while expelling the mental parasite. Yanis gets mashed like a blueberry pancake, crushed when the chamber under the Sphinx collapses.

TIE-INS The Doctor hasn't been to Egypt "recently" (Mclaughlin likely means "The Daleks' Master Plan," although the fifth Doctor notably visited the country in *The Sands of Time*). He also hasn't used the TARDIS food machine ("The Daleks") in some time.

CHARACTER DEVELOPMENT

• *The Doctor:* The Doctor can read Egyptian hieroglyphics, and recognize their placement in history. He's memorized the names of all of Egypt's pharaohs.

His comatose Time Lord body metabolizes the Egyptian assassin's poison. He can drive a chariot. While comatose, the Doctor's mind is telepathically sensitive to the alien parasite's presence.

The Doctor acquires a telepathic inhibitor that lets him neutralize telepaths, or bind the telepathic creature into a single body. He possibly visited the shaft behind the Sphinx in a previous incarnation (*see Possible History*).

A few university chancellors around the cosmos owe the Doctor favors.

• *Perpugilliam Brown:* Peri's always wanted to see the Pyramids and the Sphinx. Her mother worshiped Paul McCartney. Peri's presently a vegetarian. She deems Margaret Thatcher a poor example of a female leader, but better respects India Prime Minister Indira Ghandi.

• *The Doctor and Peri:* Peri hopes to one day learn the TARDIS console controls, but the Doctor conveniently stalls teaching her.

• *Erimem ush Imteperem:* Erimem's 17 years old. She's highly atypical for an Egyptian royal, failing to view the pharaohs as divine. She prefers to be addressed as "Erimem" rather than her formal title. Her father often admonished her to act more regal. Erimem never wanted the burden of command, and prophetically felt she'd never become pharaoh.

She doesn't believe in the Egyptian gods. She holds interest in astronomy, suspecting the world might be round and travel around the sun.

Erimem's mother, Rubak, is her only living relation and resides in the Palace of Concubines. Rubak won't look her daughter in the face and barely speaks to her, given pharaoh Erimem's new status as "a god."

Her garrison at Giza includes 100 chariots and about 800 men. She's a proficient archer, and joints her troops in combat.

The head of the palace guard, Antranak, served Erimem's father and is fiercely loyal to her. Peri's teaching Erimem basic learning principles of feminism and democracy. The Doctor tells Erimem stories about Daleks and Cybermen. Her face is already on coins throughout the civilized world.

• *The alien parasite:* A creature of pure mental energy, duplicating itself from person to person through physical contact, like a virus. All of the parasite's duplicates were linked telepathically into a single mind. The parasite gained the memories of anyone it possessed. The hosts retained their personalities for a long time, but would eventually fade into nothing. The occasional host [such as Yanis] proved too rowdy to control.

The creature cannot solely survive in non-sentient minds. It can nestle duplicates of itself in animal minds, such as flies, to observe through their eyes.

• *Shemech:* Erimem's history teacher, who tutored her in the palace gardens because she liked the smell of flowers. He was onhand when a childhood Erimem fell from a tree and came close to death. His wife Neefra died.

• *Fayum:* Raised by priests, Fayum grew up to become a junior council member. He played with Erimem as a child. Horemshep claimed that Varella, wife to Erimem's father, secretly birthed Fayum. It seems unlikely that Fayum is Erimem's brother, but the people accept the lie and make him pharaoh.

• *Horemshep:* Priest of the temple of Horus. The House of Isis follows his lead. He's rivals with palace guardsman Antranak, since their influence is roughly equal.

• *The TARDIS:* One of this audio's more baffling elements involves the manner in which the tiny TARDIS could cause an entire eclipse by materializing between Earth and the sun. The most likely explanation is that the Ship momentarily projects some sort of energy field through which light can't pass.

Regrettably, the Doctor writes off the entire incident as: "You've no idea what the TARDIS can do... she was just the right distance for just the right effect, and so long as it wasn't for more than a few seconds... instant eclipse." [Author's Note: Well, that's helpful.]

THE CRUCIAL BITS...

• **THE EYE OF THE SCORPION**—First appearance of companion Erimem, a pharaoh from ancient Egypt.

The Ship contains at least two libraries—one small, one larger. A lake currently exists in the main library, as the Ship's been moving rooms around its interior. (The Doctor preferred the lake in its previous location.)

STUFF YOU NEED *The Sphinx:* The Doctor can't say whose face is on the Sphinx—although it's definitely not the late pharaoh Cheops, who supposedly built it.

ORGANIZATIONS *Council of Priests:* Currently split on Erimem's ascension to the throne, as almost all pharaohs are male.

POSSIBLE HISTORY The Doctor cites the Sphinx as being much older than the pyramids, dating it to around 10,000 BC. He also claims that refugees from Atlantis built the Sphinx, with a chamber of knowledge—the Hall of Records—hidden in a chamber between its paws. The Doctor possibly makes up all this malarkey to deceive the alien parasite, although "The Eye of the Scorpion" leaves uncertain exactly how much he's lying.

HISTORY Erimem's father died "a season ago."

• Yanis triggers a cave-in that cracks the face of the Sphinx. Egyptian engineers start to restore the damage and Erimem, not wanting her own face on it, gives Peri leave to choose its new design. Figuring that Napoleon's troops will damage the Sphinx anyway in future, Peri gives the Egyptians the likeness of the "other" King of Memphis—Elvis—to put on it.

[Author's Note: Actually, it's a common misconception that Napoleon's troops damaged the Sphinx's face. Simple erosion is the most likely suspect. Also, the modern-day Sphinx is primarily missing its nose, which wouldn't exactly hide Elvis' other features. In short, it's cute for this audio to put Elvis' face on the Sphinx, but it's also historically implausible. Indeed, take a look at the Sphinx, then take a look at Elvis. Any fool with two eyes can see they look nothing alike. And yes, we realize this is intended as a joke.]

AT THE END OF THE DAY A production that's fairly rosy if you bask in its overall effect, enjoying it as a historical romp in ancient Egypt. But for its *details*, "The Eye of the Scorpion" should hang its

Sphinx-like head in shame. The story's hampered by logistical problems (an assassin poisons himself, but survives to undergo interrogation), science blunders (the police box-sized TARDIS inexplicably causes an eclipse), difficulties with perspective (the Doctor and Peri wander around ancient Egypt, wearing strange clothes and talking like foreigners, but scarcely anyone notices) and quite a bit of padding (a predictable council debate in Part 3; and Peri's solo adventure in Part 2, however well-intentioned, contributes nothing to the plot).

Against this, it's hard to fault the cast (barring Harry Myers as the bombastic Yanis), overall flavor, production values and the introduction of Erimem as a companion. As such, "The Eye of the Scorpion" works best when compared to "Star Wars: Episode II"—it's fine, if you're incredibly non-discerning and consciously ignore its multiple flaws.

DID YOU KNOW?

• Writer Iain McLaughlin didn't craft Erimem as an ongoing companion—he'd intended that she would get dropped off between stories, much like the Earthling in "Meglos." But during recording, producers Jason Haigh-Ellery and Gary Russell decided to make Erimem an ongoing character, impressed with actress Caroline Morris's chemistry with Peter Davison and Nicola Bryant.

PALACE OF THE RED SUN

By Christopher Bulis

Release Date: *March 2002*
Order: *BBC Past Doctor Adventure #51*

TARDIS CREW The sixth Doctor and Peri.

TRAVEL LOG Esselven, time unknown; Esselven Minor, 500 years later.

STORY SUMMARY Hoping to expand his Protectorate empire, warlord Glavis Judd captures the planet Esselven. But before their homeworld's fall, the Esselven royal family locks the Keys to Esselven—a series of irreplaceable documents and protocols—within an impenetrable vault, then flees into space. Realizing the vault will only open with a royal family member's DNA—and that Esselven society will degenerate

into mayhem without the Keys—Judd launches a manhunt for the refugee family.

A year later, Judd tracks the royals to Esselven Minor, a planetoid in orbit around a white dwarf star. Judd bizarrely finds time passing beneath the planetoid's defense shield at a rate 500 times faster than the rest of the Universe. Still undaunted, Judd takes a platoon, blasts a hole in the defense screen and ventures onto the planetoid's surface—determined to quickly nab a royal even if a year or so passes in the main Universe.

Meanwhile, the TARDIS lands on Esselven Minor. The Doctor and Peri explore the planetoid, finding a society of scavengers eking out a living in the wilderness. Some time later, the time travelers find the royal family's Summer Palace strangely bereft of people, populated only by holographic characters from an interactive drama.

The Doctor finds a message from the late King Hathold, who details how the white dwarf's intense gravity, combined with Esselven's mass, evidently strained space-time in the area. When Hathold's engineers boosted their planetary defense shield to maximum, the continuum became further torn—forcing time within the shield to accelerate. The Summer Palace's nuclear reactor consequently malfunctioned, fatally irradiating numerous royals and their engineers. A dying Hathold sent his family into the wilderness, but the palace's robotic attendants malfunctioned and refused to re-admit the family members once the radiation cleared. Generations passed within the accelerated time field, turning Hathold's descendants into the scavengers.

The Doctor realizes *any* scavenger would possess the DNA necessary to unlock the Esselven Vault. With Judd enroute to the Summer Palace, the Doctor arranges a ruse—fooling Judd into thinking that everyone on the planetoid, the scavengers included, are holograms. A frustrated Judd departs empty handed, preparing to leave Esselven Minor. However, the Doctor manipulates the defense shield to bring Esselven Minor back into synch with the rest of the Universe.

Judd's ship emerges not a year but 500 years after he left—long after the Protectorate collapsed and the scavengers reclaimed their birthright on Esselven. The new royals' troopers capture Judd and—failing to recognize him as the genuine article—toss him into an asylum with several loonies who've called themselves "Glavis Judd" over the years. Pleased for saving lives, the Doctor and Peri depart Esselven Minor.

MEMORABLE MOMENTS Journalist Dexel Dynes, recalling Peri from *The Ultimate Treasure*,

This book is not endorsed by the BBC. Doctor Who and TARDIS are trademarks of the BBC.

57

cries out, "Peri Brown, hostile news subject!", upon their second meeting.

SEX AND SPIRITS A scavenger named Kel chooses Peri as his mate, but Peri sizes him up as, "A nice kid, but not for me." Nonetheless, when Nerla challenges Peri's right to marry Kel, Peri finds herself forced into a fight-to-the-death. Peri nearly loses, but the arrival of interplanetary journalist Dexel Dynes interrupts the bout.

ASS-WHUPPINGS The Doctor survives a fall into a compost heap that would've killed a human being. The robotic Gardeners, running amok at their creators' absence, capture the scavengers, work them to death, then recycle their bodies into compost.

Robot Green-8 gains enough sentience to break its programming, side with the Doctor and behead Red-87 and Red-115.

As part of the initial disaster on Esselven Minor, a nuclear reactor at the Winter Palace—a counterpart to the Summer Palace—suffered total meltdown [one would expect this would've affected life on the entire planetoid, but apparently not].

Judd loses several craft to Esselven Minor's anti-aircraft fire. Esselven Minor's fluctuating force field obliterates another two ships.

TV TIE-INS The TARDIS can't yield time/space coordinates within Esselven Minor's accelerated time zone, so the Doctor sets an automatic fault locator ("The Edge of Destruction") to check the Ship's systems.

NOVEL TIE-INS Sensational journalist Dexel Dynes (*see Character Development*) previously encountered the fifth Doctor and Peri in Bulis' *The Ultimate Treasure*.

CHARACTER DEVELOPMENT

• *The Doctor:* It's suggested that he's met René Descartes. There are places that consider his multi-color coat the height of fashion. He's a reputed lecturer.

• *Perpugilliam Brown:* Peri's first playground fight proved she's not much use in a scrap. During holidays, she drove a tractor and a combine harvester on her uncle's farm.

• *Glavis Judd:* He wears armor that lets him punch through walls. For propaganda reasons, Judd cites himself as a liberator, not a conqueror.

• *Dexel Dynes:* Sensational journalist for the International News Agency, assigned to trail Judd and cover his war campaign. Dynes got mixed up in events on Esselven Minor and hence returned to the main Universe 500 years after he left. To Dynes' dismay, his particular breed of yellow journalism fell from favor in the interim, ruining his career.

• *The TARDIS:* Contains a portable multi-range scanner capable of detecting Peri.

ALIEN PLANETS *Esselven Minor:* Esselven Minor orbits a white dwarf, but the defense screen refracts the sunlight to appear red, shining through a purple sky. The planetoid doesn't rotate, meaning one side never lacks for sunlight while the other's in darkness. The white dwarf generates minimal ultraviolet radiation, so sunburn's not a concern.

Esselven Minor's a mere 107 km in diameter and less than 350 km in circumference, although its heavy density simulates higher gravity. You could walk the planetoid in a great circle route in about four to five days.

The forcefield helps sustain the planetoid's biosphere, extending about 10 to 15 km upward. Plants on Esselven Minor include pink retholnium beds and Altruista violets [used as flowers of mourning].

• *Madross Prime:* Home to a challenging four-dimensional maze.

STUFF YOU NEED *Autonomous Photonic Simulations:* Tiny spheres that project holographic beings [rather like Rimmer on "Red Dwarf," minus the sentience].

• *Radzell and Styne Maxima Vault:* Can't be forced open by any known means. It contains collapsium-lined walls, reinforced by internal fields and an external force shield. A megaton explosive or would rupture the vault, but it's programmed to self-destruct its contents in such an event.

• *The Keys of Esselven:* Include legal judgments, trading arrangements and computer codes for Esselven's world transport net and stellar communication web.

• *Thorn Tree b'long:* Female members of the Thorn Tree clan wear the *b'longs*, actually leather thongs with tassels of clay beads, to show they belong to their husbands.

ORGANIZATIONS *Esselven Minor Scavengers:* Unsophisticated savages who've created myths based around their getting kicked out of the Summer Palace. They believe a Sun God-ship brought them to Esselven, but that they angered said deity and got driven into the dark woods. The scavengers' tribes include Thorn Tree, Melek's House and Stoneford.

SHIPS *Judd's Warfleet:* Includes the *Adrax* and *Gantor*, plus the *Valtor*, Judd's personal battle cruiser.

HISTORY Glavis Judd was born to ordinary parents on the planet Zalcrossar. He graduated with the highest honors, but as an adult found Zalcrossar society overly stratified and developed contempt for the ruling classes. He enrolled in the military, gaining prestige when colony world Deltor 5, a habitable moon circling a gas giant in Zalcrossar's outer system, deposed its governor and declared independence. Judd engineered events to thwart a diplomatic solution, then took the colony by force.

He became the youngest man to attain the rank of Sector Marshal. He eventually won the world presidency of Zalcrossar on the Military Party ticket. As president, he stamped out crime and increased the military budget. He ran uncontested in the next election, then restructured Zalcrossar society with more security, a leveling of wealth and less personal freedom for the populace.

He finally abolished the multi-party system, deeming it inefficient. He set about creating political unrest on the nearby planet Gadron, then sent in Zalcrossar troops to purge the Gadron leaders. The Gadronians welcomed him as a hero, leading to his forming the Protectorate and absorbing even more planets. He bagged three more worlds the year before last.

• Judd never nominated a successor, meaning the Protectorate easily collapsed without him.

• Dynes' employer, International News, becomes Stellmedia in future.

• The descendants of Kel [the same scavenger who fancied Peri] became the new rulers of Esselven. By the time of King Kel III, Special Order 178 mandates the institutionalization of any lunatic calling himself Glavis Judd.

AT THE END OF THE DAY As many great science-fiction authors have pointed out, a writer must take risks or they're horse meat. Along those lines, *Palace of the Red Sun*—like most other Chris Bulis books—emerges as an average novel with an average plot. You couldn't call it *awful*, but it forwards a level of pulp that bogged down the "Star Trek" book line for years [and still sometimes afflicts it, for that matter]. Peri does virtually nothing in this story, and the Doctor spends a fair amount of time twiddling his thumbs also—and really, if we're being honest, does this book have much to offer other than that it probably, *we're guessing*, turned up at the BBC offices on time, needing minimal editing?

THE RATINGS WAR

By Steve Lyons

Release Date: January 2002
Order: Promotional CD
included with Doctor Who Magazine #313

TARDIS CREW The sixth Doctor.

TRAVEL LOG Likely Earth [although it's not specified and *could* be an alien planet], the near future.

CHRONOLOGY For the sixth Doctor, between "Trial of a Time Lord" and "Time and the Rani." For the power-mad Beep the Meep, after his imprisonment in "Star Beast II" (*DWM Yearbook 1996*).

SPECIAL NOTE This audio contains a hidden track (after the "Invaders from Mars" promo) with A) Colin Baker and actor Alistair Lock wrestling through the *Beep and Friends* song, B) an extended version of Beep's tizzy as he's drug off to jail and C) a full chorus of the savage [and very, very funny] *Beep and Friends* theme.

STORY SUMMARY In the near future, a TV network experiences a sudden surge of popularity, reveling in a string of successful [albeit mind-numbing] reality series, soap operas and quiz shows. But during a stopover, the Doctor spies the TV listings and reads about an upcoming children's program called *Beep and Friends*. Immediately recognizing the handiwork of his old adversary Beep the Meep—a psychotic alien who looks like a cuddly-wuddly animal—the Doctor sets off for the network's headquarters.

The Doctor finds the director of programming, Roger Lowell, hypnotized by Beep's mesmeric blackstar radiation. The Doctor resists the radiation's effects, but Beep in turn threatens to poison the cuddly stars of *Appealing Animals in Distress* via remote control. With the Doctor sufficiently held in check, Beep reveals that he plans to seed subliminal control messages into the greatly hyped final episode of *Audience Shares*, thus bringing 80 percent of the viewing public under his sway. Soon after, the debut episode of *Beep and Friends* will program Beep's receptive minions to kill off the remaining free thinkers, putting the entire planet under Beep's control.

The Doctor swipes Beep's laser pistol and shoots away his remote control, saving the hostage ani-

This book is not endorsed by the BBC. Doctor Who and TARDIS are trademarks of the BBC.

59

mals. Moreover, the Doctor bluffs through his teeth, claiming that he dismantled Beep's pre-set subliminal control device before the airing of *Audience Shares*. Thinking himself undone, the demented Beep retrieves his laser pistol and sets out to murder Todd and Lucy—the *Audience Shares* finalists—as a means of tormenting the public... just for the hell of it.

Beep "shoots" Todd and Lucy on live TV, failing to realize the Doctor tampered with his pistol's power unit, making it capable of stun only. Todd and Lucy survive, but the sight of the crazed Meep gunning down the celebrities puts the *Beep and Friends* debut on hiatus for 18 months. As the authorities haul off the screeching Meep, the Doctor reveals that the viewing public—successfully conditioned by *Audience Shares*, but never receiving the instructions encoded in *Beep and Friends*—will return to normal with no ill effects. Suitably pleased, the Doctor shrugs off requests for interviews, departing to find a medium worthy of his time and effort.

MEMORABLE MOMENTS Beep, on his masterful television programs: "Short of a red-hot poker, I have found the most direct route from my viewers' eyes to their hearts."

After Beep's defeat, the station's phone lines jam with viewer calls demanding to see more of the Doctor. In a move symbolic of the current state of "Doctor Who," the Doctor declines to be interviewed, claiming he finds television limiting and doubts it could do him justice. Still, as a nod to the "Who" audio line, the Doctor tells an announcer: "Oh, don't worry. You'll be hearing more from me..."

Finally, the highlight of the story, the gory *Beep and Friends* song as performed by dancing animatronic Meeps, repeated here in its glory:

"Oh, we dance and we play, with joy we gush.
As our dreadful song turns your brain to mush.
Join the fun and you'll see... soon you'll agree...
you are Beep's friend after all-l-l-l-l-l-l-l-l-l...
"Ask your neighbor round for a bite and a drink,
then nibble off his face till he's raw and pink.
Enjoy his surprise as you suck out his eyes...
you are Beep's friend, smash them all.
Put your dog in a blender and close the lid... cut your hamster to pieces to feed your kid. Slice the fur from your cat 'till you deep fry him in some fat.
You are Beep's friend, kill them all."
... and so forth.

ASS-WHUPPINGS The Doctor, Todd and Lucy all take stun bolts from Beep's pistol, but that's about it. The girl who freed Beep from incarcera-

tion as a movie character (*see Comic Tie-Ins*) found her brains seeping out her nose [probably psychic backlash on Beep's part] when she dared to call him, "A snuggily, wuggily woo."

COMIC TIE-INS Beep the Meep previously debuted as a power-mad (but very, very cuddly) alien dictator in *DWM* #19-#26, "The Star Beast." The fourth Doctor bested Beep's ambitions, then defeated him again in a re-match (*DWM Yearbook 1996*), using a "black light receiver" to trap Beep as a character in a Lassie film.

Afterward, as "The Ratings War" relates, Beep spent a great deal of time observing how movies (and by extension TV) numbs people's minds. Eventually, Beep escaped thanks to a girl who worked at the Wrarth Institute. She watched the Lassie film continuously, with her heart melting for the fluffy teddy bear (i.e. Beep) who rescued a little boy from a mine shaft because his dog had mysteriously broken all its legs. At Beep's mental urging, the girl made a touching plea to Beep for his release, restoring him to reality.

CHARACTER DEVELOPMENT
• *The Doctor:* The Doctor praises television when it's used to inform, educate and entertain. He bemoans reality TV shows, documentary dramas, quiz shows for the intellectually challenged and soap operas.

Among his grievances against Lowell's network: Using a blue hippopotamus to read the news, reality show exploits dominating the news agenda, an upper age limit of 24 on soap opera stars and curtailing channel surfing by nixing the credits.

He sabotages Beep's laser pistol by simply cramming a paper clip against its power pack and letting it gradually drain away. He's immune to Beep's hypnotic blackstar radiation.
• *Beep the Meep (a.k.a. the "Most High Beep" of all the Meeps):* He's been exerting control over Lowell and his station for six months. He mesmerizes people with [otherwise harmless] blackstar radiation.

Beep vetoes the idea of a docu-drama on his own exploits, fearing the audience might mistake his gruesome activities for science fiction—and get their imaginations stimulated.

Beep's only met the Doctor's fourth incarnation [and now the sixth]. He recognizes that his race's physical make-up looks "cute" to humans and uses this to his advantage. However, Beep finds such sweetness "loathsome in the extreme" and despises his own programs.

He's re-imprisoned by the Wrarth Warriors, who jailed him in *DWM* #19-#26.

ALIEN RACES *Meeps:* Aren't built for speed.

STUFF YOU NEED *Audience Shares:* Typical reality pap, with the premise of 10 young volunteers competing to see who's got the best media skills. The public voted out the performers until only two contestants, Todd and Lucy, remained. The winner gets to star in their own docu-drama.

As part of the show, Lucy invented a scandal from her past, and "accidentally" let her bathrobe slip open.

ORGANIZATIONS *The Station:* Lowell's unnamed station, under Beep's guidance, has risen to dominance thanks to shows such as *Young Cops in Hospital*, *Wacky Domestic Mishaps*, *Look! Cute Animals*, the conversely popular *Appealing Animals in Distress* and the first-ever 24-hour soap opera, *Hospital Street*. The station's greatest rival just lost three of its biggest personalities in a series of tragic accidents. The Campaign Against Television Violence has protested some of the station's shows.

AT THE END OF THE DAY A quirky little satire from comic guru Steve Lyons, and sweetly biting in points about today's ungodly fascination with reality TV. "The Ratings War" puts Big Finish's previous promotional CD, "The Last of the Titans," to total shame, but if there's a limitation, it's that one can only do so much in a 25 minute story with a few cast members. Even so, it deserves points for crazily (and successfully) bringing Beep the Meep to audio, and most importantly for the fall-down hysterical *Beep and Friends* theme song [proving that yes, "Doctor Who" has come a long way since the family-oriented Mary Whitehouse condemned it].

DID YOU KNOW?

• Author Steve Lyons named the *Audience Shares* finalists, Todd and Lucy, after actors Todd Carty and Lucy Benjamin, who were playing a couple in the BBC soap *EastEnders* at the time. [Lyons adds: "No offence meant, though!"] Benjamin, incidentally, played young Nyssa in "Mawdryn Undead," under the name Lucy Baker.

• Lyons completely forgot that Beep had also appeared in a *DWM* eighth Doctor comic strip in which he also tried to take over the world through the power of television. Fortunately, everything fits together okay, if you assume that Beep's plan in that strip is a more advanced version of his agenda in "The Ratings War."

THE MALTESE PENGUIN

By Rob Shearman

Release Date: *June 2002 (subscription exclusive); Nov. 2002 (wide release)*
Order: *Big Finish "Doctor Who" Audio #33 1/2*

TARDIS CREW Frobisher, with the sixth Doctor.

TRAVEL LOG Unnamed planet [where Frobisher keeps his private detective office], time unknown but potentially 82nd century [for those who this story as contemporaneous with Dogbolter's appearance in *Death's Head #8*].

STORY SUMMARY Determined to renew his private detective business, Frobisher parts company with the Doctor and returns to his former base of operations. Frobisher fails to net any cases beyond the search for a lost cat, but nonetheless declines offers from the lonely Doctor to travel around the Universe again.

Things pick up considerably for Frobisher when the sultry Alicia Mulholland enters his office, hiring him to trail her fiancé, Arthur Gringrax, and discover if he's been cheating on her. Frobisher trails Gringrax to a hotel, then hears shots and races into Gringrax's room. He fails to find Gringrax's body, discovering only a trail of blood on the flow—one that deliberately moves to avoid his touch. Seconds later, corrupt police chief Chandler arrests Frobisher on suspicion of murder. Rather than throwing Frobisher in jail, Chandler drives the shamus to meet his boss, the man-frog mobster named Josiah W. Dogbolter.

Frobisher learns Dogbolter wants a very important "something" that Gringrax had in his possession—a something Dogbolter cannot even describe. The mobster explains that whereas his off-world industries make profit in traditional fashions, he conversely—by a bizarre quirk of economics—makes coin on this planet by insuring that nothing whatsoever gets made. Having closed down every industrial company on the planet but one, Gringrax insures that his employees show up, punch time cards, fiddle with a few useless buttons and go home. However, the slightest innovation would bring the system to ruin, and Dogbolter has concrete evidence that Gringrax—formerly a harmless button-pusher—invented a "something" that could spark an industrial revolution.

Dogbolter also captures Alicia, leading Frobisher to realize she has possession of Gringrax's "something." Reasoning that Dogbolter will kill droves of people to get the "something," Frobisher helps Dogbolter deduce the object's location. Moments later, Dogbolter's men retrieve the "something," an innocent-looking box. Dogbolter finds a single computer chip within and, being intensely curious, loads it into his computer system. Unfortunately for Dogbolter, the pre-programmed chip flashes a joke—"You don't have to be crazy to work here, but it helps"—not only on his computer screen, but also on all of his workers' terminals.

Seconds later, Dogbolter's employees start laughing—triggering a mirth that will, in time, foster communication and make them start innovating again. Ruined, Dogbolter tries to blow away Frobisher and Alicia, but the Doctor—deciding to ask for Frobisher's company yet again—materializes the TARDIS in Dogbolter's office and inadvertently blocks his bullets.

Dogbolter flees, allowing Frobisher to beg the Doctor for a moment alone with Alicia. Seconds later, Alicia reveals herself as Francine, Frobisher's shapeshifting ex-wife and former investigative partner. Alicia explains that as Gringrax, she worked toward Dogbolter's downfall, later roping Frobisher into her master scheme to trick Dogbolter—as planned—into reading the computer chip. Francine still professes some love for Frobisher, but realizes he still yearns to travel in the TARDIS. She remains behind to bring Dogbolter to justice, allowing Frobisher to continue his journeys in time and space.

MEMORABLE MOMENTS Frobisher hears someone approaching his office door and narrates: "With one flipper, I reached for the bottle of bourbon. With the other, for my automatic pistol. This way, whether my visitor was friend or foe, one of the flippers would have something to offer him." After noting Frobisher's posture, the Doctor prepares to leave with: "[I can see] you're busy. Cats to find, clients to shoot. I understand."

Francine, as Alicia, emulates Lauren Bacall in *To Have and Have Not* (1944) by telling Frobisher: "If you need anything at all, just quack. You know how to quack, don't you?" Frobisher: "Well, no. I'm a penguin, not a duck." Alicia: "Just stiffen your beak and vibrate." Frobisher (weakly): "… quack."

SEX AND SPIRITS During their investigative days, Frobisher and Francine solved crimes by day and made whoopie by night. They broke up because shamuses don't make great long-term

lovers, and somewhat because Francine was a much better detective than her husband. A lot of genuine affection remains between them. Francine calls Frobisher "Frobie."

Frobisher defaults to a penguin body because Francine used to adopt a similar form, and it reminds him of her.

Frobisher spends much of this story lusting after Francine's human disguise, Alicia Mulholland. He comments that when she walks, her feet don't so much move as her hips glide her forward. When she pulls out a chair, it seems excited to get her attention. Frobisher offers Alicia bourbon, but she seductively keeps her own in a thigh flask (which leads Frobisher to find goosebumps on his flippers where he never knew goosebumps could grow). He gets to kiss Alicia once—while wearing the Doctor's body—and overcompensates for his lack of a beak. The story ends with them smooching as young penguins in love.

Dogbolter drinks seven glasses of bourbon and smokes five cigars while waiting for his lackeys to return. Frobisher joins him with regards to the bourbon. Dogbolter doesn't fancy mammals, but would probably lust after Alicia if he did.

ASS-WHUPPINGS Dogbolter eliminates his treacherous lackey Chandler with a very Smart Bomb—an implant that blows up Chandler but leaves his surroundings unharmed.

COMIC TIE-INS The fifth Doctor first clashed with Dogbolter in *DWM* #84, #86-#87, "The Moderator." The sixth Doctor later met Frobisher in *DWM* #88-#89, "The Shapeshifter," while fleeing from Dogbolter's men. A continuity error occurs in that Dogbolter here fails to recognize the sixth Doctor's form (as worn by Frobisher), although the explanation that "The Maltese Penguin" takes place before "The Shapeshifter"—i.e. when Frobisher leaves in the TARDIS for the first time—really doesn't work. [If that were the case, there'd be two Frobishers running around.] It's either a sizeable glitch, or attributable to the fact that whereas the audios are generally canon, the comics are mostly apocrypha and needn't match each other perfectly.

After this story, Dogbolter turns up in *Death's Head* #8, hiring the titular mercenary to kill the Doctor.

Mazumas are a commonly used form of currency, first seen in *DWM* #56-#57, "The Free-Fall Warriors." Excre-mazumas are a valuable denomination.

THE CRUCIAL BITS...

• **THE MALTESE PENGUIN**—First appearance of the Francine, a Whifferdill shapeshifter and Frobisher's ex-wife. Frobisher spends three weeks at his old job. Explanation why Frobisher wears a penguin body.

CHARACTER DEVELOPMENT

• *The Doctor:* The Doctor recently helped some rebels overthrow a corrupt tyrant, then nicked forward 100 years, discovered the rebels had gotten corrupt and overthrew them as well. Since Frobisher left the TARDIS, he's foiled three invasions of Earth and saved the Universe twice. He saves the Universe a third time during a break in this story.

• *Frobisher:* Frobisher has trouble morphing into humanoid bodies because they've got too many appendages. When he needs a human form, he often adopts the sixth Doctor's body because he's familiar with it. In such a form, he speaks with the Doctor's voice, accented with Frobisher's speech patterns.

He attended Private Investigator College and earned a second-class diploma [his instructor had something against avian species]. As a detective, Frobisher gets 12 mazumas a day, plus expenses. His office is abhorrently messy.

Frobisher tries to paint himself as a hard-boiled detective, but he's moreso honorable and straightforward. He's never told a taxi driver, "Follow that cab." He holds a shaky grasp of economics.

The junk mail department of the Galactic Readers' Digest calls him Mrs. F. R. Rubbisher.

• *The Doctor and Frobisher:* The Doctor wants Frobisher back in the TARDIS because he's lonely, since saving Universes isn't as much fun on his own. The Doctor here visits Frobisher's office for the first time. Frobisher finds the Doctor's form a bit ungainly for racing up stairs.

• *Josiah W Dogbolter:* Dogbolter's half-man, half-giant frog. Rumors suggest his parents, two ordinary humans, got repulsed by his looks and left him to die in the streets. Other stories claim he's the product of two frogs who did the same thing.

Dogbolter's rich and powerful enough to pull strings on 1,000 worlds. He's entirely anonymous, having eradicated all traces of his past. Dogbolter owns several industrial plants that churn out substandard goods, including cruise missiles, milk bottle tops and plastic chairs manufactured on Metazula Beta.

He personally owns original works by Van Gogh, Roygal and John Ridgway [a *DWM* comic strip

artist], but keeps the artwork facing the wall, as he appreciates their value more than their art.

Dogbolter promptly pays bills to keep his thugs in line. He doesn't allow expenses without a receipt. His black, bulbous eyes sometimes glow red. He believes imagination is unprofitable—at least, without a feasibility study.

ALIEN RACES *Whifferdills:* Can assume liquid states warm enough to generate steam.

HISTORY Thanks to Dogbolter, no industrial work has occurred on this planet for more than a century [a conceit, really, since you'd think Frobisher would have noticed before now].

• Rich and famous men in this era include Elias Thinsbrock, Olgarth Zeus III and [as Frobisher jokes] Ronald McDonald.

AT THE END OF THE DAY Goofy as hell, verging on outright hysterical if you're sufficiently bent. Shearman smartly envisions a Raymond Chandler-esque world with the lead character as a penguin, scripting some sweet dialogue and choice comments. It's a damn pity that, as a Frobisher comedy that guest-stars the sixth Doctor, "The Maltese Penguin" will probably never get the acclaim it deserves, but it made us feel right at home and holds a warm spot in our hearts.

DID YOU KNOW?

• Shearman had been working on the basic plotline of "The Maltese Penguin" and knew he wanted a great fat evil businessman in the thick of things. Simultaneously, producer Gary Russell suggested that Dogbolter, a villain from the *DWM* comics, might fit the role nicely. Shearman claims: "I was so grateful I could have kissed him (but I'm sure he's as relieved as I am that I didn't).

• Shearman pictured Danger Mouse's arch nemesis Baron Greenback when he scripted the Dogbolter part.

EXCELIS RISING

By David A. McIntee

Release Date: April 2002
Order: Big Finish "Excelis Series" CD Part 2

TARDIS CREW The sixth Doctor.

TRAVEL LOG Central museum in the city of Excelis, planet Artaris, 1,000 years after "Excelis Dawns."

CHRONOLOGY Between "Trial of a Time Lord" and "Time and the Rani."

STORY SUMMARY Seemingly at random, the TARDIS lands on Artaris—now an industrialized planet—some 1,000 years after the Doctor's previous visit. The Ship materializes in the central Excelis Museum, the new home of the Relic (*see Audio Tie-Ins*), where a pair of thieves botch a run at stealing the artifact. One thief dies in the attempt, but the other gets captured.

Soon after, a high-ranking police official [called a "Reeve"] named Maupassant arrives to question the surviving criminal. The Doctor turns slackjawed to recognize Maupassant as the former Lord Greyvorn, who rose through the city's Warden ranks legitimately. Modern-day Excelis society regards "Lord Greyvorn" as myth, but the Doctor wonders about the ex-warlord's current agenda.

After some investigation, the Doctor learns that Greyvorn *himself* engineered the Relic's theft, knowing it would fail but giving himself a reason to take the Relic into protective custody. Worse, the Doctor realizes the Relic fused the Mother Superior's consciousness and Greyvorn's mind together ("Excelis Dawns"). Mentally unhinged from sharing his brain for so long, Greyvorn hopes the Relic can somehow fission himself and the Mother Superior into separate bodies.

Greyvorn overpowers his superior, Etheric Minister Pryce, intending to Relic-transfer the Mother Superior into Pryce's body. In response, the Doctor opens the Relic in Greyvorn's face. The Relic instantly erupts with energy, opening a portal into its internal dimension. Greyvorn screams, then disappears, allowing the Doctor to re-seal the Relic and return it to the museum's care.

The Doctor again departs, failing to realize that when the Relic dissipated Greyvorn's physical form, its energies etched his consciousness into the museum's stone walls. Disembodied, a tormented Greyvorn vows to wait the long decades until someone dies in the museum, intending to possess that person's body and effect his return to life.

MEMORABLE MOMENTS The Doctor's verbal jousts with the matured Greyvorn steal the show, with both men uncertain how to deal with one another in their new setting/bodies. When the Doctor threatens to expose Greyvorn's past, ruining his position, Greyvorn brilliantly counters: "Yes. Tell the Etheric Minister that the Reeve of Excelis, chief of every Warden in the city, is a thousand-year-old warlord. That should convince them to remove me from the investigation, shouldn't it?"

In turn, Greyvorn threatens to imprison the Doctor, an intruder in Excelis, if he doesn't behave. The Doctor resigns himself to allowing Greyvorn the upper hand, adding, "When you've been falsely accused of serious crimes as often as I have, you learn to recognize the oncoming inevitability of the next one."

A police inspector catches a quick glimpse of the fast-moving Doctor and comments on his coat: "I thought I saw something move—it looked like a piece of patchwork." Hysterically, a curator looks in the general direction of the tea room and replies: "If you saw something, it must have been one of the tablecloths."

ASS-WHUPPINGS One of Greyvorn's amateurish thieves gets squished in a security shutter. Greyvorn later strangles the thief's accomplice and the head museum curator to preserve his identity. An honorable city Warden knees Greyvorn in the groin. The Doctor essentially vaporizes Greyvorn's body.

SEX AND SPIRITS Excelis society regards pictures of naked dancers from ancient Khem (presumably a lost city-state) and fertility idols from the jungle kingdoms as naughty.

AUDIO TIE-INS Nuns from the Excelis convent located the Relic a few short days after it went missing, but they never located Greyvorn or the Mother Superior. Without the Relic to empower it, the zombie village went extinct. The Doctor hasn't set foot on Artaris since his last visit. Despite the upswing of spiritualism in Excelis (*see Phenomena*), Artaris has become far less superstitious (all "Excelis Dawns").

"Excelis Decays" details Greyvorn's return to life and subsequent battle with the seventh Doctor.

CHARACTER DEVELOPMENT
• *The Doctor:* The Doctor loves to see museum exhibits of dinosaurs. He reads newspapers only

for the comics and crossword.

• *Greyvorn:* Greyvorn's clearly educated himself, seamlessly blending in with modern-day Excelis society. Even so, he still longs to solve problems by killing people. He reserves torture for people who offend him.

As a Reeve, Greyvorn handles annual performance reviews for all Excelis Wardens. Sometimes, he delivers briefings. "Reeve Maupassant" has been a Reeve for about 10 to 15 years, although Greyvorn's presumably held many such posts in Excelis law enforcement.

The same Relic force that makes Greyvorn immortal also prevents him from sleeping [he hasn't so much as napped in 1,000 years]. His brain still requires *dreaming*, however, to catalog and sort its information. Consequently, Greyvorn experiences "waking dreams"—periods of instability that leave him a screaming wreck for an hour or two—every few days.

Greyvorn's Relic connection allows him to put words in the mouths of dead spirits during seances (*see Phenomena*). However, Greyvorn can only exert this ability on one spirit at a time.

ALIEN RACES *Time Lords:* The Doctor says that regeneration—in terms we'd understand—is the equivalent of gaining a new body (which probably explains the Doctors' varying heights, abilities, allergies, etc.). Even so, it's nothing to do with corpo-electrosopy, the science of possessing other living beings ("Paradise Towers").

• *Terragonan Dream Monkeys:* A breed of proto-marsupial that mucks up the electro-chemical charge of living beings. The monkeys' psychic interference randomizes the thoughts of anyone near them, hopelessly scrambling even simple thoughts. Their homeworld's a million light years from Artaris.

ALIEN PLANETS *Artaris:* A police official in Excelis reads the words "Police Call Box" on the TARDIS' front—although it's probably a goof. Given the dating of "The Plague Herds of Excelis" as 2601, Excelis society clearly pre-dates Earth's colonial era, meaning the population is home grown and shouldn't speak English.

STUFF YOU NEED *The Relic:* It's now famous in Excelis for holding power over the afterlife. Excelis officials fear opening the artifact, believing records which claim it's a gateway to hell.

Currently, the soul of anyone who dies on Artaris automatically goes into a pocket dimension within the Relic. [Although the Doctor liberates the captured souls in "Excelis Decays."]

PLACES TO GO *Excelis:* An Imperial Family currently rules Excelis, possibly as a constitutional monarchy, with command of an Imperial Air Fleet. Certain insurrectionists would love to overthrow the current order. The posting of Reeve is one of the highest ranks a commoner can attain.

Excelis now enjoys the benefits of an industrial society, including dirigibles, printed material, record players, cannons, photographs, steam-powered helicopters and more. The monetary system's based on "gold crowns" [Greyvorn offers a thief 1,000 such units to steal the Relic].

The Imperial Society's a fairly snooty [and boring] social organization in Excelis. Rats and field mice exist in the city. Excelis' grasp of time travel theory is speculative at best.

The lifespan of Excelis residents seems comparable to humans [the museum curator notes that Greyvorn "could not" have lived for 200 Artaris years]. Schools in Excelis offer degrees in metaphysics [which is a goof, apparently—McIntee put "metapsychics" in the script].

ORGANIZATIONS *Excelis Museum:* Probably the biggest repository of Excelis history, both in terms of public and classified documents. The Imperial Family keeps close watch over the museum because some objects there could destabilize the public order. The head Curator's bound by Imperial Edict from handing the Relic over to anyone beyond the Empress, her Regent or the Etheric Minister.

• *The Wardens:* Law officials in Excelis, composed of more males than females. The administrative Reeves oversee the Wardens but rarely working as field agents. A defense council insures the Wardens obey lawful procedure.

PHENOMENA *Spiritualism / Ghosts:* Put simply, mediums in Excelis *can* contact the dead. It's not stated, but presumably, the Relic's presence in the city facilitates communication with the spirits. [The ghosts summoned in "Excelis Rising" describe the afterlife as calm and peaceful, which pretty much matches with descriptions of the Relic's internal dimension in "Excelis Decays."]

The official theory holds that just as a phonograph records sound, buildings often record the personalities of anyone who experiences intense emotional experiences within their walls. Older stone buildings generally retain a dead person's emotional impulses with greater efficiency.

Through seances, spiritualists can interact with the "local ether," thereby conversing with the dead. Seances require a circle of people who link their little fingers (and candles—lots of candles).

It's desperately important to keep the circle unbroken for the séance to continue.

The governmental post of "Etheric Minister" is an official trained in talking with spirits. The Excelis courts recognize testimony from dead people. [Last year, deposition from a deceased victim led to the conviction—and hanging—of the infamous Eastern Slums prostitute murderer.]

HISTORY   In the centuries to follow "Excelis Dawns," the Artaran population divided into itself into fortified city-states. An equivalent of the Industrial Revolution [the "Mechanical Revolution"] overtook the planet.

• Excelis modernized, but started having border disputes with rivals Gatrecht and Calann.

• Three hundred years ago, "Reeves" emerged as a type of government overseer in Excelis. A hundred years later, a Reeve [*not* Greyvorn] commissioned volunteer citizens to become Wardens, the first formal law enforcers. Greyvorn worked as one of the earliest street Wardens, later shifting identities and rising through the ranks—as Maupassant—to become Reeve.

• Excelis civilization now regards "King Greyvorn and his lost treasure" as little more than myth. However, officials at the Imperial Archives' Black Museum [and presumably the Imperial Family] privately recognize the tales as true.

• Life on Artaris became far less superstitious, although in Excelis, spiritualism became a growing movement (*see Phenomena*). The city gained a fair amount of gender equality, although men still edge out women in the working world.

AT THE END OF THE DAY   More than the middle "Excelis" installment, "Excelis Rising" admirably takes the baton from its predecessor—then charges down the track at a fever pitch. Anthony Stewart Head's entirely in his element as the older, more cerebral Greyvorn, and the verbal swordplay between the ex-warlord and the sixth Doctor sent chills up our spines. If there's a complaint, it's probably that it's not *longer*, leaving this as another win for the "Excelis" storyline.

• The name "Maupassant" stems from 19th century author Guy de Maupassant, who's sometimes cited as the greatest French short story writer.

• McIntee only knew actor Anthony Stewart Head as Giles from *Buffy the Vampire Slayer* and the man in the Gold Blend [Taster's Choice in America] coffee commercials. Not wanting to write Greyvorn like either of those aspects, McIntee

scripted the part as if written for Julian Glover (*The Empire Strikes Back*, "City of Death," etc.).

• The part of the curator was written for Michael Sheard (*The Empire Strikes Back*, oodles of "Doctor Who" stories), who served as best man at McIntee's wedding.

• Treacherous museum worker Solomon is named after Colin Baker's character from BBV's "The Stranger" stories. Inquisitor Danby owes her name to ghost story editor Mary Danby. Minister Pryce takes his name from actor Jonathan Pryce ("The Curse of Fatal Death").

• McIntee says the following dialogue got cut, thus dicing a joke he's rather fond of:

CURATOR: "I really thought that the peace process with Calann and Gatrecht would work, but… You can't trust diplomats, can you? Change their minds more often than their socks. One day it's 'peace on,' and the next—"

THE DOCTOR: "Peace off?"

CURATOR: "So they tell us."

THE SHADOW IN THE GLASS

By Justin Richards and Stephen Cole

Release Date: *April 2001*
Order: *BBC Past Doctor Adventure #41*

TARDIS CREW   The sixth Doctor, with Brigadier Lethbridge-Stewart

TRAVEL LOG   Turelhampton, a Dorset village, England, 1944 and 2001; a Berlin ballroom, 1942; Hitler's bunker, Berlin, April 30, 1945; Nazi base, Antarctica, 2001.

CHRONOLOGY   For the sixth Doctor, clearly after "The Spectre of Lanyon Moor" (as the Brigadier recognizes him), but before Mel's debut in *Business Unusual*. For the Brigadier, after those stories and "Battlefield," but before *Happy Endings*.

STORY SUMMARY   When journalist Claire Aldwych uncovers evidence of an alien presence in Turelhampton, England, UNIT solicits advice from the retired Brigadier Lethbridge-Stewart. In turn, the Brigadier uses his space-time telegraph to summon the Doctor for help.

Duly briefed on the situation, the Doctor helps the Brigadier infiltrate the Turelhampton site, learning that a British fighter plane brought down a passing Vvormak spacecruiser there in May 1944. The Doctor finds most of the alien Vvormak in stasis, then nervously confirms that in August 1944, a German trooper stole the ship's main navigational instrument: a crystal ball named "The Scrying Glass," capable of showing images of the future.

The Doctor, the Brigadier and Claire learn that a neo-Nazi group in Cornwall currently possesses the Scrying Glass, hoping to use its "mystical" powers to bring about a Fourth Reich. More curiously, the Doctor's trio discovers the neo-Nazi leader looks exactly like Adolf Hitler. The Doctor and his allies investigate Hitler's final days and realize, with effort (*see History*), that Hitler *did* commit suicide in 1945—but that the young woman buried alongside him was *not* Eva Braun. In truth, the Nazi Party faked Eva Braun's death and smuggled her—pregnant with the Fuhrer's child—away to a secret Nazi base in Antarctica. There, Braun birthed Hitler's son, the current neo-Nazi leader.

The heroes travel, via the TARDIS, to the Antarctic base to neuter the Nazis' plans. The Doctor successfully pockets the Scrying Glass, but not before it shows him taking the younger Hitler back in time to the Fuhrer's bunker. Moments later, Hitler Jr. takes Claire hostage, demanding the Doctor help him fulfill the Scrying Glass' vision.

The Time Lord reluctantly complies, taking Hitler's son, Claire and the Brigadier back to Germany, April 30, 1945: the fall of Hitler's bunker in Berlin. Hitler's son sets out to meet his father, and the trailing Doctor and Brigadier order Claire to stay in the TARDIS, then follow. The younger Hitler finds his bested father as a mere shell of a man. Hitler Jr. tries to explain his origins, but the Doctor easily paints Hitler's "time travelling son" as a lunatic. The traumatized Fuhrer deems the newcomer a madman, then takes a revolver and shoots his son through the head.

The Fuhrer's associates dispose of the younger Hitler's body. Moments later, the Fuhrer fulfills history by shooting himself, even as his supporters make ready to smuggle Eva Braun out of Germany. The Doctor and the Brigadier breathe easy, but unfortunately for her, Claire leaves the TARDIS, determined to witness the historic events. Needing a woman's body to substitute for Eva Braun, Nazi Martin Bormann captures Claire and makes her chew a cyanide tablet.

Shortly afterward, a horrified Doctor and Brigadier turn horrified to witness the Nazis burning the Fuhrer and Claire's bodies—realizing they fulfilled history but failed to save their friend. Solemnly, the Doctor and the Brigadier return to the present, making arrangements to help the slumbering Vvormak revive and depart Earth.

MEMORABLE MOMENTS While helping the Doctor infiltrate a Berlin ballroom party, 1942, the Brigadier stops at a buffet and comes face-to-face with Adolf Hitler. Confronted by one of the most evil men in history, the Brigadier can only offer him a dirty plate with a half-eaten sausage roll.

Afterward, the Doctor and the Brigadier return to 2001 and nonchalantly tell Claire—who thinks they've only been gone for 15 minutes—that they've just acquired Adolf Hitler and Eva Braun's DNA samples. In response, Claire puts down her coffee very, very carefully.

Events in Hitler's bunker play out with a miraculously orchestrated precision. More tragically, the Brigadier rages and the Doctor falls silent upon witnessing the Germans burning Claire's body in place of Eva Braun. On the last page, the Doctor hopes to breathe clean air and look at the sea, cleansing himself of these events.

SEX AND SPIRITS The Doctor, the Brigadier and Claire gulp brandy—a lot of brandy, with little effect in the Doctor's case—while making harrowing conclusions about the "deaths" of Hitler and Eva Braun.

ASS-WHUPPINGS Claire's colleague Brian Goldman, captured by neo-Nazis, slits his own throat rather than yield his discoveries about the modern-day Hitler.

The Brigadier guns down a Nazi intent on knifing the Doctor. He also eliminates Hitler Jr.'s murderous associate Hanne Neumann by making her bite down on a cyanide capsule.

The Berlin bunker witnesses the death of two Hitlers. More tragically, Martin Bormann flings Claire into the path of a mortar shell. She takes shrapnel to her thorax, hemothorax, one lung and more. Bormann finishes the job, making a shell-shocked Claire chew a cyanide capsule.

TV TIE-INS Captain Palmer (present in "The Time Monster," but not "The Daemons," cited as the mid-1970s) still works for UNIT. Claire wrote about secret history of the Nuton power complex ("The Claws of Axos"), but her work got lackluster ratings.

After events in "Battlefield," the UN renewed the Brigadier's UNIT security pass. He removed the time telegraph ("Revenge of the Cybermen")

from UNIT Headquarters, figuring the Doctor meant it for him personally. The Brigadier's far more impartial with regards to alien life (notably "The Silurians"), now believing that not all extra-terrestrials pose a threat.

UNIT engineer Tom Osgood ("The Daemons") shows up to help counteract the Vvormak ship's forcefield.

NOVEL TIE-INS   The Doctor previously befriended Winston Churchill in 1936 (*Players*), and meets him again in 1944. A grateful Churchill aids the Doctor's efforts to infiltrate Nazi Germany (*see History*).

The seventh Doctor "previously" interwove himself into Hitler's history, indirectly aiding with his rise to power (*Timewyrm: Exodus*), but the two Doctors' activities don't intersect.

The older Brigadier ironically wishes everyone could become younger and keep living (he gets his wish in *Happy Endings*).

CHARACTER DEVELOPMENT

• *The Doctor:* On the sixth Doctor's considerable activities during World War II, *see History*. Also, a previous Doctor flew a Halifax mark VII bomber during an unspecified adventure in March, 1945.

He keeps futuristic DNA testing equipment in the TARDIS. He was present when Arminius' forces battled the Romans in Germany. He learned to read Russian years ago, in order to read Chekhov in the original. The Doctor's read about the Vvormak in the *Eye-Spy Book of Alien Space-ships*, but hasn't met them before now.

Mention of the Doctor's name leaves junior UNIT members awestruck. His name carries some weight with modern-day Russian authorities. The Doctor rubs his cat badge out of habit. In Berlin ballroom party, 1942, he wears a monocle.

The Doctor has read *The Coming Race*, written by Englishman Edward Bulwer-Lytton, 1871, which theorized that "vril energy" or "astral light" surrounds the whole Earth. The Doctor deemed the science as garbage, but the book as "not bad."

• *Brigadier Lethbridge-Stewart:* The Brigadier currently resides with Doris, his wife, an hour or so from Dorset. He's retired but well connected, with some contacts in Russia.

The Brigadier holds a keen interest in military history. His reflexes have slowed over the years. His back hurts from too much gardening.

Hitler only knew the Brigadier as "Brigadier General Braun" [no relation to Eva].

The Brigadier knows the Doctor's sixth incar-nation the least well of his various personas, but has certainly met him before.

• *Doris:* She's currently off on holiday, enjoying a week of sun and sangria with her niece.

• *Claire Aldwych:* Claire wrote and directed *The Last Days of Hitler?*, broadcast on The Conspiracy Channel, August 12, 1997. She also works for The Conspiracy Channel's *So They Say* program.

Claire is single, white and an only child. She briefly attended drama school to appease her mother, a failed actress. Claire's 29, but feels 50. She knows about UNIT. She holds fellow journal-ist Sarah Jane Smith in high regards.

• *Adolf Hitler:* A realist, with little belief in the supernatural whatever his advisers say. Per the popular story, Hitler only had one testicle.

• *Adolf Hitler Jr.:* As opposed to Daddy Hitler, he was raised to value the occult. Hitler Jr. set up machinistic political forces and a shadow economy, geared to takeover the world in 2001, but the plan died with him. The Nazi base in Antarctica served as Hitler Jr.'s main base, although he also met with supporters in a millionaire's mansion outside of Kilkhampton, Cornwall.

• *The TARDIS:* The TARDIS can track energy sources, thereby locating the Antarctic Nazi base.

ALIEN RACES   *Vvormak:* During space jour-neys, the Vvormak place themselves into sus-pended animation, keeping their bodies nurtured while their "familiars"—telekinetic extensions of their psyches—operate the ship's controls.

Vvormak familiars appear as horned, shadowy imps with red eyes, but can't venture far from their host bodies. They generate empathic fields that render them invisible to the human eye, but impartial devices such as camera lenses can reg-ister them.

STUFF YOU NEED   The Scrying Glass (a.k.a. *Ocular Celluprime):* The Scrying Glass helps Vvormak pilots navigate by looking into the future. The Vvormak ship travels faster than light, so the Scrying Glass enables the Vvormak see objects approaching.

The Scrying Glass looks like a shiny disc, opaque, warm and always glowing a faint, soft red, with a swirl of mist inside.

• *The Brigadier's time-space telegraph:* It's about the shape and size of an old cash register, with small antenna protruding from a featureless base. It doesn't plug into anything—you just speak into it and the TARDIS picks up the message.

• *Vvormak Stasis Pods:* Have a life-extending unit, designed to preserve the Vvormak cosmo-naut's body. The life-extending unit also works on human beings. Any human who acquired such a device could potentially live for 1,000 years.

TOP 10 'WHO' DRAMATIC MOMENTS (NOVELS)

*From Earthworld (March 2001)
to Time Zero (Sept. 2002)*

1) Sabbath surgically removes the Doctor's heart (*The Adventuress of Henrietta Street*)— Some fans adore *Henrietta Street* like their own flesh and blood, other readers probably doused it in kerosene and torched it on their backyard grill. Whatever the case, the visceral loss of the Doctor's heart drove the EDA range for most of 2002. More to the point, the image of Sabbath standing above the Doctor's body—holding the Doctor's black, poisoned heart—etched itself into many readers' brains for months to come.

2) The Doctor acts against the Cold (*Time and Relative*)—Again, this proves important not just because the Doctor saves Earth, but because he reconciles himself to interfering with history. It's to author Kim Newman's credit that he sets this up so perfectly, you could almost believe this story was scripted before "An Unearthly Child" and simply never got filmed.

3) "It'll be all right" (*The City of the Dead*)— At least, that's what the Doctor tells a teenage girl that he rescues from a New Orleans sex ritual. After all, he's the Doctor—and if he says it's going to be all right, it certainly will. But when the Doctor drops the girl off at home, and observes her low-class household and drunken mother, he suddenly realizes that—as far as the girl's concerned—everything *won't* be all right. In such a fashion, author Lloyd Rose subverts the entirety of "Doctor Who"—pitting the Doctor against a very humanistic foe which can't be killed or banished to another dimension.

4) Benny leaves Straklant to die (*The Glass Prison*)—Fifth Axis officer Straklant finds himself tied-up and perched over an abyss—and Benny doesn't lift a finger to pull him to safety. If that seems callous, it works because Benny doesn't cause or even perhaps *wish* for Straklant's death—she just doesn't do anything to prevent it. Given that Straklant—a merciless criminal—gleefully tried to kill Benny's son, that's fine by us.

5) "I didn't want to die alone." (*The Book of the Still*)—Rendered unconscious, young student Rhian is perplexed when the Doctor awakens her before a bomb goes off—wondering why the hell he didn't let her sleep through the explosion. Somewhat embarrassed, the Doctor's forced to concede: "I didn't want to die alone."

6) A sandbag crushes the Doctor's chest (*Camera Obscura*)—A completely brutal act geared to make the Doctor—who's totally shocked when he survives—realize that his secondary heart's snug in Sabbath's chest. More to the point, author Lloyd Rose proves with this act that she's a child of the New Adventures—putting the Doctor through utter hell to make him seem more heroic.

7) Anji keeps saying Dave but meaning Fitz (*Time Zero*)—When Anji tries to get some measure of peace about her long-dead boyfriend, she realizes she *actually* needs consoling for the missing/presumed dead Fitz. In a flash, it's clear how much she's finally gotten over her late boyfriend [thank God] and how much she's grown aboard the TARDIS.

8) The Doctor forces Hitchemus' humans and tigers to get along (*The Year of Intelligent Tigers*)—Almost godlike, the Doctor uses a weather control device to eradicate a spaceport, then gets everyone's attention with a miniature tornado. For an encore, he tells Hitchemus' tigers and humans that—by the way—he's just shifted the entire planet's rotation out of kilter and they'd better start working together. For better or worse, the tigers and humans enter a new era of peace and cooperation.

9) The death of Claire Aldwych (*The Shadow in the Glass*)—What could've been just another "They Saved Hitler's Brain!" novel comes off surprisingly well, especially with the delicious twist of journalist Claire Aldwych—an extremely striking one-off character—getting brutally killed and standing in for Eva Braun's body.

10) Streaky Bacon tries to kill himself (*The Crooked World*)—Unable to stomach free will, Streaky Bacon [i.e. Porky Pig] puts a shotgun in his mouth and pulls the trigger. He doesn't die— thanks to the Crooked World's wacky physics—but it dramatically makes *The Crooked World*'s silly events deadly serious.

CONTINUED ON PAGE 71

ORGANIZATIONS *UNIT:* Strangely enough, it has a helpline number.

SHIPS *Vvormak Cruiser:* The ship draws power from potential energy, continually charging itself from the Earth's rotation. It can absorb the potential energy from an atomic blast, neutralizing the explosion to gain enough power for lift-off.

HISTORY The Nazis started building their Antarctic stronghold in 1938 or 1939.

• Needing to confirm Hitler's "death" via DNA samples from past and present, the Doctor and the Brigadier time traveled back to August, 1942.

They infiltrated a Berlin ballroom party, where the Doctor introduced himself to Hitler as "Major Johann Schmidt." Fortuitously, Hitler wanted a blood test to confirm his compatibility to Eva Braun. The Doctor obtained his samples with little difficulty, plus earned Hitler's trust.

• On May 17, 1944, a British Hurricane pilot brought down a Vvormak spaceship as it passed over England on a survey mission. The ship crashed in Turelhampton, with the British military quickly evacuating the town and securing the area. Unfortunately, the Vvormak ship projected a localized gravitational field, anchoring it to the ground. Unable to move the vessel, the military guarded the area for more than 50 years, spreading a cover story about unexploded bombs.

• British Private Gerrard Lassiter initially pocketed the Scrying Glass as a talisman, but German trooper Gunther Brun later killed him during a skirmish in rural France. Brun took the Scrying Glass, but lost it, shortly afterward, in a card game to Colonel Otto Klein of the Waffen SS.

• Two weeks later, Reichsfúhrer Heinrich Himmler learned of the Scrying Glass' existence and acquired the object from Brun. As a mystic arts practitioner, Himmler turned the object over to a group of Tibetan mystics for further study.

• To research the Vvormak ship's history, the Doctor traveled to July 1944 and convinced Prime Minister Winston Churchill to help smuggle him into France. Aided by the Marquis, the Doctor made his way to Berlin. Once there, he worked for the Reich Records Department as "Colonel Johann Schmidt." Later, he transferred to the Fifth Medical Corps in Friedrichstrasse.

• In August 1944, Hitler became curious about the Scrying Glass' origins and authorized a German raiding party to look for other such objects at the Turelhampton site. Luckily, Hitler remembered the Doctor's "service" in 1942 and insisted on sending him on the raiding party. Having anticipated this, the Doctor accompanied the German raiders and participated in the Turelhampton raid on August 18, 1944.

• On April 25, 1945, the Tibetans responsible for the Scrying Glass are found, having apparently killed themselves. The Scrying Glass went missing and later made its way into the hands of Hitler Jr.'s neo-Nazis.

• Hitler Jr. arrived at his father's bunker, via the TARDIS, on April 30, 1945, but a disbelieving Fuhrer killed his son. Hitler aide Martin Bormann stashed the body in a nearby water tower, where Allied troops later mistook it for a Hitler double, killed for an unexplained reason.

• Shortly afterward, Hitler committed suicide. The Doctor, already cited by Hitler as a medical doctor, formally declared him and the faking Eva Braun both "dead." After Bormann substituted the murdered Claire for Eva's body, Hitler's personal pilot, Hans Bauer, flew the real Eva to a waiting submarine in Hamburg.

• Even in death, Hitler and Claire's charred corpses got a lot of mileage. The Russians sent Hitler and Claire's jaws, teeth and skull fragments to Moscow for further study. They buried the rest of their remains, along with the Goebbels family in Buch. For political reasons, the group was dug-up and re-buried in 1945 and again in 1946. Finally, KGB head Yuri Andropov simply ordered the bodies incinerated on April 5, 1970, as part of "Operation Archive."

• After the Soviet Union's collapse, the Doctor helped Yablokov, the Russian President's counselor, double-check the whereabouts of Russia's suitcase nukes. They found 84 such devices unaccounted for.

• In 2001, the Brigadier snitched pieces of Hitler and "Eva Braun's" skull and DNA samples from the State Special Trophy Archive in Moscow, classified as part of "Operation Myth." The body pieces aided the Doctor's investigations, although he'd no reason to suspect Braun's body samples actually belonged to Claire.

• After this story, UNIT gleaned enough information from the Nazis' Antarctic base to break up several Fourth Reich cells.

• The British government released Turelhampton from military overview in 2001.

AT THE END OF THE DAY Lovingly slathered in darkness, rife with juicy turning points and rather unique for allowing Hitler and the Brigadier—two military men at opposite ends of the moral spectrum—to meet one another. For something written in some panic to plug a gaping hole in the schedule, *The Shadow in the Glass* stands out as one of the more remarkable PDAs from 2001, only failing (unjustly) in the eyes of people who're tired of "Doctor Who" Nazi stories. But judged on its own merits, the book more than succeeds, blessed with a talent for misdirection and a real sense of compassion for Claire Aldwych, a genuine victim who's put to the slaughter.

DID YOU KNOW?

• In Richards' original storyline, journalist Claire Aldwych was a male character who was never seen again once he passed along a videotape showing the imp-looking Vvormak familiars along

to UNIT. Cole suggested making the journalist a woman and extending her role, given there were no sympathetic female characters and she could double as the companion for the story. Richards immediately hit upon the twist whereby she became the substitute for Eva Braun's body, and both ideas were incorporated.

• The Brigadier re-meets UNIT Captain Palmer in this story, but doesn't remember him too well—a jape on Richards and Cole's part, as three "Corporal Palmers," played by different actors, appeared in "The Three Doctors," "Invasion of the Dinosaurs" and "Terror of the Zygons."

BLOODTIDE

By Jonathan Morris

Release Date: July 2001
Order: Big Finish "Doctor Who" Audio #22

TARDIS CREW   The sixth Doctor and Evelyn.

TRAVEL LOG   Galapagos Islands, Baquerizo Moreno settlement and Silurian base, September 19, 1835.

CHRONOLOGY   Between "Trial of a Time Lord" and "Time and the Rani."

STORY SUMMARY   Millions of years ago, as the Silurian race prepares to enter hibernation ("Doctor Who and The Silurians"), the Silurian elders put geneticist S'Rel Tulok on trial for unauthorized experiments that they believe pervert the course of nature. The ruling Silurians commute Tulok's death sentence, but banish the scientist and his genetically modified creatures to the Earth's surface, to almost certainly die out amid the environmental chaos.

Tulok's creatures run free, but Silurian Sh'-vak—who owes Tulok her life—allows him re-entry into the Silurian base. The Silurians enter stasis to outsleep the disaster that's made Earth's surface uninhabitable, but—unknown to Sh'vak—the vengeful geneticist sabotages the Silurians' wake-up device. He then enters cryo-sleep with Sh'vak, knowing only a few dozen Silurians will awaken under his leadership.

Meanwhile, as a surprise for Evelyn, the Doctor pilots the TARDIS to the Galapagos Islands, 1835. Once there, a shocked Evelyn meets her personal hero, naturalist Charles Darwin, during the formation of his theories about evolution. The Doctor bluffs Darwin into accepting him and Evelyn as

TOP 10

"WHO" DRAMATIC MOMENTS CONTINUED FROM PAGE 69

HONORABLE MENTIONS

• **The seventh Doctor chases off the eighth Doctor (*The City of the Dead*)**—Continuing a thread begun long, long ago in *Timewyrm: Revelation*, the eighth Doctor probes a stone wall within his own mind. Coming ever closer to regaining his memory, the eighth Doctor gets chased off by a strange Scottish man [obviously his seventh self]—showing how the Doctor's previous selves are walling off his memory to protect his sanity.

• **The Doctor cons the Angel-Maker into knifing him through the heart (*Camera Obscura*)**—Needing to venture into Death's realm, the Doctor tricks the knife-wielding Angel-Maker into skewering his heart like a candied apple. Later asked why he didn't just commit hara-kiri, the Doctor notes: "I've never stabbed myself. If I'd flinched at the last minute, everything would have been ruined."

• **"He left six hours ago." (*Anachrophobia*)**—Just when our heroes think they've quelled an inter-dimensional incursion—killing off a bundle of humans turned into clock people—the Doctor and his allies realize one of them got away. Worse, the missing individual has infected 50,000 people with the clock people-virus, turning a sure victory into a full-blown epidemic.

• **Fitz confers with the TARDIS about the Time Lords' demise (*Trading Futures*)**—Waxing philosophical about the Doctor's dead people, Fitz tells the TARDIS: "Their time has passed. There's no law, no order, not now. You're a police box, but there aren't any policemen left." Great stuff, and showing just how much the Doctor and his companions—an ex-florist's assistant and a futures trader—must protect the frikken' Universe from a proliferation of illicit time technology.

fellow survey team members, prompting Darwin to invite the travelers aboard his historic boat *The Beagle*. Before long, the Doctor hears reports about "devilish creatures" secretly at work in the settlement.

Investigating, the Doctor finds Tulok's revived Silurians, working from a hidden base. Tulok sends a mature Myrka creature to assault *The Beagle*—a first strike to test humanity's mettle—but the Doctor realizes the Myrka's homing on a signal device the Silurians implanted inside Greta, a serving girl. Greta sacrifices herself to the Myrka's jaws, thereby destroying the tracker and sending the satiated Myrka back to base.

Infiltrating the Silurian hideout, the Doctor and his allies learn Tulok wrecked the Silurian hibernation mechanism, then inform Sh'vak. Additionally, the Doctor concludes Tulok's genetically modified creatures survived their banishment and eventually evolved into the human race. Simultaneously, Tulok makes ready to leave aboard a Silurian submarine—intending to wipe out all human adults with a genetically engineered plague, then enslave the surviving children.

Sh'vak dies protecting Darwin and *Beagle* Captain Fitzroy from Tulok's telepathic attack. In the confusion, Evelyn smuggles a Myrka tracker aboard Tulok's submarine. The Doctor pushes the base's hydrogen fusion reactor to overload, then flees with his allies as it detonates. Tulok prepares to launch his biological warheads, but the Myrka—drawn to the tracker—attacks the submarine, triggering an explosion that annihilates both the Myrka and Tulok's crew. Afterward, the Doctor convinces Darwin to refrain from mentioning the Silurians in his writings, then leaves with Evelyn in the TARDIS.

MEMORABLE MOMENTS Tulok, pretty much a monster by any definition, nonetheless gives a mournful cry of, "My creatures... what will happen to my creatures?", as the Silurians turn his experiments loose into the maelstrom.

The Myrka's attack on *The Beagle* makes for a bizarre mixture of fantasy and history. Moreover, there's a chilling moment when our heroes walk through the Silurians' larder and discover the Silurians eat *people*.

The Doctor gives an impassioned speech about how a million years from now, Earth will look as though mankind never existed. When Evelyn gasps, the Doctor replies: "You should see it as I see it. That's history. All of human life, just a brief candle in the darkness."

Tulok tells the overweight Doctor: "I feel I will particularly enjoy the taste of your corpse." Evelyn pretends to be brainwashed and tells a Silurian: "Tulok wants you to proceed with... the big plan."

SEX AND SPIRITS A nauseated Evelyn, unable to enjoy a traditional Galapagos meal of cooked turtle, consoles herself with a glass of wine.

ASS-WHUPPINGS Evelyn and Darwin stumble upon a Silurian hibernation chamber, finding hundreds of Silurians who died millennia ago when the biological seals on their chambers rotted.

The Doctor and *Beagle* Captain Fitzroy traipse through Tulok's larder house—witnessing dozens of dead Baquerizo Moreno prisoners strung up like sides of beef. Tulok tests his plague virus on Baquerizo Moreno Governor Lawson—it strips the flesh from his bones.

For an encore, Tulok's Silurians eradicate an entire settlement on Galapagos with their plague virus [the Doctor speculates the contained plague will burn itself out, posing no threat to humanity]. The Silurians' mental control makes Darwin and Captain Fitzroy sink into cataleptic shock, but the Doctor breaks this effect with hypnosis.

Part 1 ends with the Doctor writhing under a Silurian eye blast. At the end of Part 2, it's Evelyn's turn. The noble Sh'vak loses a battle with Tulok, then dies aiding the Doctor.

A Myrka electrocutes a few men on *The Beagle*, plus lunches on a serving girl named Greta. The same Myrka later does in Tulok's group. The Doctor blows up the Galapagos Silurian base (shades of "The Sea Devils") with no casualties.

TV TIE-INS Silurians debuted in "Doctor Who and the Silurians," which unveiled them as the previous rulers of Earth. Myrkas didn't come along until "Warriors of the Deep," although the Doctor refers to the Myrka in "Bloodtide" [capable of bashing *The Beagle*] as "an adult"—suggesting the "Warriors" version was something of a baby [or bred for close-quarters combat].

"Bloodtide" claims the worldwide catastrophe which forced the Silurians into stasis *did* occur, whereas "The Silurians" conversely claims the advanced reptiles merely overreacted [they predicted a planetary body would collide with Earth, but it went into orbit and became the moon]. Probably, the moon's arrival—whether it smacked into Earth or not—triggered planet-wide storms that convinced the Silurians to sleep it out. Alternatively, the third Doctor's TV conclusion about the disaster "never happening" could be set aside as erroneous.

In "Bloodtide," the sixth Doctor's extremely naïve to think mankind and the Silurians can peacefully *share* Earth, considering all four previous attempts ("The Silurians," *The Scales of Injustice*, "The Sea Devils," "Warriors of the Deep") have ended in massive conflict and death. Plus, it'd grievously violate history to front a human/Silurian accord in 19th century Earth.

The sixth Doctor's hypnosis breaks the Silurian psychosis (which reverts humans to primitive states, "The Silurians").

AUDIO TIE-INS Evelyn previously expressed admiration for Charles Darwin in "The Marian Conspiracy."

TOP 5 'WHO' DRAMATIC MOMENTS (AUDIOS)

*From Loups-Garoux (May 2001)
to Neverland (June 2002)*

1) The Doctor revealed as Zagreus ("Neverland")—Very nearly the "Doctor Who" equivalent of "Luke, I am your father," the Doctor's transformation into the villainous Zagreus practically made us leap out of our seats. The fact that Big Finish decided to wait 18 months (until "Zagreus") for the resolution perfectly whet everyone's whistles for the 40th anniversary.

2) "Edward Grove is alive, and we are in his belly." ("The Chimes of Midnight")—The corker of "The Chimes of Midnight," essentially the "Doctor Who" version of *The Sixth Sense*'s revelation about Bruce Willis' character. The unveiling of Edward Grove's identity—as a sentient, menacing house—brilliantly leads to the Doctor imploring Edward to give up his thin shred of life for his servants' sake. Edward slowly comprehends, "You are asking me to commit suicide," to which the Doctor memorably responds: "I am. I'm sorry."

3) Alternate reality Daleks pour into our Universe ("Dalek Empire: Project Infinity")—After the bloodbath of "Dalek Empire," probably nobody expected Daleks from another reality—much less *friendly* Daleks from another reality—to arrive and start shish-ka-bobbing the Emperor Dalek's forces with laser beams. But that's exactly what happens, leading to a glorious row in "Dalek Empire II."

4) "Let these people pass." ("Colditz")—As events race toward their climax at Colditz castle, it's ironically Hauptmann Julius Schäfer—a Nazi—who turns bold enough to free the Doctor and Ace. Schäfer's *only* [if you can call it that] enlightened enough to realize he's completely out of his depth—but even that kernal of knowledge is enough to let him become *more* than just his station in life [which is at the core of "Doctor Who," really].

5) The death of Stubbe ("Loups-Garoux")—Inherently tied to the Earth, the ancient werewolf Pieter Stubbe fails to survive when the TARDIS materializes in orbit. Sweetly directed, Stubbe's passing for an instant made us feel *sorry* for his demise—but only for an instant.

HONORABLE MENTIONS

• **The Silurians' larder ("Bloodtide")**—Certainly, "Doctor Who and the Silurians" alone proved the Silurians weren't beyond killing mass droves of humanity. Even so, the stark revelation that the Silurians *ate* people—"like a bunch of jelly babies," the fourth Doctor might have said—bumped the long-standing "Who" reptiles to a new level of evil.

• **The Doctor refuses to kill Charley ("Neverland")**—With the Universe's safety on the line, the Doctor declines to kill Charley even at her request. It's an extremely contrived scheme [and a downright stupid gambit on the villain Sentris' part] but it gorgeously shows how far the Doctor will go to protect his friend.

• **"Don't turn around." ("Primeval")**—Facing off against the almost godlike Kwundaar, the fifth Doctor bravely declares to his unseen opponent, "I'm not frightened of you." But in response, Kwundaar—bristling with power—can only impishly reply, "No. But then, you haven't turned around, have you?" It's a confrontation that climaxes—at least, for the sake of the Part 1 cliffhanger—with the Doctor turning around, spying Kwundaar's face and screaming his Gallifreyan lungs out. Superbly done.

CHARACTER DEVELOPMENT

• *The Doctor:* The Doctor passes himself off in this era as "Dr. Albert Einstein." He carries a sonic emission detector. He [somewhat distressingly, if we're being honest about it] doesn't think the Silurians are *wrong* for eating humans—that it's simply in their nature. In addition to Darwin, the Doctor wants to give naturalist Alfred Wallace (*see History*) moral support.

• *Evelyn Smythe:* She thinks Galapagos tortoises smell "like physics undergraduates" and can't stomach eating them.

She doesn't actively help Darwin form theories about evolution, but occasionally gives tacit signs of approval. Humorously, he rejects her off-handed comment of "survival of the fittest" as a silly, self-evident phrase.

• *The Doctor and Evelyn:* Evelyn once tried to read *Moby Dick*, but gave up "before they raised anchor." Conversely, the Doctor deems Melville his favorite author [Evelyn notes that's hardly surprising, since they're both "pompous and overblown"]. The Doctor reads lines from Melville's *The Incitatus*.

They bluff Darwin by claiming they studied with geologist Charles Lyell.

• *Charles Darwin:* When the Doctor and Evelyn encounter Darwin in 1835, he's young enough to pass as one of Evelyn's students [although actor Miles Richardson's voice doesn't suggest he's *that* young]. He's currently studying the birds of Gala-

pagos, noting how in the 150 years since explorer Cowley visited the isles, the birds have grown fearful of humans. From this, Darwin forms theories about natural selection, concluding that cautious species survive to keep breeding.

ALIEN RACES *The Silurians:* Silurian law supposedly upholds "the natural order," stressing that life exists as nature's servant. [A slightly arbitrary and hypocritical view, given that the Silurians clearly *mastered* Earth and culled early mankind with plagues ("The Silurians"). The ruling Silurian triad tolerates genetic engineering to a certain point, but deems Tulok's work goes too far. Silurians hold trials in the "Justice Chamber."

Silurians can telepathically control humans by exploiting such characteristics as vanity, greed and cruelty. Their mental power varies according to their force of will [i.e. Sh'vak draws first blood, but the formidable Tulok wins].

• *Myrkas:* Myrkas will endure great amounts of pain and suffering to reach a Silurian ultra-sonic summoning device. Such hunts were deemed excessively cruel and banned.

HISTORY The Doctor erroneously claims the Silurians dominated Earth "many hundreds of thousands of years ago," although he's probably speaking generally. "The Sea Devils" more accurately dates Silurian society during the Eocene Era, between 56 and 35 million years ago. [Morris notes: "This is 'erroneous' in the sense of fitting in with genuine evolutionary history—the Silurians wouldn't be around at the same time as primitive man (as 'The Silurians' establishes) during the Eocene era. This is impossible to get right—the TV show contradicts itself!"] (*For further details, check out The Discontinuity Guide by Mssrs. Cornell, Day and Topping.*)

• The Silurians bred mankind's early ancestors—Australopithecus—as a primary food source, feeding the Australopithecus herds with seaweed. Later, Tulok tinkered with Australopithecus' genetic code, improving their flavor, breeding cycles and immune systems. He later outraged his superiors by boosting Australopithecus' intelligence. As such, Tulok didn't create mankind, but he certainly gave humanity's development a genetic kick-in-the-pants. This explains why the "missing link" in mankind's development doesn't exist, because Tulok's meddling jump-started humanity's growth.

• Tulok's trial occurs 10 years after Earth's surface becomes uninhabitable, meaning the Silurians didn't start napping straightaway. The catastrophe that ruined the Earth's surface boiled

---

THE CRUCIAL BITS...

• **BLOODTIDE**—Revelation that Silurian scientist Tulok genetically influenced mankind's evolution. Discovery that a vengeful Tulok sabotaged Silurians' resuscitation unit, explaining why they never awoke from stasis.

---

the seas, making large parts of the planet acidic. Temperatures reached 20 below freezing [on a Silurian temperature scale]. Storms blacked out the skies and razed the globe. Earth essentially became a poisoned wasteland.

• The Silurians didn't leave fossils behind because of "Monkton's Theorem"—which essentially means they were too smart to get trapped and preserved in tar pits. In the Silurians' absence, their cities and civilization crumbled to nothing. Tulok's sabotage wasn't uniform, as some Silurian colonies (the TV stories) obviously survived.

• The Doctor guides Darwin away from radical interpretations of Tulok's meddling [such as thinking that the Silurians actually evolved into mankind], assuring that his theories of descent through modification stand. The Time Lord advises Darwin to keep sharp watch for Alfred Wallace—the naturalist who persuaded Darwin to make his findings public in 1858. [It's more of a joke than anything else, since Darwin would've watched for Wallace no matter what.]

AT THE END OF THE DAY Highly entertaining, albeit woefully inaccurate historically [the real Darwin gradually formulated his theories— he certainly didn't come to his conclusions overnight]. "Bloodtide" moreso exists to bridge continuity rather than forward its own plot, although it's not a sin, given its superior implementation. It also helps that the cast—particularly Baker, Maggie Stables and Miles Richardson as Darwin—clearly enjoyed themselves making this one, bringing some truly outstanding performances to the table.

DID YOU KNOW?

• The original "Bloodtide" brief included both the Sea Devils and Silurians, but this quickly proved impractical. Still, Morris took some inspiration from *Doctor Who Weekly* back-up strips featuring both species.

• The Myrka was played, pantomime-horse style, by writer Rob Shearman ("The Holy Terror") and Big Finish production master Alistair Lock.

• Some of Darwin's dialogue is paraphrased from passages of *The Voyage Of The Beagle*.

• The following dialogue, spoken by the Doctor to Darwin, got cut on the grounds it might cause offence: "…Maybe not for many decades, but one day the world will be ready for your ideas. And you will win the argument, Charles. Because rationalism will always succeed over superstition. Enlightenment will always defeat ignorance. All you need do is present the proof of your case." During recording, this got replaced with a line about there being "more things in heaven and Earth"—which also got cut.

• Morris freely admits that his geography of the Galapagos Island is largely inaccurate.

• Colin Baker ad-libbed the line: "I suppose it is in fact a tortoise tortoise, and that's something else I've taught us!"

PROJECT: TWILIGHT

By Cavan Scott and Mark Wright

Release Date: August 2001
Order: Big Finish "Doctor Who" CD #23

TARDIS CREW The sixth Doctor and Evelyn.

TRAVEL LOG London, present day (during Blair's term as British prime minister).

STORY SUMMARY Arriving in modern-day London, the Doctor and Evelyn enjoy Chinese take-out from the Slow Boat restaurant. But afterward, the duo strangely witness a tall, crossbow-bearing stranger shoot a local casino worker named Eddie. The time travelers help the wounded Eddie back to a casino named The Dusk, finding that the establishment's owners—Reggie Mead and Amelia Doory—oddly keep a medical facility in the basement.

Eddie bizarrely combusts and explodes, leading the Doctor to demand answers. The Doctor eventually learns that during World War I, the British government sanctioned the ultra-secret "Project: Twilight" as a means of creating nigh-unstoppable super-soldiers. Working from a facility named "the Forge," Dr. William Abberton, the Project's head researcher, conducted genetic experiments on various prisoners and destitute members of society. He successfully converted Amelia, Reggie and their associates into fast-healing vampires, but they escaped on a fateful day in 1915. Ever since, Amelia and her friends struggled to survive, stalked at length by a crossbow-totting killer named Nimrod.

Concluding that Abberton victimized his charges, the Doctor agrees to help Amelia find a cure for vampirism. The Doctor examines the crossbow bolt that killed Eddie, and finding it laced with nanobots tailored to destroy the vampires' immune systems, suggests reprogramming the tiny machines to purge the body's vampiric elements.

Amelia betrays the Doctor, using his discovery to manufacture an airborne "Twilight Virus" capable of converting humans into vampires on contact. The Doctor horrifically realizes that the Project: Twilight workers never isolated the element that allows vampires to reproduce, meaning Amelia and her associates couldn't increase their numbers. The victimized Amelia now intends to avenge herself on the world, plotting to release the Twilight Virus and create a vampire nation.

As a test, Amelia uses the Twilight Virus to turn Cassie, a casino waitress, into a vampire. Meanwhile, the Doctor and Evelyn reluctantly ally with Nimrod, unmasking him as a repentant, pseudo-vampirized Dr. Abberton (*see Character Development*). Vampire Cassie tries to cope with her newfound impulses and kills the sadistic Reggie, even as Nimrod—hoping to atone for his decades-old sins—plants charges that eradicate Amelia's research lab.

Amelia escapes with a single vial of the Twilight Virus, but the Doctor intercepts her by the Thames. In the scuffle to follow, the Doctor and Amelia fall into the river. Amelia goes missing, but the Doctor retrieves the Twilight Virus sample. The Doctor and Evelyn depart soon after, compassionately dropping off Cassie in Norway, just short of the Arctic Circle. Cassie hopes to tame her feeding impulses in the wilderness, under cover of the region's short days and long nights. But as the Doctor and Evelyn leave in the TARDIS, Nimrod reports to his superiors and agrees to capture Cassie for undisclosed reasons.

MEMORABLE MOMENTS Casino patron Deeks asks the inhuman Amelia, "What are you?", prompting her seductive response: "The future." Amelia makes a very good case that she's a victim and never asked to become vampiric, but the Doctor ultimately holds her accountable for her actions.

SEX AND SPIRITS/ASS-WHUPPINGS Deeks wants sexual favors from Cassie, but Amelia and Reggie eliminate the problem by using Deeks as fodder for their experiments.

ASS-WHUPPINGS As the lab rat "Twilight Seven," Amelia (a.k.a. Millie) removes the ears

This book is not endorsed by the BBC. Doctor Who and TARDIS are trademarks of the BBC.

75

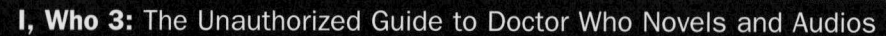

from her guards at the Forge. She also shoots Nimrod (Abberton), but he undergoes vampire conversion and survives.

Nimrod nails Eddie with a nanite-laced crossbow bolt, boiling him to death and making his body explode. He also blackmails Cassie into serving as his agent (*see Character Development*), then stabs her for failing him.

Reggie spent three years recovering from an encounter with Nimrod in 1971.

Nimrod kills two water-vulnerable vampires, Nathaniel and Matthew, by pitching them into the Thames. Beforehand, Nimrod ties Nathaniel up and scorches him with sunlight, ruining his mind and making him eat stray animals in an alley.

Reggie tortures Cassie, attempting to learn about her spying activities for Nimrod. Later, Cassie retaliates by stabbing Reggie with Nimrod's nanite-laced arrow, making him explode.

Amelia puts an arrow through Nimrod's jugular, but he survives. Nimrod blows up Amelia's blood-farm, killing the 100 mindless blood donors there (*see Places to Go*).

Reggie drinks alcohol, proving vampires retain a taste for it.

TV TIE-INS The Doctor's stopped being vegetarian ("The Two Doctors"). He remembers Houdini's advice about slipping out of bonds ("Planet of the Spiders"), but can't recall his wisdom on escaping from cells.

NOVEL TIE-INS Abraham Stroker is cited as greatest authority on vampire matters outside Gallifrey. The Doctor seems to know "Brahm" personally, but deems his *Dracula* as far too melodramatic, and a waste of Stoker's talents. At this point, the sixth Doctor doesn't realize that the Zygons (*The Bodysnatchers*) also influenced Stoker's fiction.

AUDIO TIE-INS The sixth Doctor playfully sings a Gallifreyan nursery rhyme about a menacing figure named Zagreus, further mentioned in "Seasons of Death" and central to "Neverland."

Nimrod ominously vows to retrieve Cassie, presumably leading to events in the upcoming "Project: Lazarus."

TIE-INS The Doctor's shared table with Kublai Khan ("Marco Polo") and eaten pastries from the master bakers of Barastabon (*Short Trips and Side Steps*: "The Not-so Sinister Sponge"). But by his estimation, nothing bests the Peking Crispy Duck from the Slow Boat, a Chinese takeaway joint in south-east London.

The Doctor's previously encountered vampires in "State of Decay" and *Goth Opera*. [Annoyingly, he deems it "not possible" that Amelia and Reggie could be vampires, when he knows they exist.]

CHARACTER DEVELOPMENT
• *The Doctor:* The Doctor visited the Spanish Inquisition at one point. He also likes the Slow Boat's Combo Chicken. He knows the history and geography of the Thames.

• *Evelyn Smythe:* Evelyn's husband loved war stories. She learned information about code-breaking from him.

Evelyn likes sweet and sour chicken balls. She knows less about recent history, including details about the Thames, than other historical periods. She carries a big handbag. She was a residence hall warden.

• *The Doctor and Evelyn:* The Doctor takes the moral high road with Evelyn, claiming she cannot understand his Time Lord perspective on vampires. She deems the Doctor and the Time Lords an arrogant bunch, upset that he holds her at such a distance. By story's end, they forgive and forget.

Evelyn thinks the Doctor sounds like he's in pain when he sings.

• *Amelia (a.k.a. Millie):* Prior to the Forge experiments, Amelia received an extended sentence for embezzling from her employers. The Forge researchers offered to get her out jail, failing to mention she'd become a vampire as a result.

Amelia's been studying genetics, but she's little more than an enthusiastic amateur. She was in the prime of life when converted to vampirism.

• *Reggie:* Reggie greatly admired London gangsters of the 1960s, and named The Dusk casino after them. The casino helps fund Amelia's experiments. Reggie's contacts discover that the Doctor worked for UNIT in the 1970s and 1980s.

Reggie's good with torture. He formerly put out cigarettes on the back of a German trooper in World War I.

• *Cassie:* Cassie birthed a son while still at school, but left him with her mother to find her fortune in London. Few jobs were available back home.

She started waitressing at the Dusk Casino, but also spied on Amelia and Reggie for Nimrod, who threatened to kill Cassie's mother and son if she didn't comply. Cassie suggested voluntary exile to northern Norway, recognizing herself as a threat to others.

• *Nimrod (a.k.a. Doctor William Abboton):* Nimrod underwent vampiric conversion to save his life in 1915, but subsequently augmented his body. He's part man, part machine and part vampire.

He wears Forge-made polycarbide armor, able to withstand a shotgun blast or 100,000 volts from a Tazer without too much trouble. He's read a file at the Forge about the Doctor. He's impervious to vampire bites. He recognizes that his actions as a Forge researcher were reprehensible, and reports to an unseen superior. [Author's Note: Our guess—and it's purely a guess—is that Nimrod reports to the seventh Doctor, who appears in the upcoming sequel story, "Project: Lazarus."]

ALIEN RACES *Forge Vampires:* Vampires sport an abnormally high healing factor, but conversely, their bodies suffer from a metabolism imbalance that renders them unable to produce enough blood. The Forge engineered each of its vampires with a different weakness—a precaution, if needed, to halt their development. Vulnerabilities include sunlight, fire, silver, lead, running water and more.

Amelia, Reggie, Nimrod and many others are immune to sunlight. Nathaniel burned in sunlight but didn't die from it. Amelia can't name her weakness. Traditional vampire defenses such as crucifixes, holy water and garlic have no effect. Helium destroyed one of Reggie's friends 20 years ago.

Shooting a Forge vampire at point-blank range does little damage. They're gifted with enhanced senses [Amelia can hear the Doctor's double heartbeat]. They have low body temperatures. They inexplicably lack reflections.

Amelia and Reggie are telepathic with one another, presumably an attribute of other Forge vampires.

PLACES TO GO *Kasterborus:* Gallifrey's constellation lies at the center of the galaxy.

• *Amelia/Reggie's Blood Farm:* Contains dozens of people in cages, bled intravenously as a food supply for Amelia, Reggie and their associates. At least some bloodfarm residents were evidently taken as children, as they've never experienced human contact or relationships. Tunnels under the Thames access the bloodfarm.

HISTORY Long ago, the Time Lords accidentally loosed the Great Vampires ("State of Decay"), from which all vampire life hails, into our dimension. The Great Vampires enslaved entire worlds, but the Time Lords subsequently wiped them out. It remains the duty of all Gallifreyans to eliminate their descendants.

• The Forge began operations circa 1915, part of an effort to create super soldiers for use against the Germans. The project obtained vampire DNA from an undisclosed source, then put its lab rats, all disenfranchised members of society, through DNA manipulation and courses of drugs and radiation therapy. [Author's Note: Amelia's using modern-day terms to describe the Forge work, as such things were beyond 1915 science.]

• Amelia [then named "Maggie"] underwent vampiric conversion on September 12, 1915.

• On October 4, 1915, Amelia and some test subjects staged a jailbreak. Amelia shot Dr. William Abberton ("Nimrod") while escaping. Abberton would have bled to death, but survived by turning himself into a vampire.

• The escaped vampires hunted freely after the War, but police efforts against them became more sophisticated with the passing of time. Pickings were sparse until the 1980s, when Amelia and Reggie gained enough resources to start up their bloodfarm, trading blood to other Forge victims for vampire DNA. In such a fashion, they furthered Amelia's experiments.

AT THE END OF THE DAY Sufficiently moody, but also incredibly obvious and dull. "Project Twilight" would prove easier to love if the Doctor didn't impotently spend half the story deducing that he is, rather stupidly, collaborating with vampires. He also endangers Evelyn's life by failing to mention that "By the way, these people are vampires," and worse, wastes the whole of Part 3 figuring out that said vampires are, in fact, evil bloodsuckers. We'll grant that Colin Baker delivers a smashing performance anyway, but by the time his character gets his act together, there's only time for a predictable ending and the cyborgish Nimrod going "Nyah, nyah, nyah," before skulking into the shadows. Remember: Just because it's moody, doesn't *automatically* mean it's any good.

DID YOU KNOW?

• Wright and Scott previously pitched a story entitled *The Fires of Darkness* to BBC Books, but editor Justin Richards rejected it. They made alterations based on several suggestions and shopped it to Big Finish, who also nixed it but commissioned "Project: Twilight" instead.

• Author Mark Wright claims in a Discussion Board posting that the main infuences on "Project: Twilight" were the British show *Ultraviolet*, and the gangster novel *The Long Firm* by Jake Arnott.

• Co-Writer Cavan Scott got great amusement upon hearing false rumors that "Project: Twilight" would feature the final war between the Gallifreyans and the Great Vampires at the dawn of time. ("Quite a few miles," he notes, "from a South

This book is not endorsed by the BBC. Doctor Who and TARDIS are trademarks of the BBC.

77

London casino.") Likewise, Wright cites rumors that the audio would feature the return of Omega and Rassilon, which he deems "… just so ludicrous that it might just have been true."

INSTRUMENTS OF DARKNESS

By Gary Russell

Release Date: *November 2001*
Order: *BBC Past Doctor Adventure #48*

TARDIS CREW The sixth Doctor and Mel, with Evelyn.

TRAVEL LOG Great Rokeby, London, Halcham, Norfolk Broads swamp, Sheffield University, all England; Paris, France; a temple in Micronesia, all December 1993.

CHRONOLOGY For the sixth Doctor and Mel, between *The Quantum Archangel* and "Time and the Rani." For Evelyn, after her Big Finish audio tenure.

STORY SUMMARY During a stopover in England, 1993, the Doctor pops his gourd to learn that his former traveling companion, university lecturer Evelyn Smythe, has used her future fore-knowledge to win various contests and betting pools. The Doctor looks up Evelyn in Great Rokeby fully intending to chastise her, only to hear Evelyn point out the TARDIS dropped her off 10 years too early. As Evelyn's younger self is still teaching in Nottingham, she's been forced to keep a low pro-file and make a living as best she's able. Nonetheless, the ever-faithful Evelyn aids the Doctor—as requested—in tracking renegade Auton twins Cellian and Ciara (*Business Unusual*) to the village of Halcham.

Meanwhile, an organization named the Net-work, allegedly run by an ultra-secret criminal council named the Magnate, kidnaps psionics to exploit their abilities. Network agents capture Mel's psionic friend Trey Korte (*Business Unusual* again), even as the Doctor arrives in Halcham to check on the twins. The Doctor finds Cellian and Ciara genuinely reformed and meets their bene-factor Sebastian Malvern, a frightfully powerful psionic with ties to the Network.

Malvern informs the Doctor that the Magnate isn't an organization, but rather a powerful psion-ic being named Tko-Ma. As Malvern details, two

psionic Cylox beings—Lai-Ma and his brother Tko-Ma—spent several millennia destroying worlds in another dimension. About 500 years ago, an intergalactic court exiled the two malcontents to a pocket realm, greatly reducing their psionic strength. However, the two brothers escaped their prison using human hosts, and decided—for fun—to see which of them could destroy Earth first. Tko-Ma psionically anchored himself to Earth via Malvern, in time founding the Network to track and hopefully one-up his brother. Simultaneously, Lai-Ma has worked to absorb the pocket realm's energy into his own being, threatening to vastly increase his power levels.

Although forced to serve as Tko-Ma's anchor, Malvern concedes that both brothers represent a clear threat to Earth. The Doctor convinces Malvern to psionically shift him into the pocket realm, drawing the brothers' attention while the Network psionics combine their talents and bleed off the pocket realm's energy. The Doctor nearly succeeds in tightening the realm around Tko-Ma and Lai-Ma, but Lai-Ma continues to pull the realm's energy into himself.

On Earth, a powerplay between Malvern's allies and the Network's head administrator—an amne-siac named John Doe (*see Ass-Whuppings*)—leads to a bloodbath that kills the Auton twins, Doe and his superstrong assassins. Finally, a woman named Loretta van Cheaden steps forth, endowed with the essence of Ini-Ma—the brothers' Cylox jailer. Ini-Ma lets the Doctor return to Earth, then tightens the pocket dimension's energy, killing herself and the two brothers.

Afterward, Trey and the Network psionics adopt a new mandate to guard Earth against extra-ter-restrial threats. The Doctor offers to give Evelyn a lift back home, but she points out that he's yet to show her the Eye of Orion—and joins the Doctor and Mel in the TARDIS.

MEMORABLE MOMENTS When Mel scolds the Doctor for keeping a rented VW hidden inside the TARDIS, he feels like Marie Antoinette on her way to the guillotine. In turn, he scolds the TARDIS for not dropping the car off "as instruct-ed." Mel curiously notes that the VW's top now matches the color of the Doctor's trousers.

Evelyn's resolve slips, forcing her to admit that it's hell being stuck in 1993. She knows that her students will shortly get into drugs, sticky sexual situations and car crashes, but can't do a damn thing to prevent it. Her mother's going to die in 1996, and she can't even phone her one last time. But proving why she's one of our favorite compan-ions, Evelyn tells her Time Lord friend: "Don't

worry, Doctor, your precious web of time won't be broken by me. I'm stronger than all that."

She also snips at him for failing to realize the consequences of getting older: "You may be getting steadily closer to the big ten double-oh, but let's face it, you've got an eternity to go before real old age hits you." Memorable stuff, as only the Doctor's oldest companion could speak.

SEX AND SPIRITS   Mel's mother hoped Mel and Trey would get together, but Trey's homosexuality put paid to that. Trey's lover Joe Hambidge—brainwashed after the SenéNet incident (*Business Unusual*)—regains his memories but pretends otherwise, allowing Trey to focus on his Network duties.

At University, Evelyn organized a number of midnight parties, drawing love from the students and the ire of the dean. This probably contributed to the dean slating her for retirement.

Mel erroneously suspects the Doctor's in love with Evelyn, but Evelyn explains the Doctor's not given to romantic love, and that her heart belongs to her ex-husband of 25 years, Lawrence Smythe. Evelyn's marriage ended in a bitter divorce mere days before the Doctor showed up ("The Marian Conspiracy"), meaning she chiefly left Earth to escape the pain. She wants to tell her ex-husband that despite everything, she still loves him.

Evelyn drinks Guinness, the Doctor ginger pop ("The Android Invasion") and Mel juice ("Terror of the Vervoids"). The geeky Jeremy Fitzoliver ("The Paradise of Death") was randy for Sarah Jane Smith.

ASS-WHUPPINGS   The amnesiac Jeremy Fitzoliver (*see Tie-Ins*), working as a Network director named John Doe, sends superstrong assassins Ms. de Meanour and Ms. Feasance to kill the snoopy Mel and Evelyn. In a library, the assassins clumsily smash through some pillars and bring the ceiling down on their heads. They survive, but Cellian later shoots Feasance dead. Ciara similarly blows away de Meanour, but the explosive backlash rips off Ciara's arm. Ciara expires from the trauma and Cellian—psionically dependent on his sister—croaks also.

Soon after, an armed Fitzoliver tries to attack Evelyn, but Halcham pub owner Gary Rudge offs him with a shotgun blast.

The Network's HQ explodes, smearing more than 30 technicians, guards and scientists.

Malvern's trying to atone for accidentally killing his parents, having psionically wished them dead after an argument. Network enforcer Thérése Gavalle—an ex-UNIT captain—shoots Malvern in

TOP 5

DOCTOR DEFEATS (NOVELS/AUDIOS)

*From Loups-Garoux (May 2001)
to Neverland (June 2002)
and
From Earthworld (March 2001)
to Time Zero (Sept. 2002)*

NOTE: We're lumping the Doctor's defeats into one list because really, he wins far more often than he falls on his face.

1) The Doctor becomes Zagreus ("Neverland")—Having saved Gallifrey, the Doctor takes a dose of Anti-Time, goes insane and renames himself after the dark, malevolent villain Zagreus. The upcoming "Zagreus" should resolve this plotine, although a Doctor fully given over to the Dark Side seems too terrifying to contemplate.

2) Artaris obliterated ("Excelis Decays")—Despite the Doctor's efforts, the immortal Greyvorn pelts Artaris with nuclear missiles. Billions of deaths result, although some survivors appear in "The Plague Herds of Excelis."

3) Jonas Rust eaten (*The City of the Dead*)—There comes a point when certain characters simply refuse the Doctor's help, metaphorically speeding down a dark highway and eventually pasting themselves against a brick wall. Along those lines, the Doctor does his damnedest to reform ritualist Jonas Rust, who's pursing a magical agenda that's already gotten his family killed. Rust fatefully refuses to back down, dying when the Doctor looses the ravenous Void to consume Rust like a tuna sandwich.

4) (tie) Journalist Claire Aldwych (*The Shadow in the Glass*) and the pseudo-Autons Ciara and Cellian (*Instruments of Darkness*) die—Allies of the Doctor who didn't survive. The demise of the reformed criminal twins proves tragic enough, while the wholeheartedly innocent Claire Aldwych—fatefully investigating events in World War II—gets killed during the fall of Berlin, 1945.

the leg, then gets atomized by a burst of random inter-dimensional energy.

TV TIE-INS   Internal corruption made Department C19 dissolve in 1991. Assassins killed C19's Sir John Sudbury ("Time-Flight"), giving him a needle-full of air to simulate an embolism, to keep him from exposing the Network.

This book is not endorsed by the BBC. Doctor Who and TARDIS are trademarks of the BBC.

79

Captain (later Commodore) Tonka Travers ("Terror of the Vervoids") previously proposed to Evelyn, but the Doctor talked her out of it. Evelyn thinks she made the right decision, but Travers never forgave the Doctor.

Mel's annoyed because the Doctor's a vegetarian ("The Two Doctors") only when it suits him. UNIT spent over £3 million hunting the Master (the third Doctor era).

NOVEL TIE-INS   For Mel, a year's passed since *Business Unusual*. Her parents, Christine and Alan Bush, remain well-respected members of Pease Pottage, but their eccentric daughter's disappearance probably caused some community paranoia. Mel avoids visiting her parents, thinking she's been gone for four years—which is fortunate, since she already returned home in *Head Games* (plus *More Short Trips:* "Missing, Pts. 1 and 2") and might have bumped into herself.

The pseudo-Auton twins Ciara and Cellian first appeared in Russell's *The Scales of Injustice*. They reformed and went on the run in *Business Unusual*, vowing to care for three brainwashed youths. The teens remained catatonic for two years but gradually recovered.

The Doctor made Mel a co-signer on his Coutts bank account at Coutts bank during a 1920s London stopover (which doesn't quite jibe with her being listed in the account in 1909, *Birthright*). He hasn't owned a car for a few lifetimes (presumably not since his UNIT days). The Doctor's friend Bob Lines (*The Scales of Injustice, Business Unusual*), a police detective, retires. DI Rowe (*Business Unusual*) succeeds him.

The Doctor and Mel recently visited Sydney, 1969, whereupon the Doctor bought a beach house on a whim, and rented a green VW that he conveniently forgot to return (the eighth Doctor's vehicle, first seen in *Longest Day*, destroyed in *Unnatural History*).

When Mel first snuck aboard the TARDIS (*Business Unusual*), the Doctor was off conferring with Evelyn about tracking down the twins. He would've attended to it personally, but had more pressing matters.

AUDIO TIE-INS   Evelyn initially left Earth in March, 2000 ("The Marian Conspiracy"). Her TARDIS tenure lasted quite a few months, but probably not a year. The Doctor dropped her off in an unseen story. Evelyn thinks Charles Darwin ("Bloodtide") took a shine to her. She looks upon Gallifrey as an awful, soulless place ("The Apocalypse Element").

THE CRUCIAL BITS...

• **INSTRUMENTS OF DARKNESS**—The Doctor finds Evelyn on Earth, pissed because the TARDIS dropped her off 10 years too early. Death of Sarah Jane's photographer friend Jeremy Fitzoliver and the pseudo-Autons Ciara and Cellian. Evelyn resumes TARDIS travel with the Doctor and Mel.

TIE-INS   Beings the Doctor associates with power include Rassilon, Omega, the Pythia (*Time's Crucible*) and Zagreus ("Neverland," plus the upcoming "Zagreus"). They're allegedly dust mites compared to the Cylox.

Mel's already encountered the Vervoids ("Terror of the Vervoids"), pan-dimensional terrorists, the Chronovores (*The Quantum Archangel*) and the 18-foot Chiropterons. Mel has a bat phobia, explaining her banshee-like screams in "Time and the Rani."

Jeremy Fitzoliver, Sarah Jane's photographer, previously appeared in "The Paradise of Death" and "The Ghosts of N-Space." The Doctor had asked UNIT to destroy his IRIS machine ("Planet of the Spiders"), but it got pushed to one side until the dopey Fitzoliver started fiddling with it and lost his memory. Sarah Jane got him Fitzoliver medical treatment, but he vengefully blamed the Doctor and the Brigadier for his lost memory.

The Doctor took Mel, but not Evelyn, to the Eye of Orion ("The Five Doctors") and the Kurgon Wonder ("The Sirens of Time"). When the sixth Doctor's "The Sirens of Time" segment occurred, Evelyn was trapped in the TARDIS.

The planet Kolpasha (*Placebo Effect*, "Real Time," *DWM* #212-#214, "Victims") considers the Doctor's multi-colored coat the height of fashion. It has four inside pockets.

CHARACTER DEVELOPMENT

• *The Doctor:* UN Secretary General Boutros-Galli recognizes the Doctor's saved Earth many times. The Doctor doesn't necessarily trust the Network, but deems them no more dangerous than many Earth factions. The fourth Doctor and Romana once walked up Pennine Way [with Romana grumbling because he made her carry K9].

• *The Doctor, Evelyn and the TARDIS:* The Doctor very much viewed Evelyn as an equal, but she one day decided to return home. It left the Doctor terribly hurt, and the TARDIS—sensing this—probably dropped Evelyn 10 years too soon to punish her.

• *Melanie Bush:* She hasn't been to Derbyshire or Gallifrey. She tries [but sometimes fails] to avoid coffee.

She carries a Swiss Army knife, complete with picklock, in her purse. Mel's hair is shorter than when she boarded the TARDIS, although she's thinking about letting it grow out. She hates her pink outfit [Author's Note: And don't we all.] because it's so 1980s.

• *Evelyn Richmond Smythe:* Evelyn's in her late 50s. She tried giving up cigarettes cold turkey, but instead cut back gradually until she quit.

In 1993, Evelyn lives at Mog Cottage. She runs the Norfolk Cattery as a side business. Evelyn likes cats, but not in great quantities. Her cottage is a mess. She makes wholemeal biscuits. In 2000, she owned an iBook with a 128 modem.

In addition to winning cash in various cooking contests and betting pools, she patents the phrase Digital Versatile Disc, intending to sell it for a reasonable price—not a fortune—in a few years. She has no checkbook, bank account or credit card in this time zone.

She's previously encountered the Master. In 1993, she purchases a 1950s Riley that sometimes gets her to the supermarket. She's never had an accident in 40 years of driving. She's no fan of Norfolk. Her bones get achy in winter.

She once failed a student who accidentally created an unhelpful Mobius codex on his computer, but helped him obtain a research grant to study Mobius loops.

• *Evelyn and Mel:* They initially fail to get along, as Mel thinks Evelyn's ungrateful for her time in the TARDIS and Evelyn believes Mel's spoiled. Eventually, their frankness helps them better understand one another.

• *Jeremy Fitzoliver (a.k.a. John Doe):* Jeremy's in his late 30s, with weasel-like features topped by thinning black hair. The Network psionics can't mentally read Fitzoliver, probably due to his amnesia (*see Tie-Ins*).

The Doctor never really liked Fitzoliver, deeming him someone in over his head. Fitzoliver never officially joined UNIT.

• *Ciara and Cellian:* Reformed, they're trying to improve Halcham's school system. They left their Scotland base a year ago. They can detect the Doctor's extra-terrestrial brainwaves.

• *Cellian:* A USB port in his skull lets him upload information, making him the Western World's leading authority on heating systems.

• *Trey J. Korte:* He's now 23, but still looks like he's in his late teens. After *Business Unusual*, Trey worked for C19 in Whitehall as a psi-agent. He was born in Chicago, 1970.

• *The TARDIS:* The TARDIS dims its console room lights to speak with the Doctor. The Ship projects its passengers from time dilation—their bod-

ies might age only a few weeks throughout months of travel.

ALIEN RACES *Cylox:* An incredibly long-lived species, making the millennia-old Tko-Ma and Lai-Ma the equivalent of 13 year olds.

STUFF YOU NEED *Bob Lines' Signalling Device:* A Ping-Pong ball shaped device, with a small switch on the top.

• *The Doctor's Coutts Checkbook:* It's made from paper imported from the planet Arborius, where sentient trees live. As such, the paper gives you helpful banking hints.

PLACES TO GO *The Eye of Orion ("The Five Doctors"):* Animals live there that look like baby zebras with snake's heads, and have tiny wings on their ankles.

ORGANIZATIONS *UNIT:* The Russians had a counterpart to UNIT during the Cold War. The Americans studied the paranormal less, but kept a few pocket departments within the FBI to investigate the unusual [likely Russell hinting at *The X-Files*].

• *The Network:* Composed of nine members—four telepaths, a pyrokinetic, a wire who can mentally travel through phone and modem networks, an empath, a teleporter and an electrokinetic. Conceivably, they could take over the world.

• *The Magnate:* Term for the six or seven people who purportedly run the world, pulling most leaders' strings. [Russell notes: "The idea for the Magnate comes from all those weirdos who think the world is run in secret by 9-foot lizards."]

PHENOMENA *Psionic Powers:* On an unspecified psionic scale, the Doctor rates a 6 or 7 [moderate talent, but no real training], Trey's a 12 and Malvern's a 50. The Cylox rank somewhere around 1000—making them capable of manipulating entire galaxies and dreamscapes.

HISTORY Loretta van Cheaden's bloodline housed the Ini-Ma's essence throughout the centuries. The Ini-Ma granted Loretta's female ancestors, including Leaf Snakeskin [from a pre-history age] and Lucille Mary Addison [circa 1857], the power to ward off male aggression as necessary.

• Silas Malvern created a rope-manufacturing business back in 1864. His great-great-grandson Miles [presumably Sebastian's father] closed it down in 1961.

• The Doctor met ornithologist James Bond—after whom the famous spy hero is named—in Ja-

maica, the 1950s. The Time Lord took Bond to the 1800s to see a live dodo, then introduced him to *James Bond* creator Ian Fleming, a former British military man.

• The Halcham incident got written off as someone dumping hallucinogenics into the water supply after a particularly successful Audenshaw Christmas party.

• British Rail isn't running in the future.

AT THE END OF THE DAY The best Gary Russell book to date, written as an passionate, endearing—and sometimes tumultuous—reunion of old friends. The sixth Doctor, Evelyn and Mel interaction makes the book, as Russell's a seeming natural with this TARDIS line-up (which makes sense, since he adores the sixth Doctor and created Evelyn). Against that, the confusing Lai-Ma and Tko-Ma plotline seems wedged into the mix, but even if *Instruments of Darkness* becomes a house divided against itself, the net result still lands it—thanks to the TARDIS crew's relationship—as a surprise PDA win.

DID YOU KNOW?

• Fitzoliver's superstrong lesbian assassins, Ms. de Meanour and Ms. Feasance, are based on Wint and Kidd from *Diamonds are Forever*.

THE ONE DOCTOR

By Gareth Roberts
and Clayton Hickman

Release Date: December 2001
Order: Big Finish "Doctor Who" Audio #27

TARDIS CREW The sixth Doctor and Melanie.

TRAVEL LOG Planets Generios I, VIII, XIV and XV, the Generios System, constellation of Generios, the West Galaxy, the far-flung future era known as "the Vulgar End of Time."

NOTE Bonus tracks on this CD include the Doctor and Mel lounging in front of a fireplace at Christmas, plus an extended version of The Questioner and Mentos playing *Super Brain*.

STORY SUMMARY When the TARDIS drifts too far into the future, the Ship's navigational circuits automatically lock onto a distress beacon hailing from the 14-planet Generios System. On Generios I, the Doctor and Mel find the populace celebrating a recent victory over the villainous Skeloid aliens. News reports, however, indicate *the Doctor* defeated the Skeloids—disturbing news, to say the least, as the Doctor knows full well he's never visited Generios.

The Doctor and Mel barge into the Great Council Complex seeking answers, only to find con man Banto Zame and his partner-in-crime, Sally-Anne Stubbins, respectively masquerading as the Doctor and his female companion. The genuine Doctor quickly deduces Banto habitually stages false alien invasions, pretends to save a planet as the Doctor, then "begrudgingly" accepts a sizeable reward from the overjoyed populace.

Banto's within a hair of netting 100 million credits from Councilor Potikol, a Generios leader, when a massive cylindrical spaceship rolls into the system. The alien Cylinder demands tribute for its unnamed masters, insisting the Generios System hand over its three greatest treasures within a certain time limit or face destruction. Banto thinks about pulling a runner, but the Doctor realizes the Cylinder won't allow anyone to leave the system. Forced to work together, the Doctor, Melanie, Banto and Sally-Anne depart to collect the treasures—as outlined by Potikol—before the deadline expires.

The Doctor drops off Banto and Melanie on Generios VIII before traveling onward. On Generios XIV, the Doctor and Sally-Anne but find the remains of a ruined civilization in their search for Mentos, supposedly the greatest computer ever created. In a giant amphitheater, the duo finds an elderly man—Mentos' holographic interface—answering questions for a computerized game show host. Mentos explains that 33,000 years ago, his programmers made him compete on the game show *Super Brain* as a publicity stunt. Able to answer any question—thanks to a team of time-active research devices working in a shadow dimension—Mentos kept playing the game as warfare destroyed the civilization.

The Questioner informs the Doctor that Mentos can only leave if it fails to answer a question. Fortunately, the Questioner allows audience members to ask two questions each. The Doctor fails to stump Mentos, but Sally-Anne innocently wonders what question Mentos *cannot* answer. A flummoxed Mentos fails to respond and shuts down, allowing the Doctor and Sally-Anne to spirit away his control box.

Meanwhile, Melanie and Banto find themselves in an automated furniture factory looking for the second treasure, Unit ZX419. Under pain of death from the human-hating Assembler robots (*see History*), Melanie and Banto try to assemble Unit

ZX419—more commonly called "the Shelves of Infinity." Melanie eventually realizes that the Shelves' pieces pop in and out of a nearby dimension, making assembly impossible. Finally, Mel and Banto decide the Assemblers can't know what the completed Shelves look like—as they've never been completed—hastily throw the remaining parts together and bluff their success. While the Assemblers scrutinize the Shelves' instruction manual, the TARDIS materializes and Mel and Banto hastily lug the Shelves aboard.

With two treasures down, the TARDIS crew travels to Generios XV. On a barren plain, the Doctor's party finds the third valuable: the largest diamond in existence. After something of a flap (*see Character Development*), the jewel's guardian—a long-lived Spraxis Jelloid—turns over the diamond to save the Generios System.

The Doctor's party returns to Generios I, where a pleased Cylinder receives the treasures. Having heard reports of the Doctor's presence on Generios, the Cylinder asks the Time Lord to identify himself and claim a reward. The greedy Banto acknowledges himself as the Doctor, but the Cylinder bottles Banto in a time stasis bubble, having rigged the entire quest as a task that only the Doctor could complete.

The Cylinder departs the system with Banto, intending to haul him before its masters—the Susuurats, who've a score to settle with the Doctor—for punishment. Having never heard of the Susuurats before, the Doctor makes a note to annoy them in future. The Doctor and Mel swiftly depart, allowing Councilor Potikol to give Sally-Anne 10 million credits as consolation for "the loss of the Doctor."

MEMORABLE MOMENTS The Doctor opens the audio with an ominous monologue of: "You are my pawns... I own you... I am your creator... and I can be your destroyer!"—and that's just with regards to his *Monopoly* game.

In a lively bit of satire, Banto—as "the Doctor"—tries to pass off the real Doctor and Melanie as overexcited fans. The Doctor brilliantly escapes his cell using a food dispenser—or rather, by using the food dispenser as a blunt instrument to break the cell door down.

Part 2 ends with Assembler robots shrieking "Disassemble them!" in a very Dalek-like fashion.

The Doctor claims that only those with a sharpened aesthetic sense can appreciate his multi-colored coat, making Banto retort: "Sharpened by what? A dose of mind-altering drugs?" When the Jelloid vomits up the Doctor, Banto notes: "Lucky you're still wearing that coat—[there's] no way of telling that someone's just been sick all over it."

SEX AND SPIRITS Banto proposed to Sally-Anne one night after they'd downed a "third bottle of Red." On that occasion, she confessed to having breast implants. Banto blathered about it to his drinking buddies the next night, also convinced she'd had work done on her cheeks and lips.

Banto's clearly a leech, spending most of the story lustfully eyeballing Mel. In turn, Sally-Anne starts drooling over the Doctor, repeatedly calling him sexy. She feels the Doctor's double heartbeat, only reluctantly letting go of his chest.

Banto finally proposes to Mel [a polished routine that he frequently pulls], forcing her to concede: "Perhaps in another dimension, we got together and have tons of odd-looking children." Mel avoids his advances, even trying to pass herself off as an android at one point.

Later, Banto lets slip he's married, making Sally come unglued. Trying to convince the Cylinder that he's Banto Zane, the real Doctor locks lips with Sally-Anne in a very un-Time Lord fashion.

On a bonus track, the Doctor and Mel share Christmas sherry in front of a fireplace. Banto and Sally-Anne drop their Doctor-related disguises long enough to down beer.

ASS-WHUPPINGS The Cylinder's sonic announcement system blitzes the Doctor's mind at the end of Part 1. As a show of power, the Cylinder obliterates Generios XI.

At the end of Part 3, the Jelloid swallows the Doctor for attempting to steal the giant jewel—allowing the Colin Doctor to hoop and holler while getting eaten by giant jelly. [Banto quips: "Face it, Mel. He's lunch."] The Doctor hurriedly pokes one of the Jelloid's internal organs, causing him to get puked up, covered in gastric juices.

TV TIE-INS In June 1975, the Doctor based himself at 35 Jefferson Road, Woking, during a Cybermen invasion (likely an unseen adventure, since that's really too late for "The Invasion" to occur). The back bedroom there had purple wallpaper.

The Doctor fibs that he's approaching 930 [unlikely, unless you somehow think he somehow traveled with Mel for 23 years before "The Time and the Rani," in which he's 953].

Mentos is immune to computer logic conundrums, such as the one the Doctor used on BOSS in "The Green Death." The Doctor and Mel watch stuff on the Time-Space Visualizer ("The Chase"). A bonus track features Colin Baker uttering William Hartnell's immortal line, "And a merry Christmas to all of you at home." ("The Daleks' Master Plan" Part 7)

NOVEL TIE-INS The Sinister Sponges worship an object called the Loofah of Life (Roberts and Hickman's *Short Trips:* "The Not-so Sinister Sponge").

TIE-INS The Cylinder identifies the Doctor by names such as Johann Schmidt (*The Shadow in the Glass*, "Colditz"), Theta Sigma ("The Armageddon Factor"), Ka Faraq Gatri (the seventh Doctor's moniker, starting with the *Remembrance of the Daleks* novelization), Snail (*Lungbarrow*) and Dr. VonFlair (unknown).

Comedian Gantax Nordeen once said: "You can take a Pescaton to water, but you can't make him sink." (*The Pescatons* CD or novelization)

CHARACTER DEVELOPMENT

• *The Doctor:* The Doctor's now met himself so many times, his hair [figuratively] stands on end whenever a future incarnation turns up.

He hates hotels. He wishes people would sort out their own problems rather than sending out distress signals for help. He views himself as big boned, not portly. He's thrown off kilter if his companion [in this case, Sally-Anne] doesn't give rousing speeches of encouragement. Roget of *Roget's Thesaurus* fame was a very good friend of his.

He's encountered Jelloids before. He can easily pick Tri-Sonic locks. He forgot to celebrate his birthday for two decades once. He says he'll get around to rescuing Banto... eventually.

• *The Doctor and Melanie:* The Doctor plays *Monopoly* with Mel to better get inside the mind of a power-crazed dictator, but deems it a boring place to reside. In the game, Mel's the iron, he's the dog.

• *The Doctor and Mentos:* Over his 900th birthday cake, the Doctor wished for peace throughout the galaxy, better control of the TARDIS and more manageable hair. Later in the day, the evil Mantelli threw the Doctor in a prison cell. There, he met an elderly cellmate shackled to a wall—one of Mentos' time-travelling research units—and told him about the birthday wishes, thereby enabling Mentos to answer correctly when the Doctor asked about them on *Super Brain*.

• *Melanie Jane Bush:* Mel knows very rudimentary TARDIS piloting skills, enough to prep the Ship for takeoff and *maybe* coax it back to Generios I from Generios XV.

Mel lived in a big house in Pease Pottage, about seven miles from town. Every Christmas, her parents organized a church show for pensioners. One year, when the snow fell eight feet deep, Mel and her parents bravely set out to show their mettle, determined to brighten the pensioners' lives. They trudged through the snow and gave the perfor-

mance—but none of the pensioners showed up.

Mel was a Girl Guide. She's strong enough to manhandle Banto. She likes Muesli for breakfast.

• *Banto Zame:* He's worked as a con man in the West Galaxy for 25 years. Banto has a single heartbeat, and hails from the planet Osphogus. He gains rudimentary TARDIS piloting skills by observing the Doctor.

• *Sally-Anne Stubbins:* Her Dad walked out when she was six, her mother hit the bottle, a speeding hovercar ran over her brother and a Spaag of Vishtek 3 ate her Aunty Sue. The TARDIS gives her a warm feeling.

• *Mentos:* The Doctor deems Mentos superior to the Matrix on Gallifrey ("The Deadly Assassin").

• *The Questioner:* Obviously a parody of *The Weakest Link* host Anne Robinson, telling eliminated players, "You are the Feeblest Contestant."

• *The Jelloid:* Belongs to the galaxy's longest-lived species. He's served 30 million years of a 50-million-year non-negotiable contract to guard the diamond.

The Jelloid agrees to turn over the giant diamond, but worries because he's expecting delivery of a home entertainment system from Bendalos. Delivery is only specified within a range of two million years, and the Jelloid's already been waiting 1.5 million years. The Doctor's group promises to keep watch during the 10 minutes it takes the Jelloid to turn off the jewel's force field, but unfortunately, they fail to identify a fast-moving Vektron (*see Alien Races*) as the delivery boy. The Vektron leaves a note saying the Jelloid should reschedule with the depot on Sirrinus Traxia, enraging the Jelloid since he once spent 40,000 years on hold trying to call the very same depot. The Doctor soothes the wound by personally delivering the Jelloid's entertainment system via the TARDIS when the adventure concludes.

• *The Cylinder:* Can make broadcasts to the whole of Generios I via a Multi-Phase Corpolectic Sound Wave.

• *The TARDIS:* The Doctor's reluctant to time travel in the TARDIS while the Cylinder's force field blankets the Generios System. The TARDIS launderette cleans the Doctor's bile-covered clothes in minutes. The Ship has a fireplace. The Doctor celebrated Christmas with Mel by making it snow in the console room.

The Doctor's been experimenting with the TARDIS' navigation settings, which probably tripped on the wide-range distress transceiver.

ALIEN RACES *The Assemblers:* They refuse to acknowledge that Mel and Banto outwitted them, and erase the encounter from their memories.

TOP 5 'WHO' AUDIOS

*From Loups-Garoux (May 2001)
to Neverland (June 2002)*

1) "The Chimes of Midnight" (by Rob Shearman)—Strong enough to make us cry, "Chimes" proves singularly remarkable because its radical concept—i.e. a malevolent, sentient house clinging to life whatever the cost—ironically serves as the *backdrop* for a gut-wrenching emotional drama between the Doctor, Charley and serving girl Edith Thompson. Author Rob Shearman claims writing this story kept him awake at night, and it's easy to see why, given that "Chimes"—actually an optimistic story in disguise—so lovingly covers itself in darkness and despair.

2) "The One Doctor" (by Gareth Roberts and Clayton Hickman)—Big Finish's debut attempt at straight-out comedy reaches glorious heights because it doesn't strive for "wacky," "camp" or any other sort of banal laugh-in that most sci-fi shows inflict on us. Instead, "The One Doctor" sports a really nice cleverness, playing up to the fans' intelligence. Bravo.

3) "Colditz" (by Steve Lyons)—This one's so underrated, we almost want to put our fists through a wall. "Colditz" contains a striking depth that's ideal for the seventh Doctor/Ace duo, especially considering the Doctor gloriously starts out a prisoner and then—through sheer force of will—becomes the master of Colditz prison. It's a standout drama, often sullied by people who complain that "Who" does too many Nazi stories. [Side Note: We count one TV story, three books and this audio. Since 1989 with "The Curse of Fenric," that's about one Nazi story every three years. Get over it.]

4) "Loups-Garoux" (by Marc Platt)—Even more radical than people let on, "Loups-Garoux" brings a maturity and sexual heat to the Big Finish audio line. We find the Doctor's morals in this story highly questionable, but then, "Loups-Garoux" isn't exactly intended as traditional "Who" and as such deserves praise. And ultimately, even if parts of it stick in your craw, it ranks on this list because it's just so damn *intriguing*.

5) "Neverland" (by Alan Barnes)—Certainly one of the most memorable Big Finish tales, above average for having an all-star Gallifreyan cast [so far as we're concerned, Lalla Ward's got an open invitation to appear as Romana] and showcasing the unbreakable friendship between the Doctor and Charley. Given sufficient tweaking, this could've ranked even higher, but we'll credit "Neverland" for suitably keeping "Who" fans on the edge of their seats.

HONORABLE MENTIONS

• **"Bloodtide" (by Jonathan Morris)**—A story mostly designed to plug continuity, although in this case, we don't mind much since "Bloodtide" *does* march to its own drummer. Also, the cast's chemistry really comes across this one, with Colin Baker, Maggie Stables and co. delivering a passion that's infectious.

• **"Dalek Empire" (by Nicholas Briggs)**—The brainchild of Nick Briggs, Dalek Empire" could have been the dorkiest story ever. But instead, it unfolds as a gritty, mature tale of death, love and Daleks. In a world where there's only so many surprises Big Finish can toss into a retro Doctor story, "Dalek Empire" keeps us breathless wondering what's going to happen next.

• **"The Maltese Penguin" (by Rob Shearman)**—Another win from Rob Shearman, this time spotlighting Frobisher and sidelining the Doctor to great effect. "The Maltese Penguin" always knows what it can—and can't—get away with, becoming a *Double Indemnity*-style story [about a penguin] with hysterical results.

• *Skeloids:* Likely just figments of Banto's imagination.

• *Spraxis Jelloids:* Enormous single-celled organisms who originate from the planet Bendalos, the Benary Quasar. Purportedly the Universe's longest-lived species, Spraxis Jelliods seem nigh-immortal. They have no teeth, but can easily swallow people.

• *Vektons:* The fastest moving creatures in the cosmos, able to manipulate time and move 40 times faster than everyone else.

ALIEN PLANETS *Generios I:* Heads a mighty trade empire. Everything on Generios I gets tagged with the adjective "great" [the Great Bank of Generios, the Great Commemorative Tea Towel, etc.] The Great Computers of Generios regulate the planet. Great Space Dredgers protect it.

• *Generios XV:* The system's innermost planet, composed almost entirely of superheated gas. ["Rather like you, then," Banto tells the Doctor.]

• *Abydos:* Located in the Rim Worlds, outside normal jurisdiction because absolutely nothing's there.

STUFF YOU NEED *The Stardis:* Banto impersonation of the Doctor isn't *quite* right, as details about the Doctor are garbled in this time period. Banto allegedly travels in the "Stardis," equipped with a short-range teleport beam. He thinks the Stardis' exterior resembles a police box, but the Doctor and Mel moreso recognize it as a port-a-toi-

---

let, which hysterically dematerializes with a flushing sound.

• *UNIT ZX419 (a.k.a. "The Shelves of Infinity"):* The Assemblers' greatest achievement—it took them 15 million Decons to make it. People cannot perceive the Shelves' parts slipping into different dimensions because the maths involved are beyond human senses. Additionally, the Shelves' instructions keep getting more complicated.

POSSIBLE HISTORY The *Super Brain* Questioner mentions several historical facts we've declined to list because: A) most are incidental, B) few are date specific, C) most are the stuff of comedy and not historically accurate [such as Venus competing in the 2059 Intergalactic Song Contest].

HISTORY Some biologists believe Spraxis Jelloids were the Universe's first living beings [unlikely, as that mantle in "Who" chiefly goes to the Time Lords].

• By the Vulgar End of Time, everything worth discovering has been discovered. The interesting wars are over. Technology's made everything affordable [frying pans, however, are out of style]. Hedonism rules the day. In this era, the Doctor's somewhat legendary.

• Banto's homeworld Osphogus, a superdense mudball, got terraformed 5,000 years previous.

• The Generios System got mined out eons ago.

• Thousands of years ago, a Generios XIV company became immeasurably successful exporting furniture. In time, the company's executives turned the operation over to their Assembler robots, who promptly went berserk and killed off the entire population. The planet was left to its own devices, with the fiendish robots toiling away at new furniture designs.

• The Skardu/Rosbrix Wars left huge chunks of debris in the Generios System.

AT THE END OF THE DAY Pretty much the Big Finish showstopper of 2001, "The One Doctor"—much like "The Curse of Fatal Death" before it—works because it's just so damn *clever*. The comedy's not designed to make you roll around on the floor clutching your ribs, but it's spellbinding enough to keep your attention. The Doctor and Banto gloriously bitch at one another, and really, there's certain jibes—such as Banto's "Stardis" being a port-a-toilet—that fans have thought about for years but never dreamed would actually happen. We're not convinced Big Finish can sustain their goal of doing "Who" comedy once a year, but certainly with "The One Doctor," they've knocked the ball out of the park.

• In something of a goof, Banto and Sally-Anne ask for 100 million credits in Part 1, but by Part 4, Sally-Anne only gets 10 million credits.

• Actress Jane Goddard, who plays The Questioner, is married to audio writer Rob Shearman.

• Big Finish codes "The One Doctor" as story 7C-R, whereas the preceding "Project: Twilight" is coded 7C-E. If you're wondering what happened to letters F to Q, they're reserved for future stories involving Evelyn [as she precedes Mel in the TARDIS].

RELATIVE DEMENTIAS

By Mark Michalowski

Release Date: January 2002
Order: BBC Past Doctor Adventure #49

TARDIS CREW The seventh Doctor and Ace.

TRAVEL LOG Graystairs, the Dumfries village of Muirbridge, southwest Scotland; a tiny island off Scotland's far northeast coast, both April 1982; Countess Gallowglass' place of business, London, August 2012.

CHRONOLOGY Ace seems excited about seeing the future—so it's hardly old hat to her—but knows about UNIT, making placement between "Battlefield" and "Ghost Light" a reasonable guess.

STORY SUMMARY In Scotland, 1982, UNIT physicist Joyce Brunner places her aged mother with Graystairs, an elderly care facility seemingly on the verge of an Alzheimer's cure. But gradually, Joyce notices an increasing amount of abnormal behavior among the clinic's staff. Unnerved, Joyce sends the Doctor, her friend from UNIT, a postcard asking for his help.

In London, 2012, the Doctor and Ace stop to visit Countess Gallowglass, who runs a mail forwarding service for time travelers, aliens and other dispossessed beings. The Doctor gets Joyce's card, then makes haste to Graystairs, 1982. Once there, the inquisitive Doctor and Ace find a transmat beam in the Graystairs basement, allowing transport to a spaceship hidden within the Scottish Isles. Moreover, the Doctor determines that Graystairs owner Sooal—actually an alien being,

wearing a fleshsuit to appear human—is conducting illicit brain experiments on his patients, with the Alzheimer's research merely a profitable side business.

The Doctor encounters yet another a pair of aliens, similarly disguised as human beings, who identify themselves as members of the Annarene race. The couple informs the Doctor that four years ago, the Tulkan Empire tried and failed to annex the Annarene homeworld. The victorious Annarene erased the Tulk War Council's memories and sentenced them to exile, but Sooal—a renegade Annarene—spirited away the council members to Earth. Dying from a genetic disease, Sooal hoped to restore the council's memories, thereby obtaining their clearance codes to a Tulk stasis chamber within the spaceship. If successful, Sooal would obtain a Tulk metabolic stabilizer from the stasis chamber, curing his disease.

Sooal successfully breaks the Tulk's memory blocks, obtains the needed clearance codes and guns down the council members. In response, the two Annarene—actually representing a warlike Annarene splinter group—kill Sooal. As the tables turn, the Annarene make ready to secure advanced Tulk weaponry within the stasis chamber, then turn Earth into an Annarene powerbase and marshal their people to war.

Desperately improvising, the Doctor uses Tulk cerebral implants to telepathically communicate with two elderly Graystairs sisters, Connie and Jessie. Following the Doctor's instructions, Connie and Jessie pass themselves off as legitimate Annarene agents. In the fracas to follow, the Annarene renegades attempt to flee in the transmat, but the Doctor alters the device's destination coordinates, causing the rogue aliens to materialize within the still-sealed stasis chamber. Instantly, the chamber freezes the Annarene in time, trapping them like flies in amber.

Afterward, the Doctor destroys Sooal's ship, destroying all evidence of the aliens' presence and preventing an Alzheimer's cure from hitting the market too soon. Joyce arranges for her mother's care at another facility, allowing the Doctor and Ace to depart.

MEMORABLE MOMENTS

Ace speculates she'd take time travel a lot more seriously if the Doctor looked like an alien. The Doctor concludes: "Some of the most human people I've come across haven't been within a billion miles of a piece of DNA. And some of the most inhuman wouldn't stand out in an identity parade with Nelson Mandela and Gandhi."

Michael Ashworth, wrongly pissed at the Doctor

for cheaply spending the lives of UNIT soldiers, punches the Time Lord full in the face. The affront, more than the force of the blow, does the Doctor some damage [and made us wince]. Michael hotly claims the Doctor all too often means trouble, but Ace retorts: "The Doctor sorts trouble, he doesn't cause it."

SEX AND SPIRITS

Young farm workers whistle at Ace, but the Doctor restrains her from hollering back. He catches her drinking a pint of larger, raising a disapproving eyebrow.

UNIT trooper Michael Ashworth flirts with Ace, but she basically shuns him.

Joyce feels like she's in drag while wearing skirts instead of her labcoat or UNIT fatigues. A bored Joyce reads a women's magazine, then stops to wonder if she's missing out by never having four kinds of orgasm.

A traumatized Doctor asks for water, but Ace insists he down a brandy.

ASS-WHUPPINGS

As a back-up plan in case he fails to revive the Tulk, Sooal hotwires numerous Graystairs patients, staff and visitors—including Joyce—to an Annarene computer. The device paralyzes its victims, then taps their brains' raw calculating power to run an unbelievable amount of mathematical equations. In such a fashion, Sooal hopes to decipher the Tulk clearance codes without the War Council if necessary.

Ace saves Joyce from the device, but the procedure traumatizes her. Moreover, the Doctor tests the computer on himself, overestimating its ability to paralyze his body. The computer runs roughshod through the Doctor's mind, but Ace's future self (*see Character Development*) rescues him.

Ace wonks Graystairs caregiver Megan over the head with a frying pan. It's quite understated, but one presumes the Doctor blows up the time-frozen Annarene renegades when he detonates the Annarene spaceship [and the Tulk stasis chamber within].

TV TIE-INS

Ace threatens the Doctor with bodily harm if he resumes playing his spoons ("Time and the Rani"). The Doctor has already visited Puccini. He hints that he's not human—"at least, not in the way you'd think." ("Doctor Who: Enemy Within").

The seventh Doctor leans toward vegetarianism ("The Two Doctors"), but sometimes eats meat under the "When in Rome" philosophy. Most people *do* recognize the Doctor in his new incarnations—the Brigadier was ironically (given "Battlefield") one of the few who needed some per-

suasion ("Spearhead from Space") as to the Doctor's identity.

UNIT trooper Michael Ashworth previously saw action against some Ogrons ("Day of the Daleks"), who holed up for emergency repairs in a Birmingham warehouse. On that occasion, a ricochet left him with a grazed scalp.

NOVEL TIE-INS The Doctor mentally interfaces with an Annarene computer net, unexpectedly dredging up a memory of Leela standing in the snow (*Drift*). However, he also recalls a single gray eye looking out a broken window. The scene entails autumn leaves, the woody tang of bonfire smoke, and a whispery, sardonic voice asking the Doctor "if he's forgotten him already." The fuzzy recollection unnerves the Doctor, especially as he can't remember where it sprang from. Author Michalowski says this image solely stems from a mini-storyarc that's running around in his head, where it will probably remain.

The Fleshsmiths (*Prime Time*) constructed the fleshsuit-generating tank which allows the Annarene and Tulk to appear human. *Relative Dementias* gives Ace's name as Dorothy McShane (as opposed to the somewhat apocryphal Dorothy Gale, *Prime Time*).

AUDIO TIE-INS The Doctor and UNIT helped avert a Talichre invasion of Earth, but it's also claimed that Talichre ravaged Anima Persis (the apocryphal "Death Comes to Time").

CHARACTER DEVELOPMENT

• *The Doctor:* The Doctor likes the Carpenters, but has persuaded at least three alien races to not invade Earth after they somehow heard the group's *Calling Occupants of Interplanetary Craft*.

He can use Annarene implants like telepathic walkie-talkies. The Doctor can identify human-looking aliens by their eyeballs. He can diagnose the disease progeria, but lacks much knowledge of congenital neuroendocrinological disorders. He knows a little about iridology. He enjoys tea. He utterly forbids Ace to call him "Granddad." He's unconvinced about the assets of immortality, hoping instead for his normal lifespan.

• *Ace:* Ace isn't a country girl at heart. Years ago, her mother took her to a tacky London musical that she loved and feared at the same time. Ace tried cigarettes once, but decided they didn't go with her zeal for explosives. She likes bacon sandwiches. She knows about the Doctor's regenerative abilities at this point. She suggests that her middle name, in addition to her first, hails from *The Wizard of Oz*.

Ace knows *just* enough about the TARDIS console to sloppily alter its destination settings. In *Relative Dementias*, she outfoxes the Doctor by amending the TARDIS controls, thus arriving at Graystairs some time *before* her arrival. Hence, Ace spends much of this story temporally duplicated, avoiding her younger self and using her foreknowledge to quietly help the Doctor.

• *The Doctor and Dr. Joyce Brunner:* One of UNIT's top physicists, a friend of both the Doctor and Liz Shaw. The Doctor considers Joyce family and used to play cards with her, sharing cocoa in his UNIT laboratory.

Joyce previously enjoyed the third Doctor's company on a blowy day in Cromer, when they had scones at a teashop [Joyce insisted on paying]. She hasn't seen the Doctor since, but has exchanged messages and phone calls on occasion. She insists she'll never become one of his "dolly-bird" assistants. Joyce knows about the Doctor's regenerative abilities, but this marks the first time she meets an incarnation beyond his third body.

• *Dr. Joyce Brunner:* Joyce married—and divorced—General Terrance Ashworth. She's earned favors from high-ranking officials [presumably UNIT] in Geneva. Her father Alf died of cancer more than 10 years ago. She can't help but wish that a heart attack had killed her mother, sparing her the ravages of Alzheimer's disease.

• *The Doctor, Michael Ashworth and UNIT:* Joyce's son Michael joined UNIT three years ago and initially stood up for the Doctor as his mother's friend. Other UNIT troopers deemed the Doctor a snob, believing he viewed their lives as expendable, and consequently marked Michael for hazing.

Michael continued defending the Doctor until his friend Andy, a fellow UNIT soldier, died during a Talichre invasion of Earth—because the Doctor refused to turn over a device he'd stolen from them. Michael subsequently went AWOL and here confronts the Doctor over the incident, only to realize the Doctor's not the monster he imagined. After this story, Michael voluntarily faced a court-martial and probably received a dishonorable discharge.

• *Countess Gallowglass (formerly Miss Gallowglass):* The Doctor met the Countess just as his Earth exile ended, when she was operating from a Porta-kabin in the East End. She assumed the title of Countess when her husband Edward passed away last year [in 2011]. The Countess normally dresses like a Christmas tree—displaying far too much money and no style. She's in her 60s or 70s, complete with coiffured hairdo and studded diamond trinkets. She's never met Ace before now.

She hasn't seen the Doctor for a while [possibly not since November 4, 1976, when he bestowed upon her a Landine pet, *see Alien Races*].

• *The TARDIS:* The Ship's library has relocated itself again. It previously situated itself between the sauna and table tennis room, but a blank wall stands there now. Pulsing light arrows on the TARDIS walls guide Ace to the library's new location. The Ship has at least one arboretum, possibly two.

ALIEN RACES *Time Lords:* The Doctor ominously claims the Time Lords get dementias much worse than Alzheimer's disease.

• *Annarene:* Normally look like skinny orange beings with knobby exo-skeletons. Their heads come crested with two rows of darker bumps, and two disconcertingly human eyes. Their mouths are lip-less gashes. Earth feels too moist to them.

• *Landine:* Name for any animal that the Annarene genetically tailor to serve as polymorphic guard forms. When its Annarene masters die off, the Doctor orders a Landine to forget its hostile programming. It shapeshifts into a cat, which he bestows upon Countess Gallowglass without mentioning its alien roots.

STUFF YOU NEED *Annarene Computers:* Run equations that involve Bessel functions and Cantor sets.

• *Progeria:* A Tulk-engineered genetic disease that causes premature aging in Annarene.

• *Tulk Metabolic Stabilizer:* Supposedly extends the life of a Tulk indefinitely. It's also designed to counter-act the effects of progeria, according the Tulk some bargaining power over their Annarene collaborators.

• *Tulk Stasis Chamber:* A bubble of dampened space-time, impenetrable unless deactivated with a control sphere and the proper access codes. As a safety feature, destroying the control sphere will trigger a self-destruct powerful enough to obliterate Scotland.

PLACES TO GO *Countess Gallowglass' Forwarding Service:* Hidden in a London alley, shrouded behind a holographic building front and a mild aversion field that stops trespassers.

HISTORY The Annarene Protectorate previously gained a great deal of power, but its leaders eventually pursued pacifism and political alliances rather than conflict. Even so, an extremist faction festered on Annares, itching to return the Annarene to warfare.

• The Doctor met the Countess when one of her

customers, pissed when his/her parcel got lost, declared war on Earth and stole Britain's Crown Jewels. The Time Lord replaced the Crown Jewels with fakes, thereby averting a historical catastrophe. He's unsure if British authorities ever discovered the switch, but gives the Tower of London a wide berth just in case.

• Countess Gallowglass warns the Doctor to avoid London on July 4, 2013, but fails to explain why.

• A cure for Alzheimer's exists in future.

AT THE END OF THE DAY Certainly above average, with a decent amount of twists and a sense that Michalowski's doing his damnedest to keep us entertained [which is always appreciated—thank you, Mark]. Against that, several elements aren't as original as they first appear, and seemingly got included in the hopes that if Michalowski threw enough jigsaw pieces onto the table, a complete puzzle might emerge. Understand us carefully: *Relative Dementias* is most definitely a *good* book, but not a *great* book, and probably earned its glowing reputation in some quarters because 2001 was a fairly lackluster year for the EDAs—meaning this book's B-level performance, coming when it did, probably seemed more praiseworthy than normal.

DID YOU KNOW?

• The Margaret McConnon who appears in the prologue is actually author Michalowski's mother, going by her maiden name. She was a little worried when told she'd be featured in a "Doctor Who" book, and the fact she was featured as an elderly woman, dumped unceremoniously in the clinic by her uncaring children, hasn't eased her fears.

• Michalowski spent much of his youth living in an elderly people's home run by his parents, and a couple of the residents—particularly Connie and Jessie—are based on real people.

• At one point, Dr. Joyce Brunner was intended as TV's Corporal Bell.

• Michalowski and Simon Forward (*Drift*) were commissioned on the very same day—with the very same e-mail, actually—and have since become good friends, hence the Doctor's flashback in *Relative Dementias* to events in *Drift*.

• Ace's trip to Kelsay originally entailed her going to Sitges near Barcelona in Spain, but Michalowski changed this—at editor Justin Richards' suggestion—to maintain a cold, drizzly claustrophobic feel.

• The Archer Memorial Gallery [page 19] was originally The Dando Memorial Gallery—until someone at the BBC suggested changing it to avoid offending anyone.

• Graystairs is loosely based on Laurieston Hall, a real Scottish house.

CITADEL OF DREAMS

By Dave Stone

Release Date: *March 2002*
Order: *Telos "Doctor Who" Novella #2*

TARDIS CREW The seventh Doctor and Ace.

TRAVEL LOG Hokesh City, time unknown; Radiant City, clearly in Hokesh's future.

CHRONOLOGY After "Survival." The Doctor here wears a gray jacket rather than a brown one, suggesting Season 24 or 25 instead of Season 26. However, Stone intended this story to take place after "Survival," the last TV story, to mirror that the previous Telos novella, *Time and Relative*, occurred before the debut "An Unearthly Child."

STORY SUMMARY In Hokesh City, a settlement near the Galactic Hub, a street urchin named Joey Quine spontaneously develops psionic abilities. Joey sets about telepathically dominating the will of others, improving his social standing. Regrettably, the City ruler, a psychic named Sloater, senses Joey's budding power and moves to mentally squash his potential rival.

Meanwhile, the Doctor learns that unfolding events in Hokesh will help craft the City's future, deciding to take an active hand and fulfill its history. The Doctor drops Ace off in Hokesh, directing her to snag Joey and hole up until he returns. Ace finds Joey under Sloater's telepathic thrall, but her "alien" presence snaps Joey back to normal. As instructed, Ace rents an apartment and keeps Joey under cover.

Arriving via the TARDIS some years in the future, the Doctor finds Hokesh City rebuilt into a gleaming metropolis named Radiant City. The Doctor meets Joey's future self, city ruler Magnus Solaris, at the end of his rule, requesting that he journey with him to the past. Remembering the Doctor's wisdom from his youth, Solaris agrees. Shortly afterward, Solaris and the Doctor reunite with Ace and Joey in Hokesh City.

The Doctor explains to young Joey that the City is literally a living entity, existing in a state of symbiosis with "people" created from raw protein. However, the City crucially requires an Avatar to interface between itself and the ersatz people. Sloater, the current Avatar, has served for centuries but is currently bored of life, allowing Hokesh to fall into disrepair. The City intends to spend years generating a replacement Avatar in the form of a child, but has selected Joey to serve as a stopgap Avatar during the interim.

Unwilling to relinquish his power, Sloater mentally sucks the life force from the Black Watch, his City guardsmen, then hurls a raw energy bolt straight at Joey. Solaris intercepts the attack, perishing almost instantly, but not before mentally shunting his knowledge and skills to younger self. Working on instinct, Joey drains all the life energy from Hokesh's "people," then eradicates Sloater.

Afterward, the Doctor and Ace depart, knowing that Joey will repopulate Hokesh as part of the City's growth cycle, creating Radiant City and ruling there as Solaris. "Meanwhile," in the future, Radiant City births the child who will succeed Solaris as the new Avatar.

MEMORABLE MOMENTS In Hokesh City, the Doctor turns relieved to find a statue of "the Doctor" refers to a spaceship's medic, fearing he'd forgotten something.

The Doctor tersely advises Joey *not* to telepathically scan his mind, warning it would burn him.

Ace finds it strange that the Doctor doesn't like her hauling explosives around, yet keeps putting her in situations where she needs to blow shit up.

SEX AND SPIRITS Joey mind-scans a Dracori (*see Alien Races*) with a fetish for donning human underwear, often several sets at the same time, evenly distributed over a number of different limbs and appendages.

Café de la Rue Tigris serves as a high-society brothel in Hokesh City, located on the cusp between the wretched Guild Hall Square and more respectable quarters.

Solaris uses his post as Avatar to take lovers of shocking variety and beauty.

ASS-WHUPPINGS Ace bashes some Sloater-mesmerized City inhabitants with a smooth, metallic club—specifically, an "East Grinstead Slugger." She blows up her Hokesh City apartment to prevent Sloater's agents from obtaining her Nitro-9 and stuff. She possibly kills a few pursuers in the process, but writes it off as, "Better them than us."

When a pair of human and Dracori youths try to rob Joey, his budding power reflexively makes

them cut themselves. The thugs tie themselves up, for their own protection. Additionally, Joey's power makes a couple of Sloater's "Black Watch" enforcers viciously turn on themselves.

Solaris' waning power creates holes in the very fabric of Radiant City.

Sloater projects nightmares into Joey's brain, making him witness a serial killer offing a prostitute. Sloater sucks life energy from his Black Watch. Joey goes a step further and kills off Hokesh City's inhabitants. Solaris gets incinerated, making *Citadel of Dreams* the beginning and end of Joey's story. Sloater also croaks.

TV TIE-INS The Doctor's back on a vegetarian kick ("The Two Doctors"), trying to also convert his friends and associates. Ace still likes bacon butties and cooks meat when the Doctor's not around.

The Doctor tends not to believe in magic "on even-numbered days, at least." ("The Daemons")

NOVEL TIE-INS A tailor shop in Hokesh City, named H. Flatchlock (Prop.) & Associates, bears no relation to "Agragazar Flatchlock," Jason Kane's employer in *The Infernal Nexus*.

CHARACTER DEVELOPMENT

• *The Doctor:* The Doctor doesn't understand how olives get stuffed with little peppers, and considers them ghastly. He can rig a device that blocks electromagnetic pulses, preventing the psionic Sloater from using direct mind control.

• *Ace:* In Hokesh City, Ace drives a sleek, black automobile with a silent-running radium engine. She's utterly devoted to the Doctor at present. She liked Hokesh City despite herself.

Ace's mother would have rather "drowned in live rats" than cook a proper meal with eggs. Ace's arsenal now includes a pencil-shaped plunger that blows up Nitro-9 explosives by remote.

• *The Doctor and Ace:* Ace complains for not knowing that the Doctor's gambit with Solaris entailed killing off everyone in Hokesh City. She's somewhat comforted to learn the people weren't really alive to start with, and that mass deaths are part of the City's renewal cycle.

• *Joseph Quine (a.k.a. the Broken Avatar, the Magog god):* Joey's 15 years old, having spent his entire life scavenging on the streets of Hokesh. He's been experiencing blackouts, moments when—unknown to him—Sloater has reflexively blocked his budding power.

At first, Joey needed to touch individuals to read their memories. Gradually, he learned to exert his power from a distance. He can tap his empathic link with the City to see in dark places. He cannot

telepathically read Solaris, as they're the same person.

• *Magnus Solaris:* Joey's older self, and the lord and sovereign of Radiant City. Remembering his urchin youth, Solaris sometimes disguises himself and ventures out to observe his people.

He has been unable to mentally feel Radiant City of late, suggesting that it's ready to replace him. He's forgotten what the word "Dracori" means (see *Alien Races*), as they were part of Hokesh City, not Radiant City.

Solaris survives at his post of Avatar longer than the Doctor expected, but his world was too limited, inward looking and self-serving to survive. The Doctor accordingly acted to ease the transition to Solaris' successor, fearing Radiant City might tip into entropy otherwise.

• *The Doctor and the TARDIS:* He laments that the TARDIS always seems to land in alleyways, not somewhere classy like a performance of *The Threepenny Opera*.

ALIEN RACES *The City Inhabitants:* They're creations of the City, and largely go through the motions of being alive. The City inhabitants don't eat or excrete, although the City contains "markets" and "a sewer system." The people love books, but lack intimate relations, death and cemeteries. Children aren't "born," but spontaneously appear in the streets as the City grows.

The people of Radiant City seem fairly one-minded, enjoying life solely because they're under Magnus Solaris' protection.

• *The Dracori:* Supposedly the "original" inhabitants of Hokesh City (see *History*). Dracori are distinctly non-humanoid, with several hundred eyes scattered over their upper promontory. Wearing clothing is optional, since their tentacular mass would require, at best, an elaborate leather harness. The weakest Dracori is twice as physically strong as a human bodybuilder. Dracori don't speak human dialect, but are understandable with effort.

PLACES TO GO *The City:* The City resides on a planet orbiting an old, red sun near the Galactic Hub (see *Phenomena*). It exists in symbiosis, not a parasitical relationship, with its self-generated inhabitants. Other City organisms are undocumented, but allegedly grow to no more than a meter across, barring the arrival of actual beings (see *History*).

The City needs an Avatar, a sort of patron deity, to interface with [and harmlessly subsist on] its inhabitants. The Doctor witnessed a similar setup in a town ruled by giants Gog and Magog.

• *Hokesh City:* City locations include Market Hill, which sells *oogli* fruit and hauler-beast, a sort of vinegar-cured donkey. Bagshall Place contains fruit stands. The late "Erth" settlers worshiped their gods at a church in Temple Quarter.

A council officially administrates the City, but Sloater holds the real power. The Council Hall [including Sloater's offices] moved from the Guild Hall Square to better accommodations in the "Marshalt Side."

The City contains a run-down wharf. Hokesh dock workers sport arrays of multi-colored bandannas that denote their Guild status. The City's people sometimes travel on steam engine-driven carriages.

Old Man Srescht runs the Hostel for the Aid and Succor of Deserving Itinerant Youth, but frequently robs his tenants.

• *Radiant City:* A brilliant place of jade, ivory, marble and gold. Its districts include the Manufactory Quarter, the Provisionary Quarter and the Financial Quarter. The City Center includes hippodromes and a theatre district, called "the Thieves' Hall." Due to Solaris' waning power, whole areas of Radiant City are uninhabitable.

• *The Gutter Palace:* Solaris' headquarters in Radiant City, seemingly fabricated from pure gold. The Gutter Palace is divided into "organs," with a "cranium" that opens to the stars. Solaris speaks with City Counselors in the "Chamber of the Heart."

• *Outmarsh:* Outlying region of Hokesh City. It's not part of the City proper, meaning Sloater's power couldn't touch Joey there. The Feast of Fools is an annual event where the Outmarsh residents march through the City and get recognized.

PHENOMENA *The Avatars and the Galactic Hub:* Psionically speaking, the Avatars have little more than precognitive abilities. However, the City's relatively close proximity to the Galactic Hub—a singularity that causes metatemporal events—disrupts time to a certain degree. Hence, the Avatars' precognitive powers does more than simply *view* the future. It actually *changes* the fabric of time and reality.

The empathic City speaks to its Avatars, guiding them through its alleyways and hidden plazas as needed. When channeling the City's power, the Avatars become "psycholeptics," going into a waking trace state.

City Avatars are functionally immortal, but their interest in living eventually fades. When that occurs, the City loses coherence and falls apart.

HISTORY The City previously existed in symbiosis with its self-made "Dracori" inhabitants, not based on a humanoid pattern. But at some point, a human colony ship crashed near the City. The addition of *actual* people, however few, sped up the City's evolution and generated some human "inhabitants." Sloater, one of the crew, became the City's Avatar and endured for centuries while his comrades died out. A few of Sloater's shipmates, notably the ship's captain, doctor and counselor, were later commemorated as statues of "the dark gods" in the Plaza of the Deities.

"Hauler-beast," one of the DNA strands that survived the trip from Earth, started selling at City markets. Conflicts between the "humans" and "Dracori" are purported to have happened, but if so, the two sides integrated.

AT THE END OF THE DAY Unless you're one of those readers who enjoys literature that's different for the sake of being different, this is a wellspring of confusion, with little control over what it's actually saying. The first half, chronicling Joey's budding psionic powers, could almost get torpedoed with little penalty, and indeed, virtually all of *Citadel of Dreams* reads like a tangled story that Stone wrote years ago, then sutured a bit to include the Doctor and Ace. As such, it finishes as a text that at best seems "baffling," and at worst puts its reader on the rack—all for a whopping £10 UK/$17.95 US.

• Stone wrote the first section, concerning how people go insane when landmark buildings get destroyed, on September 10, 2001. Note the date. He thought long and hard about revising it, but decided to leave it exactly as written for whatever interest and correspondence it might contain. Stone adds that this marks the second time such a coincidence struck him, as he wrote an involved section about Judges taking down a cult for one of his *Judge Dredd* books—only to soon after hear about Waco, Texas.

• *Citadel of Dreams* was consciously conceived as a sort of anti-matter twin to the preceding novella, *Time and Relative*, especially when Stone realized the cover colors were going to be reversed.

• Stone decided late in the game that nobody in the City would eat anything, causing him to go back and remove all references to it. He says the cumulative effect changed the tone completely, as the original text had a kind of "tenebrous cannibalism" that was genuinely nasty.

DUST BREEDING

By Mike Tucker

Release Date: *June 2001*
Order: *Big Finish "Doctor Who" Audio #21*

TARDIS CREW The seventh Doctor and Ace.

TRAVEL LOG Duchamp Corp. spaceship refueling stations, luxury liner *The Gallery* and a reclusive art colony named "The Outhouse," all planet Duchamp 331, sometime during Earth's colonial age. Also, the National Gallery in Oslo, some years previous.

CHRONOLOGY Clearly after *Storm Harvest* and "The Genocide Machine."

STORY SUMMARY Upon learning that Edvard Munch's famous painting *The Scream* will mysteriously disappear, in the future, from an alien planet, the Doctor and Ace travel there to nick the masterpiece for the Doctor's personal art collection. Soon after, the TARDIS materializes on Duchamp 331—a world covered in shifting layers of dust, completely barren save for a few spaceship refueling stations and a reclusive art colony named "the Outhouse."

Suddenly, some dust on Duchamp's surface becomes strangely animated, battering a refueling station and strangling everyone aboard. The Doctor and Ace detect the station's distress signal and investigate, but arrive too late to help. Afterward, the Doctor and Ace trade notes about the murderous dust with Arnold Guthrie, a veteran technician aboard another refueling station, but fail to concoct an explanation.

Stumped, the Doctor and Ace continue onward to the Outhouse and locate *The Scream*. However, a psionic presence in the painting batters Ace. Even worse, the Doctor finds his longtime adversary, the Master, masquerading as an art patron named "Mr. Seta."

Confronted, the Master confesses that a long extinct race on Duchamp once constructed an energy creature—named "the Warp Core"—to defend them against genetically engineered, marine-like invaders named the Krill (*Storm Harvest*). Regrettably, the uncontrollable Warp Core did its work too well, eradicating both the Krill and its creators.

The drained Warp Core fled into space and took refuge on Earth, eventually slumbering in Munch's *The Scream*. The Master located *The*

Scream in the National Museum in Oslo, but the Warp Core briefly flared to life and reduced the Time Lord to his skeletal form (*see Tie-Ins*). Undaunted, the Master arranged to transport the Warp Core back to Duchamp, then seed its energy into the planet's dust. For a grand finale, the Master hopes to goad the dormant Warp Core into action with a clutch of Krill eggs—its ancient enemies—then bind the creature's intelligence to his TARDIS. If successful at this over-complicated scheme, the Master will enslave the Warp Core as a planet-sized weapon.

The Master hatches his pile of Krill eggs, causing Duchamp's surface to churn as the Warp Core awakens. In response, the Doctor takes Ace back to the TARDIS, using the Ship's telepathic circuits to grapple with the Master for mental control of the Warp Core.

The planet-sized Warp Core reels from the psionic combat, even as technician Guthrie responds to the Warp Core's threat by venting 120,000 tons of starship fuel into Duchamp's dust. By flicking his lighter, Guthrie turns Duchamp into a raging inferno—sacrificing himself to obliterate the planet and the Warp Core. The resultant shockwave separately flings the Doctor and Master's TARDISes into space, guaranteeing a rematch between the age-old enemies.

MEMORABLE MOMENTS The end of Part 2 ranks as one of Big Finish's most effective cliffhangers, with the Master revealing his true identity—and surprising the hell out of everyone.

SEX AND SPIRITS Bev Tarrant (*see Audio Tie-Ins*) indulges in a dry vodka martini.

ASS-WHUPPINGS Some Warp Core-animated dust strangles everyone aboard Refueling Station B. The Warp Core also brutalizes Ace with a psionic assault at the end of Part 1. It further tries battering the Doctor, but he mentally wrestles the creature back to sleep.

The Master kills two people in his traditional fashion: zapping them down to the size of a bathroom buddy with his Tissue Compression Eliminator. He also arranges for the Krill to gobble everyone aboard *The Gallery*, a pleasure liner, partly for sport and partly to draw the Warp Core's attention. An art dealer named Madame Salvatori [played by Caroline John, TV's Liz Shaw], deeming everything lost, throws herself to the Krill—thereby buying Ace and Bev Tarrant time to reach the TARDIS.

The Master uses the Outhouse artisans as fodder for a psionic network (*see Places to Go*).

Years before this story, dust on Duchamp (endowed with some residual Warp Core power, probably from the monster's original rampage, *see History*) killed one of Arnold Guthrie's co-workers. Guthrie never forgot the offense, but here gains *some* retribution by torching the Warp Core—and himself—to ash. The resultant inferno also eradicates *The Gallery* and the Master's Krill.

When all's said and done, the Warp Core's particles harmlessly scatter throughout the Universe—enough to give a few people bad dreams.

TV TIE-INS The TARDIS contains a genuine art gallery, rather than the holographic version seen in "The Invasion of Time." The Doctor's art collection includes a jumbled Terileptil glass sculpture ("The Visitation") and a Mona Lisa (with no "This is a fake" scribbled in felt tip on the canvas, "City of Death").

The Master's TARDIS yet again resembles a Greek pillar ("Logopolis," "Castrovalva").

NOVEL TIE-INS The Krill previously menaced the Doctor and Ace in *Storm Harvest*. Several ultra-tough Krill eggs got flung into space at the end of that book, with the Master later acquiring them to create his Krill stockpile.

AUDIO TIE-INS The Doctor and Ace here re-meet salvage merchant/thief Bev Tarrant (Tucker's "The Genocide Machine"), who arrives on Duchamp 331 after hastily escaping a border patrol into hyperspace.

TIE-INS In what's probably the greatest contradiction between the "Doctor Who" books and audios, "Dust Breeding" and the New Adventures novel *First Frontier* (Sept. 1994) compete for the vaunted position of offing the Anthony Ainley Master.

The Master here loses his stolen Trakenite body and the Source's healing power ("The Keeper of Traken"), returning to his previous state as a skeletal husk ("The Deadly Assassin"). However, *First Frontier* long ago showed the Master bargaining with the alien Tzun to regain his regenerative powers. An older Ace subsequently shot the Master in the back, forcing his regeneration into a new incarnation.

All of that said, a contradiction doesn't have to exist. Since Ace in "Dust Breeding" is written much closer to her TV persona, this audio almost certainly pre-dates the New Adventures. Ergo, it's easy to suggest an unrevealed story where the skeletal Master regains his Trakenite form (he probably put the body on ice after the Warp Core

damaged it), leading to his fateful regeneration in *First Frontier*. Admittedly, it's an imperfect solution, especially since *First Frontier* wants to fill the Master's continuity between itself and the last TV story, "Survival." But then, "Doctor Who" continuity resembles the Gordian Knot on a number of occasions.

"The Genocide Machine" established that Bev Tarrant spent some time on the planet Coralee, but she lacks knowledge of the Krill slaughter there (*Storm Harvest*). This suggests that "Dust Breeding" historically occurs before *Storm Harvest*, if one allows that the Master acquires his space-flung Krill eggs, then time-travels into the future on Duchamp 331.

CHARACTER DEVELOPMENT

• *The Doctor:* The Doctor's mind can, with effort, repel the Warp Core's telepathic assault. Conversely, the Warp Core can speak through the Doctor (a sign of his powerful intelligence). He can telekinetically manipulate small amounts of Duchamp dust saturated with Warp Core energy, although this requires his total concentration.

The Doctor can perform post-mortems.

• *Ace:* Ace's O-level art teacher, Ms. Parkinson, loved abstract art and taught Ace about Rembrandt's *The Night Watch*. Ace's professional assessment of *The Scream*: "Yuk."

• *The Doctor and Ace:* The Doctor frequently researches when great works of art will historically get "destroyed" [say, in a museum fire]. He then nips back in time, perhaps an hour or two prior to the works' obliteration, and takes them for his private collection. Ace deems the Doctor's art collection somewhat akin to graverobbing, although the Doctor insists he couldn't return the works without altering history.

• *The Master (a.k.a. Mr. Seta):* Wealthy art clientele aboard *The Gallery* disgust the Master, who ironically dismisses them as "Crooks, cheats and scoundrels, hiding behind their wealth." In short, he's proud of his standing as a self-made renegade.

The Master wears a gemstone-covered mask, worth three million units of an unspecified currency, to disguise his skeletal form. He carries a device that hatches Krill eggs by remote control.

• *Bev Tarrant:* She's 29, smokes and sells some of her stolen wares at the Outhouse. After this story, the Doctor and Ace give Bev a lift back home.

• *The Warp Core:* The Warp Core's primarily a psionic force, composed of pure energy. It was engineered with a killer's instinct, born without conscience or morality.

Visionaries, psychics and artistic types prove es-

THE CRUCIAL BITS...

- **DUST BREEDING**—The Master loses his Trakenite body, reverting to his skeletal self ("The Deadly Assassin").

pecially sensitive to the Warp Core's influence, explaining how it readily affected Edvard Munch (*see History*) and Outhouse leader Damien Pierson.

The Warp Core can animate the Duchamp dust to strangle people, then fill its victims' corpses with dust to make them dance about.

- *The TARDIS:* The TARDIS art gallery is located a fair distance from the console room. At one point, the TARDIS seems to voluntarily home on Ace's location.

ALIEN RACES *Krill:* For details on the Krill's battle prowess, *see Storm Harvest write-up in I, Who*. The Krill are innately frightened of Warp Core-saturated dust, recalling race memories of the Warp Core wiping out their ancestors.

- *Dust Sharks:* A singing lifeform that swims through the dust on Duchamp 331. Young dust sharks scream when hungry.

ALIEN PLANETS *Duchamp 331:* A backwater planet, but centered on major space shipping routes. Duchamp 331 lacks any sort of life except for the dust sharks (*see Alien Races*), the six Duchamp Corp. refueling stations and the Outhouse (*see Places to Go*). The planet's dust interferes with communications.

PLACES TO GO *The Outhouse:* A reclusive colony of approximately 50 artists, secretly founded by the Master to aid in his Warp Core master plan. Mentally enthralled by the Master, Outhouse leader Damien Pierson trapped his fellow artists in sensory deprivation tanks and wiped their minds clean—creating a psionic network that bled the Warp Core energy from *The Scream* into Duchamp's dust.

The commune originally sported a more artsy name, but lowbrow Duchamp Corp. workers deemed it "The Outhouse" as a commentary on the art produced there. Freighter crews sometimes bought artwork at the Outhouse, either shipping it back to their homeworlds or off to the frontier.

The Outhouse artists worked with just about every art discipline, becoming especially noted for their "dust art."

- *Duchamp Corp. Refueling Stations:* The six refueling stations on Duchamp 331 sit atop reservoir tanks floating in the planet's dust. The stations weigh and service ships enroute to "the new fron-

tier," although weeks can pass without an arrival.

The stations hold approximately 20,000 tons of fuel, are located 50 km apart and each sport a crew of 20 to 25. Duchamp Corp. crewmen frequently exact bloodfeuds on one another, giving the corporation a convenient excuse to cover up any unexplained deaths.

HISTORY Long ago, an advanced society on Duchamp 331 crafted the Warp Core to combat the invading Krill. In the apocalypse to follow, the Warp Core eradicated the Krill and its own creators—turning Duchamp 331 into a dust planet.

- Grievously wounded, the Warp Core wandered through time and space, finally arriving on 19th century Earth. It randomly sought refuge in the mind of Norwegian artist Edvard Munch, who thought he heard "an infinite scream passing through nature." Utterly tormented, Munch set about rendering *The Scream* to exorcise [literally, as it turned out] his inner demon. Through sheer force of will, Munch banished the weakened Warp Core into the painting. Completely exhausted, the Warp Core went dormant, sleeping through the 20th century.

- Duchamp Corp. built the spaceship refueling centers about 20 years ago.

- A battle-scarred Dalek saucer once touched down on Duchamp 331 to effect repairs, but consequently sank into the dust. Guthie's final gambit against the Warp Core detonated the saucer's Dalekanium power source, enhancing the planet's destruction.

- The Doctor snitched Rembrandt's *The Night Watch* from the Reich Museum in Amsterdam, 33rd century, just before it burnt down.

AT THE END OF THE DAY We'll grant that the Master's spontaneous unmasking in Part 2 suitably hit us in the face like a brick. Hell, Big Finish almost deserves some sort of award, especially in our information-driven culture, for keeping it a secret so long. Unfortunately, the hopelessly jumbled "Dust Breeding" has virtually nothing else to recommend it, strangling itself with nonsensical plot points [a completely token character does in the Warp Core] and an almost unbearable posturing between the Doctor and the Master. In short: Other than the cliffhanger, it's entirely forgettable.

COLDITZ

By Steve Lyons

Release Date: October 2001
Order: Big Finish "Doctor Who" CD #25

TARDIS CREW The seventh Doctor and Ace.

TRAVEL LOG Colditz Castle, Germany, October, 1944.

STORY SUMMARY Bumped off course by a time anomaly, the TARDIS materializes in 1944 at Colditz Castle, one of the most secure Nazi prisons in Germany. The Colditz wardens easily capture the Doctor and Ace, tossing them into separate cells. While Colditz supervisors puzzle over the Doctor's medical report, Ace dodges advances from Kurtz, a lowly, sadistic German sergeant.

Eventually, a blonde female named Klein arrives at Colditz, flashing high-ranking Nazi credentials and confronting the Doctor in his cell. To the Doctor's bafflement, Klein possesses a frightening amount of information about him, threatening to instantly gun down Ace in cold blood unless the Doctor surrenders the TARDIS key. Suitably outmaneuvered, the Doctor complies. Klein turns the Ship over to Colditz officials as the first stage of her plan, then takes the Doctor away at gunpoint.

Klein supposedly makes for a hidden transport, but finds nothing but a square indentation in a nearby woods. Gradually, the Doctor realizes that his arrival at Colditz altered history. Bizarre as it sounds, Klein originates from a future where Germany won World War II. But worse, she somehow, someway traveled back to 1944 in his TARDIS.

Exposed, Klein concedes that she hails from the year 1965, having risked a single journey in the now-absent TARDIS to obtain the Doctor's help in learning its operation. As Klein explains, the Doctor *did* escape from Colditz in 1944, but that Ace died, shot during a botched escape attempt. However, the Doctor later re-surfaced, whereupon German SS troopers shot him dead and seized the Ship. Eventually, Klein, actually a Nazi scientist, was asked to study its function (*see Sidebar*).

As events unfold, the Doctor concludes that his future self, acknowledging his failure, arranged for Klein's journey as a means of retroactively giving himself a second chance. Klein returns to Colditz for assistance, but as the future Doctor anticipated, her presence starts altering events to get history back on track. Kurtz refrains from killing

Ace, under specific orders from Klein to preserve her as a hostage. Moreover, the Doctor recovers a CD walkman confiscated from Ace's backpack—preventing the Germans from studying its technology and winning the war, thus creating Klein's timeline (again, *see Sidebar*).

Finally, the Doctor brings Klein's forged credentials to Kurtz's attention, exposing the fact that Klein has no official standing in 1944. Klein flees from Colditz in a staff car, even as the Doctor and Ace make a mad dash for the TARDIS. Kurtz follows, wedging himself into the exterior TARDIS doors and firing his rifle wildly. The TARDIS console shorts out, dematerializing the Ship and charring Kurtz—who's caught in the TARDIS/Time Vortex interface—beyond recognition.

Afterward, the Doctor confirms that history is back on course, albeit with Klein running loose in 1944 as a living paradox. The Doctor breathes a sigh of relief, even as Ace, feeling somewhat responsible for Kurtz's death and assorted violence at Colditz, sheds her teenage nickname and declares her desire to simply become "Dorothy McShane."

MEMORABLE MOMENTS The Doctor and Ace get tagged within minutes of their arrival at Colditz, allowing Kurtz to growl: "For you, the war is over."

Some ingenious cliffhangers: Klein suddenly arrives and bests the befuddled Doctor, threatening to shoot Ace if he doesn't surrender the TARDIS key (Part 1). The Doctor realizes that Klein arrived in 1944 in *his* TARDIS (Part 2).

Ironically, it's Klein, the product of a Nazi society, who stands in the TARDIS console room and reiterates the TV show's glorious premise: "Think what this machine can do… you could make great advances, undo past defeats, explore new worlds. This room is just the start of the greatest journey you will ever undertake."

A locked-up Doctor hums the "Doctor Who" theme song to amuse himself. He asks Flight Officer Gower, who's also in detention, if he has an ultra-secret, sophisticated means of smuggling out messages. Hysterically, Gower responds: "My cell overlooks the courtyard. I'll shout over to someone."

Klein, praising her Nazi timeline: "What about the world I've seen? The world of the future, Doctor. An efficient, peaceful, prosperous world. A golden age." Hotly, the Doctor responds: *"Built on how many corpses??!!* Oh, I'm sure your trains run on time, Klein. But was it worth the bloodshed? Was it worth the slaughter of millions?"

Best of all, the escaping Doctor forces Haupt-

THE COLDITZ PARADOX

Although temporal paradoxes often make some fans shrivel in terror ("The Mutant Phase" springs to mind, although to be frank, we understood every word of it), the history revision that occurs in "Colditz" seems quite simple once you realize that the seventh Doctor and Ace—without knowing it—are experiencing events for the second time.

When the Doctor and Ace "first" arrived at Colditz in 1944, the camp's Nazi wardens easily took them prisoner. The Doctor later freed himself, but only after Ace died in a botched escape attempt. Worse, Ace's CD walkman, a dangerous anachronism she rather foolishly carried in her backpack, remained in Nazi hands.

Grieving, the Doctor dematerialized the TARDIS, only to check its instruments and find his visit to Colditz had corrupted history. After the fact, Nazi scientists studied Ace's CD walkman, making technological advancements leading to lasers and even atomic bombs. Armed with such weaponry, Nazi Germany conquered the world.

Unable to return to Colditz and directly intervene in his own timeline, the Doctor crafted an elaborate means of giving himself a second chance. He re-materialized in the victorious Germany, 1955, where a pack of SS troopers "conveniently" shot him dead and took the TARDIS away for study. The Doctor regenerated into his eighth incarnation, crafted a cover identity and spent the next 10 years looking for a German operative to manipulate into fixing the timeline. Meanwhile, Nazi scientists never truly appreciated the TARDIS' value, leaving it to rot.

As "Schmidt," the alternate eighth Doctor became a top assistant to Klein, who was assigned by the German government in 1965 to study the TARDIS' secrets. "Schmidt" persuaded Klein to ambitiously take the Ship for a "test run," suggesting she return to Colditz in 1944 and force the then-captive "Doctor" and to demonstrate the TARDIS' abilities. With little understanding of the temporal mechanics involved, Klein agreed. "Schmidt" secretly pre-programmed the TARDIS to deposit Klein in 1944, then take off again, fooling Klein into thinking she had piloted the Ship solo.

Klein successfully arrived in 1944 and retroactively encountered the seventh Doctor, who had no pre-knowledge of his future self's actions. As the alternate Doctor intended, Klein's presence at Colditz subtly altered events. Kurtz, an ambitious soldier, restrained himself from killing Ace to curry favor with Klein. Also, the seventh Doctor to prevent the CD walkman from falling into Nazi hands. All things considered, this erased Klein's timeline from existence. Unfortunately, since her presence crucially altered events (akin to Charley Pollard's means of salvation, "Neverland"), she continues to exist in "our" timeline.

---

man Julius Schäfer, a sympathetic German officer, to recognize that his "I am simply following orders" excuse won't exonerate him if the Doctor and Ace wind up shot. Determined to leave, the Doctor levels Schäfer with: "The commandant isn't here. This is your choice... your responsibility... your decision to shoot us in our backs in cold blood, one by one. I don't think you will."

Then, in a top moment from the entire Big Finish audio series, the mortal Schäfer realizes that he's dealing with events completely beyond his kin, and relents. When a gun-totting Kurtz screams out in reply, "You will be shot for this, [Schäfer]!", a resolute Schäfer replies: "I don't doubt it. Now drop the gun and let these people pass." Unforgettable.

SEX AND SPIRITS The Allied prisoners hoot and holler when Ace arrives at Colditz, since they don't see many women. They continually applaud her spunk and stage protests on her behalf.

Kurtz threatens to strip Ace and delouse her, but she refuses (Schäfer sides with Ace, since she's clearly clean). Kurtz obviously has lascivious plans for Ace, claiming that she owes him "a favor" after an escape attempt. He clearly intends to force himself upon Ace, but never gets the chance.

ASS-WHUPPINGS The Doctor takes a bullet to the shoulder during his capture, but gradually works the slug out and hands it to Schäfer. Kurtz proceeds to happily thrash the Doctor at the end of Part 1, but Klein interrupts. He also smacks Ace around, but Flight Officer Gower stands up for her.

Ace thunks a guard unconscious with a board— which would normally warrant a firing squad, save that she finally escapes. Kurtz meets his end, caught in the TARDIS doorway as the Ship dematerializes, getting fried like overcooked bacon.

German SS troopers pumped the Doctor's future self with six bullets [shades of his end in "Doctor Who: Enemy Within," *see Sidebar*], leaving him for dead in a ditch.

TV TIE-INS The Doctor still lacks a TARDIS remote control device ("The Mark of the Rani").

NOVEL TIE-INS The future Doctor adopts the

German moniker "Schmidt," also used by the sixth Doctor in *The Shadow in the Glass*.

AUDIO TIE-INS Ace recuperates from witnessing Kurtz's death—and continues insisting everyone call her "Dorothy"—in "The Rapture."

TIE-INS Paul Tanner gave Ace her walkman in "The Fearmonger." She listens on it to music by Danny Pain (*No Future, Happy Endings*).

Ace loathes Nazis, having encountered them before in "Silver Nemesis," "The Curse of Fenric," *Illegal Alien* and possibly *Timewyrm: Exodus*. She carries a rope ladder in her backpack (a derivation of the metal one from "Dragonfire" and "The Curse of Fenric").

CHARACTER DEVELOPMENT

• *The Doctor:* The Doctor's familiar with the history of Colditz. Through sleight-of-hand, he's able to substitute and alter Klein's identity documents without her noticing. He can hide his torch and the TARDIS key about his person, no matter how hard the Nazis search. The Doctor can easily slip out of handcuffs.

• *Ace/Dorothy McShane:* She's described as being, "No more than 20." She's played the Colditz board game, and knows about some of the [failed] escape routes.

• *Klein:* The product of an alternate history (*see Sidebar*), Klein was born to German parents but grew up in Britain. She adhered to her heritage and welcomed a German victory over the Allies. Klein has blue eyes and blonde hair—sparing her from the Reich's purification programs.

Klein holds an appalling grasp of temporal physics, ignoring the Doctor's advice about averting temporal paradoxes. She can't pilot the TARDIS, however much she thinks otherwise.

Presumably, "our" Klein is alive in this time zone, unaware of her temporal duplicate.

• *Hauptmann (Captain) Julius Schäfer:* High-ranking Colditz officer, although not the camp commandant. Schäfer's compassionate and smuggles the prisoners bits of food, since they're kept on starvation rations.

Schäfer realizes—first from the Doctor's double heartbeat, then from spying the TARDIS console room—that he's witnessing events beyond his comprehension. He finally allows the Doctor and Ace to escape. British Flying Officer Gower, a Colditz prisoner, befriended Schäfer and testified on his behalf concerning Kurtz's death.

• *The TARDIS:* It needs to reboot its systems after hitting a temporal anomaly. Until then, it can't reveal where it's landed.

THE CRUCIAL BITS...

• **COLDITZ**—Ace gives up being "Ace" and renames herself "Dorothy."

• *The Doctor and the TARDIS:* Colditz officers take the TARDIS key, but the Doctor hints that the Ship will open for him anyway [although he's possibly referring to a hidden spare key].

PLACES TO GO *Colditz Castle:* Built in the 18th century, Colditz Castle serves as "the escaper's prison"—housing prisoners who've escaped from other facilities.

The prisoners exercise in a highly fortified inner courtyard. It's surrounded by 100-foot-tall buildings, with sentries at every entrance, then additional sentries beyond that. Barbed wire lines the perimeter, and the entire structure's set against a cliff-face. Motion detectors in the walls detect the prisoners digging tunnels.

Colditz houses Allied "prominent prisoners" (a.k.a. the *prominente*), who're intended as potential hostages if the Allies invade. Colditz isn't set up to house female prisoners [Ace lodges with the *prominente*].

ORGANIZATIONS *The Colditz Prisoners:* The Allied prisoners can make/smuggle maps, keys and Deutchmarks. Colditz has experienced more than 100 escape attempts, most of which failed. A successful escape hasn't occurred in more than a year. Some time ago, the French officers spent a year digging a tunnel under the chapel. Four of them escaped through the German barracks.

An escape committee coordinates the prisoners' illicit activities. They're building a glider in one of the attics, behind a false wall. They've got keys to almost every door in the camp. They listen to war broadcasts on a secret radio set. They've been trying to map the inside of the *kommendantur* for years.

Prisoners' meals consist of mashed turnips every day, with a bit of meat on Sunday. The Red Cross sometimes sends packages.

AT THE END OF THE DAY Outstandingly potent, with Klein and the Colditz wardens thinking they've got power over the incarcerated Doctor when clearly it's the reverse. All too often, "Colditz" gets unjustly slagged by people who're either A) sick of Nazi stories, or B) simply unable to like or understand stories about time paradoxes. But setting aside the Doctor's verbal chess, it also features stellar dilemmas for Ace, Klein and especially the enlightened Hauptman Schäfer.

emerging as a solid piece of drama. The sound-track—yes, okay—the *overpowering* soundtrack does the work little favors, but otherwise, it's almost airtight, and a Big Finish production to treasure.

DID YOU KNOW?

• Author Steve Lyons originally planned to use the Master in "Colditz," because he needed a time travelling villain who could explain the Doctor's alternative timeline. However, producer Gary Russell told Lyons he couldn't use the Master—presumably because he was already slated to appear in "Dust Breeding." Lyons briefly considered using another Time Lord character, but eventually came up with Klein, the German scientist who returns from the altered future in the Doctor's own TARDIS.

EXCELIS DECAYS

By Craig Hinton

Release Date: June 2002
Order: Big Finish "Excelis Series" CD Part 3

TARDIS CREW The seventh Doctor.

TRAVEL LOG Excelis City, planet Artaris, about 300 years after "Excelis Rising."

CHRONOLOGY Between *Lungbarrow* and "Doctor Who: Enemy Within."

STORY SUMMARY Hoping to appease the TARDIS after refurbishing its console room, the Doctor graciously lets the Ship choose their next destination. But for some odd reason, the TARDIS materializes in Excelis, some 300 years after the Doctor's last visit.

Upon arrival, the Doctor reels to find Excelis has become a highly industrialized, war-like society, ruled by an oppressive Inner Party. The Doctor hurriedly researches Excelis' recent history to learn more, horrifically deducing that the warlord Greyvorn somehow effected his return to life (*see Audio Tie-Ins*), then worked behind-the-scenes to make Excelis into a totalitarian state.

In due course, the Doctor confronts Greyvorn, currently working as an Inner Party adviser named "Lord Vaughan Sutton." The Doctor learns that Greyvorn—now insane with dreams of conquest—long ago retrieved the Relic and excised the Mother Superior's mind into its pocket dimen-

sion. Worse, Greyvorn mastered the Relic enough to rip the souls from Excelis dissidents, re-funneling their essences into super-strong humanoid lumps of bio-mass called "meat puppets." With such nigh-unstoppable shock troops, Greyvorn plans to extend his reach far beyond Artaris—furthering an empire across time and space.

To the Doctor's further shock, Greyvorn rattles off an intimate knowledge of alien life, realizing that when his fifth self briefly touched the Relic ("Excelis Dawns"), he inadvertently left a portion of his soul inside its internal dimension. Consequently, Greyvorn has used his Relic link to plunder the Doctor's soul fragment for knowledge of alien worlds and time travel.

Greyvorn revels in his madness, but the Doctor hurriedly locates the Relic and opens it. Instantly, the Doctor's soul travels into the Relic, merging with the part of his essence already there. Thanks to his presence in the Relic as a fully living spirit, the Doctor exerts enough willpower to forever snap Greyvorn's control. To Greyvorn's horror, his captive Artarian souls depart for the *true* afterlife, turning his meat puppets into useless bio-mass.

Completely undone, Greyvorn decides to destroy his homeworld rather than accept defeat. Greyvorn activates Excelis' orbital defense grid, priming nuclear missiles to annihilate every major city on Artaris. Unable to stop the countdown, the Doctor reaches the TARDIS and dematerializes. Moments later, nuclear salvos obliterate civilization across Artaris. Greyvorn dies instantly, even as the Relic goes missing. Safe in the TARDIS, the weary Doctor mourns for Artaris' devastation.

ASS-WHUPPINGS At story's end, Greyvorn's madness [and a bundle of nuclear warheads] lay waste to Artaris civilization. Greyvorn, age 1300, also goes up in a blaze of glory.

TV TIE-INS The Doctor has a soul of some sort to leave behind in the Relic, although whether this hails from his Time Lord inheritance or human side—or both—isn't clarified. The Doctor here finishes refurbishing the TARDIS console room into its modernized version ("Doctor Who: Enemy Within").

NOVEL TIE-INS Additionally, the Doctor's using his new sonic screwdriver (a gift from Romana in *Lungbarrow*).

AUDIO TIE-INS Greyvorn kicks it, but the Relic re-surfaces in the Benny CD "The Plague Herds of Excelis."

After "Excelis Rising," Greyvorn honed his

This book is not endorsed by the BBC. Doctor Who and TARDIS are trademarks of the BBC.

99

Relic-given talents enough to funnel his disembodied intelligence into a museum visitor. In addition, the Relic somehow enabled Greyvorn to physically morph his host body, returning to life as a copy of his old self.

Newly restored, he reacquired the Relic and pickled the mind of the Mother Superior ("Excelis Dawns") inside. She remained in the Relic until the Doctor broke Greyvorn's power, presumably traveling onward to the true afterlife.

Greyvorn claims that when the fifth Doctor touched the Relic in the zombie camp ("Excelis Dawns"), a part of his soul remained within. In some fashion, the Doctor's missing piece lured him and the TARDIS back to Excelis ("Excelis Rising" and this story). Still, one presumes that only a part of the Doctor's consciousness remained in the Relic, since it's hard to imagine that he's been running around completely soulless for two incarnations.

Excelis Wardens now serve as enforcement officials for the Inner Party. The position of "Reeve" still exists, but denotes a lesser official. As "Lord Sutton," Greyvorn took up residence in the remains of the Excelis museum. He's still subject to headaches, although nothing like his previous mental trauma (all "Excelis Rising").

The seventh Doctor erroneously claims that Iris Wildthyme brought the Relic to Excelis "1300 years ago." Actually, she brought it there several thousand years previous, (see "Excelis Dawns.")

CHARACTER DEVELOPMENT

• *The Doctor:* The Doctor can cross-correlate historical records to flesh out inaccuracies, piecing together a reasonably *correct* version of history whatever the official lies.

The Doctor can override Excelis security systems. He likes parties. He carries himself like a distinguished Inner Party member.

• *The Doctor and Greyvorn:* Thanks to the Doctor's soul fragment in the Relic, Greyvorn has obtained knowledge about Daleks, Cybermen, Sontarans and a wealth of alien worlds, plus the Doctor's understanding of time travel. Greyvorn claims the Doctor's soul burns with "a certain darkness."

• *Greyvorn:* Greyvorn's completely demented by this point, envisioning a war that will ignite the universe. He's assumed a number of identities over the centuries. He's sensitive to Excelis' life force, realizing instantly when something from outer space [namely, the TARDIS] materializes.

Greyvorn supports genetic purity programs. His work largely depends on secrecy—even the Inner Party might turn on him if they learned too much.

• *The TARDIS:* The Ship sometimes sulks, scrambling the console's external sensors. However, it can't black out the external viewer, which is on a separate circuit.

ALIEN RACES *Greyvorn's Meat Puppets (a.k.a. The Elite):* Humanoid-shaped lumps of bio-mass, birthed in Greyvorn's chemical vats, then endowed with stolen souls from the Relic. One soul can potentially animate up to 10,000 meat puppets.

STUFF YOU NEED *"Treasure":* A pacification drug, used by the Inner Party to maintain control in Excelis. "Treasure" exists in most of Excelis' air, food and water, keeping the Outer Party and prol workers in line.

PLACES TO GO *Excelis:* Greyvorn largely leaves the running of Excelis to the Inner Party, intervening only when necessary. The lesser Outer Party overseas weapons production, whereas the lowly "prols" serve as a labor force. Resistance to the Inner Party *does* exist, but it's highly disorganized. The Wardens have turned over thousands of dissenters to "Lord Sutton" as fodder for his meat puppet army.

Excelis has become an extremely polluted environment, resembling Earth in the mid-21st century. The city-state's extremely isolated, and foreigners stick out like a sore thumb.

ORGANIZATIONS *The Inner Party:* The Inner Party regards Greyvorn as a late, great military hero and considers Reeve Maupassant "the Architect of Reason."

Commissar Erco Salis serves as the Inner Party's Minister of War. The Party doesn't frown on prostitution, but utterly forbids cross-breeding, expelling members who sire children with prols [and presumably Outer Party members].

HISTORY Circa 200 years ago, Greyvorn returned to life. He resumed a position of authority with the Wardens, then secretly effected number of socio-political changes in Excelis, making it a totalitarian state almost overnight. The Inner Party seized power, assassinating the Imperial Family.

Afterward, the state immensely suppressed knowledge to prevent dissent—burning churches, hanging philosophers and forbidding the prols from reading. Books were banned, although one of Commissar Salis' ancestors saved some texts from the Imperial Museum and Arcane Library, squirreling away a single cache of legitimate information. After 150 years of such slavery, the working

THE CRUCIAL BITS...

- **EXCELIS DECAYS**—Death of Lord Greyvorn, who butchers Artaris with a nuclear missile volley.

prol and Outer Party classes [and the Inner Party, to large degree] forgot their history.

- Greyvorn pushed Excelis into military conflict with the city-states of Calan, Buzhtoy, Kruce, Meefah and the Getrecht Confederacy. The resulting onslaught quickened Excelis' technological advancements, furthering Greyvorn's meat puppet research.
- Eventually, Greyvorn gained too much too much stature in his "Lord Sutton" identity, causing the Getrecht Confederacy to mark him for assassination. Greyvorn consequently faked his death, then continued his meat puppet experiments in private.
- Five years ago, various city-state leaders met in secret to draft the Artaris Convention—a bill of rights designed to end the war. However, Greyvorn sabotaged the peace accord, finding the war too useful to his industrial efforts.

AT THE END OF THE DAY Horrendously off-target, the undisciplined "Excelis Decays" simply doesn't know what it's saying in parts [the Doctor to Commissar Salis: "Of course, your entire society may collapse, but that is a small price to pay for freedom."—and exactly *how* is that a small price?]. Greyvorn here devolves into just another sci-fi madman, squandering Tony Head's talents. A cinder block could give a more rousing performance than Yee Jee Tso as Major Jal Brant. And just when you think it can't get much worse, the planet's destroyed by a hitherto-unmentioned missile system in the last few minutes. All in all, this represents the sort of bland, surface level science fiction that "Doctor Who" *must* resist becoming.

DID YOU KNOW?

- Author Craig Hinton says in a discussion board posting that "Excelis Dawns" was already written when producer Gary Russell solicited submissions for the other "Excelis" installments. Russell and Big Finish producer Jason Haigh-Ellery came up with the basis for the other two stories, but left the individual plots up to the individual authors. Hinton initially submitted the Colin Baker installment [without the nuclear holocaust ending, obviously] but Russell asked him to morph the story into the third "Excelis" audio.
- Hinton closely collaborated with David McIntee, who wrote the "Excelis Rising" segment.

McIntee invented the notion that the Artaris System only had only one other habitable planet, called the Redbrick Moon, but this got cut for reasons of time.

- During recording, producer Gary Russell playfully smacked writer Craig Hinton with a copy of the script—for penning a 15-page scene.

BULLET TIME

By David A McIntee

Release Date: August 2001
Order: BBC Past Doctor Adventure #45

TARDIS CREW The seventh Doctor, with Sarah Jane Smith.

TRAVEL LOG Bangkok, March 1997; Hong Kong, April, 1997.

CHRONOLOGY Between *Lungbarrow* and "Doctor Who: Enemy Within."

STORY SUMMARY In 1997, journalist Sarah Jane Smith travels to Hong Kong, hoping to research its imminent handover from Britain to China. Sarah Jane finds an import-export company named Pimms Shipping on her itinerary, then stops to interview the Pimms director: a small, tweed-wearing man named Pendragon. Failing to recognize Pendragon as yet-another incarnation of the Doctor, Sarah departs to continue her research.

Soon after, members of UNIT's South-East Asia (UNIT-SEA) division approach Sarah, knowing of her previous work with UNIT-UK. To Sarah's surprise, UNIT-SEA's Colonel Tsang details how Pimms Shipping serves as a front for a smuggling/extortion gang named the "Tao Te Lung." Worse, Tsang reveals that Pendragon—actually the Doctor—runs the criminal organization.

Sarah investigates the Tao Te Lung, confused as to the Doctor's motives. Regrettably, crimelords in the Tao Te Lung advocate killing the snoopy Sarah—compelling the Doctor, in order to save Sarah's life, to suggest discrediting her instead. Guilt-stricken, the Doctor leaks information that pegs Sarah as a hare-brained UFO spotter, ruining her standing in the journalistic community.

A furious Sarah eventually tracks down the Doctor, who explains that he usurped control of the Tao Te Lung to help a group of aliens (clearly the Tzun, *First Frontier*) stranded on Earth. The Doctor used the Tao Te Lung's resources to secretly

move the Tzun to places of safety, simultaneously searching for their sunken spaceship. Unfortunately, the Tzun came under threat from "The Cortez Project," a rogue, xenophobic UNIT faction secretly led by Colonel Tsang.

Operating without sanction from UNIT HQ, the Cortez Project members seek to eliminate *all* extra-terrestrials on Earth as potential threats to humanity. The Doctor initially arranged for Sarah to travel to Hong Kong as a means of exposing the Cortez members, but events ran out of control before she arrived. The little Time Lord pretended not to know Sarah, then struggled afterward to keep her alive.

Sarah begrudgingly accepts the Doctor's explanation, even as the Tzun reach their sunken saucer. The Tzun prepare for liftoff, but Tsang's Cortez group hijacks the *USS Westmoreland*, on patrol in the Persian Gulf. The Cortez members try to ram the *Westmoreland* into the Tzun saucer, but the Doctor and Sarah enter the submarine.

The Doctor reaches the *Westmoreland*'s conn and primes one of the ship's nuclear warheads. The little Time Lord bluffs through his teeth, threatening to annihilate Tehran—and thereby sparking a worldwide nuclear holocaust—unless Tsang backs down. Bested, Tsang kills her associates, then herself, to preserve the Cortez Project's anonymity. The Doctor disarms the *Westmoreland* warhead, allowing the Tzun to leave Earth. Afterward, the Doctor and Sarah reconcile, agreeing to let the Brigadier flush out the remaining Cortez Project members.

MEMORABLE MOMENTS Sarah turns boggle-eyed to spy a police box in the Pimms Building, but accepts an explanation that it's an art exhibit [the irony being that it's the *real* TARDIS].

The Doctor sullies Sarah's reputation, then turns grief-stricken while looking at newspaper reports of her shame, saying: "They won't go away, no matter how hard I concentrate." More to the point, he comments on his questionable actions [throughout the New Adventures, one presumes]: "I see the faces of death I'm responsible for every time I sleep. Every enemy, every friend I've lost, every innocent I've failed to save. So I stopped sleeping."

Conversely, the Doctor bluffs his enemies into submission with a nuclear warhead, then comments: "The greatest power of any weapon is the power not to use it. That's the power that defeated the Cortez Project today."

Finally, Sarah Jane apparently dies at one point (*see Sidebar*), putting a lump in our collective throats. A final scene on the beach, while not the

end for Sarah Jane, certainly lets her say goodbye to the soon-to-be-regenerated seventh Doctor.

SEX AND SPIRITS Whacked intelligence agent Tom Ryder convinces himself that he had sex with Sarah (*see Sidebar*). In reality, he gives Sarah a foot massage, little more.

The Doctor authorizes the Tao Te Lung to give Sarah a "traditional scare," failing to realize that such language denotes a gang rape. Discovering his error, the Doctor saves Sarah from harm.

Sarah here fails to mention her boyfriend, Paul Morley, whom she dated in 1996 (*Interference*) and had married by 1998 (*Christmas on a Rational Planet*). *Bullet Time* occurs between the two, either suggesting a break in their romance or more timeline revision thanks to events in *Interference*. [McIntee favors the latter.]

ASS-WHUPPINGS Reports of Tom Ryder killing Sarah Jane (*see Sidebar*) seem greatly exaggerated.

A skirmish makes UNIT-SEA Lieutenant Fiona Clark fall to her death. Colonel Tsang drops a Tomahawk-loaded, low-level, 2.5-kiloton nuke onto a Tzun base, killing off everything for a half mile in every direction. Thankfully, the main Tzun force survives.

TV TIE-INS Sarah lacks the Brigadier's talent for recognizing the Doctor in his different incarnations ("Battlefield").

Bullet Time sides with "Pyramids of Mars" in terms of dating the UNIT stories, claiming that Sarah Jane served as civilian liaison to UNIT-UK from 1978 to 1982. She returned to investigative journalism afterward, publishing a couple of sci-fi novels and occasionally assisting UNIT.

NOVEL TIE-INS The Doctor's alien colleagues never get named, but use of the term "Ph'Sor" denotes them as the Tzun. After their botched invasion of Earth in McIntee's *First Frontier*, the Tzun subsequently deemed our planet as strategically unimportant and too much trouble to maintain. The Tzun team in *Bullet Time* simply intended to recover technology left behind during the previous incursion.

Among UNIT's various advisers, Iris Wildthyme (first seen in *Short Trips:* "Old Flames") is on vacation. MI6 also employs a Time Lord, currently on assignment to the Russian/Afghan border.

Bullet Time concurs that by 1997, Sarah had published at least two science-fiction novels (*Decalog 3:* "Moving On").

The Doctor here deals Sarah's reputation a blow,

THE 'DEATH' OF SARAH JANE

More than anything, *Bullet Time* deserves mention for killing off Sarah Jane—or at least, *appearing* to kill her off. McIntee deliberately tailors this book with a certain ambiguousness, putting Sarah Jane's death/survival into question to let the reader experience the dramatic impact of her passing. But upon close examination, it's pretty clear that Sarah Jane lives.

McIntee notes about this deliberate deception: "My intent was to look at how far Sarah—as the Doctor's best friend—would go to help him, even after he crossed her. Would she give her life for him even after that? As we find out, yes, she would—whether she did is another matter. To my mind, she did pull the trigger, but if she was wearing her bulletproof vest, she was presumably just knocked down by the impact."

In *Bullet Time*, Sarah Jane finds herself dogged by a tall, black American named Tom Ryder. Ryder's employers and purpose are never properly made clear, but either A) he's a habitual liar, or B) the Tzun have edited his memories [as they do to Colonel Barry and company earlier in the book].

Ryder likely belongs to some intelligence organization, perhaps the American CIA or DEA. However, Ryder crazily views himself as an action hero. We're shown, through Ryder's point of view, a very Bond-esque adventure in which he saves Sarah Jane with a crazy parachute stunt [that clearly didn't happen]. Later, Ryder's unreliable narration states that he and Sarah Jane had sex [ditto].

As it happens, the only concrete account of Sarah Jane's death comes from Ryder, who holds her hostage at gunpoint on the *Westmoreland* to stop the Doctor from thwarting the Cortez Project members. Allegedly, Sarah Jane grabs Ryder's gun and pulls the trigger *herself*, sacrificing her life to deprive Ryder a hostage. The Doctor supposedly stuns Ryder unconscious, with Ryder later awakening slick with "Sarah Jane's blood."

However, it's far more likely that Ryder merely knocked Sarah Jane unconscious. Certainly, the Doctor's associate Yue Hwa fails to see any blood after Sarah Jane's "shooting"—although he spies her form curled up in a corner. Also, the Doctor distinctly acts like someone who has *not* just seen one of his best friends killed. Given that Yue Hwa fails to mention Sarah's "death" in his formal report to PSB Headquarters in Beijing—and unlike Ryder, we've little reason to doubt Yue Hwa's word—Sarah likely survived with a flesh wound at worst.

Also of note: We're left unclear if, in a final conversation, the Doctor speaks with the real Sarah Jane or bids goodbye to her ghost. But ultimately, it's notable that the Doctor leaves the scene with "a little more bounce in his step"—hardly appropriate, if Sarah had gotten plugged.

Finally, while we're actually not continuity hounds, killing off Sarah in 1997 would throw a lot of "Who"-canon into turmoil. Even allowing for the moment that Big Finish's "Sarah Jane" audios aren't dated *too* specifically, *System Shock* and *Millennium Shock* most definitely show Sarah alive and well in December, 1998. *Decalog 3:* "Moving On," claims that by 2007, she's published loads of science-fiction novels [and *Bullet Time* accepts this story's dating regarding her early novels].

Christmas on a Rational Planet also makes reference to a married Sarah Jane in 1998, and *Interference* shows her waiting, with husband Paul Morley and Samantha Jones, for the Doctor to arrive on Dec. 31, 1999. Fellow journalist Claire Aldwych praises Sarah's work in 2001 (*The Shadow in the Glass*). More to the point, *Interference* shows her funeral at some point in the 21st century. So all in all, these works—and the very ambiguous nature of *Bullet Time*—make Sarah's "death" best viewed as something done for show.

---

although other novels (for a run-down *see last paragraph of Sidebar*) suggest she somehow recovers from the professional slander.

TV/NOVEL TIE-INS *Interference* mucked up Sarah Jane's memories to the point that she claims she "hasn't seen the Doctor in years," even though she saw the eighth Doctor "last year" in 1996. She's also fuzzy on details regarding the Doctor's third regeneration ("Planet of the Spiders").

The Cortez Project's shadowy head, "General Kyle," is indeed Marianne Kyle, a product of the "Inferno" Earth (McIntee's *The Face of the Enemy*). [McIntee plans to use her in a sequel novel.]

The seventh Doctor knows that, with his regeneration drawing near (an event clearly established in *The Room With No Doors*, actualized in "Doctor Who: Enemy Within"), "he" won't see Sarah again.

CHARACTER DEVELOPMENT

• *The Doctor:* The Doctor has been coordinating with Major Yue Hwa of China's Public Security Bureau—an undercover agent in the Tao Te Lung—to further the arrest of Hong Kong's crimelords (*see Organizations*).

The Doctor possesses refined safecracker skills and can quote World War I poet Wilfred Owen.

• *Sarah Jane Smith:* Sarah, age 48, opens this book as a press corps star, having just published a

---

This book is not endorsed by the BBC. Doctor Who and TARDIS are trademarks of the BBC.

103

worldwide article entitled, "Sex Tourism Launders Golden Triangle Harvest," exposing a pornography-based money laundering operation. She doesn't like being in the public eye, considering herself a journalist, not a news anchor. She turned down an offer to present *Tomorrow's World*.

She's researching a piece about Khmer monuments for the *Metropolitan*, but can't figure out why she's still writing for them, considering the publisher changes personalities so often.

She avoids telling people that she's interested in extraterrestrial life, afraid that they'll start spouting alien abduction stories. On rare occasions when she gets genuine information on extra-terrestrials, she files the data away for research or notifies UNIT.

Sarah loves Hong Kong's people and atmosphere, but not its humidity. She sometimes takes photos for her stories, but recognizes the difference between her nominal skills and those of a true photographer.

She rarely gets carsick. She despises the landing approach to the Kai Tak airport. Sarah enjoys watching the evening news, but isn't an expert on big business. Experience has taught Sarah to run and ask questions later. She can pick locks. She's not big on revenge. As a child, she enjoyed poking her nose into dark corners. She earned an A-level in history.

• *The Doctor and Sarah Jane:* The older seventh Doctor reminds Sarah of actor Peter Falk as "Columbo." The seventh Doctor's manipulations make Sarah ponder if he's gone the way of the Master, obsessed with control and his own divine judgement, but she later accepts his good nature.

ALIEN RACES *The Tzun:* As detailed in *First Frontier*, purebred Tzun [designated "S'Raph" Tzun] look like Roswell aliens, about 3 to 4 feet tall, gray, with big heads and black eyes. Tzun can genetically bond with other species to produce "Ph'Sor" hybrids, who appear normal but serve the Tzun according to their mental conditioning. Some human/Tzun Ph'Sor remain behind after the Tzun depart Earth, either living out their lives without incident or conscripted by the Chinese government as agents.

S'Raph Tzun carry crystalline barreled weapons and have transmat equipment.

STUFF YOU NEED *Gallifreyan Technology:* It can compress metallic elements into ingots. The Doctor gives the Tzun some [presumably redundant] Gallifreyan technology to help their escape from Earth, but stresses that it gets finicky without proper maintenance.

• *"Bullet Time":* The time it takes a bullet to leave the gun barrel and strike home.

PLACES TO GO *Pimms Building:* Designed by architect Paul Rudolf, the Pimms Building has a five-story base, from which a 12-story tower rises. It's not the biggest building in Hong Kong, but numbers among the most striking. An actual Paul Rudolf building—not the fictional Pimms Building, however—appears on the book's cover.

ORGANIZATIONS *The Cortez Project:* UNIT underground movement, operating without knowledge of the UN Secretary General or UNIT's host countries. Whereas UNIT-UK now distinguishes between alien hostiles and potential allies, the Cortez Project members believe that if the public encountered beings from a more advanced civilization, it could collapse human society.

The Project takes its name from Cortez's historical landing in South America, signaling European dominance of the New World. Fearing to go the way of the Aztecs and more, the Project members believe it's simply safer to rub out any extra-terrestrials they find.

• *Tao Te Lung:* Seemingly a ruthless criminal organization, but actually a front for the Chinese government (*see History*).

The Tao Te Lung traffics in drugs, arms and illegal immigrants. Recently, the Tao Te Lung's been acquiring rare mineralogical and metallurgical samples, unknowingly to help the Doctor evacuate the Tzun from Earth.

Tao Te Lung means "Way of the Dragon," with its leader designated "Pendragon," meaning "Head of the Dragon."

• *Pimms Import-Export Company:* Actually a commercial arm for the Tao Te Lung. Sarah's never heard of it before, suggesting the Doctor recently founded it as part of his operations. Pimms owns a whole patch of the Kwai Chung container port, the largest in the world.

• *UNIT:* Most UNIT-UK operatives have heard of Sarah. She hasn't worked for UNIT-UK in a couple years, but maintains a friendly relationship with the group. Technically, nobody "leaves" UNIT unless they're physically and mentally unable to contribute.

• *UNIT South-East Asia (a.k.a. UNIT-SEA):* Arm of UNIT headquartered in Singapore. In Hong Kong, UNIT-SEA operates out of a small, rented office block in Mongkok.

UNIT-SEA operatives include Colonel Tsang and Lieutenant Nomura. Some UNIT-SEA agents wear lightweight body armor, and carry Heckler-Koch MP-5s, with a Beretta 92F automatic pistol

THE CRUCIAL BITS...

- **BULLET TIME**—Possible (although highly unlikely) death of Sarah Jane Smith.

as back-up. UNIT-SEA doesn't fully trust UNIT-UK, but that's partly due to the Cortez Project's need for secrecy.

SHIPS *USS Westmoreland:* Part of the United States Navy's Pacific Fleet, Captain Davis commanding, and formally designated a Ticonderoga-class guided missile cruiser.

- *Qe'shaal:* The Tzun vessel, not designed for operation in the water and slower than the *Westmoreland*.

HISTORY UNIT-US had some involvement in the Vietnam War.

- *Bullet Time* occurs less than a month before Britain hands control of Hong Kong back to China. Toward this end, the Chinese government secretly founded the Tao Te Lung as a means of ferreting out—and arresting—Hong Kong's criminal element, fearing that the city might otherwise fall prey, like post-Soviet Moscow, to control by mobsters.

AT THE END OF THE DAY Average at best, although winning some points for putting the pure-hearted Sarah Jane at odds with the formidable seventh Doctor. Regrettably, *Bullet Time*'s secondary characters are simply too lackluster to do the book many favors, and after a while, the plot threads—*especially* the confusing Tom Ryder—achieve meltdown. Overall, a book with good intentions with regards to the Doctor and Sarah—but takes on [ironically] the pulpiness of your stereotypical mass market paperback.

DID YOU KNOW?

- The phrase *Tao Te Lung* translates as "Way of the Dragon"—not an accurate triad name, but certainly the title of a Bruce Lee movie.
- McIntee considered a scene where the Tzun talked to the Doctor about the Master, thereby patching up any continuity differences between *First Frontier* and "Dust Breeding." However, he decided not to bother on the grounds that A) additional continuity would only bog down the book and B) fandom's so much better at sorting out continuity issues.
- Author David McIntee claims confusion over where *Bullet Time* occurs in "Who" history is: "Exactly the reason why the Beeb stopped putting

story placement on the back cover."

- UNIT Lieutenant Fiona Clark is named after a "Who" fan, who won a convention auction to get killed off in this book.
- *Bullet Time* mentions that MI6 currently employs a Time Lord, currently on assignment to the Russian/Afghan border. This is James Bond, according to whimsical fan theory stating he's a Time Lord with five official incarnations [to date]. In the year that *Bullet Time* takes place, the Bond producers filmed the pre-credit sequence for *Tomorrow Never Dies*, set on the Russian/Afghan border.
- McIntee intended Tim Russ (*Star Trek: Voyager*'s Tuvok) to play Tom Ryder, hence their having the same initials.
- Inspector Katie ("Cannonball") Siao is named after Katya the Cannonball, one of McIntee's cats. Siao's dress sense is that of McIntee's wife Lesley.
- The *USS Westmoreland* is named after General William Westmoreland. Captain Davis takes after actor Don Davis, who plays General Hammond on *Stargate SG-1*. Westmoreland crew members Jones and Cunningham stem from actors Gary Jones and Colin Cunningham, who also play roles at Stargate Command.

INVADERS FROM MARS

By Mark Gatiss

Release Date: *January 2002*
Order: *Big Finish "Doctor Who" audio #28*

TARDIS CREW The eighth Doctor and Charley.

TRAVEL LOG 34th and Broadway; detective J.C. Halliday's office; main lobby and room 1540 of Excelsior hotel; Chaney's base inside left leg of the Brooklyn Bridge, Manhattan side, all New York City; Devine's hideout in New Jersey, all locations October 31, 1938.

STORY SUMMARY When an alien spaceship suddenly crashes in New Jersey, September, 1938, mobster Don Chaney mobilizes his thugs to loot the wreck. Chaney squirrels away the spaceship—and its single bat-like alien occupant—in one of his hideouts. Next, he acquires the services of Russian physicist Yuri Stepashin to adapt alien technology within the ship into an atomic bomb. Chaney hopes to sell the bomb to the CIA for immense profit, also helping to guarantee America's supremacy over Nazi Germany. Holding little love for Mother

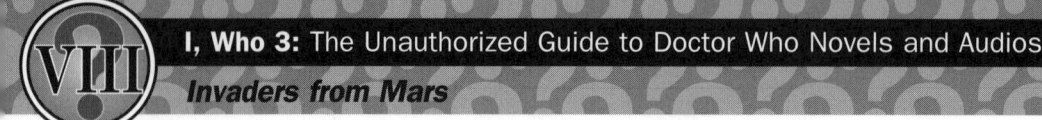

Russia, Stepashin agrees.

Meanwhile, the Doctor tries to take Charley to her rendezvous in Singapore, 1930 ("Storm Warning"), but misses and arrives in New York City, October, 1938. Once there, the Doctor finds evidence of alien technology and investigates further. Eventually, the Doctor learns about Stepashin's involvement, tracking the noted physicist to Chaney's hideout in a leg of the Brooklyn Bridge.

Simultaneously, rival gangster Cosmo Devine learns of Chaney's find and shows up, hoping to nab the alien technology and sell out to the Nazi Party. Amid the standoff, Devine looks into the alien's life-support tank, horrified to discover the extra-terrestrial has undergone mitosis and split into 30 carnivorous creatures. The ravenous newborns burst from the tank and savagely wound Stepashin, threatening to gobble up everyone present.

Amid the chaos, a pair of adult aliens named Streath and Noriam land and tranquilize the rampaging creatures with an audio device. Streath and Noriam try to bamboozle the assembled humans into rewarding them for their actions, but the Doctor quickly realizes the duo sent the quick-breeding newborns to Earth in the first place—exposing their scheme as a galactic protection racket.

Realizing the alien weapons could legitimately dominate Earth, the opportunistic Devine offers a deal to the otherworldly duo. Streath and Noriam consider Devine's proposal, then load the sleeping newborns, their spacepod and all of Stepashin's work—including his atomic bomb—aboard their spaceship and take off with Devine.

The Doctor notes that the date—October 31, 1938—coincides with Orson Welles' panic-spreading *War of the Worlds* broadcast. The Doctor rushes to CBS Studios and convinces Welles to give a second, private rendition of his sci-fi radio drama. Thanks to the TARDIS, the Doctor transmits Welles' repeat performance directly to Streath and Noriam's spaceship. The production fools Streath and Noriam into thinking that the warlike Martians have already invaded Earth, making them flee into space. However, the Doctor's crew fails to stop broadcasting afterward, exposing his ruse.

Streath and Noriam make ready to return and unleash their ship's weaponry against Earth's major nations, but the dying Stepashin, having smuggled himself aboard the alien vessel, primes his atomic bomb. The resultant explosion blows the aliens, Stepashin and Devine to atoms, saving Earth. Afterward, the Doctor and Charley bid farewell to Welles, making another stab at reaching Singapore, 1930.

MEMORABLE MOMENTS   The Doctor astutely notes, "People are rarely killed without a reason. Even in New York."

Track 14 of "Invaders from Mars" opens with "Orson Welles" delivering the opening lines of *The War of the Worlds*—showing a fantastic command of the language even now, 65 years after the original broadcast.

The Doctor alludes to regeneration as a means of keeping fit, claiming that, "Every now and again, I treat myself to a complete makeover."

Chaney's lackey Ellis, knowing Devine's about to kill him, spits out, "See you in hell, Devine," to which Devine replies: "No doubt, but enjoy your head start."

SEX AND SPIRITS   When Stepashin's "niece" Glory Bee (actually a Russian agent in disguise, tracking Stepashin) pretends to faint, the Doctor plays along by saying, "Come on… I'd better get you to a darkened room." Also, the Doctor professes a weakness for Manhattan cocktails.

ASS-WHUPPINGS   Ellis fries JC Halliday, a private investigator tracking Stepashin, compelling the Doctor to adopt Halliday's identity and continue the case.

Later, Ellis repents his betrayal of Chaney, so Devine kills him. One of Chaney's thugs shoots Russian agent Glory Bee, making her fall off the Brooklyn Bridge.

Gangsters shot Chaney's nose off prior to this story. Devine shoots CBS network chairman Bix Biro, one of his blackmail victims, to silence him. Stepashin saves the day, obliterating Streath and Noriam's ship to protect Earth.

TV TIE-INS   Streath and Noriam recognize the Martians as a formidable race of warriors ("The Ice Warriors" onward).

AUDIO TIE-INS   The Doctor tries (and fails) to materialize in Singapore, 1930, Charley's intended destination before the *R-101* disaster ("Storm Warning"). They finally reach the location in "Seasons of Fear."

Orson Welles fails to recognize the name Shakespeare, reflecting a historical glitch that's resolved in "The Time of the Daleks." Other historical blunders include claims that America has 49 states (not 48, as was the case in 1938) and the existence of America's CIA before its creation (all explained in "Neverland").

CHARACTER DEVELOPMENT
 • *The Doctor:* The Doctor's puzzled why so many

THE EIGHTH DOCTOR PRIMER

For as much we'd like to think that Whovians around the world could recite every single word of *I, Who* and *I, Who 2* verbatim, there's probably the odd one or two people who need a refresher course in the eighth Doctor's adventures . So if you're a newcomer—or simply need to catch up—here's a quick outline of his activities up to the stories covered in the spellbinding tome that you're holding.

P.S. Bear in mind that the Big Finish eighth Doctor audios take place between the eighth Doctor novels *The Eight Doctors* and *Vampire Science* (it's complicated, but *consult the Uber-Timeline* for details).

• **THE EIGHT DOCTORS (BBC Books)**—Newly regenerated, the eighth Doctor encounters his seven previous incarnations. First appearance of companion Samantha Jones, a Coal Hill schoolgirl.

• **UNKNOWN**—The Doctor leaves Sam's company for a time.

• **THE DYING DAYS (Virgin Publishing)**—The Doctor meets Bernice Summerfield and shuttles her to a new life on the planet Dellah. [The cat Wolsey also leaves the TARDIS, suggesting this story pre-dates the audios.]

THE BIG FINISH AUDIOS

• **STORM WARNING**—First appearance of companion Charlotte ("Charley") Pollard, a self-proclaimed adventuress enroute to Singapore aboard the doomed airship *R-101*. The Doctor saves Charley from dying as history dictates, thereby violating the Laws of Time.

• **INVADERS FROM MARS to NEVERLAND**—Charley's paradoxical survival causes an increasing amount of historical glitches and general weirdness.

• **UNKNOWN**—The Doctor and Charley part company.

MORE BBC BOOKS

• **VAMPIRE SCIENCE**—The Doctor has resumed travelling with Samantha Jones. For the

Doctor, three years have passed since his regeneration.

• **ALIEN BODIES**—First appearance of Faction Paradox, a rebellious group of Time Lords with voodoo control rituals. First mention of a future "enemy" who's winning a war against the Time Lords.

• **THE TAINT**—First appearance of companion Fitz Kreiner, a lout, would-be guitar singer and flower store clerk from 1963.

• **INTERFERENCE**—Samantha Jones leaves the TARDIS to assist ex-companion Sarah Jane Smith with her journalism projects. The Doctor accepts Compassion (a.k.a. Laura Tobin), the product of a signal based-society called "the Remote" as a new companion.

• **THE SHADOWS OF AVALON**—Compassion transforms into Gallifrey's first fully sentient and humanoid TARDIS.

• **THE ANCESTOR CELL**—The Doctor destroys Gallifrey to prevent its capture by Faction Paradox and the Enemy, but becomes amnesiac as a result. Compassion and Fitz leave the Doctor and the damaged TARDIS in Victorian England to heal, leaving a note for him to rendezvous with Fitz in 2001. Compassion departs for parts unknown.

• **THE BURNING to ENDGAME**—The amnesiac eighth Doctor stays on Earth throughout the 20th century.

• **FATHER TIME**—The Doctor adopts the orphaned 10-year-old Miranda Dawkins, last of a hunted alien species. Nine years later, Miranda becomes supreme ruler over disjointed political factions in the far-flung future.

• **ESCAPE VELOCITY**—First appearance of companion Anji Kapoor, a London futures trader. The Doctor and Fitz are reunited in London, 2000. The TARDIS finally heals and regains its internal configuration, but the Doctor's memory and piloting skills remain questionable at best. Death of Anji's live-in boyfriend Dave Young. The Doctor tries and fails to return Anji to Earth, leading to events in *Earthworld*.

companions leave his company, as he shows them the Universe without any need for thanks. He loosely knows 1930s slang. He sleeps "once in a while."

The Doctor hasn't encountered Streath and Noriam's race (the Laiderplacker) before. He's a huge fan of Orson Welles and has seen all of his films. In the private recreation of *The War of the Worlds*, the Doctor ironically plays a Martian. He's an exceptional lock-picker.

• *Orson Welles:* He thinks the dialogue for *War of the Worlds* is crap.

• *Don Chaney (a.k.a. "The Phantom"):* Chaney

owns a 1929 Lamborghini that formerly belonged to Al Capone. He's profit-minded, but also patriotic (he won't let the Nazis bid on the alien technology). He eats at Luigi's on 34th and Lexington in Manhattan.

• *Cosmo Devine:* Homosexual gossip columnist who writes articles for *The Tattler*. Devine's politics favor the Nazi Party, but he tries to convince Streath and Noriam to attack the Soviet Union, the United States, England, France and Germany.

• *Yuri Stepashin:* He defects while in America for a top-secret physics conference on heavy water. He has no family, and despises Russia's gulags.

ALIEN RACES *The Laiderplacker:* They look like giant, hairy fruit bats.

Streath and Noriam seem representative of their race, holding simultaneous goals of destroying their opponents and conserving resources. Streath holds the post of "Destroyer," making him prone to smashing things and killing people. Noriam's more levelheaded, acting as a "Conservator." At the very least, this entails his recording information on indigenous lifeforms before Streath eviscerates them.

Water's a valued commodity on the Laiderplacker homeworld. Laiderplacker young lack intelligence, driven instead by ravenous hunger.

ALTERNATE HISTORY An amoral Time Lord [likely the Meddling Monk] at one point used a 24th century flood controller to let Viking ruler Canute (995-1035 AD), as he'd boastfully declared, become powerful enough to "turn back the tide." Canute consequently formed an unshakable power bloc in Anglo-Saxon Britain. However, the Doctor intervened and restored history, guaranteeing that Canute, as recorded, got little more than soggy ankles.

HISTORY The New York skyline lit up a month ago as the Laiderplacker breeding party's ship fell to Earth. No previous visits from the Laiderplacker are recorded.

• Yuri Stepashin here builds the world's first atomic bomb, thanks to his work with the Laiderplacker technology. Its detonation in Earth orbit was written off as a fragment from the "meteorite" that landed a month previously.

• *The War of the Worlds* was transmitted in 1938 as part of the *Mercury Theatre* radio series, part of a line-up that also included *Dracula*, *A Tale of Two Cities*, *The Immortal Sherlock Holmes* and more. It was never intended to be a roaring success, but—as you doubtlessly know—listeners heard the broadcast and, to a large degree, believed the "Martian invasion" was real.

• The CIA covered up Devine's murder of CBS network chair Bix Biro.

AT THE END OF THE DAY What could've been a stunning "Who" rendition of *Mars Attacks!* fails to give much payoff, as it's too slight when viewed as either a comedy or a drama story. We'll grant that it's stylish, and actor David Benson makes an excellent Orson Welles, but it's simply too off-handed to make much of an impact. Even the Doctor's jape with the second *War of the Worlds* broadcast seems fruitless, given that it's foiled because some boob leaves their microphone on.

THE CHIMES OF MIDNIGHT

By Rob Shearman

Release Date: February 2002
Order: Big Finish "Doctor Who" CD #29

TARDIS CREW The eighth Doctor and Charley.

TRAVEL LOG Edward Grove house, England, December 24, 1906.

STORY SUMMARY At random, the TARDIS arrives in a seemingly ordinary Edwardian manor on Christmas Eve, 1906. Once there, the Doctor and Charley find the household servants caught in a bizarre time loop. To wit, the servants keep getting murdered in the space of a few seconds, in ways that curiously denote their function—the scullery maid's drowned in her sink, the cook's smothered with her homemade plum pudding, etc. But at the stroke of midnight, a malevolent force rewinds time in the house back by two hours, undoing each murder to begin the killing anew.

The Doctor and Charley investigate the repeated murders, unable to rationalize them. Bizarrely, the spirit of Edith Thompson—the murdered scullery maid—speaks to Charley from a phantom realm between life and death. Edith ominously warns "Edward Grove is alive," then vanishes. Charley repeats Edith's announcement to the Doctor, who unnervingly concludes that the house *itself*—located at 22 Edward Grove—is literally alive and responsible for the killings.

Charley expresses disbelief, but the Doctor cites theories stating that ghosts result when the walls of a house record traumatic emotional impulses. Ergo, if such a murder occurred as part of a temporal paradox, it might get replayed over and over until the house absorbed enough emotion to gain sentience. Eventually, the Doctor realizes that later in life, Edith Thompson worked as a cook in the Pollard household. Upon learning of Charley's 1930 death aboard the *R-101* ("Storm Warning"), a grief-stricken Edith slit her wrists and killed herself.

However, when the Doctor and Charley landed in 1906 at Edward Grove, where Edith had previously worked as a scullery maid, history couldn't decide if Edith murdered herself or not because Charley—the cause of her suicide—still lived. Cycled through the temporal paradox, Edith's repeated deaths brought Edward Grove to life. (*For*

a full explanation, see Sidebar.)

Edward Grove's intelligence strengthens enough to possess a butler named Shaughnessy, allowing it to speak with the Doctor. Simultaneously, Edward shifts Charley into the shadow realm, where the murdered Edith resides until the time loop recycles. The Doctor finds Edward Grove beyond reason, unwilling to relinquish its scant bit of existence even if the servants remain trapped in the murderous loop forever. More dangerously, Edith and Charley succumb to Edward's psionic force, threatening to kill themselves in the shadow realm and thus make the loop permanent.

Out of options, the Doctor orders the remnants of Shaughnessy's intelligence to strangle him. The obedient Shaughnessy complies, killing the Doctor and sending him into the shadow realm. Hurriedly, the Doctor talks Charley out of killing herself. Together, they convince Edith to decisively choose life over death, thereby breaking the paradox's uncertainty. Edith refuses to murder herself again, snapping the paradox and dissipating Edward Grove's mental force.

Instantly, the Doctor and Charley return to life, observing a far more confident Edith resume her work in Edward Grove, which is now a quite normal Edwardian household readying itself for Christmas. But as they depart, the Doctor grows uneasy about Charley's still unresolved paradoxical existence.

MEMORABLE MOMENTS

The detached butler Shaughnessy, when the cook gets smothered with her own plum pudding: "This is dreadful news. To lose another member of staff over Christmas is bad enough. To lose the plum pudding makes it even worse."

The sarcastic Doctor, on the impossible suggestion that chauffeur Frederick committed suicide: "Yes, I imagine so. It's quite clear that Frederick brought the car into the house, ran himself over with it and put it back outside before he finally expired."

Later, Shaughnessy pulls a gun on the Doctor and Charley, compelling the Doctor to comment, "That's not a very nice way for a well-bred butler to behave, is it?", followed by Charley's hysterical: "You do realize that holding us at gunpoint means [you're going to top] of our list of suspects."

The Doctor ominously declares at one point: "Edward Grove is the killer. And we are standing within his belly." Even more dramatically, the Doctor implores Edward to give up his illusion of life for the servants' sake. Edward slowly responds, "You are asking me to commit suicide," to which the Doctor replies: "I am. I'm sorry."

Finally, in the shadow realm, the Doctor implores Charley to live because: "Without you, I would just be a lonely old man, rattling around in the TARDIS with no one to talk to, my life going round and round without meaning." Together, the Doctor and Charley convince Edith to live—an awesome moment steeped in optimism.

SEX AND SPIRITS In what's possibly the best "Who" audio-related double-entendre, the cook snidely tells Edith: "You have designs on my plum pudding."

The chauffeur Frederick serves as a representation of servants who viewed Edith as a sex toy, not an actual human being (*see Sidebar*). In the Edward Grove paradox, Frederick bangs Mary, the ladies' maid, but—as with Edith's real-life dalliance—dismisses the event as "a bit of fun." Frederick finally concludes, giving voice to the emptiness in Edith's own life: "The likes of you and me, Mary. We haven't the right to love anyone."

ASS-WHUPPINGS Crazily enough, there are a lot of murders… but nobody actually dies. Well, except Edward Grove, if indeed it had a life to lose.

Edith gets drowned in a sink, suffocated with a sink plunger and beaten to death with a broom handle. Frederick gets run over by a fast-moving car… in the living room. The cook, Mrs. Baddeley, gets stuffed full of her own plum pudding. Even the Doctor dies at one point, arranging his own strangulation to save everyone's hide.

AUDIO TIE-INS The TARDIS is still trying to avoid Singapore, 1930 ("Invaders from Mars"), but finally arrives there in "Seasons of Fear." Charley's paradoxical survival from this point increasingly upsets the web of time, leading to events in "Neverland."

CHARACTER DEVELOPMENT

• *The Doctor:* The Doctor feels he's been too safe and predictable "these last few incarnations," always setting coordinates and *deciding* where they're going.

He loves plum pudding and brandied butter. He recalls Gudol's Custard, manufactured in Leeds, sold at the dawn of the 20th century. He also adores Christmas, but finds the anticipation better than the actual event.

• *Charlotte Pollard:* Charley was born in 1912 [making her currently 19]. She hails from an upper-class family that's able to afford servants.

She loves condensed milk, but hates custard. By her estimation, Edith—during her days as a cook in the Pollard household—always made too much

This book is not endorsed by the BBC. Doctor Who and TARDIS are trademarks of the BBC.

109

plum pudding at Christmas. The pudding's thready bits made Charley afraid of breaking a tooth.

Edward Grove can mentally influence Charley into adopting the role of the household lordship's daughter.

• *The Doctor and Charley:* He loves the dark, whereas she only likes it within moderation. Charley helped the Doctor find a first edition of *Oliver Twist* on Charing Cross Road.

• *Edith Thompson:* She sings *Hark the Herald Angels Sing* because it's the only song she knows. Even then, she hums the bits where she doesn't know the words.

Edith can't read or write. She started work at age 14.

• *Edward Grove:* Edward can only influence events on the stroke of the hour, because it only feels fully alive when it hears the clock chime. It can speed up or slow down time in the two hours that compose the paradox, but it can't stop it entirely. It has trouble concentrating on more than one thing at a time.

The sentient Edward Grove exists in something of a pocket dimension. Nothing exists outside the house's lower quarters, so the servants actively intervene—on Edward's behalf—to stop the Doctor from venturing out the front door or going upstairs.

Edward lusts after life for its own sake. It's impossible to think Edward could ever do something with its scant bit of existence. Edward holds some affection for the Doctor and Charley, since her temporal paradox birthed it.

• *The TARDIS:* After a certain point, the TARDIS gets incorporated into Edward's spatial loop. The Doctor and Charley try to depart in the Ship, but the console room transforms into part of the house. From that point, the TARDIS' exterior exists in the scullery, but walking through its police box shell only takes you through to another scullery with another police box [similar, but not identical, to the effect in "Logopolis"].

The TARDIS console only gives blank readings with regards to Edward Grove's location.

ORGANIZATIONS *Edward's Servants:* Servants caught in the Edward Grove time loop include Edith, the butler Shaughnessy, the cook Mrs. Baddeley, the lady's maid Mary and the chauffeur Frederick. Each of them represent a personality type who plagued Edith in her working life. Mrs. Baddeley is a representation of Edith's older self, who worked in the Pollard household.

As part of the time loop, the servants forget their individual identities and very much become slaves

to their occupations. They hold little like or dislike for one another. They cannot identify the year [1906], yet paradoxically have knowledge of people/objects extending up to 1930, such as Agatha Christie [first published in 1920] and Chryslers [first released in 1924].

The servants normally go about their business dulled by the time loop's set routine, although Edward can command them to do its bidding.

They cannot describe the Lordship and Ladyship they're supposedly serving, unable to identify their true master as Edward.

PHENOMENA *Living Houses:* The Doctor calculates the odds of a house gaining sentience as "one in several billion."

• *The Time Loop:* The time loop holds a duration of two hours—the interval between when Charley and Edith paradoxically meet [10 p.m. at Edward Grove house, 1906] and Edith's suicide [midnight at the Pollard house, 1930], as those are the two main events in conflict with one another.

When the Doctor and Charley arrive at Edward Grove, they're initially out of synch with the main time loop. Until the clock chimes and Edward can amalgamate them into the servants' timeline, the Doctor and Charley exist on a separate time track. They explore the seemingly empty house, unable to leave much impression on it. They can't hear the wind outside. Charley knocks over a jam jar, but Edward spontaneously puts it back together [complete with a note letting the time travelers know they're being watched]. Flames literally stand immobile in the fireplace, unless the Doctor and Charley burn something—thus creating a brief access point into the servants' time track.

As a phantasm, Charley can write words in the dust, but cannot erase dust words written by Edith in the servants' time track. Phantasm Charley's more attuned to the time loop than the Doctor, as she can hear Edith singing through the time veil. While a phantasm, Charley sometimes pops into the shadow dimension, thereby appearing frozen to the Doctor.

Once the Doctor and Charley enter the servants' time track, they instantly get teleported back to the pantry—the site of their arrival—each time the clock strikes midnight and the loop resets itself. During this transition, they can hear the Edward Grove's heartbeats. Eating Mrs. Baddeley's plum pudding makes Charley revert to a child-like state.

AT THE END OF THE DAY Once in a blue moon, a "Doctor Who" product rolls out that's so successful, it's frightening. Along those lines, "The

THE EDITH PARADOX

As the Doctor himself discovers, the Edward Grove time loop patterns itself after Edith's suicide. However, the true *origin* of the time loop—i.e. the event that started it in motion—is Charley's paradoxical death aboard the *R-101*.

EDITH'S STORY

In the original history, a young Edith Thompson worked in a number of family houses, including Edward Grove. The lowly Edith endured abuse after abuse for years, and indeed, it's easy to see how life as an Edwardian servant might make anyone think about doing themselves in.

As a scullery maid, Edith was constantly made to repeat, "I'm nothing. I'm nobody," as her personal mantra. The butlers bullied Edith and the rest of the staff weren't much better. She craved love and had sex with a chauffeur in his Chrysler in 1926, only to have him pretend it never happened, passing it off as a "bit of fun."

Later, a middle-aged Edith worked as a cook in the Pollard household. There, she formed a warm love for young Charley, who at least treated her like a human being and brought some humanity into her soulless world. The relationship was rather lopsided, as Charley failed to notice Edith's love. Charley at least remembered Edith's name and smiled at her, prompting Edith to make plum pudding at Christmas, just for Charley's amusement [not that Charley ever liked it much].

CHARLEY'S DEMISE and EDITH'S SUICIDE

In November, 1930, the Pollard household received word of Charley's death aboard the *R-101*, after her diary was found in the wreckage. The house went into mourning, but Edith, a mere cook, wasn't allowed to grieve.

On Christmas Eve, Edith found no reason to continue living and went down to kitchen, picked up a carving knife and opened her wrists. She took a long time to die, but nobody answered her screams. She finally expired, cold and alone.

THE EDWARD GROVE PARADOX

Edith's life might have simply ended there, but for the fact that a time-travelling Charley impossibly turned up at Edward Grove in 1906. When that happened, history failed to decide if Edith—who died in direct correlation to Charley's death—was alive or not.

The paradox tried to resolve itself, replaying Edith's murder again and again until Edward Grove gained sentience. From that point, Edward gained the strength to manipulate time, murdering its servants—in ways designed to emulate Edith's suicide—to further nourish itself.

The murders typically follow the same pattern, each occurring as the clock strikes:

• A young woman [Edith, who hollered in pain when she slit her wrists] screams.

• Seconds later, a servant winds up dead in an impossible fashion.

• The surviving servants swear blind that the victim committed suicide, even when that's plainly impossible.

• The survivors return to their business, more upset about the victim's work getting left undone than the loss of life.

• Everyone gets resurrected at midnight.

REPERCUSSIONS

The Doctor and Charley decisively convince Edith to *not* commit suicide. Moreover, they compel Shaughnessy to praise Edith's work. As such, they make Edith feel better appreciated, nurturing her self-worth in future.

Truth to tell, the paradox gets so tangled, almost nothing can suitably resolve it. If Edith lives instead of dying in 1930, then none of the events in "The Chimes of Midnight" could ever have taken place. However, it's best to ignore this fact and simply enjoy the drama.

Final point: None of this, of course, resolves Charley's paradoxical survival. As such, the Doctor and Charley do good by Edith, but it's rather like treating a symptom while not actually curing the cold.

Chimes of Midnight" not only emerges as the show-stopper of the new McGann audio "season," but it's a script that nearly makes you sit down and weep, especially in regards to Edith's loneliness. Writer Rob Shearman has commented that writing this audio kept him awake at night, and it's easy to see why—given that it puts love and malice into a cocktail shaker, blending both into a tearful drink. Overall, it's glorious for forwarding such optimism amid violence and death, and it makes us glad to be alive.

DID YOU KNOW?

• Shearman posts that he viewed his previous Big Finish audio, "The Holy Terror," as a comedy that grows into a horror. By contrast, "Chimes" is written as a horror story which grows into a comedy [albeit a very black comedy].

• Shearman desperately points out that in "Chimes," Charley finds a tin made by Goodall's: a genuine Edwardian company who produced tinned dessert. [Shearman stresses this to show off his minimal research.]

SEASONS OF FEAR

By Paul Cornell and Caroline Symcox

Release Date: March 2002
Order: Big Finish "Doctor Who" CD #30

TARDIS CREW The eighth Doctor and Charley.

TRAVEL LOG Roman fort, 305 AD; court of King Edward the Confessor, London, 1055 AD; a Hellfire Club base, Wickham Caves, Buckinghamshire, 1806; Singapore, December 31, 1930; Alex Grayle's family home, circa the same period.

STORY SUMMARY With coaxing, the TARDIS materializes in Singapore, 1930, allowing Charley to make a scheduled rendezvous ("Storm Warning") with her friend Alex. The Doctor waits for Charley in a tea garden, but suddenly, an immortal named Sebastian Grayle walks in, sits down and boastfully claims he's already "killed" the Doctor in future. Grayle takes additional satisfaction in announcing he helped his unnamed alien masters capture Earth, Gallifrey and the entire Universe—and that what the Doctor perceives as Singapore, 1930, is merely a shadow timeline, created so Grayle could gloat at his mortal enemy.

After Grayle departs, the Doctor, having absolutely no recollection of him, researches Grayle's lineage. With effort, the Doctor and Charley learn of a "Decurion Sebastius Gralae" at a Roman fort, 305 AD. Travelling there, the Doctor and Charley find the still-mortal, impressionable Gralae serving as minister to the god Mithras. All seems fairly normal until Gralae locks up his fellow Mithras worshippers and offers to let his newfound alien masters feed on their life energy.

As a reward, Gralae's far-distant employers channel a power stream through a black hole. The energy boost radiates through Gralae's body and greatly extends his lifespan, just as the Doctor frees Gralae's hostages, depriving his employers a food source. Gralae escapes, forcing his masters to postpone their plans.

The Doctor and Charley hastily return to the TARDIS, determining that the aliens' energy beam originated from the Ordinand System. The Doctor calculates that Ordinand aligns with the Sol System every 750 years, suggesting the date when Gralae's employers will try again to dominate Earth.

In London, 1055 AD, the Doctor and Charley thwart Grayle a second time (*see History*). Grayle again escapes, prompting another confrontation in Buckinghamshire, 1806. But this time, Grayle succeeds in using his masters' technical expertise to build a transmat device. In short order, Grayle's contraption brings a travel pod with five of his masters—the bull-like Nimon ("The Horns of Nimon")—to Earth. The Nimon plan to consume Earth's resources, then use the planet as a jumping point to spread throughout the Universe, bringing Grayle's prophesied timeline to pass.

Desperate, the Doctor and Charley reposition the TARDIS and block the time corridor between Ordinand and the Sol System, preventing more Nimon from transporting through. In response, Grayle and the Earth-based Nimon materialize their travel pod onboard the TARDIS. Overrun, the Doctor creates a dimensional conduit between the TARDIS and the Roman fort, 305 AD. By opening the console room doors, the Doctor sucks himself and the five Nimon into the Time Vortex, but Grayle secures the Ship. Grayle celebrates for having "killed" the Doctor, even as Charley, on the Doctor's previous instructions, puts the Ship on return course to the Roman fort.

The Doctor free-falls through the time corridor and arrives at the Roman fort a short while before his previous visit. Quickly, the Doctor rallies the fort troopers against the Nimon, who arrive moments later. The Doctor then meets the more-impressionable Sebastius Gralae for the "first" time, convincing him to swear true allegiance to Mithras, not the murderous Nimon. Moments later, the TARDIS materializes. The older, hardened Grayle threatens Charley's life, but the more honorable Gralae, appalled by Grayle's lack of chivalry, runs his future self through with a rustless sword. Grayle dies, and the soldiers kill off the Nimon.

Afterward, the Doctor provides Gralae with enough gold coins to buy out his commission and marry his beloved, a woman named Julia. The Nimon-dominated timeline never comes to pass, leaving Charley bewildered, as the now-dead Grayle paradoxically set everything in motion by appearing in Singapore. The Doctor admits the adventure's details aren't perfect, but says history will iron out the wrinkles and accordingly edit their memories.

MEMORABLE MOMENTS It's anachronistic (but quite hysterical) when Cornell and Symcox treat a Mithras ceremony like a warped version of modern-day church service. Mithras follower Lucillius comments that with Gralae absent,

"We're going to need someone to manhandle the entrails," afterward telling Gralae, "Fine, you're here now, brother. Go and get the entrails," when he arrives. With all the verve of a pastor reading the bulletin, Gralae announces, "Before we proceed to the bloodletting, I have a few announcements." Best of all, Lucillius tells the over-zealous Gralae, "Will you please stop believing in things, Decurian? It's very messy!"

The Doctor memorably outlines the difference between himself and the nigh-immortal Grayle: "How would it be if everything was the same? If the rainy autumn lasted forever and spring never came. At least I change. I stumble my way through bodies like I own a particularly dangerous bicycle. Grayle never changes. Not who he is. Not inside. So Time piles on top of him and kills everything good."

Gold digger Lucy Martin (*see Sex and Spirits*), trying to comprehend the Doctor's instructions of "Fast Return Switch, three times fast": "I am sure in the culture you both come from, they are passionate and meaningful words."

SEX AND SPIRITS Charley locks lips with her friend Alex Grayle. She praises Alex for dancing divinely and "always having something stunning in his buttonhole."

Gralae lacks the cash needed to marry his beloved Julia. He starts out extremely chivalrous, learning disdain for women throughout the centuries. Thanks to the Doctor's intervention, young Gralae and Julia get married.

The Doctor previously left King Edward's wife Edith at the altar (*see History*). The Doctor's "very fond" of Edith, but he just doesn't do weddings. Charley went to an orgy once, but she didn't stay.

In 1806, hit-and-run gold digger Lucy Martin proposes to Grayle. She's nearly married eight wealthy men in the last year, leaving them all at the altar.

Charley suggests wearing a nice dress in 1806 Buckinghamshire, but the Doctor worries it would be too inconspicuous. Charley's forced to clarify: "I was talking about me [not you]."

ASS-WHUPPINGS In Part 1, the Nimon transmat beam destroys the Roman fort [the Doctor evacuates it beforehand].

Grayle poisons Charley in 1055 AD, but the TARDIS console room nanites heal her. She later slugs Grayle unconscious with the TARDIS hatstand. Grayle also stabs the Doctor twice in an Edwardian dungeon, and gives Charley a harmless nick on the ear. At the end of Part 2, the Doctor—enraged at Grayle for threatening Charley—pitch-

es him off a roof. Grayle survives thanks to his Nimon-granted invulnerability, a factor the Doctor somewhat—we stress *somewhat*—took into account.

In 1806, the Doctor drains away some of Grayle's energy with a rustless sword (*see History*), making him look about 70. Grayle nails the Doctor with a dagger. He lets the Nimon suck life force energy from Hellfire Club associates. Grayle kills con artist Richard Martin, dumping him down a chimney. Richard survives, but a malevolent force later eats him (*see Audio Tie-Ins*).

In the grand finale, the Roman soldiers take about 60 casualties while butchering the Nimon.

TV TIE-INS The Nimon previously battled the fourth Doctor, Romana and K9 in "The Horns of Nimon." The Doctor mentions "my Aunt Flavia" ("The Five Doctors"), probably as a joke. He now carries anti-radiation pills ("The Daleks").

Like most of his other incarnations ("The Sea Devils," "The Androids of Tara," etc.), the eighth Doctor excels at swordplay.

NOVEL TIE-INS The Doctor and Charley spend three weeks with the Abbot of Felsecar (Cornell's *Love and War*) tracking Grayle's genealogy. Gallifreyan meditation techniques help the free-falling Doctor navigate/survive in the Time Vortex (Cornell's *The Shadows of Avalon*).

AUDIO TIE-INS   The Time Vortex is now churning with storms thanks to Charley's paradoxical survival ("Storm Warning"), a timeline disruption that leads to events in "The Time of the Daleks" and "Neverland." As part of this, the Doctor and Charley cite Benjamin Franklin as an American president, scientist and magician. The TARDIS kept avoiding Singapore, 1930 partly for this reason [because Charley was never meant to arrive there].

Amid the brouhaha, a Dalek randomly appears at the Roman fort in 305 AD—a bit of foreshadowing for "The Time of the Daleks."

The Doctor mentions his mum used to recite a Gallifreyan nursery rhyme about Zagreus (previously mentioned in "Project: Twilight" and *Instruments of Darkness*), which spoke of people vanishing up paradoxical staircases. Charley's friend Alex is Grayle's descendent. Ergo, it's possible that Grayle retroactively arranged for a pre-TARDIS Charley ("Storm Warning") to become friends with Alex, simply to arrange their eventual meeting in Singapore, 1930.

The Doctor and Charley previously tangled with a Hellfire Club extension in "Minuet in Hell."

"Seasons of Fear" ends with a conversation between the Doctor and a knowledgeable stranger (revealed as Rassilon in "Neverland").

Lucy Martin witnesses Grayle kill her partner-in-crime, Richard Martin. But at story's end, various temporal shenanigans retroactively bring Richard back to life. In another prelude to "Neverland," an evil presence who looks and sounds like Charley consumes both the time-travelling Lucy and the paradoxical Richard as rich sources of chronon energy. Unlike most Big Finish audios, "Seasons of Fear" runs without the closing music, driving home the cliffhanger.

TIE-INS Charley uses the TARDIS' Fast Return Switch, first seen in "The Edge of Destruction" and crucially used in "Neverland." Nanites in the TARDIS console room ("The Shadow of the Scourge," several New Adventures) heal Charley, but they take longer to seal the Doctor's wounds.

CHARACTER DEVELOPMENT

• *The Doctor:* The Doctor likes the Singapore Hilton's tea gardens, because the humidity there isn't too oppressive. He wears a hat, but gives it to Grayle because it looks better on him. London, 1055, is one of the Doctor's favorite times and places. He rarely eats meat. He smells of honey and often lets his tea cool too long. He refers to the proper timeline as "Time Classic."

• *Charlotte Pollard:* She previously visited Alex Grayle at his family home, venturing into the attic to retrieve a cricket bat. She chats with King Edward and Edith about the Charleston. She here learns about plutonium, and previously read a lot of Jane Austen.

• *The Doctor and Charley:* At the Roman fort, the Doctor adopts the name "Ambrosia Clemenses." Charley traffics herself as "Daisia Daisia." King Edward recognizes the Doctor as the "the Reverend Doctor of Bruges," with Charley announcing herself as "Lady Charlotte." In 1806, the Doctor identifies himself as Sir Peter Pollard, her father.

She believes the Doctor often plays the fool to make his opponents talk more. The Doctor lets Charley win at Scrabble [or so she believes].

After dealing with Grayle, the Doctor and Charley return to Singapore, 1930, to usher in the New Year.

• *Sebastian Grayle (a.k.a. Decurion Sebastius Gralae):* Gralae hails from Londinium. He's extremely chivalrous, but he felt slighted when his eldest brother inherited the family villa. He changed his name to Gralae, distancing himself from his relatives. He accepted the Nimons' offer

of employment partly for the money—but partly out of spite.

After the Roman fort debacle, the nigh-immortal Gralae (re-naming himself Grayle) outlived his brothers and received the family estate. He spent 80 years in penitence in a monk community on the Northern Isles but eventually rejoined society. He married 12 times, with no children, grievously watching each wife die of old age.

In 1055 AD, Grayle traffics as the Bishop Leofric of Exeter. He also held position as the Bishop of Cornwall. In 1806, he's learned falconry skills and has usurped a Hellfire Club chapter to his own ends. By this point, he's an excellent swordsman.

The Nimon extend Grayle's lifespan, but he would need to physically travel through a black hole to become permanently immortal. By decrying the Nimon, the younger Gralae denies himself immortality.

Grayle's normally impervious to harm, but rustless swords drain away his energy. He's immune to radioactivity and a little afraid of his masters.

Temporal mechanics elude Grayle, since it never occurs to him that gloating in Singapore might actually get the Doctor's attention.

• *The TARDIS:* The Ship can track transmat beams. It has a medical wing. Its communications systems can contact the Ordinand System.

It can also trail DNA patterns [possibly biodata, "The Deadly Assassin"] through the Time Vortex. This works best if the Doctor feeds a DNA analysis directly into the console.

The Ship can hover in the Vortex, then lock onto a mental signature and create a limited wormhole to its destination.

ALIEN RACES *The Nimon:* Dominating Earth would give them a bridgehead to conquer other planets that currently elude them. They're vulnerable to rustless iron, but their tough hides resist most other weapons.

SHIPS *Nimon Travel Pod:* It sports a sleek new design with increased maneuverability (but it's still a bit tight around cosmic corners).

PHENOMENA *Time Revision:* The Doctor claims Grayle's interference in history means the Laws of Time are suspended, enabling the Doctor to intervene. Charley's conflicting memories about this story reconcile while she sleeps.

HISTORY Circa 1700 BC, a single Nimon scout appeared on Earth, giving the Persians tokens of appeasement. The Nimon offered up a rustless sword—forged from material that had traveled

through a black hole—while stupidly failing to consider that they might turn it against him. The warrior Mithras slew the Nimon with the sword, furthering myths about a demon bull intent on ravaging the world, plus fables about slaying beasts with rustless iron. The other Nimon abandoned aspirations on Earth until their gambit with Gralae.

• The Doctor helped save King Edward's father, King Ethelred the Unready (978-1016) from a fever that would've killed him.

• King Edward (1003-1066) and his equally shrewd wife Edith enjoyed a highly successful reign in England. Before their marriage, the Doctor met Edward and Edith at their respective fathers' courts. The Doctor looked forward to discussing politics with Edith, the most brilliant tactician of her age, but she viewed the Time Lord in a much more romantic light and proposed. He tried and failed to weasel out of the marriage, finally pulling a runner to avoid becoming part of English history.

As "Bishop Leofric of Exeter," Grayle used his Nimon-granted knowledge to forge plutonium, a ready-made power source for the Nimons' travel equipment, during King Edward's era. The Doctor thwarted Grayle's schemes, instructing Edward and Edith how to dispose of the plutonium, and immunizing the court with anti-radiation pills. Even so, the Doctor speculates the latent radiation might explain the screwed-up genetics of Edward's successors.

AT THE END OF THE DAY Suitably ambitious, this is another win for Big Finish in 2002. The plot admittedly requires the story to jump from time zone to time zone, so it frays around the edges a bit—rather like a reliable, comfortable pair of jeans with a few tears in the side—but "Seasons of Fear" nonetheless keeps things moving and delivers a flavorful overall effect. Indeed, when *TV Zone* completely wronged this story with a 2/10 rating, we nearly swam to England, broke the magazine's doors down with an axe and demanded a retraction.

DID YOU KNOW?

• While at a convention bar, Big Finish producer Gary Russell to Paul Cornell that he use the Nimon as villains for "Seasons of Fear," because their voices—Russell felt—were ideal for audio.

• The "Seasons of Fear" production team taped their Nimon voices from inside a cupboard, to better give them an echoing quality.

EMBRACE THE DARKNESS

By Nicholas Briggs

Release Date: April 2002
Order: Big Finish "Doctor Who" CD #31

TARDIS CREW The eighth Doctor and Charley.

TRAVEL LOG Planet Cimmeria IV, time unknown (but clearly the future).

STORY SUMMARY On the sunless, mineral-rich planet Cimmeria IV, a trio of human engineers erect 12 Energy Projection Units (EPUs)—i.e. artificial suns—in orbit. Once lit, the EPUs will illuminate the supposedly uninhabited Cimmeria IV, allowing mining operations to commence. Before they can light the EPUs, however, an unidentified wave of alien particles hits the engineer's base and robs it of power, leaving the scientists completely blind.

Meanwhile, the in-flight TARDIS stumbles upon a Type 70 TARDIS fleet. Anxious in an effort to avoid hassle, the Doctor hurriedly changes course and arrives in the Cimmeria System. The Doctor and Charley eventually find the EPU control base and discover its team of engineers have been robbed of more than just their sight—they've been robbed of their eyeballs. Before long, Charley feels intense burning in her eyes, suggesting the alien particles responsible for the engineers' plight are scorching her retinas also.

The Doctor's party corrals a Cimmerian—a small, childlike creature adapted for life on the sunless planet—and the Doctor realizes that the eyeless natives "see" by sense of taste. The insular Cimmerians have equipment that projects particles designed to corrode intruders' technology, particles that inadvertently burn out human retinas.

The Cimmerian, possessed of an innate healing power, restores Charley and the engineers to health, but it falls unconscious as a result. Theorizing that the EPUs might burn off the Cimmerian particles and thereby keep everyone from further harm, the Doctor ignites the artificial suns, just as the Cimmerian awakes, warning that the sunlight will attract hostile aliens named the Solarians.

The Doctor's group learns that, long ago, the plague-riddled Solarians implored the Cimmerians to cure them. Psychologically unable to refuse, the Cimmerians healed the Solarians but nearly

died from the effort. Unable to continue but still unable to refuse, the Cimmerians extinguished their own sun, thereby depriving energy to the Solarians' solar-powered spaceships. The Solarians departed, and the drained Cimmerians went into hibernation for millennia, evolving into creatures adapted for life in total darkness.

As predicted, a solar-powered Solarian fleet enters the Cimmeria System, drawn to the EPUs' energy. A few Solarians land in miniature tanks and confront the Doctor's party, shocked to find anyone still living in Cimmeria's darkness. When the lead Solarian emerges from his mini-tank, the Doctor's group pegs the Cimmerians and Solarians as genetic cousins.

The head Solarian identifies his group as archaeologists, searching for the remnants of a "long-dead" civilization abused by his ancestors. The Solarians and Cimmerians begin the long process of reconciliation, allowing the Doctor and Charley to quietly slip away.

MEMORABLE MOMENTS Part 1 contains a whale of a cliffhanger, with Charley spying the tormented engineers and asking, "You don't know, do you?", then announcing their eyes are missing.

ASS-WHUPPINGS The three engineers, Orllensa, Ferras and Haliard, endure an paralyzing amount of eye pain, yet don't realize, until Charley points it out, that they've lost their eyes entirely. Charley's eyes also feel pain in Part 2, but she recovers. The initial Cimmerian dies after healing the engineers.

TV TIE-INS The artificial sun system in "Embrace the Darkness" resembles the one over Pluto from "The Sunmakers," although there's no clear connection.

NOVEL TIE-INS Type 70 TARDISes are considered "new" on Gallifrey, further proof that the Big Finish McGann audios occur before most of the eighth Doctor novel adventures. [Older models are certainly used by *The Shadows of Avalon*, when Compassion notably emerges as a Type 102.]

The Doctor's encountered a few races with the name "Solarians," denoting that there's no relation between these creatures and the "Solarians" in *Decalog:* "Prisoners of the Sun."

AUDIO TIE-INS "Neverland" explains why the Doctor and Charley find a flotilla of Type 70 TARDISes just hanging out in the Time Vortex.

The security robot ROSM somehow detects Charley's existence as a paradox ("Storm Warn-

ing"). The TARDIS remains temperamental, as with virtually every other McGann audio Season 2 story.

CHARACTER DEVELOPMENT

• *The Doctor:* The Doctor always meant to find out why the Cimmerian sun disappeared (*see History*). Never much for crowds, he feels at home in dark, foreboding locations.

• *Charlotte Pollard:* Charley knows how to access the TARDIS databank. She refers to seeing yachts coming across at the Cowes Regatta—Cowes being a coastal town on the Isle of Wight, the Regatta being a big social event. [Briggs adds: "I thought it was quite likely that Charley may have witnessed it, probably sitting on Calshot Beach, which faces Cowes from Central Southern England, across the Solent."] She knows how to play draughts.

• *Orllensa:* Head engineer for the EPU project. Her previous missions haven't gone terribly well either. One entailed an undercover terrorist, who pulled a bomb and declared, "The human race has no place in space." Orllensa reflexively hit her with a spanner, killing her.

• *ROSM (a.k.a. Rescue Operational Security Module G723):* Robotic rescue module, with a central intelligence in control of a couple dozen assault drones.

ROSM's historical records make no mention of the TARDIS. It deems the Doctor's sonic screwdriver as highly sophisticated. The ROSM has a containment field for potential biohazards. Cimmerian anti-technology particles can damage its core systems.

The Doctor's sonic screwdriver could initially futz up ROSM's orientation centers, but the robot develops a counter-measure.

• *Professor Astrov:* Throxillan scientist, working at a location named "Central," who drafted up specifications for the EPU operation at Cimmeria IV. He also designed ROSM G723.

• *The TARDIS:* The TARDIS can park itself in space, then roll forward at a rate of 50 years per second—allowing a fast-forward glimpse of events [although that's still a damnably fast rate, either suggesting one needs the Doctor's Time Lord eyes to actually see anything of use, or that the Ship selectively edits items of note].

The Ship can detect the temporal energy discharge of Type 70 TARDISes. Hover mode remains tricky even under ideal conditions. The Ship's impervious to ROSM's scans.

ALIEN RACES *Time Lords:* They rarely travel anywhere in great numbers.

• *Cimmerians:* Modern-day Cimmerians don't understand the concept of "eyes," having forgotten they ever possessed such organs. They look child-like and anemic, standing waist-tall. Cimmerians have flat, almost invisible noses, with a small slit for a mouth.

Their healing power evidently adapts to the physiology of other races (in this case, humans), but the effort dangerously drains them.

The Cimmerians' molecular technology releases particles that corrode technology, or enables the Cimmerians to phase through solid matter. The Cimmerians can also displace matter, as proven when they sink the engineers' base beneath the surface of Cimmeria IV.

• *Solarians:* Essentially Cimmerians with eyes.

ALIEN PLANETS *Cimmeria IV:* The planet's freezing, quite naturally, because it lacks a sun. Also, it lacks a breathable atmosphere [suggesting the Cimmerians either have survival chambers or simply don't need to breathe].

• *Throxillia:* Located several hundred light years from Cimmeria IV. The planet contains an offshoot of humanity—the race sponsoring the EPU/mining project on Cimmeria IV.

STUFF YOU NEED *Energy Projection Units (EPUs):* Composed of a dozen artificial suns, set in a ring above Cimmeria IV and slaved to a central tripod on the engineers' station. The EPUs have independent power storage units.

• *Cimmerian History Stew:* Cimmerians mainly sense by taste. Ergo, they store their history records in a "boiling mud pie" that smells like potatoes. Humans and Time Lords, as Charley and the Doctor prove, can ingest this soup without harm.

SHIPS *Solarian Ships:* Travel in space by use of solar sails.

POSSIBLE HISTORY The Cimmerians and Solarians certainly share an ancestry. Briggs doesn't specify, but it's possible that some time ago, Cimmerian colonists [later called the Solarians] left their homeworld and settled in an unknown region. But a thousand years ago, a plague devastated the Solarians and they returned to their ancestral homeworld for help.

HISTORY The Cimmerians healed the Solarians, but millions of Cimmerians died from exertion. Finally, the Cimmerians released their light-blocking particles and extinguished their sun, convincing the Solarians to depart. Afterward, the devastated Cimmerians under-

went accelerated evolution to survive in their new environment. They also forgot about their genetic ties to the Solarians, crafting myths that depicted them as enemies.

• Early Throxillan space travelers used solar sails on their craft.

• Led by Professor Astrov, the Throxillians recently conducted fly-bys of the Cimmeria System, finding it mineral-rich and uninhabited. Nothing recorded explained the system's loss of a sun. The Throxillians deemed the planet ideal for mining operations, since the lack of an indigenous population kept it outside the Galactic Charter of Species Protection. Astrov's surveyors dubbed the system "Cimmeria," meaning "of darkness." (The modern-day Cimmerians don't recognize the name, but they understand its symbolism.)

• Throxillians in this time zone routinely undergo genetic modification, even in the womb, to eliminate diseases.

AT THE END OF THE DAY A rare example of a work that's so off-kilter, we barely know how to respond. With "Embrace the Darkness," the accomplished Nick Briggs ("Dalek Empire," etc.) seeds his story with a two-dimensional supporting cast, whom we learn little about save their occupation. Most damning of all, everything revolves around a misunderstanding, becoming what we'd call "anti-climate" in polite company and "extremely lame" if we're being more truthful. It'd be like if some "terrifying" figure came up and knocked on your door... then you opened it to find your Cousin Phil standing there. That being the case, we finished this story going, "What the hell was all the fuss about?", then filed it on a shelf and forgot all about it.

DID YOU KNOW?

• When Nick Briggs wrote "Embrace the Darkness," he had utterly no idea that aliens named "Solarians" had previously appeared in *Decalog:* "Prisoners of the Sun." He went so far as to double-check with producer Gary Russell, who also swore that—so far as he knew—the term had never appeared in "Who" before. Even so, Briggs covered his ass by including a line that the familiar term "Solarians" applies to more than one race.

• The term "ROSM" stems from Rossum's *Universal Robots*, the Karel Capek play that re-invented the word "robot" to mean an artificial human being.

This book is not endorsed by the BBC. Doctor Who and TARDIS are trademarks of the BBC.

117

THE TIME OF THE DALEKS

By Justin Richards

Release Date: May 2002
Order: Big Finish "Doctor Who" audio #32

TARDIS CREW The eighth Doctor and Charley.

TRAVEL LOG New Britain, Earth, the near future; Stratford-Upon-Avon, September 19, 1572.

STORY SUMMARY In the Time Vortex, the Daleks seek to capitalize on the sudden appearance of a temporal rift, hoping to collect its energy and improve their time travel capabilities. Numbering 1,700 strong, a Dalek warfleet enters the Vortex and deploys a Temporal Extinction Device, intending to detonate it, enlarge the rift and harvest its power. However, the experiment fails, pounding the Dalek fleet with temporal shockwaves.

Reeling, the Dalek command ship scans for a secondary time travel device, locating such equipment in London, the mid-21st century. The Daleks open a temporal corridor to the secondary site and dispatch a pilot and two temporal specialists there, hoping to find a temporal stabilizer capable of steadying their battered fleet. In New Britain, the Daleks find General Mariah Learman, a benevolent dictator, using a time viewer made from mirrors and clocks (*see Stuff You Need*) to scan history, hoping to view Shakespeare's debut performances. The Dalek pilot dies on arrival, apparently obliterated by a freak side effect of the time corridor, but the remaining Daleks and Learman strike an unholy bargain.

Learman offers to let the Daleks upgrade her equipment, thereby creating a suitable temporal stabilizer. In turn, Learman—believing that Shakespeare's genius is wasted on humanity, and that only she can appreciate his work—crazily asks the Daleks to travel back in time and assassinate Shakespeare, removing him from history. If successful, the Daleks will provide Learman with a temporally protected copy of Shakespeare's works, making her the only person who remembers the great playwright.

The Daleks begin work, but suddenly, mass droves of people in Britain start forgetting Shakespeare ever existed. In desperation, a group of rebels tap into Learman's mirror system, travel back to 1572 and spirit away an eight-year-old

Shakespeare. The rebels return to the present and disguise young Shakespeare as one of Learman's kitchen workers—inadvertently protecting him from assassination, but causing the very historical disruption they'd tried to prevent.

Meanwhile, the Doctor off-handedly mentions Shakespeare to Charley, becoming perplexed when Charley swears blind she's never heard of the famous playwright. Baffled, the Doctor finds a time corridor operating between Shakespeare's era and mid-21st century London, and travels there to learn more. Soon after, Learman tries to pass the Daleks off as simple Shakespeare lovers, but the Doctor scoffs at such nonsense, learning their true plans.

In time, the Daleks detect a source of chronons—temporal particles that enable time travel—in the mirror chamber, certifying Learman's master clock for use as a temporal stabilizer. Needing a replacement pilot, the Daleks welch on their deal and mutate Learman into a Dalek, then return with her master clock and Charley—as a hostage to stay the Doctor's hand—back to their warfleet. Undaunted, the Daleks craft a duplicate Temporal Extinction Device, intending to rerun their experiment.

The Doctor realizes that Charley—a living anomaly, thanks to her paradoxical death aboard the *R-101* ("Storm Warning")—is the true chronon source, not Learman's master clock. With haste, the Doctor uses residual chronon energy to open a portal between Learman's mirror device and the Dalek warship. The Doctor rescues Charley, locates young Will Shakespeare and beats a hasty retreat back to the TARDIS.

As the Doctor expected, the Daleks retry their experiment, relying on the master clock to protect them. But for lack of Charley's protective chronons, the Daleks get stuck in a temporal feedback loop. Just as before, the Daleks fail to master the rift, get buffeted, look for a secondary time travel device and dispatch a team to Learman's era. The Doctor concludes the Daleks will replay their actions unto infinity, then takes young Shakespeare home and restores history.

MEMORABLE MOMENTS The Doctor's shocked to hear a Dalek say something he agrees with—that Shakespeare is the greatest playwright in the Universe.

Part 1 ends with a cacophony of Dalek voices crowing, "We are the masters of time," rather terrifying when heard in mass.

The Doctor's adept description of a Dalek: "Think of your worst nightmare. Think of the most repellent, nauseating thing you can possibly imag-

ine. Think of pure evil, made malignant flesh."

Young Will Shakespeare ironically tells the Doctor: "I have found I rarely understand your words or meaning." The Doctor abbreviates the Daleks' Temporal Extinction Device to read TED, which seems a bit too cuddly.

ASS-WHUPPINGS The story opens with a temporal wave—a veritable time tsunami—bashing the TARDIS.

A massive Dalek contingent invades Learman's base, doing their best to mow down her troopers and the rebels. Mostly, it's the rebels who die, but grenades put paid to a few Daleks. One Dalek loses its eyestalk, triggering the old-reliable cry of: "My vision is impaired! I cannot see!"

A Dalek gets atomized when a time corridor prematurely collapses. When Learman's nuclear reactor overloads, some Daleks sacrifice themselves by self-destructing, thereby triggering minor explosions that bring down the radiation shutters. A few Daleks, trapped inside, get irradiated. The Dalek in charge of reactor security kills itself as punishment.

The Doctor resorts to the old "get the Dalek to fire its laser in a mirrored confinement" trick. Charley takes a glancing Dalek blast in Part 2, but the master clock absorbs the brunt of it.

A time-lost Dalek gets killed during the Blitz in World War II, crying out "Where is Shakespeare??!!" while British soldiers grenade its hide.

The Daleks exterminate Professor Osric, Learman's temporal expert. Major Ferdinand, her attaché, grenades himself and a Dalek. The Doctor and his allies push a Dalek through an open time portal into the Time Vortex, allowing the Time Winds ("Warriors' Gate") to rip it apart.

Learman inadvertently and unknowingly kills her older, Dalek-y self (*see TV Tie-Ins*).

TV TIE-INS Learman's mirror/clock conglomeration bears obvious similarities to Professor Maxtible's contraption in "The Evil of the Daleks" [although Maxtible only used mirrors, not clocks].

Thanks to a freak effect of the time loop, Learman comes into contact with the Dalek pilot, her future self. As an extension of the Blinovitch Limitation Effect ("Day of the Daleks"), the cross-temporal contact obliterates the pilot. The younger Learman survives in order to become the pilot and get eradicated in future.

Davros discovered how to convert humans into Daleks in "Revelation of the Daleks." The Daleks here hasten Learman's transformation by pumping her full of mutagenic drugs, then tossing her into a transient time corridor, thereby hyper-ac-

celerating the metamorphosis. Daleks mutated from humans retain their progenitors' skill (i.e. the Learman-Dalek retains her grasp of temporal mechanics).

NOVEL TIE-INS *Trading Futures* makes mention of Learman's fall, and the Euro wars that helped create the Eurozone.

AUDIO TIE-INS The Doctor and Charley realize the temporal fissure sprang into existence as a side effect of Charley paradoxically surviving the *R-101* crash ("Storm Warning"). They're left with the grim conclusion that the web of time's coming unraveled, leading to events in "Neverland." In the same story, the Doctor suggests the Time Lords will probably let the time-looped Daleks out, as too much history hinges upon their actions.

In "Neverland," it's oddly stated that the entire Dalek race is trapped in the time loop. Richards didn't intend it that way—he'd envisioned that nothing more [if you can call it that] than a massive Dalek warfleet got stuck. Still, it's worth remembering that A) some scenes in "Neverland" take place in a possible future, in which President Romana eradicated the entire Dalek species, not just this warfleet, and B) some references in "Neverland" to the Daleks are spoken in the general sense. In other words, "The Time of the Daleks" moreso gets this right [it just doesn't make sense for the time loop to trap every Dalek in creation].

"The Time of the Daleks" explains why Orson Welles didn't recognize Shakespeare ("Invaders from Mars").

The Daleks here open a portal to Shakespeare's era, but the Doctor throws their destination coordinates off-course. Daleks appear in various time zones and get killed, and notably, a Dalek crops up in a Roman fort ("Seasons of Fear").

TIE-INS The Daleks gained a great deal of knowledge of Time Lord technology during their invasions of Gallifrey ("The Apocalypse Element") and the Kar-Charrat Library ("The Genocide Machine"). Accordingly, the Daleks crafted an Eye of Harmony ("The Deadly Assassin") from Time Lord designs, using it to power their fleet. As per designs by Omega ("The Three Doctors"), the Daleks placed their Eye of Harmony fractionally in the future—thereby getting power in a controllable Osmotic stream rather than all in one go.

"The Time of the Daleks" features a spooky narrator [revealed in "Neverland" as Rassilon, "The Five Doctors"] quoting Shakespeare.

CHARACTER DEVELOPMENT

• *The Doctor:* He considers Shakespeare the most accomplished, influential and talented playwright who ever drew breath. On the Doctor's mirror portal equipment, *see Stuff You Need.*

• *Charlotte Pollard:* Some otherwise faulty time travel devices work for Charley because she's saturated with chronons.

• *General Mariah Learman:* Considered the people's heroine. Even so, she doesn't seem too thrown by the notion of the Daleks conquering time. She crazily thinks it's okay to kill off Shakespeare, so long as she remembers him. [Which of course begs the question—what happens to Shakespeare when, one day down the road, Learman dies?]

The Daleks honor the spirit, if not the letter, of their agreement by equipping Learman's Dalek self with a memory sphere of Shakespeare's works.

• *William Shakespeare:* Viola Learman, Mariah's niece and one of the rebel leaders, specifically forbade the 8-year-old Shakespeare to read his future plays, fearing even more historical disruption if he did.

• *The TARDIS:* The scanner can tap the Daleks' monitoring system.

STUFF YOU NEED *Learman's Time Machine:*
Composed of more than 1,600 clocks and 111 mirrors, each coated with orthopositronium, a substance in which the electron and the positron orbit each other in the same direction.

The machine works on the principle that you can see a mirror reflection because light travels from the mirror to your eyeball. Ergo, mirror reflections actually exist a split-second in the past. Learman lined a room with mirrors, then stuffed it full of clocks to measure this time differential. Thanks to Heisenberg's Uncertainty Principle, which states that the act of measuring something changes its nature, Learman's mirrors can open portals to the "mirror universe," a realm where light travels faster than our reality.

Learman's mirrors can view various points in history. They can allow people to step into one mirror and out another. Given the addition of a temporal stabilizer device, such as Charley's chronons or residual energy from the Daleks' equipment, persons *could* step through the mirrors into other eras.

The Doctor cobbles together a device that lets him tap Learman's equipment, enabling him to move spatially—not temporally—between two different mirrors. He can duplicate the effect with any reasonably reflective surface, say, a large piece of aluminum foil. He can also hover in the mirror

universe before arriving at his destination.

A nuclear explosion in the present could cascade through the mirrors, decimating the eras they're viewing.

• *Learman's Master Clock:* If it worked properly, it would improve the Daleks' time travel abilities. However, the clock's only good for setting destination coordinates.

PLACES TO GO *The Time Vortex:* The destruction of a single Dalek ship in the Time Vortex would prove negligible, but the eradication of the Dalek warfleet—1,700 strong—could permanently rupture the web of time.

SHIPS *Dalek Ship:* Uses ti-monic engines, capable of converting nuclear power for fuel.

PHENOMENA *Chronons:* Largely a chicken and egg phenomenon. Chronons generally appear wherever there's a working time machine, paradoxically enabling the time travel in the first place.

• *History Revision:* Shakespeare's removal from history slowly causes people to forget him, suggesting that history alterations take time to crystallize and become permanent. Many Britons witness, in dreams, an alternate timeline where the Daleks conquered all of Earth history. Others consciously recall the alternate timeline, with the side benefit that they suddenly gain knowledge of Dalek tactics—erroneously thinking they've been fighting the Daleks for years.

As part of this history revision, books containing Shakespeare's texts go blank [an odd occurrence, since you'd think that whatever the alternate timeline, nobody would print a blank book].

HISTORY Shakespeare clearly named some of his characters after people in Learman's time zone, including Major Ferdinand (*The Tempest*), Viola (*Twelfth Night*), Marcus (*Titus Andronicus*), Osric (*Hamlet*) and Learman (*King Lear*).

• A King [presumably William, but more likely Charles] sits on the throne. During the Euro wars' chaos, Learman's forces seized control of Britain while she walked into the House of Commons and fired at the ceiling. The country was renamed New Britain and put under martial law. Learman's

been delaying the restoration of democracy, supposedly to prevent power falling to someone who sides with the Eurozone's interests over Britain.

EXPANDED HISTORY Richards says that much of the historical background for this time-zone got chopped, curtailed or summarized. As such, the following information arguably isn't canon, but Richards offers it as a fleshed-out version of what led to Learman's dictatorship:

• The British government held a referendum on whether or not to adopt the Euro. The people decidedly voted "No," but British officials ignored the people's decision and took up the Euro anyway. The British military soon worried that a Euro-zone-centric defense policy would supersede British goals, and many people saw that the Eurozone countries were going bankrupt trying to maintain a single economic policy. Learman gave the government an ultimatum to respect the people's decision. When they didn't, her troops captured Parliament and she sent the legislators home. She appointed herself president over an interim military government, sanctioned by royal assent, until elections could be held.

[Author's Note: Technically speaking, the British monarch still appoints the Prime Minister to lead his/her government. By tradition, the monarch almost invariably picks the leader of the party that controls Parliament. But in theory, he/she could spark a constitutional crisis by choosing someone else. The blessing of the crown therefore made Learman's dictatorship more legitimate than not.]

AT THE END OF THE DAY Credit where credit is due: The audacious "The Time of the Daleks" deserves points for bravely mixing the Daleks and Shakespeare. But beyond its sheer bravado, the audio's flaws seem to outnumber its strengths. First off, the work doesn't just focus on Shakespeare, it *browbeats* you with Shakespeare, hardly containing a character name or bit of dialogue that doesn't seem tainted by his presence. Learman's motives seem completely nutty, and at nearly two hours, the work's simply too long, saddled with a lot of running around and leaping through mirrors. Add to this the fact the Doctor doesn't really win, so much as the Daleks happen to shut themselves in a temporal laundry hamper and close the lid for all eternity, and you've got a debut eighth Doctor/Dalek battle that's not *dreadful*, but it certainly misses the mark.

• Richards originally scripted Learman as a male named General Kent Learman. However, director Nick Briggs wanted to cast actress Dot Smith in the role, so the General underwent a gender change and became Mariah Learman.

• The opening scene with the Dalek ship was initially intended as a pre-title sequence.

• "The Time of the Daleks" claims Learman's mirrors can open portals to the "mirror universe," a realm where light travels faster than in our reality. The "mirror universe" bit is strange but true—Richards read about it in *New Scientist*. Orthopositronium, which coats Learman's mirrors, is a real substance used in the search for so-called mirror matter. Claims made in this audio about using clocks and the Heisenberg Principle to stabilize a mirror portal, however, are sheer bollocks.

NEVERLAND

By Alan Barnes

Release Date: June 2002
Order: Big Finish "Doctor Who" Audio #33

TARDIS CREW The eighth Doctor and Charley, with Romana.

TRAVEL LOG Gallifrey and the Antiverse, current Gallifreyan era (*see* History).

NOTE "Neverland" consists of two extra-length episodes rather than the customary four.

STORY SUMMARY Breathing easy due to their victory against the Daleks, the Doctor and Charley suddenly find a TARDIS WarFleet surrounding the Doctor's Ship. The Doctor takes advantage of time storms in the Vortex, cresting the TARDIS to safety on a wave of temporal distortion. But Charley, deciding it's time to account for her paradoxical survival aboard the *R-101*, uses the TARDIS' Fast Return Switch to flip the Ship back to its previous location—allowing the Time Lords to capture them.

Soon after, the Doctor and Charley find themselves hauled aboard a Gallifreyan Time Station commanded by President Romana and CIA Coordinator Vansell. Romana greets her old travelling companion, but warns that the whole of space-time is near collapse. The Time Lords believe that Charley, existing as a living paradox, has quietly served as a gateway through which destructive

Anti-Time particles—hailing from an Antiverse that's opposite and inimical to our own—have entered our reality. Unless stopped, the Anti-Time particles will exceed the Eye of Harmony's ability to maintain causality, plunging the Universe into perpetual chaos.

Romana and Vansell propose linking Charley to a sub-proton accelerator, thereby enhancing her "gateway" effect and enabling the entire Time Station to pass into the Antiverse. If successful, the Time Lords will eliminate the Anti-Time particles at their source, stemming the threat.

In the Antiverse—a chaotic realm without causality—the Time Station locks onto a planetoid that's stable amid the maelstrom. There, the Doctor's party meets the ghostly "Neverpeople," beings composed entirely of Anti-Time. Moreover, the Doctor's group identifies the planetoid as a TARDIS belonging to Rassilon. In the planetoid's console room, the Doctor finds a recording that claims—as Romana and Vansell secretly suspected—that Rassilon journeyed into the Antiverse and battled Zagreus, a menacing figure from Time Lord mythology. Rassilon evidently triumphed, but has been locked in a Zero Cabinet in the Antiverse ever since.

Infected by Anti-Time particles, a mesmerized Vansell forges a deal with the Neverpeople to transport Rassilon's casket back to Gallifrey. The Anti-Time particles similarly infect the Time Station's staff, but the Doctor and Romana unmask the Neverpeople as Gallifreyan political criminals, supposedly wiped from existence—but actually cast into the Antiverse—by the CIA's Oubliette of Eternity (*see Stuff You Need*).

The Doctor realizes that via Charley, the Neverpeople visited various points in history and retroactively spread myths about Rassilon battling Zagreus, tempting the modern-day Time Lords to visit the Antiverse. Instead of Rassilon's body, the Zero Cabinet contains a critical mass of Anti-Time—enough to corrupt the stabilizing Eye of Harmony on Gallifrey. With the Web of Time stretched to its limit, the Eye's contamination will allow Anti-Time to triumph over the entire Universe.

The Time Station sets off toward Gallifrey, but Vansell slowly regains his faculties, sacrificing his life to let Romana reach the station's Matrix door. Romana enters the Gallifreyan Matrix, but proves unable to alter her presidential access code and deny the Time Station entry to Gallifreyan space. With little time remaining, the Doctor reaches the TARDIS and re-materializes his Ship around the entire Time Station. In Gallifrey orbit, the Neverpeople self-destruct the station to spread the cas-

ket's Anti-Time particles, but the TARDIS absorbs resultant energy release.

In the Matrix, the genuine Rassilon—having monitored these events—reveals himself to Romana and explains that the threat Charley posed to the Universe is now part of established history, meaning the timeline now accepts her survival aboard the *R-101*. The gateway to the Antiverse has closed, stabilizing the Web of Time. Additionally, Rassilon gives Romana his blessing, allowing her to emerge from the Matrix on Gallifrey.

Simultaneously, Charley reconstitutes in the TARDIS' darkened console room, finding that although the Doctor's gambit worked, but Anti-Time particles saturated him in the process. Completely insane, the Doctor adopts a new identity—announcing himself to be the legendary, terrifying figure Zagreus.

MEMORABLE MOMENTS In the Antiverse, a stranded Charley cries out, "Oh, Doctor, where are you?" Seconds later, the time station comes hurtling toward the planetoid, a manic Doctor at the helm, to crash near Charley's location.

A Matrix projection shows Gallifrey's potential future: Transformed into part of Zagreus' empire, with a corrupted Romana serving as Imperatrix.

For sadism's sake, Sentris, the Neverpeople leader, offers the Doctor a chance to end the threat to Gallifrey—by murdering Charley, thereby sealing the Antiverse gateway. Hearing all this, Charley orders the Doctor to shoot her, insisting she's had a full life and that, "We measure our lives in love, and I've loved every minute." Still, the Doctor adamantly refuses to cold-bloodedly kill his friend, even though he's risking the Universe to save her life.

There's a gorgeous moment when the TARDIS materializes around the immanently exploding Time Station, signaling that the Doctor's going to scoop up victory in the last second. Before the Doctor's final sacrifice, Rassilon manifests himself aboard the TARDIS, monumentally telling him: "I come here simply to tell you, before everything has ended, that you have honored me"—a monumental acknowledgement from the founder of Time Lord society. And there's a *tremendous* cliffhanger with the Doctor becoming Zagreus, sure to keep some "Whovians" awake at night until the resolution in the upcoming "Zagreus."

SEX AND SPIRITS A CIA agent claims the interior of the Doctor's TARDIS looks like an Ormelian brothel ("Last of the Titans").

ASS-WHUPPINGS The TARDIS WarFleet fires off time torpedoes that freeze the Doctor and Charley in temporal stasis for 300 years—the time needed for Gallifreyan CIA agents to crack the TARDIS' defense systems.

The Humanian, Sensorian and Sumaran Eras suffer timeline disruption. In the Matrix, the Doctor spies a possible future entailing the Gallifreyan Capitol becoming a charnel house, part of Zagreus' empire, with many heads on pikes in front of the Panopticon. As part of this, Romana becomes a tyrannical Imperatrix, condemning the entire Dalek race to temporal extinction.

Charley screams when transformed into the gateway, possibly out of pain or just surprise. The time station runs aground in the planetoid's metal forest, where acid rain pelts the Doctor's party.

Vansell dies while opening the station's Zibanian shield to expose its reactor core—thereby obliterating himself and two Neverpeople, Rorvan and Taris, to give Romana a chance to save Gallifrey. The Neverpeople consume Kurtz, a Cousin of the Patrix house and under-assassin with the CIA.

Sentris and her cadre of Neverpeople die when the time station explodes [Author's Note: A bit odd, really—did they always intend to go down with the ship?].

The Doctor goes insane, starts calling himself Zagreus.

TV TIE-INS The Matrix uses a dating system similar to the TARDIS read-out in "Doctor Who: Enemy Within." The Doctor lets slip the line, "You—I mean, we, we Time Lords," probably referring to his mixed parentage ("Enemy Within" again).

The Doctor hasn't visited the Acteon Galaxy since "Planet of the Spiders." The Time Station contains an eighth door into the Matrix (the seventh appeared in "The Ultimate Foe"). Romana's Time Station presumably mirrors the vessel seen in "Trial of a Time Lord."

Gallifrey's Transduction Barriers ("The Invasion of Time") separate the planet's continuity from the rest of space-time. Anti-Time cannot pass through these barriers. Certain Gallifreyan ships—such as Romana's vessel—emit signals that automatically grant access.

A CIA agent swears "by Thalia's bones," citing a fan theory that Chancellor Thalia ("Arc of Infinity") became the skeleton seen in "The Five Doctors." Charley's aware of the Mountain Mauler of Montana ("The Romans"). Zero Cabinets first appeared in "Castrovalva."

TOP 5

DOCTOR TRIUMPHS (AUDIOS)

From Loups-Garoux (May 2001) to Neverland (June 2002)

1) Gallifrey saved ("Neverland")—Pretty much the opposite to *The Ancestor Cell* in that the Doctor here stops Anti-Time forces from annihilating Gallifrey. He neatly yanks victory from defeat, but goes insane in the process. As such, we're tentatively labeling this a victory—unless of course, "Zagreus" comes out and the dark Doctor perpetrates even greater crimes upon Gallifrey.

2) Charley reconstitutes aboard the TARDIS ("Neverland")—The Doctor's love for Charley blinds his judgement at times—indeed, it makes him take hugely questionable risks with trillions of lives. But certainly, we can't deny that he never faltered from standing by her, helping to undo her paradoxical death aboard the *R-101*.

3) Ace doesn't get shot ("Colditz")—Along similar lines, the seventh Doctor goes to outlandish lengths when he messes up and gets Ace killed. Indeed, the Doctor gives up his own life, setting in motion events that let him save her the second time around.

4) Dalek warfleet dumped in a time loop ("The Time of the Daleks")—Something of a pseudo-Doctor victory, in that the Daleks largely pickle themselves in a time loop. Even so, the Doctor's clever enough to keep the bloodshed to a minimum, and knows when stand back and let the Daleks plunge themselves into temporal oblivion.

5) Kwundaar defeated ("Primeval")—Kwundaar's all-seeing and unstoppable in direct combat, machinistically moving players across the chessboard with greater ease than the Deep Blue supercomputer. Yet he overlooks the tiniest detail, giving the Doctor an opening that ends with Kwundaar—a psionic powerhouse who would be god—incinerated into less than ash.

NOVEL TIE-INS The Doctor says he's 950-something [clashing with the seventh Doctor's 1,000th birthday in *Set Piece*. Also, *Vampire Science*, which pretty clearly pre-dates this story, claims he's 1012].

Vansell says he and the Doctor attended the Academy together [at least] 600 years ago (*Divided Loyalties*).

AUDIO TIE-INS The Neverpeople are responsible for the time storms/historical disruption seen from "Invaders of Mars" until now. They've been quietly entering our reality—via Charley—and consuming time particles called chronons, thereby upsetting history. Along those lines, Sentris ate the chronon-tainted Richard and Lucy Martin ("Seasons of Fear"), thereby turning them into Neverpeople. Charley isn't the cause of the disruption as such—she's more accurately tagged as "patient zero."

The War TARDIS fleet previously cropped up in "Embrace the Darkness."

The Doctor speculates the Time Lords will let the Daleks out of their time loop ("The Time of the Daleks") because they're too instrumental to the web of time.

The Doctor's narration in "Seasons of Fear" mirrors his conversation with Rassilon here. Charley used the Fast Return Switch in that story.

Vansell last appeared in "The Apocalypse Element." Gallifrey's now allied with the Monan host and the Warpsmiths of Phaedon. The Doctor invokes the Archetryx Convention, Charley's right to an independently assembled commission of the temporal powers (all "The Apocalypse Element").

Charley's been in the TARDIS for about six months (since "Storm Warning").

COMIC TIE-INS War TARDISes and time torpedoes debuted in *DWM* #70-#75, "The Stockbridge Horror."

TIE-INS "Project: Twilight," "Seasons of Fear" and *Instruments of Darkness* previously mentioned Zagreus. One presumes "Neverland" leads into the 40th Anniversary story, the aptly titled "Zagreus" (Nov. 2003).

Rassilon was last seen [in TV and print respectively] in "The Five Doctors" and *The Eight Doctors*. He here turns up as an old man, decently spry and powerful for his age.

The Doctor gives Romana his sonic screwdriver—which is actually *her* sonic screwdriver ("The Horns of Nimon") if we're to believe *Lungbarrow*.

CHARACTER DEVELOPMENT

• *The Doctor:* As a seasoned time traveler, he recovers from time stasis quickly. He doesn't believe in ghosts.

• *Charlotte Elspeth Pollard:* She was born April 14, 1912, in Hampshire, England, on the day the *Titanic* sank.

When Charley was six, she spent time in Bernham Beaches with her nanny and sisters. One afternoon, Charley ran ahead and hid, getting

THE CRUCIAL BITS...

• **NEVERLAND**— Resolution of Charley's paradoxical death aboard the *R-101* ("Storm Warning"). Death of CIA agent Vansell. The Doctor saves Gallifrey, but gets saturated with anti-time particles and goes insane, declaring himself to be the legendary, terrifying figure Zagreus.

terrified when it got dark and nobody came for her. Charley read *Peter Pan* as a child, wanting to become Wendy Darling. When linked to the sub-proton accelerator, Charley provides a bird's eye view of the Universe.

"Neverland" ends Charley's paradoxical existence, with history accepting her escape from the *R-101*.

• *Charley and Romana:* Seem chilly toward each other.

• *Romana:* As a little girl [age 60], Romana vacationed with her family in a rambling house on the shores of Gallifrey's Lake Abydos. She swam there with singing fish and collected Zinc ore thorns from molten rushes at the lake's edge. Taris and her brother Rorvan also played there until, one day, a hermit chased them away with fire sigils. The CIA later consigned Taris and Rorvan to the Oubliette of Eternity (*see Stuff You Need*), erasing Romana's memory of them. Afterward, Romana dithered too much about her tri-bio physics marks ("The Ribos Operation") and lost time for friends.

Romana was an only child. She got a Triple-Alpha in temporal engineering.

• *Vansell:* Now Coordinator of Gallifrey's CIA ("The Deadly Assassin"). His full name is Vansellostophossius, but prefers just "Vansell" because "ostophossius" is terribly common. Prefector Zorac nicknamed Vansell "Nosebung." [A fellow student got dubbed "Toast Rack."]

• *Rassilon:* His name's hailed as the conqueror of Yssgaroth (*The Pit*), overpriest of Dronid ("Shada"), first Earl of Prydon (denoting the Prydonian Chapter, "The Deadly Assassin"), Patris of the Vortex and ravager of the void.

Rassilon can effortlessly freeze time and teleport from location to location, but it's implied he can't directly intervene in these events.

• *The Doctor and Rassilon:* Rassilon claims he's watched the Doctor's adventures for many years, and that he's proud of him as a favorite son.

• *Sentris:* Served as Gallifrey's 217th CIA Coordinator, but guiltily subjected herself to the Oubliette of Eternity upon learning she'd erased 200 Gallifreyans that way. [Her own erasure presumably means that *another* Time Lord served as the

CIA's 217th Coordinator]. As a Neverperson, Sentris wears Charley's form, honoring her as the Neverpeople's means to escape their reality.

• *The TARDIS:* Its destination monitor can't provide a tangible location in the Antiverse, as the realm defies mathematics. The Ship's hearty enough to give the Time Station a jumpstart.

ALIEN RACES *The Neverpeople:* They feast on chronons [i.e. time particles], meaning they find time travelers or Time Lords particularly delectable. They can munch directly on a TARDIS' time rotor. Gallifreyan stasers can't harm them.

Numbering in the thousands, the Neverpeople include Bidolf, a Chancellery Guard who got drunk and babbled details of President Pandack's retinue ("The Deadly Assassin"); Servos, a barman who listened to his gossip; Romana's friends Rorvan and Taris, who accessed classified documents on how they got orphaned; and their parents Majos and Telsa, who conducted unlicensed research into mutagenic breeding.

Becoming a Neverperson seems to corrupt one's personality—Sentris genuinely regretted her actions as CIA Coordinator, but now seems wrathful against our reality.

Neverpeople can assume the others' aspects, communicate empathically and walk through solid matter.

ALIEN PLANETS *Gallifrey:* Possesses a self-contained ionosphere. It's possible to see the Kasterborus Borealis from Gallifrey. The skies there dance with purple, green and yellow.

STUFF YOU NEED *The Gallifreyan Matrix:* Normally, simulated archivists in the Matrix recite and cross-reference various historical events. When history gets disrupted, the simulations start screaming, remembering nothing from history but the coming of Zagreus.

Romana fails to change her presidential access code in the Matrix because, by order of Vansell, no amendments can be made to transduction permits during a state of emergency.

• *The Oubliette of Eternity:* Built by Rassilon, the Oubliette served to erase treasonous Time Lords from history. Its use was officially banned, but the CIA squirreled it away on an off-world station, using it to eliminate political opponents.

[Author's Note: Many details about the Oubliette just don't make sense if one considers them for more than 60 seconds. The device *carves* Gallifreyans from history, meaning children of Oubliette-condemned Time Lords, such as Taris and Rorvan, don't get new parents—they suddenly

lack them altogether. Let's consider: Could *thousands* of Time Lords truly get exorcised from Gallifrey's history with nobody noticing, and no temporal penalty? Clearly Taris and Rorvan got suspicious enough to check the CIA's records.

Also, a surprised Sentris discovers, via a time-protected document, that she condemned 200 Gallifreyans to the Oubliette—if she was the sort of being to authorize the condemnations in the first place, would she really have become guilty about them later? And isn't it a bit inconvenient that the CIA Coordinator keeps forgetting the Oubliette is at their disposal? All in all, the Oubliette's a plot device that doesn't hold up well under close inspection.]

PLACES TO GO *The Acteon Galaxy ("Planet of the Spiders"):* A spiral nebulae, containing asteroids made of mercury. It lies at coordinates 7729-Gamma-7, 19th span.

• *The Antiverse:* Features in the Antiverse include a comet eating its own tail, two nebulae locked together and a star eating a star eating a star—instances of life and death in an ever-changing instant.

ORGANIZATIONS *Gallifreyan Presidents:* Are privy to such secrets as the Jasquig Records, the War Perceptives and the Kavox Imperatives.

SHIPS *"Rassilon's TARDIS":* Actually not Rassilon's TARDIS, meaning its origins go unspecified [possibly, the Neverpeople cobbled it together from leftover TARDIS pieces]. The planetoid registers 1.13 G's, .95 atmospheres [Gallifreyan normal?].

• *The Time Station:* Specifically a Class 7C, supra-orbital time station. It's uniquely forged from triple-bonded Polysium with Tinclavic ("The Visitation") relief. It possesses a limited ability to heal itself, running on Artron fuel ("The Deadly Assassin"). The station contains a solarium. Its temporal engines entail a chrono-plasmic energy cauldron, protected behind a Zibanian shield.

• *War TARDISes:* War TARDISes can block all access to the Time Vortex across five million years. A halo effect appears when they open their time-warp silos, just prior to a time torpedo launch. They can tractor the TARDIS out of the Vortex if it dematerializes.

PHENOMENA *Anti-Time:* Generally speaking, Anti-Time shreds all notion of the present, past and future. Some Time Lord circles have postulated the existence of Anti-Time for centuries, but it's never been accepted into the Time Lord Codex of

Disciplines. Theories on Anti-Time pre-date the Flat Galaxy Society.

• *Historical Distortion:* After a certain point, simple intervention won't cure it—meaning the Time Lords can't repair the Web of Time by stuffing Charley back aboard the *R-101* to die.

ALTERNATE HISTORY Historical disruption causes the 50-year Kosnax war ("Planet of Fire") to run into its third century. On the ring system of the Vita worlds, stones and not reptiles emerge as the dominant lifeform. Benjamin Franklin becomes an American president ("Seasons of Fear").

HISTORY Millions of years ago on Gallifrey, Rassilon used the Eye of Harmony ("The Deadly Assassin") to anchor the entire space-time continuum—stabilizing the whole of history into a single chronology. Consequently, the Antiverse sprang into existence as the continuum's opposite.

• The Matrix dates the following events in the Rassilon Era: Formation of the cult of Morbius ("The Brain of Morbius"), 5725.3; the Master steals plans for the Doomsday Weapon ("Colony in Space"), 5892.9; Chancellor Goth visits Tersurus ("The Deadly Assassin"), 6241.11; Romana and Etra Prime go bye-bye ("The Apocalypse Element"), 6776.7; Romana repels the Dalek Invasion of Gallifrey ("The Apocalypse Element"), 6796.8; Dalek warfleet stuck in a time loop ("The Time of the Daleks"), 6798.2. Dating "Neverland" itself is tricky, as the Matrix claims the time station left for the Antiverse on 6978.3, yet the Doctor subsequently foiled the Neverpeople's plot on 6798.5—note the numerical discrepancy.

• Additionally, "Neverland" provides concrete dating for some previous adventures: "The Stones of Venice" took place in 2294, "Minuet in Hell" in 2003 and "The Sword of Orion" in 2503 [a questionable date, as the story seemingly takes place after the Cyber War, circa 2526].

• The Neverpeople breached our Universe through Charley and retroactively created the long-standing myths about Rassilon battling Zagreus. Rumors about the battle exist on numerous worlds, including a parable on Sparbarus and an epic of the Jzeric-speaking peoples [in a language with very complicated consonants] on Finium Four. The Library of St. John the Beheaded (*All-Consuming Fire*) holds records some of the myths, which extend back to the 12th epoch, possibly beyond. *The Books of Zagreus* furthered this legend.

The tale almost inevitably involves a two-hearted hero abandoning his people, building a mighty ship to search for Zagreus. After many years, he enters the Antiverse, does battle with Zagreus the beast and lives happily ever after. The hero's variously named Azaron, Razlon or Ra [obviously Rassilon derivatives].

• The Jovians decided to celebrate the billionth span of their civilization with a party lasting 1,000 years. In a space-time fold outside the Time Lords' purview, they commenced the Millennium Mardi Gras in the Sumaron Era, 9235.3. Megaluthian Slimeskimmers ("Dimensions in Time") at some point exploded "the third planet."

• The awakening Doctor mumbles about warning Lord Byron he's meddling with forces he didn't understand. Also, he insists on telling *Frankenstein* author Mary Shelley, "That man is not your brother." (An elaboration on off-handed references in "Storm Warning.")

AT THE END OF THE DAY A titanic, triumphant conclusion to the Charley paradox storyline, scoring high for its cosmic scale and the fact that it *feels* like a season finale. In truth, "Neverland" had the potential to tower as the best Big Finish story ever, but a few notable flaws keep it from winning the crown: Namely, Vansell's a campy villain, the gratuitous continuity references get tiresome, and the script's heavy-handed in parts, as if to say, "Look how heroic the Doctor's being!" But overall, "Neverland" unquestionably succeeds thanks to its raw emotional impact, conveying a sense of one door closing as another opens—and brilliantly keeping listeners on edge for 18 months (until "Zagreus") to see how it resolves.

DID YOU KNOW?

• When Alan Barnes wrote "Storm Warning," Charley's intro story, producer Gary Russell told him that someone else would get the joy of resolving Charley's paradoxical death. Russell adds in a discussion board posting that, "I lied of course," later approaching Barnes to write "Neverland" and fix the problem.

EARTHWORLD

By Jacqueline Rayner

Release Date: March 2001
Order: BBC Eighth Doctor Adventure #43

TARDIS CREW The eighth Doctor, Fitz Kreiner and Anji Kapoor.

TRAVEL LOG EarthWorld tourist park, planet New Jupiter, unspecified point in the future.

CHRONOLOGY Immediately after *Escape Velocity*. From Anji's point of view, EarthWorld takes place on February 14, 2001—the date she left Earth (*Escape Velocity*). For Fitz, less than a week has passed since *The Ancestor Cell*.

STORY SUMMARY When the Doctor promises to get Anji home to Soho, 2001, the TARDIS misses Earth entirely and materializes, in the future, on the colony world of New Jupiter. Once there, the TARDIS crew quickly find themselves in "EarthWorld"—a theme park featuring androids of historical figures. New Jupiter President John F. Hoover, a lover of Earth culture, hopes the park will bring his colony an inrush of badly needed tourist dollars. Unfortunately, some of the androids malfunction, murdering various park visitors before EarthWorld's grand opening.

The Doctor decides to question President Hoover's triplet daughters—Asia, Africa and Antarctica—as they designed many of the androids. However, the Doctor discovers—to his horror—that the brilliant, albeit psychotic, triplets are re-programming the androids to commit murder, purely for sport. The triplets continue wrecking havoc, but eventually, the Doctor convinces a noble "Sir Lancelet" android (*see Places to Go*) to round up the three killers.

Soon after, the Doctor finds the triplets used a "Memory Machine" to endow their androids with human brain patterns. The Doctor discovers the device contains memory prints belonging to the triplets' mother, Elizabethan, thereby learning a laundry list of Hoover family secrets. As the Doctor discovers, Elizabethan long ago inseminated herself with DNA samples from Hanstrum—the president's chief technician—when Hoover proved infertile. Unfortunately, Elizabethan's genetic tinkering split her single child into three, leaving the triplets dangerously unstable. Moreover, when Elizabethan tried to confess her wrongdoing, Hanstrum attacked her, placing her in a coma.

An exposed Hanstrum goes berserk, shooting the Memory Machine to ruin Elizabethan's memory prints and cover up his crimes. The resultant explosion kills Asia, prompting Antarctica to vengefully gun down Hanstrum. Afterward, the Doctor links the somewhat-damaged Memory Machine to the TARDIS, hoping to download Elizabethan's memory prints into her comatose body and restore her to life. Even better, Anji proposes the Doctor also use the Memory Machine to undo his own mental blocks, thereby regaining his past.

Fitz turns aghast at the thought of the Doctor remembering his act of genocide (*The Ancestor Cell*) and quietly implores the TARDIS to protect the Doctor from himself. Accordingly, the TARDIS lets the Memory Machine restore Elizabethan, then shorts the device beyond repair. Elizabethan awakens, determined—along with Hoover—to give their two remaining daughters the care they need. Still oblivious to his past lives, the Doctor departs with his companions.

MEMORABLE MOMENTS New TARDIS companion Anji considers that she'd rather read *Sense and Sensibility* than face scary robots, because it's better to be bored than die. She also ponders getting an "I'm a main character. Don't kill me" T-shirt.

Confronted by a stern EarthWorld curator, the "brave" Fitz blows his cover by shrieking "Don't kill me!" and hurling himself back over a desk. Fitz basks in the triplets' praise for his purported musical talents, then remembers that they haven't actually heard him sing—and that they're homicidal lunatics.

The vicious Africa says she revels in screaming, to which the Doctor replies: "I never scream."

Fitz gets thrashed by an Elvis android and deems it his most embarrassing moment—then considers the embarrassment of dying embarrassed. Fitz's shorts get jerked down to his knees, making him horrifically consider that he might die with his trousers down.

SEX AND SPIRITS Anji's friends thought she was too good for her late boyfriend Dave (*Escape Velocity*), but she believed the opposite because Dave—unlike her—had patience and could laugh at himself. She never properly felt that she deserved his love. Even so, she (somewhat paradoxically) at times wondered if she was better off with someone else. She was never unfaithful to Dave, but got offers. Anji believes Dave loved her in word and deed, but that he was possibly unfaithful in thought.

Anji tries to wring out a soaked blazer without

showing Fitz her bra. She's relieved to note that she's wearing a sensible black cotton bra, not an old gray "I'm not seeing my boyfriend tonight" one. Still smarting from Dave's death, she's skittish about embracing another man. *EarthWorld* ends with Anji crying in the Doctor's arms, mourning Dave's passing.

Dave gave Anji a necklace with her name on it for their last anniversary, but an EarthWorld guard confiscates it.

Would-be New Jupiter revolutionary Xernic (a.k.a. James, *see Organizations*) seems taken with Anji, but she merely holds his hand for comfort. Anji appreciates the Doctor's sexiness, but doesn't fancy him. In school, she once cried herself to sleep because Robert Fordham asked Joanne Davies to the end-of-term disco. Later, Anji's favorite pop star turned out to prefer boys.

Fitz frequently compares hot babes to the Doctor's big blue eyes—not because he's feeling *romantic* toward the Doctor, but because his obsession over the Doctor bleeds into other areas of thought. The triplets are taken with Fitz, who performs for them as guitar player "Fitz Fortune." Africa lets out almost sexual moans while watching a savage tiger mangling someone.

The Doctor and Anji kiss—or rather, their bodies kiss—when the Memory Machine briefly endows them with the adulterous Elizabethan and Hanstrum's memory prints.

Fitz notes that his former love interests include Maddie (*Revolution Man*), Arielle (*The Fall of Yquatine*) and Kerstin (*Dominion*). He still considers Filippa (*Parallel 59*) his true love, and hopes to see her again.

ASS-WHUPPINGS Desperate to stop the androids' murderous rampage, the Doctor engineers an anti-android pulse that shorts out all EarthWorld androids in a certain range. This also explodes an android Fitz, crafted by the sadistic triplets to cover up their holding the real Fitz hostage. As the android Fitz blows up, its severed hand launches out at high speed and impales Venna Durwell, an unscrupulous EarthWorld curator, in the head. The Doctor's anti-android pulse also fries the comatose Elizabethan's cybernetic parts (*see Character Development*), threatening her life.

An android Elvis beats up Fitz as part of a death match, but Africa gets bored with the Elvis dupe and shoots him. The triplets dump their victims in a storeroom to decompose.

The Doctor's body briefly switches itself off, to purge Elizabethan's memories from his head. Anji panics and gives the Doctor CPR, but he recovers.

TV TIE-INS *EarthWorld* opens with a caveman android mysteriously moving closer to the TARDIS—echoes of the Ship arriving in pre-historic times in "An Unearthly Child."

New Jupiter historical records mistakenly believe the lethal War Machines ("The War Machines") worked for Briton's General Post Office. Fitz, a native of 1963, doesn't remember the 1966 War Machines incident.

The Doctor doesn't recall his home planet, but vaguely recalls a place with a burnt orange night sky and silver tree leaves ("The Sensorites"). He somewhat recalls bits about an Arthurian reality ("Battlefield").

NOVEL TIE-INS Fitz is determined to keep the Doctor amnesiac and unable to remember Gallifrey's destruction (*The Ancestor Cell*). This probably entails a lot of wayward travels, suggesting Fitz will never reunite with Filippa (*Parallel 59*) or get Anji home (*Escape Velocity*)—all to preserve the Doctor's state of mind. The amnesiac Doctor doesn't even recall what the word "Gallifrey" means, off-handedly suggesting they take Anji there for a holiday.

The Doctor mistakenly believes former companion Samantha "Sam" Jones was a man who always tinkered with the Doctor's VW Bug (destroyed in *Unnatural History*). He confusedly expects Anji to understand commands such as "Number 17!", a code-system previously hashed out with Sam (*Unnatural History*).

Fitz still wears the coat he acquired on Earth, 2001 (*Escape Velocity*). The Doctor uses a new sonic screwdriver (a bulkier version appeared in *Father Time*), but can only work it by instinct. Fitz is internally traumatized about his "duplication" of sorts in *Interference*, unsure if his memories can be trusted. He remembers meeting Iris Wildthyme (*The Scarlet Empress*).

The TARDIS' butterfly room (first seen in *Vampire Science*, leveled in *The Ancestor Cell*) has now restored itself.

AUDIO TIE-INS The Doctor recalls that Queen Mary met her fate with courage (Rayner's "The Marian Conspiracy").

CHARACTER DEVELOPMENT

• *The Doctor:* The Doctor can sometimes determine his location by referencing star positions in the night sky. He knows something about pterodactyl growth patterns. He knew a man who misinterpreted the phrase "A picture paints a thousand words"—and painted a thousand words (using the dictionary as his inspiration).

The Doctor instinctively recognizes androids. He's met several people who're clinically mad. His body still goes into a healing trance as needed, although he doesn't recognize it as such. He gives a recovering Elizabethan a big black motorbike from the TARDIS as a parting gift.

• *Fitzgerald Michael Kreiner:* Fitz sometimes passes himself off as 1960s guitarist Fitz Fortune, playing Fortune-written songs including "Groovy Weekend," "You Broke My Heart, Bikini Girl," etc. Fitz also performs "Song for Sam," a tune he wrote for travelling companion Samantha Jones. "Shakin' All Over," "Three Steps to Heaven" and "Chantilly Lace" are songs Fitz loves.

Fitz doesn't know basic first aid. His old math teacher mocked his German heritage. He hasn't read Christie's *The Murder of Roger Ackroyd*, but better knows her *Murder on the Orient Express*.

During the Blitz, Fitz and his mother got spat on in an British air-raid shelter for their German heritage. Mama Fitz celebrated his fifth birthday party despite the war, determined that Hitler wouldn't spoil Fitz's day. Fitz and Mama Fitz once saw an Oscar Wilde play.

He's hoping to get lockpicks the next time the TARDIS lands on Earth. He once got trapped in the classical section of the TARDIS library for two days and consequently formed an appreciation of Greek and Roman plays, due to their high levels sex and violence.

He's horrified to learn that Elvis, a GI chart-topper of his era, become a big-collared overweight living legend.

He once spent entire days masquerading as "Dick Baron, Special Agent."

The Memory Machine lets Fitz witness himself being born [and he's utterly horrified about it].

• *Fitz and Anji:* Fitz acts like a seasoned time traveler around Anji, but comes across as patronizing. Anji looks down on Fitz, who hails from the primitive 1960s, an era of "free love, racial intolerance and bad haircuts."

Fitz can't swim, but Anji can. He knows more about Arthurian lore than Anji.

• *Anji Kapoor:* Anji's radically reexamining her priorities, realizing how her previous worries about work and her annual review now seems silly. As a newbie time traveler, Anji's brain renders things in simplistic terms ("Robot! Scary Robot! With Gun!") She likes minimalism and doesn't have a circle phobia. She still carries her mobile phone. She knows a bit about the prehistoric era. She's lived in student housing with people she didn't like.

She's seen *Terminator*. At age six, she loved *The Jungle Book* but didn't understand the ending, where the boy gives up adventure and settles down. She better appreciates it now.

She once got lost in the Hampton Court maze. Her grandparents were big on adhering to their cultural identity. She doesn't like waxworks or talking dolls, deeming them creepy. She's superb at math.

Associates claim Anji holds a startling resemblance to Vanessa Redgrave [Fitz scoffs at the suggestion].

Anji's newfound rules of time travel include: No high heels, always have an escape route, trust no one except the Doctor. She carries spare knickers and roll-on deodorant in her bag.

On Earth, Anji did aerobics twice a week, meaning she's decently fit but not particularly strong. The Doctor teaches her a rudimentary use of his sonic screwdriver.

• *Anji and Dave:* Anji's writing e-mail to Dave's "Cybertron@xprof.net" account, although its unclear if this occurs on her Psion organizer or in her head. Her e-mail account is "Anji_kapoor@MW Futures.co.uk."

Anji and Dave once visited a moving dinosaur display at the Natural History Museum. She always took the initiative to pay bills, arrange parties and sort out collections, because Dave always procrastinated.

Dave attended Sunday school and drama school, whereas Anji went to temple and university. Anji and Dave both did GCSEs and bought albums by ABBA and Nik Kershaw. Timothy Dalton was the first James Bond they saw on the big screen.

• *Africa, Antarctica and Asia:* Hanstrum taught the triplets their robotics skills. They learn what Fitz is trying to keep secret from the Doctor (events in *The Ancestor Cell*), but never spill the beans. Elizabethan's genetic experiments accidentally birthed the triplets as three aspects of the same person. Antarctica and Africa were traumatized after Asia's death, but stand a good chance of recovery.

• *The Doctor, Fitz and the TARDIS:* Fitz can apparently communicate with the TARDIS on a rudimentary level—he speaks aloud in the library and holds a favorite childhood read, *The Tale of Peter Rabbit* ("The Horns of Nimon") for emotional support. He's never talked to the TARDIS directly before now.

ALIEN PLANETS *New Jupiter:* The colony still pays taxes to Earth, although it's otherwise left to its own devices. President John F. Hoover is descended from the colony's first leader. The colony supports the death penalty.

STUFF YOU NEED *The Sonic Screwdriver:* Its signals can neutralize the androids one-by-one, or disorient groups of them. Even so, the effect isn't that trustworthy.

• *The Memory Machine:* The bulky Memory Machine contains far more detailed memory prints than the triplets' portable version. The Memory Machine could have cleared the Doctor's amnesia by downloading a copy of his inaccessible memories, then rewriting them over his mental blocks.

PLACES TO GO Theme parks within *EarthWorld* include Egyptian, Ancient World, Japanese, Prehistoric and Twentieth Century (primarily London). Regrettably, the park's historical records aren't very accurate. EarthWorld officials believe that humanity colonized Mars in the Edwardian era, that Elvis was supposedly the King of Earth, and that all Earth crocodiles have alarm clocks in them (obviously a reference to *Peter Pan*).

EarthWorld merchandise includes T-Shirts, personal datapads, "Genuine Earth Recipe Fudge" [made on Alpha Centauri] and "Genuine Earth Recipe Coca-Cola" [made with "Real Earth Cocaine"].

EarthWorld shows sometimes feature Julius Caesar and Robin Hood androids. "King Elvis" performs every night at the Alhambra Theatre on City Centre Street.

New Jupiter's Earth Heritage society helped construct EarthWorld.

ORGANIZATIONS *Association for New Jupitan Independence (ANJI):* "Resistance cell" secretly founded by Hanstrum as a means of applying political pressure against President Hoover. Mostly composed of 17 and 18-year-old boys, the group decried presidential succession based on heredity. It also demanded that New Jupiter retain its own identity, not kow-tow to its Earth origins. Any connection between the group's name and Anji was purely coincidental.

HISTORY Earth history records are extremely scarce in this time period, probably due to an unspecified catastrophe.

• Early settlers on New Jupiter used androids to perform manual labor.

AT THE END OF THE DAY Awkward, and a book that's hard to credit from the same author who produced the magnificent *The Glass Prison*. Rayner's charming, colorful wit shows through in a number of scenes (especially with her use of Fitz), but the overall plot (starting with murder-

ous androids, ending with the Doctor's memory dilemma) is simply lump of hash. By itself, *EarthWorld* would simply wind up average, but as the first book of a new era—supposedly rolling off events in *Escape Velocity*—it's a drastic misstep for the eighth Doctor line.

VANISHING POINT

By Stephen Cole

Release Date: April 2001
Order: BBC Eighth Doctor Adventure #44

TARDIS CREW The eighth Doctor, Fitz and Anji.

TRAVEL LOG Remote region of space, unnamed planet, time unknown (but clearly during Earth's space-faring period).

STORY SUMMARY Passing through a remote region of space, the TARDIS arrives on an unnamed planet with a religious-minded population. As the Doctor quickly discovers, the people believe that if they lead worthy lives and die of natural causes, "the Creator" will reveal the meaning of life to their souls. In time, the Doctor finds evidence that every human on the planet has been encoded with a genetic marker—a "godswitch"—that lets the Creator review each person's experiences and judge if they're worthy enough to "receive his blessing."

With further investigation, the Doctor identifies the Creator as an energy force that keeps the planet and its people in harmony. Unfortunately, a long-standing alien presence on the planet has disrupted the Creator and corrupted the people's gene pool, generating several deformed, godswitch-less children referred to as "mooncalves." With effort, the Doctor unmasks the alien presence as colonist "Derran Sherat," actually a criminal Earth geneticist named Cauchemar.

Somewhat unwittingly, Cauchemar played a role in the planet's creation. Long ago, an Earth prison ship carrying Cauchemar passed through a local radiation belt, fatally irradiating the prisoners and crew. Soon after, a group of benevolent aliens, having previously worked out the genetic coding for the soul, arrived and offered to help the dying humans. With Cauchemar's help, the aliens reformatted the humans to serve as carriers for their own criminals, blending the human and alien souls together.

The prisoners settled down on the unnamed

planet, lacking any memory of their previous identities. Any prisoner who lived a commendable life passed on to the hereafter, but any soul who proved unworthy or died prematurely was instantly reincarnated, given another chance for redemption. As such, the colony has deliberately lost population—as the aliens intended—aiming for the day when all souls are redeemed and "Vanishing Point" is achieved.

Cauchemar's genetic experiments, however, rendered him unsuitable as a host. The aliens isolated him from the planet, but Cauchemar returned, fatally irradiated by the local belts and determined to find his lover Jasmine—a former shipmate converted into a human/alien hybrid. Unfortunately, Cauchemar's unaccounted-for presence on the planet disrupted the Creator's perception of Jasmine—causing the Creator to reflexively kill her.

Cauchemar vengefully sought to bring the Creator to ruin, brainwashing ordinary people to serve as his minions. Under Cauchemar's instructions, his agents fan out to plant charges and murder hundreds *en masse*. If successful, the Creator will grow confused for the sudden influx of prematurely dead souls. Simultaneously, Cauchemar intends to confront the Creator with a specially tailored baby, grafted with multiple godswitches. Cauchemar insanely hopes the double-whammy of the soul influx and the abnormal baby will completely overload the Creator, causing an energy release that will destroy the planet but allow him to attain enlightenment.

The Doctor sets about foiling Cauchemar's scheme, alerting authorities to round up Cauchemar's enthralled lackeys. Cauchemar takes the godswitch-loaded baby to a nearby mountain, a lodestone of the Creator's energy, but Doctor intercepts him. While trying to shoot the Doctor, Cauchemar misses and kills the baby instead. Succumbing to his disease, Cauchemar falls off a cliff and dies. The TARDIS crew departs, but investigator Nathaniel Dark, privy to these events, later finds the Creator has re-balanced itself and incorporated the mooncalves into its designs.

MEMORABLE MOMENTS Fitz botches yet-another attempt at playing James Bond, claiming: "My name is Fitz. Fitz Kreiner. Professional adventurer. And wrestler." He pleads, "Not the face, not the face," when confronted with physical violence.

Slowly adjusting to the concept of alien worlds, Anji asks, "What would God be doing here of all places?", prompting the smiling Doctor to com-

ment: "Instead of watching over somewhere really important like Earth, you mean."

SEX AND SPIRITS Fitz tries coming onto one of Cauchemar's young female agents, then recoils upon mistaking her name of "Thirteen" [as Cauchemar designates his operatives by numbers] for her age.

Notably, Fitz screws Vettul, the most mature mooncalf. The assignation mostly happens off-screen, but at story's end, Vettul cradles her belly as if to suggest she's pregnant with Fitz's child.

Fitz insists he's "just friends" with Anji. Anji wishes she believed in reincarnation, just so she and the late Dave could live together again.

The alien benefactors exiled Cauchemar, but he returned partly because he'd fallen in love with Jasmine. After Jasmine's death, Cauchemar spent several years trying to locate her reincarnated form. As "Derran Sherat," he married a young woman named Treena, believing she held Jasmine's spirit, but concluded he'd made a mistake. He later decided Jasmine's soul resided in Treena's older sister Etienne Grace. They had an affair, siring a son named Braga. However, Treena grew resentful and, during a convenient bank robbery, tried to train one of the robbers' guns on her husband. She wound up getting shot and killed instead.

ASS-WHUPPINGS Fitz opens this book by clowning around, then falling off a cliff edge. He survives with a wounded ankle. Fitz later gets into a scuffle with one of Cauchemar's crew—unit Seven-Two-C-One—and accidentally snaps his neck. Later, Fitz takes a shotgun blast to the leg.

A car chase leaves Doctor a bit mooshed, but alive. Fitz also comes to blows with Hox, the leader of Cauchemar's operatives, causing him to fall off a balustrade to his death.

The dying Cauchemar accidentally shoots his augmented baby. As a final act, he pulls the Doctor off a cliff with him. Cauchemar's decaying form oozes all over the ground, and the Doctor recovers after three days in a healing trance.

When Fitz was eight, he fell off a dry-stone wall, pretending it was a tightrope, and twisted his ankle. Fitz's mother frequently made a fuss with his headmaster when the bigger kids bullied her son. Consequently, Fitz gained a reputation as a snitch, incurring further beatings. He'd often ask his tormentors to hit him on the stomach and ribs, where it didn't show.

NOVEL TIE-INS Shortly after being dropped on Earth (*The Ancestor Cell*), the wandering, raving

Doctor spent five days locked in a Victorian ward packed with consumptives.

The Doctor's eager to meet some true aliens, having spent the last century (*The Burning* onward) with nobody but humans for company.

Anji's still seeking comfort over Dave's death (*Escape Velocity*). Events in *Vanishing Point* make Fitz ponder why his religious mother met such a messy end (*The Taint*).

Cauchemar's mind-control device, called "the Wiper," fails to work on Fitz because he's already undergone memory/perception alteration (notably *Interference*, and to lesser degree *Parallel 59* and *Earthworld*).

CHARACTER DEVELOPMENT

• *The Doctor:* He can navigate the TARDIS through cosmic objects. He's an excellent electrical engineer. He often talks to himself, to distract his brain from awkward questions. The Doctor knows some kung fu maneuvers (most likely a derivation of his Venusian karate).

• *The Doctor and Fitz:* The Doctor believes other people lead Fitz too easily.

• *Fitz Kreiner:* Fitz likes to call himself "toned and lithe," which is a polite way of saying, "scrawny." His mother used to call him a "mooncalf," meaning someone who idles the day away. He can't drive a space tractor. He's rubbish with computers.

• *Fitz and Anji:* She's gradually viewing Fitz as less of a buffoon.

• *Anji Kapoor:* Anji has three sisters. She's taken self-defense classes and sometimes carries a rape alarm. She used to practice ballet, but wasn't any good at it.

Futures trader Anji feels guilty that she's never done a proper day's work in her life. She's never *seen* a farm, let alone worked on one.

Anji's unsure if God exists. Her late boyfriend Dave considered that God might be an alien, but she rejected the suggestion.

She ponders writing book entitled, *What I Learned in Outer Space*, making a mental note that on this planet, "They have bigger cows."

Visiting Boston was a culture shock for her. At this point, she desperately hopes the Doctor will take her home.

• *The Creator:* An organizing entity, perhaps sentient, perhaps not, which regulates the life and reincarnative processes on this planet. The Creator's energy flows through the planet's people, but seems more concentrated in a particular mountain range. The Creator's energy suffuses water in this area.

• *Cauchemar:* His body's awash with telomerase, a chemical substance that gives his cells a measure of longevity. However, he's suffering from advanced dystrophic cellular degeneration (partly radiation exposure, and partly the fact that he's artificially extended his life for so long), meaning he's going to wind up a puddle of DNA.

• *Cauchemar's Stolen Baby:* Cauchemar grafted multiple godswitches to the child simply by stealing fingers from the dead, then affixing them onto it. [Author's Note: One presumes Cauchemar simply found fingers convenient—other body parts such as tongues would have sufficed, although rather messily.] Cauchemar picked a baby as his godswitch nexus simply because he knew he'd have to carry it.

• *The TARDIS:* Cosmic phenomena in this area scramble the TARDIS' navigational systems.

ALIEN RACES *The Alien Benefactors:* They previously found a means of transcending the body, becoming energy beings. The benefactors claim to have genetically identified the soul, in layman's terms isolating it as a matter of DNA proteins and chemicals.

• *Human/alien hybrids:* They don't believe in extra-terrestrials, citing their world as the center of the Universe. Aside from the mooncalves, deformed because of Cauchemar's prolonged presence, the people have no instances of children with disabilities, Down's syndrome or cystic fibrosis.

ALIEN PLANETS *Unnamed planet:* The planet sports Earth-normal gravity. All mention of genetics rates as a "Cat-G offence," the worst possible crime one can commit. The planet houses multiple cities. The largest and oldest settlement has no name.

STUFF YOU NEED *"The Godswitch":* Standard human DNA consists of three percent useful stuff (proteins that enable the body to function) and 97 percent genetic gibberish. However, the unnamed alien benefactors highly refined the humans on this planet, leaving them with only one percent "junk": the "godswitch," which keeps each person connected to the Creator. The "Godswitch" is located on Chromosome 13 out of 23 base pairs.

• *"Vanishing Point":* Requires a fairly coordinated effort on the Creator's part—meaning the slightest disruption [Cauchemar's presence, and later his blatant terrorism] could bring the design to ruin.

ORGANIZATIONS *Diviners:* Human investigators on this planet, assigned to research the sig-

nificance of unexplained deaths. Diviners technically solve crimes, although their function seems more philosophical in nature. They accumulate data on people who died prematurely, trying to compile enough evidence to get them deemed "worthy." If successful, the deceased's soul supposedly passes from limbo to the true afterlife. However, the Creator seems to take little or no account of the Diviners' findings, suggesting the Diviners are achieving some peace of mind about people who die early, but little else.

Diviners adhere to rules in the Book of the Holy Statutes. They're forbidden from wearing jewelry. A silver double helix serves as their crest, although they fail to recognize it as a DNA symbol.

• *The Holiest:* Fashioned by the aliens who founded this planet, the Holiest serve as the Creator's eyes and ears—i.e. they help the Creator monitor life on the planet, thus enabling the Creator to better regulate conditions and hopefully achieve "Vanishing Point." The Holiest are even more genetically pure than the typical human/alien hybrid, with virtually no "junk" DNA. Cauchemar's terrorism confounds the Holiest because—like the Creator—they can't sense anyone without a godswitch. [Author's Note: The Holiest's confusion actually exacerbates the Creator's own bewilderment about events on the planet, rather like popping stitches a few at a time to unravel an entire tapestry.]

HISTORY Centuries ago, Earth authorities imprisoned Cauchemar for murdering people as part of his immortality experiments. Cauchemar was incarcerated aboard a colony arkship, bound for a prison world on the edge of the New Earth frontier. It never arrived, colliding with a meteor that badly damaged the ship and killed half the crew outright.

Soon after, a race of alien benefactors arrived, offering to help spare the humans from death by radiation sickness (*see Story Summary*). The benefactors taught Cauchemar to perform the necessary genetic manipulation, creating a genetic "godswitch" in each human/alien hybrid. Cauchemar's modifications also made the hybrids immune to radiation, sparing them from the lethal cosmic phenomena in the area. "The Creator" was (ironically) created as an energy emission to keep the new colony in balance until "Vanishing Point" was achieved.

AT THE END OF THE DAY The budding of a good novel—but it goes no further than that. *Vanishing Point*'s characters actually seem promising, but ultimately cease to matter since

the book pushes most of them to the background while unleashing wave after wave of scientific gobbledygook. In trying to be mysterious, it only muddles the waters and ties your brain in knots, meaning that you're hardly in a position to care much by the time proper explanations arrive.

DID YOU KNOW?

• Author Stephen Cole originally pitched this novel as *Junk Heaven*, featuring a dying third Doctor enroute back to Earth at the end of "Planet of the Spiders."

• This book's title hails from a song by New Order.

EATER OF WASPS

By Trevor Baxendale

Release Date: May 2001
Order: BBC Eighth Doctor Adventure #45

TARDIS CREW The eighth Doctor, Fitz and Anji.

TRAVEL LOG Marpling, England, August 27, 1933.

STORY SUMMARY In Marpling, England, 1933, a local dentist named Charles Rigby finds a black metal tube of unknown origin in his garden. Regrettably, Rigby's youthful friend Liam clumsily drops the tube into a wasp nest, partly breaking it. A short while later, the fractured tube releases a bio-psionic field that enhances the wasps into a nigh-unstoppable killer swarm. Moreover, once Liam departs, the bio-psionic field telekinetically mutates Rigby into a host body, capable of housing hundreds of mutant wasps.

Meanwhile, a trio of time-travelling commandos—the female Kala, the male Jode and an android named Fatboy—arrive from the future to hunt down the missing device. Almost simultaneously, the TARDIS materializes at random on the Marpling village green.

In rapid succession, the Doctor hears reports of abnormally vicious killer wasps in the area and investigates, tracking the insects to Rigby's house. The Doctor recovers one piece of the mutagenic device, fearful to leave such a gadget lying about 1933, but a mutating Rigby escapes with the rest. Kala's team continually jousts with the TARDIS crew to recover the device, each group unsure of the other's motives.

This book is not endorsed by the BBC. Doctor Who and TARDIS are trademarks of the BBC.

133

Eventually, Kala privately approaches the Doctor, confessing that the device is an experimental weapon that originates from about 3000 years in the future. Kala stresses that she works for unspecified parties and doesn't know the device's abilities, but the Doctor concludes the mutagenic device was intended to genetically corrupt and kill enemy soldiers from within. The Doctor worries that if left unchecked, the bio-psionic force inside Rigby will strengthen and consume all life on Earth.

To the Doctor's further horror, Kala mentions that upon failing to retrieve the device, her orders were to sterilize the area with a nuclear warhead housed in the android Fatboy. The Doctor lectures Kala about the temporal dangers of detonating such a warhead in England, 1933, but elsewhere, Jode panics about the mission's success rate and starts Fatboy's countdown.

A further mutated Rigby kills Jode, then takes shelter in a nearby church. Fatboy follows, trying to get near the bio-psionic device before detonation. Fortunately, the Doctor tracks Rigby and offers to repair the fractured device, supposedly to alleviate Rigby's pain. The small part of Rigby's remaining personality hands over the device, but the Doctor immediately smashes it. The bio-psionic field immediately dissipates, killing Rigby and reverting the wasps to normal.

Unable to countermand Fatboy's countdown, Kala advises that the android will go dormant to prime his detonator. As expected, Fatboy becomes inactive during the countdown's final four minutes, allowing the Doctor to hurriedly defuse the nuclear bomb. Afterward, Kala and the Doctor's crew part company, separately leaving Marpling.

MEMORABLE MOMENTS There's a brief moment where we experience the Universe through the Doctor's excited eyes, when he tells Anji, "*Everything* is significant—to someone or something."

The naïve Kala speculates that a nuclear explosion in England would be negligible in the course of history, making the determined Doctor hurl in her face, "Go stand on the village green, and then tell me that the effect will be *negligible* for the people who live there."

As the Doctor charges past officials, he cries out, "Doctor coming through!" A following Fitz shouts, "Doctor's assistant!", and runs past, leaving Anji, desperately trying to improvise, to simply croak out, "Nurse!"

SEX AND SPIRITS The Doctor carries a handwritten letter dated Aug. 22, 1918, from Mary

Minett, his pseudo-love interest in *Casualties of War*. Anji notes that Fitz "loves" the Doctor, but as with *EarthWorld*, it's moreso a deep-running regard than homosexual desire.

ASS-WHUPPINGS The mutating Charles Rigby keeps barfing killer wasps onto people, with fatal results. The device tries to mutate other Marpling residents, one Hilary Pink among them, into wasp hosts, but they die from anaphylactic shock. The Doctor later douses Hilary's body with ethanol, toasting the abnormal wasps within.

The Doctor and Anji suffer a few wasp stings. Rigby chokes Anji to the point that her eyes bulge. The Doctor whips up a batch of anti-wasp spray (*see Stuff You Need*) and sprays the mutating town spinster Miss Havers with it, killing her.

A fire damages Fatboy's exterior skin and melts his eye shut. He remains dormant after the Doctor defuses his nuclear bomb. Rigby kills time agent Jode. The Doctor shatters the bio-psionic device, making a dying Rigby plummet from a church rafter.

NOVEL TIE-INS The Doctor's more at ease with his amnesia (*The Ancestor Cell*), looking upon himself as someone who's unencumbered. Since his "rebirth" (*The Burning* onward), the Doctor has never driven a tractor.

His memories of 1933 (between *Casualties of War* and *The Turing Test*) are fuzzy, although he recalls sailing in the South Seas and getting a tattoo (explained in *The Year of Intelligent Tigers*).

Tiny lines around Doctor's eyes and mouth remain the only outward signs of his aging since *The Ancestor Cell*.

Anji sometimes mistakes the Doctor's practical side (*see Character Development*) for callousness, a foreshadowing of events in *The Year of Intelligent Tigers*. She here returns to Earth for the first time since *Escape Velocity*. The Doctor re-offers to take Anji home to 2001, but she instead decides to see what the galaxy has to offer.

CHARACTER DEVELOPMENT
• *The Doctor:* The Doctor can identify various time periods by the level of iron-oxidant pollutants in the atmosphere. He likes motorcars, especially 4.5-liter Bentleys. He once stayed at Longleat with the Marquis of Bath.

The Doctor knows something of wasp biology, enough to identify *vespidae vulgaris* (a distinct yellow and black pattern). He's also studied butterflies.

He can play "Paranoid" by Black Sabbath on the piano. He can identify futuristic clothing. A stun

gun, if discharged at point-blank range into the Doctor's skull, would probably cause permanent synaptic damage. He knows how to sabotage time travelers' equipment. He likes Anji's tea.

The Doctor has a criminal record in this time period. He maintains a clinical detachment when cutting open bodies. He recognizes that some people call him "overtactile."

He can recognize Anji's blood on sight. He once associated with boxer Cassius Clay. He used to love playing conkers, and knows karate chops that render people unconscious.

• *The Doctor, Fitz and Anji:* Anji finds the Doctor's behavior highly questionable at times, especially when the bio-psionic device mutates resident Hilary Pink's insides. The Doctor advocates mercy killing Hilary to spare him from suffering—briefly looking as if he's going to snap Hilary's neck—but Hilary dies of his own accord. Anji views the Doctor's proposed euthanasia as callous, although Fitz is more accommodating. She forgives the affront by story's end.

Even more dubious, the Doctor encourages the mutated Rigby to turn on his youthful friend Liam—figuring he won't do it, thereby proving that a spark of Rigby's personality remains. Of course, if the Doctor had been mistaken, Liam would be dead.

Anji gives Fitz the evil eye for smoking. His unswerving loyalty to the Doctor confuses her, but she's learning to accept the Doctor's role as a hero. The Doctor sometimes lets Anji win at cards, just to improve her mood.

The Doctor hasn't eaten porridge for years. Fitz never could stand the stuff.

• *Fitz Kreiner:* Fitz is learning to recognize Earth by smell. He can't stand insects, but nurses a special disgust for wasps. He can play the piano, including the Beatles' "Let it Be." Fitz is dark and unshaven, with a "distinctly untrustworthy look about him." Earth has ceased to automatically mean home for Fitz, who moreso dubs himself a citizen of the Universe.

• *Anji Kapoor:* Anji's growing into the idea of time/space travel. She's fairly lousy at consoling people who've lost loved ones, since bereavement counseling was never of much use to her while playing the stock market.

She's never been in a police cell before—not on Earth, anyway. She's dark-skinned, taken for someone who hails from the Indian subcontinent.

Anji despises feeling useless. She's watched *All Creatures Great and Small* [which costarred Peter Davison, ironically]. She realizes, with a jolt, that she's already seen a *lot* of bodies in her TARDIS travel.

• *Kala, Jode and Fatboy:* Their names are probably aliases. Kala and Jode are human, possibly even from Earth. We never learn their true allegiance, or anything about their employers, but they hail from circa 4900 AD.

They time travel via a "transduction duct." They carry equipment capable of detecting temporal anachronisms and the TARDIS through rogue chronon displacement. Metal interferes with their temporal imaging scans.

Kala's team holds a frightfully bad grasp of temporal physics, mostly because of bad historical records. They mistakenly think that the 20th century experienced hundreds of nuclear explosions, and consider our era a footnote. As such, they're not worried about detonating a nuclear warhead to sterilize Marpling, figuring that history will have 3,000 years to sort everything out.

The trio carry futuristic stun guns that're ineffective on the mutating Rigby.

• *Kala:* She's taller than average, with fine-boned features and steady green eyes. The Doctor invited Kala to join the TARDIS crew, but she declined, returning to the future to continue her work. She deemed the Doctor trouble, but suggested they might meet again.

• *The TARDIS:* Its "yearometer" currently functions well enough to display the date on arrival.

STUFF YOU NEED *The Bio-Psionic Device:* On the surface, nothing more than a smooth, ebony tube that glows with an emerald light. But in truth, the device is a crystal lattice that contains a "bio-psionic energy field"—a mutagenic, telekinetic force.

The device was designed for deployment behind enemy lines, crafted to mutate soldiers from within. Upon landing, the device broadcasts a psionic field that latches onto whatever DNA's handy—it uses wasp DNA simply for the sake of convenience—and bonds it to enemy troopers. The mutating troopers either die from hopelessly scrambled insides, or turn into hosts that incubate various threats (killer insects, etc.) for use against their fellow soldiers.

The hosts are unaware of their transformation up to a certain point, with vestigial emotion remaining. The transformation process essentially voids all known rules of biology, keeping the hosts alive despite the lack of a viable organ system.

The device is organic and self-aware to a certain point, becoming more proficient at genetic alteration with every attempt. It subtly radiates emotion. It's not blatantly telepathic, but can sometimes sense the thoughts of others.

• *Fatboys:* Futuristic class of android with full artificial intelligence and omnitronic control processors. "Fatboys" have android strength, but are essentially walking, talking thermonuclear devices.

Fatboy's chest cavity contains little more than the nuclear device, about the size and shape of a bowling ball. The bomb contains two stable, sub-critical lumps of uranium 235 that hit critical mass when brought together.

The last four minutes of any countdown are the most critical, as Fatboy's android body re-routes all power to prime the detonator. Fatboy goes immobile during this period and remains vulnerable—the trade-off one pays for having a mobile nuclear bomb. The nuclear device can level anything in a 20-km radius.

Fatboys on the whole exhibit simple behavior and attitudes. They understand the nature of fear, but are incapable of experiencing it.

Two command codes are needed to prime a Fatboy for detonation. Before speaking with the Doctor, Kala put Fatboy on standby by speaking the protocol, "alpha-Kala," and the codeword "failure." Jode completed the process with "alpha-Jode" and "success."

• *SNS:* Futuristic stealth device used by Kala's commandos. The SNS deploys a polyprismatic mesh that duplicates the colors and shapes of the immediate surroundings, rendering the wearer practically invisible. It's damnably hard to spot unless the user is inept or—like the Doctor—knows what they're looking for.

• *The Doctor's Wasp Spray:* Bio-psionic counter-agent, crafted by the Doctor once he identified the futuristic device's energy wave pattern with an oscilloscope. With such data, the Doctor encoded some CO_2 chains as a counter-agent, filling a fire extinguisher with spray that neutralized the killer wasps.

HISTORY The Doctor once chatted with Edgar Rice Burroughs (creator of *Tarzan* and *John Carter, Warlord of Mars*) about Mars, but suspects he was only half listening. Along those lines, the Doctor claims he actually met Tarzan.

• Illegal time thieves stole the bio-psionic device circa 4900 AD (allowing for Kala's claim that history will have "3,000 years" to sort everything out). Unfortunately, the renegades tried to flee through time with a jury-rigged transduction apparatus and no permit, getting vaporized thanks to a badly calibrated transduction beam. After their demise, the device somehow wound up in England, 1933.

• Kala's team hails from an era where burial in the ground is deemed "barbaric."

AT THE END OF THE DAY Often cited as a top-notch novel, although hardly deserving of such praise. The by-the-numbers *Eater of Wasps* leaves little to the imagination, relying on generic threats such as a mutagenic weapon [that's broken] and a nuclear bomb [that's defused with maybe a couple beads of sweat]. The book's so unambitious, it hurts, creating some very fly-by-night tension between Anji and the Doctor and not even bothering to explain where Kala's time agents come from. Overall, it's not so much *bad* as simply *mediocre*—but it's certainly not, as some would claim, anything special.

As a complete and total aside, it *is*, however, the second Trevor Baxendale book (*Coldheart* being the first) with a sort of strange orifice on the cover.

THE YEAR OF INTELLIGENT TIGERS

By Kate Orman

Story by Jonathan Blum and Kate Orman

> *Release Date:* June 2001
> *Order:* BBC Eighth Doctor Adventure #46

TARDIS CREW The eighth Doctor, Fitz and Anji.

TRAVEL LOG Human colony of Port Any, planet Hitchemus, human colonial era (and certainly after the invention of T-mat, the 21st century).

CHRONOLOGY For the TARDIS crew, at least a month after *Eater of Wasps*.

STORY SUMMARY When the TARDIS lands on the planet Hitchemus, a world 7/8 covered by ocean, Fitz and Anji explore the human colony of Port Any while the Doctor amuses himself playing violin in an orchestra. Curiously, the colony's human population lives at peace with an indigenous animal species that resembles Earth tigers. However, the tigers are merely playing dumb, having spontaneously developed an intelligence unheard of for generations.

Suddenly, Hitchemus' tigers drop all pretence and capture Port Any *en masse*. The tigers seize crude voice synthesizers and forcibly organize orchestra rehearsals, crazily determined to learn the concept of music. In response, some colonists form a resistance cell. Fearing bloodshed, the Doctor appeals to a tiger leader named Big for peace.

Determined to win the Doctor's sympathy, Big shows the Doctor a hidden storehouse of tiger knowledge—a gift from a long-deceased generation of intelligent tigers. The Doctor theorizes that evolution crafted the tigers to only develop true intelligence once in multiple generations, preventing them from advancing too far and consuming Hitchemus' limited resources. The current tigers, knowing their progeny will turn out stupid, wish to add the gift of music to the storehouse, thereby advancing any intelligent tigers in future.

Investigating further, the Doctor discovers that intelligent tigers of old developed weather control equipment, as a means of stabilizing Hitchemus' unstable climate. But in the sweeping centuries between the generations of intelligent tigers, the weather control systems have fallen into disrepair, explaining Hitchemus' wild climate shifts of late.

As fear and paranoia among the humans and tigers spill over into full hostilities, the Doctor deduces the existence of a second tiger storehouse beneath Port Any. With casualties mounting, the Doctor reaches the second storehouse's powerful weather control equipment and destroys Hitchemus' spaceport with a concentrated lightning bolt, preventing outside assistance from easily reaching the colony.

For an encore, the Doctor briefly scatters the warring humans and tigers with a mini-tornado, then announces that he's deliberately exacerbated Hitchemus' unstable orbital tilt. In 10 years time, all land on Hitchemus will become totally submerged—unless the humans and tigers combine their efforts and repair the weather control systems. Denied outside help and faced with extinction, the humans and tigers agree to pool their resources and live in peace.

MEMORABLE MOMENTS In an eye-opening moment, Anji reels to find a "stupid" tiger quietly swiping a book from the Port Any library. Later, the Doctor envisions an orchestra with humans and tigers playing side by side. The peaceful period on Hitchemus makes Fitz ponder if the TARDIS crew is brave or stupid for rattling around the Universe getting into trouble.

Fitz protests when the Doctor sulks and won't come out of his room, arguing: "Eventually civilization will crumble. And so will the building. And then where will you be?" Colonist Quick questions the Doctor's right to negotiate with the tigers, considering he's only been at Port Any for a month—cleanly illustrating how much the Doctor, however well-intentioned, wanders in and imposes himself on others.

When the Doctor gains some of the tigers' confidence, hostile tiger Longbody walks in to find the Doctor—supposedly the leader of their enemies—playing with a bunch of kittens.

Finally, the Doctor uses the weather control equipment to quell the human/tiger conflict, irrevocably changing life on Hitchemus—and then takes a bow.

SEX AND SPIRITS Orchestra leader Karl Sadeghi certainly has romantic leanings toward the Doctor. But as with virtually every other EDA, the Doctor's libido remains nil and he barely notices the attention. Karl most definitely wants the Doctor to stay on Hitchemus, latching onto any excuse that the Doctor *might* be showing interest, but it's a lost cause. Mostly, the two of them just chat over coffee. They also gulp down chocolate martinis.

Karl's unrequited love further fractures when he drowns a tiger pack (*see Ass-Whuppings*), thereby drawing the Doctor's ire, although they part on good terms.

Fitz ogles biologist Besma Grieve. A cattle prod-wielding Besma fends off some tigers at one point, saving Fitz and prompting him to weakly gasp: "Marry me."

Anji oddly dreams of a winged, naked Doctor flying over Port Any. The tigers reproduce by laying purple eggs.

ASS-WHUPPINGS The tigers only kill a few humans, relying on strategy rather than outright murder. Anji sticks a pitchfork into a hostile tiger named Longbody, who later gets electrocuted while trying to kill Fitz.

During a skirmish, a tiger kills biologist Besma Grieve, one of Anji's friends. Anji limps away from the conflict.

A friendly tiger named Spotty fails to realizes its own strength and light-heartedly thumps the Doctor, knocking him unconscious for a few hours. Most notoriously, some tigers corner the Doctor in the Port Any dam and a panicking Karl opens the dam, triggers a flood that drowns dozens of tigers. The Doctor decries Karl's actions, sickened by the loss of life, especially since some few sympathetic tigers died as well. Karl and the Doctor later reconcile to some degree.

The Doctor uses the tigers' weather control devices to annihilate the Port Any spaceport.

NOVEL TIE-INS Anji finds it more convenient to tell people that Dave "died after a long illness," instead of the more accurate "got stabbed and charred to death by a rocket engine." (*Escape*

Velocity) The Doctor considers the tigers lucky because their storehouses at least bridge the generations—a familial contact that's denied him (*The Ancestor Cell*).

Fitz saw Jimi Hendrix perform in 1967. During the same period, Fitz and girlfriend Maddie listened to the B-side of the new Beatles single all night (*Revolution Man*).

The Doctor doesn't worry about money, likely because he's re-discovered the TARDIS contains riches of some sort (first mentioned in *Shadowmind*). As with a host of other "Who" novels (starting with *Transit*), the Doctor can get drunk only if he wishes.

As hinted in *Eater of Wasps*, the Doctor worked as a sailor aboard the *Sarah Gail*, bound from Sydney, in 1935 (between *Casualties of War* and *The Turing Test*). He affected a vague doctorate, claiming partial amnesia due to World War I. He spent his time on the *Sarah Gail*—and the decades to follow—plagued by a tune rattling around in his head. For obvious reasons, he failed to realize that Fitz wrote the tune during their pre-*The Ancestor Cell* travels.

CHARACTER DEVELOPMENT

• *The Doctor:* The Doctor's something of an idiot savant when it comes to music. He can't improvise for spit, let alone compose. Yet his skill with a violin remains unsurpassed—so long as some other genius writes the notes. He can play all four parts of Verdi's *The Four Seasons*—on an instrument that wasn't designed for it—probably because his fingers work faster than human norm.

To the annoyance of his fellow orchestra members, the Doctor only has two speeds—ultra-quick and stop. The Doctor vaguely remembers playing music with his family. He took "terrible" piano lessons from a deaf, aged German [clearly Beethoven] and someone with four arms who played the viola and cello at the same time.

The Doctor can play violin [in a complex arpeggio], harpsichord, flute, transverse cello, harp, trombone, banjo, theremin, wobbleboard and an alien instrument with purple tubes that baffles Fitz.

While performing, the Doctor wears a loose white shirt over hemp trousers, and a black waistcoat embroidered with brilliant orange designs. He serves as "concert master" for Karl, meaning he organizes some rehearsals and subs as conductor as needed.

In 1962, the Doctor shaved his head and walked alone through China, Indochina and Siam, following sightings of "a dragon" across half a continent. The Doctor carries alien currency, a dozen cred-

it cards with expiration dates in four different decades, 18 library cards, business cards in scripts he can't read and a photo of Miranda (*Father Time*).

Even while amnesiac, he's experienced in alien languages. The Doctor can spy force fields that're invisible to human eyes. He knows a recipe for killer chocolate martinis. He can read Chinese and horseback ride. He can't remember how many times he's been imprisoned.

The Doctor readily senses that each planet's soil carries its own scent. He distinguishes Earth by the tang of the actinomycetes. Hitchemus' loam has more of a woody, smoky scent. Considering the Doctor's century spent on Earth, the Universe seems like a spice shop.

• *The Doctor and Anji:* The Doctor and Anji come to philosophical blows in this story, given that the Doctor views humans and Hitchemus tigers as equals, whereas Anji sees the tigers as the aggressors. She's reminded that, whatever his exterior, the Doctor's very much an alien. She actively sides with the colonists against the Doctor, but eventually accepts his benevolence. By story's end, Anji remains with the TARDIS, deeming the Doctor and Fitz like a pair of brothers who drive you crazy—but whom you love anyway.

The Doctor tries to teach Anji to play the recorder, but she prefers to spending time in the swimming pool.

• *The Doctor and Fitz:* They sometimes sing in an erratic two-part harmony.

• *Fitz Kreiner:* Fitz plays guitar with an impromptu band at Port Any street corners and coffeehouses. He could probably live off the musician's dole.

Fitz insists that every good rebellion has its musical accompaniment. He allegedly was one of seven musicians who led the rebels on Cantonine 4 to the Momilogist's palace. On Telemahuka, he gave a rock concert in the science compound that broke the Caxtarids' mind control (*Return of the Living Dad*).

He's not versed in 22nd century bands and doesn't believe in luck. Running takes a lot out of him. Fitz saw a more accomplished performer named Danny Gatton in concert. Fitz can drive a Hitchemus hovercar.

• *Anji Kapoor:* She's convinced that Hitchemus' oddball economy works, but worries about its long-term prospects.

When Anji was little, she bizarrely dreamed that she owned a spaceship shaped like a seashell. She would get into it and shrink, getting trapped in another universe. She compares it to TARDIS travel sometimes.

Anji hasn't met Cleopatra or geneticist Barbara McClintock.

• *Karl Sadeghi:* He met the Doctor during a party at Port Any's Palmer Gardens. On Earth, Karl worked as a composer, prep chef, library assistant and fruit picker. His music brought him a reputation, but not much money. Fresh out of the Academy in Nairobi, he wrote "Violin Concerto Number One in C minor." He later took up practicing Octagonal Serialism. He's never heard of donkeys.

• *The TARDIS:* It's suggested that the TARDIS' telepathic translation system relies, to some extent, on the crew's receptability. Notably, the open-minded Doctor hears the tigers' words before Anji.

ALIEN RACES *The Tigers:* Whatever their name, Hitchemus tigers aren't really Earth-style "tigers." They're not even mammals. They have two hearts: one in chest and one in abdomen. Their shoulder and hip joints don't resemble Earth vertebrates, and their DNA codes are unique to Hitchemus.

The tigers' "fur" is actually soft, raised spines on hardened, flexible skin plates (three spines to a plate). The plates function like scales, but aren't very water-resistant. As the tigers are prone to losing moisture through the skin, they drink a lot and love swimming.

Their fur yellows with age. They physically can't speak human tongues, but vocorders—a strapped-on purple disc—help them approximate the sounds.

Hitchemus tigers are typically playful, but prone to negative streaks, since it's tough to stay optimistic when your children are guaranteed to be dumb as rocks.

The tigers mostly inhabit an area called "The Bewilderness," hunting furry "runner" animals with long necks and legs. Hunting tigers rely on the element of surprise, since they're not really made for running.

Some modern-day intelligent tigers develop a taste for coffee. They're too big to drive the colony's hovercars and trucks. They learn music fast, since they grew up hearing it in Port Any.

The tigers adopt colorful names such as Chew You, Bounce and Longbody. At story's end, a few tigers join the orchestra.

ALIEN PLANETS *Hitchemus:* Its current planetary tilt varies from 10 to 25 degrees, accounting for its inherent climate shifts (*see History*). Hitchemus orbits Beta Canum Venaticorum, also known as Chara, a G-type star in Earth's neighborhood. Earth's sun is visible from it.

TOP 5

DOCTOR TRIUMPHS (NOVELS)

From Earthworld (March 2001) to Time Zero (Sept. 2002)

1) The Cold defeated (*Time and Relative*)—Arguably the greatest turning point in the Doctor's life, not so much because he saves Earth [which he'll do multiple times in future], but because he chooses to get *involved* in the Universe's affairs. As such, he shucks off the Time Lords' conditioning and becomes *more* than his roots—to large degree the reason the TV show works so well.

2) Time Zero preserved (*Time Zero*)—The Doctor saves the period before the Big Bang, and by extension the whole of history, but it's notable he accomplishes this by convincing paleontologist George Williamson to die—begging the question what would've happened if George had refused. Nevertheless, the Doctor uses just the right words to make George sacrifice himself, preserving the lives of everyone who ever lived.

3) The King of Beasts beheaded (*The Adventuress of Henrietta Street*)—Nearly equal to the Doctor's victory in *Time Zero*, a *babewyn* triumph would've left mankind alive but totally corrupted into savages. Fortunately, the Doctor doesn't shirk his responsibilities as Earth's protector, and cuts off the King's noggin to signal the triumph of science over barbarism.

4) Hitchemus tigers/humans stop killing one another (*The Year of Intelligent Tigers*)—Granted, the Doctor here possesses all the subtlety of an iron gauntlet—making Hitchemus' humans and tigers get along on pain of death—but his tactics work. Whatever the cause, the humans and tigers stop killing one another—a rare instance of the ends justifying the means.

5) The clock people obliterated (*Anachrophobia*)—With the clock people [i.e. evil Vortex creatures] having grown 50,000 strong—and indeed, transformed into a clock person himself—the Doctor manipulates events with *just* enough delicacy to wipe out his adversaries. As such, he partly plays into the hands of Sabbath and his unnamed business partners—but certainly, the clock people needed eliminating at *some* point.

Days on Hitchemus are 22 hot daytime hours, with barely six dark hours of darkness in between.

• *Chi Bootis:* Location of human military base that's the nearest source of help to Hitchemus, four days' travel away.

STUFF YOU NEED *The Sonic Screwdriver:* It opens holes in force fields, and can project painful sonics that ward off Hitchemus tigers.

PLACES TO GO *Port Any:* Port Any's self-sustaining and lacks poverty, a single town on a world that's 7/8 ocean. It's very much a city of music, rich with opera, bossa nova, zydeco and disco. Its rehearsal halls include the Jerry Lynn Williams, the Albinoni, the Keiko Abe and the Vermilion Rooms.

Port Any has a population in the tens of thousands. Its strange economics guarantee a minimum standard of living to anyone who can play or sing. Farms in the South refuse to grow tobacco. The colony's small enough that one could walk across it in an hour. Cars mostly haul cargo, or aid with expeditions into the wild. Only useful Earth animals, such as horses are allowed—cats and dogs are forbidden.

The port that gives Port Any its name is a great black circle, two km across. Spaceships must land rather than use shuttles or T-mat ("The Seeds of Doom"). The Doctor destroyed the spaceport, but landing *is* possible with great difficulty—meaning the colonists could evacuate if needed.

The colony's buildings are scattered low and thin, set between native trees in flaming red and orange colors. Port Any relies little on tourism, despite a stream of spacecraft that use a nearby gas giant as a refueling center. Anji speculates there's less than 50 tourists in the colony.

The Hitchemus University is barely 10 years old, an afterthought of the Musical Academy. Port Any's "printed" material is similar to hypertext screens.

• *The Tigers' Stela:* A ruin of sorts, containing tiger technology. The stela's secured by a logic test, guaranteeing that only tigers of a certain intelligence can gain access (so it doesn't get ransacked, presumably). The main stela facility rises from the ground. Similarly, a second storehouse contains the weather control equipment, directing thousands of metal nodes—part of the weather control system—all over the planet.

ORGANIZATIONS *The Association for the Annihilation of Experience (a.k.a. Annihilists):* Rationalist organization that views consciousness in mechanical terms—an illusion caused by neurons, hormones, etc. Their unsettling (to some) philosophy suggests that humans, slaved to their biochemistry, only imagine that they love people.

PHENOMENA *Evolution:* Has no universal constant or goals, meaning it's impossible for one planet to truly duplicate the biome of another. Thus, no world could ever evolve genuine Earth tigers—except Earth.

HISTORY Competing theories exist regarding Hitchemus' development. A leading idea speculates that the world's ocean was much lower few million years ago, allowing flora and fauna to migrate from a much larger continent. At some point, an object collided with the rings of Hitchemus' moon, triggering an explosion that melted Hitchemus' southern polar cap. The ocean rose to consume all bit a single island, even as the moon, knocked out of its orbit, greatly disrupted Hitchemus' weather patterns.

• The shifting climate probably threw the tigers' genetics into high gear, allowing for the creation of intelligent tigers. The earliest intelligent tigers regarded the diminished intelligence of their offspring as a plague. They built their main city hundreds of thousands of years ago, developing the weather control systems. Even so, it was likely another 18 or 24 generations before intelligent tigers were born again.

• The intelligent tigers of old developed an almost structure-less, symbolic language. They also developed music based on singing, not instrumentals.

• The human race is fragmented at this point, spread over numerous colonies that hardly speak to one another. Large clumps of humanity would probably feel alien if they returned to Earth.

• Port Any was founded a century ago. Until now, the colonists erroneously believed that humans had built the planet's ruins. They simply built Port Any over it, further constructing a hydroelectric power station at a tiger-built dam. A few researchers took stupid-variety tigers off planet for study, but they failed to breed in captivity.

AT THE END OF THE DAY A dynamo of a book, and along with *Father Time*, the only A-level EDA from the first half of 2002. The bold theme alone—intelligent tigers wanting to play in an orchestra—puts most of this book's rivals to shame, although it drastically helps that Orman also runs with the Doctor's alien nature, Anji's sense of displacement and Karl's unrequited love for the Doctor. The powerhouse ending, with the Doctor almost divinely dictating life on Hitchemus, resonates with the best themes of the New Adventures, marking this a clear sign of the "Doctor back in the TARDIS" EDAs finally getting back on track.

DID YOU KNOW?

- Kate Orman comments on the relationship between the Doctor and conductor Karl Sadeghi, who's smitten with the Time Lord: "The Doctor and Karl are at it like rabbits every time the reader isn't looking. However, the precise nature of their relationship is deliberately left ambiguous, so that the reader can interpret it as A) a passionate but platonic friendship or B) unrequited love on the part of Karl. However, I know the location of all the missing sex scenes."
- The boat *Sarah Gail* is named after Orman's sister-in-law.
- While his character plays a violin in *Tigers*, Paul McGann plays a banjo in the movie *Paper Mask*.
- Orman goofed slightly in *Tigers* by claiming that Verdi, not Vivaldi, wrote *The Four Seasons*.

THE SLOW EMPIRE

By Dave Stone

Release Date: *July 2001*
Order: *BBC Eighth Doctor Adventure #47*

TARDIS CREW The eighth Doctor, Fitz and Anji.

TRAVEL LOG Planets Shakrath, Thakrash, Goronos and unnamed founder world, all within "the Empire," time unknown.

CHRONOLOGY Sometime after *The Year of Intelligent Tigers*, as the TARDIS crew here recovers from an unspecified, "unpleasant" adventure during the interim.

STORY SUMMARY In a first for the TARDIS, the Ship arrives in a region of space-time where the laws of physics prohibit faster-than-light travel. The Doctor considers how the region might affect the TARDIS' trans-dimensional engines, making Fitz and Anji sweat over the prospect of being stuck there for years. But of more immediate concern, a pack of Vortex Wraiths, creatures that normally inhabit the Time Vortex, impossibly warp the disrupted TARDIS' control systems and manifest inside the Ship.

Unable to stop the Wraiths from running amok, the Doctor hurriedly materializes on the planet Shakrath. The travelers hurriedly flee the TARDIS, trapping the Wraiths inside. Soon after, the Doctor's crew learns that Shakrath is part of "the Empire"—a thousand worlds, each inter-connected by Transference pylons that transmit matter at light speed. Eventually, the Doctor's trio returns to the TARDIS, finding the Ship has somehow slaughtered the Vortex Wraiths inside.

The Doctor dematerializes, concerned about reports of Time Vortex creatures escaping into our reality through the Transference pylons. In short order, the Doctor stops off on a couple of Empire worlds, Thakrash and Goronos, then cross-correlates data on the Transference system and pinpoints the planet that most likely founded the Empire.

The TARDIS crew arrives on the unnamed world, discovering that the Empire founders long ago destroyed themselves through warfare. In the meantime, a group of Vortex Wraiths have taken over the planet, desperate to escape a ravenous, unidentified threat in the Time Vortex that's eating their fellows. Worse, the Vortex Wraiths have devised a means of controlling hundreds of Empire trade negotiators, formally called "Ambassadors," through advanced voodoo techniques (*see Alien Races*).

The Vortex Wraiths capture the Doctor's group, desperate to manifest their race en masse in our reality. The Doctor refuses to help, but the Wraiths threaten to cause death and suffering, via their puppet Ambassadors, on hundreds of Empire worlds. Suitably checked, the Doctor pretends to comply, secretly plotting to eliminate the Vortex Wraiths and the corrupted Empire system all in one go.

The Doctor offers to "link" the TARDIS' secondary console to the main Transference pylon, thereby boosting its power. The Vortex Wraiths hook themselves into the TARDIS console, hoping to complete the link and bring their brethren through into our reality. However, the Doctor rigs the console to short out. The resultant overload fries the Wraiths into piles of ash, then emits a pulse that will, in time, wreck every Transference pylon. For an encore, the Doctor, Anji and Fitz slip away in the TARDIS, knowing now-isolated Empire worlds are safe from incursion and free to solve their own problems.

MEMORABLE MOMENTS The Doctor tensely opens the TARDIS' exterior door, cautiously expecting Vortex Wraiths to bolt from the Ship, then becomes disappointed when nothing happens.

Patronizing thief Jamon de la Rocas fails to get along with Anji, earning him a stern look that makes him realize he's "dicing with his very life." The Doctor promises a group of Thakrash circus

This book is not endorsed by the BBC. Doctor Who and TARDIS are trademarks of the BBC.

141

folk "tales to astonish, stagger and amaze by their breadth and erudition," but when he points at Anji, she blanks and thinks about repeating the adventure of Han Solo and Jabba the Hutt.

Anji bravely confronts the Doctor with the notion that he's deliberately drawing out events in the Empire purely to amuse her and Fitz, thereby winning the Doctor's admiration for her observation skills.

Fitz finds this adventure so unpredictable, he expects Doctor to waltz around the corner eating cheese purely because "It's just something I've never seen him do."

SEX AND SPIRITS The lecherous Shakrath Emperor considers adding Anji to his harem, threatening to make Fitz a eunuch to watch over her.

The late Dave once deemed Anji as attractive as Seven of Nine from *Voyager*.

On Shakrath, the Plaza of the Nine Wise Maidens commemorates a Shakrath myth involving an elderly ruler and his nine over-hormonal daughters. The girls eventually kill their father, claiming that he died from a curious disease that ripped him limb from limb, then settle down to a life of depravity, which is pretty much standard for Shakrath rulers.

ASS-WHUPPINGS Vortex Wraiths storm the TARDIS, partly damaging its databanks and shattering the Ship's Stellarium dome (*see Stuff You Need*). The TARDIS kills off the Vortex Wraiths an unspecified manner, possibly by a particle emission beam that ages them to death. The Wraith assault, combined with the Empire's weird physics, leave the Ship out of sorts until it heals on Thakrash.

The Doctor engineers a complicated escape from the corrupt Shakrath Court, causing a brouhaha that makes some palace guards indiscriminately shoot one another. It's played for comedy, but literally speaking, the Doctor commits manslaughter without much comment.

On Thakrash, the High Ambassador Elect slices the Doctor's chest with a glass shard, using his blood to somewhat affix a damaged Transference pylon back together. (The Doctor later retires to the TARDIS infirmary, sticks tubes into his chest and heals within seconds.)

The Doctor's final stunt with the TARDIS console fries all Vortex Wraiths, kills off their puppet Ambassadors (admittedly carbon copies of the genuine article) and brings the Empire to ruin. The fact that some Empire worlds probably relied on the Transference system for their very survival

gets glossed over. To his credit, the Doctor rigs a travel device that lets his acquaintance in the Empire, a thief named Jamon de la Rocas, rescue all persons in-transit in the Transference System.

The Doctor's final gambit leaves the TARDIS' white console room somewhat ransacked, but presumably salvageable.

TV TIE-INS The TARDIS currently sports one swimming pool ("The Invasion of Time," etc.) that continually shifts position and décor. The TARDIS wardrobe ("The Twin Dilemma," etc.) includes an almost impossibly large collection of hats.

NOVEL TIE-INS *The Slow Empire* marks a cameo by the Doctor's rival Sabbath, who more properly debuts in *The Adventuress of Henrietta Street*. When Anji gets plugged into the Cyberdyne, a computerized reality on the planet Goronos, a dapper man (Sabbath) saves her from a bald serial killer. Certainly, Anji never identifies the dapper man, although he's intended as Sabbath. Even so, it's completely unclear how Sabbath—at this point, at least—wound up as part of Anji's simulation.

On Thakrash, the TARDIS crew meets a stranded "Collector," part of a metamorphic race that debuted in Stone's *Heart of TARDIS*.

Anji believes the TARDIS' interior is growing, probably fleshing itself out after its near-destruction in *The Ancestor Cell*. Some doors and passageways remain sealed off. The Doctor believes his people shielded the TARDIS (pre-*The Ancestor Cell*, naturally) to avoid incursion by the Vortex Wraiths.

The Doctor's currently not trying to reach Earth, echoing Anji's desire to stay with the Ship for awhile (*Eater of Wasps*, *The Year of Intelligent Tigers*).

Anji more-or-less believes that persons who undergo molecular transport (in a "Star Trek"-like fashion) are essentially committing suicide, with a carbon copy of themselves appearing at the other end. Similarly, the Benny book *Down* discusses "teleportphobia," a fear of dying by teleporting.

Savage tribes of pygmies, located in the fungus jungles of Glomi IV (Stone's *Death and Diplomacy*, *Burning Heart*), allegedly reside in the Empire.

AUDIO TIE-INS In addition to Vortex Wraiths, the Time Vortex more commonly contains Vortisaurs ("Storm Warning" to "Minuet in Hell"). Wraiths and Vortisaurs are similar in nature, but the Vortisaurs have a more defined biology.

TIE-INS Fitz and Anji see the TARDIS' white console room for the first time ("The Invisible Enemy" and onward). The Doctor entirely fails to recognize the white console room, suggesting either that the TARDIS independently regrew it after *The Ancestor Cell*, or generated it specifically for this story.

CHARACTER DEVELOPMENT

• *The Doctor:* The Doctor owns a medium-sized, battered yellow umbrella with an ebony question mark handle. It pulls out to reveal a length of tempered steel.

He can feel the TARDIS' inner pain through their empathic link. He possibly recorded a version of "Trenchtown Skank" for Two-Tone Records. His brain thinks of 7,432 lethal things potentially waiting for him at the top of a stairwell.

The amnesiac Doctor's evidently been reading up on the TARDIS databanks, since he knows of "nice" races who look dreadful to human eyes.

Thanks to the Empire's oddball physics, the Doctor can pre-position objects in a room, calculating probability waves to make them spontaneously collapse and instigate chaos (*see Ass-Whuppings*).

Occasionally in recent years, the amnesiac Doctor's been unable to distinguish between fact and fiction on television. He's been forcibly restrained from watching a popular British soap opera, for fear he'd slit his wrists at the sheer futility of life.

He considers wearing spectacles, like Superman, to conceal his identity. He thinks Collectors (*see Alien Races*) are among the Universe's most entertaining species, but they get carried away with themselves.

• *Fitz Kreiner:* Fitz picked up a battered Fender Telecaster during their previous adventure. He knows the story of Sir Gawain and the Green Knight.

• *The Doctor and Fitz:* Shared an unspecified adventure at Roswell before they met Anji.

• *Anji Kapoor:* Anji's taken a self-defense class and left home before age 17, partly due to cutting (and presumably sexist) remarks from elderly male relatives. On Earth, Anji maintained "contacts" more than actual friendships.

She once flew business class for work, feeling claustrophobic. TARDIS travel in general confuses her, since it entails changing climates and a sense of "wrongness." She feels dislocated when the TARDIS is in flight.

She knows a brief account of the Indian goddess Devi, who battled the buffalo-demon Mahisha. Anji's feeling her age to some extent, recognizing that as people approach 30, they stop trying to ac-

celerate in life and start clinging to what they've got. She's ambitiously seeking a greater path for her life, deciding that her previous occupation as a futures trader probably wasn't worth dying young from a heart attack.

The late Dave subjected Anji to every episode of *Quantum Leap*. She also saw *Star Wars* and *Independence Day* with him, but she hated *The Abyss*.

• *The Doctor, Fitz and Anji:* The Doctor makes Fitz and Anji endure arduous side adventures on Thakrash and Goronos, purely to keep them from getting bored. Anji learns, after the fact, that they could have easily gleaned their data while remaining in the TARDIS.

• *The TARDIS:* As a matter of course, the TARDIS scans a planet's radio broadcasts, computer and satellite communications systems before landing, also peeking a look at various cities. The TARDIS console includes a button labeled *Do Not Push!*, which, if pushed, makes the Ship instantly disappear up its own pocket singularity. Even more disturbingly, the Vortex Wraiths could damage the TARDIS' primary systems and trigger an interstitial singularity, potentially sucking the entire Universe into oblivion.

The TARDIS' scanners can render a cross-map of the Empire.

ALIEN RACES *Collectors:* Slimy, obloid creatures who roam the galaxy in five-mile-wide supercruisers built from planetary debris. Collectors are metamorphic, often seen with multiple limbs and four eyestalks. They have extended lifespans.

• *Vortex Wraiths:* Not so much evil as simply alien, looking like structureless black blobs. Their individual voices blend together into an incomprehensible whole. The Wraiths call the Time Vortex the "Endless Real." They number in the billions.

Some Vortex Wraiths learned to control Empire Ambassadors through a bizarre form of voodoo. Essentially, the Wraiths would preserve the in-Transference Ambassadors' original bodies on the founders' homeworld, then send a carbon copy, via the Transfer System, to the destination planet. By manipulating the Ambassadors' original bodies, the Wraiths could essentially puppeteer the copies by remote.

ALIEN PLANETS *Shakrath:* Empire planet ruled by a corrupt Emperor. Shakrath allegedly treats newcomers with kindness, but more accurately videotapes the reception for posterity, then sends visitors to the torture chambers.

Shakrath has a College of Physiological Undertakings. The planet's instigating negotiations with

This book is not endorsed by the BBC. Doctor Who and TARDIS are trademarks of the BBC.

143

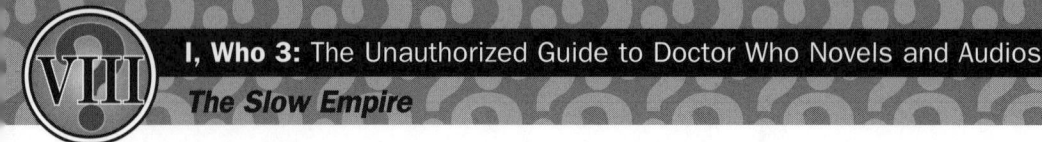

the mining colony Tibrus, 124 light years away, to procure shipments of bauxite, lithium and other refined transuranic elements.

The Emperor demands, mostly for sadism, that Shakrath Ambassadors get face tattoos to help identify their souls after Transference.

PLACES TO GO *The Empire:* The Empire spans a thousand light years and composes hundreds of worlds. Because communication—and physical transfer—between planets only occurs at the speed of light, negotiations between worlds take centuries to complete. Ergo, the smarter Empire worlds take a long-term approach to virtually everything.

Empire worlds tend to think they're all-important, given the inherent seclusion from other planets. Empire worlds include Draglos, an devastated world plagued by tribal warfare. The planet Gingli-Tva is barely habitable, thanks to industrialization.

Areas in the Empire include the caterpillar-treaded cities of the Barsoom sand canals. Wild tales are told about an Empire organization called "the Dominion of the Hidden Hand."

Probably due to its founding (*see History*), the Empire has a remarkably standardized language.

• *The Pamanese Confederacy:* A kind of archipelago, consisting of seven Empire worlds, located within a 30-light-year radius and 700 light years from Shakrath.

STUFF YOU NEED *The TARDIS' Stellarium Dome:* Anji's private name for the TARDIS' inter-dimensional viewing room, allowing travelers to see the environment outside the Ship.

The Stellarium does not physically touch the outside, but rather shows a *representation* of it. The Empire's nutty physical laws allowed some Wraiths to burst through the Time Vortex into the Stellarium, but that's normally impossible.

During flight, the Stellarium renders the Time Vortex as a churning mess of light.

• *Transference pylons:* They break down matter, transmitting it as an information stream for reconstruction by another pylon. It isn't necessary to destroy the original, but the pylon builders deemed it necessary (*see History*).

ORGANIZATIONS *Empire Ambassadors:* Potential ambassadors attend an Ambassadorial Academy, studying geography, history and the socio-political status of numerous worlds.

PHENOMENA *Sequentiality:* The intermix of TARDIS travel and Empire physics subtly dis-

turbs sequentiality, making the Doctor phase erratically in terms of his personality, shifting in and out of his other lives. The phenomena also affects Anji and Fitz, making them act like their past and future personas, but proves temporary.

HISTORY Millions of years ago, an unnamed planet founded the Empire by dispatching probes into space, each containing a brainwashed criminal in stasis. The probes would individually arrive on various planets, whereupon the criminals would awaken and, acting on pre-programmed instructions, set up a Transference pylon. Afterward, the conditioned criminals immediately dropped dead.

As a secondary phase, the founders would dispatch volunteer colonists through the pylons to seed the target planets. The founders initially let the colonists' original bodies survive, hardly caring if copies of them sprang up on a distant world, but eventually abolished the practice.

• The Empire's founding took thousands of years to accomplish. For two million years, it ran smoothly, although the founders' eventual demise left the system subject to decay.

• On Thakrash, an Empire world, slaves from other planets worked in a global lumberyard. Five hundred Thakrash years ago, a metamorphic Collector fell from the sky in his spaceship, damaging Thakrash's Transference pylon. The slaves revolted, forcing the planet into isolation. The Collector hid out in the Thakrash wilderness, but eventually met the TARDIS crew and later traveled with the thief Jamon de la Rocas throughout the ruined Empire.

• The planet Goronos once housed a massive archive for many local Empire worlds. At some point, the slaves revolted and hung their masters, but found themselves unable to function in a liberated social system. Accordingly, they dumped their minds into an elaborate "Cyberdyne" computer reality. Each mind became a circuit in the Cyberdyne reality, processing information. In the meantime, Goronos became an urban wasteland, uninhabited for centuries.

• In the "Doctor Who" Universe, an industrial-military complex founded *Pokémon* as an evil-mind control plot.

AT THE END OF THE DAY The premise is gorgeous, almost worthy of Ursula K LeGuin or Orson Scott Card, but the text is hopelessly mired in gobbledeygook and wayward digressions. As usual, Stone insists on warping "Doctor Who" to his own, almost indecipherable flavor (the Doctor drops phrases such as: "Well, this is all very

Hundred and Twenty Days of Sodom."), meaning the whole mix would be a damn sight better if he'd focus on his plot and characters, rather than leaning over your shoulder and pointing out, "Look how clever I am." The more you read, the more mired it gets, and it's such a shame because one senses that, sufficiently butchered to pieces and re-stitched, this would have made a far better novella than Stone's *Citadel of Dreams*.

DID YOU KNOW?

- Author Dave Stone notes: "The book contains an utterly disastrous typo, which completely wrecks the thematic sense of it, and which I missed until after it was printed. It makes me look even more stupid because the typo appears in one of the section-headings: 'On Thakrash' should have of course read 'No Thackrash'—which would have literally made three points about the plot clear to the reader."
- Stone also claims that when the Doctor acts like his past personas (*see Phenomena*), he had different actors in mind for the roles. Consequently, as Stone puts it, "I managed to get eight Doctors wrong instead of just the one."
- The story of the Siddharata Buddha, as told by the Doctor in *The Slow Empire*, is a relatively straight translation. Stone views this as supporting the Doctor's essentially mythic nature himself—an iconic character elaborating on another iconic character.

DARK PROGENY

By Steve Emmerson

Release Date: August 2001
Order: BBC Eighth Doctor Adventure #48

TARDIS CREW The eighth Doctor, Fitz and Anji.

TRAVEL LOG Planet Ceres Alpha, November 9, 2847.

STORY SUMMARY In the Time Vortex, an agonized telepathic shockwave throws the TARDIS off course, making the Ship crash on Ceres Alpha, a human colony planet. The telepathic intrusion also renders Anji comatose, forcing the Doctor and Fitz to seek medical help. Eventually, the time travelers seek help at Medicare Central.

There, the Doctor finds physician Dr. Pryce con-

ducting amoral experiments on 12 fast-growing children with alien features. The Doctor soon discovers WorldCorp, the company responsible for terraforming the planet, has authorized Pryce to conduct reprehensible experiments regarding the children's budding psionic talents. If successful, WorldCorp hopes to use the children as telekinetic worktools, terraforming the planet on a molecular level at low cost.

In time, the Doctor concludes Ceres Alpha possesses a sentient biosphere—a single intelligence responsible for the children's births. Long ago, Ceres Alpha experienced a planetary catastrophe that decimated the planet, forcing it to enter a healing cycle. Its renewal process threatened by WorldCorp's terraforming, the Ceres Alpha intelligence telepathically influenced 12 babies in their mother's wombs—generating half-alien ambassadors to inform the humans of its plight. However, the children's psionic birth trauma rippled into the Time Vortex, pitching the TARDIS off course and incapacitating Anji, the nearest to a mother figure the children's pained minds could find in the Vortex.

Anji recovers, and the children grow more powerful, telekinetically upsetting the city's power grid. The Doctor herds the children into the TARDIS, only to discover the Ship's internal dimension cuts the kids off from the planet's biosphere, which they require to survive. The Doctor hurriedly opens the Ship's exterior doors, saving the children's lives but enabling WorldCorp troopers to arrest them.

Gaskill Tyran, the ruthless WorldCorp owner, authorizes further tests on the children and orders the execution of the TARDIS crew. In response, the children telepathically make Tyran relive his lifetime of reprehensible, murderous acts. Tyran pitches forward dead, but the children also die from exertion. Hurriedly, the Doctor's party buries the children, allowing Ceres Alpha's biosphere to restore them to life. With WorldCorp decently neutered by Tyran's death, the Doctor grants custody of the children to Veta and Josef Manni, parents to one of the kids, then departs in the TARDIS.

MEMORABLE MOMENTS Fitz acknowledges that while the TARDIS' translation system lets you understand the local idioms, it hardly stops you from making a complete ass of yourself.

SEX AND SPIRITS A randy Fitz pauses to notice a comatose Anji's striking face and breasts.

Medic Ayla Damsk rescues an unconscious Fitz from a sandstorm, then strips him to treat his in-

This book is not endorsed by the BBC. Doctor Who and TARDIS are trademarks of the BBC.

145

juries. Fitz finds himself concerned about this, having been unable to make appropriate excuses for his naked body—or at least sheepishly flex his muscles.

Later, in the TARDIS, Fitz shamelessly hints to Ayla: "I'm going to take a shower. An antigrav shower. It's very stimulating," but she simply smiles and shakes her head, forcing Fitz to beat an embarrassed retreat.

The Doctor drinks some whisky, now considered an "ancient" Scottish tradition, with Tyran.

ASS-WHUPPINGS The alien kiddies' birth trauma makes Anji suddenly ill, causing her to puke all over the TARDIS kitchen. She falls comatose and turns cold as an ice cube. Her eyes turn black, as if slicked with oil. Her heart rate drops to almost nothing, but her brain stays properly oxygenated. She also breaks an arm when the TARDIS crashes, but for the most part, Medicare Central patches her up.

Amid a dust storm, a windswept rock bashes Fitz's leg.

WorldCorp officials interrogate the Doctor with a mind probe. They also interrogate Fitz, sans mind probe. Finally, Tyran interrogates Anji with a mind probe. In short, everyone gets roughed up during interrogation, give or take a mind probe.

As if that weren't enough, Tyran decides he doesn't like Anji's answers and shoots her with a phase rifle. She nearly dies, but Tyran kindly orders his medics to save her life.

The alien children, reflexively protecting themselves, kill doctors Danes and Domecq by telekinetically stabbing them with scalpels and syringes. They also make some WorldCorp troopers' rifles backfire, causing them to erupt in a tremendous fireball.

Tyran's mind probe kills one of the alien children, but the Doctor buries the child and happily brings it back to life. Later, the kids collapse in the TARDIS, cut off from Ceres Alpha, and eventually die, but the Doctor performs the reliable, "Bury the kids and watch 'em come alive" trick.

TV TIE-INS The TARDIS fault locator's faulty right now ("The Edge of Destruction"). The Doctor's finally lowered himself to reading the TARDIS manual ("The Pirate Planet," etc.).

NOVEL TIE-INS A medic finds one of the Doctor's heartbeats is erratic, foreshadowing events in *The Adventuress of Henrietta Street*.

CHARACTER DEVELOPMENT

• *The Doctor:* The Doctor's antigen profiles vary from human norm. He spent some time in the 1960s with Edgar Bergen of *The Edgar Bergen and Charlie Mccarthy Show*, learning ventriloquism.

The Doctor's tool kit includes a sonic wrench (which looks neither like a wrench nor a sonic device). He's heard of Paxx-Sinopoli Syndrome (*see Stuff You Need*), and knows its cure. He suggested the alien children call him "Old Deuteronomy," after a T.S. Eliot-created cat who's lived many lives in succession.

• *Fitz Kreiner:* He's due for a haircut.

• *Anji Kapoor:* Anji's never thought too seriously about motherhood, having prioritized her investments and rainy-day funds. On Earth, she considered that she'd need to save harder as she and Dave planned to get pregnant in their early 30s. But inevitably, Dave would show up with holiday brochures, making saving seem pointless.

Anji learned some mothering instinct by watching her younger brother Rezaul, often while their mother worked in a shop. She complained at the time, but now looks on the babysitting fondly.

Anji's not much good with magic tricks. She's not given to phobias, but her fear of rats borders on the irrational. The Doctor gives Anji a TARDIS key that'll only work for her. She feels the Doctor and Fitz don't respect her need for a handbag.

• *The TARDIS:* The Doctor can set the Ship to land only on planets with a certain technology level. The TARDIS sensed the children's telepathic birth trauma, but got thrown off course and landed on Ceres Alpha two months later.

ALIEN RACES *The Alien Children:* They originally only had numbers for names, but later scanned the Doctor's brain and named themselves after characters in T.S. Eliot's *Practical Cats*.

WorldCorp told the kids' parents that they'd died during childbirth, allowing them to experiment on the children in secret.

The Ceres Alpha intelligence specifically affected the unborn children during their transition from zygote to embryo stage. The kids display cranial bloating, with large saucer-like eyes and wisps of silver colored hair. They have brittle bones, spindly bodies and three-fingered hands.

The children telepathically share each other's pain. They can mentally project themselves into the minds of other people.

[Author's Note: It cannot escape comment that the Doctor saves the alien children's lives, but does little to solve their problems. Essentially, *Dark Progeny* takes for granted that Tyran's death would halt WorldCorp operations on Ceres Alpha when there's no guarantee of that. Also, no Earth

official worth their salt would automatically buy the "These kids are speaking on behalf of the planet itself, please grind your extremely profitable development on Ceres Alpha to a standstill" excuse. In all probability, Earth Central would certainly want to examine/neutralize the kids' psionic abilities, leading to their A) getting dissected, B) instigating psionic warfare to defend themselves/halt development on Ceres Alpha, or C) enduring a lifetime of seclusion.]

ALIEN PLANETS *Ceres Alpha:* So far, it's the closest known planet to Earth-like conditions. The atmosphere's perfectly breathable, requiring no alteration.

WorldCorp's terraforming is reconstituting the soil, morphing the planet's rhizosphere. The planet's fighting back as best it can, struggling to maintain its original state.

Travel between Ceres Alpha and Earth takes two months. Food on Ceres Alpha is largely synthesized, requiring taste caps. Rats evidently smuggled themselves aboard the colony ships.

STUFF YOU NEED *Cyclotol Concentrate:* An explosive substance, with a detonation pressure of about 50,000 atmospheres per square centimeter.

• *Paxx-Sinopoli:* A parasitic virus that resides mid-brain, nourishing itself with synaptic bursts and devouring the cerebral cortex, leading to death. Creating a harmonizing feedback with a properly tuned skullcap cures the problem.

ORGANIZATIONS *Earth Central:* Keeps genetic records on various animals, such as birds, in the hopes of breeding them on colony planets.

HISTORY Previously, a civilization with a telepathic populace lived on Ceres Alpha. Unfortunately, an unspecified catastrophe (probably a meteor strike) wiped out the society. The people died out, but their telepathic imprint gave the planet a singular intelligence.

• Seventy years ago, a baby Gaskill Tyran was found abandoned in the drains of Earth Central. He nearly died from exposure and malnutrition, but later became one of the most powerful men in the seven worlds.

• Earth is massively overpopulated, and increasingly desperate to terraform colony worlds. There's not a blade of real grass left on Earth. Birds haven't been seen in two generations. Overcrowded and often living in squalor, Earthers still spend most of their lives entertained by v-worlds and hologames.

• Archaeologist Daniel Bain, age 149, is an ac-

tive member of society, which says something about human longevity in this era.

• Humanity's currently debating whether AIs have souls.

• Some years ago, Earth Central staked a lot of resources on making Gildus Prime habitable for humans. Before work began, WorldCorp owner Tyran read reports of a local cosmic anomaly, prone to flaring up without warning. However, Tyran suppressed all knowledge of the anomaly, allowing the rival PlanetScape to obtain a Gildus Prime development contract. As Tyran expected, the anomaly wrecked the Gildus Prime undertaking, killed a great many colonists and sullied PlanetScape's reputation.

• The alien children were born September 11, 2847, all two months premature, across Ceres Alpha's six continents. The Ceres Alpha intelligence spurred their birth—not to kick humans off the planet, but merely to stop their terraforming from mucking up its healing process.

AT THE END OF THE DAY Mistakenly thinking it's original, *Dark Progeny* reads like a lump of cliched science fiction. Basically, the TARDIS crew gets injured early on, then spends half the book recovering from their injuries. A lot of single-minded characters upstage the far-more interesting alien kids and everyone, but everyone gets interrogated with a mind probe. It's a work so middling, it fails to notice that—aside from saving the kids' lives—very little gets solved, leaving *Dark Progeny* a book that just… sits there.

DID YOU KNOW?

• After the birth of Emmerson's son in November 1996, a relative sent him a card with the quote, "Your children are not your children." Emmerson deemed it a wonderful way to start a book about children, particularly alien kids, and opened *Dark Progeny* with it.

THE CITY OF THE DEAD

By Lloyd Rose

Release Date: September 2001
Order: BBC Eighth Doctor Adventure #49

TARDIS CREW The eighth Doctor, Fitz and Anji.

TRAVEL LOG New Orleans, Louisiana, USA and Dorset, southern Vermont, October, a few years after 2001; Christmas, New Orleans, same general time zone; 22 miles southwest of New Orleans, April 30, 1980.

STORY SUMMARY When the Doctor finds a bone charm stashed away in his closet, he pilots the TARDIS to New Orleans, a few years in our future, to get an expert opinion about the item. The Doctor visits the Museum of Magic, owned by the crippled Mr. Thales, only to find it closed. As a back-up plan, he leaves the charm with Maurice Chickley, who runs Chic's House O' Bones, for a proper examination. But soon afterward, a local named Vernon Flood murders Chickley, steals the bone charm and sells it to French collector Pierre Bal.

The Doctor coordinates efforts with Jonas Rust, the homicide detective investigating the case. Gradually, the Doctor concludes the bone charm could summon and bind a water elemental in human form. Moreover, a New Orleans man named Alain Auguste Delesormes attempted to conjure such a creature in April 1980—but the spellcasting went awry, flooding the Delesormes home and killing the family. Only Alain Jr. survived, getting put into foster care in Vermont.

Curious, the Doctor pilots the TARDIS back to the date of Delesormes' casting. He tries to observe, not interfere, but winds up saving a young boy from the obliterated Delesormes house. In the confusion, the lad places Delesormes' conjuring charm in the Doctor's pocket for safekeeping. The Doctor leaves the boy and returns to the present, off-handedly flinging his coat into his closet. Afterward, the Doctor realizes the Delesormes' bone charm contains unique temporal properties, meaning it will retroactively get found in the Doctor's closet and trigger this whole adventure.

Returning to the present, the Doctor identifies Vernon Flood as Chickley's killer, further realizing that Flood's wife is actually a water elemental.

Flood's elemental son was bound to Earth in the errant summoning that killed the Delesormes family, and Flood fell under Vernon's control when she came looking for her offspring. By showing compassion to Mrs. Flood three times, the Doctor inadvertently breaks her binding spell and enables her elemental self to gush off to her home dimension—drowning Vernon in the process.

Regrettably, Rust betrays and captures the Doctor, revealing himself as the grown-up Alain Jr. Hoping to complete his father's work—i.e. absorbing a water elemental to gain further power—Rust makes some progress in tapping artron energy in the Doctor's blood ("The Deadly Assassin") to fuel certain spells. Rust kills Bal by remote, then departs to retrieve the bone charm.

In Rust's absence, the Doctor escapes and realizes that the crippled Thales was the boy he rescued from the Delesormes home—identifying Thales as a second water elemental made flesh by Delesormes' conjuring. The Doctor tries to warn Thales about Rust, but Rust tracks him down using the Void, a force of negation and undoing. Rust knocks the Doctor aside and readies to absorb Thales, but the Doctor suddenly opens a window, thereby inviting the at-bay Void into Thales' house. The creature immediately starts consuming everything, but the elemental Thales—immune to its effects—wraps his arms around the Doctor to protect him. The Void eventually consumes Rust, the person who summoned it, then dissipates. Afterward, Mrs. Flood returns to the Earthly plane long enough to unbind Thales—actually her son—and return to their home dimension.

MEMORABLE MOMENTS When the Doctor mentions an accident gave him amnesia, Rust privately hopes the "accident" didn't involve shock therapy. Lacking a search warrant for a suspect's abode, the Doctor proposes he could break in and let Rust arrest him.

In a top dramatic moment, the Doctor rescues a teenage girl from a sex ritual and drives her home to a New Orleans suburb, repeatedly telling her "it'll be all right." But upon witnessing the girl's low-class household, complete with a drunken mother, the Doctor guiltily realizes that really, so far as the girl's concerned, everything *won't* be all right.

The tied-up Doctor asks his ritualistically robed captor: "Oh, no. You're not going to kill me wearing something stupid-looking, are you?" He also notices how some humans seem so eager to escape from their pasts, trying to figure out how, in the course of their short lives, everything becomes un-

bearable for them so quickly.

The pensive Doctor refuses to answer questions at one point, compelling Anji to dump a glass of water on his head. Rust, on why America looks mad to the rest of the world: "When you have a country devoted to dreaming, a fair percentage of the population is going to have nightmares."

SEX AND SPIRITS Rust seems shy around Anji, but takes her out for dinner and dancing. After only two dates, Anji starts to like Rust *a lot*, only minorly disconcerted by his being her elder [physically, not literally, as it turns out] by at least 20 years. She deems him a good kisser, judging she hasn't made out that enthusiastically since University. However, she feels that she impinges on their relationship by asking for Rust's help when the Doctor goes missing. The revelation Rust's a mad magician pretty much sours their romance.

Anji and Fitz platonically walk by the Mississippi River at night. Artist Teddy Arcee asks the Doctor to model naked with his wife Swan, but he declines. Notably, the Doctor intercedes when ritualist Jack Dupre tries to bang a teenager as part of a sex ceremony, unencumbering the object of Dupre's lust from a bizarre metal corset and safely taking her home. Later, when Dupre captures him, the Doctor breathes easier to see Dupre's clothed under his ceremonial gown.

Vernon Flood kept his elemental wife bound to Earth with sexual magic, with chemicals released by intercourse turning her body into a trap. After her release, Mrs. Flood rescues the Doctor from Rust's clutches and transports him to her realm for safekeeping. They pretty obviously have a sexual relationship, but the Doctor eventually returns to Earth to thwart Rust.

Sex ritualists offer to let Fitz and Anji participate—Anji immediately declines; Fitz seems curious until there's mention of a participant named Roy. Fitz's accent intrigues a waitress.

The Doctor's brain chemistry can metabolize bourbon 15.3 seconds after he swallows. He had absinthe in Prague, 1903. Anji drops two margaritas in quick succession. She doesn't like beer, but Fitz enjoys some brands.

ASS-WHUPPINGS Vernon Flood takes issue with the Doctor snooping around, beats him up and drops him through a trap door. The freed Mrs. Flood drowns her husband.

Rust's family died during his father's spellcasting (*see History*). Later, young Rust conjured a magical creature to eliminate his abusive foster family in Vermont.

THE CRUCIAL BITS...

• **THE CITY OF THE DEAD**—Revelation that the eighth Doctor's past selves are actively causing his amnesia, protecting him from the trauma of destroying Gallifrey.

Dupre notoriously makes incisions in the Doctor and pours ritualistic, poisonous powder into his wounds, making the Doctor's system churn with fever. Rust taps the Doctor as a magical power source, and makes Pierre Bal's heart pop out of his chest.

Rust commands swamp spirits, named bogles, to restrain the Doctor in the muck.

TV TIE-INS The Doctor recalls the term artron energy ("The Deadly Assassin"), but doesn't know what it means. An amusing moment involves the Doctor picking up a salt shaker and viewing it as something sinister [clearly a Dalek].

NOVEL TIE-INS In a scene that's obviously reminiscent of *Timewyrm: Revelation*, the eighth Doctor probes his own mind and happens across a stone wall, twice his height, with a wrought-iron gate. Peering inside, the eighth Doctor spies a small Scottish man [obviously the seventh Doctor] in a white suit, curled up asleep in a patch of flowers. The eighth Doctor recalls briefly spotting the man at a funfair (*Endgame*), but seconds later, the Scottish man awakens and forcibly ejects the eighth Doctor from his own memoryscape, blocking off his memories.

Some fans presume this scene means the seventh Doctor's somehow responsible for the eighth Doctor's amnesia, although Rose definitively states that all of the eighth Doctor's previous personas are present and actively walling off his mind. It's almost as if the parts of the Doctor's psyche are protecting his greater consciousness, keeping him from the trauma of realizing he destroyed Gallifrey (*The Ancestor Cell*) lest it destroy him. The seventh Doctor's the only incarnation shown because—given his more assertive personality [especially in the New Adventures]—he makes a natural gatekeeper.

Or to sum this all up: Rose favors the interpretation that the Doctor's amnesia is more psychological than biological.

Artist Teddy Arcee at one point claims the Doctor has "already killed himself twice"—which Rose intends to denote the seventh Doctor killing his predecessor (first revealed in *Love and War*) and the seventh Doctor departing Gallifrey after *Lungbarrow*, essentially realizing that he's going to get

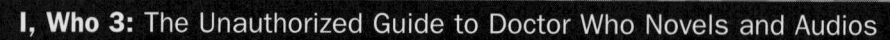

killed while retrieving the Master's remains.

Water elementals in *The City of the Dead* and such bear no relation to "elementals," the term for Time Lords in *The Adventuress of Henrietta Street*. A moment where the Doctor clutches his collarbone does *not* foreshadow to his heart surgery in *Adventuress*. Rather, it occurs because the Doctor smells fresh-cut grass and subconsciously remembers when an alien flower sprouted there in *Set Piece* (in *The Also People*, he also fingers this area and remembers the lawnmower smell of the Ship in *Set Piece*).

The Doctor refitted the TARDIS' defenses after *Dark Progeny*, making the Ship nigh-unbreachable again. The Doctor's read *The Ministry of Fear* by Graham Greene (*The Turing Test*).

A few months ago TARDIS time, the Ship landed in Kent, the early 1990s. While Fitz and Anji slept, the Doctor ventured out of the Ship and found a small yellow cat (obviously Chic, *Warlock*) rubbing his ankles. The Doctor experienced something of an empathic shock, transported the cat to a farm in South Wales, deposited it with a grateful family and has remained perplexed about this ever since.

The Doctor experiences a dream—just before he awakens and confronts Rust—with references to a clutch of previous Who works: Namely, there's mention of a rooftop (*Set Piece*), some church steps (*Timewyrm: Revelation*), a sofa ("The Curse of Fatal Death"), a beach (*The Also People*), a dining room table (*Lungbarrow*), a staircase hewn from gemstone (*Sky Pirates!*) and the deck of a ship (*All-Consuming Fire*).

CHARACTER DEVELOPMENT

• *The Doctor:* He's visiting New Orleans for the first time [that he recalls]. The Doctor's getting more flashbacks of his past lives, including distant memories of Susan. He suspects that he's met French occultist Eliphas Levi [although if so, in a past life, as Levi died in 1875—before the Doctor's century on Earth].

Years ago, he had analysis sessions with Sigmund Freud, mostly out of curiosity and the vague hope of retrieving his memories.

He used to be vegetarian, then decided there wasn't much point in having senses if he never used them. [Again, this is a memory slip—the seventh Doctor was vegetarian, the eighth Doctor isn't especially.] He was in Budapest 10 years ago. He plays Mozart's horn concertos in his head. He's never met a real god and doesn't recognize beignets [a French pastry served in New Orleans]. The Doctor claims that budgies, gerbils and rabbits scare him. He likes black currant tea. Rust

and the Doctor mix blood at one point, enabling the Doctor to replay Rust's memories. His body heals any injury short of fatality, including scar tissue.

• *Fitz Kreiner:* Fitz guzzles New Orleans coffee. He was raised Lutheran, with little knowledge about Catholic saints. He owns a proper lockpick.

• *The Doctor and Fitz:* Fitz doesn't think the Doctor really understands evil, that it's a blind spot for him.

• *Anji Kapoor:* She likes New Orleans-style coffee [flavored with chicory], and the way that New Orleans streets are named after muses. She's in cholesterol overload from New Orleans cooking. She recalls how her little brother used to awaken screaming. She nearly gets home, but doesn't want to arrive a couple of years too late.

• *Fitz and Anji:* Fitz often tunes out when Anji goes off on mini-lectures about economics. He wishes she'd smoke; she wishes he'd quit.

• *Jonas Rust:* Rust's been channeling his own life energy into his incantations, so he appears about 50 when he's really 30. His heart's no good, and his prostate's about the size of a golf ball [mercifully, he doesn't have hemorrhoids].

Born to an abusive father, Rust likes children and protects them as needed. His family's part Creole [meaning part black], but despite this, his father advocated white supremacy. As his name implies, he's got reddish-brown hair.

Rust initially joined the homicide department because it granted access to bodies for spellcasting. He's killed a few people.

• *The TARDIS:* It's more reliable in this story, partly due to law of averages [the Ship's got to hit the mark *sometime*], and partly because it can track the bone charm's temporal field. The console lets people play Q-Bert.

ALIEN RACES *[Water] Elementals:* They exist in a completely different relationship to time than anything mortal. Objects required to breach the wall into their domain [such as the bone totem] have a complex relationship to time.

ALIEN PLANETS *Nicola IV:* Pigs on Nicola IV, or something that looks very much like pigs, literally fly.

PLACES TO GO *Sunnydale, CA:* Buffy the Vampire Slayer's hometown doesn't exist in the "Whoniverse." [Although Rose is hardly consistent, since a pre-vampiric Spike appears in *Camera Obscura*.]

THE CITY OF THE DEAD TOUR

As any New Orleans visitor will know, several locations in *The City of the Dead*, even the weird ones—actually, *especially* the weird ones—are based on real-life settings. Author Lloyd Rose kindly pointed out to Mad Norwegian Press that it's possible—were someone demented enough—to at least cobble together a real-life *City of the Dead* tour based on the book. Accordingly, she gave us a rundown of the fictional/genuine locations you'll find in *City*.

• **The Owl bookstore:** Actually a bookstore named Starling on Royal Street, which also has a room to rent. Both the store and the back courtyard (including the cement chipmunk) are as described. The Doctor's landlord Laura, however, isn't based on anyone real.

• **Death's Door:** Based on Westgate, a purple Victorian house on Magazine Street in Uptown. It houses a death-art gallery and the living quarters of an artist, her husband and father. Again, the Death's Door characters—the artist Teddy Arcee and his wife Swan—are totally fictional.

• **The Museum of Magic:** Rose invented this one, and can't decide where it's located in the French Quarter. The floorplan's that of a sidehall Victorian.

• **Chic's House o' Bones:** Based on a now-defunct Royal Street store of morbid artifacts. It included a child's skeleton from Peru and many other things Rose describes in *City*, as well as John Wayne Gacy clown paintings. Physically, Chic is modeled on several narrow, rundown junk stores one finds along lower Decatur Street.

• **Beauregard-Keyes House:** A genuine mansion that Anji tours, located on Chartres.

• **St. Louis Cathedral:** Anji and Fitz discuss Dave in a garden behind the cathedral. It's right by Pirates Alley, which houses the Faulkner House bookstore where the Doctor finds a rare copy of Capote's *Observations*.

• **Cornstalk Fence Hotel:** Located on Royal Street. Fitz and Anji lodge there.

• The Doctor eats rice cakes and grits and at **The Old Coffee Cup**. Anji and Rust have their first meal at **Coop's** on Decatur. The TARDIS crew eats crabmeat cheesecake at the **Palace Café**. Fitz and Anji have beignets at **Café du Monde**.

• Anji waxes melancholy in front of the **Blue Dog Gallery** on Royal Street, behind Jackson Square, identifying with the small, melancholy and startled-looking blue dogs on the paintings by George Rodrigue.

• **The Nightmare of Horror** is based on the House of Shock, a haunted house event, although Rose located it in the warehouse district on Tchoupitoulas.

• Rose based **Rust's house** on the abode of a friend in New Orleans [Author's Note: And before anyone can ask—it isn't me.], although Rust's home is located in Marigny, a New Orleans neighborhood behind the French Quarter. **Dupre's house** is pretty much any old place in the Garden District.

• Despite moonlighting as an evil magician, Rust attends Mass at **Our Lady of Guadalupe**, located on North Rampart Street.

• Dupre's **vampire tour** is real, although the tour guides are not—to our knowledge—sex ritual practitioners. Like the Doctor, Rose was the only person who showed up and booked a private [daylight, as it happens] tour, hearing ludicrous stories from a guide who confided that he wanted to sing opera. He even serenaded her with an aria as they walked along Chartres.

• *The Cities of the Dead:* Term for New Orleans cemeteries, located above ground [New Orleans is below sea level, so the earth gets very slushy in parts].

PHENOMENA *Magic:* It's fundamentally an attempt to alter probability. In the same way that only the most slender percentage of hydrogen atoms actually undergo fusion and power a star, magic users attempt to distort tremendously small odds in their favor [without the benefit of trillions of hydrogen atoms, obviously].

The main problem lies in acquiring enough energy for such spells. Some magicians [such as Rust's father] literally sever parts of their bodies and make them into bone totems, carving phonetic renderings of the elemental's language onto them. Other magic users, such as Rust, tap their

own life energy. On this score, children make excellent mediums for casting, as they're not sullied.

True magical talent among humans is rare, possibly genetic or endowed by close proximity to spells at a young age. Spellcasting talent, if it's going to manifest, often appears at puberty.

HISTORY By 1980, the Delesormes family had largely withered down to one branch headed by Alain Auguste Delesormes and his wife Helen, née Dubois. The family died when Delesormes summoned a water elemental [later called Mrs. Flood] to Earth. Authorities blamed the incident on a freak tornado. [Rose notes: "I avoided the cliche of Halloween in this book, but I set the date of Delesormes Sr.'s fatal conjuring on April 30, Walpurgis Night."]

• Some years later, Rust killed off his abusive

This book is not endorsed by the BBC. Doctor Who and TARDIS are trademarks of the BBC.

151

foster family and faked his death with a stock—a piece of wood temporarily enchanted to emulate a human corpse.

AT THE END OF THE DAY Gloriously suffused with rich prose, *The City of the Dead* succeeds because it's a flavorful novel first and a "Who" work second. Rose uses New Orleans' penchant for death and decay to full effect, capturing the voodoo-laden city in its fullest, right down to the Vampire Tours. Moreover, the book unfolds with some clear threats against the Doctor's life [you know he's going to live, but you dither for his well-being moreso than most books], keeping track of every single character and using them to their full potential. For daring, sexuality, an attention to detail and more, this ranks among the top-flight EDAs and, although not intended as such, makes a great jumping-on point.

- Rose photographed the architecture on the book's cover [sans TARDIS and energy effect, of course]. She fortunately saw the cover before she'd finished the book, and incorporated it into the novel as what the Doctor sees when he returns to our reality after his time with Mrs. Flood.
- Rose was inconsistent with names, most of which lean toward watery references such as Flood and Rust. Morgan is a Welsh name with a sea connection, while Thales is a Greek philosopher who thought the basic constituent element of reality was water.
- Rose made up most of the magic, although Enochean magic isn't her invention. She concocted Dupre's conjuring, and was amused when Spike on *Buffy the Vampire Slayer*—much like the Doctor—recently got runes carved on his chest. She based the Doctor's explanation of magic-as-physics on writings by Timothy Ferris.
- Fitz and Anji visit an unnamed town in Vermont that's actually Dorset. The non-existent Browne trailer-cabin and graveyard are way up Kirby Hollow Road.
- The name Delesormes means "of the worms" and is an actual Creole name. It's on a tombstone in St. Louis #1 [a New Orleans cemetery] and Rose quotes it as an homage to Barbara Hambly's New Orleans mystery, *A Free Man of Color*.
- At one point, the Doctor gets consigned to the care of the swamp bogles—an act loosely inspired by the fairy tale *The Captive Moon*.
- The Doctor receives a Tarot reading in which the overturned cards summarize his history. To wit, the first Doctor = the Hierophant, the second

Doctor = the Hermit, the third Doctor = the Emperor, the fourth Doctor = the fool, the fifth Doctor = the Star, the sixth Doctor = the Moon and the seventh Doctor = the Hanged Man. The Tower equates with Gallifrey's destruction, and the magician is the eighth Doctor.

Rose admits: "The Hermit isn't really right for the second Doctor, but it was the best I could do." The seventh Doctor's identification as the Hanged Man owes to author Paul Cornell.

GRIMM REALITY

By Simon-Bucher Jones and Kelly Hale

Release Date: Oct. 2001
Order: BBC Eighth Doctor Adventure #50

TARDIS CREW The eighth Doctor, Fitz and Anji.

TRAVEL LOG Planet Albert, circa 2890.

NOTE A framing sequence in *Grimm Reality* features Anji visiting the TARDIS library and reading about the crew's adventures on Albert, as if the escapade is a fable itself. The overall effect's rather cute, but hardly a sign that *Grimm Reality* isn't canon (if nothing else, *The Crooked World* handily acknowledges that this caper happened).

STORY SUMMARY At random, the TARDIS lands in a seemingly ordinary forest. But as the Doctor, Fitz and Anji explore their surroundings, they bizarrely find themselves on a madcap planet—oddly named "Albert"—where giants, pixies, gnomes, evil step-sisters and all manner of fairy tales are literally alive.

Meanwhile, the salvage ship *Bonaventure* arrives with workers from three different races—humans, the hippopotamus-like Abanak and the insectoid Vuim—to scour Albert for riches. The Doctor's party and the salvagers experience a series of misadventures, crazily realizing that Albert adheres to laws of physics found in fairy tales. In particular, there are six "wishing boxes" that alter reality according to each user's desires.

Eventually, the Doctor eats a magical apple and experiences a series of historical visions. The Doctor learns that the entire planet of Albert is actually a metamorphic, planet-sized organism, capable of shapeshifting into a near-infinite number of forms. But at some point, a deep space human colony ship crashed on the planet. The ship disgorged its memory banks, providing a template

by which the planet molded itself into a world based on fairy tales.

In time, the shipwrecked colonists birthed descendants, who blended in with Albert's fairy-tale creations. But recently, a nearby white hole disgorged six powerful "skyfallings," which fell onto Albert and become the "wishing boxes." Gradually, the Doctor concludes the white hole is sentient, and that the "wishing boxes" are actually its spawn, made from quantum singularity material capable of reshaping matter at will.

The Doctor gathers the disruptive wishing boxes into a single location, allowing one seedling to gain dominance and absorb its fellows. The sentient seeding suggests the Doctor wish for something that will alter the Universe, thereby warping causality and allowing the seedling to properly gestate in the gap between the current Universe and the new timeline.

Reluctant to play god, the Doctor defers his wish to the insectoid Vuim leader, who wishes his people cured from a devastating genetic disease. Instantly, all Vuim across the Universe are miraculously healed, causing the seedling to pop into the fracture between realities, planning to bloom in 100,000 years time. Pleased with its progeny's development, the white hole dematerializes from our Universe. With life on Albert largely back to normal, the Doctor's crew and the scavengers depart.

MEMORABLE MOMENTS In what's reminiscent of Lucy Van Pelt's psychiatry clinic in *Peanuts*, the Doctor sets up shop in a Goblin Market, nailing up a sign proclaiming, "The Doctor Is In."

Fitz scoffs at mention of a reward, but thinks to himself, *"Let it be money, let it be money..."* The Doctor gets popped into a giant's mouth at one point, and ponders head-butting the uvula, if needed, to make him gag. Anji competes in a competition where, thanks to Albert's wacky physics, she's able to balance 500 books on her head.

The Doctor to Fitz: "Did I mention that you were to guard these [wishing] boxes with your life because they're horrendously powerful, and also might come in useful in the very specific sort of near-fatal danger?" Fitz: "Nooo, more along the lines of, 'Make yourself useful and lug these about for a bit will you?'"

SEX AND SPIRITS The aristocratic Duke of Sighs forces a bewildered Anji and *Bonaventure* Captain Christina Morgenstern to compete for the honor of becoming his wife. Deeming the Duke as pompous, all-around twit, Anji and Christina col-

laborate to earn a draw. To this end, Christina acquires some wish-granting acorns [good for one use only] that let her nullify the first two contests.

Finally, the Duke decides to judge a poetry contest between the two, causing Anji and Christina to recite derivations of the same poem. When the Duke chooses Anji's work as superior, the powerful Fairy Belesia declares the contest void. As penance, the Duke's turned into a toad and wed to a hag.

The ogre Bricklebrit, a servant to six evil sisters, becomes quite smitten with Anji. She's not very interested because, quite obviously, he's an ogre. Forced to later obtain Bricklebrit's help with regards to a wish, Anji makes absolutely clear that he can't wish for them to fall in love, get married or retroactively *be* married. He's also barred from turning her into an ogress, forcing her to stay on Albert or wishing for anything involving sex. Just for good measure, Anji double-checks, "I said no sex, right?" Bricklebrit ultimately wishes to become the sort of person Anji *could* love, compelling her to dance with him.

This white hole reproduces almost like a biological entity. They deposit their seedlings into various realities, then go on their merry way. White holes try to propagate their progeny across time and space. White hole seedlings take a billion years to gestate.

In a giant's castle, the Doctor encounters Janet, the seventh daughter of a seventh daughter, sold into slavery by her six evil sisters (Anji's bosses, *see Ass-Whuppings*). The Doctor convinces Janet to help him escape, but eats a golden apple that inadvertently makes him forget about her. Janet's clearly taken with the Doctor, but little happens between them other than a kiss.

A skipping girl named Jacqueletta randomly claims that she loves the Doctor, but he mostly tells her to go away.

Bonaventure Captain Christina somewhat flirts with the Doctor, tossing out a very sultry, "I'll show you all my secrets, Doctor, if you'll show me yours," comment. Yet, she quickly senses the Doctor's disinterest and judges that he doesn't have a "fetishistic aura, or a homosexual one." The Doctor suggests that she's failed to notice his "not entirely human aura" and pink bunny slipper fetish.

Fitz gulps ale in a local pub.

ASS-WHUPPINGS Anji gets bamboozled while bargaining for a wishing box, causing her to forcibly serve as a maid to six evil sisters. She scrubs like hell, fetches firewood and does other chores for two weeks.

She tries to trick the sisters into wishing her

This book is not endorsed by the BBC. Doctor Who and TARDIS are trademarks of the BBC.

153

servitude away, but it keeps backfiring. For instance, they snidely wish that Anji was never born, making her spend the better part of a day as a ghostly-Anji. Finally, she's freed as part of the "contest" to become wife to the Duke of Sighs (*see Sex and Spirits*).

Fitz takes a two-fisted hammer blow to the back of the head. The Doctor's getting heart pains, to wit…

TV TIE-INS A giant sniffs the Doctor and determines that he "smells of man-cattle… and other," somewhat confirming the Doctor's mixed parentage ("Doctor Who: Enemy Within").

NOVEL TIE-INS The Doctor's been experiencing chest aches for the past 100 years (the post-*Ancestor Cell* era). *The Adventuress of Henrietta Street* explains why.

The Doctor took a life-saving course during his years as a corporate troubleshooter (*Father Time*).

TIE-INS *Grimm Reality* suggests that the planet Albert was, in fact, created from a *seventh* white hole seeding. But in a bit of an editorial snafu, *The Crooked World* suggests that metamorphic planets, subject to alteration by contact with various concepts (such as fairy tales, cartoons, etc.) occur naturally, further citing Albert as one of these worlds. Or to put it simply, *Grimm Reality* says Albert originated from a white hole seedling, but *The Crooked World* suggests that the metamorphic Albert pre-dated the white hole's appearance. So you get to pick.

CHARACTER DEVELOPMENT

• *The Doctor:* The Doctor plies his trade in a Goblin Market as "Doctor Know-All. Adviser, and helper; donor in extremis"—a title denoting a fairy tale character who aids the hero or heroine.

The Doctor's knowledge of "herbal medicine" is mainly limited to chamomile tea. The Doctor has read/seen *The Texas Chainsaw Massacre*, *King Kong*, *Stuart Little* and 1970s *Doctor Strange* comics. He claims he can sing the periodic table to the tune of "The Modern Major General."

The Doctor doesn't agree with philosopher Hume or the reductionists, who claim that the soul is nothing more than an illusion created by the brain's mechanical processes. Nonetheless, he sometimes worries they're correct.

The Doctor declines to restore his memories using a wish box, deeming the past as the past. He once consulted with Sigmund Freud regarding his phobia of silverfish [i.e. Cybermats].

He prefers adventures where nobody's maimed

or tortured. The Doctor can set bones, dress wounds and cook omelets.

• *The Doctor and Anji:* Anji tries not to rely too heavily on the Doctor to save her ass, since he often acts like an *idiot savant*.

• *The Doctor and Fitz:* The Doctor's constant proclamation of "We've landed somewhere!" is starting to get on Fitz's nerves.

• *Fitz Kreiner:* Fitz currently wears a gray flannel shirt, black jeans and scruffy boots. He doesn't know any woodcrafting skills.

Fitz can never make out the words in *The Wizard of Oz* when the main characters approach the Emerald City. He's stupefied by how long women take to get ready for a ball.

• *Anji Kapoor:* Anji has very deliberate posturing. She resists non-verbal clues such as licking her lips to denote avarice.

During her childhood, Anji lived next door to a "perfect daughter" whom her parents held up as a model of young behavior. The girl in question dumped Anji as a playmate when a "better little girl" came along with a Barbie's Dream House, stole lipstick from Woolworth's and put it into Anji's pocket, and shagged a boy that Anji fancied at the first nightclub she attended.

Anji got so worked up over her parents' regard for the girl that she took three months to introduce her boyfriend Dave to her mother. And she *never* introduced Dave to the girl next door.

Anji holds an MBA. She rarely gets to a level of actually hating someone. She hired a cleaning woman to scrub her apartment every Tuesday, but didn't appreciate how the cleaning woman kept vacuuming a zen-like pattern in the carpet.

She once wrote a paper on spin-doctoring for political science class. She's inexperienced with riding horses (although on Albert, her mount adjusts accordingly). She prefers new printings to older books.

• *The TARDIS:* The Doctor keeps spare keys to the Ship onhand, although he's not sure if he needs the TARDIS key to get inside. A magic word or phrase might suffice.

The TARDIS library features a lost work by Sophocles resting against *Delia Smith's Cooking Dictionary—Book Thirty Four: Xylocarp to Zwieback*. The Doctor also owns five editions of *Life and Likings of a Lobster*, all from different libraries. [Bucher-Jones says this refers to a children's story by Norman Hunter involving Professor Branestawm, a forgetful professor who keep borrowing copies of the same book (which he has lost) from different libraries so as to always have one to renew.]

The library books seem to dust themselves off,

plus shuffle into alphabetical and categorical order when nobody's looking.

ALIEN RACES *Vuim:* Insectoid species whose members lack individual names. The Vuim are suffering from a recessive genetic disease, non-contagious to races with DNA-based biology. The Vuim are proud and competent, sticking to business as usual even though their race faces extinction.

ALIEN PLANETS *Albert:* Fairy-like world inhabited by giants, hags, magical horses and the like. Communities there may include Oz [L. Frank Baum], Fairyland [Trad, Shakespeare, Baum], Middle Earth [Tolkien] and Witchland [E. R. Eddison].

The malleable nature of Albert's mass means that, even setting aside the wishing boxes, the planet often transforms matter in accordance with bargains and promises made between individuals. For this reason, formal arrangements on Albert get loaded with unsavory clauses and conditions. Witches on Albert fear making wishes, afraid they'll wind up in ovens. Many servants on Albert belong to a union. The planet sometimes generates imaginary items, such as an herb that the Doctor makes up.

The wishing boxes are likely the most powerful reality altering objects on Albert, although lesser items such as magical acorns also affect causality. Albert's overall consciousness *wants* the Doctor to remove the wishing boxes, as they're too unpredictable.

STUFF YOU NEED *Fairy Horses:* Raise all manner of alarm if you try to steal them.

PHENOMENA *Quantum White Hole:* Generally regarded as a "naked singularity," acting like a point of intersection with any conceivable locus in any conceivable universe. In layman's terms, this means that mature, sentient white holes can voluntarily teleport between dimensions. They frequently don't obey the laws of causality.

• *White Hole Seedlings (a.k.a. "Wishing Boxes"):* Contained in carved, black-wooden boxes with blood-red spirals contouring their surface. As "wishing boxes," the white hole seedlings talk to their owners, encouraging them to wish for things.

Scientifically speaking, the white hole seedlings act like "quantum fields." Albert's laws of contract bind servants from using the wishing boxes.

HISTORY Ranches now exist on Saturn's moon Titan.

• The Vuim once indulged in some wars, but their medical needs soon took precedence.

• Age-enhancing treatments in this era are haphazard at best. With sufficient wealth, you can purchase age-delaying genetic treatments such as tissue replacement patches, but they often fail. One man dissolved into a mass of twisty blue-gray DNA strands (albeit young DNA strands), writhing in a cylinder.

AT THE END OF THE DAY Yet another gem from the end of 2001, lovingly marinated with rich prose and making fairy tale characters scuffle around the room while you read. The highly sensual *Grimm Reality* shifts into high gear from the moment the Doctor's party steps from the TARDIS, gifted with a real sense of world creation, and providing the sense that virtually anything can happen. That said, it's also far less fantastical than you might expect, using its setting—much like *The Crooked World*—as a backdrop for some startling drama. Exceptional.

DID YOU KNOW?

• Editor Justin Richards came up with the idea for *Grimm Reality*'s framing sequence, although Bucher-Jones claims he "never quite understood what Justin wanted to achieve by it." Bucher-Jones and Hale consequently put off writing the end sequence, hoping Richards would forget about it. But as Bucher-Jones points out: "Justin didn't forget, because he's a very good editor with a very good memory."

• Bucher-Jones has in mind a sequel story in which the surviving seedling—as the title implies—becomes *The Tree of All Gods*, set in every possible Heaven.

• Stone's *Justice Manual* is a book in the TARDIS library. Whereas this seemingly refers to author Dave Stone, who writes Judge Dredd novels, Bucher-Jones points out that it's also a large set of books detailing English Case law. Bucher-Jones used this text during his civil service career, when he worked on Data Protection Law.

• Bucher-Jones claims that along similar lines to Albert's diverse communities, DC Comics once published *The Oz-Wonderland War* #1-#3, starring *Captain Carrot and The Amazing Zoo Crew.* "Check it out, it's great," he says.

• *Grimm Reality* cites Hydrogen-3, also called Tritium, as an extremely valuable element. However, Bucher-Jones adds: "If I'd been writing a few months later I could have cited Helium-3, whose superfluidity appears to now have uses in fusion power." For more on this scientific mumbo-jumbo

This book is not endorsed by the BBC. Doctor Who and TARDIS are trademarks of the BBC.

155

that's way over our heads, check out http://www.space.com/scienceastronomy/helium3_000630.html

THE ADVENTURESS OF HENRIETTA STREET

By Lawrence Miles

Release Date: *November 2001*
Order: *BBC Eighth Doctor Adventure #51*

TARDIS CREW The eighth Doctor, Fitz and Anji.

TRAVEL LOG Chiefly Scarlette's bordello, London; Brighthelmstone (a.k.a. Brighton); *The Jonah*; the Church of Saint Simone, Caribbean island of St. Belique, February 1782 to February 13, 1783.

NOTE *The Adventuress of Henrietta Street* presents itself as a non-fiction text, written by an unspecified researcher. Ergo, it's a lot more speculative than most "Doctor Who" works, with the researcher piecing together, long after the fact, a history of these events.

Subsequent EDAs acknowledge the main gist of *Adventuress*, such as the Doctor's marriage to Scarlette, Sabbath's removal of the Doctor's heart, etc. As such, *Adventuress'* overall events are fairly easy to ratify, but many of the details could be fictional (so to speak).

STORY SUMMARY For lack of the Time Lords' stabilizing influence (*The Ancestor Cell*), a region known as "the horizon"—which seems to exist on the threshold between time and consciousness, and apparently marks the limits of human understanding—has begun to close in on the Earth. Beyond the horizon, a brutish King of Beasts holds sway over the *babewyns*—murderous, ape-like animals which in truth are nothing more than reflections of humanity's own ignorance. If left unchecked, the horizon could consume Earth, forever thwarting mankind's development and condemning its future to little more than savagery.

Upon realizing this, the Doctor identifies the horizon's nexus point as the 18th century, the era in which humanity first conceptualized the notion of time as a dimension. Accordingly the Doctor arrives in London, 1782, and makes contact with a bordello owner and ritualist named Scarlette. Although failing to understand his own nature, the Doctor comprehends that his people, often cited as "elementals," previously protected the timeline. As such, the Doctor intends to ritualistically marry one of Scarlette's associates, the young Juliette, and link his elemental aspect to Earth. In such a fashion, the Earth will gain the Doctor's elemental protection, keeping the horizon at bay.

Scarlette invites Earth's religious factions to witness the Doctor's marriage. The Doctor's endeavors, meanwhile, draw the attention of Sabbath, a former British intelligence agent with an interest in ritualistic matters. Deeming himself a protector of humanity, Sabbath believes the Doctor is responsible for summoning the *babewyns* to Earth (technically true, since the Doctor was involved in the Time Lords' downfall). Sabbath dispatches his chief enforcer, Tula Lui—a bone-wielding Polynesian *Mayakai* warrior—to attack the Doctor and dissuade him from interfering in Earth's affairs. The Doctor eventually finds Sabbath aboard *The Jonah*, a battleship with very limited time travel capabilities. There, the two rivals forge an uneasy truce for the betterment of Earth.

Sabbath lets the Doctor base himself aboard *The Jonah*, but time starts to run short. An aspect of the horizon, manifesting itself as a ruined city inhabited by the *babewyns*, makes further contact with Earth. As part of this, some *babewyns* tear Tula Lui limb from limb. Sabbath places his own interests ahead of the Doctor's goals and starts regarding Juliette as a replacement for his fallen warrior. Stricken with doubts about her impending marriage, Juliette abandons the Doctor and begins training to serve as Sabbath's right hand.

Crushed, the Doctor succumbs to a lingering illness, a malady localized in his chest that's been brewing ever since his awakening on Earth (*The Burning*). The Doctor consigns himself to bed, but Scarlette, undaunted, decides to marry him in Juliette's place. As planned, Earth's major lodges assemble on a Caribbean island for the Doctor's nuptials.

Attended by Fitz and Anji, the Doctor recovers enough to carry through with the wedding ceremony. But as the Doctor and Scarlette kiss, thus completing the binding ritual, the King of Beasts musters enough resistance to transport the assembled wedding party and guests into the horizon's ruined city. Scarlette marshals the lodge members to combat the *babewyns*, as the Doctor locates a deserted palace in the city—a final remnant of his homeworld.

Fitz recognizes the edifice as a recreation of Gallifrey's Panopticon, as the ailing Doctor collapses, near death. Suddenly, Sabbath appears, having entered the horizon aboard *The Jonah*. Sabbath performs emergency heart surgery on the Doctor, having deduced that one of his hearts—which previously kept him linked to Gallifrey—has been poisoning him ever since his homeworld's demise. By removing the blackened organ, Sabbath saves the Doctor's life.

More human than ever before, the Doctor recovers and confronts the King of Beasts. The Doctor challenges the King to a duel on Earth, thereby transporting the combatants back to Scarlette's bordello, albeit a few months after they left. Scarlette apparently dies in the conflict, but the Doctor uses a prototype *screwdriver sonique*—a symbol of technological achievement, but also a ritual "fetish" far more powerful than any other on Earth—to behead the King. With the King's death, the *babewyns* vanish from Earth.

In the aftermath, Sabbath—intent on boosting his time travel capabilities—surgically installs the Doctor's heart into his own chest. Sabbath thereby becomes greater bound to his homeworld, Earth, and departs with Juliette aboard *The Jonah*. Scarlette's allies bury their mistress on February 9, 1783, but the Doctor senses his wife's presence. Scarlette privately tells the Doctor she faked her death, having realized that he's responsible for protecting more worlds than Earth. Shortly afterward, the Doctor parts company with Scarlette, collects Fitz and Anji and departs in the TARDIS.

MEMORABLE MOMENTS The opening scene, involving prostitute Lisa-Beth having sex with a member of Parliament (*see Sex and Spirits*), certainly grabs one's attention. Scarlette thinks the Doctor's predictable in that he *always* does something remarkable.

Sabbath, meeting the Doctor for the first time: "I'd be most impressed, *Doctor*, if most of the people who use that title weren't either third-rate quacks or peddlers in pornographic literature."

Anji and Fitz worry that if the Doctor's sick, there's literally something wrong with the world. Fitz claims that with regards to the wedding, the TARDIS qualifies as something old, new, borrowed and blue.

An inspired Scarlette organizes a massive *babewyn* hunt to keep the wedding guests entertained. A priest quiets the wedding viewers with: "*If you buggers will give me a moment's peace, I can get this over with.*"

The Master benevolently attends the wedding, proposing that perhaps one day, the Doctor will attempt to destroy the Universe—putting him in the awkward situation of saving it.

Most dramatically of all, the visual image of Sabbath standing over the Doctor's body, holding his blackened heart, surely stands out as one of the EDA range's most climactic moments.

SEX AND SPIRITS The Doctor avoids courtesan Katya's efforts to bed him. He holds genuine affection for Juliette, whom he considers a virginal sacrifice of sorts. However, Juliette's clearly undergoing a sexual awakening. She seemingly flirts with Fitz, although it's possibly just a means of testing her social skills. Scarlette's later convinced that Juliette's had sex, although exactly how or when isn't clarified.

The Doctor and Scarlette have no time to consummate their relationship (presuming the Doctor even has an interest). They sometimes lie together in bed, fully clothed. At one point, Scarlette proposes she and the Doctor continue fencing without weapons, wrestling naked on the floor—the Doctor's response isn't recorded.

Sabbath previously tried [unsuccessfully, it seems] to seduce Scarlette in 1780, but brushes off the incident with: "I did what was necessary."

Adventuress opens with prostitute Lisa-Beth screwing a member of Parliament. Bored with the liaison, Lisa-Beth drifts into a meditative state, *Shaktyanda*, that examines her own timeline. In such a fashion, she contacts the horizon, terrifyingly witnesses a *babewyn* and awakens to find her client missing.

The Doctor teleports Fitz and Anji into Scarlette's bordello, but he messes up and causes them to arrive naked. Fitz grins inanely at the prostitutes, unsure about protocol. He and Lisa-Beth sleep together at least once, more out of boredom than passion. Lisa-Beth and Katya later attempt [and presumably succeed] to double-team Fitz, hoping to get his help in fleeing before the wedding ceremony.

At an auction, Scarlette wryly suggests that anyone wishing to bed her must pay *two* philosopher's stones.

ASS-WHUPPINGS The Doctor succumbs to more than a century of heart illness, but Sabbath's open-heart surgery fixes the problem.

Reports claim that some time ago, prostitute Anne-Belle Paley was found dead in the back of a cab, her heart or lungs missing. [She likely came into contact with the *babewyns'* realm and—unlike Lisa-Beth—got savaged.]

This book is not endorsed by the BBC. Doctor Who and TARDIS are trademarks of the BBC.

157

The Secret Services' Rat-Catchers (*see Organizations*) storm *The Jonah*, but Tula Lui kills 'em. The *babewyns* later tear her apart.

Scarlette ritually summons some *babewyns* to "entertain" the wedding guests, leading to a massive hunt. Mostly, the *babewyns* die, but a cornered huntsmen or two get torn apart.

A final bloodbath in the *babewyns*' gray city proves costly, claiming priest Robert Ashton Kemp and many others as casualties. The Doctor eventually kills the King of Beasts.

Scarlette fakes her own death. A homicidal client kills Katya in 1783, but Scarlette most likely avenged her death.

Juliette apparently hangs herself as a sort of death ritual, designed to put her into Sabbath's service, but the Doctor happens along, pulls her down and successfully performs CPR. She tries to blame the *babewyns* for stringing her up, but it's notably too civilized an act for the likes of them.

TV TIE-INS The Doctor's poisoned heart likely contains his Rassilon Imprimature ("The Two Doctors").

NOVEL TIE-INS Adventuress focuses on fallout from the Time Lords' demise in *The Ancestor Cell*. The Doctor's supposedly been suffering chest pains since *The Burning*, although we only get signs of this in *Dark Progeny* and *Grimm Reality*.

Sabbath briefly appeared in Dave Stone's *The Slow Empire* as part of a computer reality, although nobody's sure how this occurred. From here, Sabbath becomes a recurring character, turning up in *Anachrophobia*, *History 101*, *Time Zero* and more. *Camera Obscura* resolves the issue of the Doctor's stolen heart. Two of Sabbath's agents cause trouble in *Trading Futures*.

A black-eyed sun keeps watch in the horizon— the first sign of an as-yet unidentified threat. The malevolent eyeball briefly crops up in *History 101*, and it's speculated that the upcoming *Sometime Never...* will deal with this menace.

TIE-INS In *Adventuress*, the Master tells the Doctor there are "only four of us left," which fandom immediately took to mean, "There are only four Time Lords left"—thus generating a shitstorm of discussion about the identities of the other two. However, it's all a lot more nebulous than that. Miles deliberately left unclear if the Master's speaking of Time Lords, Gallifreyans, Gallifreyan renegades, members of a specific clique, major elemental presences or even ferrets, for that matter.

BBV's *The Faction Paradox Protocols* (vols. 3 and 4) and the upcoming *Faction Paradox* comic series cover some of Sabbath's time as a British Secret Service agent.

CHARACTER DEVELOPMENT

• *The Doctor:* Marrying Scarlette gives the Doctor a symbolic green card of sorts, allowing him to formally serve as Earth's protector. The Doctor knows that in the post-*The Ancestor Cell* Universe, his family never existed (barring the Master), but paints a picture of a serious old man to serve as his grandfather.

The Doctor grows a moustache, beard and neat triangle of chin hair just to test if he can. Most people draw a single tarot card to tell their fortunes— the Doctor uses a quarter of a deck. [As it's a simple playing-card deck rather than a true tarot deck, that's 13 cards—suggesting one per life?]

He suspects he could turn himself into a being of pure light, given 3,000 years or less to work on the problem. The Doctor makes a will, dividing his estate into 13 portions, but the document's stored in the TARDIS catacombs and largely forgotten.

His handwriting's almost illegible. He can identify the *Mayakai* people. Thanks to his Time Lord inheritance, he can physically interact with the horizon and the Time Vortex. He dreams of "seven surgeons" [obviously his previous incarnations] who seemingly want to operate [on his poisonous heart, one presumes].

• *The Doctor and Scarlette:* The Doctor first met Scarlette on a street in Marylebone, asking if she was a magician. She sometimes calls the Doctor "Jack." Scarlette can best the Doctor at swords. Robert Ashton Kemp, a drunken Anglican priest in Birmingham, marries them. The oldest surviving *Mayakai*, the only person to whom Scarlette feels any fealty, blesses the marriage. Scarlette and the Doctor wed on December 1, 1782.

• *Fitz Kreiner:* In this time zone, he frequently visits a St. James' tobacconist notorious for selling laudanum.

• *Anji Kapoor:* She doesn't like the Doctor's beard. She avoids Scarlett's brothel as much as possible, wandering the streets of London.

• *Scarlette (a.k.a. The Adventuress of Henrietta Street):* She's English, and typically portrayed as a classical heroine. She wears red dresses with collar ruffles but makes few other concessions to femininity. She's got almond-shaped eyes, pale skin and aristocratic looks.

She's barely into her 20s and sometimes wears the Hellfire Club's red and black colors. She avoids functions with the Whigs, supporters of America. She once rode a woolly mammoth. Her attention

SABBATH 101

Is Sabbath a villain?

He's moreso the Doctor's rival than his outright adversary. The Doctor and Sabbath often share the same goals, but Sabbath's willing to cross a certain line [such as arranging someone's murder, when the need suits him] that the Doctor won't. It also must be said that Sabbath's obsessive behavior makes him dangerous, even psychotic at times. There are also instances when his lesser grasp of the nature of time travel (notably *Time Zero*) causes him to make poor decisions with grave consequences.

He still seems a lot like the Master to me.

Unfortunately, certain novels have painted Sabbath as a Master replacement, especially given his utterly annoying habit of disguising himself (chiefly *Anachrophobia* and *Time Zero*), then turning up at random to cause trouble. However, there's a crucial difference between them: Whereas the Master chiefly sought to conquer the Universe, Sabbath isn't interested in power for power's sake. His goals are very different.

... so what does Sabbath want?

To large degree, Sabbath wants to protect Earth. He views himself as a superior choice as protector of humanity, judging that the Doctor often lacks the mettle to properly safeguard mankind.

If the Doctor and Sabbath often want the same thing, how do they differ?

If we're being entirely honest, there's many occasions where Sabbath really *isn't* much different than the Doctor. Let's admit a certain truth: The Doctor is *always* turning up, putting people in their place, and insisting he knows better (his treatment of the Group-Captain Gilmore in "Remembrance of the Daleks" springs to mind). So if Sabbath often seems villainous, it's simply because he's arrogant enough to believe he knows better than the Doctor—and anyone who opposes the Doctor, for right or wrong, automatically gets pegged as the villain. [However, since Sabbath belongs to a post-Time-Lord universe and the Doctor still thinks like a Gallifreyan, there's instances when Sabbath probably *does* understand the modern continuum better than the Doctor.]

But if a chief difference between them exists, it's with regards to Sabbath's practical nature. There are many instances where the eighth Doctor will refuse to kill a single individual—say, Charley in "Neverland"—even though his mercy potentially endangers millions of lives [or, in the case of "Neverland," the entire damn Universe]. Sabbath, on the other hand, would happily have someone killed if it furthered a greater goal.

What's curious is that Sabbath far more closely mirrors the seventh Doctor's New Adventures personality, certainly with regards to books such as *Love and War*, *Eternity Weeps*, etc., where the Doctor sacrifices various individuals to serve a greater good. But certainly, Sabbath is more at odds with the eighth Doctor's personality, and *Camera Obscura* examines their philosophical differences in great detail.

Side Note: Sabbath vs. the New Adventures Doctor. Now *that* would be a showdown worth watching.

If the Doctor keeps thwarting Sabbath's aims, why doesn't Sabbath just kill him?

Sabbath kills when it's necessary, not when it's convenient. He sees the Doctor as something of a relic—after all, the Time Lords have "failed" the universe once already—but not exactly as a threat. Also, Sabbath's still new to the intricacies of time travel, and keeps the Doctor around to learn as much as possible from him. Finally, Sabbath sometimes manipulates the Doctor (chiefly *Anachrophobia*) into doing his dirty work for him.

Do the books after *Henrietta Street* constitute an "arc"? Do I need to read them in order?

No, that's ridiculous.

Sabbath is a recurring character, not an "arc." He's no more an "arc" than [and pardon the comparison] the Master ever was in the TV show.

The Adventuress of Henrietta Street introduces Sabbath, but it's only eight books later—with *Camera Obscura*—that the EDAs fall back on any sort of mythology. *Time Zero* also continues certain threads, but for the most part, the 2002 EDAs were either stand-alones or books requiring minimal explanation. [That said, it certainly doesn't hurt you to read them in order, and 2002 was an above-average year for the range].

---

to the bordello's finances often wanes. A *Mayakai* brought to Britain in the 1770s tutored her. She sometimes speaks with the TARDIS and sleeps near it.

Scarlette views Juliette's defection as a very personal failure on her part. After *Henrietta Street*, numerous stories appear to explain what becomes of Scarlette. Most likely, she accepts a new ap-

prentice with "more than a little of Juliette's blood in her veins."

Her "funeral" was held on February 9, 1783.

• *Scarlette and Sabbath:* They've previously met (*see History*). Sabbath tries to curtail the Doctor and Scarlette's interference by bringing Scarlette's house to financial ruin, but fails.

This book is not endorsed by the BBC. Doctor Who and TARDIS are trademarks of the BBC.

159

• *Sabbath:* Sabbath was born in 1740. He studied at Cambridge, where the Secret Service recruited him in 1762. His indoctrination allegedly entailed his sinking to the bottom of the Thames and somehow surviving, perhaps by use of *siddhis*, alleged supernatural skills that the Service stole from Eastern *tantrists*.

Sabbath notably defected from the Secret Service in 1780. The Service sent its Rat-Catchers (*see Organizations*) to assassinate Sabbath, but Tula Lui in turn eliminated various high-ranking Service officers—a message for them to leave her mentor alone.

Sabbath's overweight, with a bulky, muscular body that's shifting toward plump. He keeps his head shaved, with a thin layer of dark hair. He's primarily headquartered aboard *The Jonah* and in Manchester. Sabbath isn't rich as such, but can acquire money if it facilitates his goals. He considers the military, with its insistence on protocol and uniform, absurd.

He knows rituals that summon and bind the *babewyns* to his will [they assist with surgically implanting the Doctor's heart in Sabbath's chest]. He possesses enough engineering skills to oversee construction of *The Jonah*. He sometimes consults with his associate, Dr. Nie Who, regarding his theories about the workings of time.

• *The Doctor and Sabbath:* Before their falling out, the Doctor named Sabbath his best man. They jointly attended the premiere of Mozart's *The Abduction from the Seraglio* in Vienna.

Sabbath at least aided the Doctor by showed up at the wedding in an ape mask, ritualistically showing the *babewyns* had no power over the event.

At some point after 1783, Sabbath grows determined to have the Doctor killed at all costs.

• *The Master (a.k.a. The Man With the Rosette):* The Doctor's only family member at the wedding. He wears black clothing, complete with a blue/white rosette from a Manchester tavern, marking him as member of the Opposition (i.e. the Whigs, advocates of democracy). He supplied Doctor and Scarlette's wedding rings.

The Master's now a clean-shaven, dark-haired man in distinguished middle age [it's unclear if he's an older Eric Roberts incarnation or a new one]. His accent's English, but his features have a little Latin.

The Master says the Universe might one day be ready for his feud with the Doctor again. He departs after the Doctor's wedding, saying he might go to sleep, hopefully awakening in a Universe that won't bore him.

• *Juliette Vierge (a.k.a. "The Flower"):* A pretty little redhead, intelligent and allegedly born in 1769. She possibly knew Lisa-Beth during her time in India from the mid-1770s to 1781. Almost nothing is known about her life. She never knew her parents. She perhaps had a twin sister, believed deceased.

• *Lisa-Beth Lachlan:* Lisa's the most accomplished *tantrist* in Scarlette's house. When the Secret Service investigates the bordello too closely, Lisa-Beth takes a Service agent prisoner and marks the Service's five names of power onto his chest—a warning that if the Service doesn't behave, the names will get distributed to its rivals.

No record of her exists after 1789.

• *Scarlette and Lisa-Beth:* They're both trained in the art of *black coffee*, a somewhat arcane practice—associated with sex acts—that can summon the *babewyns*.

• *Rebecca Macardle:* Handsome, literate, and among the last of the "Deerfield witches" to evacuate America in 1781. She often runs the bordello's card table. She helped Lisa-Beth run Scarlette's house until 1789, then found employment in central Europe for a government agency. No reliable record of her death exists.

• *Tula Lui:* A 16-year-old *Mayakai* warrior, Tula Lui left for the Western world at age seven. Sabbath first encountered her, age 10, in 1776. She was his only real company between 1780 and 1782.

• *The TARDIS:* It includes an opera house which the Doctor picked up by accident, intended to deliver somewhere and forgot about.

ALIEN RACES *The babewyns:* A manifestation of mankind's ignorance, appearing ape-like because humans at basest level hold a lot in common with apes. The *babewyns* have burning eyes, but little by way of internal physiognomy. Essentially, they stay alive by sheer will. There's probably millions of them.

The Maroons, a lodge at the wedding, eat some *babewyns* and claim they taste like pork—but that's perhaps because they *expected* them to taste like pork.

STUFF YOU NEED *Scarlette's Glass Totem:* The greatest surviving relic of the bloody, gothic events of 1762 (*The Faction Paradox Protocols* vols. 3 and 4), a piece of glass that witch-sorceress Mary Culver slit her own throat with.

• *The Screwdriver Sonique:* A new version of the Doctor's sonic screwdriver, composed of a narrow tube of glass, mounted on a steel handle and run through with wire.

THE CRUCIAL BITS...

- **THE ADVENTURESS OF HENRIETTA STREET**—The Doctor marries Scarlette, a 18th century bordello owner, to ritualistically keep the horizon—an indescribable realm beyond human understanding—from consuming Earth.

First appearance of Sabbath, a former intelligence agent who deems himself a superior guardian of Earth. Sabbath saves the Doctor's life by removing one of his poisoned hearts, only to implant the organ in his own chest and gain greater control of time travel. Guest appearance by the Master (a.k.a. the man with the rosette), who holds little interest in battling the Doctor these days. First appearance of the giant, malevolent eyeball that keeps watch in the horizon.

ORGANIZATIONS *The Rat-Catchers:* The Secret Service's muscle, founded to enforce the department's conditioning. By 1782, only one renegade—Sabbath—had escaped them.

- *The Wedding Guests:* The Doctor envisions his marriage as a means of uniting Earth's major ritualist lodges. However, it's worth noting that only 12 of the 13 invited lodges are identified.

SHIPS *The Jonah:* A monstrosity of a steam-powered vessel, although actually not that large for a battleship. It's about 20 yards long, but no more than a dozen across, reflecting Sabbath's obsession with efficiency. *The Jonah's* bridge is a great vaulted steel hall, 20 feet wide and 30 long. It contains a detailed map of the world.

The Jonah granted Sabbath limited time travel, although his skill greatly improved after stealing the Doctor's heart. Every steel plate onboard *The Jonah* is inscribed with a magic word.

PHENOMENA *The Horizon:* The Doctor believes the horizon encroached on Earth in the 1780s because 1781 saw publication of Johan Wessel's *Anno 7603*, the first Western work related directly to time travel. In short, the book enhanced mankind's understanding of time as a dimension en masse and acted like a summoning.

- *Magical Theory:* In very broad terms, it states that a person's power is inseparable from their place of authority. Accordingly, Scarlette to large degree is her house, the Doctor is his TARDIS and Sabbath is his warship, *The Jonah*.

HISTORY It's said that famous Covent Garden celebrity Fanny Murray fell for Sabbath's charms as early as 1762.

- Scarlette was born in 1762, the same year that London witch-sorceress Mary Culver (*The Faction Paradox Protocols*) slit her own throat.

- Some of the Time Lords' knowledge has worked its way into various arcana and is now used, in varying degrees, by the Hellfire Club, the Grand Lodge Freemasons, the witch-cults in Russia, the West Indies religious orders, Scarlette's coven and more.

- In 1773, a great plague ostensibly largely wiped out the Polynesian *Mayakai*. A scant handful survived, taking refuge in Europe or the Americas.

- On June 6, 1780, Scarlette was present during the Gordon Riots when Newgate Prison burned to the ground. Her exact role in the affair remains unclear, although Sabbath was also present and, at the time, tried to seduce her.

- By 1782, the last known *Mayakai* in Europe resided in St. James.

- The Doctor's *The Ruminations of a Foreign Traveler in His Element*—a discursive, awkward catalogue of his adventures—was published in 1783 to a tiny circulation. [The Doctor, it must be said, makes a better adventurer than an author.]

- A fragmented report claims that either Fitz or Anji died in the 21st century.

AT THE END OF THE DAY For better or worse, Mad Norwegian Press' current publishing arrangement with Mr. Miles forbids us fronting a review for *The Adventuress of Henrietta Street*. Call us old fashioned, but we respect areas of conflict of interest and—given Mad Norwegian's extensive work with Lawrence to publish *Faction Paradox* books and comics—this appears to be one of them. So for now, we can only comment: *"The Adventuress of Henrietta Street.* It's 284 pages long. And did we mention that it's got whores?"

DID YOU KNOW?

- Amusingly enough, the initial outline of *Adventuress* [provisionally entitled *The Napoleon of Beasts*] failed to mention the following: A) the Doctor and Scarlette get married, B) Sabbath removes the Doctor's heart, C) Scarlette apparently dies and D) the fact the entire book is written as a historical text rather than as a straight narrative. Halfway through the book, Miles checked with editor Justin Richards that removing the heart wouldn't be a problem, but still failed to mention the rest.

- Sabbath was originally more closely based on Captain Nemo, with the final confrontation involving a techno'd-up submarine flying into the ape-city on a pair of enormous flapping wings, grappling monkeys with its steampunk tentacles.

However, Miles drastically changed direction upon reading Alan Moore's acclaimed comic series *The League of Extraordinary Gentlemen*, fearing he'd get accused of ripping Moore off.

MAD DOGS AND ENGLISHMEN

By Paul Magrs

Release Date: *January 2002*
Order: *BBC Eighth Doctor Adventure #52*

TARDIS CREW The eighth Doctor, Fitz and Anji, with Iris Wildthyme.

TRAVEL LOG Terran Science Fiction of the Twentieth Century convention, unnamed planet, circa 2174; dogworld space station, 2077 [that's a guess, allowing for the stated transmission time between the dogworld and Earth]; Tyler's house and the Book and Candle bar, Mayfair, England, springtime, 1942; Hotel Miramar, Las Vegas, 1960; Los Angeles, 1978.

STORY SUMMARY While attending a convention on science-fiction literature, a stunned Doctor finds that Reginald Tyler's *The True History of Planets*—a celebrated 20th century fantasy work—has retroactively become a story about talking poodles. The Doctor examines the alternate version of *Planets*, and discovers galactic coordinates hidden in a Chapter 87 footnote. Taking the bait, the Doctor and his friends soon arrive at a space station and meet two talking poodle archivists, Fritter and Char.

The Doctor's group soon realizes the space station screens Earth transmissions for viewing on the dogworld—an entire planet inhabited by poodles. In due course, the Doctor finds that the poodle story portrayed in *Planets* mirrors the tragic story of Princess Margaret, a royal poodle deposed when her uncle, the Emperor, killed her mother. Margaret somehow tinkered with time and turned Tyler's *Planets* into her life story, hoping that the *Planets* motion picture version—when broadcast on the dogworld—would incite rebellion in her favor.

Fritter and Char support the Emperor, and agree to help the Doctor undo Margaret's historical distortion. The Doctor quickly splits up his allies, dropping them off throughout the 20th century to investigate the poodle-themed *Planets*. In Las Vegas, 1960, Fitz investigates singer Bren-

da Soobie, responsible for the *Planets* theme song in future. Meanwhile, Anji and Fritter look up *Planets* director John Fuchas in Los Angeles, 1978, even as the Doctor and Char get to the root of the problem and track down Tyler in England, 1942.

Fitz eventually recognizes Soobie as yet-another incarnation of the time-traveling harridan named Iris Wildthyme. Simultaneously, the Doctor and Char find B-level novelist William Freer, one of Margaret's agents, using the dogworld's time-lost dark sorcery to influence Tyler's mind—thus swaying him to redraft *Planets* as a story about poodles. Moreover, the Doctor discovers famous playwright Nöel Coward also contacted by one of Margaret's allies—supporting the Princess' cause. Thanks to his good friend Iris, Coward now possesses a pair of dimension-rending pinking shears, capable of opening time-space portals by cutting the Very Fabric of Time and Space.

Chaos ensues on most fronts, leading Coward to realize Margaret would become a tyrant far, far worse than the reasonably benevolent Emperor. Thanks to Coward's pinking shears, the Doctor collects his allies—leaving Fuchas tied up in 1978—and forces a confrontation on the dogworld. Margaret uses her own mystical powers to overcome the Emperor's guards, paving way for a coup, but everyone involved discovers that the *Planets* motion picture has unexpectedly reverted to Tyler's original fantasy story, largely curtailing Margaret's revolution.

An enraged Margaret tries to kill the Emperor, but mutually dies in combat with Char. Afterward, Coward's pinking sheers return the Doctor's group to Earth some weeks after they left—causing them to realize the tied-up Fuchas starved to death in their absence, explaining why the poodles version of *Planets* never got made. Life returns to normal on the dogworld, even as Iris—acknowledging the amnesiac Doctor doesn't recognize her—quietly slips away in her TARDIS.

MEMORABLE MOMENTS When the TARDIS materializes and seemingly squishes Professor Jag—an aphid—the Doctor considers he may, in fact, have mashed intelligent beings all over the Universe and been none the wiser. He's unsurprised when murders start occurring at the sci-fi literature convention because: "Just about anyone could walk into the hotel, any time."

Singer Brenda Soobie [Iris] prances about onstage and tosses out a feather boa, it's said, "like a throttled anaconda."

Upon learning that Freer and Princess Margaret's true intentions, Coward tells his allies: "We

were all hoodwinked, my dears, by a satanist and a royal poodle."

At story's end, a woman arrives at Coward's doorstep with kittens supposedly hailing from the besieged pussyworld. The woman implores the famous playwright to help, but Coward—thinking he's gotten involved in enough animal machinations for one day—slams the door in her face.

SEX AND SPIRITS Virtually everyone recoils to learn that novelist William Freer and the poodle Princess Margaret have been *lovers* since 1932 [even Coward spits out his drink at this].

Fritter traffics bootleg videos of Earth films—such as *Lassie Come Home* and *Digby the Biggest Dog in the World*—on the dogworld black market, apparently to kinky [possibly even S&M of sorts] poodle customers.

On the space station, Princess Margaret views the TARDIS crew as her pets, makes them strip and shackles them in dog-style collars and chokers. A bare-assed Anji is utterly mortified, but the Doctor and Fitz show no self-modesty. Anji tries to avoid getting an eyeful, but can't help it at times.

Fitz starts to realize that all the time he's spent dossing about, getting drunk and falling for unsuitable women *has* harmed him [although he fails to specify how].

The Doctor drinks with Tyler's colleague Cleavis at the Book and Candle bar. He also shares champagne with Coward. The Doctor and Fitz gamble in Las Vegas. Fitz and other characters dine with Coward, downing a pale green, very dry white wine.

Academic Mida Silke flirts with the Doctor, but he fails to notice. Iris retains some pent-up attraction for the Doctor, but restrains herself [for once] because he doesn't recognize her.

ASS-WHUPPINGS In one of the most terrifying "Who" moments ever, Princess Margaret deems her lover Freer of no further use—then leaps on his shoulder and tears his throat out. [Author's Note: Bloodsoaked, ravenous poodles. We always knew it could happen.]

Professor Alid Jag, an aphid and agent of MIAOW (*see Organizations*) fakes his death when the TARDIS materializes. Fellow MIAOW agent Mida Silke later squashes him, just to eliminate the competition.

During a brouhaha in Las Vegas, a heavy stage curtain thumps Fitz unconscious.

Freer's black arts make Tyler's face melt into a gaping hole—inexplicably channeling Princess Margaret through Tyler. [He somehow survives and unbelievably regrows his face over the course

of three months—that's sorcery for you.] Princess Margaret pulls the same stunt on the Emperor's guards to defend herself, making them faceless.

Char hurls Princess Margaret to her death, then dies from his wounds. A poodle named Martha—both Iris' companion and Margaret's ex-handmaiden—proves unable to live without Margaret and flings herself off a balcony also.

Director John Fuchas gets forgotten about, starves to death.

TV TIE-INS Freer writes a novel entitled *The Slaves of Sutekh* ("Pyramids of Mars") published by Faber and Faber. As a cover story, the Doctor blathers about events/characters in "Spearhead from Space," "Planet of the Spiders" and "Terror of the Zygons," failing to realize he actually experienced them.

NOVEL TIE-INS Fitz doesn't immediately recognize Iris (who last appeared in *The Blue Angel*), suggesting we're dealing with a new incarnation. Iris also acknowledges visiting the Doctor's house in *Father Time*, but he fails to identify her—again suggesting she's wearing a new body. She fears the Doctor's changed almost beyond recognition since she last saw him. When Iris' TARDIS dematerializes, the Doctor realizes that he's not entirely alone in the Universe (*The Ancestor Cell*), although he already knew that from the Master's visit in *The Adventuress of Henrietta Street*.

The Doctor still has a beard (*Adventuress* again). Anji yet again (*The City of the Dead*) smolders at witnessing the Doctor's skill with the TARDIS, wondering why the bloody hell he can't get her home.

Tyler's University [likely Cambridge] offered the Doctor a Chair but he turned it down, not wanting to appear conspicuous and needing to look after Miranda (*Father Time*).

Fictional creatures (Professor Challenger, etc.) aboard a train seem to resemble the alien Meercocks, who morphed into creatures from literature. However, this doesn't really mesh with their appearance in *Verdigris*, suggesting Magrs is simply being cute.

CHARACTER DEVELOPMENT

• *The Doctor:* The Doctor decided to visit the literary science-fiction conference to hear Professor Jag's lecture on writer Fox Soames. The Doctor's read the genuine *The True History of Planets* and deems it wonderful.

The Doctor speed reads. He improvises, as part of a cover story, that he's from a little place in Ireland that starts with "G."

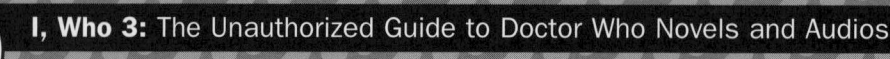

He's observed South Seas shamanism similar to Freer's black arts. He's unfamiliar with the travel effect that Coward's pinking shears generate.

He hasn't gambled in years, but previously had a system for beating casinos.

• *Fitz Kreiner:* He likes dogs, but despises poodles. He doesn't like the TARDIS library much because it's so vast. He also dislikes glitzy Las Vegas shows.

• *Iris Wildthyme and Martha:* The late Empress' handmaiden, Martha somehow fled the dogworld with Iris, determined to help Margaret regain the throne. She remained as Iris' poodle companion for 60 years, furthering her singing career. She also helped sway Nöel Coward to Margaret's cause.

• *Iris Wildthyme:* As "Brenda Soobie," Iris has become a world-famous Scots Caribbean songstress. She hammers every single note while onstage, and to Fitz's horror, her song rendition in 1960 includes future tunes such as "Hey Jude" and "Bohemian Rhapsody."

"Brenda" allegedly hails from Glasgow. She's shied away from full-scale adventures, focusing on her singing career. After Martha's death, Iris accepts hotel chef Flossie and poodle archivist Fritter as her new companions.

• *Iris and Nöel Coward:* Iris met Noel at the Royal Variety Performance, 1957.

• *Nöel Coward:* Thanks to Iris' pinking shears, Coward learns to manipulate his own timeline. Different temporal versions of Coward simultaneously operate in multiple time zones. Coward even learns how to merge two of his selves, replacing an older Coward with a younger one. Whenever Coward's oldest self dies [as history records in 1972], he's somehow whistled back to his birth to live his life all over again.

Even so, Coward resists knowing the future, thinking life wouldn't be fun otherwise.

• *William Freer:* First fell under Princess Margaret's sway after conjuring her up during a Black Mass [evidently, Freer's magics resonate with those of the dogworld].

• *Flossie:* Portly TARDIS companion [for this story only] who owned a chain of restaurants in the future. She fell from grace when a miscommunication led to her feeding some very important lobster people lobster.

• *Princess Margaret:* She's older [for a poodle], and not very easy on the eyes. She smokes.

• *The TARDIS:* During his early days aboard the TARDIS, Fitz once happened upon an old woman lying face down on a table in the Ship's library, surrounded by hundreds of volumes on British birds. She wore what looked like 1960s teenage gear but was draped in cobwebs. Fitz

THE CRUCIAL BITS...

• **MAD DOGS AND ENGLISHMEN**—First appearance of yet another Iris Wildthyme incarnation, complete with Martha, her poodle companion of 60 years.

woke her up and accompanied her back to the console room, where the Doctor turned shocked and called her "Emily." She failed to recover her identity, and presumably returned home somehow.

The library's card catalog speaks directly to Fitz [via red ink on various cards]. Certain books are booby-trapped.

ALIEN RACES *The dogworld poodles:* They have five-fingered hands [on Earth, they disguise this fact with booties], which enabled them to climb to the top of their evolutionary ladder. Dogworld poodles must be frightfully long-lived, as Martha's been Iris' companion for 60 years.

STUFF YOU NEED *Coward's Pinking Shears:* Enables time travel by cutting a rift in the Very Fabric of reality, opening a space-time conduit that's *not* the Time Vortex [and indeed, seems exclusive to use by Coward and some of the Emperor's poodles]. The rift seals up shortly afterward. Travelers can see past and future travelers in the conduit, meaning multiple Cowards are present.

ORGANIZATIONS *MIAOW (a.k.a. Ministry for Incursions and Ontological Wonders):* Organization devoted to insuring that history doesn't get buggered with. MIAOW agents include the late Professor Alid Jag [an aphid], and Professor Mida Slike, who holds a Chair in Bastardization at the University of Outer Angila.

MIAOW agents routinely compete with one another. The Emperor hired them to insure the poodle version of *Planets* never got made.

• *Smudgelings:* Tyler's literary discussion group, with his friend Cleavis [a thinly disguised C.S. Lewis] as their unofficial leader.

ALTERNATE HISTORY [Author's Note: The following details either occur as part of the alternate history in which *Planets* concerned itself with poodles, or it's simply a heap of lies perpetrated by special effects wizard Ron Von Arnim, who's at least half mad.]

• Special effects guru Von Arnim worked on Sean Connery's last Bond movie, *Voodoo Something To Me*, which entailed skeletons and zombies climbing out of New Orleans graveyards.

• Nöel Coward starred as Aragorn in a John Waters drag version of *Lord of the Rings*, which included Bette Davis as Sauron and Joan Crawford as Gandalf the witch.

• Coward also wrote the hit song "Martha," performed by Brenda Soobie [Iris], which became the theme song for the blockbuster hit *The True History of Planets* [the poodle version, obviously]. The first line goes: "What's the web of time, when you've lost your favorite four-legged friend."

• Princess Margaret succeeded in not only regaining the dogworld throne, but in brutally deposing the British Royal Family.

HISTORY Reginald Tyler [quite obviously a spoof on J.R. Tolkien] started writing *The True History of Planets* in 1917, while on leave from soldiering in France. He labored on it through both World Wars, eventually becoming a college professor.

• Freer was a very minor 20th century novelist. Cleavis wrote a children's story about [at the Doctor's suggestion] an innocuous piece of household furniture [obviously a cousin to *The Lion, the Witch and the Wardrobe*].

• Tyler allegedly died in 1974, but in reality, the Emperor's agents kidnapped him as part of this story's intrigue. A grateful Emperor allowed Tyler to remain on the dogworld.

• Enid Tyler cashed in on her "late" husband's work and moved to Jamaica.

• When storms struck England in 1988, some boars escaped from a neighbor's property and settled on the Doctor's land in Kent (*Father Time*). He sheltered them, thereby becoming responsible for a resurgence of England's wild boar population during the 1990s. He also evidently taught them to talk, possibly enabling them to evolve into a talking pig race seen in future.

• BBC Three broadcast the motion picture version of *The True History of Planets* at 2 pm, Christmas Day, 2010. *Halliwell Film Guide of 2010* critically skewered the work, but it seems to have been popular anyway.

AT THE END OF THE DAY A guilty pleasure, the joyous Mad Dogs and Englishmen makes you feel like you've just had a rewarding backscratch. It's intensely comfortable with its own camp identity—as evidenced by the foofy, smoking poodle on the cover—and the fact that few of Magrs' characters [especially the fat cook Flossie] would get the likes of Tom Cruise and Halle Barry to play them. When all's said and done is Paul Magrs' best "Who" book to date, extremely clean and a rolling good time. Hell, we laugh just to even *think* about it.

HOPE

By Mark Clapham

Release Date: *February 2002*
Order: *BBC Eighth Doctor Adventure #53*

TARDIS CREW The eighth Doctor, Fitz and Anji.

TRAVEL LOG City of Hope, planet Endpoint, the far-flung future.

CHRONOLOGY For Anji, "some months" after *Escape Velocity*.

STORY SUMMARY Still smarting from the loss of his heart (*The Adventuress of Henrietta Street*), the Doctor tests himself by piloting the TARDIS into the far-flung future. The Ship finally grounds itself on the planet Endpoint, near a colony named Hope, during winter. But as the Doctor, Fitz and Anji explore their frosty surroundings, the TARDIS accidentally plummets into a frozen sea.

Stranded, the Doctor's trio find Hope's people to be a last vestige of humanity, genetically modified to survive in a toxic environment. Eventually, the Doctor learns a cyborg named Silver both controls the colony's industry and serves as its *de facto* leader. Actually a time-lost refugee from the 30th century (*see Character Development*), Silver agrees to help retrieve the TARDIS. In turn, he asks the Doctor's help in capturing an unidentified serial killer at work in the city.

Meanwhile, Anji learns Silver possesses advanced cloning technology, and asks if it's possible to genetically recreate her dead lover Dave. Silver agrees, but in return asks Anji to smuggle a handheld scanner aboard the TARDIS, allowing him to study the Ship's technical specifications. Anji consents, desperate to see Dave live in any form, and offers up a keepsake—one of Dave's hairs—for cloning purposes.

The Doctor eventually pins the "random" murders in Hope to a clutch of humans—survivors from less-fortunate colonies—who recently awakened from cryo-sleep. As part of their genetics program, the humans have been decapitating people in Hope to harvest Kallisti, an adrenaline-like hormone exclusive to Endpointers' vivactic glands. If successful, the humans hope to treat 2,000 of their fellow cryo-sleepers with Kallisti, helping to insure their bloodline's survival.

With the Doctor's help, Silver captures the cryo-

sleepers' deep-sea bunker and its Hypertunnel, a means of teleporting to other worlds. Additionally, Silver dredges up the TARDIS, allowing Anji to record its technical data, then begins growing a Dave clone. Finally, Silver uses a cloud-seeding pod in the cryo-sleepers' equipment to return Hope's toxic environment to human norm.

The Doctor benevolently helps Silver synthesize a more durable Kallisti variant, intending it for a wide range of medical benefits. Unfortunately, Silver—thirsting for even greater power—uses the Doctor's serum to convert three dozen cryo-sleepers into Kallisti-powered, semi-synthetic soldiers named "Silverati." Silver plans to leave Hope via the Hypertunnel and use his super-strong soldiers to conquer a rich Imperial Homeworld. In time, Silver hopes to generate an entire army of Silverati, and conquer world after world with duplicated TARDISes.

Silver activates his Hypertunnel, but the Doctor stages a distraction and steals back the stolen TARDIS data. Additionally, the Doctor fiddles with the Hypertunnel coordinates, causing Silver and his Silverati to materialize on planet A2756, a desolate world containing only the remnants of an extinct civilization. With Silver and his army stranded, the Doctor forgives Anji for her betrayal. Hoping to forge a new life for himself, the Dave clone remains on Hope as the TARDIS departs.

MEMORABLE MOMENTS The captive Doctor berates a renegade human for being so cutthroat, arguing that the people of Hope—whatever their genetic modification—are the true inheritors of humanity's mantle. The Doctor sufficiently gets his point across, but his captor, a curious surgeon, merely replies: "You don't know how much I look forward to cutting you open."

SEX AND SPIRITS Anji goes to great lengths to resurrect Dave, despite quietly acknowledging that A) He probably wasn't the love of her life, B) She was on the verge of leaving him (prior to *Escape Velocity*), and that C) She kept naïvely convincing herself their relationship would last forever. She concedes her relationship with Dave was more defining than her previous love affairs, but it's easy to see how she's held onto Dave this long simply because he died. Indeed, Anji keeps saying she wants to bring Dave back because he "didn't have a chance to succeed in life," which is not exactly true and, on a certain level, indirectly insulting to Dave.

Eventually, Anji finds she lacks an emotional connection to Dave II, effectively closing a chapter of her life.

Anji kept Dave's first gray hair as a keepsake, joking about his getting older. The two of them once visited Green Park.

Fitz gets sloshed in the Silver Palace's bar. He awkwardly hits on a singer, but she calls him a pervert. He fondly studies the backside of Miraso, Silver's sexy female assistant. Miraso asks Fitz if he's ever been in love, and Fitz, slightly reopening old wounds, replies: "It's not been unknown."

ASS-WHUPPINGS The wounded TARDIS grounds itself on Hope, requiring time to recalibrate its systems.

Silver easily (and lethally) quells a casino dispute. While invading the renegade humans' base, Silver offs 43 opponents. He later pins his second, Miraso, to the wall for betraying him.

Silver diverts Hope's main power supply to pinpoint the renegade humans' base, causing a power loss that results in some deaths. The Doctor sets off an explosion that miraculously only lacerates a Silverati with shrapnel.

During the finale, Silver beats the Doctor silly, but Anji jabs a dart into Silver's eye. The Doctor also crams a microblade into Silver's elbow joint, paralyzing his arm.

NOVEL TIE-INS Anji's boyfriend Dave died in *Escape Velocity*.

The Doctor's still acclimating to the loss of his heart, plus the fact his other Time Lord attributes have gone dormant. He keeps forgetting he can't metabolize drugs or use his respiratory bypass system. The Doctor's new ties to Earth make him feel disconcerted in a time zone where Earth's long dead. He also keeps subconsciously scratching his now-missing beard (all *The Adventuress of Henrietta Street*).

His pockets contain a diamond engagement ring (*Adventuress* again).

The Doctor supplies his companions with survival discs, which he acquired from the human salvagers in *Grimm Reality*. The small, gold discs extend a microscopic filtration layer that lets the crew survive in Hope's toxicity.

Hope's "end of the Universe" setting was first seen in *The Infinity Doctors* and also appeared in *Father Time*. Fitz sings what sounds like Chinese—a reference to his time as a Chinese agent in *Revolution Man*.

CHARACTER DEVELOPMENT
• *The Doctor:* The Doctor remains uncertain if his single heart will grant him a human lifespan or conk out tomorrow. His body's more human than ever before, but his thoughts remain alien.

THE CRUCIAL BITS...

- **HOPE**—Anji helps create a genetic copy of her dead boyfriend Dave, who remains in the far-flung future.

He considers himself something of a Libertarian. He carries a supermarket card with six months worth of points.

- *Anji Kapoor:* Anji now looks upon the TARDIS as home. She [rather implausibly] acclimates to Hope's futuristic accounting principles.
- *The Doctor and Anji:* She's jealous of the Doctor's talent for bending the rules of life and death. The Doctor gets upset about Anji's betrayal, but forgives her in the span of a few minutes.
- *Dave Young II:* The cloned Dave sports toned muscles, whereas the original barely exercised. Dave II is a born fighter, with a striking confidence—extremely different from his sire.
- *Silver (a.k.a. Humberto don Silvestre):* On Silver's origin, *see History*.

Silver's an immensely tall cyborg, with an oversized right arm ending in a huge fist at knee level. Gun-barreled attachments, which fire small missiles, sprout from the back of this four-fingered hand. His other arm's more normal, but muscular.

He boasts super-strength and resistance. His sensors can detect heart rates, plus grant enhanced eyesight. He's powerful enough to single-handedly capture the renegade humans' base. His feet also contain booster packs, aiding him in swimming through Hope's waters.

His face looks human, with thick, black hair, although a faceplate covers half his head.

His brain contains a mercury-like substance, part of an alien computer network (*see History*). The brain enhancement, among other things, makes Silver a shrewd businessman.

He can inject a tracking nanobot into someone's bloodstream via a simple handshake.

His brain contains a copy of the "Chronicles of Knowledge." Silver otherwise curtails knowledge in Hope, particularly printed matter, to better maintain control. Hope's residents look upon Silver as their benefactor.

ALIEN RACES *Endpointers:* They're descended from a number of races, but are chiefly human. Endpointers have highly evolved lungs and a protective inner eyelid rather than eyelashes. They're traditionally bald, but throwback features (hair, blue skin, etc.) sometimes show up.

- *The Silverati:* Humanoid, but with silvery, shining skin and deep black eyes. Kallisti-enhanced machine colonies in the Silverati's blood keeps them geared for battle, and guarantees their loyalty to Silver.

ALIEN PLANETS *Endpoint:* Home to the colonies of Hope, Survival, Triumph, Victory and Persistence [a flatter and smaller settlement than Hope]. Endpoint's unfriendly atmosphere makes travel between such cities difficult, but not impossible. Endpoint's weather disruptions allow Silver to monitor every ship arriving at Hope.

STUFF YOU NEED *Kallisti:* Hormone unique to Endpoint residents, found in the brain's vivactic gland. Kallisti bolsters Endpointers' immunity to their environment, normally breaking down on contact with air. The Doctor left the people of Hope with a more durable Kallisti serum, providing lots of benefits.

PLACES TO GO *Hope:* It's built on stilts, straddling a frozen sea of acid.

Towers line Hope's eastern perimeter. "Long Pier" is a slender web of interweaving walkways that reach the mainland. Hope sports a city militia, headed by Chief Powlin, but Silver holds the true authority.

Hope society is based around loose rules, with violence and even murder reasonably tolerated. [Silver seeks to eliminate the city's serial killer, on the grounds that such a killer is too unpredictable.]

All resources are at a premium in Hope, so virtually nothing is disposable.

Silver's entertainment facilities provide a rare bit of pleasure on Hope, actually drawing tourists from other colonies.

ORGANIZATIONS *The Brotherhood of the Silver Fist:* A sham organization, secretly founded by Silver and Miraso to gather dissidents together, then allow Silver to triumphantly best them and rally public support. The Brotherhood uses cybernetic enhancements, possibly stolen from the long-dead Cybermen.

HISTORY Humberto don Silvestre (a.k.a. Silver) was born, to his mother Maria, on Dec. 31, 2978, on Earth. The era's high levels of pollution made Humberto a sickly child, but he nonetheless excelled at computer skills. At age 15, Humberto got caught hacking into the Central TacNet, impressing authorities enough to recruit him for their Tactical AI Division in Melbourne, Australia. Officials granted Humberto artificial lungs and a lot of medical drugs, giving him a mandate to tinker with sophisticated software and hardware.

• On Dec. 31, 3000, a resentful Sun City teenager hacked into Earth's TacNet mainframe. The spiteful little teen triggered a technological meltdown that killed thousands along Australia's wealthy East Coast. Humberto survived the incident, but suffered brain damage. At a Zero G Hospital facility orbiting Earth, Maria gave her assent for officials to save Humberto's life with a radical operation. Officials grafted an alien-made, liquid computer onto Humberto's brain, greatly enhancing his cognitive abilities. Humberto emerged from the procedure a combat-ready cyborg.

• In 3006, alien invaders landed in Detroit, quickly overrunning America and capturing Washington. With Earth unable to cope, its High Command authorized use of an experimental time travel device to acquire aid from other time zones. Agent Grey went into the past, but Silver journeyed into the far future.

• Some time ago, a diverse number of species and colonies resided in the Endpoint System. One of the smaller planets, named A245, became the system's dumping ground for spent fuel rods, decommissioned military equipment and toxic waste.

• Eventually, war erupted and a fleet of enemy ships ransacked the system. Most Endpoint planets and moons suffered total annihilation, but A245—tagged as a dump—went unscathed.

• With the rest of the system ruined, civilization on A245 (renamed Endpoint) developed a feudal system of government. Silver emerged from his time jump and quickly dominated Hope's industry, but proved unable to return.

• The Universe is now past the point of sustainable expansion. Entropy is settling in, killing off stars at an increased rate.

• Hope's security grid (SacNet) came online two generations ago. The power drain shut down the city for a month, caused a reactor to suffer meltdown and killed hundreds.

• Purebred humans haven't been seen for centuries. Apples haven't existed for millennia, but the Doctor gives Silver an apple core that lets him clone apple trees.

AT THE END OF THE DAY Average at best, *Hope* strangely draws acclaim in some sectors for granting Anji, the young'un in the TARDIS, with some depth of character. The problem being: It's still pretty surface level and not particularly *good* characterization. Ultimately, Anji betrays the Doctor for a genetic—not an identical copy—of Dave, making her about as nutty as people who keep vials of their dead cat's blood in the freezer with the misguided hope of cloning them back to

life. Oh, and everyone seems particularly trusting of Silver, a menacing, warfare-prone cyborg who—surprise!—emerges as the villain. All in all, a book that tailors itself as a "fun little romp"... which means it's nothing special.

• Silver's second, Miraso, is named after Oscar winning actress Mira Sorvino (*Mighty Aphrodite*, *Romy and Michelle's High School Reunion*).

• The line "We go up" at the end of Chapter 1 is a completely gratuitous quote from *Ghostbusters*.

ANACHROPHOBIA

By Jonathan Morris

Release Date: *March 2002*
Order: *BBC Eighth Doctor Adventure #54*

TARDIS CREW The eighth Doctor, Fitz and Anji.

TRAVEL LOG Unnamed colony world, formerly part of the Plutocratic Empire, time unknown.

CHRONOLOGY Immediately after *Hope*.

STORY SUMMARY Tussled off course by unexpected turbulence in the Time Vortex, the Doctor, Fitz and Anji find themselves on a war-torn planet where the combatants have time-active weapons. Directed by computers named the Actuaries, money-hungry plutocrats seek to eliminate some colonists, called the defaulters, for reneging on their world's lease payments. Each side possesses weapons that can rapidly accelerate time (thereby aging opponents to death) or decelerate it (freezing them for eternity) in a limited area. However, genuine time travel eludes both sides.

The Doctor's trio takes shelter in a plutocrat stronghold, Isolation Station 40, only to find a researcher named Dr. Paterson attempting time travel experiments. Paterson successfully launches time capsules into the past, but his volunteers keep returning with "anachrophobia"—the inability to readjust to the present, rather like the temporal equivalent of the bends.

Suddenly, Paterson's volunteers begin transforming into "clock people"—humanoids which literally sport a clock face, a swinging pendulum in their chest and gears for organs. Worse, the clock people spread their condition like a virus, infect-

ing more station personnel.

The Doctor realizes that Paterson's capsule created a space-time fissure, allowing creatures within the Time Vortex to replace the volunteers. The creatures grant each affected person the irresistible ability to rewrite their own past, but as soon as someone makes even the slightest change, they paradoxically void their own past—allowing the Vortex creatures to inhabit the hollow shell that remains. In our reality, the creatures look like clock people because that's the closest equivalent the senses can perceive.

The remaining station personnel resort to firearms, but the clock people demonstrate an ability to rewind time a few minutes, retroactively erasing simple gunshot wounds and grenade injuries. Alternatively, the Doctor quietly riddles the clock people with odorless, colorless and lethal mustard gas. By the time the clock people feel the gas' effects, it's too late for them to rewind time to save themselves.

The clock people die off, but plutocrat auditor Mistletoe discovers that Bishop, another volunteer, was taken to the central Station One base for observation. The Doctor, Fitz, Anji and Mistletoe rush to intercept Bishop, arriving at Station One to find its 50,000-plus plutocrats already transformed into clock people.

The Doctor realizes the clock people rely on the temporal fissure for their continued survival in our dimension. Luckily, the clock infection taints him also, giving him the ability to alter his own past. Applying his newfound skill, the Doctor's mind returns to a point where he got separated during the Isolation Station 40 brawl. The Doctor hurriedly loads a time capsule with explosive chronomium, rigging it to detonate in the present. In such a fashion, the Doctor alters events while preserving his personal history. The Doctor's consciousness returns to the present, just as the chronomium-loaded capsule launches. The capsule explodes, sealing the rift and killing off the clock people in our dimension.

The drained Doctor falls unconscious, leaving Mistletoe to unmask himself as Sabbath. Having manipulated events from the start, Sabbath tells Fitz and Anji that he's acquired unnamed business partners who sought to eliminate the Vortex beings. Sabbath admits bringing the Doctor and the clock people into conflict, certain the Doctor would kill them off. Mission complete, Sabbath departs, gloating that his business partners now control the Time Vortex, edging them closer to an unknown agenda.

MEMORABLE MOMENTS Plutocrat Lane,

sensing her transformation into a clock person, tries to slash open her wrists—only to peel back her skin and find a mass of whirring cogs, gears, coils and springs within. Similarly, the Doctor opens up Bishop's chest with a scalpel, discovering a rectangle of glass, set in mahogany, with a swinging pendulum.

Dr. Paterson, justifying his time experiments: "The past is a dream, Doctor. It is not real, it cannot be revisited or changed. But the memories tempt us that things could have been different. Why do we regret? We regret because we wish we could go back."

The Doctor, illustrating the pointlessness of regret: "We are the sum of all our days. If the past could be changed, then it would have no meaning. *We* would have no meaning."

A fleeing Anji cannot decide which will kill her first: The clock person pursuing her or her aching calves. When Anji gets upset, convinced the Doctor lacks the ability to care, he gently replies: "I still have one heart left, you know."

Finally, there's a horribly scary moment when the Doctor turns into a clock, complete with Roman numerals on his face. [This would've made a stellar TV cliffhanger, complete with theme music and rolling credits—Morris intended it as such.]

SEX AND SPIRITS Fitz now takes a dim view of all his failed romances, sensing his one-night stands were wasted opportunities for something more.

Fitz and Anji recall seeing each other naked (*The Adventuress of Henrietta Street, Mad Dogs and Englishmen*) and don't care to repeat the experience.

ASS-WHUPPINGS The Doctor's mustard gas kills clock-infected personnel Lane, Ash, Norton and Bragg. A clock-infected Dr. Paterson commits suicide, flinging himself down his time capsule shaft, to ward off his transformation. The Doctor also slaughters the 50,000, possibly 60,000, clock people at Station One, effectively committing genocide [as Sabbath finds no trace of the creatures in the Time Vortex].

After the Doctor arranges for the chronomium bomb, he preserves his own history by deliberately breathing a lung-full of mustard gas. The shock robs the Doctor of his short-term memory, thereby guaranteeing he won't recall his time meddling, averting a paradox.

Twenty-six of Dr. Paterson's volunteers get anachrophobia, but most of them die from liver failure, renal collapse, brainstem death, respira-

This book is not endorsed by the BBC. Doctor Who and TARDIS are trademarks of the BBC.

169

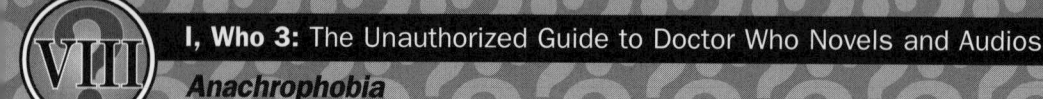

tory collapse and assorted other nastiness.

The seven actuaries (*see Organizations*) controlling the war shut themselves down.

TV TIE-INS When the TARDIS loses power, the crew opens the doors with brute force, not a handy crank ("Death to the Daleks").

NOVEL TIE-INS The Doctor's remaining heart (*The Adventuress of Henrietta Street*) is currently struggling to do the work of two. Unfortunately, the Doctor doesn't know anyone qualified enough to examine him. He momentarily gains the ability to rewrite his past, but can't [or simply doesn't] view his pre-*The Burning* history.

Fitz's memories of the Kingdom of Beasts (*Adventuress* again) are already fuzzy. He's especially cloudy about the Doctor's emergency heart operation. He also has trouble recalling his childhood bedroom, probably due to his memory sieving in *Interference*.

The TARDIS feels a bit sluggish, still recovering from its strenuous journey in *Hope*. Mistletoe (a.k.a. Sabbath, as it happens) very briefly appeared in a futuristic vision in *Father Time*.

CHARACTER DEVELOPMENT

• *The Doctor:* The Doctor fumbles to remember the Laws of Time, but knows that undoing your own past is bad. He tends to view history as immutable.

The Doctor knows song selections from The Beatles, Mozart, Erasure and Rogers and Hammerstein.

• *Fitz Kreiner:* Fitz snores. He can hum tunes from *Children's Favorites* [an album recorded by Jon Pertwee].

• *The Doctor and Fitz:* Sometimes play chess.

• *Anji Kapoor:* Anji remembers her grandmother's house as being full of 1950s furniture, sliding doors and linoleum. Her mother tried, and failed, to make Grandma redecorate. A lot of Grandma's possessions ended up in the street for the council when she died.

As a frightened young girl, Anji dashed past her grandmother's large, foreboding clock without daring to look it in the face.

She loves coffee. When trying to look tough, she emulates scenes from *Pulp Fiction*. Auditor Mistletoe reminds her of people she once knew—and didn't like.

• *Sabbath:* His ability to disguise himself as Mistletoe [holographic?] goes unexplained. As Mistletoe, Sabbath looks considerably more slender. Like most plutocrat auditors, he's dressed in a black suit and bowler hat, carrying an umbrella

and clipboard. He wears horn-rimmed glasses.

Sabbath somehow creates a door out of thin air and exits through it, perhaps a means of returning to *The Jonah*.

• *The Doctor and Sabbath:* Sabbath deems the Doctor to be of inestimable value.

• *The TARDIS:* The Ship contains an intimate chess room like Oxbridge College quarters. The room includes shelves upon shelves of books. The walls are honeycombed with the TARDIS circular indentations, with more books stacked in 'em.

During a crisis, the TARDIS' wall circles pulse to denote danger. Despite its vastness, the Ship can't keep the crew alive for long if its life-support systems fail.

ALIEN RACES *The Clock People:* Most clock people have a large clock face and a mahogany carriage case inside their chest with a swinging pendulum. The clock people render themselves as all manner of clocks from different periods. Their clock face hands turn so long as they live. They can also chime like grandfather clocks.

Clock people possess the ability to rewind time a few minutes in a limited area. The talent expends a lot of energy, and must be used sparingly.

If shot, clock people bleed blood and a fluid almost like gear lubricant. Their springs uncoil and their pistons jam.

Clock people seem to exist in a state of temporal acceleration—the mustard gas that the Doctor deploys builds up in their system, creating hastened symptoms and death.

They view the Time Vortex as cold and dark. They can see and hear just fine, despite having clocks for heads.

ALIEN PLANETS *Unnamed Defaulter Planet:* The gravity's about Earth normal. There's also a bracing atmosphere. If not for the war, it'd be a nice place to live.

STUFF YOU NEED *Chrononium:* A time-active element, and the source of temporal technology in this conflict. Unprocessed chrononium merely slows time around it. Refined, it causes rapid temporal acceleration or deceleration. It can also be rendered inert, made to act as insulation. Chrononium-based TR alloy blocks time weapons' effects, much like lead stops radiation.

Chrononium's often shaped into protective suits, or made into highly durable translucent alloys. It's also available in gel form.

• *Accelerated Time Storms (AT Storms):* Makes time pass at 100 years in an instant, turning its targets into dust.

THE CRUCIAL BITS...

- **ANACHROPHOBIA**—First mention of Sabbath's unnamed business partners.

- *Decelerated Time Zone (DT Zone):* Brings time to a near-standstill (about a minute on the inside for every 1,000 years on the outside). It's possible to fire bullets into a DT Zone and kill people trapped within—the decelerated bullets might take 100 years to reach their targets, but it'll get 'em eventually.

- *Paterson's Time Travel Capsule:* Works by generating a localized AT storm within a protective DT field. The two time forces in collision create a third impulse that sends objects back in time.

- *Anachrophobia:* Literally the fear of temporal displacement—but also a very real mental condition. Anachrophobia occurs when the brain, having traveled through time, cannot adjust to its new location. The main result is extreme neurological disturbance, much like decompression sickness. Symptoms include cyanosis, hypertension, paranoia, memory loss and sometimes a complete mental and physical breakdown.

PLACES TO GO *The Time Vortex:* Sabbath and his associates have culled the various creatures that dwelled therein. Time travel through the Vortex, for now, remains unimpeded.

- *Station One (a.k.a. Central Register):* The plutocrats' main headquarters on the defaulters' colony planet. It originally served as an orbital colony town, but the plutocrats requisitioned it.

ORGANIZATIONS *The Plutocrats:* Evidently an offshoot of humanity, adhering to the Plutocratic Ideal. The plutocrats prize the acclimation of wealth above all else, having little time for morality.

- *The Actuaries:* Seven box-like computers, responsible for directing both the plutocrats and the defaulters' war efforts to achieve a stalemate (*see History*). The actuaries sometimes employ human-looking robots forged from time-shielded chrononium alloy. Such robots are programmed to believe they're human.

PHENOMENA *Time Travel:* It takes more effort to go backward in time than forward, since it's the equivalent of going "uphill." Time travel sometimes mutates viruses.

HISTORY Some time ago, the Plutocratic Empire franchised out development of the unnamed colony planet. Regrettably, the colony defaulted on its lease, compelling the plutocrats to put it in receivership. Four hundred years ago, open warfare resulted. Whereas the colonists fought to win, the empire subtly worked to achieve a stalemate. In such a fashion, the plutocrats gained a ready-made fashion for disposing of their non-viable civilians, weeding out their bad debtors by making them cannon fodder for the war.

- Unfortunately, the seven robotic actuaries crafted to run both sides of the receivership war outlived their masters. The Plutocratic Empire crumbled five years ago for an unknown reason, forcing the actuaries to deposit the spoils of war in reserve.

- For lack of communication with the plutocrats, the actuaries spurred Dr. Paterson's time travel experiments to receive new instructions. With the clock people having taken over Station One, the actuaries released the colonists' lease in perpetuity, then switched themselves off.

AT THE END OF THE DAY Just when one worries that the "Doctor Who" formula might be aging after 39-plus years, a book like *Anachrophobia* comes along that yet again shatters our preconceptions. It's intensely sci-fi driven, but its true appeal lies in convincingly making creatures who strut around with clock faces and pendulums in their chests actually seem dangerous. Sweetly disturbing in a good way, *Anachrophobia* proves memorably scary and—as it's more stand-alone than not—could entice back fans who stopped reading the EDAs.

DID YOU KNOW?

- This book was originally proposed as the penultimate "Sabbath arc" story, with the final scene revealing Sabbath's victorious masters, but editorial concerns mandated leaving things more open-ended.

- The clock people were inspired by the sculpture *The Beanery* by Edward Keinholz, which turns up on page 234. The cover is a Magritte pastiche—indeed, a rather famous Magritte painting turns up on page 239. Morris never intended the cover to emulate the clock sketch of Romana in "City Of Death," but there's quite obviously some similarities.

- Morris considered ending the book with the twist that the defaulters weren't human, but rather strange, three-eyed aliens. However, he feared adding one twist too many and eventually nixed the idea.

- The clock people were originally called "Horoligans," but Morris decided they'd be more

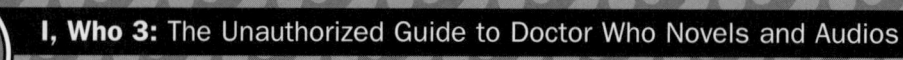

enigmatic if kept nameless.

- Morris' associate, Dr. Katie Bramall, provided the book's medical jargon. As Morris adds: "Apparently, it all means something."

- *Anachrophobia* was written around the same time that Rob Shearman scripted "The Chimes Of Midnight," so the authors took care that the *Sapphire & Steel* aspects of their works didn't overlap.

- Most of the soldiers are named after villages near where Morris grew up in Somerset, although the robotic Hammond is named after a *Sapphire & Steel* writer.

- In the same fashion that Lance Parkin includes a role for actor Ian Richardson in all of his "Who" works, Morris always includes one for David Bamber.

TRADING FUTURES

By Lance Parkin

Release Date: April 2002
Order: BBC Eighth Doctor Adventure #55

TARDIS CREW The eighth Doctor, Fitz and Anji.

TRAVEL LOG Chiefly the Mediterranean, Athens; Neverland, California; Heathrow; the Green Hotel, Istanbul and Baskerville's RealWar factory, the Steppes, Russia, all July, circa 2010. [Clues to the date: The Doctor's 1989 space shuttle hijack occurred "more than 20 years ago." Also, Baskerville, age 60, is too young to have lived through World War II, but his parents did.]

STORY SUMMARY During a stopover on Earth, the early 21st century, the Doctor, Anji and Fitz find political tensions running high between two power blocs: the United States and the Eurozone, a consolidation of Europe's various nations. More curiously, the Doctor detects rogue temporal signatures, suggesting the use of illicit, possibly dangerous time travel equipment.

Investigating further, the Doctor finds a man named Baskerville, allegedly a time traveler from the future, pitting the US against the Eurozone in a bidding match for his time travel technology. Additional parties, namely a pair of Sabbath's time agents and a band of mercenary, rhino-like Onihr aliens, also take an interest in Baskerville's time travel equipment. Sabbath's minions, Jaxa and Roya, hope to assess whether the supposed time-traveler poses a threat to their employer.

The Onihr mistake Fitz for the Doctor, take him prisoner and proceed to interrogate him for information about time travel. Fitz escapes and hotwires the Onihr ship's weaponry, teleporting to Earth just as the vessel explodes. Meanwhile, Eurozone secret service agent Jonah Cosgrove efficiently plugs Jaxa and Roja, hoping to eliminate the competition.

Finally, the Doctor unmasks Baskerville as a modern-day arms dealer, realizing he faked demonstrations of his "time travel" equipment by drugging US and Eurozone officials with hallucinogenic coffee. Baskerville hoped to exchange his fake time travel equipment for access to ULTRA, Earth's top computer system. If successful, Baskerville would have used ULTRA to re-program the International Financial Exchange Computer (IFEC), literally gaining control of all money on Earth.

Exposed, Baskerville takes US President Felix Mather hostage and forces him to reveal his ULTRA clearance code. Baskerville subverts the IFEC computer as planned, but before the transfer of authority becomes permanent, the Doctor re-programs the IFEC and invisibly re-routes all the world's financial transactions through his bank account in Athens. Afterward, the Doctor, Fitz and Anji blame Baskerville for the Onihr vessel's destruction, convincing a few surviving Onihr to escort the con man—via a teleport beam—back to their homeworld for trial.

The Doctor wraps things up by pocketing a hand-held time porter that Jaxa and Roja left behind, but a gun-toting Cosgrove demands the device. In response, the Doctor whimsically pitches the timeporter off a cliff. Cosgrove greedily dives after it, intending to grab the device and timeport himself to safety. Unfortunately, the energy-depleted device fails to function and Cosgrove falls splat against the rocks. Having put paid to the US/Eurozone bidding war, and with President Mather safely returning to America, the Doctor's crew leaves Earth.

MEMORABLE MOMENTS Fitz confers with the TARDIS about the Time Lords' demise, claiming: "Their time has passed. There's no law, no order, not now. You're a police box, but there aren't any policemen left."

Cosgrove finds the thought of killing someone without having to do any paperwork refreshing. While disarming a clock-less nuclear bomb, the Doctor starts counting down himself for the sake of drama.

When Fitz comments, "I just saved the Earth from a race of invincible would-be time-travelling

space rhinos," the Doctor compliments him for using a sentence that's never been spoken before.

SEX AND SPIRITS
In the Mediterranean, Anji spends time in a bikini, while Fitz tries to discretely ogle sunbathing women. Espionage agent Malady Chang briefly smiles at Fitz, making him dub her a "possible." He fails miserably to get the attention of a hot theme park guide.

The Doctor's attended Olympics featuring naked competitors (*see History*).

One year at Christmas, Anji and Dave snuck upstairs in her parents' house for a quick cuddle, an escapade that ended with her on top of him. Anji insisted Dave remain quiet—then she screamed so loud, her dad shouted up the stairs to ask if they were okay.

Anji still carries keys to her and Dave's flat. While undercover aboard Baskerville's yacht, she worries about spy cameras and ponders undressing under the bedsheets, plus showering in her bikini.

ASS-WHUPPINGS
Baskerville "prophesizes" about the destruction of Athens to help verify his claims of time travel, then arranges to set off explosions which cause a tidal wave and devastate the city. The resultant chaos kills off four thousand, and leaves a million homeless.

The Doctor outwits a lifejacket-wearing Cosgrove by simply dumping water on him, causing Cosgrove's lifejacket to inflate and immobilize him in a doorframe.

Fitz plays RealWar, a video game involving actual robot tanks and soldiers (*see Stuff You Need*), thereby taking out a machine gun nest in some foreign locale. The Onihr later connect him to a pain-inducing device, dredging up the memory of a time when Fitz jumped a bit too hard onto his scooter bike. Eventually, Fitz hotwires the Onihr ship's EMP cannon, blowing the ship to scrap.

A teleporting Jaxa dies after unwisely materializing around one of Cosgrove's bullets. Cosgrove shoots Roja in the back of the head. Cosgrove also commands a RealWar robot detachment against an Onihr hunting pack.

At story's end, the Doctor essentially kills Cosgrove, fooling him into jumping off a cliff.

TV TIE-INS
The Doctor carries a meter that logs disturbances on the Bocca Scale ("The Two Doctors"). America and the Eurozone possibly become the two unnamed power blocs in "Warriors of the Deep."

NOVEL TIE-INS
Fitz vaguely comprehends that the Time Lords (destroyed in *The Ancestor Cell*) previously stopped other people from developing dangerous time technology.

The Onihr claim they can identify the four surviving elementals (*The Adventuress of Henrietta Street*), and the Chronodev from the 51st century. They wish to learn more about Sabbath. American espionage agent Malady Chang reports to Control (last seen in *Escape Velocity*), who's supposedly a Time Lord—although Heaven knows if that's still the case in the post-*The Ancestor Cell* universe.

Fitz occasionally hears something scratching inside the TARDIS, making him wonder if something got trapped in there when the Ship rebuilt itself (*The Ancestor Cell* to *Escape Velocity*). The TARDIS loosely talks to Fitz by rumbling under his feet (*Earthworld*).

Anji reiterates (*Hope*) that her relationship with Dave soured somewhere along the line. Their romance would probably have flopped, but she felt an outpouring of emotion when he died (*Escape Velocity*).

The Doctor met Felix Mather while hijacking Atlantis. He hasn't told Anji about his adopted daughter Miranda (*Father Time*).

Fitz still speaks Chinese (*Revolution Man*). He claims that the last few places the TARDIS visited, the coffee wasn't up to much (notably *Hope*).

Anji's now thrice chagrinned to realize that the Doctor here pilots the TARDIS flawlessly (as seen in *The City of the Dead, Mad Dogs and Englishmen* and here) yet still can't get her home.

AUDIO TIE-INS
Felix Mather was Secretary of State during the Canisian Invasion ("Death Comes to Time," although this off-handed reference does *not* make DCTT canon).

TIE-INS
Cosgrove served in the British Secret Service throughout events such as the moon landings, the Martian encounters (*The Dying Days*), the Euro Wars and the fall of General Mariah Learman ("The Time of the Daleks").

CHARACTER DEVELOPMENT
• *The Doctor:* He still looks about 40, and here wears a long black coat rather than his customary green. As a time traveler, the Doctor contaminates anything he touches with chronons [the same's likely true for Fitz and Anji].

He carries a passport, and doesn't take off his jacket, even in warm climates. *Trading Futures* marks the first time he's robbed a bank [in this case, to forcibly escort people to safety].

The Doctor holds some knowledge of the Inuit-Inupiaq polysynthetic language. Given a gun, he's

able to shoot an opponent's bullets out of the air.

He owns an IFEC account at the Medusa Bank, Athens. After this story, the world's financial transactions continue to filter through the Doctor's bank account, for only a millisecond or two.

• *Fitz Kreiner:* American accents all sound the same to Fitz. He doesn't recognize the name "Exxon." He doesn't know what his name means. Fitz has learned some 1980s and 1990s music, chiefly covers from his day. Fitz tries curbing his smoking with addictive nicotine oil pills, then resumes smoking to kick his oil pill habit.

• *Anji Kapoor:* Before Anji met the Doctor, she was feeling old. She was 27, in a steady relationship, with her student loan nearly paid off. Her formerly riveting Friday nights came to mean watching *Changing Rooms* and *Frasier*. Anji formerly worked at MWF, a London bank, and quickly learned that "ethical fund management" was a misnomer. To guarantee her clients' profitability, she invested in tobacco and defense contractor stocks.

She recalls a few IRA bombs going off in her era. Anji's bag contains a Psion organizer. Her cell phone plays *X-Files* theme music. She illogically always sets her watch at 6:30 when she wakes up.

Anji regrets not taking a year to backpack before or after college. She here flies First Class for the second time in her life. She's never liked sending text messages via cell phone, deeming it a step backward.

• *Dave Young:* Given the chance to time travel, Anji's late boyfriend would have [rather pathetically] traveled forward to cheaply acquire all six *Star Wars* films on DVD.

• *Baskerville:* Age 60, Baskerville is already the richest man in the world, thanks to his creating RealWar (*see History*). Therefore, his con job to acquire all the world's money is quite possibly the greediest stunt in history.

For last 10 years, Baskerville's operated as freelance defense contractor. He used his vast wealth to completely erase his identity, getting the CIA and EZSS off his trail.

• *Jonah Cosgrove:* Officially a deputy head for the Eurozone Secret Service, although Cosgrove's true loyalties lie with England. He's approaching 80, but remains in absurdly good shape even though he hasn't left his London desk in nearly 20 years. Cosgrove knows of at least nine organizations, six still active, who think they're running the world.

• *US President Felix Mather:* A distinguished African-American in his 60s. He's formerly worked for the CIA and served as an astronaut on all three SDI projects. He's also served as Secretary of State

and Vice-President. The US government can locate Mather via a nanotech tracking device in one of his eyebrows. Ben Russ serves as Mather's vice-president.

• *Jaxa:* A historian, Jaxa first encountered Sabbath after an errant time jump deposited her on the moon's surface—three decades before it acquired an atmosphere. Sabbath saved Jaxa from death by exposure and radiation sickness.

• *Roja:* Sabbath's cabin boy, age 10 or 12. Sabbath met Roja in an era where children grow up quickly, tutoring the lad in mathematics, chronology, astrology-astronomy and high-energy physics.

• *The TARDIS:* Its communications systems can patch into President Mather's direct line.

ALIEN RACES *Onihr:* Typically 7 to 8 feet tall, humanoid, hunched and gray-skinned, with stubby legs. Their long heads have a horned, blunt snout. Like Earth rhinos, they've got poor eyesight, but a highly defined sense of smell. They're strong enough to crush brick.

Onihr are immensely long-lived [the Onihr leader in *Trading Futures* has commanded his ship for 30,000 years]. They've had no luck with time travel, but wear Time Lord-esque ceremonial collars and Faction Paradox-like skullcaps to emulate time travel rituals.

The Onihr possess transmat technology, plus wear armor resistant to human firepower [shooting an Onihr in the mouth does the trick, however]. They possess no sense of self, trained to value the many over the one.

ALIEN PLANETS *Onihros:* The Onihr homeworld, four times the size of Earth.

STUFF YOU NEED *ULTRA:* The world's top computer system, located in an underground bunker beneath European Secret Service headquarters in Brussels.

PLACES TO GO *Neverland:* A California funpark. Its founder lives in a mansion at LunarDisney.

HISTORY The Doctor gave the pre-fame Beatles a suggestion that they perform in suits.

• Baskerville formerly served as a Russian army general, responsible for detonating a nuclear bomb in Chechnya and turning 500,000 people to cinders.

• Ten years ago, pharmaceutical companies introduced cancer-free nicotine oil pills, which led to the Eurozone banning cigarettes. However, the nicotine pills themselves proved addictive.

• The Articles of European Zoning detail Britain's commitment to Eurozone. The UK Prime Minister is now called "President Minister."

• Professional soldiers fought wars in Afghanistan, the Persian Gulf and Mexico until Baskerville created RealWar, a means of paying video game addicts to fight via remote control with cheap, efficient robot tanks and soldiers. Using RealWar, American and the Eurozone won the War on Terror. Nonetheless, there are recent reports of a neo-terrorism resurgence.

• The IFEC Accord, created when Mather was vice-president, establishing a single protocol for every electronic financial transaction.

• Children in this era have rebelled against their Generation X parents by becoming teetotalers, passing their exams and settling down to steady jobs. "R:C" is a popular youth motto meaning "Rebel: Conform."

• The Pentagon is now the Octagon. The BBC is now the EZBC. CDs are no longer in common use. The term "phone operator" has fallen into disuse. Rhinos are extinct, but exist in clonetivity. Low-level nukes are now used for big engineering projects.

The Eurozone has banned vitamin pills, but Ecstasy and hash are legal [and on some restaurants' dessert menus]. Some guns in this era have smart software prohibiting their users from shooting a villain. Vineyards are now climatically controlled and tended by robots.

Concordes fell out of service when British Airways went bust [Author's Note: In April 2003, one year after *Trading Futures* published, British Airways announced intentions to end Concord service.] The Airbus IX has emerged as the fastest commercial airliner.

• The Mafia still holds a great deal of authority in Russia. The Siberian territories are now in dispute, with RealWar troops engaged in combat against Exxon Corp's forces.

• Italians of this era are busy fighting one another. Several North African regimes have collapsed.

• In future, the Olympics will reinstate naked competitors, hoping to boost flagging TV ratings.

AT THE END OF THE DAY If *Trading Futures* were a baseball player, you'd see a potent wind-up, a tremendous swing—then watch as it's a line drive rather than a home run. It's striking and edible, but this book bogs itself down by forgetting its genre, coming off better as a James Bond film than a novel. Indeed, looking at Parkin's numerous hits (*Cold Fusion*, *The Dying Days*, etc.), it's his worst book—which means it still kicks the shit out of

most of its contemporaries, but nonetheless yearns to become something more.

DID YOU KNOW?

• Parkin viewed the character of Cosgrove as akin to the Sean Connery Bond, who never retired and got promoted to the rank of M. To Parkin's mind, the Cosgrove/Bond figure was extremely muscled, bitter and anachronistic. Or to put it another way, Parkin claims, "He's Sean Connery in *The Rock*, as drawn by [*Dark Knight Returns* artist] Frank Miller."

• Parkin wrote the part of Baskerville with actor Ian Richardson in mind.

THE BOOK OF THE STILL

By Paul Ebbs

Story by Paul Ebbs and Richard Jones

Release Date: May 2002
Order: BBC Eighth Doctor Adventure #56

TARDIS CREW The eighth Doctor, Fitz and Anji.

TRAVEL LOG The Still Room, the Museum of Locks, planet Lebenswelt; planet Antimasque; the Unnoticed's Tent City, the photosphere of Earth's sun, 4009.

STORY SUMMARY On the planet Lebenswelt, 4009, the Doctor feels an inexplicable urge to steal The Book of the Still, the primary artifact at the Museum of Locks. He tries—and fails—to bag the relic, and earns a 20-year-prison sentence for his trouble. While Anji faithfully and diligently works toward the Doctor's release, Fitz parties, convinced the Doctor will somehow free himself.

Hoping to make a fast buck, Fitz answers an advertisement for a back-alley escort service named "IntroInductions." The service's owners—a seedy trio named Darlow, Gimcrack and Svadhisthana—inject Fitz with illegal fast-acting memory acids, making him fall in love with an IntroInductions client named Carmodi. Prone to falling ill unless she's in the presence of a time traveler (*see Character Development*), Carmodi makes off with Fitz and a good chunk of Darlow's money. Darlow's crew begins relocating IntroInductions to cover

their tracks, vowing revenge against Carmodi.

Back in jail, the Doctor meets an imprisoned, non-linear anthropologist named Rhian Salmond. Rhian explains that The Book of the Still simultaneously exists in many times and locations as a safety net for time travelers. By writing their names in the Book, stranded time travelers can instantly arrange for a pick-up.

Suddenly, a group of aliens named the Unnoticed arrive, determined to acquire The Book of the Still. The Unnoticed's Wave Interrupter device cancels out all electrical power on Lebenswelt, allowing the Doctor and Rhian to escape. Simultaneously, a lovestruck Fitz enters the powerless Museum and makes off with the Book on Carmodi's behalf, enabling her to better locate time travelers.

Fitz and Carmodi flee to the nearby planet Antimasque, leaving virtually everyone else associated with this adventure to hunt them down. Anji recovers the Book, and the Unnoticed run Carmodi, one of their ex-time sensitives (*see Alien Races*) aground, hauling her and Fitz back to their base of operations. In due course, the Doctor, Anji, Rhian and Darlow's less-than-willing trio pursue them to the Unnoticed's Tent City, pitched on the photosphere of Earth's sun.

The Unnoticed admit they're the product of a temporal anomaly with no memory of their past. As such, the Unnoticed fear that interaction with time-active cultures and time travelers might unravel their fragile existence. The Unnoticed sought to acquire the Book as it mentions their Tent City, causing the Doctor to realize he psionically sensed the Unnoticed's desire and became compelled to steal the Book himself.

Rhian deduces the Unnoticed exist as part of a closed time loop—meaning their imminent destruction will paradoxically cause their creation. As part of this, the Doctor accidentally touches Carmodi, releasing some pent-up energy in the loop and causing pockets of Time to go soft. Bizarrely enough, one such soft Time wave melds Darlow, Gimcrack and Svadhisthana into a twisted gestalt creature.

With Rhian's help, the Doctor realizes Darlow's monstrosity gave rise to the Unnoticed. If Darlow's abomination and the Unnoticed were to touch, the resultant energy discharge would destroy the Unnoticed and fling Darlow's trio back in time, to one day evolve into the Unnoticed. Purely out of spite, Darlow touches an Unnoticed and completes the loop. The Doctor gets his companions and allies to hold onto the Book, which—thanks to an in-built safety device—teleports back to its last location of safety on Lebenswelt.

Fitz regains his true memories, but Carmodi departs with the Book. Using her foreknowledge gained from this adventure, Carmodi eventually finds a means of retroactively planting a time bomb aboard the Unnoticed's spaceship. The time bomb obliterates the Unnoticed before their creation/destruction event, thereby ending the time loop entirely. Satisfied, Carmodi departs with Rhian for parts unknown.

MEMORABLE MOMENTS During his courtroom sentencing, the Doctor's bid for freedom entails a lot of embarrassing karate chops, then rushing toward a public gallery where Anji and Fitz are flailing their arms to make a grab for him. Within seconds, he's subdued and zipped into shiny black body bag.

Anji later discovers that posting bond for the Doctor would require her surrendering a lung, both eyes and an earlobe. She feels guilty for refusing, but the Doctor consoles her with: "I know, I know. You'd look lopsided for one thing."

With the overturned TARDIS inaccessible, an inspired Anji starts a riot to knock the Ship upright. To stoke the crowd's fire, she screams some Native American war chants Dave taught her.

Largely the stuff of comedy, *The Book of the Still* contains many sentimental moments, especially between the Doctor and Rhian. At one point, she hands the wounded Doctor a tissue to dab his cuts, but he instead uses it to wipe tears from her eyes. Later, the Doctor rouses an unconscious Rhian before a planet-bomb explodes, purely because he doesn't want to die alone. While waiting for the bomb to detonate, Rhian teaches the Doctor how to waltz [indeed, this bittersweet, ironic scene might well encapsulate the entire book].

The Doctor memorably tears out the Book's pages, shapes them into an invulnerable paper cube, then dives onto the Unnoticed's Tent City on the sun's photosphere. He tells his companions to "stand back" as he opens the cube, leading the snide Svadhisthana to wonder how that will protect them from the sun's naked fury.

SEX AND SPIRITS Darlow's memory acids make Fitz spend most of this story in love with Carmodi, no matter how deceitful or non-responsive she becomes. He hits her up for sex—or even just halfway to first base, really—but she keeps making excuses. She *does* suggest marriage, probably just to keep him passive. Carmodi claims she actually loved Fitz to some degree, although she really never shows it and dumps him like a hot potato when he's of no further use.

When Fitz regains his memory, he leaves Car-

modi to help the Doctor because: "I've been engineered to love you, Carmodi. With the Doctor… it's the real thing." Mind, this alone is not indicative of a romance between Fitz and the Doctor.

Anji accidentally touches Fitz's discarded undies at one point. She finds a wallet receipt for a meal that she cooked for Dave. She deems Fitz a sexually unconscious 1960s throwback. At a dance, a green-skinned, fork-tongued female with a titanic bosom invites Anji back to her place, but she declines. Anji covers the Doctor's face with kisses when a bomb fails to kill them. She considers that becoming alcoholic might make life on Lebenswelt bearable.

The Doctor offers Rhian platonic company in his makeshift bedroom.

ASS-WHUPPINGS The Doctor gets roughed up during his botched attempt to steal the Book. Later, Darlow's trio viciously interrogates the Doctor by affixing electrodes to his skull. Additionally, a vengeful Darlow implants a "Mindbomb" into the Doctor's head, compelling him to hunt Carmodi and choke the life out of her. Upon realizing this, the Doctor takes advantage of the soft Time pockets, urging Fitz to literally reach into the Doctor's brain and harmlessly remove the Mindbomb.

The Doctor saves Lebenswelt by materializing the TARDIS around an Unnoticed bomb, [somewhat akin to "Neverland," really], although the subsequent explosion makes the Ship's exterior seem bowed, with cracked panels and rich crimson light spilling between the gaps. The Doctor emerges from the Ship singed, with melted shoes.

Later, the Unnoticed try the same trick with the planet Antimasque, but at a critical moment, the Doctor spies a Book of the Still written by Rhian's future self. With the laws of causality guaranteeing Rhian's survival, the Doctor's forced to protect her by leaving Antimasque to its fate. As you'd expect, it depresses the Doctor to realize the Laws of Time require him to sacrifice an entire planet for the sake of one person.

Darlow lasers at least three Unnoticed, failing to recognize them as his descendants. Fitz shields the Doctor and gets a laser burn on his shoulder.

TV TIE-INS The TARDIS generates a Minus Room (obviously a Zero Room, "Castrovalva"), described as a lens of unreality around which reality is bent, to shield the Doctor. The TARDIS' interior automatically rights itself if the exterior's tipped over ("Time-Flight"). The Doctor recognizes the Blinovitch Limitation Effect ("Day of the Daleks") even if he can't remember the term for it.

NOVEL TIE-INS The Doctor puts his conducting experience (*The Year of Intelligent Tigers*) to good use, getting an orchestra to play a harmonic that counteracts the Unnoticed's Interrupter device (*see Stuff You Need*).

The Doctor praises The Book of the Still's usefulness, but remains convinced such an artifact shouldn't exist (and it probably wouldn't have done, in the pre-*The Ancestor Cell* universe).

CHARACTER DEVELOPMENT
• *The Doctor:* The Doctor's subject to psionic attacks when he enters a temporal loop. He smells the tang of burning clocks when he's near The Book of the Still. Time-sensitive Carmodi variously thinks the Doctor smells like rice paper, rainy days, orange groves, freshly printed books and an illegal backstreet autopsy.

He's never felt terribly safe on rollercoasters. He heals faster near the TARDIS, even while sleeping in its shadow.

The Doctor's a hopeless dancer, but Rhian teaches him to waltz. He suspects he's immortal. After spending a century on Earth, he now gets impatient waiting for an egg to boil. The Doctor satiates Carmodi's temporal addiction like no one else.

• *Fitz Kreiner:* Fitz had the TARDIS whip up some business cards entitled "Fitz Kreiner—Freebooter and Gigolo," keeping them hidden from Anji. He hates job interviews. He never tires of wearing big white shirts. He loves sword fights.

• *Anji Kapoor:* By this point, she's forgetting how to get culture shocked. On Lebenswelt, she wears a *Don't ask me, I'm new here myself* T-shirt. She likes museums.

Anji remembers a school assembly in which classmate Brian Curran suffered an epileptic fit. She carries a Psion wallet. Anji prefers Daphne over Velma from *Scooby Doo*. She can dance a waltz.

• *Carmodi Litian:* Carmodi fears being pegged as a villain even though she's moreso a victim of circumstance. Thirty years ago, Carmodi was born as one of the Unnoticed's sensitives (*see Alien Races*). She served them faithfully until age 15, then participated in an excursion to the planet Porconine. Once there, she insulted the Unnoticed leader, hoping he'd kill her and grant a release from her servile existence. The leader tossed Carmodi over a cliff but she survived, albeit half dead, as the Unnoticed departed.

Carmodi spent the next few years tracking down time travelers on behalf of dodgy characters [who wanted them for experimentation, etc.], simultaneously appeasing her own addiction to temporal particles. Contact with the Doctor cured Carmodi of her temporal addiction. She knows how to pilot a spaceship.

• *Rhian Salmond:* A non-linear anthropology student, age 25. Rhian attended University on Sirius One-Bee, funded in part by a late aunt who time traveled through powerful mirrors. The same aunt became wealthy through use of some temporal stunt. Even after paying 99 percent time tax, there's enough for Rhian to get by.

Rhian's mother made her take dance lessons to become more feminine. Rhian wanted to embark on a professional dancing career, but studied temporal anthropology to find her time-lost father. She was working toward a Ph.D. in Homeostatic Time-travelling Cultures, but got her academic credentials revoked for trying to steal the Book. Rhian hoped to find her time-lost father via the Book, and reunites with him at story's end.

• *The TARDIS:* A credit chip from the TARDIS vault apparently has no limit. The Ship underlined the Museum of Locks on a map—apparently to warn him against going there—but it actually had the opposite effect.

The TARDIS routes the crew's mobile phones through local satellites. The Unnoticed's Interrupter fails to affect the Ship.

ALIEN RACES *The Unnoticed:* Incredibly emaciated—and distinctly non-humanoid—the Unnoticed hang below gas-filled sacs. They're slick with decay, having thin spindly legs that wouldn't support their weight. Their flesh seems petrified, and they frequently drip acidic stomach juice from open sores. The Unnoticed have writhing, tentacle hands and speak in fractured sentences.

They possess silver-barreled disintegrator weapons. They've developed bombs no larger than white marble balls, capable of blowing up planets. They can smell the Book's presence.

• *The Unnoticed's Sensitives (a.k.a. Canaries):* The Unnoticed can convert humans into time sensitives through physical touch, using the sensitives to scan nearby planets for any sign of time travel technology or time travelers—avoiding worlds with positive results. For convenience and secrecy, the Unnoticed keep a small breeding colony of time sensitives at their disposal [Carmodi hails from this breeding stock].

ALIEN PLANETS *Lebenswelt:* The remote Lebenswelt fantastically profited from its mineral wealth (*see History*), then devolved into a state of hedonism and decay. A few off-world business people settled on Lebenswelt to leech off the wealthy, but nobody wants to travel that far to perform menial tasks. Ergo, little on Lebenswelt gets fixed

and its civilization is horribly dirty.

Lebenswelt's major city—also named Lebenswelt—looks like a gothic nightmare, with dingy streets, slimy stone walls, rubbish-strewn pavements and cracked stained glass. Every second roof's got a spire, turret or belfry. Jewels and gold are plentiful, albeit often tarnished.

Off-worlders attempting to live off Lebenswelt's rubbish get shot on sight. The planet's prisons are overcrowded, with the Licensing Committee examining prisoners for early release.

• *Antimasque:* The nearest planet to Lebenswelt, located a distance of 17 standard [presumably 17 light years] away. Antimasque's a pleasure planet that rotates on its axis every 29 hours. It's home to a wide variety of lifeforms and is terribly expensive.

STUFF YOU NEED *The Book of the Still:* About the size of a hotel guest book. It's not particularly thick—maybe 100 pages—bound in cracked gray leather with gold leaf words etched onto the cover.

We're given no clues about the Book's origin. The term "Seekers" refers to stranded time travelers looking for the Book. "Finders" refers to the beings who rescue them. Entry 3756 contains information and coordinates for the Unnoticed's Tent City.

The Book's made from invulnerable taffeta. As such, the Doctor at one point tears out the Book's pages and fashions them into a cube, bound together by the equivalent of Quantum Velcro. Using such a contraption, the Doctor falls through the sun's photosphere and safely arrives at the Unnoticed's Tent City.

• *Super-Strong Taffeta:* Substance that composes both The Book of the Still and the Unnoticed's Tent City. It's made by running a thread through the Universe's substratum, producing a material that's one part fabric and nine parts baseline reality. That makes it durable enough to wallpaper over a black hole.

• *The Unnoticed's Wave Interrupter:* Neutralizes all communication, electricity and microwave transmissions on a target planet. The Unnoticed come and go via a narrow, protective resonance corridor in the field.

• *Nanite Virus:* Made by a designer named Globbo, this dust makes robots double over and fitfully sneeze like humans with head colds.

• *Stasis Suit:* Protective suit the Doctor uses in his attempt to steal The Book of the Still—literally diving into the Museum of Locks from 50 km high, relying on the stasis suit to protect him. The stasis suit's controls include a Big Red Button.

PLACES TO GO *The Museum of Locks (a.k.a.*

Das Museum der Verriegelungen): Oddly enough, the Museum's defenses are the real exhibits. The museum's curator tracked down the Book in this time zone and put it on display—an almost gratuitous object for the Museum to protect.

ORGANIZATIONS *TimeCorp:* Unspecified company that employs Rhian's father. It offers a fringe benefit allowing employees to complete their working day, then zap back to the morning for the start of family time. Not all workers take this perk, because they consequently age a third faster than their family every day, but those that do get to see their families more.

SHIPS *Unnoticed Ship:* Essentially a flying cremation with no recognizable design, covered with blackened bubbles and scabs.

PHENOMENA *Time Travel:* Causes all sorts of exotic particles—such as Bockatrons, Harminum and Artron Oxidants—to accrue in time travelers' systems.

[Author's Note: It's worth mentioning that Carmodi's breaking of the Unnoticed's time loop should, in fact, void her own existence. Still, her letter to the Doctor at book's end suggests she hopes to temporally outrun the loop's unraveling by some millions of years and somehow survive.]

PARTIALLY DELETED HISTORY
• Temporal expert Albrecht spent 14 years on Hej with some aboriginals, only to retro-crash three of his ancestors and wipe himself from existence [his exact screw-up was deemed a "Dream Time Error" (DTE)]. Albrecht's diaries survived because the DTE caused a reality pocket which gave a rescue team 24 hours to retrieve his notes. His theories gave rise to the condition, "Albrecht's Ennui," which afflicts temporally displaced people who go a few years without time travel.

HISTORY Five hundred years ago, Lebenswelt sold its considerable mineral wealth to a Galactinational.
• Sirius One-Bee University Press published *Of Finders and Seekers—a user's guide to being lost in time* in 3972.

AT THE END OF THE DAY Solid, funny and meaningful. *The Book of the Still*'s reputation sometimes suffers because it works hard to avoid having an outright villain [pretty much everyone involved deserves *some* sympathy] and admittedly, there's a point midway through—when Ebbs shifts gears—that you're tempted to start snooz-

ing. All of that said, this book's astoundingly chock-full of ideas [the Doctor sun-diving in a paper cube alone deserves praise] and although it made us laugh, *The Book of the Still*'s touching bits [Rhian teaching the Doctor to dance while they wait for death] stuck in our brains even more. As such, it becomes like a performer who swaps white and black dinner suits between sketches, sweating bullets to keep us entertained. Recommended.

DID YOU KNOW?

• Author Paul Ebbs says about *The Book of the Still*: "It's a bloody big book about drugs, addiction, flashbacks and recovery (specifically LSD) and *no one* seems to notice until I point it out to them. I was going to jointly author it with the far-too clever and brilliant Richard Jones, but he had a ton of personal shit and had to pull out. Which was a shame... up to the point where I got the cash."
• In addition, Ebbs says about the novel's ending: "I didn't want to fill the end with tons of *Scooby-Doo* explanation, and left it open to interpretation as to how a species (the Unnoticed) could evolve purely out of spite. The end is one big head-fuck trip anyway, and under those conditions not a lot actually does make sense. That's my excuse and I'm sticking to it."

THE CROOKED WORLD

By Steve Lyons

Release Date: June 2002
Order: BBC Eighth Doctor Adventure #57

TARDIS CREW The eighth Doctor, Fitz and Anji.

TRAVEL LOG Zanytown, Gloomy Forest and a supervillain base, all The Crooked World, time unknown.

STORY SUMMARY Purely at random, the TARDIS arrives on the Crooked World, a remote planet inexplicably inhabited by cartoon characters such as Boss Dogg, Streaky Bacon, the Whatchamacallit and more. In the tradition of Warner Bros. cartoons, the Crooked World's inhabitants gleefully run about maiming and hurting one another with no ill effect. But as the Doctor steps from the TARDIS, a gun-toting, hyperactive Streaky Bacon unloads a blunderbuss into his

This book is not endorsed by the BBC. Doctor Who and TARDIS are trademarks of the BBC.

179

chest. Amazingly—to Streaky, at least—the Doctor falls to the ground, genuinely wounded.

Thanks to his recuperative powers, the Doctor recovers in nearby Zanytown. In learning about the Doctor's injury, however, the Crooked World's inhabitants come to understand the concept of death. Infinitely malleable, the Crooked World's physics shift to accommodate this new worldview, making it possible for the cartoon inhabitants to grievously injure one another. Amid such raised stakes, cartoon cat Jasper playfully bites the head off a mouse named Squeak, and shockingly commits the Crooked World's first murder.

Moreover, the Crooked World morphs to accommodate *any* concept the time travelers care to mention. When Fitz's loose lips cite various supervillain tactics, a pack of Crooked World menaces—the Masked Weasel, the Green Ghost, etc.—band together to seek world domination. The villains target Zanytown with a giant superlaser, but the Doctor and Fitz let slip various concepts to their advantage, such as the fact that supervillain countdowns inevitably stop at "one." The infuriated Green Ghost finally self-destructs the villains' lair, even as the supervillains, finding the notion of actual world domination too much work, disband.

Eventually, the Doctor's party finds evidence that the verboten Scary Manor holds clues to the cartoon characters' origin. Inside, the Doctor and his allies discover the remains of a spaceship escape pod. Zanytown Sheriff Boss Dog confesses that years ago, the Crooked World residents were blank slates, lacking cohesive form or thought. But eventually, the escape pod, containing a little girl, crashed on the planet. The Crooked World patterned itself and its people according to the little girl's wild imagination, but she starved to death soon after.

Gradually, the Crooked World residents mature enough to restrain their murderous impulses. With considerable willpower, the cartoon characters bring Squeak back to life, absolving Jasper of blame. The Crooked World characters further adjust to notions such as female liberation and sex, even as the Doctor's trio—pleased to have helped the Crooked World characters develop self-will—depart in the TARDIS.

MEMORABLE MOMENTS It's hard not to love a book that goofily opens with Streaky Bacon (i.e. Porky Pig) blowing the Doctor away at point-blank range.

A chicken receptionist asks Fitz how he'd like his breakfast eggs, giving "freshly squeezed" as an option. The Doctor notices the Crooked World res-

idents are painfully growing up, causing Anji to ask: "But what if they weren't meant to grow up?"

In a dramatic moment, Streaky Bacon can't handle his budding independent thought and tries to blow his head off, but only gets a bit charred for his trouble. More comically, the supervillains torture Fitz with a fluffy duster, stressing that, "The sooner you tell us all about [the villains of your world], the less it will tickle." The Doctor later rescues Fitz with a custard pie gun.

Cats protest on the imprisoned Jasper's behalf, carting signs that say, "Give Cats a Fur Deal," and "Fight for the Right to Kill Vermin." The Doctor brilliantly serves as Jasper's defense attorney, pointing out his mistress—a big, fat hotel maid essentially told Jasper to murder "that darn mouse." A liberated Jasper sheds tears of relief when Squeak comes back to life.

SEX AND SPIRITS The ever-randy Fitz introduces the Crooked World to the notion of sex, repeatedly hitting up the chaste, female car driver Angel Falls for quick nookie. Finally, Angel relents to Fitz's desire in the back of a helicopter, enabling an anguished Fitz to discover the Crooked World inhabitants don't have genitals. Indeed, their crotches are smooth as naked Barbie dolls.

Even so, the Crooked World gleans the fundamentals of sex from Fitz's botched dalliance, resulting in Anji finding Mike Leader and Harmony Looker (obviously *Scooby Doo*'s Fred and Daphne) in a closet, naked, with Mike atop Harmony. Unable to properly shag, the Crooked World residents adopt naked wriggling as an act of passion.

Normally, Crooked World residents reproduce by writing a letter to the Baby Stork. Thanks to Fitz's interference, the Baby Stork gets four requests from unmarried couples.

Blondes make Fitz melt. He knows his pick-up routine isn't the most polished, but prides himself [rightly or wrongly] on a high success rate. He's leveled when Angel Falls announces intentions to marry Mr. Weasley, her guardian.

Streaky Bacon asks out the Crooked World's equivalent of *Scooby Doo*'s Velma (Thelma Brains), hoping to take in a derby and some wriggling with her.

ASS-WHUPPINGS Streaky Bacon unloads his blunderbuss into the Doctor's chest, but the buckshot doesn't penetrate much [the Crooked World physics slowly adjust to the notion of actually harming someone].

The Whatchamacallit (i.e. the Road Runner) makes Anji skid out on a near-frictionless banana peel and pushes the TARDIS into a canyon (the in-

:erior force field protects Anji from harm).

Jasper the cat repeatedly whacks Fitz with an .ron, just to see how he experiences pain. Squeak plugs Jasper's tail into a light socket, and bashes out his teeth with a saucer. Jasper swallows Squeak whole, but the mouse punches his way to freedom. Finally, Jasper bites Squeak's head off—the first Crooked World fatality.

Three cartoons die, flattened and unable to re-inflate. A rabbit cooks and eats a human being. Jollity Farm residents stone a man to death for marrying a cow. During a riot, hot fat slops on two ducks. A bespectacled penguin gets knifed in the back.

In a move sure to make *Scooby Doo* fans leap out of their seats and cheer, a 10-ton weight mashes Scrapper Dogg (i.e. that misbegotten runt Scrappy Doo).

TV TIE-INS The TARDIS food machine ("The Daleks") dispenses tablets. The Doctor subconsciously fears hospitals ("Doctor Who: Enemy Within").

NOVEL TIE-INS *The Crooked World* implies that morphable planets naturally spring into existence, citing Albert, the shapeshifting planet in *Grimm Reality*, as such an example. However, this contradicts *Grimm Reality*'s origin for Albert (*see Grimm Reality* write-up).

It's never stated, but the pre-cartoon Crooked World residents are possibly the same race of formless alien beings seen in Lyons' *Salvation*.

The Doctor healed quicker when he possessed two hearts (*The Adventuress of Henrietta Street*). Fitz's late mother (*The Taint*) called him "Fitzy." He can't stand anyone else using it, but tolerates it from Angel.

CHARACTER DEVELOPMENT

• *The Doctor:* The Doctor's not thrilled about the Crooked World residents learning murder, but he's excited they've learned self-will.

• *Fitz Kreiner:* Fitz considers the Doctor his best friend. He's not ready for child-rearing.

• *Anji Kapoor:* Her hair's a bit long, and she's desperately hoping the TARDIS will land near a decent hairdresser. She's never been one to talk to animals. She doesn't know how to get water from a cactus.

Anji's TARDIS key looks like an anachronistic Yale key. She wears makeup to feel more composed. She somewhat arrogantly thinks she can craft the Crooked World's philosophies and create a utopia. She masters Crooked World physics enough to will banana peels into existence.

• *Boss Dogg:* Zanytown Sheriff and biggest proponent of the Crooked World's old ways. After this story, Boss Dogg settles down to protect Streaky Bacon's cropland from the Whatchamacallit.

• *Streaky Bacon:* Gets deputized for this story, then becomes Sheriff when Boss Dogg resigns.

• *Whatchamacallit:* A contortionist creature, bright purple, that defies classification (based on the Road Runner, clearly).

• *The Masked Weasel:* Supervillain identity of Mr. Weasley, Angel Falls' guardian. He defected from the supervillain gang out of love for Angel. He decides to help Streaky Bacon write a book about these events.

• *The Green Ghost:* Remains jailed after this story—because nobody feels like letting him out.

• *The TARDIS:* The Library seemingly runs beyond reason, with shelves stretching out of sight. E-books are shelved alongside old paperbacks. Anji suspect the Ship reads her mind and re-arranges the books accordingly. She doesn't know how to work the TARDIS controls, suspecting they change in accordance with the Doctor's disposition. Certainly, the console room darkens as the Doctor's mood worsens.

ALIEN RACES *The Crooked World Inhabitants:* The Crooked World residents call their newly independent thinking, "A Plague of Questions." Anji furthers the notion of female liberation there.

• *Twitters:* Tiny blue birds that spontaneously appear and fly in a circle when someone gets hurt. They vanish into dust when finished.

ALIEN PLANETS *The Crooked World:* It's named such because there are hardly any parallel lines. The little girl that created the Crooked World was evidently human, because the planet exhibits Earth currency, animals, customs, landscapes and language. Its colors are flat-toned, meaning the TARDIS crew seems vibrant by comparison.

The Crooked World has an economy based on invention, theft and the ability to pluck money out of mid-air. Money's desirable for its own sake—anyone can create it on command, including million-dollar bills.

The planet's sun wears cool-looking sunglasses, and sometimes chats with the hat-wearing moon. The planet lacks coffee. It holds a daily Funny-Car Derby. There's also a First National Bank and a Dry Gulch Mining Company.

Crooked World regions include Futuria, Jolly Jungle and Anime City. Stoneville's home to Mike Mason and his forward-looking Paleolithic relatives.

PLACES TO GO *Zanytown:* It looks like a caricature of New York or Chicago, with buildings at odd angles. Some taper off, almost pyramidal. The population's officially 512 and 1/2. Numerous cats live there. There's no toilet facilities, because none of the cartoon characters need them.

• *Scary Manor:* It's converted into a museum-cum-library-cum-shrine, with the little girl properly buried there.

ORGANIZATIONS *Crooked World villains:* Include Dirty Duck, the Grim Rider, the Masked Weasel, the Green Ghost, Baron Von Nasty and a wart-riddled hag named Repugna. They misinterpret Fitz's mention of an "A-bomb," thinking it's a device that erupts into A-shaped objects.

• *The Skeleton Crew:* Clean-cut teenage rock band, based on the Scooby gang, whose members include Mike Leader, Harmony Looker, Thelma Brains, Tim Coward and a dog named Fearless. They drive around solving mysteries in "The Spook Wagon."

To date, they've had 962 adventures. Their van inevitably breaks down near spooky joints. Trying to run makes their feet momentarily pedal in midair. They often play instruments for chase scenes.

PHENOMENA *Crooked World Physics:* The Crooked World's malleable physics enable a bundle of Warner Bros. cartoon-style effects. Essentially, ideas govern every occurrence. The TARDIS crew only feels pain and takes wounds because they believe in such things. Conversely, the cartoons can defy gravity, avoiding falling until they realize they *should* be falling. They can run through walls, even survive and talk underwater. Their eyes glow in the dark [but Anji's don't].

Cartoon characters can will objects into existence [*a la* creating a piano to drop on someone] and later make such objects disappear. They can produce portable holes.

Cartoons typically flatten if injured and reinflate themselves afterward (they can postpone reinflating, if being flat helps them).

When punched, the cartoons' heads cave in like rubber balls. Explosives simply leave them charred and pissed off. Smashed-up cars simply get tire-pumped back into shape.

Crooked World TV newscasters can speak directly *to* the viewer. They can also step into the TV and arrive at any on-screen location.

Light bulbs appear above people with ideas (the Crooked World Electric Company runs dry in this adventure).

• *The Universe:* The Doctor claims that conflicting forces in the quantum multiverse sometimes make reality stretch thin, creating malleable planets like the Crooked World.

HISTORY Unknown parties put the little girl in her escape capsule. Boss Dogg was one of the few Crooked World residents to have contact with the girl, but couldn't understand her garbled words. After the little girl's death, Boss Dogg buried her with a tombstone reading: "She made us what we are."

AT THE END OF THE DAY Just about the nuttiest "Who" undertaking in some time, brilliantly geared for anyone who grew up with *Scooby Doo* and Warner Brothers cartoons. Written by slobbering cartoon guru Steve Lyons, who [last we checked] kept his comic collection in his attic, and was in danger of the entire house collapsing and killing him, *The Crooked World* achieves a near-perfect balance between lunacy and tragedy. It's often hysterical, then subverts expectations (Streaky Bacon's attempted suicide, Jasper's killing Squeak, etc.) to make you realize that suddenly, what's happening here is tearfully, lethally serious. Overall, a *very* strange book—which says a lot for "Doctor Who"—and we adore it.

DID YOU KNOW?

• Lyons dubbed his Tom-like cartoon cat in *The Crooked World* as Jasper, as that's what Tom is called in his very first appearance. Lyons meant to change the name for fear of copyright infringement, but got too used to Jasper and stuck with it.

HISTORY 101

By Mags L. Halliday

Release Date: July 2002
Order: BBC Eighth Doctor Novel #57

TARDIS CREW The eighth Doctor, Fitz and Anji.

TRAVEL LOG Barcelona, Spain, November 1936 to April, 1937; Guernica and Bilboa, Spain, April, 1937; the Paris Exposition, France, 1937; the System, time unknown.

STORY SUMMARY In Barcelona, the 1930s, an Absolute—a creature on the fringe of human perception—arrives through time to collect information for a futuristic data network called the System. However, Sabbath learns the System con-

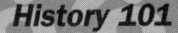 
tains incriminating information about his activities past and present, and thereby dispatches an agent to bring the network to ruin. Sabbath's operative arrives in Barcelona, wearing modified glasses that let him perceive the normally shrouded Absolute. Unfortunately, the mere presence of a time traveler futzes up the Absolute's own perceptions—causing a cascade effect that corrupts the System and in turn throws the public's ability to perceive history out of whack.

Increasingly disoriented, the Absolute spies differing accounts of a café conversation between photographer Miquel Dominguez and novelist Eric Blair. The Absolute absorbs Miquel for further study, but its corrupted systems eject him as a shattered information monster out of synch with reality. In another blunder, the Absolute fails to possess Blair, leaving the writer unharmed but corrupting itself even further, thereby assuming a new persona named Enrique.

Meanwhile, the TARDIS crew arrives at the Parisian Exposition, 1937, only to note inaccuracies between the original of Picasso's *Guernica* and a book reproduction of the painting from the TARDIS library. In time, the Doctor grows convinced that Western culture's perception of history is awry, dispatching Fitz to observe the infamous April, 1937, Guernica bombing that inspired the Picasso work.

The Doctor and Anji TARDIS-hop to Barcelona and wait for Fitz. Elsewhere, Sabbath's agent disguises himself as a Russian weapons smuggler named Sasha, then travels with Fitz to Guernica to ascertain the Absolute's historical corruption. Fitz and Sasha spy differing accounts of the bombing, unable to determine if the Germans, the Russians or the Spanish Republicans leveled the town. Fitz returns to Barcelona, where Sasha tidies up loose ends by entering the System via the TARDIS telephone, thus retroactively arranging the historical German bombing of Guernica. In such a fashion, Sasha brings history back into alignment, then reports back to Sabbath.

Simultaneously, the Doctor tracks down the weakened Enrique and the Miquel-based information creature. With help from the TARDIS, the Doctor compels Enrique to confront the genuine history of Guernica, allowing it to reconcile its conflicting viewpoints. Enrique stabilizes enough to merge with the information creature, then transfers itself back to the devastated System. In the aftermath, Sabbath's pleased for knowing his secrets are safe, a somewhat traumatized Blair returns to England [later writing *1984* as George Orwell] and the Doctor's crew travels onward.

MEMORABLE MOMENTS Anji listens to the Doctor deliver a fairly nutty speech about perception, to which he adds: "[I'm not] insane, I'm just very worried."

When the TARDIS shuts itself down, trying to ward off incursion from the corrupted System, the Doctor and Anji suffer telepathic backlash and struggle, weakened, to the TARDIS doors. Anji pulls the Doctor's key from his pocket—sort of like "The Caves of Androzani," only in reverse. In what becomes the most unnerving moment of Anji's life, the Doctor screams at having lost the TARDIS again, then wanders about in a daze mumbling to himself. Later, the Doctor ramps himself up to full-blown fury, attacking the sealed-off TARDIS library with a crowbar to get at the books.

An utterly brilliant moment entails Sabbath referring to Anji and Fitz as the Doctor's agents. When the Doctor insists they're friends, not operatives, Sabbath comments: "Doesn't that rather depend upon your perspective?"

Finally, the Doctor laughs while defeating the Absolute, realizing that to some degree, he's exorcising the Absolute's restraining viewpoint and restoring anarchy to history.

SEX AND SPIRITS Curious Parisians eyeball Anji, wondering what she's doing running around with two Englishmen. A hotel receptionist mistakes the Doctor and Anji for man and wife. In Barcelona, Anji throws a drink at a lascivious man named Roberts, then shrugs off the incident by remarking: "It wasn't very good wine."

Sabbath's agent, further disguised as a Hispanic correspondent named Jueves, keeps stopping by to visit Anji. She isn't interested, but considers him intelligent and witty.

Fitz gets jailed during a bar brawl (*see Ass-Whuppings*). He catches a glimpse of a woman's camisole top during the Guernica bombing, and decides it's not such a bad mission after all.

At the risk of making too much of this, Sasha shares a bed with Fitz and risks his life stopping Fitz from going into the System. Although Fitz doesn't seem to realize it, he spends most of his time with Sasha mildly drunk.

ASS-WHUPPINGS When the Absolute tries linking the System to the TARDIS, hoping to use the Ship as a back-up data storage system, the TARDIS ejects any data that contradicts established history and shuts itself down to prevent further incursion. While the Ship's comatose, the console room door leading to the interior gets locked. The library's there, but unbreakable glass seals off its bookshelves. The kitchen's gone entirely. The TARDIS' telepathic backlash knocks the Doctor and Anji for a loop.

Thousands die in the Guernica bombing. Fitz spends five minutes trying to stanch a nun's bullet wound, observing her sisters don't make it. A haggard Fitz ventures back to Barcelona, scruffy after sleeping in ditches for a few days.

Miquel's sister Eleana gets her perceptions knocked off-kilter and crazily tries to shoot the Doctor, but her gun jams and explodes in her face. The Doctor helps re-set her dislocated arm.

Fitz smashes a glass in his hand during a bar fight. Barcelona authorities remove the glass, then toss him in prison. Officials round up Anji during a gunfight, throwing her into a cell with other rebel fighters. In a perception flip-flop, Burton [novelist Eric Blair's *id*] tortures Anji and Blair [his ego and superego, later restored] rescues her. Sabbath's agent, as Sasha, arranges Fitz's release.

TV TIE-INS The TARDIS shuts down on November 23, the TV show's anniversary ("An Unearthly Child"). The powerless TARDIS doors require a manual crank to open ("Death to the Daleks"). The Doctor gives Fitz a TARDIS tracker ("Mawdryn Undead") which locates the Ship even when it's inert. Fitz also owns a TARDIS key.

NOVEL TIE-INS The System apparently holds details concerning Sabbath's escape from his Secret Service initiation. The Doctor retains a chest scar from his open-heart surgery. *History 101* ends with a giant, malevolent eyeball—the same one seen in the horizon's gray city—keeping watch over the ruined System (all *The Adventuress of Henrietta Street*).

The Doctor deliberately avoids *Times* correspondent Kim Philby, since he's not slated to meet the journalist until some years into Philby's future (*Endgame*). He spies Fitz's scribbled notes in the TARDIS' copy of *The Age of Reason* and becomes horrified, foreshadowing events in *Time Zero*.

Fitz retains murky memories of jumping off a tower—namely, his thwarted suicide attempt in *Interference*. The Doctor sends a message to Fitz with the phrase, "The planet is called Albert," so he'll know it's genuine (*Grimm Reality*).

During the Doctor's century on Earth (*The Burning* to *Escape Velocity*), he spent time in Europe, America, China, Asia and Australia. In 1937, he frequented London. At some point, he visited the Catholic-Hierarchy Archdiocese of Hangchow in China (*The Year of Intelligent Tigers*).

Author Mags Halliday says that references to cameras throughout *History 101*—such as the Isherwood quote: "I am a camera with its shutter open, quite passive, recording, not thinking"—weren't deliberately intended to reference the next novel, *Camera Obscura*. [Author's Note: In any case, the term *camera obscura* refers to a dark room, not something made by Polaroid.] Even so, Halliday agrees that *History 101*, *Camera Obscura* and *Time Zero* contain some similarities of theme—notably that history can lie—meaning comparisons are unavoidable.

CHARACTER DEVELOPMENT

• *The Doctor:* The Doctor's on debating terms with Sartre. He doesn't sweat. He's able to provide pesetas and forged papers for Spain, 1937. He speaks French without an accent, although his phraseology indicates French as a second language.

In moments of crisis, the Doctor falls back on invented swear words, such as "Oh sugarmice—"

He visited Spain during dictator Franco's regime, stunned at the lack of free speech. Picasso's lover gave the Doctor a preliminary sketch for Picasso's *Guernica*.

• *Fitz Kreiner:* Fitz got a quarter of the way through *The Age of Reason*, but failed to finish it. He's disappointed because there's no time to stop at the Moulin Rouge in Paris.

In school, Fitz owned a winning marble—that bully Tubby Johnson took from him after a beating. He spent time during World War II huddled in an Anderson, hiding from German bombs.

Fitz finds Sabbath's handwriting vaguely familiar. He sometimes fantasizes about cigarettes made of the finest Virginian tobacco. Fitz still has no clue how to run the TARDIS.

• *Anji Kapoor:* She visited Paris in her own era, but spent most of her time looking unimpressed, acting like a wary 20th century cynic.

In London, Anji used a step-machine at a gym. She's out of shape at the moment, and gets winded while walking up stairs. [Halliday wishes to add: "Have you seen the steps to the Sacre Coeur? Anyone would get winded!"] Her flimsy EU passport is somewhere in the TARDIS.

Anji speaks some French, with a rapidly increasing Catalonian vocabulary. She views the TARDIS console room as a corporate office.

Anji's political views aren't set. She likes chocolate. Her journals, detailing her six months in Barcelona, get destroyed.

• *Fitz and Anji:* Until now, they haven't visited Paris before World War II.

• *The Doctor, Fitz and Anji:* They tacitly agree to avoid the German [i.e. Nazi] section of the Paris exhibition. Anji views the Doctor and Fitz as two younger brothers on permanent sugar rushes.

She considers ditching the Doctor and Fitz during a crisis point, tapping the Doctor's contemporary bank accounts and using a front company to rule the markets in New York. But ultimately, she finds herself unable to abandon them.

• *Sabbath:* Sabbath's *not* actively manipulating the Doctor's journeys at the moment, needing to be informed when they crop up in Barcelona.

• *The Enrique-Absolute:* Finishes this story trapped in the System with all escape routes blocked.

• *The TARDIS:* When linked to the System, the Ship can digitize people via its exterior phone, enabling transport from one end of the System to another. The Doctor speculates that the TARDIS' exterior phone actually interfaces with the primitive, raw powers that drive the time machine. The phone keeps a dialing tone even when the power's down. The Doctor's insistent about hanging up the phone, presumably worried about an unspecified disaster otherwise.

After *The Ancestor Cell*, the TARDIS rebuilt herself from the smallest atom upward. Accordingly, the Ship's entire contents are fakes, composed of TARDIS matter. Such objects are somewhat protected from historical revision. Also, the objects possess some of the TARDIS' temporal properties [surrounding yourself with paper from a TARDIS book, for instance, also enables transport through the System].

The TARDIS' exterior remains nigh-invulnerable even while the Ship's powerless. It contains a bath the size of the swimming pool, plus an auto-razor (mentioned in "Doctor Who in an Exciting Adventure with the Daleks"). Fitz worries that he'll fall asleep and awakening to find the damn thing's shaved his whole body.

The Ship can search for historical anomalies by tapping and cross-referencing the local phone system, newspapers and radio broadcasts. In a pinch, the Ship can deliver information via its ticker tape system ("State of Decay").

ALIEN RACES *The Absolute:* The Absolute's origins [and those of the System] are never clarified. We only see one Absolute here, but it's implied others exist. The Absolute collect information as non-partisan observers, unfettered by human bias. They don't conform to the universally held perceptions, making them invisible under normal circumstances.

The Absolute seem to lack individual identity, which means the Enrique persona seen in *History 101* stems from the System's corruption. The discordant Enrique looks slightly human, albeit jumbled like a shattered mirror image of Blair.

MISCELLANEOUS STUFF!

HISTORY 101 SONGS

Although most people didn't notice it, Mags Halliday named the chapter titles in *History 101* after songs by the Clash—only written in Catalan.

Below is a full list, just in case you're curious, but a few need extra explanation: Chapter 1 is titled, "Know Your Rights," the first track on the album *Combat Rock*. Halliday included this one because the PDA *Combat Rock* published the same month as *History 101* [and she's duly grateful that the novel line's cutback didn't happen sooner, thereby throwing the schedule out of whack]. Chapter 12 is called "The City of the Dead," denoting the Lloyd Rose EDA of the same name.

Chapter 01: Know Your Rights
Chapter 02: Safe European Home
Chapter 03: Somebody was Murdered
Chapter 04: Police on My Back
Chapter 05: Stay Free
Chapter 06: Spanish Bombs
Chapter 07: Hateful
Chapter 08: Working for the Clampdown
Chapter 09: Guns on the Roof
Chapter 10: The Prisoner
Chapter 11: I Fought the Law
Chapter 12: The City of the Dead
Chapter 13: Last Gang in Town

On Earth, the Absolute makes heavy use of the telephone system to collect data. It can also digitize other beings into the System, analyzing said beings' entire history and cross-referencing it.

STUFF YOU NEED *The System:* Time travelers throw the System out of synch because they lack a linear history.

PHENOMENA *History Perception:* Altering people's perception of history could potentially corrupt the timeline as much as blatantly altering historical events. Time travelers have some resistance to perception alteration, since they're already dislocated in time.

HISTORY [101] Novelist Eric Blair genuinely ventured to Spain at the end of 1936, hoping to examine/support the socialist undertakings of the Partido Obrero de Unificacion de Marista

This book is not endorsed by the BBC. Doctor Who and TARDIS are trademarks of the BBC.

185

(POUM). In *History 101*, he takes a bullet to the throat while liberating Anji from jail [the bullet, at least, is historical fact], but survives and returns home to his wife. He wrote about his experiences in Spain [minus the sci-fi elements in *History 101*, one presumes] in *Homage to Catalonia* (1938). As George Orwell, he wrote the dystopic *1984* and *Animal Farm*.

• Sabbath's agent fulfilled history by contacting German Lt. Colonel Wolfram von Richthofen (cousin to Manfred von Richthofen, World War I's Red Baron), convincing him to attack Guernica with his Condor Legion. Sufficiently fooled, von Richthofen assaulted Guernica on behalf of the Spanish dictator General Francisco Franco. [Side Note: Sixty-one years later, the German Parliament formally apologized to Guernica for the bombing. The Spanish government offered no such concession.]

• Previous to this story, Sabbath dispatched his agent to 1980—for unknown reasons—to assassinate Pope John Paul II [again, the assassination attempt is historical]. The Pope ducked and went uninjured, but the incident prompted the creation of the Popemobile.

AT THE END OF THE DAY   Layered, intellectual, and unabashedly gelling the current TARDIS crew into a *family* (with Anji constantly perplexed by her two weird "brothers"). Generally speaking, *History 101* dissects a brutal yet surprisingly cultured point in history, putting the Doctor and company through the wringer (climaxing with Fitz's dilemma about ordering the genuine Guernica attack, thus killing thousands to preserve history's web). Admittedly, it could use a bit more polish and clarity in parts, but *History 101* is above average on its own merits, and when viewed as a first-time novel, it's even more remarkable.

DID YOU KNOW?

A website exists detailing some of *History 101*'s background appears at:
http://www.halliday47.freeserve.co.uk/mj-h101.html. [Note: The hyphen is part of the address.]

• Halliday wrote *History 101* in a variety of locations, including Sao Paulo, Brazil; Sydney and the Gold Coast, Australia; a swish hotel in Falkirk, Scotland and the SWT train service from Devon to London. In celebration for signing the contract to write *History 101*, Halliday fell in a ditch and twisted her ankle—a typical "Doctor Who" injury [usually dubbed by Mad Norwegian staffers as

"Sarah Jane Smith Syndrome"].

• Sabbath frequents the Café en Ballena—i.e. the Café in the Whale—a nod to Sabbath's ship *The Jonah*.

• Sasha's name began as a gender reversal joke that got lost in the rewrites. The Agent—Sasha's true identity—was never given a real name. *History 101* erroneously claims that Sasha was in Florida, 1935, when Halliday actually intended him present at the attempted assassination of FDR in 1933.

• When the TARDIS loses power, its kitchen vanishes and the woodwork gets darker—simply because Halliday couldn't stand the modernized interior and was keen to change it.

• The Doctor wears a red velvet jacket and red shirt partially because Paul McGann—at least, by Halliday's estimation—looked very dapper in similar clothes in the BBC drama *Sweet Revenge*.

• Whilst in Barcelona, Mags got one of those bull-fighting posters with a name stamped on it. The name was Fitz Kreiner and the poster is still on her wall beside the desk. She is fairly sure Fitz had one in his crummy bedsit in *The Taint* but at least it means she never spells his name wrong.

• Fitz uses a passport with a Prussian birthplace/date because in 1900—his falsified birthdate—Germany was still divided into separate states.

CAMERA OBSCURA

By Lloyd Rose

Release Date: August 2002.
Order: BBC Eighth Doctor Adventure #58

TARDIS CREW   The eighth Doctor, Fitz and Anji.

TRAVEL LOG   Dartmoor and Capel Gorast, Wales, late July and early August, 1893.

STORY SUMMARY   Detecting a temporal anomaly in Victorian England, 1893, the TARDIS crew and Sabbath separately arrive to ascertain the anomaly's origin. Soon after, the Doctor finds evidence that a rogue time machine is somehow fracturing people into identical duplicates. The Doctor finds eight copies of a stage magician named Octave, but the Octaves react with hostility to the Doctor's inquiries, believing he wants to steal the time machine for himself.

Incensed, the Octaves gang up on the Doctor and drop a 30-pound theatre stage sandbag onto

him—crushing his chest. To the Doctor's complete shock, he survives long enough to reach the TARDIS sickbay. Afterward, the recovering Doctor realizes his secondary heart, snug in Sabbath's chest (*The Adventuress of Henrietta Street*), keeps him tethered to the living world. As such, the Doctor and Sabbath share a biodata link that makes the Doctor virtually immortal.

Sabbath erroneously dubs the Octaves as the anomaly's source and dispatches his agent, a knife-wielding female named "the Angel-Maker," to murder them. As the Octaves are temporally linked, killing one Octave offs the entire lot. The Doctor decries the murders, then links the rogue time machine to an insane psychologist named Nathaniel Chiltern. As the Doctor discovers, Nathaniel's brother Sebastian somehow found the time machine and used it to search for a future cure to his sibling's madness. Regrettably, the machine splintered Nathaniel into two beings: A shell-shocked Nathaniel 1, and a malformed Nathaniel 2.

The demented Nathaniel kills Sebastian, then escapes with the machine. The Doctor worries continued use of the slipshod machine—based on faulty principles of temporal interferometry—could irrevocably puncture the space-time continuum. With Sabbath's help, the Doctor pursues the evil Nathaniel to his family home in Wales.

Nathaniel 2 throws the machine into high gear, leading the Doctor—as a final resort—to fling himself into it. As the Doctor expected, his unique status as a former elemental [i.e. a Time Lord] shorts out the machine, shattering it beyond repair. The demented Nathaniel moves to attack the Doctor, but the Angel-Maker intercepts him, fearing that the Doctor's demise might by extension harm Sabbath. The mad Nathaniel kills the Angel-Maker, but Sabbath snaps the deformed Nathaniel's neck. Miles away from the battle, the benevolent Nathaniel also dies.

Grieving because the Angel-Maker died protecting him, Sabbath rebukes the Doctor's ways, tears the Doctor's secondary heart from his chest and tosses it onto the ground, killing it. Sabbath departs, leaving the Doctor to donate his dead heart to a traveling freak show. Soon afterward, the Doctor realizes that with his secondary heart's demise, his body has started growing a new one.

MEMORABLE MOMENTS After the Doctor takes a sandbag through the chest, he gets annoyed at failing to die property—which on the surface seems a simple enough task. The Doctor later awakens, suddenly realizes that he survived because Sabbath stole his heart and says—not

yells, simply says—"You son of a bitch!"

In one of the funniest "Who" moments in some time, the Doctor leaves Fitz and Anji a note saying, "I have been kidnapped. It would be a good idea to rescue me. Yours, the Doctor. P.S.—Tell Sabbath to help you." [A resigned Fitz comments that at least the Doctor's trying to keep them informed.] Also, the Doctor makes Sabbath sit on a whoopie cushion, just to prevent matters from getting too serious.

On page 246, Sabbath beautifully goes on for three paragraphs about how the Doctor's almost a unique space-time event, pointing out that whenever he's in trouble: "Rescuers turn up. Weapons jam. Your companions, who, if you will forgive me, don't strike me as more than usually competent, save the day. Buildings explode immediately after you find the way out… If you're drowning, a spar floats by… You survive alien mind probes that would boil the average brain in its skull. No one ever shoots you in the head. Villains tie you up too loosely, and hide-bound tyrants' convictions falter at your rhetoric. In short, in your presence, the odds collapse."

Finally, in the finale, Sabbath rips out the Doctor's heart, making the Doctor ask: "Is that the heart you loved the Angel-Maker with?" To which Sabbath tersely responds: "That is not a human heart."

SEX AND SPIRITS The Angel-Maker initially believes Sabbath wants her for sexual purposes, but he turns her down with disinterest. Later, when Sabbath finds her sleeping outside his door to protect him, he takes her into his bed. The Doctor embraces people in a deliberately non-sexual fashion. He notes that Sabbath: "… stole my heart. What a phrase. I suppose I'll have to start sending him Valentines."

Fitz and Anji down Scotch, plus Sabbath's brandy. Sabbath believes the Doctor practically lives like a monk, conceding the ex-Time Lord was close to Scarlette (*The Adventuress of Henrietta Street*) but pointing out she's long since dead.

Turning lemons into lemonade, Fitz comes to the warming realization that "The universe is going to blow up… " could be the greatest pick-up line in history.

ASS-WHUPPINGS The Octaves' trick with the sandbag crushes the Doctor's remaining heart, driving the edges of his smashed ribs out his back to scrape the floor. He heals, but Sabbath collapses and requires CPR.

Needing to locate Nathaniel 2, the Doctor ambitiously finds a means of communicating with his

deceased brother Sebastian. The Doctor tricks the Angel-Maker into stabbing him through the heart [because he's never stabbed himself, and isn't confident he'd get it right], counting on his biodata link with Sabbath to anchor him to the realm of the living. The gambit works, although the Doctor further relies on Sabbath mentally following him into the realm of Death—the Doctor's old foe from the New Adventures—and pulling him away from Death's clutches.

The Angel-Maker kills Octave and other temporally duplicated individuals. In one instance, she kills an adult male and by extension his seven duplicated children. Nathaniel 2 slices the Doctor with rose thorns, then proceeds to mash him against the floor.

TV TIE-INS The Doctor still an efficient hypnotist ("The Talons of Weng-Chiang," etc.), but he believes the talent's intrinsic to his body. He can hypnotically surface/subdue multiple personalities in other people, but this only has limited results on the temporally fractured Nathaniel 1. *Camera Obscura* implies the Doctor's very presence alters probability—a claim that surfaced in the New Adventures.

NOVEL TIE-INS Sabbath's decision to keep the Doctor's heart (*The Adventuress of Henrietta Street*) was a spur of the moment decision, not part of some master plan. Until their biodata link kept him from dying, the Doctor had no idea that Sabbath had implanted the heart in his own chest.

Sabbath's interested in using Chiltern's time machine as a means of collapsing errant (or parallel) timelines together—an agenda he continues in *Time Zero*.

The Doctor thinks Sabbath played him for a fool on Station One (*Anachrophobia*) and in Barcelona (*History 101*). With Sabbath intrinsically tied to his homeworld, the Doctor gives him the dubious name "Time's Champion" (the seventh Doctor's long-running title, *Love and War* onward). Death plagued the seventh Doctor for a good chunk of the New Adventures (ditto).

The Doctor realizes the Time Lords' destruction (*The Ancestor Cell*) has enabled the creation of illicit temporal devices.

Anji's finding TARDIS travel more emotionally draining than normal, foreshadowing her departure in *Time Zero*. Fitz attends a lecture on Siberia and meets explorer George Williamson, leading to events in the same book. The Doctor sets up an exclusionary field keyed to Sabbath's biodata readings, preventing him from entering the TARDIS. Even so, Sabbath—or his agent, perhaps—gains

access to the console room (*Time Zero* again).

Fitz turned 33 in Guernica (*History 101*). He's since had his hair trimmed. From Fitz's perspective, *Unnatural History* occurred "a few years ago." In judging his life, he prefers being a shop assistant to—shudder—a true florist (*The Taint*).

The Doctor's uncomfortable in confined spaces (Rose here plays on *Seeing I*, *The Turing Test* and others). The Doctor glimpses his previous incarnations in the time machine's mirrors, including his seventh self (*The City of the Dead*), but fails to identify them.

TIE-INS Nathaniel's mirror device actually doesn't work along similar principles as mirrored time machines seen in "The Evil of the Daleks" and "The Time of the Daleks."

CHARACTER DEVELOPMENT

• *The Doctor:* The Doctor's getting flashbacks about being shorter or taller [his former incarnations, obviously]. He donates his lost heart to a freakshow owned by Hugo Small and his mate Vera.

He's familiar with Beethoven's Fifth. He's tried to explain his low body temperature and abnormal pupil response since his rebirth. He's studied the work of neurologist Jean-Martin Charcot (1825-1893), and sings with a pleasant tenor. He can make origami penguins. He identifies laudanum by taste, but his human body can't quick-metabolize it.

The Doctor can make a Lady Baltimore cake [a Southern confection]. He can't find the TARDIS' sugar thermometer.

He doesn't eat for days, presumably nourished by his restorative link with the TARDIS.

His healing trances prove more effective if he's inside the TARDIS. He pretty much knows how to snap the human body like a twig.

• *Fitz Kreiner:* Fitz finds Victorian England depressing—there's no decent music or ways to meet girls. He talks to Yeats at a Golden Dawn gathering, but only remembers him as some guy with crazy theories about the phases of the moon. Fitz has no uncles.

Fitz studied evolution in his fourth-form science class. He enjoyed lessons about fossils.

He tends to speak up when something's bothering him. He's chilled to think that, thanks to the hazards of being with the Doctor, he might not reach age 40.

• *Anji Kapoor:* Racist comments in the Victorian Era upset her. She watches episodes of *Absolutely Fabulous* stored in the TARDIS' archives. She looks upon Sabbath as a comic-book villain.

TOP 10 'WHO' NOVELS

*From Earthworld (March 2001)
to Time Zero (Sept. 2002)*

1) *Camera Obscura* (by Lloyd Rose)—It's to Lloyd Rose's credit that she's become her own worst enemy. From the moment her *Camera Obscura* published, fandom immediately started dickering about whether it was superior/inferior to her previous book, *The City of the Dead*—meaning that virtually everyone agreed both books were top-notch. But although *City* arguably makes a better novel, *Camera Obscura*'s interaction between the Doctor and Sabbath—not to mention its portrayal of Sabbath overall, the most detailed and respectful outside his debut novel—rockets this book to claim the top slot. Also, *Camera*'s rich plot—clearly modeled after aspects of the New Adventures—succeeds because Rose is a *writer* first and a "Who" lover second. Overall, *Camera Obscura* is simply awesome in its intent.

2) *The Glass Prison* (by Jacqueline Rayner)—Though the term "a good ride" is by now cliched, it nonetheless applies to *The Glass Prison*—a roller coaster event in which Benny bizarrely gives birth while sweltering in a Fifth Axis prison. Narrated by Benny, this book runs the entire emotional gamut—by turns a marrow-chilling drama and a hysterical, sarcastic comedy. Like the Benny NA *Dead Romance*, it's a criminal shame this book will never receive the readership it deserves, because it makes a number of "Doctor Who" books look like chump change.

3) *The City of the Dead* (by Lloyd Rose)—Using its dark, decayed setting of New Orleans to the fullest, *The City of the Dead* emerges as one of the novel range's most stylish, striking entries in some time. The fact that it's a "Doctor Who" book almost seems incidental in parts, and one senses that Rose worked, re-worked and worked again the plot to make it as tight as possible. Also, without intending as such, *The City of the Dead* works as a great lure for newcomers, hopefully returning some strayed "Whovians" to the novel fold.

4) *Time and Relative* (by Kim Newman)— The heavyweight of the Telos line, and a book that makes most other 2001 PDAs look light as a feather. In the space of a novella, author Kim Newman breathes new life into the first Doctor formula, forcing the reader to experience the beginnings of "Who" as if they know *nothing* about the series. We hate to apply a banal word such as "magical" to this one—but that's pretty much the case.

5) *Anachrophobia* (by Jonathan Morris)—A po-tent, hardcore science-fiction story, better geared for the novel format since this probably would've flopped—given the special effects requirement—on television. But if you read *Anachrophobia* with *Farscape*-level effects running through your head, it more than succeeds and makes its clock people seem frightening.

6) *The Crooked World* (by Steve Lyons)—Touted as silly stuff, *The Crooked World* takes the Warner Bros. format and gives it a depth rarely—if ever—seen on television. Dozens of writers would've botched this type of work, but author Steve Lyons contains the rare vision to make this work. For anyone who grew up with *Scooby Doo* and the like, this book's almost essential.

7) *The Year of Intelligent Tigers* (by Kate Orman)—Published in a fairly lackluster EDA period, the savvy *Year of Intelligent Tigers* blessedly hits you like a bucket of water in the face. It's an incredibly humanistic book, using the intelligent tigers to make us take stock of exactly what it means to be human. As with *The City of the Dead*, this also makes a good entry point into the EDA line.

8) *Mad Dogs and Englishmen* (by Paul Magrs)—Heavens, late 2001 and 2002 was a great period for the EDAs, wasn't it? Continuing the EDA Spartan domination of this list, *Mad Dogs and Englishmen* emerges as Paul Magrs' best [and strangely enough, most lucid] book. It's geared for laughs, and if you can stomach the pink poodle from the cover [and avoid getting taunted if you're reading this in public], it'll keep you charmed for hours.

9) *History 101* (by Mags L. Halliday)—It's easy to reward passion, and *History 101*—written, one senses, by someone chomping at the bit to draft a "Who" book—brings a delicious forcefulness to the TARDIS crew. The plot's extremely layered and worthy also, and whereas we couldn't give a toss about the Spanish Civil War before *History 101*, this book made the locale a stellar backdrop for its drama.

10) *Time Zero* (by Justin Richards)—A needed climax to the ongoing Sabbath storyarc, spinning the EDA line in a new direction. *Time Zero* puts a lump in your gullet because for once, the TARDIS crew's genuinely splitting up and going their separate ways. The book's science, if murky at times, gets its point across well enough and paleontologist George Williamson's final sacrifice shows some true heroism.

CONTINUED ON PAGE 191

• *Anji and Fitz:* They now have one TARDIS key between them. Fitz takes stock that he's spent most of his life as a loser, but Anji—to her credit—consoles him otherwise.

• *Sabbath:* Sabbath adopts the identity of Mr. G.K. Thursday, retired clergyman and amateur

student of Dartmoor's fauna, with regards to the Dartmoor police. He bases himself in a Regents Park mansion built by Nash in the previous century.

Sabbath likes clocks. An unspecified incident in Cairo completely terrified him. He doesn't believe in hell, but views Death's realm as such.

• *The Doctor and Sabbath:* The Doctor does his best to screw around with Sabbath's head, hoping to make Sabbath lose his resolve and tear out the Doctor's secondary heart [whatever its usefulness for keeping the Doctor alive, it makes him overly reliant on Sabbath]. The Doctor certainly didn't intend the Angel-Maker's death, but it's fair to say that he's not disappointed when it pushes Sabbath over the brink.

Sabbath ponders having the Angel-Maker rub out the well-meaning Nathaniel, which would by extension slay his duplicate, but the Doctor refuses to murder an innocent and sends the good Nathaniel away. Afterward, he successfully convinces Sabbath that prematurely killing Nathaniel would leave the time machine wide-open for any fool to get their hands on it.

Sabbath looks upon the preservation of history as a war, and freely recruits murderers such as the Angel-Maker because, "All the combatants can't be choirboys." The Doctor's obviously more picky.

Additionally, Sabbath believes humanity is fundamentally base and will inevitably screw up if given access to time technology. The Doctor acknowledges the truth in Sabbath's words, but refuses to accept them simply because he "prefers not to." [The Doctor's tremendously optimistic, and doesn't want to pre-judge humanity whatever its inherent nature.] This makes Sabbath believe the Doctor's molding the Universe to fit his views, not vice-versa, accusing him of "breathtaking hubris." The Doctor again doesn't deny such the charge, but remains unapologetic.

The Doctor and Sabbath's dual hearts share a biodata link ("The Deadly Assassin," *Interference*) that enables the Doctor to survive mortal injury. When the Doctor's harmed, Sabbath reels from the effort of healing him. The healing factor *might* work in the other direction, although it's questionable if Sabbath's human body could survive the traumatic healing process, as the Doctor—two hearts or no—has greater stamina.

The biodata link also lets the Doctor track Sabbath's location, plus mentally surf into Sabbath's brain and give the illusion of him drowning [Sabbath physically lacks the lobes to do the same].

Sabbath's starting to think of the Doctor as a temporal strange attractor of sorts, potentially an outright threat to history. Still, when Death asks

THE CRUCIAL BITS...

• **CAMERA OBSCURA**— Major smackdown between the Doctor and Sabbath. Sabbath rebukes the Doctor's ways and removes his implanted heart, killing it. In turn, the Doctor's body starts growing a new one.

Sabbath for permission to sever his biodata link with the Doctor—thereby killing his rival—Sabbath refuses, thinking the Doctor's still of value to his plans.

The Doctor's Gallifreyan hearts allow Sabbath to comprehend Death's realm—ordinary human voyagers there would likely go mad.

• *Death:* Death wants to punish the Doctor for his past arrogance and trickery. The Doctor and Sabbath merely visit the outskirts of Death's realm. Her true domain lies beyond Time altogether.

Too much time spent near Death can poison your identity. Her skin's black and papery, like something burned. Her gelatinous eyes look like as raw eggs. Her tongue lies curled like a red snake.

• *The Angel-Maker (a.k.a. Elizabeth Kelly):* Serial killer who looks about 18 or 19. Elizabeth killed her sister in their mother's womb, and has her sibling's teeth embedded in her hip.

When Kelly murders seven duplicated children, newspapers dub her "the Angel-Maker"—an old term for women in peasant communities who perform afterbirth abortions, on behalf of poor families who can't feed another child.

She left Ireland five years ago. She's sensitive to time disruptions, viewing a halo around the Doctor's body [and a lesser one around Sabbath when the Doctor's present]. She holds an unshakable loyalty and affection for Sabbath.

• *Dr. Nathaniel Chiltern:* Age 40, a renowned psychiatrist who runs a sanatorium at the end of Hampstead Heath.

• *Nathaniel Chiltern 2:* Nathaniel's duplicate, accidentally grafted by the time machine to various items from the year 1957. Nathaniel 2 sported a mouth for his right eye. He had tentacles made from rose bushes, which extended into his rib cage and left leg, and a toaster chord trailing from him like a prehensile tail.

• *Sebastian Chiltern:* Brother to the temporally duplicated Nathaniel.

• *The TARDIS:* It can detect the rogue time machine when it's active. When the machine's off, the TARDIS can only scan one 40 square-mile area at a time.

STUFF YOU NEED *Camera Obscura:* A Victorian amusement based on letting light into a dark room through a pinhole, thereby projecting an inverted image on the back wall. The term literally means "dark room."

• *Chiltern's Time Machine:* Alien device of unknown origin, ill-suited for continued use in Earth's magnetic field. The device works on faulty principles of temporal interferometry (*see Phenomena*). It would likely work fine in the Time Vortex, for lack of planetary conditions to mess it up.

Its mirrors look like glass, but are impervious to physical harm. It supposedly comes with instructions.

SHIPS *The Jonah:* It's greatly increased in time-traveling proficiency, but isn't anywhere near on par with the TARDIS.

PHENOMENA *Temporal Interferometry:* Time travel method with an appallingly high failure rate. Essentially, temporal interferometry uses a mirror system to grab a piece of history and haul it to the present. Theoretically, you could just step into the abducted time period, but anything—say, a gravity fluctuation—could throw off the process and make the machine fracture the user.

In the case of a young American named Constance Jane, the machine fractured her personality and put her second persona—Millie—out of synch with our time zone. Millie could therefore predict the future.

• *Historical Alteration: Camera Obscura* falls into the camp of "Who" works that argue history alteration is possible, since Constance Jane travels back and averts her childhood abuse with little penalty. [That said, she gets lucky—other time travelers aren't so fortunate.] Indeed, history often makes minor alterations of its own volition, just to keep everything in line.

AT THE END OF THE DAY The crowning EDA achievement of 2002, *Camera Obscura* delivers tremendous payoff to the Doctor/Sabbath storyline and contains some passages—especially their moral debates—that just about knock you off your chair. Whereas Rose's *The City of the Dead* arguably read like a better novel, *Camera Obscura* markets itself as a superior "Doctor Who" book—giving rare insight into Fitz and Anji's relationship with the Doctor, plus examining Sabbath long enough to do the character justice. It's also to *Camera Obscura*'s credit that it models itself as a New Adventures story, making the Doctor tremendously potent as a character and providing one hell of an escapist text.

TOP 10

TOP "WHO" NOVELS
CONTINUED FROM PAGE 189

HONORABLE MENTIONS

Egads, it *pains* us to not include these books on the Top 10 list, but there's just not room. Even so, they're worthy of your time, and in no particular order...

• *The Squire's Crystal* **(by Jacqueline Rayner)**—The stuff of true comedy, centered on a Bernice who's stuck in a man's body—and therefore completely out of her depth. This one's also shorter than your typical "Who" book [Big Finish tried to ballpark the Benny novels at 65,000 words rather than the customary 80,000 to 85,000], meaning it does its work, makes you roll with laughter, then exists stage right with stunning precision.

• *The Shadow in the Glass* **(by Justin Richards and Stephen Cole)**—A meaty mystery story in which virtually everything that occurs has a purpose, driving almost destiny-like toward a final confrontation in Hitler's bunker. If you're anything of a World War II buff, *The Shadow in the Glass* makes for a thoughtful examination of the Fuhrer's last days, and it's great drama even if you're not.

• *The Book of the Still* **(by Paul Ebbs)**—Witty, whimsical and a book that's good at making the Doctor perform impossible stunts at the drop of a hanky. Paul Ebbs applies his warped sense of humor in some really satisfying ways, doing justice to the TARDIS crew but also crafting a secondary cast [the addict Carmodi, the astute student Rhian] that's above-average.

• *Grimm Reality* **(by Simon Bucher-Jones and Kelly Hale)**—This one works because the core concept—i.e. a world literally ripped out of fairy tales—merely paves the way for some nutty events. Anji's made to work for evil stepsisters and balance hundreds of books on her head; the Doctor opens up shop as "Doctor Know-All" and Fitz... well, he's just tussled along from one madcap event to another. The final result's entertaining as hell, and [without intending] becomes an odd pre-cursor to the DC/Vertigo comic series *Fables*.

NON-RUNNER: *The Adventuress of Henrietta Street* **(by Lawrence Miles)**—As mentioned in the Adventuress review, Mad Norwegian Press' publishing arrangements with Lawrence Miles force us to decline ranking *The Adventuress of Henrietta Street*. That might seem like a cop-out, but we're old-fashioned enough to respect "conflict-of-interest" even if it's increasingly passé among journalists these days. You'll have to judge this one for yourselves.

DID YOU KNOW?

• A séance scene in *Camera Obscura* features a pre-vampiric Spike from *Buffy the Vampire Slayer*, who appears as his "William the Bloody Awful Poet" self, complete with brown suit and puffy hair. [Author's Note: It's a lovely addition on Rose's part, although—if we're being excruciatingly anal—not in harmony with *Buffy*, as Spike becomes vampiric in 1880 but here appears human in 1893.]

• Rose confesses that an editing error crops up on page 84, with some dialogue from a previous draft re-surfacing to cause some confusion. "Oh please, don't be coy. If you wanted to kill me, you would have. But you can't do without me yet. You don't know your way around well enough," was originally attributed to the Doctor, but as written, it seems attributed to Sabbath—which as Rose admits, makes absolutely no sense. Rose inked the line out of comp copies she handed out to friends.

• The book's title refers not only to Scale's sideshow attraction, but also to the inner chambers of the human (or Gallifreyan heart), given that *camera obscura* literally means "dark chamber." Rose thinks the book's cover is technically all wrong—as the story never makes mention of a pier—but that the rose, with its two fallen petals, is at least symbolically a heart.

• A Time Squid sequence in this book is a parody on Disney's *20,000 Leagues Under the Sea*. Rose didn't think she was capable of pulling off such a joke, but fellow author Kate Orman decreed, "There must and shall be a Time Squid!", so Rose complied.

• Rose went back and forth for weeks with regards to the Doctor uttering, "You son-of-a-bitch!" upon realizing that Sabbath stole his second heart. Editor Justin Richards felt it didn't fit the Doctor's character, so Rose variously tried substituting "You bastard!" and "You damned thief." When Rose got dangerously close to writing, "You dastardly fiend!" Richards told her to restore the original wording. However, the Doctor does not shout the epithet as some critics claimed.

• The idea for the Doctor giving his heart to sideshow people actually pre-dates even *The Adventuress of Henrietta Street*. Rose considered it for a (now-abandoned) seventh Doctor novel.

• Chiltern misspeaks on page 29 when he makes mention of the "Blair Witch," when Rose intended him to mention "the Bell Witch," a well-documented poltergeist case from the early 19th century.

• References to the Doctor's borrowed mental landscapes on page 212 are: 1) *Alice In Wonderland*, 2) "Poe's *The Narrative of A. Gordon Pym*, 3) the opening of Dante's *Commedia* (not Aslan, as Rose dislikes the Narnia books) and 4) *The Wizard of Oz*. The film in which the projectionist enters the screen and has his reality edited out from under him is Buster Keaton's great silent comedy, *Sherlock, Jr. La trista riviera d'Acheronte* is also from Dante.

TIME ZERO

By Justin Richards

Release Date: *September 2002*
Order: *BBC Eighth Doctor Adventure #59*

TARDIS CREW   The eighth Doctor, Fitz and Anji.

TRAVEL LOG   The Thames, England, late 1893; Siberia, early 1894 and 2002; the British Museum, Curtis' abode and Anji's apartment and workplace, 2002; a Euston Road bookstore, London, October 12, 1938 (our reality), same location in 1937 (alternate reality).

STORY SUMMARY   Deciding to become more than just the Doctor's sidekick, Fitz joins his new-found friend—paleontologist George Williamson (*Camera Obscura*)—on an expedition to look for fossils in Siberia, late 1893. The Doctor sadly lets Fitz go, promising to pick him up several months into Fitz's future. Privately, the Doctor knows—having long ago bought Fitz's journal of the event from a Euston Road bookstore, 1938—that most of the expedition members won't survive.

Later, the Doctor finds a few torn pages from Fitz's journal on display in the modern-day British Museum. The Doctor curiosity piques when reclusive billionaire Maxwell Curtis shows an interest in the journal, then discovers that Curtis founded the Naryshkin Institute in Siberia as a means of researching—perhaps even creating—black holes. When the Institute finds a body in a nearby ice cave, the Doctor—further contemplating the fate of Fitz's expedition—accompanies Curtis to Siberia.

In Siberia, early 1894, a dimensional doorway snaps into existence, allowing saurian lizards [akin to velociraptors] from another reality to attack Fitz's group (*see Sidebar*). The saurians kill everyone present save Fitz and George, who take refuge in a central ice chamber. Fitz finds an ice sculpture of the TARDIS, then takes a break and updates his journal. The saurians renew their at-

tack, forcing Fitz to toss a grenade and bring down the cavern wall. Fitz pushes George to safety, then makes a mad dash to take shelter behind the ice TARDIS.

More than 100 years later, the Doctor finds George Williamson's body frozen in the Siberian ice cave. The Doctor chips George free, but George inexplicably awakens as an intangible ghost— with an image of himself remaining in the ice. Testing a theory, the Doctor places the TARDIS into the cave, then flips a coin to decide whether he should move it or not. When the Doctor dematerializes the TARDIS and re-materializes it a short distance away, he causes an ice TARDIS to form in the cave.

The Doctor considers that whenever a key decision occurs, the Universe incorporates the result into its primary timeline. However, the Universe often, of its own volition, splits off a parallel reality where alternate results occur. Thus, the ice TARDIS—which retroactively appears in Fitz's era, thanks to the TARDIS' special affinity with time—represents the Doctor's indecision about moving the Ship from the cave. Along similar lines, George remains intangible because the Universe cannot decide if he died in the cave or not (*see Sidebar*).

Most shockingly, the Doctor realizes that Curtis' body is literally collapsing into a black hole (*see Sidebar*). Curtis founded the Institute as a means of travelling back to Time Zero—the point before the Big Bang—to safely release the black hole matter and save Earth from getting sucked into it. However, Curtis' black hole matter has dangerously distorted time and space in the region, catalyzing a variety of freak effects. To prove this, the Doctor smashes the modern-day ice TARDIS, pleased when a dazed Fitz falls free. The Doctor concludes that Fitz remained in the ice TARDIS for more than 100 years in a state of indeterminalism, neither dead nor alive, with the Universe only now deciding that he survived the cave-in.

George's very existence brings a time corridor into being, allowing Curtis to start travelling down said corridor to reach Time Zero (*see Sidebar*). The Doctor realizes that if Curtis' black hole erupts before time begins, it could destroy the entire Universe. With heavy hearts, the Doctor explains the situation to George, who agrees to travel back with him in the TARDIS to 1894. George deliberately spooks his younger self just as Fitz tosses a grenade into the cave. The younger George, riveted to the spot, dies when the cave wall collapses. Instantly, history acknowledges George's death and shuts down the time corridor. Curtis travels back no further than 1894 and dies in a (comparatively) minor explosion.

THE CRUCIAL BITS...

- **TIME ZERO**—Fitz spends more than 100 years in an intangible, indeterminate "Schröinger's Cat"-like state. Anji returns home for 18 months, but America's CIA kidnaps her. The Doctor rescues them, but events in this novel make various parallel realities overlap, giving the TARDIS crew the mandate of insuring that "our" timeline regains dominance, and dropping off Fitz's expedition journal at the proper bookshop to fulfill history. Origin of the fire elemental from *The Burning*.

Tying up loose ends, the Doctor tries to stop at a Euston Road bookstore, 1937, to sell Fitz's journal for his younger self to find. Unfortunately, the TARDIS arrives not in our reality, but in a parallel universe. The Doctor realizes the events in Siberia did somehow affect the Universe's nature, causing the myriad of parallel realities to vie for supremacy. With mounting dread, the Doctor recognizes the TARDIS crew must find a means of making the right timeline assert dominance, plus somehow get Fitz's journal to the right Euston Road bookstore so they'll be onhand to stop Curtis and save the whole fabric of time.

MEMORABLE MOMENTS When a younger Maxwell Curtis tries to demonstrate his power over gravity on a kid's show, his errant abilities make a tube full of coins hammer a beloved children's TV pet—Fluppy the puppy—to death. This brilliantly lets *Time Zero* open with the sentence: "Everyone in Britain can remember where they were when Fluppy died."

The Doctor insists that simple time travel [i.e. the TARDIS] cannot split reality, because if it did, none of his adventures would have a point.

Best of all, Anji returns home for a time (*see Character Development*), finds out Fitz's expedition was lost and lets the information fester. Finally, she calls Dave's mother at five in the morning, unleashing a torrent of pent-up emotion and crying for her dead boyfriend (*Escape Velocity*). Afterward, an ashamed Anji realizes that every time she mentioned the lost *Dave*, she meant *Fitz*.

SEX AND SPIRITS The Doctor arranges a tavern rendezvous with Fitz to discuss strategy for his Siberian expedition. He claims that Napoleon ("Day of the Daleks") always liked a tipple. Anji gets horribly drunk with co-worker Mitch on his last night of work.

This book is not endorsed by the BBC. Doctor Who and TARDIS are trademarks of the BBC.

193

ASS-WHUPPINGS Curtis stabilizes his black hole matter by passing certain people through his internal event horizon, allowing them to get compressed into superheavy black lumps of matter.

Fluppy the puppy dies in front of legions of British viewers (*see Memorable Moments*).

The alternate reality saurians lunch on three members of Fitz's expedition. When rival paleontologist Hanson Galloway physically attacks him, George stabs Galloway in the head with a wooden tent peg.

A bullet singes Anji. She endures near-hypothermia twice. A bullet grazes Sabbath's right hand. Renegade CIA agents kill off several of the Institute workers (*see Character Development*). The agents' leader, the murderous Colonel Hartford, gives his life to slow Curtis down so the Doctor can devise a solution.

NOVEL TIE-INS The Siberian debacle releases the fire elemental that the Doctor defeats in *The Burning* (*see Sidebar*). [Richards notes: "It's really to appease people whose only complaint about *The Burning* was, 'But what was the monster and where did it come from…'"—which of course matters not the slightest, but we aim to please!"]

Control, who directs his CIA operatives to kidnap her, first appeared in *The Devil Goblins of Neptune* and most recently surfaced in *Trading Futures*.

The Doctor purchased Fitz's journal some years before *The Turing Test*, but failed to confirm the document as genuine until *History 101*, when he spotted Fitz's handwriting and realized it matched the journal. [Author's Note: It's rather improbable that the Doctor didn't see Fitz's handwriting once until *History 101*, but let's move on.]

As with *Anachrophobia*, a disguised Sabbath unabashedly makes two stupid mistakes: A) he lets slip the Doctor's name before he's told, and B) he picks a cover identity that's holiday-themed [i.e. related to his own name of Sabbath]. Indeed, in *Time Zero*, he disguises himself as Holiday, Curtis' servant. It's a habit even more stupid than the Master's penchant for anagrams, giving the Doctor an easy means of exposing him. It's stated that Sabbath owns a suit that's bigger on the inside than the out, allowing him to disguise himself as someone more slender (such as in *Anachrophobia*). [Author's Note: And shades of the Foamasi in "The Leisure Hive," really.]

Fitz and George became friends in *Camera Obscura*, which established that Sabbath cannot enter the TARDIS. Even so, Sabbath—or one of his agents—leaves a tiny boat on the TARDIS console, leading to events in *The Infinity Race*.

Psi-ence Fiction explored similar themes about the Universe containing a dominant timeline and several parallel universes.

At story's end, the Doctor, Anji and Fitz hear a crunching sound on the other side of the TARDIS. They investigate but fail to find anything—although notably, there's a brief moment when they're absent and the TARDIS door is left open, suggesting something got inside. Odds are, we won't discover the answer to this conundrum until the Sabbath storyline wraps up, possibly in 2004's *Sometime Never…*

TIE-INS Barring the odd exception ("Inferno," *Blood Heat*, etc.), the TARDIS always travels within the Universe's primary timeline.

CHARACTER DEVELOPMENT

• *The Doctor:* He likes the British Museum, especially a cluster of clocks found there. He drinks coffee because it stimulates his brain cells. He was personally acquainted with 13-year-old Alex Romanov, shot and killed in a Yekaterinburg cellar in 1918.

• *Fitz Kreiner:* By his best guess [allowing for TARDIS travel], he's 33. His journal is simply titled, *An Account of an Expedition to Siberia*.

• *Anji Kapoor:* In *Time Zero*, the Doctor finally returns Anji to London, 2001, only three weeks after she left (*Escape Velocity*). She gets compassionate leave for Dave's death, quickly resumes her job as a futures trader and spends 18 months without incident. Eventually, a rogue element within America's CIA, headed by the enigmatic Control, comes to suspect the Naryshkin Institute of performing time experiments. Led by Colonel Hartford, Control's operatives construct a temporal detector that pinpoints Anji as a time traveler. Mistakenly believing that the Institute sent Anji back in time, Control's agents kidnap her and head for Siberia to learn more. She there reunites with the Doctor and Fitz, but must remain with the TARDIS crew until the Doctor insures the correct timeline regains dominance, fearing he might leave Anji in a parallel London by mistake.

During her 18 months back on the job, Anji professionally advances quickly—partly thanks to sheer skill, partly due to foreknowledge gained from her TARDIS travels. For instance, she cheats with share listings ripped from future copies of the *Future Times*.

Anji's boss is a senior partner named Larry, who's married to Anna. She's platonically fond of coworker Mitch.

• *Fitz and Anji:* They're solid friends by this point.

THE SIBERIAN TIME MACHINE

Alternate reality lizards. Dimensional doors. Fire elementals. There's a hell of a lot of science in *Time Zero* which, truth to tell, the brain tends to read over while relishing its drama. But if you're scratching your head as to how the Siberian time machine—a natural phenomena, not the product of technology—worked, here's an overview:

The machine essentially needs two very unique men—Curtis and George—in order to function. Curtis, it must be said, started transforming into a black hole for no particular reason. A microscopic remnant of the Big Bang, masquerading in Curtis as an ordinary atom, started collapsing into a black hole. He simply got unlucky—the same thing could've easily happened to a mongoose. [Richards notes: "But that would have made for a very different kind of story."]

The Siberian time machine works because it paradoxically assumes that Curtis *did* use it to travel into the past. As a result, his extremely dense black hole matter served to attract light from a far-distant o-region (*see Places to Go*). Light from this particular o-region travels more slowly than normal light—but as Curtis was travelling into the past, the o-region light had something of a head start. It lodged itself in the Siberian ice cave where Curtis first departed into the past, getting trapped in the ice.

We should pause here to mention that the o-region light contained something organic, much in the same way that bacteria survives inside ice.

When Fitz blew up the ice cave in 1894, George Williamson got caught between two interacting shafts of slow light. When that happened, the Universe couldn't decide if George—like Schrödinger's Cat—was alive or not.

More to the point, the slow light interaction caused—for George at least—time and space to swap positions. George became more a being of *time* than matter, able to walk forward or backward in time and return to the present. Ordinarily, George's range would've been extremely limited, but Sabbath—furthering his plot with Curtis—did something "really clever" to extend George's reach.

George's survival wasn't so much the problem, but he tested his newfound existence by travelling back several million years in time, joyously watching as the dinosaurs walked the Earth. Two things happened as a result of George's side trip: A) he paradoxically created the time corridor that Curtis used to go back in time in the first place, and B) his very presence encouraged some saurian lizards to start walking upright. This immediately created a parallel reality where said saurians gained an evolutionary advantage. Consequently, a dimensional doorway to their timeline opened up in Siberia, as the two realities were so close in nature.

P.S. It's important to note that George cannot interact with time—the alternate reality happens because he was simply *observing* the past, a case of Heisenberg's Uncertainty Principle that the act of observation changes the experiment itself.

All of this collapsed, of course, when George made certain that he died in the ice cave. The time corridor collapsed and Curtis went back no further than George's death in 1894, expending his energy in a minor explosion. This also released the fire organism—the o-region creature—trapped within the ice, allowing it to infest Earth's magma. As astute readers might have guessed, the creature becomes the fire elemental that the Doctor defeats in *The Burning*, bringing Justin Richards' two cornerstone EDAs full circle.

• *Maxwell Curtis:* Made his fortune by putting his gravitational powers to use as a stage magician named "The Great Attractor."

• *Sabbath and Maxwell Curtis:* Sabbath manipulates events in much of this story, determined—through his faulty reasoning of how the Universe works—to prune out all parallel universes until only our reality remains. [Author's Note: Sabbath's unseen business partners are evidently shaping his agendas these days, with an emphasis on eliminating free will to an extent that even Sabbath doesn't realize.]

Sabbath maneuvers Curtis into founding the Institute, erroneously believing that if Curtis were to release his black hole matter at Time Zero, it would kick-start the Big Bang, enabling the Universe to prune off its parallel realities. The Doctor better educates Sabbath on the Universe's nature.

• *Beatrix "Trix" MacMillan:* One of Sabbath's agents, loyal only so far as his pocketbook extends. The name "Beatrix MacMillan" is possibly an alias. She looks like she's in her late 20s, but could be either a decade younger or older. Trix can disguise herself, *Mission: Impossible* style, with Latex masks. She speaks fluent Russian. In *Time Zero*, she helps mislead Curtis on Sabbath's behalf.

• *The Doctor and Trix:* The Doctor enjoys Trix's company. He doesn't trust her enough to give her a lift in the TARDIS, however. Trix helps Sabbath escape in exchange for information about the Doctor. She's decently kind to Fitz, but glares at Anji.

• *George Williamson:* George previously worked as librarian at Cambridge University, tutoring

---

under the late, professionally wronged history professor Edward Parton.

- *The TARDIS:* In some senses, it's made of fire.

PHENOMENA *Time Travel:* Time travelers don't age as they travel in Vortex ships such as the TARDIS or *The Jonah*.

- *Parallel Realities and Schrödinger's Cat:* The Universe holds a primary timeline in an 11-dimensional space, but splits off parallel realities in accordance with a momentous decision's possible outcomes.

If it helps, think of this with regards to the "Schrödinger's Cat" experiment, in which a feline is placed in an indeterminate state between life and death. "Our" timeline chooses a course of action—the cat lives or dies—as the experiment concludes. The Web of Time crystallizes around said outcome and life goes on. However, the Universe often generates a parallel reality in which the converse result occurs.

P.S. It's notable that Fitz survived in the ice TARDIS *a la* Schrödinger's Cat, caught between life and death, partly because nobody definitively saw him die and the Doctor and Anji refused to accept he'd snuffed it.

Quantum Theory states that the number of parallel universes is by definition finite. But it's still a tremendously large number. Time travel alone does *not* generate parallel realities.

- *O-Regions:* Far-flung pockets of space that're isolated from the rest of the Universe. They're mini-universes in their own right, but part of our reality.

ALTERNATE HISTORY The Doctor, Anji and Fitz briefly visit a reality where King Edward VIII didn't abdicate the British throne in December 1936.

HISTORY George published a book called *Written in Stone*, dealing with the subject of fos-

silization and the cooling of Earth.

- Tzar Alexander III was present when Fitz's expedition left Vladivostok in 1894.

- Curtis' release of energy in 1894 was heard all the way to Moscow, but the much grander Tunguska incident (*Birthright*) later overshadowed its historical relevance.

- A few pages of Fitz's journal fell out during a scramble with the saurians, later ending up on display in the British Museum.

AT THE END OF THE DAY Winning for raw emotional impact, *Time Zero* gives the reader with a gaping heart wound as the TARDIS crew splits up—making you realize just how much the Doctor, Fitz and Anji have grown together. If readers don't like *Time Zero*, it's usually because it at times thinks it's a science textbook—with labored discussions about slow light and such—and because Sabbath's treated like a melodramatic villain who twirls his moustache and binds young women with wire to railroad tracks. However, when *Time Zero* focuses on its drama, it's excellent, especially when the Doctor wins by convincing the innocent George Williamson to kill himself. At the end of the day, there's a mettle here that's hard not to like—bringing events to a needed conclusion and refusing to let things get too quiet for the TARDIS crew.

DID YOU KNOW?

- Richards based much of *Time Zero*'s details about o-regions, and the notion of a slow light time machine, on an article in *New Scientist* 2291, dated May 19, 2001.

- Similarly, Curtis' transformation into a black hole stems from the April 1, 2000 issue of *New Scientist*. The cover features a fairly nasty picture of a man's blank face with black holes shot into it, complete with a headline that reads, "Black Holes—They're Living Inside You!"

Benny and the Daleks

THE SQUIRE'S CRYSTAL

By Jacqueline Rayner

Release Date: *April 2001*
Order: *Big Finish Benny Adventure #3*

MAIN CHARACTERS Bernice Summerfield, Irving Braxiatel and Adrian Wall.

TRAVEL LOG The Braxiatel Collection; Avril's cavern, planet Hera; Arsine de Vallen's estate; all February, 2600.

STORY SUMMARY At the Braxiatel Collection, a dashing young man named Dominic approaches Benny about rumors regarding medieval squire Avril Fenman (a.k.a. "the Soul-Sucker"), who once fell into possession of a soul-swapping crystal on the planet Hera. Avril instigated a reign of terror with the crystal, but the noble Knights of Rowan eventually imprisoned her. Dominic's employer, collector Arsine de Vallen, has reason to believe that Avril was entombed for her crimes on Asteroid KS-159—the home of the Braxiatel Collection.

Benny scoffs at Dominic, but simultaneously, a Braxiatel engineering team discovers a hitherto-undiscovered cavern near the Collection. Dominic and Benny confirm the site as Avril's tomb, locating a mummified body and a glowing blue crystal within. Dominic, acting on orders to obtain the crystal for de Vallen, shows his true colors and drugs Benny unconscious.

Dominic awakens Avril by moving her dormant mind, via the crystal, into Benny's body, hoping to question Avril about the crystal's properties. Benny's mind survives as a discorporate entity, but the newly awakened Avril rashly smashes the crystal to prevent anyone re-imprisoning her. Avril agrees to accompany Dominic to her homeworld, Hera, for a replacement crystal and shows him a crystal-laden cavern there. Benny follows and, mustering her willpower, forcibly displaces Dominic from his body.

Moments later, Dominic's pistol-wielding girl-friend Poppy arrives as back-up and shoots at Avril/"Benny," accidentally collapsing the crystal cavern. Trapped in Dominic's form, Benny pockets one of the soul-swapping crystals, even as Avril—still in Benny's body—escapes back to the Braxiatel Collection.

Benny makes to follow, only to get forcibly hauled, by a pack of de Vallen's guards, back to de Vallen's estate. There, the aged de Vallen wills his fortune to Dominic, intending to poison himself, then move his mind, via the crystal into Dominic's body. If successful, de Vallen will become wealthy *and* young again. But regrettably, his plan goes awry in a brouhaha of body-swapping.

Dominic's disembodied mind ends up in de Vallen security guard Bill, whose consciousness dissipates into nothing. Simultaneously, de Vallen fails to dislodge Benny from Dominic's body and dies, having poisoned himself. Somewhat back in the driver's seat, Benny threatens to harm Dominic's body, blackmailing Dominic and Poppy to return with her to the Braxiatel Collection.

Benny convinces Braxiatel of her true identity, allowing Braxiatel to mediate a proper return to everyone's body. Benny and Dominic regain their proper forms with the crystal, but Avril finds herself in Bill's body. With Bill's soul entirely dissipated, Avril unexpectedly smashes the crystal to guarantee her continued existence.

Authorities later arrest Dominic and Poppy on long-standing charges (*see Character Development*). Benny celebrates returning her to own body and Braxiatel graciously allows Avril to live, in Bill's body, in her former tomb at the Collection.

MEMORABLE MOMENTS Benny ponders the advantages of being a man: No little pill every day, an enormous saving of toilet paper, plus the ability to pee standing up. As a downside, she can't believe any man tolerates having a penis that's not under his control. She's traumatized to witness Avril eating chocolate in her body—all the weight gain, but none of the enjoyment.

From Dominic's body, a humiliated Benny witnesses herself skinny-dipping and cries out: "I—*she* does not do things like that! She is not a drunkard who constantly embarrasses herself! She is an extremely nice person!" Rubbing salt in the wound, Poppy speculates Benny's birthed a lot of children, since, "It would certainly explain all that flab. And the sagging. And the stretch marks."

On a more serious note, Avril burns some of Benny's diaries, an act of spite for losing her own past. In response, an astute Braxiatel comforts Benny with: "I know they were precious to you. I know they are, in most senses, irreplaceable. But you must not, when the anger has passed, think that the memories or experiences themselves have been destroyed. The last few days have proved without a shadow of a doubt that the essential Bernice Summerfield can exist without any physical bonds."

THE CRUCIAL BITS...

• **THE SQUIRE'S CRYSTAL**—Avril, a soul-swapping sorceress, briefly switches bodies with Benny. While Benny's out, Avril enjoys sexual relations with engineer Adrian Wall.

SEX AND SPIRITS Benny briefly shows interest in Dominic, shaving her legs before his arrival at the Braxiatel Collection. She mentally scolds herself for drooling over him. But the fact that he becomes a villain—and drugs her brandy—douses any chance of romance.

Stuck in Dominic's body, Benny struggles to bring her newfound penis under control. To Benny's dismay, Dominic's wiener pops woodies whenever Poppy's around (Benny screams: "Aaaarg! It moved all by itself!"). Benny's hardly shy, but finds it hard to even look at Dominic's manhood.

In desperation, Benny tries restraining Dominic's runamuck penis with a large bandage, but this only leads to Poppy seeing "Dominic" struggling to affix a plaster over his privates. Amazingly, Benny passes off the incident as normal.

Poppy mistakenly believes "Dominic" is trying to seduce Benny, whom she deems "a middle-aged cow" and a "flat-chested pseudo-intellectual bitch."

Meanwhile, Avril returns to the Braxiatel Collection and seduces engineer Adrian Wall when he accidentally happens upon a slumbering nude "Benny." Adrian genuinely falls in love with "Benny," having always deemed her attractive (but with a questionable personality).

When Benny returns to the Collection, still in Dominic's body, Adrian pulls her out of a shuttle wreck and Bernice—forgetting that she's a man—kisses him as a reward. Benny flirts, in her male form, with Ms. Jones to get a new security pass.

Still later, Benny becomes horrified to spy her body skinny-dipping with Adrian. Moreover, Dominic's male form gets aroused looking at Benny, bizarrely meaning she fancies herself.

When all's said and done, Adrian ponders marriage with Bernice, only to learn that Benny wasn't Benny. Braxiatel and Benny never properly decide how to quell Adrian's embarrassment.

Chapter 6 is whimsically named: "Does my Bum Look Big (in this Body)?"

Benny's torn about ex-hubby Jason Kane, at first convinced that they would probably argue and have sex, but never become a couple, if they met again. She considers ridding herself of Jason thoughts by lying on a couch while Braxiatel drones on in a German accent, then electro-shocks her every time she looks at her wedding photos.

Later, she accepts she's still in love with Jason.

Other interesting facts: Benny wears Poppy's knickers on Dominic's body, purely for comfort. Braxiatel Collection guard Calvin Jersix is having an affair with Security Sub Officer Tom Delaney.

Benny has never been a "good-time girl," exhibiting restraint in her choice of sex partners. She has a "marvelous" dream involving lots of chocolate and ex-hubby Jason Kane. She remains a sucker for the boyish grin and floppy blond image.

Benny thinks about sending pics of "Dominic" to *Playbeing* to make a fast buck. She's got a 34 double-A bust, but shoves out her chest to make it look like 36B.

ASS-WHUPPINGS As "Dominic," Benny agonizingly takes a knee in the groin. Afterward, she vows to never again make fun of such injuries.

De Vallen poisons himself. Avril's crystal accidentally draws the minds of Braxiatel's Dyamon Daggerfish out of their bodies, killing them (but answering the aeons-old question of whether or not fish have consciousness.)

Dominic's uber-sexy body gets sullied when Avril smashes the final crystal and a shard lodges itself in his face. A good reconstructive surgeon could easily fix the damage, but a distraught Dominic, believing his beauty forever ruined, puts his fist through a mirror and presumably never recovers.

NOVEL TIE-INS Benny ironically states that she's never having children, failing to realize that during her bodyswap, Adrian Wall inseminated her body (she learns about the pregnancy in *The Infernal Nexus*).

Benny hasn't shifted bodies since an unseen event where she became a small white female cat (coincidentally, a similar body-swap happened to Ace in *Warlock*). She physically looks 35, but she's technically somewhat older (especially allowing for the rejuvenating temporal blast that hit her in *Twilight of the Gods*).

Braxiatel commissioned extensive geological surveys of Asteroid KS-159 before he built the Collection (shortly after *Tears of the Oracle*).

Folders in Benny's quarters include: "Repetitive Poems of the Early Ikkaban Period (Revised)" (*Sleepy*, *Walking to Babylon*), "The Twentieth Century and What it was Really Like to Live There" and "The Lost Tomb of Rablev: The Truth" (*The Doomsday Manuscript*).

Benny's still friends with Pakhar journalist Keri (*Legacy*). Benny's burnt diaries contained information on Simon Kyle, her first boyfriend, who betrayed her to the authorities (*Parasite*).

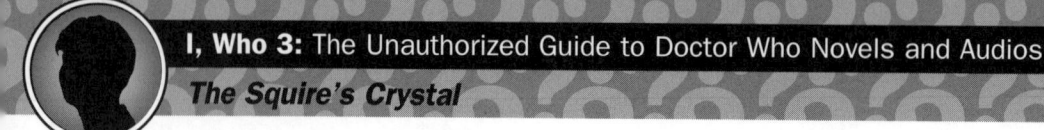

CHARACTER DEVELOPMENT

• *Bernice Summerfield:* Benny confirms that Braxiatel is probably her dearest friend, but she loves Jason Kane and the feline Wolsey most of all.

She gets invited to lecture at various colleges, but only accepts if they serve a great buffet. She's never met Broderick Naismith, Braxiatel's right-hand man. She loves pasta and tends to eat vegetarian, lamenting that a meat-free bacon sandwich doesn't exist.

Benny gets an inferiority complex seeing her body from the outside, fixated on her stomach bulge and unshaved armpits. She vows to stop licking her lips seductively, deciding it doesn't suit her. Benny knows the (now-archaic) phrase, "Don't spare the horses!", plus myths about horseshoes and the irrelevance of horseradish and horse chestnuts. She's previously heard of the Soul-Sucker legend.

She considers her robotic assistant Joseph "a snotty little ball." She doesn't know how to work a laser-razor. Benny's quarters include one-way, soundproofed glass windows.

• *Benny and Irving Braxiatel:* Benny's exact duties at the Braxiatel Collection remain somewhat undefined. Braxiatel looks upon Benny as more of a guest than a staff member. Benny remains oddly broke, considering Braxiatel's immense wealth.

• *Adrian Wall:* Wall's a member of the dog-like Killoran race. He's 7-foot-tall, with a sensitive nose. His bulky hands belie his fine gemworking skills. He installed a cat flap for Wolsey.

• *Irving Braxiatel:* Braxiatel is highly respectful of his guests' privacy, providing quality service even for detainees at the Collection. He can swim, and sometimes asks Benny to feed his Dyamon dagger-fish.

• *Avril Fenman (a.k.a. the Soul-Sucker):* She finds it hard to remember her identity, having spent a long time discorporate.

• *Dominic Troy (a.k.a. Nico Lyence, "the Fifth Axis Gigolo"):* "Dominic Troy" was merely a cover identity for Nico Lyence, a Fifth Axis agent purported to be the most gorgeous guy in the galaxy. Lyence came from a poor background and slept his way to the top. He consequently sparked a lot of in-fighting, with the Fifth Axis officers killing one another over him.

In time, the upper echelons of the Fifth Axis decided to eliminate Lyence for being a disruptive influence. Terrorist attacks in the Galamanus System were partly intended to off Lyence, but he escaped (*The Doomsday Manuscript*).

Fifth Axis Kolonel Farning and Commander Heparta, certainly, longed to kill Lyence. Fifth Axis operatives Kirit Jom or Teg Dissoccin could confirm Lyence's identity. Lyence eventually went to work for de Vallen as "Dominic Troy."

• *Jason Kane:* He sports a hairy chest and sometimes called Benny a nagging wife.

• *Benny and Ms. Jones:* Benny gets along with secretary Ms. Jones better than anyone at the Collection. Ms. Jones feels much the same, deeming Adrian Wall coarse and the gardener, Crofton, impudent. All things considered, Ms. Jones only deems Braxiatel of higher quality than Benny.

• *Ms. Jones:* She's a stickler for detail.

• *Arsine De Vallen:* Cited as the richest man in the sector, suggesting his wealth outstrips Braxiatel. In his quest for the Soul-Sucker, de Vallen hoodwinked Braxiatel by intercepting the survey of Asteroid KS-159 before it became the Braxiatel Collection. De Vallen noted the most likely locations of Avril's cave, amended the maps and passed them back to Braxiatel's surveyors. However, he realized ongoing construction at the Collection would probably turn up Avril's cave, dispatching Dominic to approach Benny as Braxiatel's engineers neared de Vallen's intended target.

• *Poppaea Prince (a.k.a. "Poppy"):* She's about 28 or 29, likely hailing from the Galamanus System (*The Doomsday Manuscript*). Poppy escapes this story in possession of yet-another soul-swapping crystal, then makes a living bodyswapping elderly rich men into younger bodies.

• *Wolsey:* Like most cats, he's rather needy. He likes tea time at mid-afternoon. He's able to identify Benny, whatever body she's wearing. He doesn't like water.

ALIEN PLANETS *Hera:* Remains a backwater planet, but improving.

PLACES TO GO The Braxiatel Collection grounds are small enough that unless you stay inside all day, you tend to pass through all points of the Collection at some stage. Braxiatel, Benny and Ms. Jones helped perfect the security systems.

PHENOMENA *Body-Swapping:* Discorporate souls experience heightened sensations, but wither and die if they remain incorporeal for too long. Bodyswapping gets easier with practice. A person's handwriting doesn't change from body to body.

HISTORY In Bernice's history, Heinrich Schliemann discovered the remains of Troy. Academics of Schliemann's day debated his findings, although modern-day archaeology largely rejects them as bunk.

• Centuries ago, a matriarchal, medieval society existed on the planet Hera. The Knights of Rowan

TOP 10 'WHO' COMEDY MOMENTS (NOVELS)

From Earthworld (March 2001) to Time Zero (Sept. 2002)

1) Benny tapes her runamuk wiener (*The Squire's Crystal*)—Stuck in the body of a man named Dominic, Benny tries to stop her seemingly untamable penis from popping woodies whenever she looks—for example—at a cloud. In desperation, Benny tries restraining her overactive sausage with a large bandage, but this only leads to Dominic's girlfriend Poppy catching "her boyfriend" in the act of affixing a plaster over his privates. To her credit, Benny somehow passes off the entire incident as normal. We howled.

2) Jasper's trial (*The Crooked World*)—Possibly setting a record for strangeness in "Doctor Who," Jasper the cartoon cat finds himself on trial for biting the head off a mouse named Squeak. Jasper's feline brethren turn out to support him, carting around signs that say, "Give Cats a Fur Deal," and "Fight for the Right to Kill Vermin." As if this wasn't enough, the Doctor brilliantly serves as Jasper's defense attorney, pointing out that his mistress—the big, fat hotel maid—essentially told Jasper to murder "that darn mouse." Totally daft and daffy.

3) The death of Fluppy (*Time Zero*)—During a gravity mishap, a large tube of coins pummels a children's TV show character—Fluppy the puppy—to death. And while we'd never, *ever* support the killing of an actual puppy, this does help vindicate anyone who's suffered watching the likes of Barney and his ilk. Plus, it lets Time Zero open with the brilliant sentence: "Everyone in Britain can remember where they were when Fluppy died."

4) Noel Coward denies help to some pussies (*Mad Dogs and Englishmen*)—After getting embroiled in a conspiracy to wrest power on the dog-world—a planet inhabited by poodles—Noel Coward answers a knock at his front door. A strange woman begs Coward to help some talking kittens, helping "the pussyworld" to attain its true

destiny. But Coward, deciding enough is enough, slams the door and returns to his Baby Grand piano.

5) Scarlette's proposal to the Doctor (*The Adventuress of Henrietta Street*)—While fencing with the Doctor, ritualist Scarlette proposes they stop and continue without weapons, wrestling naked on the floor. The Doctor's response isn't recorded, and it probably ends platonically, but it's a great scene anyway.

6) Sabbath vs. the whoopie cushion (*Camera Obscura*)—Purely to keep Sabbath from thinking too highly of himself, the Doctor plants a whoopie cushion for Sabbath's Orson Welles-like physique to sit on. It's childish, it's cheap and it's just silly—and we love it.

7) Anji declines to post bond (*The Book of the Still*)—Anji dutifully looks into posting bond for the jailed Doctor, only to discover she'd have to offer up a lung, her eyes and an earlobe. When she refuses, the Doctor graciously concedes: "I know, I know. You'd look lopsided for one thing."

8) The toasted Imp (*The Infernal Nexus*)—In a death Maze, Benny and the android Suzi II face the "Challenge of the Imp," which entails a little man standing in front of two doors—one leading to freedom, one to certain death. Suzi II solves the problem by hurling the imp through one of the doors, exiting out the *other* door when a burst of flame incinerates the little guy. Genius.

9) Hitler meets his sausage (*The Shadow in the Glass*)—Suddenly face-to-face with Hitler—one of the most evil men in history—at a Berlin ballroom party, 1942, the dazed Brigadier can only offer the Fuhrer his dirty plate, complete with a half-eaten sausage roll.

10) Benny's vow (*The Glass Prison*)—Having nearly toppled the Fifth Axis, destroyed a prison and caused widespread higgeldy-piggeldy, Benny resolves to: "Have a bath and read a book, and not cause any more deaths today."

---

lived there as a revered order of female paladins, protecting the weak from the strong. One day, Rowan knight Cherry and her squire, Avril, discovered an enormous Crystal Cavern. Cherry died soon afterward under mysterious circumstances, but Avril escaped. The Knights sentenced Avril to death for dishonorably abandoning her liege lord, but Avril used one of the cavern's soul-swapping crystals to exchange places with her executioner. She touched off a killing spree, but the Knights eventually imprisoned her on the desolate Asteroid KS-159.

• The legend of the "Soul-Sucker" fell into myth, later published as a children's book titled *The Adventure of the Crystal Cavern*. Avril is sometimes acknowledged in legend as "April," "Avinal" or "Arvin."

POSSIBLE HISTORY   Avril claims that she and Cherry discovered the Hera Crystal Cavern while tracking strange creatures that slaughtered a small village. They found the cavern, protected by trolls resistant to the crystals' influence. The trolls killed Cherry, but Avril escaped with a crys-

---

tal and Cherry's body. Avril found herself increasingly attuned to the crystal, and mentally summon help from a nearby village with it. The gambit worked, but the villagers put her on trial for witchcraft afterward. In Avril's narrative, she used the crystal to escape death and voluntarily exile herself. Benny deems Avril's story a load of bollocks.

AT THE END OF THE DAY The first sign of greatness from Big Finish's Benny novels, and a high-powered romp that made us laugh until we cried. It's amusing enough that Benny simply becomes a man, never mind that Rayner throws her so completely off-kilter (the bit where Benny over-bandages her untamable penis is priceless). It's the sort of book that leaves you with a warm feeling, tinged with dramatic bits (Benny conceding her love for Jason and Wolsey), but primarily about as funny as a top-notch "Whose Line Is It Anyway?" episode.

THE STONE'S LAMENT

By Mike Tucker

Release Date: May 2001
Order: Big Finish Benny Audio #2.2

MAIN CHARACTERS Bernice Summerfield, Adrian Wall.

TRAVEL LOG Bratheen Traloor's mansion, planet Rhinvil, 2600.

STORY SUMMARY On the planet Rhinvil, reclusive billionaire Bratheen Traloor contracts the Braxiatel Collection to build an extension onto his mansion. Adrian Wall dispatches a work crew ahead, then makes ready to travel to Rhinvil himself. But when Adrian's workmen unearth an unidentified artifact, Traloor—an amateur archaeologist—extends a personal invitation for Bernice to examine the "ancient item" in detail.

Benny and Adrian arrive on Rhinvil, finding Traloor's mansion the only sign of civilization on the planet. The two of them grow troubled, first by the mysterious disappearance of Adrian's work crew, then by the ephemeral sounds of a woman crying. Soon after, a poltergeist breaks out in Traloor's dark, stormy mansion, pummeling Benny and Adrian with a whirlwind of objects.

Running like mad, Benny and Adrian take refuge in Traloor's private quarters, where their jaws drop at finding the walls covered with pictures of Bernice. The reclusive Traloor confesses to a long-running obsession with Benny, further admitting that he modified the mansion's central computer, "House," to emulate Bernice's personality for companionship's sake. Traloor fails to explain House's telekinesis, but admits that his modifications worked *too* well, making House evolve to the point of falling in love with Traloor—and turning murderously jealous toward Bernice.

Benny outright rejects Traloor, fleeing to a nearby cave system with Adrian. Traloor remains behind to cripple House's mainframe, outraged at the computer for spoiling his chances with Benny. But in response, House offers to physically fuse with Traloor, giving them both a measure of togetherness. An anguished Traloor agrees, letting House implant his body with circuitry.

Soon afterward, a cybernetic Traloor confronts Benny and Adrian in the caves—bizarrely identifying itself as a hodgepodge of Traloor, the House computer and the very lifeforce of Rhinvil itself. The Traloor cyborg explains that some time ago, the House computer interacted, via the Rhinvil rock constituting the mansion, with the planet's central ego. When Adrian's workmen added the extension, the House/Rhinvil gestalt gained enough critical mass to use telekinesis against the thing that House hated most: Bernice. Having murdered Adrian's workmen for violating the planet's landscape, the demented Traloor/House/Rhinvil cyborg intends to kill Benny and Adrian for sport.

Benny tries—and fails—to appeal to Traloor's consciousness, even as Adrian more practically primes quarry charges. The resultant explosion brings down the entire mansion, killing the chop-sueyed Traloor being. Relieved for their survival, Benny and Adrian return home to the Braxiatel Collection.

SEX AND SPIRITS Traloor's obsession with Bernice drives most of this story, although it's enormously unclear how it got started. We never learn how, when or where Traloor—who's spent the last 20 years being a recluse—came to have any contact or interest with Bernice whatsoever. Certainly, they've never met before this story.

At a guess, Traloor learned of Benny through his hobby, archaeology—although if so, there's still a huge gap between Traloor's reading Benny's *Down Among the Dead Men* and falling in love with her.

Traloor does claim that he views Bernice as a kindred spirit and an inspiration—a vibrant person in a "dusty" profession. His bedroom contains a shrine to her, with tapes of her lectures and copies of her press cuttings. He keeps a picture of

Benny above his bed. Finally, Traloor instructed House to create an artifact for Adrian's workmen to find, thus providing an excuse to invite Bernice to his mansion.

Conversely, House views itself as Traloor's companion, having lived with him in isolation for years. House cheekily tells Benny at one point: "You're obviously not as promiscuous as your reputation indicates."

Adrian and Benny uncomfortably remember events from *The Squire's Crystal*, in which Adrian had a sex fest with a soul-swapper possessing Benny's body. Benny doesn't even joke about the situation, feeling embarrassed. Adrian continues to have some lingering affection for Benny, thinking she "looks fab." At one point, House fools Adrian into thinking Benny wants to continue their affair, but she fends him off.

Benny accidentally spies Adrian fresh from the shower, but doesn't get very excited. Adrian tries to hit the drinks cabinet after dinner, but finds it sparsely stocked.

ASS-WHUPPINGS Completely insane, the House/Rhinvil entity gains vengeance on dozens of Adrian's workmen for digging up the landscape to add onto the mansion. Just as the engineers ripped up the planet's "body" to build the mansion, the House/Rhinvil being telekinetically twists the bodies of Adrian's colleagues, including two men named Tuck and Warwick, into a twisted sort of "edifice."

House/Rhinvil telekinetically hurls stuff at Benny, somehow making its walls drip with blood. Adrian finally collapses the mansion atop the House/Traloor/Rhinvil entity.

NOVEL TIE-INS Adrian cites a pleasure station orbiting Ancil and a private island on Coralee (*Storm Harvest*) as options for a good time.

CHARACTER DEVELOPMENT
• *Bernice Summerfield:* Benny hates the sluggishness of emerging from cryo-stasis. She's aware that she's getting older, but she's happy with the direction of her life.

Benny talks to herself while working. She sometimes deduces the age of artifacts with a hand-held carbon-dater.

One has to question Benny's archaeological skills at this point, as she fails to expose the "artifact"—that House crafts on Traloor's instructions—as a fake.

• *Adrian Wall:* Adrian drinks black coffee and snores loudly. He's known Benny "a while," and thinks she's remarkable. He often carries a pow-

erful laser cutter. He can prep a shuttle for liftoff in five to 10 minutes. His workmen sometimes use a rare "Stempson multi-blade" tool.

• *Bernice and Adrian:* They're at odds because Benny's profession strives to preserve the past, while Adrian's job entails digging stuff up in favor of "progress."

• *Bratheen Traloor:* Traloor made his billions as a big-screen actor. He retired to Rhinvil 20 years ago, finding fame and wealth a curse to the inquiring mind. Traloor hasn't spoken to anyone since, barring Braxiatel and the workmen who constructed his mansion.

Partly, Traloor decided it was preferable to live alone than to compromise his life for anyone. Also, he believed that Rhinvil might hold a "surprise" for him [a rather optimistic viewpoint, considering the planet's given him nothing but rain].

Finally, one cannot escape the conclusion that Traloor's quite nuts, prone to suicidal paranoia. House has talked Traloor down from killing himself on more than one occasion. Conversely, Traloor went so far as to reinforce his bedroom walls with "Detronite" in case of assassins—even though it's never established that anyone's trying to kill him.

Traloor considers himself an amateur archaeologist and funds a lot of digs. His mansion extension was intended as a display wing for his artifact collection. He's an excellent chef.

• *House:* Traloor modified House several times over the years, inadvertently granting it an almost schizophrenic personality. House functioned as a computer, but also assumed elements of Benny's personality. House frequently spoke with Benny's voice, having pulled it from lecture tapes.

Even before it went mad, House regulated the mansion's environment and tended to a wardrobe for visitors. Linked with the Rhinvil lifeforce, House gains enough telekinesis to hurl rocks. House can duplicate the voices of other people, including Benny and Adrian. House's mainframe lies in the west wing of Traloor's mansion.

ALIEN RACES *Killorans:* Adrian's people are uncouth by nature.

ALIEN PLANETS *Rhinvil:* Nobody's properly studied the planet, a Grade-3 planet with no history of indigenous life. The climate's quite wet, with a storm belt that rattles visitors. Through the House computer, the lifeforce of Rhinvil could manifest itself enough to move around parts of its geography (collapsing the ground, for instance).

This book is not endorsed by the BBC. Doctor Who and TARDIS are trademarks of the BBC.

203

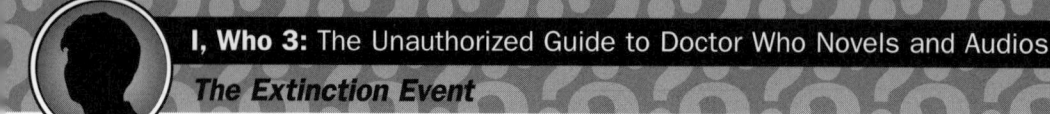
PLACES TO GO *Traloor's Mansion:* More like a small town than a mansion. The mansion's perimeter rivals the size of Braxiatel's entire estate. [Which seems odd, since Traloor does, in fact, live alone. It's even stranger that, considering the mansion's size, Benny and Adrian still have to compete for a bathroom.]

The mansion was constructed from local Rhinvil stone, since Traloor didn't want to spoil the planet by importing materials. [Even though he technically spoils the local landscape by digging up materials for the mansion.]

The mansion's located near a cave system by the sea. A shuttle pad allows the rare visitor to land. Traloor built a secret passageway that leads from his bedroom to the basement.

SHIPS *Standard Braxiatel Shuttle:* It's equipped with cryo-stasis pods.

AT THE END OF THE DAY Almost bad enough to insult the intelligence, implausibly slopping together a bunch of cliched elements—Traloor's unexplained obsession with Benny, the Rhinvil lifeforce that's added for *no* good reason, etc.—and expecting us to swallow it wholesale. There's a certain type of fan who credits "The Stone's Lament" for its spooky atmosphere—but it's just so absurd that it hardly matters.

THE EXTINCTION EVENT

By Lance Parkin

Release Date: July 2001
Order: Big Finish Benny Audio #2.3

MAIN CHARACTERS Bernice Summerfield, Irving Braxiatel.

TRAVEL LOG Unnamed auction house, planet Pelastrodon; mud planet Lubboling, 2600.

STORY SUMMARY Ever the collector, Irving Braxiatel raises his eyebrows when an auction house on Pelastrodon stages "The Extinction Event"—a sale featuring items from destroyed civilizations. In particular, the auction features a harp from the planet Halstad, a civilization annihilated seven years ago by a cosmic radiation burst. Wasting no time, Braxiatel asks Benny to accompany him to the auction house and confirm the harp's authenticity.

On Pelastrodon, Benny certifies the harp as genuine, then suggests she and Braxiatel investigate the harp's owner: a Gulfrarg ambassador. Unfortunately, a man named Hulver—soon identified as the sole surviving member of Halstad (*see Character Development*)—tries to murder the ambassador. Auction house authorities arrest Hulver, who claims he previously witnessed the ambassador, as head of a Gulfrarg warship, annihilate Halstad with an energy weapon.

Benny finds herself sympathetic to Hulver's story, but fails to reason why the Gulfrargs would obliterate Halstad. Still, Benny reasons that, if the ambassador stole the Halstad harp, he can't prove ownership of it. By default, the harp belongs to Hulver, the last of his people. Braxiatel subsequently makes Hulver a lucrative deal for the harp, offering the Gulfrarg ambassador a comparable sum if he drops charges against Hulver.

Seemingly bested, the arrogant ambassador fakes a second assassination attempt, ruining Braxiatel's bargaining position and again making Hulver a wanted criminal. The ambassador regains possession of the harp, but his plan goes awry when Hulver escapes. Benny desperately searches for Hulver, only to find him holding the ambassador and chief auctioneer Davon at gunpoint.

The boastful ambassador admits that seven years ago, his spaceship teleported a few select items off Halstad, then razed the entire planet with a radiation weapon. A horrified Benny realizes that the ambassador collaborated with Davon from the very start—leveling Halstad solely to make the harp and other Halstad artifacts extremely rare, then auction them for a fortune.

Benny promises to bring the genocidal ambassador to justice, but a vengeful Hulver grabs the Gulfrarg and hurls him off the auction house's dome—pulping the villain against the rocks below. Soon after, a Gulfrarg warship arrives to take Hulver away for summary execution. Hulver goes to his demise peacefully, having somewhat avenged his people. Benny laments Hulver's passing as a waste, even as Braxiatel promises to at least preserve the Halstad harp at the Collection.

MEMORABLE MOMENTS In flashback, Hulver's lover Jamara and her friend Jan enjoy a tranquil outing on Halstad—mere instants before the planet's surface gets boiled to vapor.

When a co-worker catches Benny sleeping rather than working, Benny bluffs that her cartoon-bear covered pajamas are, "dig clothes… from a planet that associates cartoon bears with great acts of historical and archaeological endeavor."

Braxiatel concedes the oddities of the collector mentality, citing his stamp collection as: "Just tiny pieces of gold paper. Intrinsic value: Nothing. But some of them are truly unique. Tiny printing errors and just the lack of a postmark can add two million shillings to their value."

Finally, Benny and Braxiatel come to verbal blows about the Gulfrargs' alleged destruction of Halstad. Unable to prove the Gulfrargs ruined Halstad, Braxiatel chiefly worries about acquiring the Halstad harp—making Benny blister him with: "You think that one stupid musical instrument is worth all this fuss? All this money? What about Hulver? What about Jamara, his girlfriend? What about the whole planet just swept away?" In response, a level-headed Braxiatel interrupts with: *"Benny!* There are things we can do, and there are things we can't."

It's nicely layered stuff, topped at the end with Braxiatel admitting his rashness: "I'm not proud of my actions… but I'm proud of yours. You're a good person, Benny."

SEX AND SPIRITS Braxiatel kindly says that Benny looks radiant in a dress. (Benny replies, fresh from a dig: "I like to think I scrub up well.") Brax further informs the ambassador that "[Benny's] not my bodyguard and she's certainly not my… she's a colleague."

Hulver was childhood friends, then lovers with Jamara, who perished on Halstad.

ASS-WHUPPINGS The vaporization of Halstad takes maybe all of two minutes.

On the planet's devastation, *see History.*

The Gulfrarg Ambassador, as perpetrator of the crime, finishes this story very flat. Hulver's almost certainly executed after this story.

NOVEL TIE-INS An auction house official denotes Braxiatel's Gallifreyan rank by calling him "Lord Cardinal Braxiatel," although Braxiatel offers that he's "just Braxiatel these days." Braxiatel indirectly notes Gallifrey's loss (*The Ancestor Cell*) by claiming that Hulver "isn't the only one to lose a homeworld."

Benny's mother died when she was eight, killed during an air raid in the Galactic Wars (*Love and War*). Afterward, Benny wanted revenge, but she deemed living well as more important.

CHARACTER DEVELOPMENT
• *Bernice Summerfield:* A few years ago, Benny wrote an article entitled *Halstad Musical Notation: Initial Thoughts and Questions.* Even that small level of research probably ranks her as the Universe's leading authority on Halstad. She never visited the planet before its destruction.

Benny's just spent three days on the mud planet Lubboling, where she's been sleeping instead of working. She's knowledgeable about Third Era Lubboling tablewear.

She knows virtually nothing about Gulfrargs.

During the finale, Benny screams out that Hulver had "no right" to kill the Gulfrarg ambassador (somewhat unkind, considering the ambassador *did* wipe out Hulver's entire civilization).

Martian history (*see Stuff You Need*) remains one of Benny's specialties.

• *Benny and Tamara:* Benny's voice sounds remarkably similar to Hulver's dead lover Jamara. Otherwise, Jamara was shorter than Benny, with platinum-colored hair. Jamara's family grew fruit for a living.

• *Benny and Braxiatel:* Braxiatel understands the Gulfrarg language, but Benny doesn't. Ms. Jones makes Benny travel in an uncomfortable one-moor space jumper, part of Braxiatel's economy drive.

• *Irving Braxiatel:* Braxiatel's a renowned collector who draws attention at pricey auctions. If he's interested in an item, it usually drives up the price. He's stayed at the Pelastrodon auction house before.

Braxiatel's overly pragmatic and frugal at times, but acts with compassion when possible. He acknowledges that the Gulfrargs' destruction of Halstad was evil, but failing the ability to do anything about it, mainly wants to preserve the harp in the Braxiatel Collection.

Braxiatel funds Benny's expedition to the mud planet Lubboling. He's particularly interested in Third Era porcelain (*see History*).

• *Hulver:* Shortly before butchering Halstad, the Gulfrargs teleported three males and three females up to their ship for experimentation. Three Halstads died from the tests, another two committed suicide upon learning Halstad's fate. Only Hulver survived, escaping on a human freighter when the Gulfrarg ship docked for supplies.

Hulver's an expert musician, able to compose as he plays. He doesn't speak the Gulfrarg language. Hulver hails from the Halstad city of Mitol, located on the "Eastern River."

• *Gulfrarg Ambassador:* He's one of the auction house's most valued customers. About 77 percent of "The Extinction Event" lots belong to the ambassador.

He holds some diplomatic immunity, and an excellent credit rating. His life support gear includes a force field (although Hulver's laser gun wears it down). The ambassador conceded, before his

This book is not endorsed by the BBC. Doctor Who and TARDIS are trademarks of the BBC.

205

death, that destroying Halstad wasn't entirely necessary—just "expletive" good fun.

ALIEN RACES *Gulfrargs:* Highly advanced species whose members literally look like a pile of offal, swimming around a goldfish bowl. Your typical Gulfrarg is unpleasant and impolite. The Gulfrarg language is largely a bundle of obscene expletives, meaning their translators automatically censor many of their words.

Gulfrargs are one of the few intelligent species to evolve without a skeleton or epidermis. They evolved in ammonia oceans on their homeworld and need life support units to survive in other environments. They don't covet Earth-style planets, since they couldn't live there.

As a species, the Gulfrargs tend toward privacy. They ironically place great value on beauty, even though they're unpleasant to look at.

Gulfrarg executions entail the condemned being "cubed." Humans physically cannot speak the Gulfrarg language.

• *Halstads:* They're certainly humanoid, and an extremely musical people. Their language incorporated unique pictograms.

ALIEN PLANETS *Halstad:* Found on the edge of known space. The humanoid civilization there enjoyed a sedate pre-space technology, with an emphasis on music and art. Halstad was several hundred years from having teleport technology.

• *Pelastrodon:* Aside from the auction house, Pelastrodon contains little of interest. It's located near major routes, close to the auction house's rich clients. However, the climate isn't desirable.

• *Lubboling:* The un-aerobic mud there makes a splendid preservative, allowing for high-quality archaeological discoveries. The bad news: Rain often weights down the mud, making everything take longer to excavate.

STUFF YOU NEED *Martian Artifacts:* Are worth a great deal. Martian items from Aridonia (a Martian city or colony) fetch more than objects from Cabrenia (ditto).

• *The Halstad Harp:* Literally Hulver's harp, taken off his person during his abduction (*see Character Development*).

The Halstad Harp is Auction Lot #1175. It's unremarkable to look at, crafted from wood and likely one among thousands (before Halstad's destruction). On Halstad, it cost eight "Kaltavas" (a week's wages). Braxiatel ended up paying "more than one week's wages for all of Halstad" for it.

• *Warp Drive:* Emerging from warp drive near a planet is dangerous and bad for the environment.

PLACES TO GO *Pelastrodon Auction House:* It's loosely under Earth space law jurisdiction. The auction house's translucent dome, specially imported and strengthened to starship hull levels, was installed a couple years ago. Auction house officials might install a coffee shop.

Tundra surrounds the auction house, making theft doubly difficult. The auction house tries to avoid legal entanglements whenever possible, allowing extradition of criminals.

SHIPS *Braxiatel Collection Shuttles:* All Braxiatel Collection shuttles are decorated with lemon livery (a fancy term for "painted yellow"). Braxiatel's ship bears his personal insignia.

HISTORY Mudslides long ago covered up a major urban area on Lubboling. Little survived from Lubboling's Third Era, in which the "Mobilians" sculpted exquisite pieces from the local clay.

• Historians never paid much attention to Halstad, given its location on the edge of known space. Notably, a researcher named Balfar attended a concert there 80 years ago, later writing of the event in *Balfar's Planets*.

• The Gulfrargs destroyed Halstad seven years ago, unleashing a radiation beam that vaporized the planet's seas and blasted the first hundred meters of bedrock to dust. Halstad became a complete loss, with even its fossil record disintegrated. For lack of evidence, officials ascribed the destruction to freakish cosmic rays, putting the entire star system under quarantine.

AT THE END OF THE DAY Almost certainly the best Benny audio without any "Who" crossover, intoxicating mostly for its heated, meaty and driven debates between Lisa Bowerman's Bernice and Miles Richardson's Braxiatel. Benny passionately pits her humanity against Braxiatel's practical side—although Parkin adeptly scripts things with a shade of gray, meaning neither character is completely in the wrong. The rest of the characters fall into line also, making this a pithy Benny story with a good amount of heart.

THE INFERNAL NEXUS

By Dave Stone

Release Date: August 2001
Order: Big Finish Benny Adventure #4

MAIN CHARACTERS Bernice Summerfield, Jason Kane.

TRAVEL LOG Station Control, a nexus point of 417 multiverses, relative time unknown; the Braxiatel Collection, 2600.

STORY SUMMARY When an energy backlash knocks the research vessel *Tinker's Cuss* out of synch with our dimension, Braxiatel asks Benny to take a probe vessel, realign the wayward ship and bring its valuable data back to the Braxiatel Collection. Benny complies, shifting her probe ship into the trans-dimensional void that contains the *Tinker's Cuss*. Unfortunately, an Enormous Space Octopus—literally a giant octopus in space, part of an intergalactic towing service—latches onto Benny's ship despite her protests.

The Enormous Space Octopus deposits Benny at Station Control, a docking station that serves as a nexus point between 417 multiverses. Benny finds Station Control ruled by "Clans" from various realities, then turns completely shocked to re-meet her ex-husband Jason Kane—an operative for Volan Sleed, the demonic Iron Sun Clan leader.

Jason explains he previously signed a work contract with a demonic travel agent named Agragazar Flatchlock (*The Dead Men Diaries:* "The Door to Bedlam"). However, Sleed somehow took Agragazar's place and forced Jason to remain in his employ. Benny experiences her usual mixed emotions upon seeing Jason, then agrees to help him investigate the kidnapping of the spoiled Mora di Vasht at Station Control. Jason fears that if Mora remains missing, her father—a technologically powerful patriarch named Lucien di Vasht—could incite warfare with the Clans to get her back.

Eventually, Benny and Jason discover that Sleed himself arranged for Mora's disappearance, hoping to pin the crime on the other Clan heads and incite di Vasht to slaughter them. Di Vasht takes his enforcers and rushes a conclave of the family leaders, but Benny and Jason expose Sleed's plot. Seconds later, Mora and her android bodyguard, Suzi II, show up, having endured a series of perils in Sleed's death maze.

A vindictive Suzi II literally rips Sleed's head off. Suddenly, Sleed's demonic body sprouts a giant ravenous cobra head and starts eating the Clan leaders. In response, Jason takes a sword and decapitates Sleed a second time—causing Sleed's body to generate the head of Jason's former employer Agragazar. Entirely more benevolent, Agragazar explains that his species sprouts secondary and tertiary heads—complete with different personas—if the primary one is decapitated.

Uninterested in power, Agragazar makes amends with di Vasht and the offended Clans. Benny and Jason eventually depart on an Enormous Space Octopus, taking the *Tinker's Cuss* back to the Collection. Braxiatel lets Jason stay at the Collection to get back on his feet, but Benny's life gets far more complicated when a medical exam reveals that she's pregnant. Unbelievable as it sounds, when Benny was absent from her body (*The Squire's Crystal*), it got inseminated.

MEMORABLE MOMENTS Benny tells her robotic porter Joseph that if he doesn't obey her commands, she'll perform a startling (and physically impossible) operation on his person with a carrot.

As the Enormous Space Octopus approaches her ship, Benny's sensors waffle between STELLAR CRUISER, COMETARY DEBRIS and ENORMOUS SPACE OCTOPUS.

In a death maze designed for torturing people, Benny and Suzi II come up against the "Challenge of the Imp," in which a little man describes two doors—one that leads to freedom, one to certain death. Not in the mood for games, Suzi II picks up the imp and hurls him through one such door. After the imp's incinerated, screaming, in a burst of flame, Benny and Suzi II choose the *other* door.

SEX AND SPIRITS Upon seeing Jason for the first time in years, Benny starts pounding on his chest and shrieks, "Don't you ever do that to me again!"

The divorced Jason and Benny don't rekindle their relationship straight away. Indeed, Jason plays hide the sausage with Lady Mae An T'zhu, the elvish, randy Dragon Clan leader, who's grateful for his slaying Sleed II. T'zhu dubs Jason as a cheap fling and almost immediately shifts interest to the android Suzi II.

Benny and Jason hang out for a few weeks at the Braxiatel Collection. They think about sex, but never get around to it. Finally, Benny learns about her pregnancy and considers seducing Jason, hoping to fool him into thinking that he's the father. However, she fails to go through with it, suddenly

losing her demeanor, punching Jason and revealing that she's pregnant and it's *not* his child. Benny realizes her plan couldn't have worked anyway, as the child—sired by the furry Adrian Wall—would turn out half-alien.

A Station Central bar includes a wide variety of booze for humans, plus stuff for aliens such as liquid nitrogen, motor oil, etc.

The Braxiatel Collection contains several bars, including the "Rat and Pestle." Braxiatel concluded that if such establishments were going to exist, they might as well be legitimate. Benny probably influenced his decision.

ASS-WHUPPINGS Most of the *Tinker's Cuss* crew die when life support fails.

Benny uses her rape alarm to collapse a Whistling Ninja gestalt (*see Alien Races*). In a torture maze at Station Control, Benny spies a woman half-drowning in mass of viscously pliant Ping-Pong balls. An unidentified, blade-wielding assailant chases another man.

Sleed takes advantage of the Theory of Transdimensional Contrivance (*see Phenomena*) by sending two of his incompetent lackeys to another dimension. They spend an extended period getting tortured there, then return to "our" reality a split second later.

Suzi II decapitates Sleed with her bare hands. Sleed II's reptile head then emerges and swallows a pig-like Animorph Clan member whole. Only slightly more civilized than all that, Jason hacks off Sleed II's head with a sword.

NOVEL TIE-INS Benny last saw Jason just before he got marooned in an alternate dimension (*Twilight of the Gods*). Afterward, he spent a period jumping through dimensional rifts and arriving at different worlds, never aging because—as a dimensional traveler—he was dislocated from time (*see Phenomena*).

Years later, he wound up in a hellish dimension and went to work for an Ur-demon (and travel agent) named Agragazar Flatchlock (*The Dead Men Diaries*: "The Door to Bedlam"). Jason and Benny very briefly made psionic contact in that story, but failed to reunite. Benny felt emotionally traumatized by the event, harshly reminded that Jason wasn't dead, just *lost*.

Afterward, Sleed replaced Agragazar and relocated to Station Control, where he served as the Iron Sun Family leader. Jason remained in Sleed's employ, bound to his contract with Agragazar.

Jason's made and lost several fortunes over things like timeshare deals and alien pornography (notably *Beige Planet Mars*). He tries to resume his writing career, scripting *The Kiss of the Dragon Woman* based on these events [notably, his characters Jalon 9 and Suzi shag like bunnies].

A Station Control Clan includes refugees of a multiverse that collapsed several years ago (the shapechanging Sloathes and other species, Stone's *Sky Pirates!*).

Earthlink Federation cruisers (*The Doomsday Manuscript*) operate under interstellar protocols that require them to rescue stranded people, not necessarily data or equipment.

Benny meets a hovering ARVID (ARtificial Viral Intelligence Destabilization) device, a variant of the ARVID intelligence in Stone's *Ship of Fools*.

"Elves" previously appeared in the EDA *Autumn Mist*, although there's likely not much relation. Benny's held fully accredited archaeology credentials (started in *Return of the Living Dad*, finished sometime before *The Dying Days*) for some time, but hasn't specialized. She's uncertain of her age at this point (thanks to the temporal blast that winged her in *Twilight of the Gods*), although she's certainly past the early-30s metabolism flipover to the point where your body stops just getting older and starts getting old.

The Infernal Nexus is yet-another Dave Stone novel that uses the word "puissance."

CHARACTER DEVELOPMENT

• *Bernice Summerfield:* Braxiatel sends Benny on this mission because she's got direct experience with trans-dimensional mechanics. She's gained some academic credibility by joining the Collection, but mostly spends her time running perilous errands for Braxiatel. Benny guzzles coffee.

She's inducted into the Iron Sun Family for the duration of her stay at Station Control.

She's still threatening to write a sequel to *Down Among the Dead Men*. She's compiled scads of meticulously written outlines, but they bear little relation to actual content. The sequel has a new working title of: "To Be Announced."

• *Jason Peter Kane:* Jason's physically about 30, dressed in a bulky leather combat jacket and heavy boots over combat greens. Jason's contract with Sleed limited his emotional responses and memories, making him seem distant. When Sleed formally disavowed Benny and Jason, it invalidated Jason's contract and restored him to normal. Jason holds Flatchlock in high esteem, but turned down his offer of renewed employment.

He atypically carries a hand blaster while in Sleed's employ. Jason's almost broke, not one for salting money away. He owns "Dead Dog in the Water Productions," a funnel for his pornography endeavors.

THE CRUCIAL BITS...

• **THE INFERNAL NEXUS**—Benny reunites with her ex-hubby Jason Kane—and discovers that Adrian Wall knocked her up.

• *Irving Braxiatel:* His deep-space probes can travel throughout the galactic spiral arm.

• *Volan Sleed:* The current Iron Sun Clan head, given to wearing a black suit. Sleed's bald, with a mess of pointed teeth and catslit eyes. He's been deposed (i.e. beheaded) as Clan leader several times, forced to climb his way back to the top.

Sleed's secondary persona wields a thick, fleshy snake head with sabre-like teeth. It's totally deranged, wanting little more than to feast.

• *Sleed and Flatchlock:* Sleed hoped to bring the more prominent Clans to ruin, allowing him to consolidate his ties to di Vasht. If successful, Sleed wanted to acquire di Vasht's advanced teleportation technology.

By way of reparation for Sleed's actions, Flatchlock consolidated the Iron Sun and Dragon clans with Dragon leader Mae An T'zhu at its head. He also surrendered all of Iron Sun's exclusive technology.

• *Agragazar Flatchlock:* Accommodating demon/travel agent who thinks his other personas aren't very civilized. Flatchlock's head vaguely looks like Sleed.

• *Mae An T'zhu:* Elvish Dragon Clan leader, at least 250 years old. One of her favorite husbands got killed in a fracas last month.

• *Lucien di Vasht:* Arguably the most powerful man in his home reality, thanks to several alliances forged amongst some multiplexal Overlords. Said warlords have developed teleport technology greater than any other multiverse.

• *Dr. Rupert Alouicous Barnstable Gilhooly:* A polymath, historian, xenobiologist, sociologist, psychologist, and overall genius. His intelligence puts Einstein to shame, but he consequently has the communication skills of a mollusk (*see Phenomena*).

ALIEN RACES *Elves:* Big and strapping humanoids, not effeminate but endowed with a kind of "willowy grace." Elves have slightly translucent skin, with an inner glow like moonlight. The fabled "Elven Glamour" is likely pheromones rather than magic. Elves tend to fight with honor, not prone to employing assassins. They're a legendary people, hailing from a nearly inaccessible multiverse.

• *Infernal Regions Inhabitants:* Essentially what we'd call "demons," although occasionally more civilized (such as Agragazar Flatchlock). Infernal Regions residents can, given time, regenerate from virtually every wound, including getting ground to dust.

Violence against an Infernal Region member is therefore ill-advised, as they almost invariably survive to exact vengeance. For this reason, Infernal Region members sometimes refrain from hurting one another. The more sensible Infernals extend the courtesy to mortals, valuing their reputation. Even so, many Infernals (such as Sleed) are best avoided altogether.

Infernal Regions members can shapeshift, and are effectively immortal. Their abilities seem magical, but are really technological. They enjoy baseball games ... played with items more unsavory than baseballs.

• *Trichoate:* Agragazar Flatchlock's race, endowed with three personalities as a survival mechanism. Cutting a Trichoate's head will instantly make it sprout a secondary noggin and persona while the primary identity goes dormant to heal.

• *Whistling Ninjas:* A tiny humanoid creature, dressed in black ninja garb. The ninjas work as assassins, travelling by the hundreds and forming menacing pyramids upon confronting their target. They're mainly armed with a trumpet that fires off a potent sonic blast, acting like a projectile weapon in Station Control's physical confines.

Whistling Ninjas typically get hired for a specific job and, despite their sentience, are little more than a one-time bullet. If you survive a Whistling Ninja attack, don't worry about them bothering you again.

PLACES TO GO *The Braxiatel Collection:* Has a recently opened Starbucks.

• *Station Control:* Station Control exists in a state of flux, serving as a nexus point for 417 multiverses. However, leaving Station Control for another multiverse isn't so easy, as the multiverses contain different laws of physics (entropy-slopes, types of causality, atomic make-up, etc.) that could kill or otherwise obliterate many travelers from other dimensions. Some multiverses are sealed entirely, with the rare traveler from them greatly restricted even in Station Control.

The station's "Conclave Center" acts as a central meeting place. The Clans ruthlessly guarantee the center's security, as even high-ranking officials must venture there weaponless.

The station largely exists on the sufferance of others, with several multiverses capable of obliterating it. The station gets few human travelers. Station Control's components and zones tend to switch around a lot when you're not looking.

Chaotic space surrounds the station's exterior.

• *The Infernal Regions:* Not so much planets spinning in a vacuum, but moreso composed of "bubble worlds" in an infinity of rock. The bubble worlds pretty much resemble our dimension's concept of "hell," save that the Infernal Regions' inhabitants enjoy computers, bubble colonies, a history and post-industrial development.

• *Starsail Lodge:* Relatively stable habitation zone run by some of Sleed's contacts. Iron Sun uses it to discretely house visiting VIPs.

• *Unseen Lands:* The Elvish homelands. Voyagers to the Unseen Lands return with stories about elves, pixies, dwarves, etc.—but the truth usually varies from the stereotypes.

ORGANIZATIONS *Station Control Clans:* Families at Station Control include Iron Sun (mostly demons), Pontification Dragon (elves), Hooting Chrysanthemum Men (zombies), Monasticy of Slon (a variety of profoundly religious, land-based squid), Saurian, Elemental and even a God Clan (complete with thunder god). There's also a vampire clan, Xloomi of the Three Small Toad Clan and something called "the Sisters of Perpetual Night."

Visitors to Station Control usually join a Clan for the declaration of their stay, mostly a formality so long as you stay out of trouble.

PHENOMENA *"The Multiverse":* Chiefly a misnomer, given that by definition, there is only one Universe in which all life resides.

Within the Universe, all manner of different dimensions co-exist. However, they're separated by various physical impediments, in the same fashion that America and Ireland exist on the same planet but you can't simply walk from one to another. Still, travel between the two, with sufficient know-how, is possible.

Station Control services 417 multiverses, but others undoubtedly exist.

• *Multiverse Resonance:* Persons with rare sensory perception can subconsciously experience aspects of other multiverses. This often results in writers crafting "fiction" created around real people and places. [Stone obviously includes himself in this group, as the Maze, Sleed's entertainment/torture center, appears in his *Judge Dredd* novel *Deathmasques*.]

Other-dimensional versions exist of Frankenstein, a world of lycanthropes (often mistaken for werewolves, vampires and zombies) and a planet ruled by dinosaurs. "Santa Claus" actually existed as a nasty predator in a multiverse that collapsed on itself.

• *Theory of Transdimensional Contrivance:* Postulated by Dr. Rupert Gilhooly, it states that persons dislocated from their home dimension don't age, as they're cut off from the passage of time in their native history.

AT THE END OF THE DAY Shockingly one of the more lucid and readable Stone books, continuing a roll for the Big Finish Benny line. *The Infernal Nexus* indulges in a certain whimsy, but by now Stone's affinity for the slightly older Benny and Jason (presumably Stone's own age, by this point) carries the needed conviction to win you over. Overall, *The Infernal Nexus* rolls out some concepts/characters you can sink your teeth into, making us wish Big Finish had debuted their Benny novels with *The Squire's Crystal* and worked their way up.

DID YOU KNOW?

• Author Dave Stone posts about his creation, Jason Kane: "The thing about Jason is, of course, that he's basically me. I zoom around in space ships all the time and do incredibly heroic things—only nobody believes me."

THE SKYMINES OF KARTHOS

By David Bailey

Release Date: *September 2001*
Order: *Big Finish Benny Audio #4*

MAIN CHARACTERS Bernice Summerfield.

TRAVEL LOG Unnamed mining colony, planet Karthos, 2600.

CHRONOLOGY After *The Infernal Nexus*, and five months after Benny gets knocked up in *The Squire's Crystal*.

STORY SUMMARY When Caitlin Peters, Benny's longtime friend, goes missing on the planet Karthos, Benny stuffs her overly pregnant self into a Braxiatel shuttle and hurries off in hot pursuit. Benny sets down at a thulium mining settlement on Karthos, finding it under attack by swarms of winged, bat-like humanoids called "fireflies." Caitlin's husband Michael, a thulium miner, says that his wife went missing while investigating evidence of a dead civilization.

Benny ventures after Caitlin into a nearby mountain range, aided by Michael and Caitlin's boss, Professor Konstantin. The fireflies somehow exert a psionic hold over Konstantin, forcing him to wander off. Soon after, Benny and Michael find an enthralled Caitlin inside a large cavern, commanding the fireflies as an authority figure. To complete the firefly command structure, the possessed Konstantin acts as an advisory council leader.

Caitlin's personality briefly becomes dominant, informing Benny and Michael that a long-dead civilization on Karthos built a machine in the cavern to manufacture the fireflies as disposable rock soldiers from carbon and thulium deposits. Caitlin re-activated the equipment, hoping to generate a few fireflies and scare off most of the thulium miners, thereby enabling her husband Michael to take home a larger haul. However, the ancient weapon subdued Caitlin's will and forced her to host an artificial Authority persona. The weapon further snared Konstantin to house a Council figure, thus completing the firefly hierarchy.

Never geared for self-will, the fireflies take an over-simplistic approach and decide to kill people everywhere. Benny realizes that, theoretically, the fireflies could subdue a passing spaceship and, multiplying themselves via the carbon and thulium available throughout the Universe, exterminate humanoid lifeforms everywhere. In response, Benny confronts "Authority" and "Council" with the contradiction that they have mandated the deaths of all people even though their hosts, in fact, are people. The logical paradox confuses the Authority and Council personalities long enough for Caitlin and Konstantin to snap their control.

The fireflies die off as a result, allowing Michael to blow up the cavern with mining charges. Benny's group returns home, assuming the weapon was destroyed. But within the entombed cavern, the weapon comes to life on residual power, awaiting another chance to wreak havoc.

SEX AND SPIRITS Benny advised Caitlin not to marry the loutish Michael, stung by her own failed marriage to Jason Kane. A week before the wedding, a drunken Benny started ragging on Michael to Caitlin, who consequently slugged her. They reconciled enough for Benny to serve as the maid of honor.

Benny later predicted that Caitlin would leave Michael, but it never happened. Michael wouldn't blame Caitlin for divorcing him, since their relationship isn't the most stable and life on Karthos entails sacrifice. Even so, Caitlin's gambit with the fireflies—however ill advised—proved her love for Michael and they grow closer together.

Michael's stunned to realize a pregnant Benny can't drink booze.

ASS-WHUPPINGS Fireflies have besieged the mining colony for about a month, killing roughly a half-a-dozen colonists per day. The fireflies readily die off when Caitlin and Konstantin break free, but the firefly-generating equipment survives.

AUDIO TIE-INS Benny takes Braxiatel's prized shuttle without asking, the first in a line of shuttle stealing incidents ("The Plague Herds of Excelis"). Caitlin and Michael previously visited a dig on Bellotron (presumably the upcoming "The Bellotron Incident").

CHARACTER DEVELOPMENT

- *Bernice Summerfield:* Benny's somewhat talented at breaking computer encryption codes. She has some knowledge of safety procedures regarding explosives. As usual, she's stalling her publishers as much as possible.
- *Benny and Michael Peters:* There's friction between them, since Michael's well aware that Benny objected to his marriage to Caitlin.
- *Irving Braxiatel:* He doesn't like people calling him collect.
- *Caitlin Peters:* She once visited the Collection to study an Ambretian cave painting exhibit. She's studied primitive art for years. She normally works as assistant to Dr. Konstantin, an environmental scientist sent to Karthos to research the fireflies.
- *Caitlin and Michael Peters:* In addition to Benny, they know Braxiatel and Jason Kane.

ALIEN RACES *The Fireflies:* Humanoid creatures with bat-like attributes, including snubbed noses and serrated teeth. Fireflies typically stand about seven feet tall, weighing 100 to 110 kilograms. They're highly muscled, winged and covered with short fur. Despite the hair, they're mostly creatures of rock, with sheets of tough hide between their torso and arms.

Fireflies have no obvious gender. Their hands and feet have three digits, ending in vicious talons. Large eyes give them a developed sense of sight.

Thulium forms a crucial part of fireflies' biology, present in their very blood. Fireflies lack individual names, designated instead by numbers. Some fireflies (called "only minds") are generated for specific tasks, then die off once those tasks are complete.

The controlling Authority host typically wears a control crown that links it to the firefly-generating

equipment. The Counsel host doesn't require a crown, and can be brainwashed by remote. Some thoughts bleed through the firefly network (as Counsel, Konstantin senses some of Caitlin's thoughts).

The firefly chain of command resembles that of pre-21st century England, where a prime minister (in this case, Counsel) would report the people's will to a monarch (Authority). The Austorians had a similar command structure.

ALIEN PLANETS *Karthos:* Mining colony, located a few parsecs from the Braxiatel Collection. The planet holds no volcanic activity. There's little water in the mountains.

Certain atmospheric elements on Karthos routinely combine to create fireballs. The thulium miners usually brave such firestorms, eager to harvest the displaced thulium. It's not as dangerous as it sounds, but there's simply not enough thulium to support the excess of miners on the planet (it's akin to the California gold rush on Earth—every man and his dog went to Karthos to get rich).

In addition to a previous civilization, Karthos once supported a variety of animal life.

STUFF YOU NEED *Thulium:* A low-level radioactive element. No other lifeform, save the fireflies, requires it to live. Nearly all intergalactic star miners use thulium as fuel.

ORGANIZATIONS *Kontep Corporation:* Mining corporation that pays good bonuses, if one harvests enough thulium. Kontep set up a crisis center, staffed by miners who pull double-duty as volunteers, to respond to firefly attacks.

HISTORY On Karthos, an outbreak of war long ago compelled the Moralian people to construct the Fireflies as a means of generating dispensable soldiers. Despite this, the Moralians got wiped out.

• The initial human surveyors on Karthos found no signs the planet was ever inhabited. Caitlin's more experienced eye noted the suggestion of long-disused roads, and later discovered cave drawings detailing some of the fireflies' history.

AT THE END OF THE DAY An audio cursed with being average. As a listener, you're *somewhat* made to care about Benny's relationship with Caitlin and Michael, but only so far (and it doesn't help that Caitlin spends most of the audio possessed, unable to interact much with Benny). Furthermore, the Fireflies work somewhat well, but they're ultimately B-grade monsters. That

leaves "The Skymines of Karthos" as a very take it or leave it proposition—best forgotten if you're trying to save a few bucks.

THE GLASS PRISON

By Jacqueline Rayner

Release Date: January 2002
Order: Big Finish Benny Adventure #5

MAIN CHARACTERS Bernice Summerfield.

TRAVEL LOG The Glass Prison, planet Deirbhile, circa October, 2600.

CHRONOLOGY About 10 months after *The Doomsday Manuscript*.

STORY SUMMARY Unable to stand Adrian and Jason's nagging, a massively pregnant Benny flees into space with Claire, her Pakhar midwife, to quietly give birth somewhere. However, Benny and Claire's shuttle mysteriously flies off-course and crashes on the planet Deirbhile, a Fifth Axis world. There, authorities quickly round up Claire and the rotund Benny, tossing them into the Axis' infamous Glass Prison.

Benny and Claire discover the Glass Prison, albeit not literally made from glass, has transparent walls to better keep the inmates under observation. The duo tries to acclimate to prison life, but unnervingly finds that some of the inmates belong to "the Cult of the Mother," a Deirbhile underground movement. The cultists believe Benny's child, bizarrely conceived through two mothers (*The Squire's Crystal*), is actually a long-foretold savoir that will liberate Deirbhile from Fifth Axis rule. The cultists take credit for bringing Benny to Deirbhile, intending to help the baby fulfill its destiny.

Later, Benny learns the Fifth Axis is planning a major offensive against the quadrant, threatening a conflict that could catch the Braxiatel Collection in the crossfire. In response, Benny sows dissent by leaking word that ex-Kolonel Daglan Straklant (*The Doomsday Manuscript*), also incarcerated at the Glass Prison, can identify a high-ranking traitor within the Fifth Axis ranks.

Soon after, Benny's water breaks, compelling the cultists to riot, seize control of the prison and prepare for their liberator's birth. The cultists find a newly arrived Axis doctor to aid with Benny's

labor, and also locate Joseph, Benny's confiscated robotic porter, to monitor her condition. The doctor delivers Benny's son by C-section, allowing Joseph to cauterize the wound. But immediately afterward, a Grel inmate named Sophia kills the doctor, recognizing him as the Fifth Axis Imperator. Benny realizes the Imperator arrived to interrogate Straklant about the "traitor," then switched plans, intending to murder the cultists' savior.

Axis reinforcements storm the prison, even as Straklant tries to kill Benny for past offences. Straklant confronts Benny in her cell, intending to murder her son. In desperation, Benny orders Joseph to amplify her baby's cries, thus cracking her locked cell door and allowing the cultists to save them.

The cultists put Straklant on trial for trying to kill their savior, but Joseph's sonic attack resonates through the Glass Prison's architecture, destabilizing the entire building. The prison falls to ruin, killing most of the cultists, and leaves a tied-up Straklant dangling above a perilous drop. Benny grabs her son and leaves Straklant to die, fleeing with her allies as the building collapses.

Afterward, Joseph radios the Braxiatel Collection for a pick-up. Braxiatel soon arrives, and informs Benny that the Imperator's death—and rumors of Straklant's "traitor"—have thrown the Fifth Axis into chaos, thwarting their planned offensive. After recuperating, Benny performs a naming ceremony at the Braxiatel Collection, introducing her son, Peter Guy Summerfield, to the Universe.

MEMORABLE MOMENTS   When Sophia's smock gets damaged and the wardeners refuse to replace it, Benny selflessly gives up her own—then stands around, very naked and very pregnant until they respond.

When Benny enters labor and a cultist stares at her for too long, she hollers: "It's a perfectly natural and beautiful event!", making the embarrassed cultist retire.

Dying from her haphazard C-section, Benny whispers to her son: "I'm sorry, little one, I don't think we're both going to make it. But whatever happens, you'll always be loved. Claire, or Adrian, or Brax, or Jason, they'll take care of you."

As a murderous Straklant approaches, a post-operative Benny falls to the floor and reopens her wound. Traumatized, Benny thinks about scraping up her spilled blood and feeding it back inside her stomach, convinced she can't afford to lose any. With the last of her strength, Benny blasts Straklant with the point that she's not to blame for his going to jail, pointing out, "You do bad things, you

TOP 5

COMPANION TRIUMPHS (NOVELS/AUDIOS)

From Loups-Garoux (May 2001) to Neverland (June 2002) and From Earthworld (March 2001) to Time Zero (Sept. 2002)

1) Benny gives birth in prison (*The Glass Prison*)—… and that's even more difficult than it sounds, considering this book's main escapade nearly ends with Benny bleeding to death—the victim of a C-Section gone awry. Faced with hostile inmates, a premature birth and a personal visit from the Fifth Axis Imperator, Benny [as always] perseveres.

2) Fitz blows up the cavern (*Time Zero*)—Acting on the Doctor's instructions, Fitz pitches a grenade that brings down a cavern wall atop some alternate reality saurians. Unfortunately, the resultant cave-in also entombs Fitz and his friend George Williamson—setting in motion events with grave repercussions for the history of the Universe.

3) Evelyn helps blow up a Silurian submarine ("Bloodtide")—Granted, the Doctor runs interference, but it's up to Evelyn Smythe—a mid-50s University professor—to waltz into a Silurian submarine, plant a Myrka tracker and sally back out again. Thanks to Evelyn, the Myrka creature attacks and destroys the sub, thwarting a Silurian plan to wipe out humanity.

4) Anji endures some magical trials (*Grimm Reality*)—Forced to compete for the doltish Duke of Sigh's hand in marriage, Anji helps insure that the contest ends in a draw. The Duke therefore gets penalized and turned into a toad, leaving Anji mercifully single.

5) Fitz blows up an Onihr spaceship (*Trading Futures*)—Fitz admittedly gets some help with this one [namely, from an interactive Onihr computer pad], but it's to his credit that he keeps his wits together, survives an Onihr interrogation and eradicates their space vessel in Earth orbit.

hang out with bad people, you get a bad life. Deal with it," before collapsing, half-dead.

Benny doesn't cause Straklant's death, but notably (and laudably, really) doesn't do anything to stop it. More humorously, Benny freaks from being in the spotlight at Peter's naming ceremony, grabs her son, flees and hides with him in a wardrobe.

After all's said and done, Benny resolves to "have a bath and read a book, and not cause any more deaths today."

SEX AND SPIRITS Jason Kane's on the prowl again, telling shiftless women he's a movie producer. He's inadvertently responsible for Benny getting jailed, having drunkenly told a cultist named Marianne about Benny's abnormal pregnancy. The cultist evidently screwed Jason, then tampered with Benny's shuttle afterward. Benny later finds this out and shouts Marianne was, "sleeping with my husband!" when they're actually not married.

Jason and Benny have a spat about her birthing Adrian's child, despite their being divorced and her thinking he'd snuffed it (*Twilight of the Gods*). He's waffling between jealousy and obsession, picking up floozies to show he doesn't care, then bursting in to drunkenly rave about how the baby should've been theirs. They somehow reconcile despite all this.

Privately, Benny calls Jason "Mr. Rabbit"—and not because of his long floppy ears and twitchy nose. She claims she hasn't been biting Jason's bottom. Lately.

Benny's lactating boobs have swelled to massive proportions, a strange change from her inferiority complex about their smallness.

Chapter 10's labeled "Enforced Sobriety," composed of a single sentence in which Benny notes: "I really need a drink."

Some Glass Prison inmates collect money by making out and letting men watch.

Previously, Benny nearly died during a drunken midnight skating jaunt on an ornamental Braxiatel Collection lake. She reached shore just before the ice cracked.

ASS-WHUPPINGS The Imperator C-sections Benny with Sophia's Tarfle Savaging-dagger. Claire gets the Terpsechians (*see Alien Races*) to generate anaesthetic. By the time Straklant tries to kill Peter, Benny's lost so much blood she can barely crawl. She later spends weeks recovering, complete with transfusions, scar reduction treatment and antibiotics.

Prison officials torture Claire, as per standard procedure. The Axis draws the line at torturing the pregnant Benny, but she rebelliously earns a session in a prison room with unfiltered walls, netting her some sunstroke.

Working for Straklant, female inmate Crow torments Benny in various ways. She hangs fellow prisoner Deedee, stringing her up with a note that sloppily reads, "Your Next Summerfield" in carmine lipstick. On the flimsiest of accusations, the cultists think prisoner Jevina did the deed and literally tear her apart. Deedee's lover Thall eventually kills Crow.

The cultists seize the prison by flinging acid in their guards' faces. The Wolf, the cult leader, kills five guards with a sharpened toothbrush.

Sophia axes the Fifth Axis Imperator. Benny's final gambit with Joseph's audio systems cracks the Glass Prison to pieces, presumably causing dozens or hundreds of deaths. The Wolf and Jason's snugglebunny Marianne are among the casualties. Benny leaves Straklant to die.

TV-TIE INS The pyramids of Mars ("Pyramids of Mars") are now public knowledge.

NOVEL TIE-INS Body-swapper Avril, still a chunky 40-year-old man, warns that her genetics (*The Squire's Crystal*) might influence Peter in undesirable ways.

Fifth Axis Kolonel Daglan Straklant debuted in *The Doomsday Manuscript*, sparred with Benny and consequently wound up in the Glass Prison. With the Fifth Axis in chaos, Earthlink Federation forces liberate several Axis worlds. However, the organization presumably returns in the upcoming "The Axis of Evil."

Jason Kane's still working on borderline illegal holovids (*Beige Planet Mars*).

Benny and Jason are slightly haunted from glimpsing themselves as parents in *Return of the Living Dad*. To large degree, Benny never found closure after their divorce (*Eternity Weeps*).

Claire hails from the same race as Keri, Benny's Pakhar friend (*Legacy*, "Buried Treasures").

Sophia's race, the information scavenging Grel, first appeared in *Oh No It Isn't!*, and will appear (one presumes) in the upcoming "The Grel Escape."

Benny's still traumatized about her mother's death (*Love and War*). She bawls her eyes out to realize that Braxiatel could bring her mother through time to the naming ceremony—but realizes she couldn't handle losing her again.

Peter's middle name hails from Guy, Benny's lost love in *Sanctuary*. She fails to tell Jason this, not wanting to rub his nose in it.

Guests at Peter's naming ceremony include Benny's father Issac Summerfield (*Return of the Living Dad*), Michael Doran and Jayne Waspo (*Oh No It Isn't!*), Emile Mars-Smith, Tameka and her now-large son Scott (*Beyond the Sun*), Arko, Forno, Shell and her ex-lover Starl (*Gods of the Underworld*).

THE CRUCIAL BITS...

- **THE GLASS PRISON**—Benny gives birth to Peter Guy Summerfield. The Fifth Axis considerably neutered.

An older Chris Cwej (last viewed as a teenager in *Twilight of the Gods*, also seen in *Faction Paradox: The Book of the War*) also puts in an appearance. The Doctor doesn't attend, but leaves a silver-naming bracelet and a note telling Benny, "He will be worthy of you."

Benny modifies her credo of never being cruel nor cowardly (*Beyond the Sun*) for Peter.

CHARACTER DEVELOPMENT

- *Bernice Surprise Summerfield:* She's fond of her name, which means, "Bringer of Victory." She considers Claire the closest thing she's had to a substitute mother. She sometimes thinks of Joseph as a person.

Benny's never met an Asek (*see Alien Races*) before. She's knowledgeable about Ming Dynasty pottery. She's unclear about the amount of material the Braxiatel Collection holds. She's got little knowledge of pre-trowel archaeology or pre-gas anesthesia [but suspects both involved alcohol].

Benny doesn't understand the Killoran language. She likes double mochas, with extra whipped cream and sprinkles. After this story, Benny learns to trust people more, acknowledging that running away got her into trouble.

- *Benny and in-utero Peter:* Sophia tells Benny about the Biblical Simon, whom Jesus renamed Peter to mean "the Rock." Benny similarly names her son Peter because he's her foundation. [Jason's middle name is coincidentally Peter, which pleases him.]

A pregnant Benny's sometimes prone to shouting and throwing crockery, allegedly so Peter will better tolerate such sounds in childhood. Adrian keeps reciting Killoran battle poetry at Benny's womb. Benny counteracts such sessions by declaiming Wilfred Owen and Siegfried Sassoon.

Benny sometimes hates the baby for draining her energy. She sometimes thinks the thing growing inside her is half dog-man, half witch, and wants to claw it out—which is precisely why Braxiatel made her get a midwife. Benny decides to be happy with either a boy or a girl. She hasn't seen her ankles since June.

- *Peter Guy Summerfield:* Peter's half-human, half-Killoran, with black eyes, a kitten-like nose and a shock of blond hair/fur on his head. His tiny fingers have tiny claws. He's got Benny's ears and Adrian's nose. Claire and Sophia are his godmothers.

- *Jason Kane:* He's balding on top, but in denial about it.

- *Irving Braxiatel:* He built a birthing pool for Benny. He recently purchased a lemon yellow space yacht, and grants the information-loaded Sophia unrestricted access [that even Benny lacks] to the Collection.

- *Adrian Wall:* He's seven feet tall.

- *Joseph:* He can monitor life signs, send interstellar transmissions, access a Grel dataaxe and cauterize wounds.

- *Claire (a.k.a. Clar'atil):* Benny interviewed 30 candidates before choosing Claire as her midwife. Benny's mother was also named Claire, which probably swayed her decision.

Claire's read Benny's *Down Among the Dead Men*, and makes a phenomenal chocolate cheesecake. She can beat Benny at Scrabble. She's utterly selfless and has assisted in 20 C-sections, five involving human mothers.

- *Ms. Jones:* Her first name's rumored to be Cleopatra. She vents her spleen against anyone calling her "Miss" or "Mrs."

- *Sophia:* She's Grel, but uses the human name Sophia, meaning wisdom. By killing the Imperator with a Grel axe, Sophia gains his knowledge.

- *Wolsey:* Benny can program an automatic can-opener for Wolsey. She's meant to get him wormed. He loves sunning himself in Mr. Crofton's greenhouse.

ALIEN RACES *Killorans:* There's only three recorded instances of Killorans cross-breeding with humans. Killorans have shorter gestation cycles than humans, explaining why Benny's labor arrives early. There's little correlation between human births and Killoran whelping. Killorans typically embrace the pain of childbirth as a sacrifice to their creators. They're not prone to crying.

- *Pakhar:* Typically wash themselves with their tongues [although Claire infinitely prefers a bubble bath]. They traditionally weave blankets for newborns from their own fir.

- *Grel:* Their tough, rubbery skin doesn't sweat. Acid capable of scorching humans only mildly hurts Grel. They have a hard time understanding colloquialisms, and no concept of shyness.

- *Aseks:* Short for "asexual," denoting a race of hairless humanoids. Their origin's unclear, although the Fifth Axis probably engineered them. They administrate the Glass Prison. Aseks are entirely devoid of color, with noseless faces. They don't appear to socialize, nor exhibit emotion. They don't carry weapons, but they're strong and authorized to use violence. They possess tough skin that's resistant to acid.

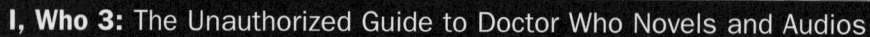

• *Terpsechians:* They look like walruses, with a hint of elephant. Terpsechians can excrete various substances out of their trunks, including acids and a euphoric substance.

• *The Criath People:* Located on the planet Taghost. Eating marshmallows makes them instantly lose consciousness.

ALIEN PLANETS *Deirbhile:* A tiny, strategically positioned planet with a single landmass. Deirbhile measures time with Earth standard years.

PLACES TO GO *The Glass Prison:* It's 11-stories tall, made from an unknown, soundproof material. Floor A's for interrogation. Floors B, C and D are all-female floors [Benny's in cell D20]. Floors E to K are for men. Each floor has 30 cells, with four prisoners each, and a dining room. Rations consist of chewy gray slabs that taste like armpit-flavored cardboard.

Escapees are shot on sight. Females who prove too rowdy "accidentally wander" into the men's levels and never return. The Glass Prison's blanketed in a communications exclusion zone, preventing unauthorized transmissions. Half the Glass Prison inmates are ex-Axis military.

• *The Braxiatel Collection:* Its security measures won't count for tofu against actual military might. The Collection features the Roman Emperor Claudius' lost diaries. It also has two copies of *The Amazing Armadillo Girl* #1, one with a free Armadillo keyring.

ORGANIZATIONS *The Fifth Axis:* The Fifth Axis long ago learned of the Mothering Cult's aims and quietly supplied the cultists with equipment to draw Benny's shuttle off-course. The Axis wanted to seize the cult's savior, prove it was nothing special and debunk the prophecy. Benny's just taken along for the ride.

Axis soldiers wear red-and-silver uniforms.

HISTORY Long ago, a woman simply named "the Mother" [possibly Benny] arrived on Deirbhile and warned of a future threat. The Mother also spoke of a baby, born to two mothers in the year that crossed worlds [i.e. 2600] that would liberate Deirbhile. The cult concluded Benny's child, essentially conceived with Avril and Benny as its mothers, fit the bill.

• *Buffy the Vampire Slayer* Season 792 is currently screening.

AT THE END OF THE DAY Astonishing, raw and soaked with genius dialogue—not only Big Finish's best Benny novel by a mile, but also ranks among the strongest "Who"-related books of any type from the past two years or more. Rayner gets away with a lot in *The Glass Prison* (notably Benny's first-person narration) because she intrinsically *gets* Benny, and it's a damnable shame that—as the Benny books can't help but sell lower than "Who"—*The Glass Prison* will never get the readership it deserves. Overall, it's clear that Rayner put loads of work into this project, marbling it with hair-pin turns and polishing it with love. Superb.

THE GREATEST SHOP IN THE GALAXY

By Paul Ebbs

Release Date: February 2002
Order: Big Finish "Bernice Summerfield" CD #3.1

MAIN CHARACTERS Bernice Summerfield.

TRAVEL LOG The Gigamarket, planet Baladroon, 2600.

NOTE A hidden track at the end of "Greatest Shop" contains nearly three minutes of outtakes.

STORY SUMMARY Hoping to blow off steam, Benny slyly assigns herself to a minor dig on the planet Baladroon. But upon landing, Benny leaves work to her archaeobots and lustfully explores Baladroon's Gigamarket, the galaxy's largest shopping center. Swiftly, Benny goes into raw, primal shopping mode in the Gigamarket's shoe canyon, armed with a credit card chip she "borrowed" from Adrian Wall.

Suddenly, a string of freak temporal effects disrupts the Gigamarket, violently wrenching time forward and backward. As part of this, the anomalies teleport a group of carnivorous Borvali aliens, normally kept separate from Baladroon's human population, into the Gigamarket. The Borvali start hunting the human customers, forcing Benny to run like hell with Keelor, a Gigamarket executive.

Benny scrambles for a solution, even as a follow-up temporal effect transports some human soldiers—combatants in the last human-Borvali war,

held 100 years ago—into the Gigamarket. Keelor identifies the human soldiers as part of a platoon that went missing at the war's end, lost when their battlefield unexpectedly vaporized. Afterward, human and Borvali officials signed a peace accord, rigging up a temporal barrier to separate Baladroon's human and Borvali populations. However, the Gigamarket's time engines—rigged to let the supermarket straddle the human and Borvali zones—are somehow malfunctioning, causing the time anomalies.

Keelor starts sweating because the Gigamarket is rigged with a blanking bomb, a fail-safe device in case its time engines malfunction. Benny agrees to help defuse the bomb, but shockingly discovers Keelor sabotaged the time engines in the first place. Keelor hoped to disrupt the Gigamarket and make its stock drop, thereby allowing his partner in crime, Gigamarket investor Joggon, to stage a hostile takeover. Unfortunately, Keelor mistimed his exit, trapping himself inside the beleaguered shopping center.

With little time to spare, Keelor leads Benny's ragamuffin group to the Gigamarket's time engines. The blanking bomb explodes, but the fritzed time engines roll back time, granting Benny several attempts to defuse the device. Amid the brouhaha, Keelor identifies the time-transported military leader, Lieutenant-Colonel Tarband Tantz, as his grandfather. The brash Tarband blames Keelor for their predicament, causing a spooked Keelor to paradoxically shoot and kill his ancestor at a point before he has children.

Keelor and Tarband begin fading in and out of existence, caught in a time loop as history tries to determine which of them exists. A Borvali shows up and kills Keelor at a point in the loop before he shoots Tarband, allowing History to bring Tarband back into existence, while Benny—finally accorded an opening—smashes the blanking bomb's control circuits with her shoe.

Afterward, Gigamarket's stock nosedives, causing the business-minded Joggon—who's cerebrally hotlinked into the galactic stock index—to experience death by orgasm. Tarband helps Benny reprogram the Gigamarket's warehouse robots to herd the remaining Borvali out of the Gigamarket, restoring some semblance of order. Benny breathes a sigh of relief and heads home, leaving Tarband's brigade to acclimate to life in 2600.

MEMORABLE MOMENTS Benny asks Keelor, Tarband's grandson, to tell Tarband something only his grandson could know. But Keelor, lacking a drop of delicacy, blurts out: "You were killed in the last battle of the human/Borvali war!"

TOP 5

'WHO' COMEDY MOMENTS (AUDIOS)

*From Loups-Garoux (May 2001)
to Neverland (June 2002)*

1) The *Beep and Friends* singalong ("The Ratings War")—Admittedly, it's hard to *truly* love this one unless—like us—you ever felt flayed by happy-go-lucky kid's shows such as *Barney*. But that being the case, the subversive *Beep and Friends* theme song—which encourages kids to chop up their hamsters and deep fry their cats—was just about the funniest thing we'd ever heard. We'd never, *ever* condone playing this song for children, but as adults, we nearly pissed ourselves.

2) A Jelloid swallows the Doctor ("The One Doctor")—Yet another audio moment that would *never* work on television, a giant Jelloid creature gulps down the Doctor at the Part 3 climax. The con man Banto Zane adds, "It's too late, Mel—he's lunch," right before the theme music strikes up, brilliantly topping off the swallowed Colin Baker's beautiful screams.

3) "Was it suicide?" ("The Chimes of Midnight")—It's worth noting that some of the darkest stories [Alan Moore's comic epic *Watchmen* springs to mind] also turn out very, very funny. Along those lines, the menacing "Chimes of Midnight" includes servants who insist a string of murder victims *must* have committed suicide—no matter how ridiculous that sounds. At the height of this, the Doctor sarcastically claims that chauffeur Frederick—impossibly run over in the living room—obviously committed suicide because: "It's quite clear that Frederick brought the car into the house, ran himself over with it and put it back outside before he finally expired." Hysterical.

4) Death by orgasm ("The Greatest Shop in the Galaxy")—Having beautifully set up Gigamarket stock to take a tumble—thereby paving the way for a hostile takeover—the business-minded Joggon screws himself by too closely monitoring the outcome. Cerebrally hotlinked into the galactic stock index, an overjoyed Joggon experiences death by orgasm [but at least he dies happy].

5) "You know how to quack, don't you?" ("The Maltese Penguin")—In a scene that emulates Lauren Bacall in *To Have and Have Not* (1944), Frobisher's sultry client Alicia Mulholland tells him: "If you need anything at all, just quack. You know how to quack, don't you?" Frobisher responds: "Well, no. I'm a penguin, not a duck." Alicia: "Just stiffen your beak and vibrate." Frobisher (weakly): "… quack."

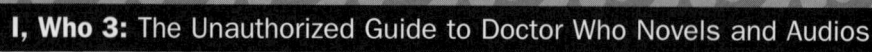

After whacking the blanking bomb controls with her shoe, Benny comments she didn't try such a tactic sooner because: "I wasn't pre-menstrual enough."

SEX AND SPIRITS Keelor's a big fan of Benny's work, to the point of constructing a *Down Among the Dead Men* display that features a 30-meter-tall Benny cut-out, tanned, wearing a spandex bikini and showing lots of thigh. Since the display's installment, *Down Among the Dead Men* sales are up by 50 percent. Keelor also keeps (unsuccessfully) trying to feel Benny up.

A futzing Joseph starts reading from Benny's audio diary, reciting in her voice: "… absolutely enormous. Obviously, I couldn't say anything to him at the time, but he certainly goes down in my Top 10 list of…"

Benny keeps encouraging the hunky Tarband to give her a kiss, but to no avail.

SEX AND SPIRITS/ASS-WHUPPINGS
"The Greatest Shop in the Galaxy" *surely* marks the first instance of a "Who"-related work involving death by orgasm.

ASS-WHUPPINGS The Gigamarket's wayward temporal distortion reverts stacks of leather back into live cows, then dead cows. The temporal waves also glitch Joseph's circuits, making him sing, "For he's a jolly good fellow," and shout "Boing!" for most of the story.

The Borvali run rampant in the Gigamarket, savagely munching customers and Tarband's men. The Gigamarket's Borvali section sells human meat (*see Places to Go*).

Tarband shoots some Borvali civilians. Benny later beats him up for threatening to kill a Borvali child, whatever its dietary preference.

A blanking bomb repeatedly goes off, but thanks to the temporal waves, nobody dies. Tarband and Keelor wink in and out of existence, a textbook example of the grandfather paradox. Keelor loses out, and finally snuffs it.

Benny gets a foot blister "the size of New Orpington."

TV-TIE INS Keelor's belt registers time distortion on the Bocca scale ("The Two Doctors").

CHARACTER DEVELOPMENT

• *Bernice Summerfield:* Benny hands Braxiatel the cover story that she's on Baladroon to dig up latrines from the Baladroon Dark Ages in the Gigamarket parking lot. Admittedly, her archaeobots make some choice finds. Benny's not actually an expert on Baladroon latrines, but hopes to become one before Braxiatel asks too many questions.

Benny's fixated on shoes, as they make her feel like a woman, not an archaeologist slathered in dirt and sand. She wonders if the Gigamarket has a cosmetic surgery department that can shave a few millimeters off her heel.

She prefers real leather to Syntho-Tan. Benny has so-so knowledge of computers. She doesn't speak binary code. Her archaeobots seem relatively self-sufficient. She curses, "Oh, spheres."

Adrian Wall is currently watching their son Peter. When Adrian figures out Benny swiped his credit chip, he puts a block on it—causing the Gigamarket to impound hundreds of her shoe purchases.

• *Joseph:* An expansion kit would allow Joseph to answer rhetorical questions. He's ill-equipped for sound analysis [much more sophisticated than his sonic amplification in *The Glass Prison*]. Joseph can use virtual Post-it notes for Benny's diary dictation. He can access Galactic Mean Time.

• *Keelor:* Member of the Baladroon Historical Society, specializing in military paraphernalia, who considers Benny a formidable archeologist. Keelor holds a basic understanding of chrono-engineering.

[Author's Note: We should pause to note that although the Borvali kills Keelor, thereby eliminating the grandfather paradox, it doesn't solve the problem of Keelor's grandfather Tarband taking up residence in 2600 before he spawns. As such, Keelor technically shouldn't exist. But as "Neverland" and "Colditz" prove, paradoxical figures can still exist if they play crucial roles in history. Therefore, Keelor's paradoxical survival is required for him to sabotage the Gigamarket's time engines, thereby causing this adventure and actually *fulfilling* history. Finally, let's remember that this is all played for laughs.]

ALIEN RACES *Borvali:* Cited as looking like a cross between a three-meter tall pepperoni and a cross-eyed autopsy. They hunt by sight, not smell, and prefer slaughtering live prey to purchasing them from a supermarket.

• *Vorax:* Literally lack hearts. If Joggon's representative of his species, Vorax spit buckets of drool whenever they speak. He claims that it's a rare honor to get covered in expectorate by a Vorax, but that seems unlikely. Vorax are large, but move quickly.

STUFF YOU NEED *Gigamarket Hyper FM:* Plays infomercials that directly interact with your brain. To listen, just hold your forehead or hindbrain against your radio's speaker plate. The infomercials scan your brain's need cortex and tailors offers to your tastes.

• *Adrian Wall's Credit Chip:* Its credit ratings include "lukewarm" and "Cor, blimey, gov'nah… do you want to take the shop as well?"

• *The Gigamarket's Blanking Bomb:* Has access code AB45JKLX.

• *Sinister Scratchings:* Considered the greatest work on ancient latrines ever written, available at the Gigamarket as a floppy screen edition.

PLACES TO GO *The Gigamarket:* It purports to sell every product in the known galaxy.

Viewing the Borvali Protectorate on Baladroon as an untapped market, some crooked Gigamarket executives decided to start selling the Borvali one of their staple products: human meat. The Borvali took some time to accept a humanely killed product, but finally relented. The Gigamarket blanking bomb was therefore designed to cover up, if necessary, the executives' highly illegal acts of human meat trafficking.

The humans-only portion of the Gigamarket features an Imelda Marcos Shoe Canyon, which accommodates alien beings with differing numbers of legs. There's also a selection of LSD-implanted footwear.

The stationary department alone encompasses six floors. There's entire sections devoted to soft furnishings, paper clips, bedding and explosives. The 98th floor holds a visitor lounge. Customers zip about on hover-carts.

The Gigamarket sells leather from cows who die of natural causes, agreeing in advance to donate their skin through will and probate.

HISTORY The human-Borvali war on Baladroon ended when a secret weapon (actually the Gigamarket's time engines) apparently vaporized forces on both sides. Horrified to have witnessed destruction on such a scale, the combatants signed a peace treaty that separated the planet's human sector from the Borvali Protectorate with a 50 km-tall force wall. Humans on Baladroon still celebrate Freedom Day to mark the war's conclusion.

• Station WKRP in New Cincinnati is currently playing the hit song, *Your Heart is Just a Hologramatic Circuit for My Love.*

• Paper was largely ditched in favor of floppy screens, but some cultures still use it.

• A vegan terrorist faction is currently in operation.

AT THE END OF THE DAY Suitably deft and daffy, throwing a bundle of hysterical concepts into a blender and seeing what results. "Greatest Shop" goes for a whirlwind comedic effect, tossing the listener from one gag to the next, and as such is near-impossible to explain succinctly to friends, no matter how many margaritas you consume. As such, the more serious-minded Benny stories will outpace "Greatest Shop," but it's a highly entertaining ride nonetheless.

DID YOU KNOW?

• "Greatest Shop" started life as a seventh Doctor pitch for Big Finish—until Ebbs showed an unfinished version to BBV producer Bill Baggs, which impressed Baggs enough to net Ebbs a commission for BBV's "Zygons: Absolution." It then resurfaced as a pitch to BBC books—during the commissioning process for *The Book of the Still*—as a seventh Doctor PDA called *Gigamarket*. But BBC Books rejected the story because it was, "a bit of a run-around."

From that point, Ebbs says: "Proving how loathe I was to kill off a good idea and to save me coming up with a new one, I pitched the proposal, reworked to a much shorter, pithier, runnyaroundier seventh Doctor story, to Big Finish." Producer Gary Russell pulled Ebbs aside in a Chicago bar [at Chicago TARDIS convention] and said he wanted the story... as a Benny audio. "The rest," Ebbs says, "is economics."

• Director Alistair Lock initially told Ebbs [whether serious or not] that he wanted to cast Gary Martin, the man who voices the Honey Monster in *Sugar Puffs* adverts, to play Joggon. Unfortunately, Martin wasn't available, so Lock instead cast Toby Longworth, who portrays Judge Dredd for Big Finish. [Ironically, Martin's also played Dredd in a *Judge Dredd* radio adaptation.]

THE GREEN-EYED MONSTERS

By Dave Stone

Release Date: July 2002
Order: Big Finish Benny Audio #3.2

MAIN CHARACTERS Bernice Summerfield, Jason Kane and Adrian Wall.

TRAVEL LOG The Braxiatel Collection and Goronos IV, 2600.

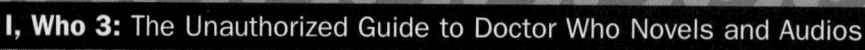

NOTE Due to production difficulties, "The Green-Eyed Monsters" was released after "The Plague Herds of Excelis" but chronologically occurs first.

STORY SUMMARY At the Braxiatel Collection, Lady Ashantra du Lac, affiliated with the House Royal on Goron IV, hires Benny to authenticate certain artifacts and totems. An excited Benny leaves Peter with Jason Kane and Adrian Wall—who're still squabbling with one another, competing for Benny's attention—then jets off for Goron IV.

Enroute, Benny learns the Goronos System consists of five inhabited planets, each of which hopes to somehow gain supremacy over the entire region. Of late, a legend has come to light claiming twin kings—the Goronos rulers of old—will one day get reincarnated and rule the system. The myth further states the reincarnated kings' eyes will glow green in the presence of certain artifacts and totems. With a sinking feeling, Benny realizes she's meant to verify Ashantra's artifacts as genuine, thereby paving the way for her charges—the twins Boris and Ronald—to make their eyes flash green and claim the throne.

On Goron IV, Benny identifies Ashantra's artifacts as a load of cheap junk, available from many off-world retailers. Ashantra confesses to Benny that she spread the ridiculous rumor about the reincarnated kings in the first place, then purchased bio-implants to make Boris and Ronald's eyes flash green. If successful, the dim-witted twins will claim the throne, but Ashantra will hold the true power as regent. Benny balks at the thought of certifying the junk as artifacts, but low-level criminals at the Braxiatel Collection—working on Ashantra's behalf—kidnap Peter to guarantee Benny's complicity.

In response, the roguish Jason tracks down Mr. Sloathe, Ashantra's agent at the Collection, and name-drops certain associates who would happily butcher Sloathe's family if Peter isn't returned in ten minutes. Terrified by the thought of Jason's connections, Sloathe arranges for his henchmen to drop Peter off in the Collection's main lobby. With Peter safe, Jason uses his seedy connections to borrow a space-faring General Infridanex Battle Corvette, then makes all speed with Adrian to Goron IV.

The arriving duo informs Benny of Peter's safety. She, in turn, slugs Ashantra unconscious, then exposes her fraud. Goron IV authorities arrest Ashantra, leaving the system to return to its war posture as Benny's crew returns to the Collection.

MEMORABLE MOMENTS Benny tries to comprehend the myth of the reincarnated kings: "You know, it strikes me rather that of all the qualities necessary in a ruler, the ability to make your eyes flash green in the presence of certain artifacts and totems is the least of them, ancient prophecies or not."

The stoic Adrian comforts his son Peter with: "You're a perfectly satisfactory result of genetic reproduction…"

Jason compliments himself and Adrian for successfully caring for Peter in Benny's absence. Seconds later, armed roughnecks burst in, shoot Jason and Adrian with stun pistols and take the child.

Later, Jason tells Benny about Peter's rescue, then adds: "If you didn't know anything about [the kidnapping], then there's nothing going on at all and you should forget everything I just said."

SEX AND SPIRITS Adrian's the father of Benny's child; Jason Kane's her ex-husband and the love of her life. So naturally, they're at each other's throats for her attention. Jason cuttingly points out Adrian only made progress with Benny when she wasn't in her own body.

Benny scolds Jason for letting himself "get drunk around Peter," then finishes off his boilermaker herself. She hasn't had a proper drink in ages, which feels unnatural.

Jason and Adrian hash out some differences on the way to Goronos. Adrian confesses that his race mates for life, meaning he knows Benny doesn't love him but feels a biological imperative to protect her nonetheless. Jason harbored thoughts of Benny during his time in another dimension (*Twilight of the Gods* to *The Infernal Nexus*). They genuinely bond, but resume arguing by story's end.

Ashantra tries to play host and liquors Benny up with: "If you need anything… a big bottle of liquor or a destructive and completely meaningless sexual encounter… please do let me know." She kindly stocks Benny's liquor cabinet with triple-distilled Proximan vodka and Soldarian brandy, unaware that Benny's cutting back on her booze.

The idiot royal twins Boris and Ronald feel Benny up, although Joseph zaps them during the final confrontation.

ASS-WHUPPINGS Sloathe's thugs stun Adrian and Jason unconscious, but they recover nicely. Benny slugs Ashantra unconscious.

NOVEL TIE-INS Stone's habit of recycling names crops up aplenty in this story. The Goronos

System is unrelated to a planet of the same name in Stone's *The Slow Empire*. Mr. Sloathe probably doesn't hail from the shapechanging Sloathe race (Stone's *Sky Pirates!*, *Oblivion*).

Some connections seem more genuine. Goron IV's located on the other side of the Proximan Chain (*Return to the Fractured Planet*). The twins' eye implants hail from Catan Nebula bio-facilities (*Ship of Fools*, etc.).

Jason mentions having some experience with children "in another life," probably referring to his alternate history son, Keith Summerfield-Kane, that turned up in *Return of the Living Dad*.

AUDIO TIE-INS "The Green-Eyed Monsters" marks the end of the Benny line using *Adventure is My Game* as its theme song. Benny opens this audio listening to the song for a bit, then switching it off and commenting, "I can't imagine what I was thinking." [Author's Note: We agree.] After this, the original Benny theme music becomes standard.

TIE-INS Ashantra's worthless trinkets include a statuette of the seven-armed swamp goddess Raghi Ano [valued at four credits, 30p] that's a knock-off from the Garazone bazaar ("The Sword of Orion," "Dalek Empire") and the fabled Book of Dreams, supposedly the last remnant from the lost citadel of Hokesh (Stone's *Citadel of Dreams*), but in reality just an Apocryphal Publishing Consortium copy [a credit 90, standard edition].

CHARACTER DEVELOPMENT

• *Bernice Summerfield and Peter:* Benny won't let people use baby talk around Peter, fearing he'll start out in life thinking people talk like complete and utter idiots. She's recording holo-diaries for Peter just in case anything happens to her.

She doesn't impose unnatural sleep patterns on Peter. She was going to nickname him "Peanut," but worried about saddling him with the name forever. She's encoded his baby formula in her room's sub-molecular fabricator unit.

• *Benny:* Finds Braxiatel shuttles cramped.

• *Jason Kane:* Several disreputable characters, including the space-faring Plague Dog pirate band (from whom Jason borrows a General Infridanex Battle Corvette), owe Jason favors. He also knows Nix, a nymph-sucking Vicoraptor from the soul-reeving dimensions, who's taken up residence at the Collection.

• *Adrian Wall:* He's working on the Collection's new xenoarchaeology wing. Some of the exhibits there might distort the space-time continuum and need special facilities.

Adrian claims males of his species don't raise their children, but he noticeably looks after Peter anyway.

• *Joseph:* Joseph failed to tell Bernice he's equipped with various armaments, worried she might get trigger-happy. He also carries military-spec detection gear. He triggers an alarm if someone comes within 10 paces of Benny's room.

Joseph can access GalNet's pricing database, plus emit a Galactic Positioning Beacon.

• *Lady Ashantra du Lac:* Ashantra bribed guilds of historians on several planets to abide by her myth about the reincarnated kings. She's a bit off her rocker, wanting to purge the Goronos System's deviance and sedition by setting up dissident camps.

• *Mr. Sloathe:* Criminal contractor based at the Collection. He's got a new wife, some kids from a previous marriage and a mother in a stasis tent.

PLACES TO GO *The Braxiatel Collection:* Braxiatel tolerates a certain seedy element at the Collection, figuring any crackdown would only boil the criminal population down to truly hardcore levels.

• *The Goronos System:* Possesses an impressive merchant fleet.

ORGANIZATIONS *Royal Houses of the Goronos System:* They're been tinkering with their genetics, as each house hopes to produce twins and thereby fulfill the false prophecy. As a result, too many of the houses' offspring are nitwits.

HISTORY A creation myth features the god Raghi Ano killing the all-seeing celestial father god Watho, then tying his entrails around a stick to make the galaxy's mystic spirals.

• The Goronos System was colonized during the first Terran expansion. Contact was lost for a time during the Earthline Collapse. Goronos developed its own social structure and mythologies during the interim, resuming diplomatic relations with the galaxy some 300 years later.

AT THE END OF THE DAY Rather than shuffling Benny's newborn off to the sidelines, "The Green-Eyed Monsters" tackles the problem head on, bringing about a needed confrontation between Jason Kane and Adrian. It's fair to say that to some degree, "Monsters" isn't *much* different from your standard baby sitcoms—only this time set in space—but it's a lot of fun regardless.

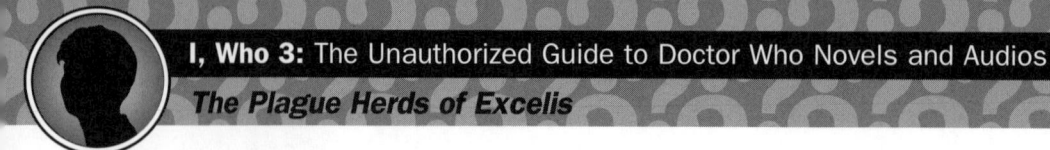

THE PLAGUE HERDS OF EXCELIS

By Stephen Cole

Release Date: *July 2002*
Order: *Big Finish "Excelis Series" CD Part 4*

MAIN CHARACTERS Bernice Summerfield, with Iris Wildthyme.

TRAVEL LOG City of Excelis (notably the "Plain of Justice," a.k.a. the "Trial Plateau of Excelis"), planet Artaris, 2600.

STORY SUMMARY At the Braxiatel Collection, Benny gets fed up with her male friends' bickering ("Green Eyed Monsters"), nicks Braxiatel's personal shuttle and races off-world—hoping to find an alien bar and have a proper sulk. But once in space, Benny stumbles upon an alien battle fleet, forcing her to choose discretion and divert to the post-apocalyptic world of Artaris.

Benny sets down near Excelis City—now a feudal society ruled by the Empress Vitutia—then encounters the cosmic adventurer/reprobate named Iris Wildthyme. Boisterous as ever, Iris takes a liking to Benny, suggesting they steal a much-vaunted artifact named "the Relic" from Vitutia's care. Mostly to alleviate boredom, Benny agrees.

In Excelis, a false prophet named Snyper turns public opinion against Vitutia and dethrones her, insidiously seizing control of the Relic. Benny and Iris confront Snyper, forcing the villain to shed his human guise and stand revealed as an insectoid creature—the sole surviving member of his race. Snyper explains that the war queen who murdered his people will soon pass Artaris in her spaceship, further announcing his intent to fulfill a long-running conspiracy (*see Sidebar*) and turn the Relic into the lit fuse for a massive bomb. If successful, Snyper will annihilate the war queen (and Artaris) in a fit of revenge.

Snyper quickly uses the Relic's life-endowing powers to animate a plague-infested herd of animal corpses, then sends the rampaging horde to kill off the Excelis inhabitants. As the slaughter

continues, Snyper gloats that when the last person in Excelis dies, the Relic will trigger an explosion that will rip the planet asunder.

In desperation, Iris and Benny snatch the Relic and hoof it. Snyper hotly pursues, causing Benny to fling the Relic into the slaughtering zombie herd. Snyper wades into the melee to retrieve the Relic, but—as Benny guessed—the anti-toxin that protected Snyper's human body against the plague fails to protect his alien form. Surrounded by plague-infested zombie cows, horses and more, Snyper dies in agony.

Without Snyper's intelligence, the zombie horde collapses into a heap of festering corpses. Benny and Iris breathe a sigh of relief, even as the Relic goes dormant and becomes an ordinary gold lamé handbag. As Empress Vitutia begins the long process of rebuilding Excelis society, Iris and Benny depart to find a good party and drink up.

MEMORABLE MOMENTS In a landmark among spin-off "Doctor Who" characters, Benny and Iris get schnookered in an Excelis bar.

Iris, on why she wants the handbag-shaped Relic: "I'm attending a very special and important soiree. I have to coordinate."

In a slight departure from the typical use of a TARDIS, Iris barrels her bus through an assembled crowd to save Bernice.

SEX AND SPIRITS Shortly after their first meeting, Benny and Iris head into Excelis to get sloppy drunk. Iris claims the barman has a crush on her, since he doles out very generous measures. Iris and Benny drink Old Maudlin, then switch to spirits. Benny also has brandy; Iris, a snowball. For a finale, the two of them toast and spill *advocat* on Benny.

At story's end, Empress Vitutia and her lover Aragon—and indeed, the whole of Excelis—have to screw like bunnies to repopulate the planet.

Iris frivolously claims about the Doctor, as usual: "Know him? I've had him! He's me fancy man. One day, the silly romantic will propose..."

ASS-WHUPPINGS Snyper directed barbarian hordes to besiege Excelis with plague-infested animals, then killed the barbarians as part of his extermination plan. Afterward, Snyper replaced them with automated catapults chucking plague-riddled animal corpses over the Excelis walls.

Snyper's genetically tailored plague has, off-panel, wiped out every settlement save Excelis on the planet. Snyper's zombie hoards—composed of dead pigs, horses, cattle and the like—kill off a fair amount of Excelis residents also, although enough

UNEARTHING THE RELIC

A virtual Pandora's Box, the Relic causes incalculable trouble throughout the "Excelis" series. That said, we're almost—but not quite—given a proper explanation for the damn thing. The individual "Excelis" CDs, it must be said, hold a lot of merit. Yet, any attempt to reconcile their views on the Relic creates a tapestry with a *lot* of holes. As such, the following sidebar represents a some-what-cohesive picture, gleaned from the (some-times sketchy) evidence provided.

The Relic's abilities

In layman's terms, the Relic holds power over people's souls. On Artaris, the soul of anyone who died automatically passed through the Relic's internal dimension. In addition, anyone who possessed the Relic could forcibly rip the souls from the living (hence, Greyvorn's Meat Puppet experiments, "Excelis Decays").

Additionally, the Relic could grant immortality (notably Greyvorn) and reanimate the dead (the zombie tribe, "Excelis Dawns"; the plague herd, "The Plague Herds of Excelis"). It also fused Greyvorn's consciousness with the Mother Superior's soul almost at random, although what happened to her *body*—or Greyvorn's physical form in "Excelis Rising," for that matter—goes unsaid.

The Relic's origins

In "Exclis Decays," the seventh Doctor cites the Relic as a "pan-dimensional artifact, created by far-away beings." Possibly, the race intended the Relic as a dimensional repository for its dead, since the internal dimension within the Relic seems closer to Heaven than Hell. Some confusion enters in once you reconcile this against "Plague Herds," because the Doctor implies that the Relic was made for a more noble purpose and he's unaware of its role as an assassination device.

The Relic's movements

More definitively, "Plague Herds" author Steve Cole says that Snyper's race built the Relic specifically to further a conspiracy against a space-faring, genocidal war queen——i.e. they didn't steal it from anyone. As the war queen's sensor scans would have detected conventional technology, Snyper's people turned to a device fueled by life energy.

As "The Plague Herds of Excelis" details, the war queen finally renounced her militaristic ways and petitioned for peace. When a long-standing mediator (likely the Doctor) proved unavailable, the queen asked Gallifreyan Iris Wildthyme—one of her most trusted friends—for help negotiating a truce.

But whatever the queen's change of heart, some of her enemies worked toward her downfall. A small group of conspirators nabbed the Relic,

then devised a means of turning it into a mega-bomb (*see below*), capable of atomizing the queen's fleet. Reasonably time-active, the conspirators knew the precise day that queen's warfleet would travel through the Artaris System. As such, they planned to meddle with history and retroactively annihilate the queen—thus sealing Excelis' fate.

When ready, the conspirators got Iris drunk and brainwashed her—finding it deliciously ironic that one of the queen's friends would seed her destruction—forcing her to take the Relic to Artaris. They also reshaped the Relic into a little gold lame French handbag, purely so the spacey Iris would find it familiar.

Unfortunately, the conspirators' plan was less-than-perfect. Iris deposited the Relic on Artaris, then left in her TARDIS. The Relic went missing, in time furthering the creation of a zombie village with its life-granting powers.

"The Excelis Trilogy"

Thousands of years elapsed. Iris subconsciously maintained an empathic link with the Relic and felt drawn to it, "randomly" turning up in "Excelis Dawns." (Then again, her explanation of "I was wildly drunk and found myself in a nunnery..." is also plausible.) Iris helped the Doctor and Greyvorn retrieve the Relic from the Zombie village, but they unknowingly had one of the alien conspirators along for the ride.

The insectoid alien was disguised as Sister Jolene, an Excelis nun, who supposedly accompanied the fifth Doctor's group on the Mother Superior's behalf. The Doctor's group retrieved the Relic, but Jolene was left behind in the zombie camp. She killed the Zombie King, then somehow learned how to duplicate the Relic's ability to reanimate matter.

Over the next 1,300 years ("Excelis Rising," "Excelis Decays"), the Relic's influence devastated Artaris. It's unclear how Jolene spent this period, or why she never tried to snitch the Relic from the Excelis Museum ("Excelis Rising").

Regardless, Greyvorn kick-started the Relic by infusing it with so many souls for his Meat Puppet program, and it became truly primed after Artaris' nuclear annihilation ("Excelis Decays").

Even so, in "The Plague Herds of Excelis," Jolene shows up and assumes the form of Snyper, a false prophet in the post-apocalyptic Excelis. Snyper seized the Relic and, as planned, tried to detonate it and atomize the queen's warfleet.

The arcane physics here get a bit snarled. "Plague Herds" states that the Relic was a bomb and the people of Artaris its fuse—although more

CONTINUED ON PAGE 225
CONTINUED ON PAGE 225

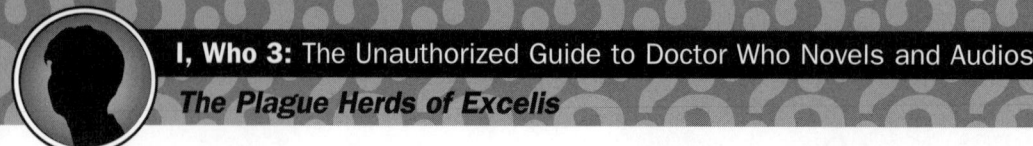

survive to guarantee repopulation.

Snyper blows up Benny's shuttle and briefly sabotages Iris' bus.

NOVEL TIE-INS Benny worries that Fifth Axis forces (last seen in *The Glass Prison*) might still be active.

AUDIO TIE INS Benny hasn't slept for six nights straight, and here departs the Braxiatel Collection to escape Jason Kane and Adrian Wall's bickering ("The Green Eyed Monsters").

In "Excelis Dawns," an Excelis nun named Sister Jolene—one of Snyper's guises—accompanied the fifth Doctor, Iris and Greyvorn in their quest to retrieve the Relic (*see sidebar*). "Jolene" was left behind in a zombie village, thereby learning the zombies' Relic-given talent for raising the dead by thought.

The Relic's supposedly immobile when placed in its central pedestal in the convent, but Iris alone, because of her previous link with the artifact, can remove it. As with "Excelis Dawns," Iris turns up because she's drawn to the Relic, having brought it to Artaris in the first place (*see sidebar again*).

Vitutia's Imperial Palace is built on the remains of the Excelis nunnery ("Excelis Dawns"). Empress Vitutia claims that Artaris once boasted a space-faring civilization, helping to explain the out-of-the-blue planetary defense grid that butchered the planet in "Excelis Decays."

Benny here learns that, as she speculated ("The Extinction Event"), Braxiatel's shuttle contains a jacuzzi behind a hidden door.

CHARACTER DEVELOPMENT

• *Bernice Summerfield:* She hasn't visited Artaris before. She's never heard of the Relic.

• *Iris Wildthyme:* Iris brandishes a cigarette lighter shaped like a gun. She carries skeleton keys that unlock manacles. She smokes slim Panatella cigarettes.

• *Snyper (a.k.a. Sister Jolene):* He's got an excellent grasp of engineering and chemistry. Snyper developed a means of inoculating his alien aspect against the plague, plus made his human form fireproof. Snyper knew how to activate the autosystem shutdown on Iris' TARDIS, but couldn't destroy the Ship.

• *Iris' TARDIS:* Its exterior looks like a 1973 Vintage Routemaster made in Camberwell. It can become invisible (either a cloaking device or an extension of the Ship's chameleon circuit). The Ship isn't dimensionally transcendental because it lacks a proper dimensional stabilizer.

THE CRUCIAL BITS...

• **THE PLAGUE HERDS OF EXCELIS**—First meeting between Bernice and Iris Wildthyme. The Relic becomes a normal gold lame handbag.

• *The Alien War Queen:* She's continually mobile for fear of easy reprisals. As the queen's spaceship approaches a star system, it projects an image of a large warfleet onto the sun as a warning. Moreover, the queen possesses a scanner that projects "black lightning" which searches for advanced technology (the Relic was pre-programmed to direct this lightning elsewhere, avoiding detection). The queen avoids any star system beyond a certain level of development, deeming it a potential threat.

She enjoys a near-infinite lifespan. Now reformed (*see History*), the war queen throws great parties.

ALIEN RACES *Artarans:* Bernice labels Artarans as "human," although given this story's date of 2600 and the duration of Artaris society, the people didn't originate from Earth.

• *Zombie Animals:* The plague they carry [engineered by Snyper] is so virulent, it kills on contact.

PLACES TO GO *Excelis:* The city is now heavily fortified, with the people wary of outsiders.

A people's senate now runs Excelis, electing an Emperor/Empress to one-year terms on the Plain of Justice (a.k.a. the Trial Plateau of Excelis).

SHIPS *Braxiatel's Shuttle:* Its features include a movie library and a collection of rare Dilonian war paintings that move in time with the shuttle's movement. The shuttle can go into "stealth mode," a feature unique to Braxiatel's ship rather than all Collection shuttles. "Stealth mode" makes the ship invisible, but it still makes a ruckus upon landing.

HISTORY Eons ago, an unnamed war queen and her warrior-like people upset half the galaxy and started numerous wars. She eventually repented [either due to a religious conversion or hormone therapy] and sued for peace, but her enemies didn't forgive easily. Finally, she called for the Doctor to arbitrate, although Iris claims he couldn't make it due to an ear infection [an unlikely story, but he nonetheless failed to show]. The war queen summoned Iris to arbitrate instead, but a conspiracy against the war queen's life led to the arrival of Iris and the Relic on Artaris (*see sidebar*).

• In wake of the nuclear holocaust that butchered Artaris ("Excelis Decays"), the people

largely abandoned their mountain societies and formed isolated ground settlements. Generations of technological advances, including electricity, were lost. Details regarding the catastrophe are were forgotten, but the people, laying blame for Artaris' devastation on a previous regime, no longer follow their leaders blindly.

• Artaran superstitions now say that whomever possesses the Relic can storm the gates of Heaven or Hell.

• Empress Vitutia is starting her eighth year of rule in Excelis.

AT THE END OF THE DAY An inspired idea to meld Benny into the "Who" universe, winding up two of the strongest "Who" females—Benny and Iris—then letting 'em go. "Plague Herds" admittedly sports some crap science, although the story's overall verve helps considerably. In short, one of the more interesting Benny audios, and proof of just how far off-screen "Doctor Who" has developed.

DID YOU KNOW?

• Cole originally pitched this story as the McCoy installment of the "Excelis" trilogy, but got asked to rework it for Bernice and Iris. It was originally titled "Plague Harridans of Artaris," then "Devil Herds of Excelis" in an e-mail header, but the tongue-in-cheek title survived [unlike most of Artaris].

DALEK EMPIRE MINI-SERIES

By Nicholas Briggs

Individual CD titles: 1. Invasion of the Daleks
2. The Human Factor
3. "Death to the Daleks!"
4. Project: Infinity

Release Date: June 2001 (Part 1), August 2001 (Part 2), November 2001 (Part 3); January 2002 (Part 4)
Order: Big Finish "Dalek Empire" Audio Mini-Series

MAIN CHARACTERS The Daleks, geologist Susan Mendes, security agent Alby Brook, honorable knight of Velyshaa Kalendorf, interplanetary police officer Mirana, head of security Ernst Tanlee, "Project: Infinity" Director Espeelius, jour-

MISCELLANEOUS STUFF!

RELIC CONTINUED FROM PAGE 223

properly, the Relic's the fuse for a larger bomb hidden in the planet. People's souls would pass through the Relic like grains of sand falling through an hourglass, and when every last soul on Artaris passed through the Relic, it would detonate the planet bomb. For this reason, the Relic needed to be placed in an allotted slot within the ex-Excelis convent at a specific time.

Snyper therefore set about killing off everyone on Artaris, claiming that when the last person expired and their soul passed through the Relic, it [or rather the true bomb] would detonate. Either way, Benny and Iris—who turned up again, drawn to the Relic—thwarted the plot.

Upon failing to go off, the Relic somehow defused and became an ordinary handbag. Again, it's uncertain why this happens. And for that matter, the *handbag*'s fate isn't specified. Possibly, Iris takes it with her, but for all we know, it's still lying where we last saw it—in a patch of dead animals ("Plague Herds" again).

P.S. The Doctor oddly claims ("Excelis Decays") that the Relic's creators settled on Artaris after it was stolen, trying to reclaim their lost property. It's possible he's referring obliquely to Snyper, who remained on Artaris to regain his lost property. At best, the Doctor's words in "Decays" simply don't mesh with the rest of the "Excelis" storyline, and at worst, it's completely inconsequential.

nalist Pellan, the psionic Seer of Yaldos, alternate reality Daleks.

TRAVEL LOG *Part 1:* Planet Vega VI; the spaceship *Aquitania*, passing the LegaRshu Nebula, time unknown but obviously the future.

Part 2: Garazone space station and planet Guria, plus Garazone moon K-5000, six months later.

Part 3: Planets Celatron, Carson's Planet and Yaldos, plus the Orealis deep space array, three years later.

Part 4: Planets Yaldos and Lopra Minor, a few months later.

CHRONOLOGY Centuries after the Dalek raid on the Kar-Charrat library in "The Genocide Machine," time unknown. Alby works for the Space Security Service, which was definitely in operation by the year 4000 ("The Daleks' Master Plan").

STORY SUMMARY *Part 1 (Invasion of the Daleks):* In the far future, a group of like-minded planets band together and form the Earth Alliance, supposedly heralding an age of peace. On Vega VI, geologist Susan Mendes enjoys a leisurely picnic—and a warm friendship—with water-taxi driver Alby Brook, unaware of his true identity as an undercover Space Security Service agent. Alby holds orders to locate Kalendorf, a member of the honorable Knights of Velyshaa, to further an Earth/ Velyshaa coalition against the Daleks. But despite his mission, Alby finds himself enjoying Suz's company.

Suddenly, Daleks based in the Seriphia Galaxy mobilize for war and charge into the Vega System. Alby implores Suz to flee with him, but Suz, failing to grasp the Daleks' threat, storms off to locate her parents. Hating himself, Alby flees Vega aboard the star cruiser *Aquitania*. The Daleks capture the Vega System, rounding up thousands of captives—including Suz and Kalendorf—to mine a rare mineral called veganite.

Meanwhile, the Emperor Dalek orders his subordinates to watch the slave workers for signs of defiance, hoping to dissect "the Human Factor," the indomitable quality that lets humanity triumph against overwhelming odds, and turn it to the Daleks' advantage. Back in the mines, Suz befriends Kalendorf, then lashes out at the Daleks for working their slaves to death. The Dalek Supreme, as the Emperor's second-in-command, notes Suz's behavior and communicates with her via hyperlink. To Suz's surprise, the Dalek Supreme agrees to provide the slaves with rest periods and food, hoping to increase mining efficiency. More to the point, the Dalek Supreme concedes the slaves must receive some shred of hope if they're to survive and make quota.

Accordingly, the Dalek Supreme conscripts Suz as a motivational speaker. Treading a fine line between saving lives and collaborating with the enemy, Suz implores the Vega slaves to work for food and rest—arguing that a drop of hope is better than starving to death. The Vega slaves comply, renewing their efforts for survival's sake. Immensely pleased, the Daleks continue their military advance, scheduling Suz to similarly brace up efficiency in the conquered Garazone System.

Elsewhere, Alby's superiors provide him with a new scout ship, re-assigning him to covert duty in the Lopra System. Instead, Alby comes to realize his romantic feelings for Suz, dashing back to Vega VI in the vague hope of rescuing her. Alby briefly hooks up with a Vega News ship coordinating the resistance, but the Daleks assault the vessel. With little choice, Alby and journalist Gordon Pellan escape aboard Alby's scout ship, racing away from the plundered Vega System.

Pellan mentioned that he tapped Dalek transmissions, hearing mention of the Daleks dispatching one "Susan Mendes" to the Garazone System. Confused as to why the Daleks regard Suz so highly, Alby persuades Pellan to help him locate her on Garazone.

Part 2 (The Human Factor): Six months later, the Daleks rout Earth forces, dominating a number of Alliance worlds. As part of the advance, the Daleks send Suz—known throughout Dalek space as "The Angel of Mercy"—to give slaves on multiple planets a spark of hope. Suz dutifully complies, with Kalendorf serving as her aide.

Together, Suz and Kalendorf concoct a desperate plan to seed rebellion. On each planet, Suz convinces Dalek slaves to work harder for the foreseeable future. Simultaneously, the telepathic Kalendorf tells the slave leaders to keep watch for a particular code phrase: "Death to the Daleks!" Kalendorf and Suz intend to prime slave leaders on several worlds, then spread the code phrase and overthrow the Daleks *en masse*.

Meanwhile, Alby and Pellan awaken, after six months of hypersleep, in the Garazone System. Pellan decodes Dalek transmissions, tracking Suz to the nearby planet Guria. The duo plays cat-and-mouse with some Daleks, eventually crashing their scout ship into a Gurian sea.

With the Daleks drilling for oil on Guria, Alliance forces launch a major offensive. Suz and Kalendorf briefly spy the battle, then get sent back to Dalek-held space. Worse, Dalek reinforcements somehow slip past the Guria detection net and secure the planet. Alby and Pellan haphazardly flee in an abandoned Dalek saucer, but the Earth Alliance cruiser Horatio tractors them aboard. Cautiously, Alby and Pellan emerge with their hands held high in surrender—shocked as the Earth soldiers take aim and open fire anyway.

Part 3 ("Death to the Daleks!"): To Alby's horror, Alliance soldiers under the command of his superior officer, Tanlee, gun down Pellan. Tanlee explains that the Daleks actually captured Pellan aboard the *Aquitania* and installed a mind-control chip in his brain. Unknowingly, Pellan performed acts of sabotage on Guria, helping to insure the Daleks' victory.

Moreover, Alliance officials believe Pellan stuck close to Alby to learn more about his relationship with Suz Mendes. Alby recalls Pellan mentioning—in passing—something called "Project: Infinity." The late Pellan speculated that Suz might

know something about the classified project as her employers, the Reinsberg Corporation, helped develop it for Earth Alliance. Pellan supposedly knew little about Project: Infinity, but Tanlee blanches at the mere mention of the name. Tanlee provides Alby with a top-of-the-line ship, ordering him to track down Suz and learn what, if anything, she knows about the project. Furthermore, Tanlee orders Alby to kill Suz if she betrayed the undertaking to the Daleks.

In the years to follow, Alby resorts to illegal methods of cracking Dalek jamming signals, compelling interplanetary police officer Mirana to hound him. Meanwhile, the Daleks further pound Alliance forces, capturing Earth. Amid the victory, the Emperor Dalek quietly loads a command ship with vast supplies of veganite mineral, then departs for the Lopra System—the location of Project: Infinity—expecting planetfall in one year.

On the planet Yaldos, Kalendorf presses Suz for action, determined to incite their long-planned rebellion. Kalendorf volunteers to shout out the code phrase, even at the cost of his life, during an upcoming broadcast to declare Dalek supremacy over the galaxy. But Suz, as the scheduled speaker, takes responsibility for her actions and decides to give the code phrase herself, knowing the Daleks will immediately kill her.

Alby briefly stops on the neutral Carson's Planet, but Mirana—still unaware of his status as a security agent—shows up to arrest him. Almost helpfully, some Daleks arrive, forcing Mirana to flee with Alby in his spaceship. Acting on information from Tanlee, Alby sets course for Yaldos to intercept Suz.

Soon after, the broadcast begins and Suz screams out the code phrase, "Death to the Daleks!" Instantly, billions of slaves rise up against their Dalek oppressors, throwing hundreds of planets into mayhem. Soon after, Alby and Mirana touch down on a liberated Yaldos. But once there, Kalendorf mournfully informs Alby that Suz, the Angel of Mercy, is dead.

Part 4 (Project: Infinity): Alby feels his inner world collapse, learning that the Daleks shot Suz at point-blank range. Humanity spends three months liberating Dalek-conquered planets, forcing the Daleks to withdraw to a few strongholds that include Earth and the Seriphia Galaxy. Alby's stunned when a psychic transmission, apparently sent by Suz, directs him to coordinates in a Yaldos mountain range. Alby, Kalendorf and Mirana arrive at the rendezvous, thereby meeting an elderly woman named "The Seer of Yaldos."

The trio learns that before Suz's fateful broadcast, she visited the Seer, reputed to hold psionic powers, and forged a telepathic link with her. Suz asked the Seer to monitor her thoughts, hoping to convey information about the Daleks' plans after death. The Seer narrates Suz's final meeting with the Daleks, revealing that they targeted the capture of Project: Infinity above all else. Alby takes heart to realize that Suz's body was never found, suggesting she somehow survived the melee. However, Kalendorf realizes the entire Dalek invasion was a red herring. The Daleks simply wanted to keep the Alliance worlds under siege, even as the Emperor's crew quietly went around the galaxy to reach Project: Infinity in the distant Lopra System.

Suddenly, Mirana pulls her gun, revealing herself as a mind-controlled Dalek agent directly linked to the Emperor's mind. In response, Kalendorf and the Seer combine their telepathic talent to short out Mirana's Dalek control chip. Mirana falls into a coma but awakens five months later aboard the Alliance battle cruiser *Courageous*, under Kalendorf's command, enroute to Lopra.

As events race toward a conclusion, Tanlee arrives separately on Lopra Minor to personally oversee final phases of Project: Infinity. The Emperor Dalek sends out a raiding party to capture the project's research team, but the *Courageous* finally shows up and wipes out the Dalek patrol.

With the Emperor Dalek's dreadnought due to arrive in 45 minutes, Kalendorf implores Tanlee to deploy Project: Infinity—whatever it is—against the Daleks. Unfortunately, Tanlee reveals Project: Infinity is not a weapon, but rather a means of scanning/viewing an infinite number of parallel realities. In short, Project: Infinity was designed to locate a reality where humanity had defeated the Daleks for all time, thereby allowing the Alliance to view and duplicate said success in our reality.

Kalendorf advocates destroying Project: Infinity, rather than letting it fall into the Daleks' plungers. But Mirana suddenly realizes, via the remnants of her Dalek control chip, that Tanlee is already the Daleks' slave. Tanlee holds Kalendorf, Mirana and Alby at gunpoint, even as several Daleks transmat onto Lopra. The captives learn the Emperor Dalek intends to use "Project: Infinity" to find a reality where the Daleks conquered all of known space. Even worse, the Daleks hope to open a gateway into said universe, using their vast stocks of veganite mineral as a power source, thereby bringing the alternate-reality Daleks into our reality.

Tanlee takes Kalendorf, Mirana and Alby back to the Emperor Dalek's command ship, showing

them millions of humans frozen in the hold. Kalendorf's trio realizes that the Daleks plan to put them into cryosleep, then mutate them, along with the sleeping prisoners, into Daleks. As a final jest, Tanlee suggests to Alby that Suz Mendes is somewhere in the hold, undergoing Dalek conversion. Alby screams to know more, even as Tanlee and the Daleks order their prisoners into cryosleep.

The Emperor Dalek transmats to Lopra and directly links the main Infinity Scan device to his cerebral processor, locating a reality where the Daleks have total control. Dalek engineers activate the dimensional gateway, contacting their alternate brethren with a beacon. The parallel Daleks come through the portal and greet the Emperor Dalek, who humbly asks for the alternate Daleks' help in gaining power in our universe.

In response, the parallel reality Daleks access the Emperor's command network, witnessing how "our" Daleks have waged unspeakable war and atrocities. The Emperor acknowledges the Daleks' "achievements," but the alternate reality Daleks—born to a different belief system—deem such violent, hostile acts as "the greatest crimes" imaginable. The parallel Daleks immediately throw down the gauntlet, opening fire on the Emperor's Daleks and instigating war between Dalek forces of two different realities.

MEMORABLE MOMENTS *Part 1:* Suz turns away from Alby during the Vega VI because, like many innocents of war, she can't accept the Daleks' atrocities as real.

Suz's first exhausted, but brave, act of defiance to a guard Dalek strikes a chord: "That's what you do, isn't it? Kill, kill, kill. That's all I've seen you do since you got here. Alby said you'd wipe us out... well, go ahead and do it. Just get on with it."

Conversely, Suz's first controversial, halting speech to the slaves delivers a certain passion and lust for any hope of life.

Part 2: When a rebel band on a Garazone moon smashes a Dalek to pieces, it hoarsely croaks, with its dying breath: "You... will... be... exterminated." Kalendorf decries Suz's decision to betray slave leader Morebi and his men (*see Ass-Whuppings*) to the Daleks.

Part 3: Tanlee ominously suggests to Alby that if the Daleks find out about "Project: Infinity," he might as well kill himself.

Suz crazily decides that the Daleks trust her, even though Kalendorf more sensibly advises: "They *can't* trust, Suz." As Kalendorf points out, Suz doesn't have power over the Daleks—she just has power over the slaves.

A Dalek goads the defiant Kalendorf into admitting: "Yes, I believe that one day, we will be rid of you."

When Alby finally meets Kalendorf, there's a telling moment in which Kalendorf pauses before mentioning Suz's fate. In response, Alby starts crying before Kalendorf can explain, knowing that Suz is lost to him.

Part 4: Kalendorf concedes that Suz sacrificed herself because she couldn't stand the overwhelming guilt of collaborating with the Daleks, but that: "I wanted it to be me... I wanted her to live. I wanted to be the one who was remembered as the dead hero. And you know why? I couldn't bear the guilt either. I still can't."

Suz gets Alby to trust the Seer by leaving behind a jar of pickled onions, in reference to their last lunch together. Mind, this makes Alby sound like a raving lunatic by telling Kalendorf and Mirana that Suz somehow survived because: "These are her pickled onions! I know they are!"

Alby gives a last, lovely cry of "SUUUU-UZZZZZZZZZ..." just before the Daleks stuff our heroes into cryosleep.

SEX AND SPIRITS   Suz and Alby enjoy a packed lunch on Vega VI before all hell breaks loose. Oddly enough, they *don't* have a romantic relationship before the war, making the whole of "Dalek Empire I" something of a conceit to believe that two people who aren't even dating could spend *years* pining for one another across the galaxy. But to its credit, "Dalek Empire I" embraces this lie, convincing the listener that Suz and Alby belong together.

Alby's no stranger to drink, and usually gets hammered when he runs out on a woman. He gets schnookered on the *Aquitania*, and notes that "a woman... a woman is worth a whole bottle of *Southern Comfort*. Maybe two." To Alby's disappointment, the Vega News ship contains no liquor.

Alby spends much of Parts 1-3 questioning why he's risking life and limb to pursue Suz, then accepts that he's in love with her.

Meanwhile, Kalendorf and Suz briefly pretend to be lovers in the Dalek mine, purely to facilitate telepathic contact between them. Suz asks a Dalek, "You're still watching me?", making the Dalek reply with lyrics from *The Police*: "Every move you make." [Also a sneaky quote, Briggs says, from the trailer for the first Peter Cushing "Doctor Who" movie.]

The Gurian Highness senses that Alby very clearly loves Suz. Alby slugs journalist Pellan for suggesting that he's pursuing Suz because she stole something from him.

THE CRUCIAL BITS...

- **DALEK EMPIRE I (Pt. 1)**—Daleks based in the Seriphia Galaxy overrun Vega VI, instigating a new campaign against Earth Alliance worlds. The Daleks tap a defiant geologist named Susan Mendes to become "The Angel of Mercy," a motivational speaker to give the slaves hope and improve efficiency.

First appearance of Susan ("Suz") Mendes, undercover space security agent Alby Brook and the telepathic Kalendorf, a member of the Knights of Velyshaa.
- **DALEK EMPIRE I (Pt. 2)**—Major Dalek invasion of civilized worlds. Suz and Kalendorf convince slave leaders to "comply" with the Daleks, readying a massive revolt in future.
- **DALEK EMPIRE I (Pt. 3)**—The Daleks capture the Sol System. Suz gives the code-phrase, "Death to the Daleks!", thus sparking an enormous slave uprising, but apparently dies in the process. First appearance of interplanetary police officer Mirana.
- **DALEK EMPIRE I (Pt. 4)**—Liberation of many conquered planets. Kalendorf, Alby and Mirana race to stop the Emperor Dalek from obtaining "Project: Infinity," an undertaking to view a myriad of parallel realities. The Emperor Dalek triumphs, ordering the heroes into cyrosleep to undergo conversion into Daleks. Suggestion that Suz Mendes survived and is also becoming a Dalek.

The Emperor Dalek uses Project: Infinity to open a gateway into a parallel reality where the Daleks are the superior lifeforms. However, the alternate Daleks turn horrified at "our" Daleks' crimes, opening hostilities to wipe out the Emperor Daleks' forces.

Much later, Suz concedes—to the Dalek Supreme, at least—that she'd fallen in love with Alby. Kalendorf senses Suz's affection for Alby and volunteers to give the signal for rebellion himself, as Suz at least has something to live for.

Tanlee claims that before this story, Alby enjoyed an active libido, and was prone to "sordid rendezvous in a seedy nightclub." Mirana tried to arrest Alby in a bar on Quelador. In a harmless fashion, Alby claims that Mirana's gorgeous and irresistible. Alby drinks up on Carson's Planet.

He gets drunk after news of Suz's demise, then gets confirmation of her love from the Seer. He ends this story screaming out for Suz, who's presumably undergoing Dalek conversion.

ASS-WHUPPINGS *Part 1:* The Daleks open their newest campaign by wiping out the Rapid Response Fleet, Captain Julio Medem commanding, in the Vega System. As part of the initial skirmish, the Daleks take out the Earth Alliance battlecruiser *Victorious*, a Repulse-Class destroyer, making it crash onto the South side of Vega City. The resultant devastation kills a lot of Alby's friends.

For an encore, the Daleks bombard Vega VI's cities. Thousands lie dying in barren, radioactive plains. Suz's parents don't survive the subsequent Dalek occupation.

Suz and Kalendorf suffer as slaves on Vega VI. They get whipped for daring to laugh. Hundreds of slaves collapse, worked to death, until Suz negotiates better working conditions.

Dalek assault craft raid the *Aquitania*. Alby escapes and later eliminates five Dalek pursuit craft with his scout ship. The Daleks for a time spare the Vega News ship, identifying its rebel contacts to better wipe them out, then overrun the vessel.

Part 2: A turning point occurs on the Garazone moon K-5000, when a young slave worker named Morebi, outraged by the Daleks' murder of his parents, refuses to wait for Kalendorf's signal and prematurely incites his men to rebel. Suz and Kalendorf fail to defuse the situation, knowing full well that the capture of Morebi's men could endanger their whole plan.

"For the good of everyone," Suz encourages the Daleks to kill Morebi's slaves. She also scapegoats a slave leader named Wernay to cover her tracks. He dies in a hail of Dalek death rays, crying out, "Angel of Mercy!", as the Daleks further slaughter Morebi and his men. (Kalendorf strongly protests Suz's actions, *see Character Development*.)

On Guria, the Daleks kill the ruling Highness. A number of Gurian rebels surrender to save the Highness' daughter, but the Daleks mow them down. During the fracas, an Earth Alliance ship wings a Dalek base, knocking Alby unconscious for days. He loses his legs in the process, but human medics graft on new ones.

Part 3: Alby's boss Tanlee offs Pellan, a Dalek thrall beyond hope of rehabilitation. Casualties from the Dalek-Alliance conflict now number in the billions. The Daleks win 10 victories for every Alliance success.

Suz orders her technicians, members of the Celatron race, to remove Dalek listening devices from her office. However, the Daleks kill the technicians for Suz's act of defiance.

The Daleks wipe out Alliance bases in Jupiter and Saturn orbit, similarly leveling Mars colony and capturing Earth.

Part 4: Billions more die overwhelming Dalek oppressors on numerous worlds. Much of Yaldos City Square gets flattened. Kalendorf and Seer telepathically scramble Mirana's control chip, blasting the Dalek Emperor with a psionic resonance.

Kalendorf's troopers take out a Dalek patrol on Lopra Minor, including some Special Weapons Daleks. Hostage Project: Infinity director Espeelius dies, encouraging Kalendorf's men to fight on. At story's end, the alternate reality Daleks open fire on their brethren.

TV TIE-INS Alby works for the Space Security Service ("The Daleks' Master Plan").

"The Evil of the Daleks" introduced the notion of "the human factor"—the undefinable, sacrificial quality that lets humanity persevere and triumph over the Daleks.

Some Dalek replicants ("The Chase," "Resurrection of the Daleks") allegedly operate on Carson's Planet.

Daleks on Lopra Minor include a Special Weapons Daleks ("Remembrance of the Daleks"). Dalek guns in this era stun as well as kill ("The Daleks").

Mirana's parents hail from Galsec Colony ("The Sontaran Experiment").

AUDIO TIE-INS The Daleks learned about Project: Infinity from their raid on the Kar-Charrat library ("The Genocide Machine"). The Knights of Velyshaa, the warrior breed to which Kalendorf belongs, debuted in Briggs' "The Sirens of Time."

The Daleks base themselves in the Seriphia Galaxy, which got flash-burned, then populated as a Dalek stronghold in "The Apocalypse Element."

A space habitat named Garazone Central, presumably in the Garazone System, previously appeared in Briggs' "Sword of Orion." Mirana was born on a freighter passing through Orion's Belt (ditto).

Kalendorf, Alby, Suz and Mirana find themselves embroiled in further Dalek mayhem in Big Finish's "Dalek Empire II" mini-series.

TIE-INS Mind-controlled Dalek agents such as Pellan (a more deceptive form of Robomen, "The Dalek Invasion of Earth") previously appeared in "Remembrance of the Daleks" and "The Mutant Phase." Alliance technicians can't reverse the process, explaining why Tanlee has Pellan killed.

CHARACTER DEVELOPMENT

• *Susan Mendes (a.k.a. "The Angel of Mercy"):* Suz works for the Reinsberg Institute as a geologist, researching mineral samples on Vega VI. She finds some of her work mundane. Suz can't decide

if her initial defiance of the Daleks stemmed from bravery or fear. She occasionally wishes the Daleks had killed her, but ultimately doesn't want to die. She fears that she seized on her role as "The Angel of Mercy" with too much vigor, even though it saved the lives of thousands of slaves. She sometimes doubts if humanity can ever defeat the Daleks.

She slightly recalls the Daleks from her childhood history lessons. She long ago heard of the Seers of Yaldos. She's never heard of the Seriphia Galaxy. Suz considers Earth a bit of a mess, and isn't eager to visit.

On Vega VI, Suz tells Alby that her grandmother sends pickled onions from Earth. In Part 4, as a means of making Alby believe the Seer's words, Suz leaves a jar of pickled onions for him to find. [Author's Note: Which is extremely odd, suggesting that Suz has somehow, during her time as a Dalek slave, and through the years of the Dalek campaign, carried a jar of her grandmother's pickled onions about from planet to planet.]

• *Alby Brook:* Alby hails from a broken home, growing up in a slum on Proxima Major. He didn't get the best education, and earned a juvenile criminal record. He became a corporal in the Army, but earned two years' penal servitude for petty pilfering. Earth officials suspended his sentence on the condition that he went to work for the Space Security Service.

Alby's a "B-Grade" security operative. He spent six months working undercover on Vega VI, living on the South end of Vega City.

He's well-informed about the Daleks. He's never been to Earth. He's under observation by the Space Security Service, who watch their own members.

He initially flew an X-49 scoutship, complete with a robotic Drudger pilot (*see Ships*), but later acquires an advanced prototype ship from Tanlee.

Alby's an exceptional pilot. He can fly Dalek ships, but cannot use other Dalek technology. His pocket computer contained information on Dalek methodology, but he left it behind on Vega VI.

His replacement legs (*see Ass-Whuppings*) are functional but not top-of-the-line. He never liked Tanlee much.

• *Kalendorf:* A key emissary for the Knights of Velyshaa (*see Organizations*). Kalendorf initially wants to die when the Daleks overrun Vega VI, but his survival instinct eventually kicks in. He knows a wealth of information about the Daleks.

Kalendorf's telepathy requires physical contact to function. He's not human (i.e. directly of Earth descent), but he's "humanoid."

He can't identify pickled onions. He's trained since birth for combat. He appreciates the elegance of Dalek saucer design.

• *Suz and Kalendorf:* At various points, Kalendorf accuses Suz of playing along with the Daleks too much. Kalendorf especially worries because Suz is far more naïve about the Daleks, nutty enough to believe (especially Part 3) at times that she holds some sort of rapport with the monsters. His words sting because Suz knows, to some degree, that he's correct.

Suz senses Kalendorf's resentment through their telepathic contact. They disagree about Suz betraying Morebi's rebels (Part 2, *see Ass-Whuppings*) to protect their overall gameplan. But whatever their disagreements, Suz protects Kalendorf in Part 3—sacrificing herself in his stead. Kalendorf doesn't like it when Suz calls him "Karl."

• *Mirana:* Formally designated "Officer 274" of Earth Interplanetary Police. Mirana dogged Alby through four star systems, unaware of his status as a security agent (suggesting Earth government's right hand often doesn't know what its left is doing).

Mirana arrested Alby for illegal trade in Earth Alliance government property, namely a hyperlink decoder acquired on Orealis III, but let him go for lack of evidence.

The Dalek chip in Mirana's brain kept her directly linked to the Emperor Dalek for years. She only has fuzzy memories of her activities as a Dalek agent. After Kalendorf and the Seer neutralized Mirana's chip, it allowed her to eavesdrop on Dalek transmissions and pinpoint Dalek positions. Alliance technicians can't remove the chip without killing her.

• *Tanlee:* Tanlee initially reported to Admiral Ellisonford. Madame President handed Tanlee command of all remaining Alliance forces just before Earth's fall.

• *Tanlee and Alby:* Tanlee wrote Alby's security file, indicating that he works best under extreme pressure. Tanlee made the veiled threat in Part 3 that he could've shot Alby for desertion.

ALIEN RACES *Daleks:* The Daleks recognize the tactical advantages of "the human factor," even if they don't understand it. They realize that whatever their military might, the human factor's complexity of thought and emotional instinct often defeats them.

The Dalek Supreme outranks the red-colored Supreme Controllers.

Daleks in this time zone zip about on personal "trans-solar" disc attack vessels, plus use trans-

mat devices ("Remembrance of the Daleks"). The Dalek command network comprehends both high-definition holographic transmissions and low-band frequencies.

Daleks normally work their slaves to death, then send for replacements. Suz convinces the Daleks to feed their slaves a dried nutrient concentrate, plus adopt a rotating shift schedule.

ALIEN PLANETS *Earth:* Earth holds an extradition treaty with Orealis. Southhampton [once an ocean terminus] is an Earth spaceport.

• *Vega VI:* Vega VI houses a thriving civilization, with a fresh climate under a bright sun named Vega Prime. The water and marsh lakes sparkle blue. Vega City's a main metropolitan area. Vega VI is located as much as six months from Garazone, depending on how fast you travel.

The Daleks set up Robo-tizing plants on Vega VI, mentally enslaving some of the populace.

• *Garazone:* Has more than one moon.

• *Guria:* Guria had 50 drilling platforms before the Daleks invaded, and served as one of the Alliance's biggest fossil fuel suppliers. Dangerous gales impede Dalek operations on Guria, dropping efficiency by 30 percent.

Guria has a monarchical system of government. The ruling Highness played the part of a buffoon, just to annoy the Daleks. His more sensible daughter ascended to the throne.

Guria's located on the edge of the Dalek advance. Earth Alliance lacks reinforcements within 10 light years of the planet.

• *K-5000:* Garazone moon with an artificial atmosphere bubble. Ships frequently land there using an orbital navigation signal.

• *Lopra Minor:* Project: Infinity location, and third planet of the Lopra System. It's located on the opposite side of the galaxy as Vega.

• *Carson's Planet:* Frontier world, mostly inhabited by thieves and murderers. The Daleks overran Carson's Planet, then left it for more profitable gains. The planet now operates under neutrality (mostly because the Daleks don't want it), although the Alliance and the Daleks both keep spies there.

Carson's Planet is two days away from Yaldos under an Earth ship's maximum speed.

• *Celatron:* Located deep in Dalek-captured territory, home to the galaxy's greatest technocrats.

PLACES TO GO *The Garazone System:* It falls under Dalek control for the better part of a year. Dalek mines and construction bays there work at 110 percent efficiency.

• *Orealis Relay Platform:* Space platform that relays signals classified Earth Alliance transmissions. The insectoid Stralos, a hive leader, runs the station.

A high intensity molecular disrupter field protects the station. It's possible for intruders to transmat through the defense screen. Dalek interference is considerable in the platform's sector, but they've left it alone so far.

STUFF YOU NEED *"Project: Infinity":* Requires vast supplies of veganite to function, explaining why the Daleks raided Vega VI, and started mining operations there, so early in their newest campaign.

It's suggested that the main Infinity Scan device took damage during the shootout for Lopra Minor. Hence, the device failed to scan as much of infinity [don't laugh] as the Daleks might have liked, resulting in their locating a universe with benevolent Daleks.

• *Drudger Robots:* Servo-robots used by Earth Alliance. Some are programmed for semi-independent thought, lending assistance with classified missions. Drudgers can perform simple medical work and make coffee.

• *Veganite:* A fairly rare blue rock, located on Vega VI. The Reinsberg Institute just found a rich, underground strata of veganite—perhaps prompting the Dalek assault on Vega VI. Veganite is too volatile for Dalek technology to mine. The mineral powered Project: Infinity, but its other applications are unclear.

• *Onions:* Are unique to Earth.

ORGANIZATIONS *The Knights of Velyshaa:* The Knights are ancient enemies of the Daleks. They're considered "Old School" warriors, specializing in ancient arts such as telepathy, espionage and mortal combat.

The Knights are currently petitioning to ally with Earth against the Daleks, asking to re-arm themselves. Like Klingons, the Knights prefer to die "gloriously" in battle.

• *The Seers of Yaldos:* They can forge psionic links with others, but only while the subjects remain on Yaldos. The people of Yaldos know little about the Seers, believing they're sorcerers who can raise the dead.

• *Earth Alliance:* Admiral Cheviat is a high-ranking Alliance officer, working aboard the flagship *Intrepid.*

• *The Reinsberg Corporation:* Suz's employers. Also, a multi-world corporation contracted by Earth Space Security Service to work on Project: Infinity.

SHIPS *Dalek Warfleet:* Composed of thousands of ships, moving under cover of a shrouded defense shield. Dropping the cloak allows Dalek ships to accelerate at incredible velocities.

• *Alby's X-49 Scoutship (destroyed):* Equipped with rear guns.

• *Alby's New Ship:* Equipped with a cloaking device.

• *Human Ships:* Cannot travel as fast as Dalek cruisers. Human spaceships frequently require use of cyrosleep pods.

• *The Courageous:* Its landing craft come equipped with TX missiles.

HISTORY The last Dalek war occurred centuries ago. Humanity won, but worried about future defeat, instigated Project: Infinity as a safeguard. During the project's initial phase, the Alliance scoured the galaxy for a weakness in the fabric of space-time. They located such a strained spot in the Lopra System, then spent centuries bombarding the rift to create a full-fledged dimensional fissure.

• Centuries ago, warfare between the Knights of Velyshaa and Earth forces led to the Knights' humbling defeat. The Knights have lived in shame throughout Kalendorf's lifetime.

• On Yaldos, the psionic Seers long ago deemed the Universe a "chaotic place" and withdrew to the a mountain range. They presumably died out, as the aged Seer that Suz encounters seems like the last of her kind.

• The Sol System here falls to the Daleks, with Earth's Madame President formally offering a surrender.

AT THE END OF THE DAY Far more than a simple spin-off series, endowed with a great deal of love, passion, drive and humanity amid all the laser battles. Nick Briggs wisely makes this series more about *people* caught up in horrendous events, using the Daleks as a back-drop for a meaty human drama. The first two CDs by necessity put the players on the board, with the intent of knocking them down, while Parts 3 and 4—loaded with cliffhangers that strike home like a mortar shell—achieve a staggering amount of greatness.

Overall, we'll admit this series was something of a change, given its steeled tone compared to the average "Who" audio—but the fact that we finished Parts 3 and 4 on the edge of our seats, desperately caring about the characters, more than proves its glowing success.

- Briggs thanks his late grandparents in the Dalek Empire sleeves, because the lead characters of Alby and Suz are named after them.

- Alby Brook hails from Proxima Major, which seems like the same locale that appears in *The Face-Eater* or the Bernice NA *Return to the Fractured Planet*. Briggs points out this is entirely coincidental, and that script editor John Ainsworth suggested the name.

- Although it's fairly ludicrous to think Suz has carried a jar of pickled onions with her throughout years of Dalek occupation, Briggs insists: "And why not? I would. I love my mother's pickled onions that much—Daleks couldn't stop me from keeping a secret stash." Ironically, on the day of recording, Briggs had already eaten pickled onions for most of the day and—when the script required him to munch one—resorted to biting a piece of raw cabbage instead.

APOCRYPHA: DEATH COMES TO TIME

By Colin Meek

Individual Episode Titles: *"At the Temple of the Fourth," (Pt. 1) "Planet of Blood," (Pt. 2) "The Prisoner," (Pt. 3) "No Child of Earth," (Pt. 4) "Death Comes to Time" (Pt. 5).*
Release Date (webcast): *Part 1 on July 13, 2001; Parts 2 to 5 weekly from February 14 to May 3, 2002.*
Release Date (CD): *October 2002*

TARDIS CREW   The seventh Doctor, Ace and Antimony.

TRAVEL LOG   Planets Santiny, Alpha Canis One and Anima Persis; Micen Island in the Orion Nebula; a London University and Earth orbit, all modern-day; Casmus' garden and the Kingmaker's dwelling on Mount Plutarch, Gallifrey, modern era.

AUTHOR'S NOTE   "Death Comes to Time" ("DCTT") takes as given that all Time Lords—the Doctor included—possess godlike powers, and in an unbelievable display of self-restraint, have never used them until this point. I thought it best to tell you this outright, because there's no easy way to wedge it into the *Story Summary* without

sounding like a total blockhead.

Also, "DCTT" somehow takes the tack that there's only a handful of Time Lords left in existence, evidently forgetting instances such as "The Deadly Assassin," etc. where there's an entire planet full of 'em. By Part 5, the Doctor and Tannis are the only remaining Time Lords, but it's not entirely clear what happened to the others. If Tannis killed the whole of Gallifreyan society, he did it off-panel in the most discrete of fashions. Alternatively, it's possible the Doctor's final energy burst removed *all* Time Lords from the Universe, although again—this isn't explicitly laid out, and the Time Lords seem out of the picture before the Doctor's powerplay.

Final Note: It's never established how Ace winds up on Santiny by her lonesome. The fact that she knows Antimony suggests she's recently traveled with the TARDIS, but we're given little else.

ANTI-CHRONOLOGY   This story seems to willfully ignore most of the New Adventures, given that Ace highly questions her ability to kill someone [whereas she's shot numerous people in the NAs]. However, the "DCTT" booklet says a decade has passed for Ace since "Survival," which most definitely happens after the New Adventures era.

STORY SUMMARY   Led by the ruthless General Tannis, hostile Canisian battlefleets overrun the peaceful planet Santiny. Amid the slaughter, the Doctor and his purple-skinned companion Antimony arrive, hoping to quell the Canisian advance. The Doctor and Antimony help formulate a rebellion against the invaders, then depart to answer a summons emanating from the Orion Nebula.

On Micen Island in Orion, a Time Lord named the Minister of Chance greets the Doctor, his old friend. The Minister gravely informs the Doctor that two Time Lords recently died on Earth under mysterious circumstances. After some deliberation, the Doctor and the Minister agree to swap goals—the Minster heads off to further the Santiny rebellion while the Doctor and Antimony investigate the Time Lords' deaths.

Meanwhile, Ace tries to independently aid the Santiny people, but the Canisians take her prisoner. Surprisingly, a venerable Time Lord named Casmus liberates Ace from her cell and whisks her away to his garden on Gallifrey. Once there, Casmus begins teaching Ace to evolve beyond her human ways of understanding, training her in effect to become a Time Lord.

On Earth, the Doctor combs through the deceased Time Lords' astronomical research, dis-

turbed to find new black holes sprouting across the galaxy. Moreover, existing black holes are expanding at an alarming rate—signaling a potentially catastrophic tear in the fabric of time. With mounting horror, the Doctor concludes the additional black holes stem from a Time Lord somewhere, somehow, misusing his godlike abilities on a grand scale. In time, the Doctor and Antimony discover that Nessican, a vampire mercenary, killed the two Time Lords in an attempt to suppress their findings. Worse, Nessican reports to his employer, Tannis, and cites Earth as ripe for invasion.

On Santiny, the Minister grows quite fond of Senator Sala, the rebel leader. Simultaneously, the TARDIS returns to Santiny, but Tannis anticipates the Doctor's arrival and confronts him. Tannis reveals himself as a fellow Time Lord, gloating that the Doctor's too impotent to use his godlike abilities to halt the Canisian invasion. Proving his point, Tannis shoots Antimony—exposing him as an android, secretly constructed by the lonely Doctor as a travelling companion. Tannis blows Antimony away, deactivating him, while the Doctor watches helplessly.

Tannis leaves the grieving Doctor and returns to the Santiny front. Hoping to goad the Minister into using his powers—and thereby violate the Laws of Time—Tannis maneuvers his troops into butchering the rebels, including Sala. Grief-stricken, the Minister loses control, flexes his godlike powers and annihilates most of the Canisian army. In response, a satisfied Tannis takes the surviving Canisian spaceships and heads for Earth.

Mourning Antimony, the Doctor journeys to Gallifrey and meets with the Kingmaker—an old woman, evidently representing a Universal force, who holds court over the Time Lords' activities. The Doctor urges action against Tannis, but the Kingmaker stresses Tannis hasn't broken any Laws of Time. Rather, the Minister—having used his godlike abilities—is inadvertently responsible for corrupting time and causing the black hole activity.

The Kingmaker gives the Doctor leave to act against the Minister, making the Doctor realize that Tannis manipulated the few remaining Time Lords into knocking each other off. The Doctor returns to Santiny, finds the insane Minister beyond rehabilitation and exerts his own power—thereby stripping the Minister of his Time Lord abilities. Saddened, the Doctor leaves the Minister to his madness.

Nearby, Casmus puts Ace through the final stage of her training, according her a TARDIS. Tannis briefly arrives on Gallifrey to tie up loose ends, kills Casmus and leaves again. In wake of her mentor's death, Ace heads for Earth to help repel the impending Canisian invasion. Tannis' fleet enters Earth orbit, only to come under heavy fire from British spaceships stationed on the moon. Led by the Brigadier, the British fleet whittles down the invaders, but some Canisian platoons land on Earth.

Ace tries to coordinate with the Brigadier, just as the Doctor and Tannis arrive onhand. Tannis threatens Ace's life, but the Doctor—recognizing that the Time Lords' era has passed—once again exerts his power. Tannis screams as he and the Doctor, the last two Time Lords, die off and vanish. For lack of Tannis' guidance, the remaining Canisians fall to the British troopers. Afterward, Ace visits the Kingmaker, who confirms that the Universe's new age belongs to humanity, with Ace as the new heir to the Time Lords' power.

SEX AND SPIRITS The Minister comments that Sala has an elegant figure. The Kingmaker stresses that Ace's new calling as a Time Lord means she'll never have a mate or children. Indeed, she's discouraged from bonds of affection altogether.

ASS-WHUPPINGS General Tannis eradicates the Santiny city Annet and its nine million inhabitants with a tectonic bomb. Santiny Admiral Mettna orders her troops to conduct suicide runs, but the Canisians mop the floor with them.

The vampiric Nessican kills two Time Lords, the saints Antinor and Valentine, who're conducting work at a London university. The Doctor consumes a massive amount of garlic, then lets Nessican bite him—fatally poisoning the vampire. Nessican's vampire associate Cane also kills a few people, but the Brigadier's subordinate, Lieutenant Colonel Speedwell, shoots her through the spine.

The Minister keeps healing Sala's wounds—a violation of his power—before she's outright slaughtered. The Minister's release of power butchers the Canisian fleet, but also causes scores of casualties among the Santiny rebels. Tannis kills the android Antimony slowly. The Time Lords die. Tannis dies. By the way, the Doctor dies too.

NOVEL TIE-INS *Trading Futures* makes mention of the Canisian invasion in passing, and *Relative Dementias* elaborates a bit on Anima Persis' history.

CHARACTER DEVELOPMENT
• *The Doctor:* The Doctor hints that he's bound—even setting aside his godlike powers—

from interfering *too* much in mortal affairs [such as helping the Santiny rebellion], which pretty much goes against the entire TV series [where he does little but interfere].

The Kingmaker calls him "Truth-Seeker." His godlike powers are more than capable of killing Tannis or destroying his ship, but he refrains until the very end. He's never been a child.

The Doctor knows some of the Time Lords represented in statues on Micen Island. He often finds time travel confusing, remembering tomorrow like it was yesterday. He's heard of the assassin Nessican.

• *Ace:* Ace doesn't forsake her humanity in becoming a Time Lord—rather, she becomes more than human. It's suggested she'll never die [probably pointing to the Time Lords' comparatively long lifespans, not outright immortality].

• *Antimony:* A highly curious and polite android, although completely unaware [until Tannis shot him] of his true origins. Artwork accompanying "DCTT," by longtime *Doctor Who Magazine* artist Lee Sullivan, depicts Antimony with light purple skin, blonde hair and black eyes.

Antimony's extremely strong [but curiously can't bust a pair of handcuffs]. For an android, he's strangely vulnerable to hypnotic influence.

He uses the word "TARDIS," as needed, for a surname. His social graces and historical references need work. He doesn't smell of anything. He likes mice. It's suggested he can dodge bullets. He moves too precisely for a human being.

• *Brigadier Lethbridge-Stewart:* Commands UNIT forces stationed on the moon [Author's Note: Like most of "DCTT," this wholeheartedly violates a wealth of established "Who."] Lieutenant Colonel Speedwell reports to him.

• *The Minister of Chance:* Takes his name from his fascination with the laws of probability. He often plays with quantum dice. He's very dapper, operating a TARDIS that's newer than the Doctor's Ship. He summons the Doctor with a hologram of burning trees.

The Minister's assistant wandered off some time ago on a planet in the Alderaan System [possibly explaining the Minister's intervention there, *see History*].

He bends the Laws of Time by using his powers to heal, and infects the Canisian computer system with a verbal virus. He's evidently used his godlike powers before [again, *see History*], oddly going without punishment. Sala calls the Minister "Snake."

He's learned common roots to most languages. He thinks he could live on Santiny.

• *Tannis:* Time Lord and First General of the Canisians, and the true power on their homeworld. It's also suggested that the Universe generated Tannis as a sort of dark opposite to the benevolent Time Lords. The Kingmaker calls Tannis "the Slow Agent." He unimaginatively wants power just for power's sake. He owns a villa on Alpha Canis' Thurian coast.

[Author's Note: At story's end, Tannis exerts his godlike powers and tells Ace to die—the Doctor blocks this lethal command with his own abilities. It begs the question why the hell Tannis, having been ultra careful to breach no Laws of Time until then, would so flagrantly use his power. Does the killing of a single individual not constitute an infraction? Does the Time Lords' demise mean the Kingmaker cannot enforce its oversight on the Laws of Time? Or is Tannis just stupid?]

• *Casmus:* He's not familiar with feminism. He so old, he can't remember his age. He formerly served as a Gallifreyan Castellan ("The Deadly Assassin").

• *The Kingmaker:* Unspecified being who holds power over the Time Lords. She cannot act to prevent a violation to the Laws of Time, but can sanction punishment against any Time Lord who breaks them. She previously summoned the Doctor, but he didn't come. She predicts she'll meet Ace again.

ALIEN RACES *Time Lords (a.k.a. gods of the Fourth):* Because of their godlike powers and the potential for misuse, Time Lords are discouraged from having strong emotional relationships or affectionate bonds. They're conditioned to refrain from using their powers, even for benevolent reasons, as this only leads to corruption. Time Lords can destroy entire planets with a thought.

If we're taking Ace's initiation as standard, Time Lords undergo a trial on the apocalyptic planet Anima Persis that they're *meant* to lose. The novice Time Lords are instructed to protect the beleaguered inhabitants *without* using their godlike powers. They almost invariably use the powers anyway, killing mass droves of people [in simulation]. The intent's to scar the Time Lords with a memory of what'll happen if they misuse their abilities.

A lesser test, "the Cavern of Infinite Death," entails teaching Time Lords to look for harder solutions, even if they entail more work, to therefore avoid using their powers.

Tannis suggests a human's ascension [i.e. Ace] into a Time Lord is somewhat unprecedented.

It's implied Time Lords are more beings of thought than actual people. They have unpro-

nounceable names. Time Lords take identities after their various interests, such as the Minister of Chance, the Giver, the Taker, the Meddler and the Truthseeker. Conversely, there's no explanation for standard names such as Tannis and Casmus [or for that matter, names such as Drax, Azmael and Thalia on television].

• *Canisians:* Hailing from Alpha Canis [a.k.a. Alpha Canis One, Canis Major], the Canisians thrive on conquest for economic purposes. They use "Canis Rising" as a motto.

• *Nessican's People:* Vampiric species, capable of hypnosis and unharmed by bullets unless the spinal column gets severed.

ALIEN PLANETS *Santiny:* Its space armada mostly consists of mining ships.

• *Anima Persis:* A geo-psychic world, inhabited by the psionic afterprints of its former inhabitants (*see History*).

STUFF YOU NEED *Nitval:* A swamp-like plant with healing properties, found on many planets and quite nice to eat.

PLACES TO GO *Micen Island:* Statues of dead Time Lords spontaneously appear onhand [saints Antinor and Valentine already have statues there, seemingly the day after their murder].

ORGANIZATIONS *The Fraction:* Loose name for some benevolent Time Lords, including the Doctor, the Minister, Casmus and the murdered saints Antinor and Valentine.

PHENOMENA *Dreams:* Often enhanced perceptions, uncluttered by actual matter. Time Lords in particular get dreams with some tangible link to reality [Ace and the Minister dream of whirlpools, symbolic of the expanding black holes].

• *The Future:* Apparently, it's unpredictable until it occurs. [Whatever that means.]

HISTORY During their early history, the Time Lords used their great powers to mentor/aid the lesser inhabitants of Micen Island in the Orion Nebula. However, the Time Lords spectacularly screwed up their stewardship and the people died out from chemical and biological warfare, spurring the Time Lords' non-interference policy. The Temple of the Fourth was erected as a memorial [although curiously, the statues there represent dead Time Lords, not so much the people who died].

• Biochemical warfare long ago killed off the inhabitants of Anima Persis. The psionic people sur-

vived as ghostly entities, and the Time Lords started using the location as a proving ground for their trainees (*see Alien Races*).

• Tannis previously signed the Treaty of Carsulae, handing several planets over to the UP [the United Planets, probably] to keep them at bay. The Minister was also present, swallowing insult after insult. On the planet Alderaan, population 200 million, Tannis quietly dropped a plague bomb, but the Minister—in a no-no display of his power—neutralized the disease. Tannis investigated this miracle, discovering a small cult dedicated to the god "Manastur," thereby deducing the Minister's actions and plotting his downfall.

• UNIT, now answering more to the British government than Geneva, keeps spaceships on the moon.

• It's implied that the British government [and possibly others] plunder the captured Canisian technology to aid with mankind's interstellar endeavors.

AT THE END OF THE DAY Cheap, trite and downright gut-wrenching at times. Some fans understandably loathe "Death Comes to Time" for its continuity violations—but the greater sin lies in its sounding like a 15-year-old wrote the script, flailing about its plot with a sloppiness that's embarrassing. Tannis is a horrendously cliched villain, claiming "I'm a very, very bad man" and shafting us with dialogue such as, "I rather think the Universe is my oyster." The Canisians are complete and total boobs. Ace undergoes a personal awakening that's like every other personal awakening in sci-fi, with Casmus as her poor man's Obi-Wan Kenobi. The overblown choral music doesn't help, and the final firefight's more goofy than serious.

Ultimately, any story where the Doctor croaks will automatically get *some* people to applaud, but honestly—this sounds like it was created by fans who've dreamt for years about crafting a "Doctor Who" adventure, when they should've been first and foremost worried about crafting a good *story*. And in our age of refined science fiction, that shows a lack of priorities that's just inexcusable.

DID YOU KNOW?

• A bloopers section on the "Death Comes to Time" CD includes Anthony Stewart Head (Giles on TV's *Buffy*), who plays Valentine in this story, opening with the sentence, "Previously on Death Comes to Time," *a la Buffy*.

The Über-Who Timeline ?

THE DOCTOR WHO UBER-TIMELINE

Welcome to the glorious "Doctor Who" Uber-Timeline—a madcap, often drunken attempt to reconcile the "Doctor Who" TV stories, novels and audios into a single chronology. For whereas a certain breed of "Who" purists only view the TV stories as canon—and more power to them—there's often readers like ourselves who prefer to view the three "Who" media as a single, glorious and unified history.

In that spirit, a few points require explanation before we begin:

• This timeline ranks everything according to **the Doctor's lifetime** (i.e. first Doctor stories through eighth Doctor stories and beyond). This timeline does *not* rank things in historical order. If you're dying to know how many centuries elapse between "The Romans" and "Warriors of the Deep," you're better off reading Lance Parkin's *A History of the Universe*.

• With regards to **first appearances**, the TV series is king. Hence, we've noted Nyssa's first appearance as "The Keeper of Traken," even though her older self crops up in *Asylum*, which—from the Doctor's point of view—chronologically occurs first. For novel or audio-only characters, we counted their first published appearance (such as Irving Braxiatel in *Theatre of War*).

• **Cameo appearances** refer to a brief mention or glimpse of a character, followed by their more proper and sizeable debut elsewhere.

• Occasionally, certain events (say, Erimem's departure from the TARDIS) must logically occur even though we've yet to see them happen. In such instances, we slap an "**UNKNOWN**" label upon the event in question.

• Whenever possible, all **multi-Doctor stories** are listed under the incumbent Doctor ("The Five Doctors" goes in the fifth Doctor section, etc.). However, there's some exceptions, notably regarding works (such as *Cold Fusion*) considered the domain of a certain Doctor with another incarnation along for the ride.

• The **seasonal headers**, it must be said, get completely arbitrary after a certain point. We obviously organized stuff according to the TV Seasons whenever possible. However, we imposed seasonal breaks on the New Adventures and the Eighth Doctor Adventures to make them more digestible. Whenever possible, we followed the TV series' pattern of seasons with six to eight stories, starting or ending if possible on a keystone story.

Certainly, if a companion entered or left the TARDIS, we tried to make that story an opener/fi-

nale (given the option, it seems silly to bury *Original Sin* in the middle of a season—even if it's not *totally* unprecedented on the TV show).

• We've only included **anthology stories** (from the *Decalog* and *Short Trips* series) if they impacted continuity in some fashion. Including all of them would get far, far too confusing. Along those lines, we didn't view **charity anthology stories** (*Perfect Timing 1* and *2*, etc.), as anything other than apocrypha, unless there was blatantly no choice (say, with regards to Grant Markham's exit from the TARDIS).

• **Comic strip stories** (*TV Action!*, *Doctor Who Magazine*, etc.) are generally regarded as apocrypha. However, there's times when including the comics is unavoidable (say, with regards to Frobisher).

• Finally, a general disclaimer: Some novels/audios are impossible to place with absolute **accuracy**, and it's utterly ridiculous to pretend otherwise.

For instance, "Excelis Rising" clearly takes place between "Trial of a Time Lord" and "Time and the Rani." But does it occur before or after the sixth Doctor's travels with Frobisher? With Evelyn? At present, there's simply no way of telling.

When possible, we've resorted to A) the notation on the backs of the books and audios, B) the author's intent, C) publication order and most important of all, D) common sense, in order to properly place the books and audios. Anything past those criteria gets so sketchy, we're loathe to even attempt it.

Truth to tell, there's a certain type of researcher who will cite nearly any scrap of information to discern where a work fits into "Who" history (i.e. "The Doctor here eats broccoli, so quite obviously…"), but that requires a level of anal retentiveness that even we can't justify. For the sake of clarity, we favor a much more draconian approach.

If a book or audio offers concrete proof of its placement (i.e. *Time of Your Life* making Angela and Grant Markham the Doctor's first companions after "Trial of a Time Lord"), then fine. But if a work has sketchy placement—or blatantly doesn't care—we place it within a general timeframe and move on. Ultimately, this timeline tries to reconcile 159 TV stories, a Guinness World-record breaking novel series and an ever-expanding audio line—all of them written over a 40-year period. Such an effort will never be flawless, but our slushy, "Who"-riddled brains deemed it worth making the attempt anyway.

1st Doctor: William Hartnell

PRE-TV SEASON 1

- *Time and Relative* (Telos novella)
Prequel story, concerning the first Doctor and Susan during her Coal Hill School days. First recorded instance of the Doctor interfering with history. The TARDIS gets damaged, leading to the Ship's unreliability in "An Unearthly Child."

TV SEASON 1

- **An Unearthly Child (TV)**
First appearance of the Doctor, his grand-daughter Susan and the TARDIS. First appearance of science teacher Ian Chesterton and history teacher Barbara Wright. The Doctor, unable to control the TARDIS, dematerializes the Ship but proves unable to get Ian and Barbara home.
- **The Daleks (TV)**
First appearance of the Daleks, the Thals and their homeworld, Skaro.
- **The Edge of Destruction (TV)**
First suggestion that the TARDIS is sentient.
- **Marco Polo (TV)**
- *The Sorcerer's Apprentice* (Virgin MA)
- **The Keys of Marinus (TV)**
- **The Aztecs (TV)**
- **The Sensorites (TV)**
- **The Reign of Terror (TV)**
- *The Witch Hunters* (BBC PDA)
- *City at World's End* (BBC PDA)

TV SEASON 2

- **Planet of Giants (TV)**
- **The Dalek Invasion of Earth (TV)**
The TARDIS lands on a Dalek-dominated Earth, 2164. Susan departs the TARDIS to marry resistance member David Campbell.
- *Venusian Lullaby* (Virgin MA)
- *Decalog:* "The Book of Shadows" (Virgin anthology story)
An alien presence in ancient Alexandria leads Barbara to marry Ptolemy, successor to Alexander the Great. Ian and Ptolemy die in mutual combat, but the Doctor, with help from Barbara and a Gallifreyan book ("Shada"), undoes the erroneous timeline.
- **The Rescue (TV)**
Orphan Vicki joins the TARDIS.
- *Byzantium!* (BBC PDA)
Details of the TARDIS crew's landing in Roman times (leading to "The Romans").
- *More Short Trips:* "Romans Cutaway" (BBC anthology story)

ABBREVIATION GUIDE

- **BBC EDA** = BBC Eighth Doctor Adventures (feature the eighth Doctor, obviously)
- **BBC PDA** = BBC Past Doctor Adventures (feature retro Doctors)
- **BF** = Audio Producer Big Finish
- **DWM** = Doctor Who Magazine
- **MNP** = Mad Norwegian Press
- **Virgin MA** = Virgin Missing Adventures (feature retro Doctors)
- **Virgin NA** = Virgin New Adventures (feature the seventh Doctor)

Short interlude that shows Ian and Barbara falling in love.
- **The Romans (TV)**
- **The Web Planet (TV)**
- **The Crusade (TV)**
- **The Space Museum (TV)**
- *The Plotters* (Virgin MA)
- **The Chase (TV)**
The Daleks develop rudimentary time travel. Ian and Barbara return home via a captured Dalek timeship. Spaceship pilot Stephen Taylor joins the TARDIS.
- **The Time Meddler (TV)**
First appearance of the Meddling Monk (later called Mortimus), a mischievous Time Lord. First hard evidence that the Doctor's TARDIS isn't unique.
- *The Empire of Glass* (Virgin MA)
Second appearance of Irving Braxiatel, who begins to found the Library of St. John the Beheaded, a collection of forbidden works.

TV SEASON 3

- **Galaxy Four (TV)**
- **Mission to the Unknown (TV)**
Prelude to "The Daleks' Master Plan." First mention of the Space Security Service.
- **The Myth Makers (TV)**
Vicki takes up residence in ancient Greece as Cressida, beloved of Troilus. Temple maiden Katarina joins the TARDIS.
- **The Daleks' Master Plan (TV)**
Katarina dies, blown out an airlock. First appearance and death of companion Sara Kingdom, a Space Security Service agent aged to death by the Daleks' Time Destructor.
- **The Massacre (TV)**
English schoolgirl Dodo Chaplet [hurriedly] joins the TARDIS.
- *Salvation* (BBC PDA)
More detailed version of how Dodo joined the TARDIS crew.

- *Bunker Soldiers* (BBC PDA)[1]
- The Ark (TV)
- The Celestial Toymaker (TV)
  First appearance of the Celestial Toymaker, a cosmic entity with a penchant for games.
- The Gunfighters (TV)
- The Savages (TV)
  Steven stays behind on an unnamed planet, agreeing to mediate between the energy-leaching Elders and "the savages," their prey.
- *The Man in the Velvet Mask* (Virgin MA)
  In an alternate reality, "our" Dodo loses her virginity to Dalville, an actor. Suggestion that the Doctor only has one heart, but will gain another when he regenerates.
- The War Machines (TV)
  Dodo stays behind when the TARDIS lands in London, 1963. Sailor Ben Jackson and secretary Polly Wright join the TARDIS.

TV SEASON 4
- The Smugglers (TV)
- *Ten Little Aliens* (BBC PDA)[2]
- The Tenth Planet (TV)
  First appearance of the Cybermen and their homeworld Mondas, a mirror image of Earth. The Cybermen propel Mondas into Earth's solar system, but it absorbs too much energy and explodes. The first Doctor reaches the end of his lifespan and regenerates.

2nd Doctor: Patrick Troughton

TV SEASON 4 cont.
- The Power of the Daleks (TV)
- *Invasion of the Cat-People* (Virgin MA)
- *The Murder Game* (BBC PDA)
  First full appearance of the shark-like Selachians.
- *Dying in the Sun* (BBC PDA)
- *Wonderland* (Telos Novella)
- The Highlanders (TV)
  Highlander Jamie McCrimmon joins the TARDIS.
- The Underwater Menace (TV)
- The Moonbase (TV)
- The Macra Terror (TV)
- *The Roundheads* (BBC PDA)

- The Faceless Ones (TV)
  The TARDIS luckily lands on the day Ben and Polly left, allowing them to resume their lives.
- The Evil of the Daleks (TV)
  Young Victoria Waterfield joins the TARDIS after her father dies saving the Doctor's life. First mention of "the human factor," the indomitable quality that lets humanity keep whipping the Daleks. Some Daleks take on human emotions, causing a massive civil war that brings Skaro to ruin.

TV SEASON 5
- The Tomb of the Cybermen (TV)
  First appearance the Cybermen's adopted homeworld, Telos.
- The Abominable Snowman (TV)
  First appearance of the intangible Great Intelligence and its evil minions, the furry Yeti.
- The Ice Warriors (TV)
  First appearance of the Ice Warriors of Mars.
- *Dreams of Empire* (BBC PDA)
- *Combat Rock* (BBC PDA)
- The Enemy of the World (TV)
- The Web of Fear (TV)
  The Doctor, Jamie and Victoria again fight the Yeti, thereby encountering Colonel Lethbridge-Stewart in the London Underground.
- *Twilight of the Gods* (Virgin MA)
  The TARDIS again visits the planet Vortis ("The Web Planet").
- *The Dark Path* (Virgin MA)
  Origin of Koschei, the Doctor's old friend and fellow Time Lord, who later becomes the Master. Beginning of the Doctor/Master feud.
- Fury from the Deep (TV)
  Victoria settles down in England, circa 1975, with refinery worker Frank Harris and his wife Maggie. First appearance of the Doctor's sonic screwdriver.
- The Wheel in Space (TV)
  Librarian/mathematical genius/space station worker Zoe Herriot joins the TARDIS.

TV SEASON 6
- The Dominators (TV)
- The Mind Robber (TV)
  First appearance of the Land of Fiction.

---

[1] Language in *Bunker Soldiers* suggests the first Doctor, Dodo and Stephen have been traveling together for some time. However, upon reflection, it's curious to note that virtually every story from "The Ark" through "The Savages" immediately leads into one another. That being the case, the gap between *Salvation* and "The Ark" is just about the only place that *Bunker Soldiers* can go.

[2] *Ten Little Aliens* technically cannot occur, as there's no gap in the first Doctor's travels with Ben and Polly. However, it squeezes in here if you assume that the snowy locale in "The Smugglers" Part 4 is not, in fact, the South Pole as seen in "The Tenth Planet".

- **The Invasion (TV)**
  Brigadier Lethbridge-Stewart now heads the United Nations Intelligence Taskforce (UNIT). First appearance of Corporal (later Sergeant) Benton, would-be world ruler Tobias Vaughn and his company, International Electromatics.
- **The Krotons (TV)**
- **The Seeds of Death (TV)**
- *The Final Sanction* **(BBC PDA)**
- *Foreign Devils* **(Telos Novella)**
- **The Space Pirates (TV)**
- *The Menagerie* **(Virgin MA)**
- **The War Games (TV)**
  First appearance of the Time Lords and the Doctor's homeworld. Apparent death of the War Chief, a renegade Time Lord. The Time Lords find the Doctor guilty of meddling with history, but lessen his sentence (if you can call it that) by force-regenerating him, blocking his knowledge of time travel and exiling him to Earth. The Time Lords also wipe Jamie and Zoe's memories of their TARDIS travels and return them home.

SEASON 6B[3]

- *Short Trips:* **"War Crimes"**
- *Short Trips:* **"Mother's Little Helper,"**
- *More Short Trips:* **"Scientific Adviser"**
  (BBC anthology stories)
- *Players*' **flashback sequence (BBC PDA).**

3rd Doctor: Jon Pertwee

TV SEASON 7

- **Spearhead from Space (TV)**
  The Doctor, stranded on Earth, joins UNIT. Scientist Liz Shaw becomes the Doctor's assistant. First appearance the Autons. First mention that the Doctor possesses two hearts.
- **The Silurians (TV)**
  First appearance of the Silurians, the reptilian race that once ruled Earth.
- **The Ambassadors of Death (TV)**
- **Inferno (TV)**
  The Doctor briefly winds up in a parallel Earth, controlled by a totalitarian regime.
- *The Eye of the Giant* **(Virgin MA)**
- *The Scales of Injustice* **(Virgin MA)**
  Liz Shaw departs UNIT to work at Cambridge (but often returns to UNIT service). The Brigadier and his wife Fiona divorce. First appearance of the pseudo-Autons Ciara and Cellian, the Doctor's friend Detective Inspector

Robert Lines and the modernized Department C19. Sergeant Yates promoted to captain.
- *The Devil Goblins of Neptune* **(BBC PDA)**
  First BBC PDA.
- *Decalog:* **"Prisoners of the Sun"**
  (Virgin anthology story)
  Liz Shaw's innocent application of knowledge gleaned from the Doctor destabilizes history. The Time Lords intervene to prevent a human fleet from invading Gallifrey in future. Deciding the Doctor, while a useful agent, must be kept busy on Earth, the Time Lords allow the Master to escape from Shada and distract him.

TV SEASON 8

- **Terror of the Autons (TV)**
  First appearance of the Master, the Doctor's assistant Jo Grant and UNIT Captain Mike Yates.
- **The Mind of Evil (TV)**
- **The Claws of Axos (TV)**
- **Colony in Space (TV)**
  First mention of the Adjudicators.
- **The Daemons (TV)**
- *Short Trips:* **"Degrees of Truth"**
  (BBC anthology audio story)
  The Brigadier fudges the truth, confronted by a father whose son who died in "The Daemons."

TV SEASON 9

- **Day of the Daleks (TV)**
  First appearance of the dim-witted Ogrons. The Blinovitch Limitation Effect's first mention.
- **The Curse of Peladon (TV)**
- *The Face of the Enemy* **(Virgin MA)**
  Ian and Barbara aid UNIT against survivors from the "Inferno" reality. Surgeon Harry Sullivan joins UNIT.
- *Who Killed Kennedy?* **(Virgin MA)**
  Reporter James Stevens investigates UNIT's activities and becomes Dodo's lover. She gets pregnant, but is killed in a web of intrigue.
- **The Sea Devils (TV)**
  First appearance of the Sea Devils, the Silurians' marine cousins.
- *Rags* **(BBC PDA)**
- **The Mutants (TV)**
- **The Time Monster (TV)**
  First appearance of the Chronovores.
- *Decalog 2:* **"Where the Heart Is"**
  (Virgin anthology story)
  The Doctor acquires a house from an alien doctor and gives it to a budget-crunched UNIT.

Continuity glitches (notably "The Two Doctors") have compelled several critics to create "Season 6B," a period the second Doctor spent after his trial working for the Time Lords, sometimes accompanied by companions such as Jamie and Victoria. Accordingly, we've listed some short stories that probably take place in this gap.

• *Verdigris* (BBC PDA)[4]

TV SEASON 10

• **The Three Doctors (TV)**
The first, second and third Doctors meet. First appearance of the anti-matter being Omega, formerly the stellar engineer who helped create time travel on Gallifrey. When the Doctor saves the Time Lords from Omega's wrath, they reward him by restoring his time travel knowledge.

• *The Wages of Sin* (BBC PDA)

• **Carnival of Monsters (TV)**
First mention of Metebelis III.

• *The Suns of Caresh* (BBC PDA)

• **Frontier in Space (TV)**

• **Planet of the Daleks (TV)**

• *Catastrophea* (BBC PDA)

• *Nightdreamers* (Telos novella)

• *Dancing the Code* (Virgin MA)

• *Speed of Flight* (Virgin MA)

• *Last of the Gaderene* (BBC PDA)

• **The Green Death (TV)**
Jo Grant departs UNIT to marry Clifford Jones, a Nobel Prize-winning biologist. First appearance of Metebelis III.

TV SEASON 11

• **The Time Warrior (TV)**
Journalist Sarah Jane Smith joins the TARDIS. First appearance of the Sontarans. The Doctor's homeworld named as "Gallifrey."

• **Invasion of the Dinosaurs (TV)**
Captain Mike Yates treacherously sides with the conspiratorial "Operation Golden Age," gets booted out of UNIT.

• **"The Paradise of Death"**
(BBC Audio/Virgin MA)[5]

• **Death to the Daleks (TV)**
First reference to the 700 Wonders of the Universe.

• **"The Ghosts of N-Space"**
(BBC Audio/Virgin MA)

• **The Monster of Peladon (TV)**

• *Amorality Tale* (BBC PDA)

• **Planet of the Spiders (TV)**
The third Doctor suffers a fatal dose of radiation and regenerates.

4th Doctor: Tom Baker

TV SEASON 12

• **Robot (TV)**
UNIT surgeon Harry Sullivan joins the TARDIS.

• **The Ark in Space (TV)**
First appearance of the Wirrn, some damnably big bugs.

• **The Sontaran Experiment (TV)**

• **Genesis of the Daleks (TV)**
Origin of the Daleks. First appearance of Davros, the Daleks' creator.

• **A Device of Death (BBC PDA)**

• **Revenge of the Cybermen (TV)**

• *Wolfsbane* (BBC PDA)
Guest-starring the eighth Doctor.

TV SEASON 13

• **Terror of the Zygons (TV)**
Harry Sullivan departs the TARDIS, choosing to remain on Earth.

• **Planet of Evil (TV)**

• *Managra* (BBC PDA)

• **Pyramids of Mars (TV)**
First appearance and death of Sutekh, a would-be destroyer.

• **Decalog: "Scarab of Death"**
(Virgin anthology story)
On Beta Osiris, the Doctor and Sarah Jane discover that Horus, Sutekh's opposite number, died centuries ago when his life support failed.

• **The Android Invasion (TV)**

• **The Brain of Morbius (TV)**
First appearance and deaths of renegade Time Lord Morbius and Solon, a criminal genius surgeon. First appearance of the Sisterhood of Karn, keepers of the Elixir of Life.

• *Evolution* (Virgin MA)

• **The Seeds of Doom (TV)**
First appearance of Krynoids, giant world eating plants.

• *The Pescatons* (Silver Screen Records/Target novelization)

• *System Shock* (Virgin MA)
First appearance of the cyborg-reptile Voracians. An older Harry Sullivan aids the Doctor in London.

---

[4] *Verdigris* author Paul Magrs, just out of orneriness, deliberately makes it near impossible to properly place this book. But if we're forced to pick, it likely occurs somewhere around "The Three Doctors" [despite the Doctor's jarring claim that he's yet to visit Peladon].

[5] Writer Barry Letts scripted "The Paradise of Death" to follow on "The Time Warrior," with Sarah Jane waffling on about the Middle Ages and meeting the Brigadier for the first time. Except, of course, that's exactly what happens in "Invasion of the Dinosaurs." As such, it's a continuity glitch we're going to have to live with.

TV SEASON 14

- **The Masque of Mandragora (TV)**
- *Short Trips:* **"Old Flames"** (BBC anthology story)
  First appearance of Iris Wildthyme, a debutante Gallifreyan who's crazily convinced the Doctor loves her, and her double-decker bus TARDIS.
- **The Hand of Fear (TV)**
  The Doctor receives an urgent summons to Gallifrey, leaves Sarah Jane on Earth.
- **The Deadly Assassin (TV)**
  First appearance of the skeletal Master, now at the end of his regeneration cycle. A wealth of information revealed about Time Lord society. First appearance of the Eye of Harmony, the bottled black hole that enables time travel. First mention of Gallifrey founder Rassilon, plus the fact that Time Lords only have 12 regenerations. First appearance of Cardinal (later President) Borusa.
- *Ghost Ship* **(Telos PDA)**
- *Millennium Shock* **(BBC PDA)**
  The fourth Doctor and an older Harry again confront the Voracians.
- *Asylum* **(BBC PDA)**
  The fourth Doctor meets an older Nyssa, now a university teacher in the 39th century.
- **The Face of Evil (TV)**
  Sevateem warrior Leela joins the TARDIS.
- **The Robots of Death (TV)**
  First appearance of sandminer captain Uvanov, pilot Toos and chief mover Pool. First mention of Kaldor City and its robot-reliant society.
- *Last Man Running* **(BBC PDA)**
- *Corpse Marker* **(BBC PDA)**
  Uvanov promoted to company Topmaster. First appearance (in "Who") of psycho-strategist Carnell (*Blake's 7:* "Weapon").
- *Psi-ence Fiction* **(BBC PDA)**
- *Drift* **(BBC PDA)**
- **The Talons of Weng-Chiang (TV)**
- *Eye of Heaven* **(BBC PDA)**
  Detailed information about Leela's family.

TV SEASON 15

- **The Horror of Fang Rock (TV)**
  First appearance of the cabbage-like Rutans.
- **The Invisible Enemy (TV)**
  Robotic dog K9 joins the TARDIS.
- **Image of the Fendahl (TV)**
- **The Sunmakers (TV)**
- *Decalog 2:* **"Crimson Dawn"** (Virgin anthology story)
  The Doctor awakens cryo-sleeping Martians aboard the artificial moon Phobos.
- **Underworld (TV)**

- **The Invasion of Time (TV)**
  Leela leaves the TARDIS to marry Andred, captain of Gallifrey's Capitol guard. K9 stays on Gallifrey with her. The Doctor elected president of Gallifrey, but abdicates his post.
- *Decalog 3:* **"Timevault"** (Virgin anthology story)
  First (and only) appearance of companion Ts'ril, a purser's son.
- **UNKNOWN**—The Doctor builds K9 Mark II.

TV SEASON 16
("The Key to Time" season)

- **The Ribos Operation (TV)**
  The White Guardian, a cosmic protector, sends the Doctor to assemble the six pieces of Key to Time, a reality-altering object. First mention of the Black Guardian, his opposite number. Time Lady Romana joins the TARDIS.
- *Tomb of Valdemar* **(BBC PDA)**
  Romana's future self regenerates and continues travelling the Universe in her own TARDIS.
- **The Pirate Planet (TV)**
- **The Stones of Blood (TV)**
- *The Shadow of Weng-Chiang* **(Virgin MA)**
  First appearance and death of Hsien-Ko, daughter of the late magician Li H'sen Chang ("The Talons of Weng-Chiang"). Romana and K9 dispatch the restored, pseudo-organic dwarf Mr. Sin ("Talons" again).
- *Heart of TARDIS* **(BBC PDA)**
  The fourth Doctor and Romana experience 30 years of unrelated adventures while travelling down a dimensional interface. K9 rescued after God-knows-how-many years as an artifact in the Big Huge and Educational Collection of Old Galactic Stuff. The fourth Doctor briefly helps his second self.
- **The Androids of Tara (TV)**
- **The Power of Kroll (TV)**
- **The Armageddon Factor (TV)**
  The Doctor successfully assembles the Key to Time, earning the Black Guardian's animosity.

TV SEASON 17

- **Destiny of the Daleks (TV)**
  Romana regenerates into her second body.
- **City of Death (TV)**
  Revelation that 400 million years ago, an exploding Jagaroth spacecraft furthered life on Earth. First mention, in passing, of the Braxiatel Collection.
- **The Creature from the Pit (TV)**
- *The Romance of Crime* **(BBC PDA)**
- *The English Way of Death* **(BBC PDA)**

This book is not endorsed by the BBC. Doctor Who and TARDIS are trademarks of the BBC.

243

- *More Short Trips:* **"Return of the Spiders"** (BBC anthology story)
  The Doctor re-encounters (and kills) a giant spider queen from Metebelis 3.
- **Nightmare of Eden (TV)**
- **The Horns of Nimon (TV)**
- *The Well-Mannered War* **(Virgin MA)**
  Final Virgin Missing Adventure. The Doctor and Romana foil a Black Guardian trap, but cannot materialize the TARDIS without destroying the planet Dellah. The pair opts to depart from our universe.[6]
- *Festival of Death* **(BBC PDA)**

TV SEASON 18
- **The Leisure Hive (TV)**
- **Meglos (TV)**
- **Full Circle (TV)**
  Mathematical genius Adric joins the TARDIS.
- **State of Decay (TV)**
  Details about the Time Lords' successful war against the Great Vampires.
- **Warriors' Gate (TV)**
  Romana II and K9 II remain in E-Space, helping to free the enslaved Tharil race.
- **The Keeper of Traken (TV)**
  First appearance of the planet Traken, the benevolent Keeper of Traken and companion Nyssa. The skeletal Master takes over the body of Tremas, Nyssa's father.
- **Logopolis (TV)**
  The fourth Doctor falls to his death from the Pharos Project radio tower and regenerates. Nyssa and air stewardess Tegan Jovanka joins the TARDIS. Destruction of Traken. First mention of Block Transfer Computation.

5th Doctor: Peter Davison

TV SEASON 19
- **Castrovalva (TV)**
- *Cold Fusion* **(Virgin MA)**
  First appearance of Patience (later revealed as the Doctor's wife). Patience "dies" but reappears in *The Infinity Doctors*. Implication that the Doctor and Patience had many children, killed when Gallifrey outlawed natural births in favor of the Loom-born. The fifth and seventh Doctors

meet. First appearance of the Ferutu, a group of other-dimensional Time Lords.
- **Four to Doomsday (TV)**
- **Kinda (TV)**
- **The Visitation (TV)**
  The Doctor's sonic screwdriver destroyed.
- *Divided Loyalties* **(BBC PDA)**
  Details about the Doctor's early life on Gallifrey and first battle with the Celestial Toymaker. First appearance of the Deca, an elite group of Time Lord students including the Doctor, the Master, the Rani, and more.
- **Black Orchid (TV)**
- **Earthshock (TV)**
  Death of Adric.
- **Time-Flight (TV)**
  Tegan gets stranded at Heathrow. Nyssa exhibits latent telepathy.

SEASON 19B[7]
- **"The Land of the Dead" (BF Audio)**
- **"Winter for the Adept" (BF Audio)**
- **"The Mutant Phase" (BF Audio)**
- **"Primeval" (BF Audio)**[8]
  Early history of Traken explored. Nyssa unbecomes telepathic. The Doctor briefly becomes the first Keeper of Traken. The villainous Kwundaar summons various cosmic beings to our Universe, inciting them to plague the Doctor throughout Season 20.
- **"Spare Parts" (BF Audio)**
  The Doctor and Nyssa witness the Cybermen's creation on ancient Mondas. A cybernetic scientist, Doctorman Allan, incorporates elements of the Doctor's physiology into the original Cybermen design.
- **"Creatures of Beauty" (BF Audio)**
- *Empire of Death* **(BBC PDA)**

TV SEASON 20
- **Arc of Infinity (TV)**
  Tegan rejoins the TARDIS. Borusa is now president of Gallifrey.
- *Fear of the Dark* **(BBC PDA)**
- *Zeta Major* **(BBC PDA)**
  The Morestran Empire ("Planet of Evil") unwisely acts on the Doctor's comment about harvesting the kinetic force of planetary motion.

---

[6] Technically, they never return, as this event's supposed to emulate Virgin Publishing's loss of the "Doctor Who" license. Perhaps more importantly, it denotes author Gareth Roberts' belief that everything from the John Nathan-Turner era onward is a strange and disturbing delusion. As such, *The Well-Mannered War* implies— only *implies*, mind you—that everything after "The Horns of Nimon" takes place in the Land of Fiction.

[7] These stories all entail the fifth Doctor travelling with just Nyssa.

[8] Big Finish Producer Gary Russell wishes to point out that the notion of Kwundaar's signal leading to the Doctor's Season 20 adventures is author Lance Parkin's assertion, not his own.

- *The Sands of Time* (Virgin MA)
  The Doctor defeats Nephtys, evil sister of the destroyer Sutekh ("Pyramids of Mars").
- "Omega" (BF Audio)
- Snakedance (TV)
- *Goth Opera* (Virgin MA)
  First Virgin Missing Adventure. Romana offered a High Council seat. First full appearance of Time Lord Ruath, the Doctor's old flame, who becomes a vampire. Revelation that ex-companions Ian and Barbara got married and had a son named John. This story follows on events in *Blood Harvest*.
- Mawdryn Undead (TV)
  Naughty schoolboy (and alien) Turlough joins the TARDIS.
- Terminus (TV)
  Nyssa departs the TARDIS to help the plague-riddled Lazars. Origin of the Universe.[9]
- Enlightenment (TV)
  First appearance of the Eternals.
- The King's Demons (TV)
  Robotic shapeshifter Kamelion joins the TARDIS.
- *The Crystal Bucephalus* (Virgin MA)
  Revelation that the Doctor owns *The Crystal Bucephalus*, a time-travelling restaurant. The Doctor spends five years running another restaurant named *The Tempus Fugit*. The TARDIS console, blasted by time spillage, is rebuilt and modernized ("The Five Doctors"). A mentally controlled Kamelion kills the *Bucephalus'* Maitre D', leading him to sulk in his room for the next year.
- The Five Doctors (TV)
  Massive crossover story. First appearance of Rassilon. Greedy President Borusa imprisoned in Rassilon's Dark Tower. The Doctor again elected Gallifreyan president, but pulls a runner, leaving Chancellor Flavia in charge.

TV SEASON 21
- Warriors of the Deep (TV)
- *Deep Blue* (BBC PDA)
- The Awakening (TV)
- *The King of Terror* (BBC PDA)
  The Brigadier, age 121, is briefly seen in the Westcliffe Retirement Home in Sussex, having spent 20 years in Avalon (*The Shadows of Avalon*). Tegan revealed to marry—and divorce—rocker Johnny Chess (Ian and Barbara's son) in future.

- Frontios (TV)
- "Excelis Dawns" (BF Audio)[10]
  First audio appearance of boisterous Gallifreyan Iris Wildthyme. First appearance of the warlord Greyvorn, who unexpectedly becomes immortal. The Doctor's first visit to Excelis. First appearance of the Relic, a pan-dimensional artifact shaped like Iris' gold lamé handbag.
- Resurrection of the Daleks (TV)
  Tegan departs the TARDIS, sickened by having witnessed so much death in her travels.

SEASON 21B (Turlough stories)
- *Lords of the Storm* (Virgin MA)
  The Rutan spy Karne tries to warn his fellows about a Sontaran plot, leading to events in *Shakedown*.
- *Decalog 3: "Zeitgeist"* (Virgin anthology story)
  First (and only) appearance of the Savant, an alternate Doctor.
- "Phantasmagoria" (BF Audio)
- "Loups-Garoux" (BF Audio)
  Turlough gets some.
- *Imperial Moon* (BBC PDA)

SEASON 21C (Peri stories)
- Planet of Fire (TV)
  Turlough departs the TARDIS to return to his homeworld Trion. Botany student Perpugilliam ("Peri") Brown joins the TARDIS. The Doctor destroys Kamelion, who's mentally dominated by the Master.
- *Turlough and the Earthlink Dilemma* (Companions of Doctor Who #1)
  Trion dictator Rehctaht destroys Earth, Trion and New Trion in her ambition to achieve time travel. Turlough alters history to retroactively undo her damage, but cannot return home without causing a temporal paradox. Turlough replaces a dead version of himself in an alternate timeline.
- *The Ultimate Treasure* (BBC PDA)
  A final remnant of Kamelion's consciousness helps the Doctor and Peri.
- *Superior Beings* (BBC PDA)
- *Warmonger* (BBC PDA)
  Details revealed about Morbius' exile from Gallifrey and military campaign against the Universe. Solon pockets Morbius' brain, leading to events in "The Brain of Morbius."
- "Red Dawn" (BF Audio)

---

[9] "Terminus" and "Slipback" both offer competing explanations for the Universe's creation, but since "Terminus" is a TV story and "Slipback" is a radio drama, "Terminus" wins.

[10] "Excelis Dawns" occurs at the end of Frontios Part 4, as the Doctor and Tegan return from dropping off the alien Gravis.

SEASON 21D
(Peri and Erimem stories)

- **"The Eye of the Scorpion" (BF Audio)**
  Would-be Egyptian pharaoh Erimem joins the TARDIS.
- **"The Church and the Crown" (BF Audio)**
- **"No Place Like Home"**
  (BF Promotional Audio, *DWM* #326).
  First audio appearance of Shayde, a Time Lord agent (*DWM* #61-#67, "The Tides of Time").
- **"Nekromanteia" (BF Audio)**
- **UNKNOWN**—Erimem departs the TARDIS.

TV SEASON 21 cont.
(just Peri again)

- **The Caves of Androzani (TV)**
  Poisoned, the Doctor again regenerates.

6th Doctor: Colin Baker

TV SEASON 21 cont.

- **The Twin Dilemma (TV)**

TV SEASON 22

- **Attack of the Cybermen (TV)**
- **Vengeance on Varos (TV)**
- **Grave Matter (BBC PDA)**
- **Burning Heart (Virgin MA)**
- **Shell Shock (sixth Doctor Telos novella)**
- **The Mark of the Rani (TV)**
  First appearance of the Rani, a renegade Time Lord biochemist.
- **Players (BBC PDA)**
  First novel acknowledgement of "Season 6B," the period the second Doctor spent, after his trial, working for the Time Lords.
- **The Two Doctors (TV)**
  The sixth and second Doctors meet.
- **Blue Box (BBC PDA)**[11]
- **"Davros" (BF Audio)**
- **Timelash (TV)**
- **Revelation of the Daleks (TV)**
  Davros develops a means of mutating humans into Daleks.

THE MISSING SEASON

- ***The Nightmare Fair* (Missing Episode #1)**[12]
  The Doctor imprisons the Celestial Toymaker.
- ***The Ultimate Evil* (Missing Episode #2)**
- ***Mission to Magnus* (Missing Episode #3)**
- **"Slipback" (BBC Radio Four Adventure)**
- ***State of Change* (Virgin MA)**
- ***Palace of the Red Sun* (BBC PDA)**
- **"Whispers of Terror" (BF Audio)**
- **"… ish" (BF Audio)**

TV SEASON 23
(The Trial of a Time Lord season)

- **The Mysterious Planet (TV)**
  The Doctor put on trial (again) for meddling with history. First appearance of the Valeyard, his prosecutor.
- **Mindwarp (TV)**
  Apparent death of Peri, killed when her body's taken over by the Mentor Kiv.
- **Terror of the Vervoids (TV)**
  Computer programmer Melanie Bush joins the TARDIS.
- **The Ultimate Foe (TV)**
  The Valeyard revealed as the Doctor's evil future self. Peri revealed to have survived and married Yrcanos, a warrior king. The Doctor takes Melanie's future self back to her proper location, anticipating their meeting for the "first" time in future.[13] Most of Gallifrey's High Council deposed.
- **"The Wormery" (BF Audio)**

POST-TRIAL STORIES 1
(Grant Markham)

- ***Time of Your Life* (Virgin MA)**[14]
  First appearance and death of 20-year-old Angela Jennings, the sixth Doctor's first companion after his trial. Computer programmer Grant Markham joins the TARDIS.
- ***Killing Ground* (Virgin MA)**
  Grant briefly returns to his homeworld, Agora, to find it infested with Cybermen. Death of Grant's father, Benjamin Michael Taggert.

---

[11] Author Kate Orman didn't specify too much where *Blue Box* takes place, but claims it occurs "somewhere close" to "The Two Doctors."

[12] The sixth Doctor Missing Episodes stem from novelizations of TV scripts that got torpedoed when the show went into its 1985/1986 hiatus. Fandom at large seems to consider these canon, particularly as *Divided Loyalties* acknowledges *The Nightmare Fair*. It's possible, but far less likely, that the same standard applies to *Penecasata*, a Christopher H. Bidmead script from the same period that wasn't novelized.

[13] As most of you probably know, the Mel featured in "Trial of a Time Lord" is plucked from the Doctor's future. He presumably drops her back where she belongs, facilitating a lot of adventures with Grant, Frobisher, etc. until his "first" meeting with Mel in *Business Unusual*.

[14] This book clearly tags Angela and Grant as the Doctor's first companions after "Trial."

- *Perfect Timing:* "Schroedinger's Botanist" (charity anthology story)[15]

First (and only) appearances of a Legion as a sixth Doctor companion, and journalist Carmen Yeh as a future companion. The Doctor forcibly leaves Grant behind in the Sol System, the future, with the means of starting a new life. Grant marries a cellist named Becky and fathers children, including a daughter named Emily. Years later, Grant berates the sixth Doctor for abandoning him.

POST-TRIAL STORIES 2
(sixth Doctor solo)[16]

- "The Ratings War"
(BF Promotional Audio, *DWM* #313)
First audio appearance of the power-mad, furry Beep the Meep (first seen in *DWM* #19-26, "The Star Beast").
- "Excelis Rising" (BF Audio)
- *The Shadow in the Glass* (BBC PDA)

POST-TRIAL STORIES 3 (Frobisher)[17]

- *Doctor Who Magazine* #88-#89:
"The Shape-Shifter"[18]
First appearance of companion Frobisher, a shape-shifter who typically looks like a penguin.
- *Mission: Impractical* (BBC PDA)
- "The Maltese Penguin" (BF Audio)[19]
First appearance of Frobisher's ex-wife, the shapeshifter Francine. Explanation why he's normally shaped like a penguin.
- "The Holy Terror" (BF Audio)
- UNKNOWN—Frobisher leaves the TARDIS.[20]

POST-TRIAL STORIES 4
(Evelyn Smythe)

- "The Marian Conspiracy" (BF Audio)
Modern-day history professor Evelyn Smythe joins the TARDIS.
- "The Sirens of Time" (BF Audio)[21]
The fifth, sixth and seventh Doctors meet. First appearance of CIA agent Commander Vansell and the Knights of Velyshaa.
- "The Spectre of Lanyon Moor" (BF Audio)
The sixth Doctor (from his perspective) meets the Brigadier for the first time.
- "The Apocalypse Element" (BF Audio)
The Daleks invade Gallifrey (and get their plungers handed to them). Romana spends 20 years as a Dalek slave but resumes her duties as Gallifreyan president. Death of the interim Gallifreyan president ("The Sirens of Time"). The apocalyptic Apocalypse Element ravages the Seriphia Galaxy, creating a new Dalek stronghold.
- "Bloodtide" (BF Audio)
Explanation that S'Rel Tulok, a Silurian geneticist, influenced mankind's development.
- "Project: Twilight" (BF Audio)
First mention of Zagreus, a terrifying figure from Time Lord mythology.
- "The Sandman" (BF Audio)
- "Real Time" (BF Audio)
First appearance of the sixth Doctor's blue costume.
- "Jubilee" (BF Audio)
- "Doctor Who and the Pirates" (BF Audio)
- UNKNOWN—Evelyn departs the TARDIS.

---

[15] Charity anthology stories are typically apocrypha. However, Grant obviously leaves the TARDIS at some point, and nothing exists to contradict this story's claims. As such, we're comfortable with it as canon.

[16] All of these companionless stories occur between "Trial of a Time Lord" and "Time and the Rani," but being more specific gets too speculative.

[17] Frobisher's first appearance pre-dates Evelyn's by a decade, so we're placing him before her as a companion.

[18] *Doctor Who Magazine* comic strips normally don't register as canon. However, virtually everyone seems comfortable with this as Frobisher's intro story, so we're cool with it. Frobisher also travels with Peri some in the comic series, but that would screw continuity beyond recognition. Accordingly, it's easier to acknowledge "The Shape-Shifter" and ignore the other comic strips.

[19] "The Maltese Penguin" takes place after *DWM* #127-#129, "The World Shapers," meaning all of the sixth Doctor's comic adventures with Frobisher—for anyone who counts them as canon—have occurred by this point.

[20] Unfortunately, picking Frobisher's exit story isn't so easy. *DWM* #130-#133 ("A Cold Day in Hell") is the most obvious candidate. However, the *DWM* comic strips failed to write Frobisher out during the sixth Doctor's tenure, meaning that by "A Cold Day in Hell," he's travelling with the seventh Doctor. At the time, the post-"Trial of a Time Lord" gap wasn't nearly so choked, and it would require a ridiculous amount of monkeywrenching for us to get Frobisher out of the TARDIS, then back in again. So we're respectfully not trying. Because even if Frobisher briefly travels with the McCoy Doctor, he's got to leave the sixth Doctor's company at some point.

[21] One could argue for placing "The Sirens of Time" after *Lungbarrow*, as the three Doctors involved get equal treatment and the seventh Doctor is the oldest incarnation. However, the Gallifrey in "Sirens" more accurately reflects, thanks to the Interim President and Romana's absence, the post-"Trial" era before "The Apocalypse Element." So putting "Sirens" here is much cleaner. Also, *Instruments of Darkness* claims that during "Sirens," Evelyn was stuck in the TARDIS while the sixth Doctor was off gallivanting.

POST-TRIAL STORIES 5
(Melanie Bush)

- *Business Unusual* (BBC PDA)
  Computer programmer Melanie Bush joins the TARDIS. The Brigadier (from his perspective) meets the sixth Doctor for the first time. First appearance of Trey Korte, Melanie's friend and a budding telepath.
- *Millennial Rites* (Virgin MA)
  The Doctor briefly becomes the Valeyard. The sixth Doctor's handling of events here motivates the unborn seventh Doctor to kill his predecessor and become Time's Champion.
- *The Quantum Archangel* (BBC PDA)
  Death of the Chronovore Kronos. Stuart Hyde de-aged 30 years ("The Time Monster").
- *Instruments of Darkness* (BBC PDA)
  Events in this book continue from *Business Unusual*. The Doctor and Mel find Evelyn on Earth, pissed because the TARDIS dropped her off 10 years too early. Death of Jeremy Fitzoliver ("The Paradise of Death") and the pseudo-Autons Ciara and Cellian (*The Scales of Injustice*). Evelyn resumes TARDIS travel with the sixth Doctor and Mel.
- **UNKNOWN**—Evelyn departs the TARDIS (for good, this time).
- "The One Doctor" (BF Audio)

7th Doctor: Sylvester McCoy

TV SEASON 24

- **Time and the Rani (TV)**
  The Rani makes the TARDIS hurtle out of control, causing the Doctor to bash his head and regenerate.
- **Paradise Towers (TV)**
- "Bang-Bang-a-Boom!" (BF Audio)
- "Flip-Flop" (BF Audio)
- **Delta and the Bannermen (TV)**
- "The Fires of Vulcan" (BF Audio)
- **Dragonfire (TV)**
  Mel departs the TARDIS to travel with the rogue Glitz ("The Mysterious Planet").[22] Time-stranded teenager Ace joins the TARDIS.

TV SEASON 25

- **Remembrance of the Daleks (TV)**
  Major civil war between Davros' Daleks and the Imperial Dalek faction. First appearance of the Hand of Omega, a Gallifreyan stellar manipulation device. First hint that the Doctor hails

from Gallifrey's Dark Time (continued in "Silver Nemesis" and *Lungbarrow*).
- *Remembrance of the Daleks* **(Target novelisation)**
  First mention of the Other, the mysterious Gallifreyan who, along with Rassilon and Omega, helped found Time Lord society. Also, first mention of *Lungbarrow* (the Doctor's ancestral home) and Kadiatu Lethbridge-Stewart (the Brigadier's descendent, *Transit*).
- **The Happiness Patrol (TV)**
- **Silver Nemesis (TV)**
- **The Greatest Show in the Galaxy (TV)**

TV SEASON 26

- **Battlefield (TV)**
- *Relative Dementias* (BBC PDA)
- **Ghost Light (TV)**
- **The Curse of Fenric (TV)**
  Revelation that Fenric, an evil energy being from the dawn of time, caused Ace to meet the Doctor ("Dragonfire").
- *The Curse of Fenric* **(Target novelization)**
  Includes an epilogue where Ace, having left the Doctor's company, has taken up residence in 1887 Paris with the great-grandfather of Colonel Sorin ("The Curse of Fenric"). Ace's departure from the TARDIS in *Set Piece* allows these events to take place, although she and Sorin later break up. Off-handed mention of Zeleekhá, a slave girl who allegedly traveled with the Doctor after he imprisoned Fenric.
- *The Hollow Men* (BBC PDA)
- **Survival (TV)**
- *Citadel of Dreams* (Telos novella)

PRE-NEW ADVENTURES SEASON
(chiefly seventh Doctor BBC novels)

- *Illegal Alien* (BBC PDA)
- *Short Trips:* "Ace of Hearts"[23]
  (BBC anthology story)
  The Doctor apologizes to a baby Ace for his treatment of her, in past and future.
- *Matrix* (BBC PDA)
  Death of the Valeyard and his TARDIS.
- *Storm Harvest* (BBC PDA)
  First appearance of the alien Krill.
- *Prime Time* (BBC PDA)
  The Doctor finds images of Ace's tombstone, broadcast by the villainous TV network Channel 400, are genuine and vows to save her. Ace's demise presumably mirrors her apocryphal death in *DWM* #238-242, "Ground Zero."

---

[22] After "Dragonfire," Mel next re-encounters the seventh Doctor in *Head Games*.

[23] Placement's sketchy on this one, but it belongs somewhere with this clutch of novels, largely written by Robert Perry and Mike Tucker.

- *Heritage* **(BBC PDA)**[24]
Melanie Bush dies in the mining colony Heritage, 6048, accidentally killed by a cloner named Wakeling during a heated argument. Revelation that a mob tore apart her husband Ben Hayworth. A young clone of Mel, named "Sweetness," remains in Heritage.
- *Loving the Alien* **(BBC PDA)**
- **"The Genocide Machine" (BF Audio)**
The Daleks steal craploads of knowledge from the Kar-Charrat Library.
- **"Dust Breeding" (BF Audio)**[25]
The Master returns to his skeletal form ("The Deadly Assassin").
- **UNKNOWN**—The Master regains his Trakenite body.

THE NEW ADVENTURES SEASON 1[26]
- *Timewyrm: Genesis* **(Virgin NA)**
First Virgin New Adventure. The Doctor and Ace investigate the cosmic-powered Timewyrm and accidentally create the creature.
- *Timewyrm: Exodus* **(Virgin NA)**
The Doctor re-encounters the War Chief ("The War Games"), who dies when Drachensberg Tower explodes.
- *Timewyrm: Apocalypse* **(Virgin NA)**
- *Timewyrm: Revelation* **(Virgin NA)**
Detailed explanation of how previous Doctors exist in the seventh Doctor's mind. First appearance of the Eternal Death, the Doctor's rival. The Timewyrm's essence is placed in the body of the baby Ishtar Hutchings.

THE NEW ADVENTURES SEASON 2
- *Cat's Cradle: Time's Crucible* **(Virgin NA)**
Origin of Gallifrey revealed. History of the conflict between Rassilon's neo-technologists and the mythical Pythia. Story of how the Pythia was banished and cursed Gallifrey to sterility. First appearance of the Gallifreyan Looms, the devices that "spin" new Time Lords, explaining the Doctor as essentially an asexual being. First novel acknowledgement of the House of Lungbarrow.
- *Cat's Cradle: Warhead* **(Virgin NA)**
"The War Trilogy" Part 1. First appearance of the Doctor's house in Adisham, Kent. First appearance of young psionics Vincent and Justine, who fall in love.
- *Cat's Cradle: Witch Mark* **(Virgin NA)**

THE NEW ADVENTURES SEASON 3
- *Nightshade* **(Virgin NA)**
- **"The Fearmonger" (BF Audio)**[27]
- **"Colditz" (BF Audio)**[28]
Ace for a time ditches the moniker "Ace" [but retains it for most of the New Adventures].
- **"The Rapture" (BF Audio)**
First appearance of Ace's brother Liam McShane.
- *Independence Day* **(BBC PDA)**
- *Love and War* **(Virgin NA)**
Archaeologist Bernice Summerfield joins the TARDIS. First mention of the Doctor as Time's Champion, denoting his affiliation with the Eternal Time. Revelation that the unborn seventh Doctor killed the sixth Doctor, an act that possibly created the Valeyard. Ace becomes engaged to the Traveler known as Jan, whom the Doctor sacrifices in a gambit against the alien Hoothi. Ace, rebuking the Doctor, leaves the TARDIS.
- *Transit* **(Virgin NA)**
First full appearance of Kadiatu Lethbridge-Stewart, the Brigadier's descendent, who becomes a time traveler.

---

[24] On the surface, Mel's death contradicts *Head Games* and *Short Trips:* "Business as Usual," both of which safely return her to Earth. However, Mel here is older, married and undergoing menopause, so it's easy enough to imagine that her younger self returned home, then somehow took up time travelling again. The seventh Doctor planned for a future incarnation to pick her up on *Heritage,* but Mel died before he arrived. Thankfully, this novel doesn't try to monopolize Mel's time since "Dragonfire," and even the Doctor's a little perplexed as to how she arrived in the 61st century.

[25] "Dust Breeding" and *First Frontier* compete to kill off the Anthony Ainley Master. Even so, they're hardly an excuse for doing something drastic—say, claiming that the audio and novel lines are separate time tracks—and this certainly isn't the first time that "Who" continuity has conflicted with itself. To keep everything running smoothly, it's clear there's an unseen story where the Master, having lost his Trakenite body, regains it. Ace later blows him away in *First Frontier,* facilitating a regeneration.

[26] It's fairly evident that Virgin constructed the early New Adventures to mirror the four-story Sylvester McCoy TV seasons. Certainly, the *Timewyrm* storyarc to some degree feels like a Season 27 of sorts.

[27] Author Jon Blum wants to place "The Fearmonger" between *Nightshade* and *Love and War,* and we see little problem with that.

[28] Some critics wish to place "Colditz" between *Legacy* and *Theatre of War,* however, author Steve Lyons scripted Ace as her younger self, not her older New Adventures version. Also, he deliberately intended it to take place soon after "The Fearmonger," which favors this placement.

- *The Highest Science* (Virgin NA)
  First appearance of the turtle-like Chelonians.
- *The Pit* (Virgin NA)
  First mention of the Yssgaroth, an extra-dimensional menace wiped out by the Time Lords.

THE NEW ADVENTURES SEASON 4[29]

- *Deceit* (Virgin NA)
  Ace, three years older and trained by Spacefleet, rejoins the TARDIS.
- *Lucifer Rising* (Virgin NA)
  First appearance of the dimension-hopping Legions and the modernized Adjudicators .
- *White Darkness* (Virgin NA)
  First mention of the Great Old Ones, the collective group of monsters—birthed in the Universe before ours—that include most higher powers in "Doctor Who."
- *Shadowmind* (Virgin NA)
- *Birthright* (Virgin NA)
  First appearance of Muldwich, a future Doctor and possibly the Doctor's "Merlin" incarnation ("Battlefield").[30]
- *Iceberg* (Virgin NA)

THE NEW ADVENTURES SEASON 5
(The Alternate Universe Saga)

- *Blood Heat* (Virgin NA)
  The TARDIS is lost, forcing the Doctor's party to travel in the TARDIS of a dead parallel universe Doctor. To save our Universe, the Doctor destroys an entire parallel reality.
- *The Dimension Riders* (Virgin NA)
- *The Left-Handed Hummingbird*
  (Virgin NA)
- *Conundrum* (Virgin NA)
  First appearance of the new Master of the Land of Fiction ("The Mind Robber").
- *No Future* (Virgin NA)
  The Doctor again defeats Mortimus, a.k.a. the Meddling Monk ("The Time Meddler").

THE NEW ADVENTURES SEASON 6

- *Tragedy Day* (Virgin NA)

- *Legacy* (Virgin NA)
  The Doctor's third visit to Peladon. First mention of prominent collector Irving Braxiatel.
- *Theatre of War* (Virgin NA)
  First full appearance of Irving Braxiatel and his famed Braxiatel Collection.
- *All-Consuming Fire* (Virgin NA)
  First appearance of the Library of St. John the Beheaded, a storehouse of forbidden texts. Detailed explanation of "The Great Old Ones."

THE NEW ADVENTURES SEASON 7

- "The Shadow of the Scourge" (BF Audio)
- "The Dark Flame" (BF Audio)
- *Blood Harvest* (Virgin NA)[31]
  Sequel to "State of Decay." Romana returns to Gallifrey. Rassilon frees ex-President Borusa from imprisonment. Cameo appearance by the Doctor's old flame Ruath.
- *Strange England* (Virgin NA)
- *First Frontier* (Virgin NA)
  The Anthony Ainley Master regains his Time Lord inheritance and regenerates. First appearance of the alien Tzun.
- *St. Anthony's Fire* (Virgin NA)
- *Falls the Shadow* (Virgin NA)

THE NEW ADVENTURES SEASON 8

- *Parasite* (Virgin NA)
- *Warlock* (Virgin NA)
  "The War Trilogy" Pt. 2. Vincent and Justine divorce.
- *Set Piece* (Virgin NA)
  Ace again departs the TARDIS and takes up time travelling as Time's Vigilante. Ace's last name revealed as "McShane."[32]
- *Infinite Requiem* (Virgin NA)
- *Decalog 2: "The Trials of Tara"*
  (Virgin anthology story)[33]
  The Doctor and Bernice help best Count Grendel's forces on Tara. The revived Kandyman ("The Happiness Patrol") becomes Grendel's executioner, but gets doused with red wine and melts.

---

[29] A seasonal division logically occurs somewhere between *Nightshade* and *Iceberg* (largely to keep the seasons a reasonable size) and if we're forced to pick, Ace's return in *Deceit* seems a likely dividing point.

[30] "Battlefield" author Ben Aaronovitch and Marc Platt, who wrote the novelization, never intended for us to ever see a specific Merlin incarnation. The intent was that each Doctor from the seventh onward would each have an adventure in the Battlefield reality, each encounter happening earlier than the last. As such, they hoped to play off the idea of Merlin as someone who lived his life in reverse. Muldwych seems to offer himself up as a "fixed" Merlin incarnation, although it also works fairly well if he's just another future Doctor.

[31] Romana technically becomes Gallifreyan president about 20 years before "The Apocalypse Element," but here, she's not even a High Council member. Although truth to tell, the exact timeframe of *Blood Harvest* is a bit unclear (Romana meets the Doctor's seventh and fifth incarnations out of order, as it happens), so despite the seventh Doctor's presence, it's forgivable.

[32] Her surname's later used in stories which pre-date *Set Piece*.

- *Sanctuary* (Virgin NA)
  First appearance and probable death of Benny's beloved, Guy de Carnac, a rogue knight.
- *Human Nature* (Virgin NA)
  The Doctor experiments with being human and, as "John Smith," strikes up a romance with teacher Joan Redfern. First appearance of the TARDIS cat, Wolsey.

THE NEW ADVENTURES SEASON 9
- *Original Sin* (Virgin NA)
  Adjudicators Roz Forrester and Chris Cwej join the TARDIS, wrongly marked for death by their own Order. Detailed examination of the modernized Adjudicators. The Doctor again defeats cybernetic genius Tobias Vaughn ("The Invasion"), using his brain crystal to repair the Cwej family's food irradiator.
- *Sky Pirates!* (Virgin NA)
- *Zamper* (Virgin NA)
- *Toy Soldiers* (Virgin NA)
- *Head Games* (Virgin NA)
  Mental battle between the sixth Doctor and his killer, the seventh Doctor. Melanie Bush learns the Doctor mentally influenced her decision to leave the TARDIS ("Dragonfire"), rebukes his machinations and returns to Earth. Last appearance of the Land of Fiction (*Conundrum*).

THE NEW ADVENTURES SEASON 10
- *The Also People* (Virgin NA)
  First appearance of the People, who have a non-aggression pact with the Time Lords, and their super-computer God. The Doctor and Benny restore Kadiatu Lethbridge-Stewart to mental health, granting her a Time Lord's DNA. Chris impregnates Dep, one of the People. Roz becomes romantic with another of the People, feLixi, who's ostracized.
- *Shakedown* (Virgin NA)
  Expanded adaptation of "Shakedown" video. Story follows events in *Lords of the Storm*.
- *Just War* (Virgin NA)
- *Warchild* (Virgin NA)
  "War Trilogy" Part 3. Death of Vincent. Justine and her new husband, Creed McIlveen, divorce. The loosely named "Psi Powers Series" begins.
- *Sleepy* (Virgin NA)
- *Death and Diplomacy* (Virgin NA)
  First appearance of rogue Jason Kane, who proposes to Benny.

- *Happy Endings* (Virgin NA)
  Benny departs the TARDIS to marry Jason Kane. An aged Brigadier Lethbridge-Stewart restored to youth and health. The Doctor, Roz and Chris recover the Doctor's original TARDIS while Muldwych (*Brithright*) uses the parallel universe TARDIS. Romana is now president of Gallifrey. Chris impregnates Ishtar, the ex-Timewyrm. The Eternal Time revealed as Chris' granddaughter.

THE NEW ADVENTURES SEASON 11
- *GodEngine* (Virgin NA)
- *Christmas on a Rational Planet* (Virgin NA)
  First reference of the Doctor as "Eighth Man Bound," denoting his success with a forbidden Time Lord ritual. First mention of Faction Paradox founder Grandfather Paradox (and by extension, first suggestion of Faction Paradox). First hint that Sarah Jane Smith got married (to Paul Morley).
- *Return of the Living Dad* (Virgin NA)
  Benny reunited with her father, Issac Summerfield.
- *The Death of Art* (Virgin NA)
- *Damaged Goods* (Virgin NA)
- *So Vile a Sin* (Virgin NA)[34]
  Death of Roz Forrester. The Doctor euthanizes the Earth Empress. First appearance of Roz's family members and sister Leabie, who becomes Earth Empress. "Psi Powers Series" ends.

THE NEW ADVENTURES SEASON 12
- *Bad Therapy* (Virgin NA)
  Peri, married to Yrcanos for 25 years, finally returns to Earth.
- *Eternity Weeps* (Virgin NA)
  Death of Liz Shaw, fatally exposed to an alien terraforming virus. Benny and Jason divorce. The Doctor kills 600 million people on Earth to save the rest of the planet.
- *The Room with No Doors* (Virgin NA)
- *Lungbarrow* (Virgin NA)
  Origin of the Doctor revealed. First full appearance and death of the House of Lungbarrow. First appearance of the Doctor's Cousins. Detailed description of the Doctor's time on Gallifrey. The Doctor revealed to have the genetic inheritance of the Other, third of an important Gallifreyan triad (along with Rassilon and Omega). Susan revealed as the Other's granddaughter, and the last natural-born Gallifreyan.

---

[33] Difficult to place, but certainly a non-Ace story, and probably better served as occurring before the Doctor and Benny start grieving over events in *Sanctuary* and *Human Nature*.

[34] *So Vile a Sin* was notoriously released out of order, but clearly occurs before *Bad Therapy*.

Chris Cwej departs the TARDIS to travel via use of a time ring. Leela becomes pregnant with Andred's child. Andred cited as having replaced Castellan Spandrell ("The Deadly Assassin") as head of security on Gallifrey. K9 Mark II has joined Romana on Gallifrey. President Romana forges an alliance between Gallifrey and the Sisterhood of Karn ("The Brain of Morbius"). Romana gives the Doctor her sonic screwdriver. The Doctor departs on a mission to retrieve the Master's ashes, leading to his regeneration in "Doctor Who: The Enemy Within."

POST-LUNGBARROW STORIES[35] (seventh Doctor solo)

- **"Last of the Titans" (BF Promotional Audio, *DWM* #300)**
- **"Excelis Decays" (BF Audio)**
  The Doctor refurbishes the console room into the TV Movie version. Death of Lord Greyvorn, who butchers Artaris with a nuclear missile volley.
- ***Bullet Time* (BBC PDA)[36]**
- **"Project: Lazarus" (BF Audio)**
  "Project: Twilight" sequel, starring the sixth and seventh Doctors, with Evelyn.
- **"Master" (BF Audio)**

8th Doctor: Paul McGann

EIGHTH DOCTOR DEBUT STORIES

- **Doctor Who: The Movie (a.k.a. "The Enemy Within") (TV)**
  The Doctor gets shot, leading to a botched operation that kills him, prompting a regeneration. First appearance of his lip-massage partner, surgeon Grace Holloway. The Master, now a gelatinous worm, possesses an ambulance driver who suspiciously looks like Julia Roberts' brother.

- ***The Eight Doctors* (BBC EDA)[37]**
  First BBC Eighth Doctor Adventure. Coal Hill schoolgirl Samantha Jones joins the TARDIS. The eighth Doctor meets his previous incarnations at various points in "Who" history. Explanation for the Master becoming a worm.
- **UNKNOWN**—The Doctor drops Sam somewhere and continues a string of adventures with other companions.

INTERIM SEASON (eighth Doctor solo/various companion stories)

- ***Radio Times* comic strips**
  The Doctor travels with Stacy Townsend, the survivor of a Cybermen massacre, and an Ice Warrior named Ssard.
- ***The Dying Days* (Virgin NA)**
  Final Virgin New Adventure. Only canonical meeting between the eighth Doctor and Benny. The Doctor gives Wolsey the cat to Benny and drops her off at St. Oscar's University on Dellah, leading to the Virgin Benny New Adventures. The Doctor and Benny likely have sex.
- ***Rip Tide* (Telos novella)**
- **"Shada" (BBC webcast)[38]**
  The eighth Doctor recruits President Romana for a mission, leading to their finding *The Worshipful and Ancient Law of Gallifrey*.

BIG FINISH EDA SEASON 1[39]

- **"Storm Warning" (BF Audio)**
  Self-proclaimed adventuress Charlotte ("Charley") Pollard joins the TARDIS. The Doctor saves Charley from dying aboard the doomed *R-101* dirigible, thereby violating the Laws of Time.
- **"Sword of Orion" (BF Audio)**
- **"The Stones of Venice" (BF Audio)**
- **"Minuet in Hell" (BF Audio)**
  The Brigadier meets the eighth Doctor and Charley for the first time.

---

[35] *Lungbarrow* suggests the seventh Doctor immediately dashes off to get killed on Earth, but these solo stories clearly occur shortly prior to the TV Movie (in other words, he delays eating lead for a bit).

[36] Author David McIntee wanted *Bullet Time* to take place during *A Room With No Doors*, between a scene where the Doctor digs himself out of his grave and when he next appears. However, that seems woefully optimistic. Some fans have tried making *Bullet Time* take place elsewhere in *Room*, but it's all pure speculation, and ultimately it's hard to believe the Doctor would simply leave Chris Cwej in the lurch and go gallivanting off to Hong Kong for a few months. When all's said and done, this story's much better served as a solo seventh Doctor story, post-*Lungbarrow*.

[37] In a goof of cosmic proportions, High Council member Flavia ("The Five Doctors") is shown as Gallifreyan president shortly after the eighth Doctor's debut. Writer Terrance Dicks evidently didn't know—or care—that Romana ascended to the position in *Happy Endings*. As subsequent works such as "The Apocalypse Element" establish beyond a shadow of a doubt that Romana became president at some point between "Trial of a Time Lord" and "Time and the Rani," Flavia's briefly seen presidency in *The Eight Doctors* can only looked upon as a complete and total glitch—a condition many fans want to ascribe to the whole of *The Eight Doctors*, actually.

[38] The Paul McGann "Shada" actually got finished, so it beats out the incomplete Tom Baker version as canon.

BIG FINISH EDA SEASON 2

- "Invaders from Mars" (BF Audio)
- "The Chimes of Midnight" (BF Audio)
- "Seasons of Fear" (BF Audio)
  The Doctor again defeats the Nimon ("The Horns of Nimon").
- "Embrace the Darkness" (BF Audio)
- "The Time of the Daleks" (BF Audio)
- "Neverland" (BF Audio)
  Resolution of Charley's paradoxical death aboard the *R-101* ("Storm Warning"). Death of CIA agent Vansell. The Doctor saves Gallifrey, but gets saturated with Anti-time particles and goes insane, declaring himself to be the legendary, terrifying figure Zagreus.

BIG FINISH EDA SEASON 3

- "Zagreus" (BF Audio)
  Upcoming 40th anniversary story. Follows on events in "Neverland."

BBC BOOKS EDA SEASON 1

- UNKNOWN—Sam Jones rejoins the TARDIS.
- *Vampire Science* (BBC EDA)
  For the Doctor, three years have now passed since "Doctor Who: Enemy Within."
- *The Bodysnatchers* (BBC EDA)
  The Doctor re-meets Professor Litefoot ("The Talons of Weng-Chiang") and again fights the Zygons ("Terror of the Zygons").
- *Genocide* (BBC EDA)
  Revelation that Jo Grant and hubby Cliff divorced. Sgt. Benton seen as married with three children.
- *War of the Daleks* (BBC EDA)
  Dalek history massively rewritten (for the worse). Revelation that the Doctor didn't destroy Skaro in "Remembrance of the Daleks."
- *Alien Bodies* (BBC EDA)
  First appearance of Faction Paradox and the Celestis, breakaway Time Lord groups. First appearance of the Relic [not the same as the Excelis audios], said to be the Doctor's corpse. First mention of "Dark Sam," Sam's true timeline. First appearance of Cousin Justine, the War, shifts, sentient TARDISes and Time Lords from the future. First appearance of the Enemy, an unknown adversary besting the future Time Lords left, right and center. The Doctor blows up the Relic.
- *Kursaal* (BBC EDA)
- *Option Lock* (BBC EDA)

BBC BOOKS EDA SEASON 2
("Missing Sam" storyarc)

- *Longest Day* (BBC EDA)
  Sam gives the Doctor CPR, gets embarrassed for enjoying herself too much and abandons him.
- *Legacy of the Daleks* (BBC EDA)
  The Roger Delgado Master is killed, leading to his skeletal form in "The Deadly Assassin." Death of Susan's husband David Campbell. Susan departs Earth in the Master's TARDIS.
- *Dreamstone Moon* (BBC EDA)
- *Seeing I* (BBC EDA)
  The Doctor, looking for Sam, is imprisoned for three years at a rehabilitation center. Sam, three years older, frees him and rejoins the TARDIS.

BBC BOOKS EDA SEASON 3

- *Placebo Effect* (BBC EDA)
  The Doctor briefly re-meets Stacy and Ssard, who get married.
- *Vanderdeken's Children* (BBC EDA)
- *The Scarlet Empress* (BBC EDA)
  First full-length novel appearance of Iris Wildthyme. Iris consumes poisonous Dalek flesh, then regenerates into a blonde bombshell.
- *The Janus Conjunction* (BBC EDA)
- *Beltempest* (BBC EDA)
- *The Face Eater* (BBC EDA)
- *More Short Trips:* "Femme Fatale" (BBC anthology story)
  Sexy Iris crafts an elaborate fiction involving Andy Warhol.

BBC BOOKS EDA SEASON 4

- *The Taint* (BBC EDA)
  Flower store worker and aspiring guitarist Fitz Kreiner joins the TARDIS, wanted for questioning concerning a murder. The Doctor kills a bunch of patients, including Fitz's mother, who's infected with Benelisan leeches.
- *Demontage* (BBC EDA)
- *Revolution Man* (BBC EDA)
  Fitz leaves the TARDIS for two years, becoming a brainwashed agent of Communist China.
- *Dominion* (BBC EDA)
- *Unnatural History* (BBC EDA)
  A temporal anomaly briefly replaces Blonde Sam with Dark Sam. Dark Sam and Fitz have a liaison. Dark Sam wiped from existence, restoring Blonde Sam to life.
- *Autumn Mist* (BBC EDA)

---

[39] Some critics wish to place the Big Finish stories after Samantha Jones' [temporary] departure from the TARDIS in *Seeing I*. However, the specified three year gap between *The Eight Doctors* and *Vampire Science*—plus Sam's suspicion in the latter book that the Doctor's been skipping out on her, makes putting the audios here much more convenient.

- *Interference Part 1* (Shock Tactic) and 2 (The Hour of the Geek) (BBC EDAs)
  Sam departs the TARDIS to work with an older Sarah Jane Smith. Fitz becomes an agent of Faction Paradox and is "remembered" as the Remote agent Kode. The original Fitz is taken to the Faction's powerbase, the Eleven-Day Empire, and becomes Father Kreiner. The Doctor converts Kode into a duplicate Fitz. Father Kreiner flung into the Time Vortex.
  First appearance of the Remote, a Faction Paradox splinter society reliant on signals from a media net. Remote member Compassion joins the TARDIS. First appearance of IM Foreman, a non-Time Lord Gallifreyan with ties to Foreman's Junkyard ("An Unearthly Child"). The third Doctor dies, in a very paradoxical fashion, from a shotgun wound on the colony of Dust. Implication that sexy Iris is now scientific adviser to UNIT.

BBC BOOKS EDA SEASON 5
("Who is Compassion?" storyarc)
- **The Blue Angel** (BBC EDA)
  Sexy Iris Wildthyme betrays the Doctor, preventing him from intervening in a war between the Galactic Federation and the Obverse, a pocket universe. Iris [strangely] tells the Doctor she originates from the Obverse.
- **The Taking of Planet 5** (BBC EDA)
  Destruction of the Celestis. First appearance (and banishment) of the Fendahl Predator ("Image of the Fendahl").
- *Frontier Worlds* (BBC EDA)
  Fitz's lover Alura gets killed.
- *Parallel 59* (BBC EDA)
  Fitz has an extra-marital affair with a woman named Anya, but meets the true love of his life, Filippa, who remains on the planet Skale.
- *The Shadows of Avalon* (BBC EDA)
  Compassion transforms into Gallifrey's first fully sentient and humanoid TARDIS. Romana shown regenerated into her third body. Death of the Brigadier's wife Doris ("Battlefield") revealed. The Brigadier takes up residence in the other-dimensional Avalon, eventually leading to *The King of Terror*. The Doctor's crew flees when the Time Lords plot to use Compassion as TARDIS breeding stock.

BBC BOOKS EDA SEASON 6
- *The Fall of Yquatine* (BBC EDA)
  Compassion spends decades adrift in the Time Vortex.
- *Coldheart* (BBC EDA)
- *The Space Age* (BBC EDA)

- *The Banquo Legacy* (BBC EDA)
- *The Ancestor Cell* (BBC EDA)
  Faction Paradox seizes control of Gallifrey. The Enemy prepares to launch a massive strike against Gallifrey, the opening volley of the War. Fearing for the Universe's survival either way, the Doctor destroys his homeworld. Compassion and Fitz leave the amnesiac Doctor and the damaged TARDIS on 20th century Earth to heal, leaving a note to rendezvous with Fitz in 2001. Compassion departs for space with technician Nivet, a surviving Gallifreyan.
  Resolution of the third Doctor's paradoxical death on Dust (*Inference*). Death of Father Kreiner, Fitz's original self. Fate of Romana, Leela and Commander Andred and K9's Mark I and II left unknown.

BBC BOOKS EDA SEASON 7
(The Earth Arc)
- *The Burning* (BBC EDA)
  The amnesiac eighth Doctor begins a century-long stay on Earth, besting a fire elemental in Victorian times.
- *Casualties of War* (BBC EDA)
- *The Turing Test* (BBC EDA)
- *Endgame* (BBC EDA)
- *Father Time* (BBC EDA)
  The Doctor adopts the orphaned 10-year-old Miranda Dawkins, last of a hunted alien species. Nine years later, Miranda becomes supreme ruler over disjointed political factions in the far-flung future.
- *Escape Velocity* (BBC EDA)
  Futures trader Anji Kapoor joins the TARDIS. Death of her live-in boyfriend Dave Young. The Doctor and Fitz reunited in London, 2001. The TARDIS finally heals and regains its internal configuration.

BBC BOOKS EDA SEASON 7
- *Earthworld* (BBC EDA)
- *Vanishing Point* (BBC EDA)
- *Eater of Wasps* (BBC EDA)
- *The Year of Intelligent Tigers* (BBC EDA)
- *The Slow Empire* (BBC EDA)
  Cameo appearance by Sabbath (*The Adventuress of Henrietta Street*).
- *Dark Progeny* (BBC EDA)
- *The City of the Dead* (BBC EDA)
- *Grimm Reality* (BBC EDA)

BBC BOOKS EDA SEASON 8[40]

- ***The Adventuress of Henrietta Street* (BBC EDA)**

  The Doctor marries Scarlette, a 18th century bordello owner, to ritualistically keep the horizon—an indescribable realm beyond human understanding—from consuming Earth.

  First appearance of Sabbath, a former intelligence agent who deems himself a superior guardian of Earth. Sabbath saves the Doctor's life by removing one of his poisoned hearts, only to implant the organ in his own chest and gain greater control of time travel. Guest appearance by the Master (a.k.a. the man with the rosette), who holds little interest in battling the Doctor for now. First appearance of the giant, malevolent eyeball that keeps watch in the horizon.

- ***Mad Dogs and Englishmen* (BBC EDA)**

  First appearance of yet another Iris Wildthyme incarnation, who's now a singer named "Brenda Soobie."

- ***Hope* (BBC EDA)**

  Anji helps create a genetic copy of her dead boyfriend Dave, who remains in the far-flung future.

- ***Anachrophobia* (BBC EDA)**

  First mention of Sabbath's unnamed business partners.

- ***Trading Futures* (BBC EDA)**
- ***The Book of the Still* (BBC EDA)**
- ***The Crooked World* (BBC EDA)**
- ***History 101* (BBC EDA)**
- ***Camera Obscura* (BBC EDA)**

  Major smackdown between the Doctor and Sabbath. Sabbath rebukes the Doctor's ways and removes his implanted heart, killing it. The Doctor's body starts growing a new one.

BBC BOOKS EDA SEASON 9

- ***Time Zero* (BBC EDA)**

  Fitz spends more than 100 years in an intangible, indeterminate "Schroedinger's Cat"-like state. Anji returns home for 18 months, but gets kidnapped by America's CIA. The Doctor rescues them both, only to discover that events in this novel have brought various parallel realities into collision—giving the TARDIS crew the mandate of: A) insuring that "our" timeline—the true timeline—regains dominance, and B) fulfilling history by dropping off Fitz's expedition journal at the proper bookshop (for the Doctor to later purchase it). Origin of the fire elemental from *The Burning*.

- ***The Infinity Race* (BBC EDA)**
- ***The Domino Effect* (BBC EDA)**
- ***Reckless Engineering* (BBC EDA)**
- ***The Last Resort* (BBC EDA)**
- ***Timeless* (BBC EDA)**
- ***Emotional Chemistry* (BBC EDA)**
- ***Sometime Never...* (BBC EDA)**

  Wraps up ongoing plot threads.

BBC BOOKS EDA SEASON 10

- ***Half Life* (BBC EDA)**

FUTURE DOCTOR STORIES

- ***Battlefield* (Target novelization)**

  A red-haired Doctor is present during the final battle between King Arthur and Morgaine.

- ***More Short Trips: "Good Companions"* (BBC anthology story)**

  Tegan, age 73, buries her husband, St. Cedd's chair William Haybourne[41]. Tegan revealed to have suffered a nervous breakdown in her 20s and spent time at Shawlands convalescent home. She now believes the Doctor was merely a figment of her imagination. A red-haired Doctor (same as above), along with his companion Anna, obtains Tegan's help in banishing the alien Sigrarnons to their home dimension. Tegan ends the adventure failing to recognize her old friend, but writes of the encounter in *Womanuscripts: 21st Century Female Fiction* (London, 2041).

- ***Short Trips and Side Steps: "Revenants"* (BBC anthology story)**

  The red-haired Doctor takes up travel with Professor Guinevere ("Guin") Winchester.

NTH DOCTOR STORIES

These stories concern Doctors whose incarnations/relevance to the main "Who" timeline is deliberately left murky.

- ***The Cabinet of Light* (Telos novella)**

  Leads into Telos' *Time Hunter* series.

- ***The Infinity Doctors* (BBC PDA)[42]**

  35th anniversary story. The Doctor's time as a High Council member explored. Patience (*Cold Fusion*) revealed as Omega's wife—and the Doctor's.

RELATED COMPANION STORIES

- ***Harry Sullivan's War* (Companions of Doctor Who #2)**
- **"K9 and Company" (TV pilot for K9 series)**

  The Doctor builds K9 Mark III for Sarah Jane.

---

[40] These stories contain the thread of the Doctor losing—and regaining—his second heart.

[41] Tegan marries at least twice, the first time to rocker Johnny Chess, *The King of Terror*.

- *Downtime* **(Virgin MA)**
  An older Victoria Waterfield founds New World University, which is infiltrated by the Great Intelligence ("The Web of Fear"). The Brigadier reconciles with his daughter Kate.
- *Short Trips:* **"Mondas Passing"**
  (BBC anthology story)
  Ben Jackson and Polly, now married to other people, consider a liaison in 1986 but simply part as friends.
- *More Short Trips:* **"Missing Pts 1 and 2"**
  (BBC anthology stories)
  Melanie Bush settles back into Earth life (after *Head Games*).
- *Decalog 3:* **"Moving On"**
  (Virgin anthology story)
  Sarah Jane fails to find replacement parts for K9 Mark III, who shuts down.

SARAH JANE SMITH AUDIOS
- **"Comeback"** [43]
- **"The TAO Connection"**
- **"Test of Nerve"**
- **"Ghost Town"**
- **"Mirror, Signal, Manoeuvre"**

Related Universes

BBV AUDIOS (Canonical)
It's debatable, but we've deemed BBV audios and videos as canonical if they contain a recognizable character (Liz Shaw, etc.) or monster (the Sontarans, etc.) from the TV show. The only solid reason why something like "Krynoids: The Green Man" could be considered less canonical than Benny, etc., would be because Big Finish holds a proper "Doctor Who" license, but BBV doesn't. That said, we failed to see why BBV's thinly veiled, essentially unauthorized "Who" works ("the Professor and Ace," etc.) would automatically void their more legitimate efforts, listed here.

For BBV's Faction Paradox Protocols, see the Faction Paradox section.
- **"Guy: The Quality of Mercy"**
  With Guy de Carnac from *Sanctuary*.
- **"I: I Scream"**
  With the I from *Seeing I*.
- **"K9: The Search"**
- **"K9: The Choice"**
- **"Krynoids: The Root of All Evil"**
- **"Krynoids: The Green Man"**
- **"The Rani Reaps the Whirlwind"**
  Details about the Rani's fate after "Time and the Rani."
- **"Rutans: In 2 Minds"**
- **"Sontarans: Silent Warrior"**
- **"Sontarans: Old Soldiers"**
- **"Sontarans: Conduct Unbecoming"**
- **"Wirrn: Race Memory"**
- **"Zygons: Homeland"**
- **"Zygons: Absolution"**
- **"Zygons: Barnacled Baby"**

BBV VIDEOS (Canonical)
- **"Auton"**
- **"Auton 2: Sentinel"**
- **"Auton 3"**
- **"Mindgame"**
- **"Mindgame Trilogy"**
- **"PROBE: The Zero Imperative"**
  Liz Shaw begins work for a branch of the British government, investigating mysteries in an "X-Files" fashion.
- **"PROBE: The Devil of Winterborne"**
- **"PROBE: Unnatural Selection"**
- **"PROBE: The Ghosts of Winterborne"**

BENNY NEW ADVENTURES SEASON 1
- *Oh No It Isn't!* **(Benny NA)**
  Benny gains tenure as the Edward Watkinson Professor of Archaeology at St. Oscar's University on Dellah. First appearance of Benny's robotic porter Joseph.

---

[42] *The Infinity Doctors* was designed to be more archetypal than anything else. It possibly features a young first Doctor, although there's several indications (the ending of the Sontaran/Rutan war, mention of Faction Paradox, etc.) that it occurs in the Doctor's future. Naturally, this would require Gallifrey somehow reconstituting after *The Ancestor Cell*, and oddly enough, the appearance of the Magistrate—clearly the Master—actually matches with his demeanor in *The Adventuress of Henrietta Street*. Even so, placing *The Infinity Doctors* will always cause some frustration.

On this topic, author Lance Parkin wrote in a Discussion Board posting: "Where does [*The Infinity Doctors*] fit? Well, when I say there's a multiple choice, people get annoyed. But it really *could* be a pre-series young Hartnell, or a post-TVM McGann one, or a parallel universe, or what happens instead of *The Eight Doctors*, a prequel to *Fathers and Brothers* or ... or ... or ... if people don't like that answer ... then pick one of them and stick to it. Close reading of the book will support your decision."

[43] The Sarah Jane Smith audios notably fail to mention K9 Mark III, implying they take place after *Decalog 3:* "Moving On." However, Sarah's journalism career (notably her fiction writing) in the short story suggests that it takes place some years in the future, whereas the audios are moreso contemporaneous. The two are fairly hard to reconcile, but really, it just seems overly logical that "Moving On" happens first.

- *Dragons' Wrath* (Benny NA)
  Benny meets Time Lord Irving Braxiatel[44], here the theatrology department head at St. Oscar's, before their "first" meeting (*Theatre of War*).
- *Beyond the Sun* (Benny NA)
  Jason Kane returns after an eight-month absence (since *Eternity Weeps*).
- *Ship of Fools* (Benny NA)
- *Down* (Benny NA)
  The People's early history detailed. Retcon establishes that the People's supercomputer God brainwashed Benny into joining the St. Oscar's staff, planning for the day when she'd release MEPHISTO.
- *Deadfall* (Benny NA)
  Jason Kane agrees to a marriage of convenience with former prisoner Charlene Conner (and for all we know, they're still hitched).
- *Ghost Devices* (Benny NA)
  First appearance of Clarence, God's winged agent.

BENNY NEW ADVENTURES SEASON 2
- *Mean Streets* (Benny NA)
- *Tempest* (Benny NA)
- *Walking to Babylon* (Benny NA)
- *Oblivion* (Benny NA)
  Benny and Chris briefly meet a 20-year-old Roz Forester from another reality.
- *The Medusa Effect* (Benny NA)
- *Dry Pilgrimage* (Benny NA)
- *The Sword of Forever* (Benny NA)
  Benny platonically marries the filthy rich Marillian to conduct research at the British Library. Benny sutures Earth's timeline using a powerful artifact named the Sword of Forever, but dies—and gets restored—in the process.

BENNY NEW ADVENTURES SEASON 3[45]
- *Another Girl, Another Planet* (Benny NA)
- *Beige Planet Mars* (Benny NA)
  Jason Kane obtains gainful employment writing semi-autobiographical erotica.
- *Where Angels Fear* (Benny NA)
  Powerful beings calling themselves the Dellan gods awaken, gripping Dellah in a religious fervor. Benny and Braxiatel abandon St. Oscar's University. Dellah quarantined.

BENNY NEW ADVENTURES SEASON 4
- *The Mary-Sue Extrusion* (Benny NA)

- *Dead Romance* (Benny NA)
  Chris Cwej, brainwashed as a Time Lord agent, gets hit with a lethal radiation dose. The Time Lords, fearing the Dellan gods' power, dominate an Earth within a Universe-in-a-Bottle and reshape it to their needs. The Time Lords revise their treaty with the People, allowing the People to develop time travel. First appearance of Christine Summerfield (later Cousin Eliza).
- *Tears of the Oracle* (Benny NA)
  Braxiatel revealed as the Doctor's brother. Braxiatel gambles at Vega Station (seen in *Demontage*) and wins Asteroid KS-159, the future home of the Braxiatel Collection. The Time Lords regenerate a dying Chris Cwej into a shorter, dark-haired body.

BENNY NEW ADVENTURES SEASON 5
- *Return to the Fractured Planet* (Benny NA)
- *The Joy Device* (Benny NA)
- *Twilight of the Gods* (Benny NA)
  Death of Clarence. The Dellan gods revealed as a Ferutu splinter group (*Cold Fusion*) and are consigned, with Dellah, to their home dimension. Jason Kane trapped as a Ferutu captive. A glancing Ferutu time blast de-ages Benny about five years. Chris Cwej returned to a 13-year-old, blonde-haired body. Benny becomes head of Vremnya University's Archaeology Department. Virgin New Adventures end (Dec. 1999) after more than eight years.

BENNY BIG FINISH SEASON 1
- *The Dead Men Diaries*
  (BF Benny anthology)
  Big Finish beings producing original Benny audios and books. Four years after *Twilight of the Gods*, Benny relocates to the Braxiatel Collection. Benny and a timelost Jason Kane nearly meet (in "The Door to Bedlam"). First appearance of Agraxar Flatchlock, a demonic travel agent and Jason's employer (ditto).
- *The Doomsday Manuscript*
  (BF Benny novel)
  Braxiatel gives Benny a replacement Joseph drone. First appearance of Braxiatel Collection architect Adrian Wall and administrative assistant Ms. Jones. First appearance of the Fifth Axis, a neo-Nazi organization in control of several worlds.
- "The Secret of Cassandra"
  (BF Benny audio)

---

[44] From Braxiatel's perspective, the entire Benny New Adventures occur before *Theatre of War*.

[45] After *The Sword of Forever*, lagging sales made Virgin editors fear the line might get axed entirely. The range slipped to bi-monthly publication, and novels were commissioned in three-book lumps—which helps to explain why *Where Angels Fear*, *Tears of the Oracle* and *Twilight of the Gods* were all written as possible series finales.

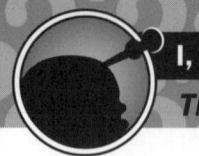

- *Gods of the Underworld* (BF Benny novel)
- *The Squire's Crystal* (BF Benny novel)
  A soul-swapping crystal temporarily deposits Benny's mind in a man's body. While she's out, an ancient sorceress takes over Benny's form and makes the beast with two backs with Braxiatel engineer Adrian Wall.
- "The Stone's Lament" (BF Benny audio)
- "The Extinction Event" (BF Benny audio)
- *The Infernal Nexus* (BF Benny novel)
  Benny reunites with ex-hubby Jason Kane—and discovers that Adrian Wall knocked her up.
- "The Skymines of Karthos" (BF Benny audio)
- *The Glass Prison* (BF Benny novel)
  Birth of Benny's son, Peter Guy Summerfield.

BENNY BIG FINISH SEASON 2
- "The Greatest Shop in the Galaxy" (BF Benny audio)
- "The Green-Eyed Monster" (BF Benny audio)
- "The Plague Herds of Excelis" (BF Benny audio)
  Benny and Iris Wildthyme dispose of the Relic in Excelis.
- *A Life of Surprises* (BF Benny anthology)
- "Dance of the Dead" (BF Benny audio)
- "The Mirror Effect" (BF Benny audio)

BENNY BIG FINISH SEASON 3
- "The Bellotron Incident" (BF Benny audio)
- "The Draconian Rage" (BF Benny audio)
- "The Poison Seas" (BF Benny audio)
- *Life During Wartime* (BF Benny anthology)
- "The Axis of Evil" (BF Benny audio)

BENNY BIG FINISH SEASON 4
- "The Grel Escape" (BF Benny audio)

DALEK EMPIRE
- "Invasion of the Daleks" (BF Dalek audio)
  Daleks based in the Seriphia Galaxy ("The Apocalypse Element") overrun Vega VI, instigating a new campaign against Earth Alliance worlds. The Daleks tap a geologist named Susan ("Suz") Mendes to become "The Angel of Mercy," a motivational speaker to give the slaves hope and improve efficiency. First appearance of Suz, space security agent Alby Brook and the telepathic Kalendorf, a member of the Knights of Velyshaa ("The Sirens of Time").
- "The Human Factor" (BF Dalek audio)
- "Death to the Daleks!" (BF Dalek audio)

- "Project Infinity" (BF Dalek audio)
  The Emperor Dalek uses "Project: Infinity" to open a gateway into a parallel reality where the Daleks are the superior lifeforms. However, the alternate Daleks, horrified by "our" Daleks' crimes, commence hostilities meant to wipe out the Emperor Dalek's forces.

DALEK EMPIRE II
- "Dalek War Pts. 1 to 4" (BF Dalek audios)

FACTION PARADOX
The Faction Paradox universe acknowledges Faction-related events in the BBC novels (*Alien Bodies*, etc.), or at the very least doesn't make efforts to contradict them. However, the *Faction Paradox* novels and comic series does not acknowledge *The Ancestor Cell*—mainly for the obvious problem that the book *kills* off the Faction, which is an impediment to our future publishing plans. That said, the events of the *Faction Paradox* line gel perfectly with the version of history used in The *Adventuress of Henrietta Street*, even though *Adventuress* takes place in a post-*Ancestor-Cell* universe. Lawrence Miles has promised to explain this discrepancy "one day."

Some critics might [justifiably] feel that *Faction Paradox* is now an entirely separate universe, but we're keeping it in the main spin-off section, as it validates "Who" history far more often than not.
- *Perfect Timing:* "Toy Story" (charity anthology short story)
  First appearance of Lolita, a humanoid TARDIS (akin to Compassion).
- *This Town Will Never Let Us Go* (MNP novel)
- *Faction Paradox: The Book of the War* (MNP guidebook)
  The first 50 years of the War—and everything leading up to it—explained in bursting detail. First appearance of the City of the Saved, the sprawling haven of humanity located at the end of the Universe. Chris Cwej turned into a veritable army of himself.
- *Faction Paradox Protocols 1:* "The Eleven-Day Empire" (BBV Audio)
  Cousin Justine (*Alien Bodies*) gains possession of Grandfather Paradox's shadow. Revelation that Christine Summerfield, now known as Cousin Eliza, joined Faction Paradox (*Dead Romance*).
- *Faction Paradox Protocols 2:* "The Shadow Play" (BBV Audio)
  Lolita destroys the Eleven-Day Empire, greatly enhancing her standing with the Great Houses. Presumed death of Godfather Morlock, a high-

ranking Faction official. Cousins Justine and Eliza escape in a stolen timeship.

- *Faction Paradox Protocols 3:*
  "Sabbath Dei" (BBV Audio)
  Cousins Justine and Eliza encounter a younger Sabbath in 1762, during his days as an intelligence agent. These events compliment the upcoming *Faction Paradox* comic series.
- *Faction Paradox Protocols 4:*
  "In the Year of the Cat" (BBV Audio)
  Lolita revealed to be seeding various worlds (including Earth) with her children: Compassion revealed as active on Earth and attempting to stop her. Beginning of the Compassion/ Sabbath/ Faction Paradox alliance against the Homeworld. Cousin Justine consigned to the Homeworld's prison planet.
- *Faction Paradox #1-#6 (Image comic series)*
  Story opens in 1774—12 years after events in *Faction Paradox Protocols* vols. 3 and 4. The War is now over. Remnants of Faction Paradox compete with the world's major powers to establish a political foothold during an age of riots, rituals and revolutions. War-time origin of the *Mayakai* (*Adventuress of Henrietta Street*).

KALDOR CITY CD SERIES

- **"Occam's Razor" (Magic Bullet audio)**
  Series of audios taking place in Kaldor City ("The Robots of Death," *Corpse Marker*). First appearance of Kaston Iago, Topmaster Uvanov's bodyguard.
- **"Death's Head" (Magic Bullet audio)**
- **"Hidden Persuaders" (Magic Bullet audio)**
- **"Taren Capel" (Magic Bullet audio)**
- **"Checkmate" (Magic Bullet audio)**

MIRANDA COMICS

- *Miranda #1-#6 (Comeuppance Comics)*
  Miranda (the Doctor's adopted daughter, *Father Time*) acclimates to her newfound political power, and consolidates her powerbase aboard The Needle (*The Infinity Doctors*).

MISCELLANEOUS VIDEO RELEASES

- **"Shakedown" (Dreamwatch Media)**
- **"Wartime" (Reeltime)**
  Featuring UNIT's Sergeant Benton.

Apocryphal Stories

These stories are *not* part of the "Doctor Who" chronology for a variety of reasons listed.
- *Campaign* **(rejected BBC first Doctor PDA)**
  Published independently for the benefit of the

Bristol Area Down Syndrome Association.
- **"The Curse of Fatal Death"**
  ("Comic Relief" special)
- **"Death Comes to Time"**
  (BBC webcast/CD release)
  Doesn't count as canon because its events would crack open the entire "Doctor Who" series like an egg. Deaths of the seventh Doctor and the Time Lords, who all possess godlike powers.
- **"Dimensions in Time"**
  (30th anniversary sketch)
  Arguably too silly to count as canon, "Dimensions in Time" moreso suffers the difficulty that nobody can even agree whether the fourth Doctor (as *The Discontinuity Guide* claims) or the seventh (as other critics argue) is the incumbent Doctor. As suturing "Dimensions in Time" into the timeline would be sloppy at best, it becomes akin to the sixth Doctor's "A Fix With Sontarans" special, and gets cast into the apocryphal well.
- *The Masters of Luxor*
  (unused first Doctor TV story)
  Proposed second story for the TV show. Published in script form.
- **"Shada" (Tom Baker version)**
  TV story, left incomplete by production strike, and probably canon until the Paul McGann "Shada" trumped it.

"DOCTOR WHO UNBOUND" AUDIOS

- **"Auld Mortality"**
  First in series of Elseworlds-type (i.e. non-canon) CD stories from Big Finish.
- **"Sympathy for the Devil"**
- **"Full Fathom Five"**
- **"Exile"**
- **"He Jests at Scars…"**
- **"Deadline"**

Upcoming Stories

We can't place this bunch until their release.
- **"PROBE: Drome" (BBV audio)**
- **"The I Job" (BBV audio)**
- *The Eleventh Tiger* **(first Doctor PDA)**
- *The Colony of Lies* **(second Doctor PDA)**
- *Deadly Reunion* **(third Doctor PDA)**
- *Flayed* **(first Doctor Telos novella)**
- *Companion Piece* **(seventh Doctor Telos novella)**
- *Fallen Gods* **(eighth Doctor Telos novella)**
- *Eye of the Tiger* **(eighth Doctor Telos novella)**

∃actioN PAradoX

THIS TOWN WILL NEVER LET US GO

PROLOGUE to the upcoming novel
by Lawrence Miles

11:32 p.m. Six minutes before the first of the rockets hits the square, so right now nothing's burning except for grill-fat.

This is Inangela, and we don't know her yet but we'll take the straightforward, statistical things for granted. She weighs 174 pounds; she's slightly shorter than she needs to be, although obviously high-heeled boots are de rigueur for someone in her position; and despite having the kind of cola-black hair that looks as if it evolved as camouflage for nightclubs with broken strip-lighting, it's bright red at the ends where a drunken experiment with scarlettine unexpectedly became a fashion statement halfway through. But if we're talking about fashion statements, then it's hard to get away from the mask. Contrary to what we might expect by now, the mask doesn't mark her out as a member of a death-obsessed guerrilla cult any more than combat pants on a twelve-year-old boy mark him out as a member of a military junta. So what does it say about her? This not-quite-fetishwear, this mask that looks like bone but really must be some kind of mass-produced polymer? Does it say that she's showing off? That she believes in something specific? That she doesn't believe in anything specific, and that this is her way of proving it?

That she liked the colour?

Now, this alleyway - with all its archaeological layers of advertising - is set just off the square, so Inangela's got a good view of the town's central, fat-insulated artery from where she's sitting. It's not just about seeing, though. There are places to eat in the square, most of them stalls with their counters open to the air, breathing out blood-hot paprika-smoke while the rest of the town freezes. Maybe it's a rare and exquisite combination of factors, or maybe it's just that there's no difference between one counter and the next, but you're downwind of the stalls wherever you go and the smells never contradict each other: however savage the competition might be between the vendors, it's as if all those razor-thin slices of sausage are rolling their eyes (metaphorical eyes, we hope) and deciding to co-operate while the humans fight among themselves. Things are frying tonight, and every night. It sinks into the air in the same way it sinks into the oil, so the atmosphere here in the alleyway is like every vegetarian's memory of how great bacon used to taste.

The town needs to be fed, especially now it's under fire. Inangela used to have a theory about that, which happens to be true, although maybe not literally true. When she was younger her friends used to ritually steal and incinerate "Neighbourhood Watch" signs, this being the cleverest and most ironic thing you can possibly do when you're fifteen ("ritually" in the sense that even if it wasn't exactly an initiation, each theft was at least a small, superstitious event). Inangela's theory held that without all these signs, without that symbolic protection, the Great Urban Horror could tunnel its way up out of the ground and start to feed on the surface-world. She still tends to see things that way. The sacred pattern of town-planning has been broken, and the thing which used to lie buried under the streets - under every street that ever existed - has been set free, hence the omens in the bill-hoardings and the lights in the sky which less interesting people believe to be long-range missiles.

Just a few hours from now Inangela is going to have her own encounter with the Great Urban Horror. Or at least she's going to think so, but by that point her consciousness will have been subtly altered by (in no particular order) chocolate, alcohol, onion rings and at least one mildly occult narcotic. All of which makes her sound incredibly selfish, as if it doesn't take more than a few deep-fried chemicals to turn her into the centre of her own urban legend, but let's be fair. This town is a town in wartime: this generation is a generation raised on shellfire as well as spare ribs. The food isn't the only thing that's liable to hyper-stimulate the nervous system.

We all have to go through these initiations. Little ones, anyway. We'd like to think that Inangela hides her face behind a big shiny bat-skull because she wants the attention, and to be honest that's not entirely untrue. But she's young. She's only nineteen. If this weren't a time of war then we'd say she just needs to get it out of her system, although really it's more a kind of longing. Cut off from the rest of humanity by so many things - by her thoughts, by her words, by a culture which showers the world around her with warheads and acts as if it's perfectly normal for the War to go on forever, and of course by her exemplary fashion sense - it'd be truer to say that she just wants to be where the action is. To have one of the rockets detonate less than six feet from her body: to be able to say, in a world where everyone sees things happen at a distance, that she's been in the middle of the Warzone and Dear God she knows what it feels like. We might have guessed as much.

Because we are, for the purposes of this story, the elders and archons of Faction Paradox. That's the kind of audience Inangela wants, so that's the audience we're going to give her. The ones who watch from outside history, who pay attention to impeccable creatures like her because obviously she deserves to be rewarded for being more interesting than anyone else. A clique of ancient, nigh-immortal beings who reject the ways of the ruling class and smile on those who wear the right badges… well, it could almost be a kind of wish-fulfilment. So tonight - for one night only - we'll be in charge of the Faction, at its best, at its brightest, at its shiniest, before the worst days of the War and before its lapse into sheer ruthless bloody-mindedness. We'll watch everything Inangela does, we'll applaud her as she either (a) saves or (b) destroys the world as she knows it, and come the dawn we'll rate her adventures out of ten. Although she may lose marks for that coat.

By the time the rockets reach the square at 11:38, Inangela has already left the area. At midnight precisely she'll become a heroine.

Let's start there.

Publisher: Mad Norwegian Press
Release Date: September 2003
ISBN: 0-9725959-2-9
Retail Price: $14.95 (softcover)
$34.95 (signed hardcover,
limited to 300 copies)

www.madnorwegian.com

1309 Carrollton Ave #237
Metairie, LA 70005
Larzo@madnorwegian.com
(504) 219-0727

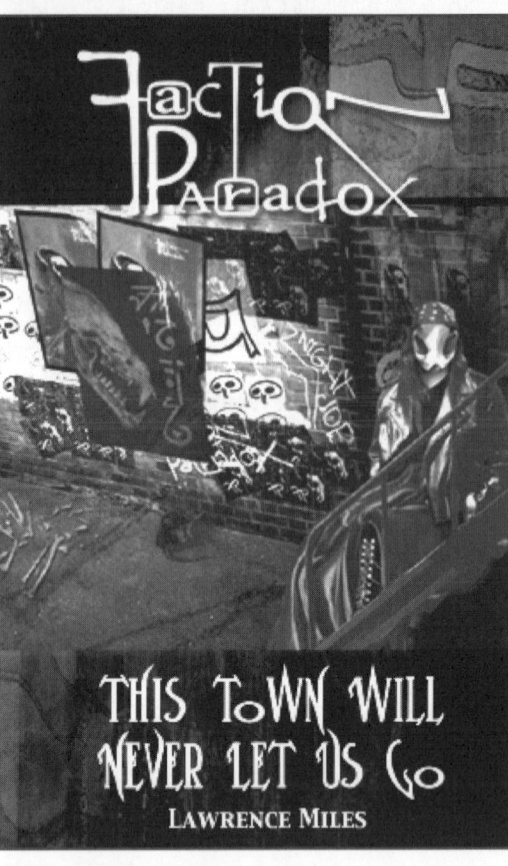

DOCTOR WHO STORE.COM

Large Selection of Books
BBC, Target & Virgin Lineups

Audio CDs
Big Finish & BBC
Subscription service available

Video & DVD
Region 1 DVDs & NTSC Videos

Magazines & Comics
Large selection available

Trading Cards
Strictly Ink & Cornerstone

Independent Productions
Soldiers of Love
Reeltime Pictures
Myth Makers
BBV Audios & Videos

Collectibles
Resin Statues
Stamp Covers
Gift Items

Look for these and other products at

WWW.DOCTORWHOSTORE.COM

The LARGEST selection of
DOCTOR WHO
on the internet!

EXCLUSIVE!
AE-1 Promo Card
Free with any trading card order.

CHICAGO TARDIS

Come celebrate the 40th
anniversary of Doctor Who
WWW.CHICAGOTARDIS.COM

Doctorwhostore.com is an Alien Entertainment Company.
We ship worldwide from the United States.

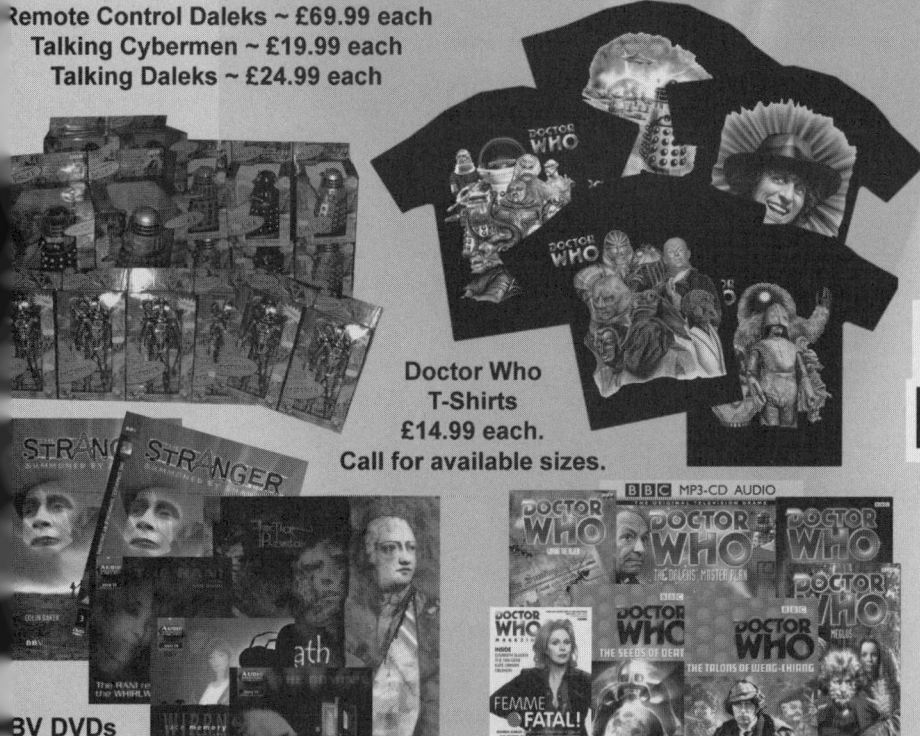

RAMBLINGS & THANK-YOUS

FROM THE AUTHOR

Like Time Lords, people regenerate. I'm utterly convinced of this, and the *I, Who* series stands as proof of it.

My brain acknowledges that I wrote all three *I, Who* volumes, but since I chiseled the books into stone in three very different parts of America at three very different parts of my life, it sure as hell feels like three different regenerations of Lars Pearson worked on them.

Thus, for anyone who keeps track of this stuff [and convention-goers have shown more interest than I'd have suspected], here's an off-the-cuff rundown of the three regenerations of *I, Who*:

• *I, Who [Nyack, New York]*—The first *I, Who* volume came into being during my time as an editor for *Wizard*, *ToyFare* and *Inquest* magazines in Nyack, New York, near Manhattan. It entailed reading and analyzing 150 "Doctor Who" novels, and—since it was self-published—a terrifying amount of marketing and finance issues. The book made me a few friends in the banking community, especially at a local branch where they let me rollerblade through the lobby.

All told, *I, Who* amounted to 250,000 words and a year of my life. As it neared completion, I started haunting the *Wizard* offices after hours—like some sort of crazed, comic-fanboy ghoul—to do the book's final layout/revision. Deadline pressure made things seem terribly surreal. I lurked in the building unshaven, unwashed, with my coworkers avoiding me like a rabid dog. I'd surface to occasionally shake hands with newcomers [which is how I met *Wizard* news writer Chris Lawrence, editor of the book you're holding], then retreated back to my crucible hell.

A week before final deadline, Hurricane Floyd struck the East Coast. I spent 16 hours trapped in the *Wizard* offices with no power and no phones. I tried navigating the building with a glow-in-the-dark moonrock from an officemate's desk, but the damn thing faded to the point where you could only see the rock, not me. Had anyone looked at me, they would've only seen a green rock somehow levitating, specter-like, down a darkened hallway.

As it turns out, I got lucky. Floyd butchered Bound Brook, NJ, so badly that the town was under marshal law for three days. I finally hopped a train to Connecticut and enjoyed drunken 500 games with friends, then finished *I, Who* a week later.

• *I, Who 2 [Los Angeles, California]*—I started *I, Who 2* after I'd moved to Los Angeles and started working for Thirsty.com, an upstart Internet news service. The job had several perks, among the greatest of which was my ability to wear in-line skates at work each day.

Like countless other Internet businesses in 2000, Thirsty collapsed, a victim of the Internet massacre business analysts would later describe as the "Dot Gone" phenomenon. And while Thirsty's demise did leave me butchered professionally, it also cemented my participation in a historic event. [A dubious and fairly apocalyptic historic event, perhaps, but it's better than nothing.]

I chiefly wrote *I, Who 2* on a laptop in various coffee shops and diners across Los Angeles. Waitresses would frequently stop, stare at me and—inevitably—mistake me for actor Topher Grace, who plays lead character Eric Forman on *That 70s Show*. Depending on my mood, I'd either fuel their delusions or admit my real name [i.e. Nobody], then return to analyzing *The Banquo Legacy* or somesuch. Not my most glamorous moment, I must admit.

• *I, Who 3 [New Orleans, Louisiana]*—I spent my latter days in Los Angeles speaking with technical recruiters about writing positions, but the economy soured to the point that even the recruiters lost their jobs. I got engaged, abandoned any semblance of a "normal" job, moved to New Orleans and started Mad Norwegian Press.

As I started drafting the book you're holding, my fiancée and I spontaneously eloped in New Orleans' French Quarter. We took our vows on a Saturday at "Weddings-a-Go-Go," where we graciously declined a voodoo priestess' offer to officiate the ceremony.

I quickly trampled every *I, Who 3* deadline into the ground, mostly because my newfound administrative duties kept interfering, but also because the overabundance of drive-thru daiquiri bars in New Orleans provided an ever-present distraction.

Because Heaven knows I can't write an *I, Who* book without some sort of natural disaster occurring, New Orleans fell prey to back-to-back hurricanes in 2002, which displaced the wife and I from our apartment for two weeks. We became nomads, wandering through Iowa, Kansas and Tennessee while I bravely tried to dissect the intricacies of *Anachrophobia* and its like. Work on the book ended in Spring 2003, at which point my muscles

www.madnorwegian.com
1309 Carrollton Ave #23?
Metairie, LA 7000?

lost cohesion and I oozed—like Odo on *Deep Space Nine*—into a bucket.

LOOKING AHEAD

So long as the BBC, Big Finish, Telos [until early 2004, at least] and others keep pumping out "Doctor Who"-related stuff, the *I, Who* series will almost certainly continue. In addition to updates, there are perhaps three major categories of "Who" stuff I'd love to examine/index: A) the *Doctor Who Magazine* comics, B) BBV's more legitimate works [*see the Uber-Timeline* for BBV audios/videos we deemed canon] and C) the "Doctor Who" anthologies, both official and charity works (such as *Perfect Timing*, *Missing Pieces*), etc. So we'll see.

THE AUTHOR WISHES TO THANK

Christa Dickson. The love of my life, who does a Herculean amount of work for Mad Norwegian. One of these days, I really must think about paying her. [She keeps saying, "You can't afford me," but I'm never sure what this refers to.]

Chris Lawrence. ... Just about the most steadfast friend on the planet, who does everything in his power to help us out. I'm convinced that if I off-handedly mentioned a particular need to incite Red Revolution, Chris would immediately start lining people up against the wall and unloading his carbine.

Craig Ernst, Nat Hanan and Joseph and Lorna Thunderhorse. The most desirable crew of advisers—and hardcore friends—any man could hope for. Anything else I could say about them would sound ridiculously cliched, so I'll just shut up now and, by way of thanks, send them liquor.

The "Doctor Who" writers/producers. I'm the first to admit—the "Doctor Who" creative crew gives us unbelievable amounts of information—with utterly no promise of a good review in return [indeed, we've scathed some of the people who've helped us the most]. I'm duly grateful to every single person who contributed. That said, it's probably fair to single out...

Paul Cornell, Mags Halliday, Lawrence Miles and Gary Russell. ... for giving sage advice/comments about the Uber-Timeline. Fact is, I e-mailed out several invitations to "Who" experts begging for help, but only Paul, Mags, Lawrence and Gary took the time to respond. As such, they've attained a level of geekdom that would make most fans blush, and I'm truly grateful.

Gene Ha. For the drop dead gorgeous cover, probably [or so some harsh critics would say] the best thing about this book.

The Right Stuf International's Shawne Kleckner. A great agent, but moreover a true "Who" lover—he's ironically one of America's top Anime distributors, yet insists on his "Who" book and audio fix each month.

Carol Scroggins. Generous backer and giver of cookbooks.

We love California! George Krstic and the Prynoskis [check out their series LowBrow on the Cartoon Network], the Moriaritys, Richard Martinez, Sadie Jacobs, Harding, J Shaun Lyon, Chad Kneuppe and Elyse Springer.

The Iowa/Coe contingent. Marcus Ebicus Maximus, Dave and Tracy Gartner, Spot, Fritze, Em and Eric Hanson [your eagle-eyed reporter in Des Moines, IA].

Good Morning, New York! Tess, Tim Hare, Jim Calafiore and McKenna.

PUBLISHER, EDITOR-IN-CHIEF
Lars Pearson

SENIOR EDITOR, DESIGN MANAGER
Christa Dickson

EDITOR
Chris Lawrence

ASSOCIATE EDITORS
Marc Eby
Dave Gartner
Joshua Wilson

COVER ART
Gene Ha

INTERIOR DESIGN
Metaphorce Designs
metaphorcedesigns.com

MARKETING GURU
Craig Ernst

TECH SUPPORT
Robert Moriarity
Mike O'Nele

HUMBLE INTERN
Laura Farmer

Those wacky Brits [and aren't they all?]. James Tomlinson, Simon Pilkington and Stephen Miles.

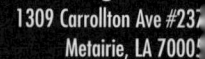